DREAM WEAVERS

DREAM WEAVERS

PHILIP SHELBY

A BANTAM TRADE PAPERBACK

BANTAM BOOKS
NEW YORK TORONTO LONDON SYDNEY AUCKLAND

DREAMWEAVERS

A Bantam Book / March 1991

Library of Congress Cataloging-in-Publication Data

Shelby, Philip.
    Dreamweavers / by Philip Shelby.
        p.   cm.
    ISBN 0-553-34895-7
    I. Title.   II. Title: Dreamweavers.
PR9199.3.S5117D74   1991
813'.54—dc20   90-48250
                                                                     CIP

Bantam Books are published by Bantam Books, a division of Bantam
Doubleday Dell Publishing Group, Inc. Its trademark, consisting of the
words "Bantam Books" and the portrayal of a rooster, is Registered in U.S.
Patent and Trademark Office and in other countries. Marca Registrada.
Bantam Books, 666 Fifth Avenue, New York, New York 10103.

PRINTED IN THE UNITED STATES OF AMERICA

BVG   0   9   8   7   6   5   4   3   2   1

For Henry and Danny, their efforts, encouragement, and
friendship . . .
And, the ladies of 320 McLain, who are always there to help.
To all, my deepest thanks.

*As well as friends who created islands of beautiful memories during
the writing:*
    Todd and Monette, Los Angeles, California
    Matt and Lisa, Orange, Australia

And, Daphne, who is my friend, my lover, and who will be my wife.

Those who dream by night in the dusty recesses of their minds wake in the day to find it was vanity; but the dreamers of the day . . . may act their dreams with open eyes, to make them possible.

— T. E. LAWRENCE
Seven Pillars of Wisdom

PROLOGUE

HAWAII, 1959

The steering wheel was slick beneath her clenched hands. In Hawaii's deep night, the wet streaks along the convertible's dash and seats appeared black. Cassandra McQueen knew they couldn't be. The color of blood was red.

Cassandra's long blond hair whipped across her face as she flung the car into a hairpin turn. The tires howled over the crushed lava shoulder, then spun as she stamped on the accelerator. The edge of the cliff, which followed the Oahu coastline, yawned ahead of her. At the last second, the tires caught and held, propelling the car back onto the asphalt.

Cassandra tried to calculate how long she had been driving. Five minutes? Ten? An eternity. The house she had fled was isolated, even by the standards of Oahu's Platinum Mile, where estates were measured in hundreds of acres. Their owners boasted that during the hunting season, one neighbor never heard another's gunshots. But whoever had tried to kill Steven Talbot—whose home, Cobbler's Point, dominated the far-flung peninsula—had not used a gun.

If they had, Cassandra thought, *I'd be dead.*

Cassandra's heart raced at the thought of the would-be killer. All around her the Pacific roiled and boomed, tossing spray high into the air where the wind carried it across the road, coating the brush and twisted trees that protruded like skeletons from the cliff wall.

I've got to slow down. If I hit a wet patch . . .

Cassandra couldn't bring herself to take her foot off the accelerator. Her eyes searched the distant hills for the faintest light, from a house or a fire-lookout station, any place that had a phone and, if she was lucky, someone to help her. Instead, her rearview mirror, once pitch-black, exploded into white.

He must have seen me! He knows that this is the only route I could take. He's been behind me all the time, waiting. . . .

Then Cassandra realized why. Just ahead was a stretch of perfectly straight road. She was driving a small English roadster, its engine already straining. The car behind her, gaining rapidly, sounded much more powerful.

He'll pull up beside me and try to run me off the road . . . over the cliff.

The distance between the cars was closing fast. Cassandra wrenched the wheel and veered into the center of the road. As long as she could prevent the other vehicle from overtaking her, she had a chance.

Her pursuer was not to be outdone. He edged so close to the roadster that Cassandra had no choice but to yield. As she pulled back into her lane Cassandra glimpsed the driver, a motionless figure wearing a cap. The reflection of his high beams in her side mirror blinded her, the night pierced by a siren's wail. Cassandra saw the flashing red light. A voice, distorted by a metal bullhorn, flooded her with relief.

"This is the police. Pull over. Repeat, pull over!"

Cassandra managed to steer the car onto the shoulder of the road, the engine stalling as she released the clutch too quickly. Quivering, she let her head fall forward onto her arms. The police! Either she had raced through a speed trap or had blundered across a routine patrol. It didn't matter. She was safe. Cassandra fumbled with the door latch and got out of the car. Her knees almost gave way.

"Officer—"

"Hold it right there!"

Cassandra shielded her eyes from the glare of the flashlight.

"Jesus Christ!"

"Officer, what's wrong?"

"Keep your hands where I can see them!"

His voice had a high, keening tremor to it. Cassandra looked down at herself and at her dress, which was covered with blood.

"There's been an accident at Cobbler's Point. I was trying to get help—"

"You were at the Point?"

"Yes! The phone was dead. Steven was . . . he'd been stabbed, he was bleeding. . . . I was going to get help!"

"Lady, you were running!"

"No—"

"Let's see some identification. And be real careful how you bring it out."

4

Cassandra wondered why she hadn't seen the gun before. It looked huge in the young patrolman's hand.

"My name is Cassandra McQueen," she said, fumbling to extract her driver's license from its plastic sheath.

The patrolman examined it carefully.

"Yeah, lady. Everybody in Hawaii's heard of you. You and Mr. Talbot didn't get along so well. Now suppose you tell me what happened—"

The officer's words were interrupted by the crackle of an incoming message on the radio-telephone.

"Move toward the car, ma'am, and put both hands on the roof."

"Please—"

"Just do it, Miss McQueen!"

Without taking his eyes off her, the patrolman reached through the open window and picked up the handset.

"Dispatch, this is Patrol Ten."

"Patrol Ten," a woman's voice answered. "Be advised a possible Code Six at Cobbler's Point. Units and ambulance on the way. Can you assist?"

The young officer stared at Cassandra. A Code 6 meant homicide.

"Someone must have found him!" Cassandra whispered.

"Don't move!" the patrolman said nervously, then asked the dispatcher to put him through to the officer in charge.

"Patrol Ten, Detective Kaneohe standing by. I'm patching you through now."

Cassandra listened as the patrolman explained the bizarre situation confronting him on the Platinum Mile.

"Yeah, she's all right," he added, glancing at Cassandra. "Blood all over the place but she isn't hurt."

The officer fell silent, listening to the message from the detective.

"What's going on?" Cassandra demanded when he finally replaced the handset.

Before she knew what was happening, Cassandra felt her arms wrenched around her back. Cold steel circled one wrist, then the other.

"What are you doing?"

"You're under arrest, Miss McQueen, for attempted murder."

Nicholas Lockwood walked beneath the high-intensity lights powered by a portable generator. He was a tall, lean man with unruly chestnut hair and the steady green eyes of a mariner. He stood across the free-form pool that dominated the back terrace of Cobbler's Point. On the other side, a doctor and two male nurses worked frantically to keep the life from draining out of Steven

Talbot. Beneath the lights, rivulets of blood snaked through the diamond-blue water.

"Is that how you found him?" asked Nicholas.

The policeman he was addressing was heavyset, with a loud, perspiration-soaked island shirt and a woven, palm-leaf fedora jammed on his head.

"Just like that." Detective Kaneohe shook his head. "They're going to have a hell of a time getting those knives out of him."

"Not knives," Nicholas murmured.

The swords imbedded in Steven Talbot's chest had curved blades topped with ornately carved handles. They were museum quality, matched by perhaps six or seven sets in the world.

"What do you mean?"

"Just that someone tried to murder Talbot in a very expensive way."

Kaneohe watched Lockwood carefully.

"Any ideas?"

Kaneohe knew that Nicholas Lockwood had, until recently, been responsible for the security of Steven Talbot's worldwide financial empire, Global Enterprises.

Nicholas watched as the two male nurses placed Steven Talbot on a stretcher. Somewhere in the distance he heard the distinctive flutter of a helicopter.

"Like any powerful man, Mr. Talbot had his share of enemies. My successor can help you with that."

"That's right," Kaneohe said softly. "You skipped over to Cassandra McQueen. So how come you just happened to be up this way?"

"Miss McQueen is in Hawaii to discuss some business with Mr. Talbot," Nicholas replied noncommittally. "I thought she might have come up here. Obviously she never did."

Kaneohe smiled, his teeth gleaming against skin the color of ancient walnut.

"Oh, she was here all right. A patrol car intercepted her heading down Platinum Mile like a bat out of hell, blood all over her, babbling that someone had tried to kill Steven Talbot."

Kaneohe was pleased by the effect of his words.

"Is she all right?" Nicholas demanded.

"She's fine. She's being taken to headquarters right now."

Nicholas couldn't believe what he was hearing.

"You think she did that?" he demanded, pointing at Steven Talbot's body as it was being wheeled toward the front lawn and the helicopter medivac.

"I read the papers, Lockwood," Kaneohe said harshly. "There was a lot of bad blood between her and Mr. Talbot. Miss McQueen admits she was here tonight. So for starters I have motive and opportunity."

"You don't have a damn thing!"

Kaneohe shrugged. "When we get the prints off the knife handles, and if Talbot manages to hang on, give us a positive I.D. . . . ."

Nicholas's thoughts raced ahead of the detective's ominous words. If Steven survived he would accuse Cassandra of having tried to murder him. That her fingers had never touched the swords wouldn't matter a damn. Steven Talbot would do everything in his power to ensure that Cassandra paid the ultimate penalty. Not only because she was poised to expose him for what he was—a madman—but because twenty-five years earlier, Steven Talbot had tried to murder her and had failed.

And now that the police have Cassandra, they won't look any further.

But Nicholas had to, because the would-be killer was still out there. Nicholas had almost lost Cassandra once. He could not imagine his life if he failed her now.

"You sure are lucky, honey. Mr. Talbot's hangin' on. You might cheat the hangman after all."

Cassandra shivered from the chill of the air-conditioning.

"My clothes . . ."

"Forget 'em, honey," the policewoman replied. "All that blood, it'll never wash out. But we'll get you something nice to wear in front of the judge. Not that it matters."

But I haven't done anything!

That's what Cassandra had been repeating ever since she had arrived at Honolulu Police Headquarters. No one had paid the slightest attention. The policewoman sat her down and began filling out the arrest sheet. Next, Cassandra was fingerprinted and photographed.

"I have a right to a phone call," Cassandra said.

"Sure you do. Later."

A policewoman escorted her into the showers and ordered her to strip and wash herself. Cassandra cringed under the ice-cold jets, then began scrubbing furiously at the dried blood on her skin. She dried herself and donned a stiff, gray prison smock.

"Now you get your call," the policewoman said, handing her a dime. "Make it count."

Taking a deep breath, Cassandra inserted the coin and dialed the number of the hotel where she and Nicholas Lockwood were staying.

Please . . . please be there!

The switchboard operator answered and put her through to her suite. Cassandra's hopes fell away as the telephone rang on and on.

Nicholas, where are you?

The operator came back on the line. Cassandra pushed her fears aside and pleaded with her to tell Nicholas that she was at Honolulu Police Headquarters and needed his help. She clung to the receiver, the dial tone ringing in her ear, long after the connection had been broken.

"Let's go," the policewoman said, prying the receiver from Cassandra's fingers.

Downstairs, she unlocked the door to the isolation block and pushed Cassandra into the first cell.

"Believe me, honey, you don't want to be in with the others," she said. "I'll be back with something to keep you warm. Better get all the rest you can. The detectives will be wantin' to talk to you when they get back."

Cassandra had no idea how much time had passed when a matron returned with a blanket. She wrapped it around her shoulders and pushed herself across the cot, her back to the wall.

Steven is alive and his would-be killer is free . . . out there somewhere.

Was that where Nicholas was too? Hunting him? Helping her the best way he knew how?

The shock of the night's events finally took hold, spilling itself into her tears. *Steven should have died*, Cassandra thought. So many people had suffered at his hands, so many dreams had been ground to ashes.

Not mine! I'll never let him take mine. . . .

But she was too tired to fight anymore. Exhaustion closed her eyes and bore her gently away, across golden fields and shining hills on whose peaks stood a glittering palace. In front of it was a young woman, a girl really, perhaps eighteen, dressed in white, like a bride. Cassandra smiled. It was Rose. It could only be Rose, the first of them, the one who had forged the code they all lived by.

PART

ONE

— | —

For as long as she could remember, Rose Jefferson had dreamed of getting married in the ballroom of Dunescrag, her grandfather's estate on Long Island, New York. Today, a peerless June day in 1907, her dream would at last come true.

Rose was standing by the railing of the third floor balcony, which ran all the way around the ballroom. Its majesty never failed to take her breath away. To build its columns and floor her grandfather, Jehosophat Jefferson, had used the finest pink marble from the quarries of Carrera. The walls were peach white, accented with lacquered ebony. Overhead were three regal chandeliers, years in the making in the shops of Venetian craftsmen. One level below, in the gallery, the orchestra musicians were tuning their instruments and arranging sheet music. On the ballroom floor, servants were making sure that the bouquets of pink roses and baby's breath that decorated the pews were just right, and that the royal-blue carpet leading to the altar was spotless.

"M'amselle! M'amselle! What are you doing running off like that? An hour to the wedding and you're still not ready!"

Mathilde Lebrun, the French seamstress who had been sent over from the House of Doucet in Paris along with the trousseau, bustled toward Rose, clucking through a mouthful of pins.

"Mathilde, don't you dare take in another centimeter!" Rose warned her. "I'm ready to burst!"

It was true. Beneath the voluminous lace and silk creation, to which ten feet of train remained to be added, Rose was wearing a Royal Worcester S-bend corset, a Reformation bodice fitted over the corset, compressing the diaphragm with a double buckle and webbing at the back, a petticoat and an overskirt. Mathilde Lebrun thought she looked stunning.

The seamstress had dressed many brides during her years at the House of Doucet but even the most exalted of them paled beside this eighteen-year-old American girl. Rose Jefferson's long black hair was piled high in coils and loops, the artful creation held in place by mother-of-pearl barrettes. The summer sunlight infused her cheeks with a radiant glow, bringing out the luster in her enormous gray eyes, accented by black brows and long, upturned lashes.

The devil's own eyes in the face of an angel, thought the seamstress. They made Rose Jefferson unique. Depending on their mistress's mood, they could fill a room with laughter and sparkle or cast angry, forbidding shadows. Alternately they reflected tenderness, determination, and stubbornness. Their one constant was a shrewd intelligence.

Mathilde Lebrun commiserated with the groom. No matter how experienced or worldly, he would have his hands full with this one.

As she waited patiently for the seamstress to make the last-minute pinnings, Rose too was thinking of her future husband. Ever since she had met Simon Talbot five years ago, when she was thirteen and he thirty, Rose had known, with all her adolescent heart, that she would one day marry him. To Rose, Simon was a fascinating man who had carved out a mighty railroad empire that was changing the face of industrial America. He was also sophisticated and charming, with a southern gallantry that thrilled her heart. As far as Rose could see, the only obstacle to her destiny was Simon's wife.

Rose hated the beautiful Nicole Talbot on sight. To Rose, Nicole had everything she didn't: poise, confidence, and an understated elegance that only highlighted her brilliant qualities. Because of Simon's business dealings with Jehosophat Jefferson, the Talbots always attended the two big parties given at Dunescrag each Thanksgiving and Memorial Day. Rose seized the opportunity to study Nicole, from the way she walked and spoke to the delicate manner with which she held a teacup and the way she lifted her chin slightly when she was about to laugh. One day, Nicole caught Rose mimicking her and burst out laughing.

"Oh, Rose, you don't have to do that! I think you're perfectly wonderful the way you are. And Simon does too!"

Rose was both furious and mortified. She wished the worst plagues upon Nicole and at night lay awake concocting elaborate schemes to steal Simon away from her. When Nicole Talbot passed away during the influenza epidemic of 1904, Rose was devastated. She was convinced that she had brought

12

about Nicole's death and that one way or another she would be made to pay for it. Her penance began when Simon Talbot stopped coming to Dunescrag.

For almost two years Rose wondered what had become of Simon—and what was going to happen to her. Although she was ardently pursued by young men from New York's finest families, Rose ignored them. She was sure that Simon's business with her grandfather would bring him back to Dunescrag. The day it finally did, she seized the opportunity with both hands. When Simon Talbot next saw Rose Jefferson, the gangly girl had disappeared. In her place was a beautiful young lady on the verge of womanhood.

Rose often wondered if Simon had been aware of her slowly seducing him. She always found a way to create moments for them to be alone together, whether at Dunescrag or in Manhattan, and used every one of the wiles she had perfected on hapless teenage boys. Over the next few years, as his visits became more and more frequent, Rose was continually on the verge of believing that Simon was falling in love with her. But just as she thought the battle won, Simon would retreat across a chasm she hadn't been able to bridge: the seventeen-year age difference between them.

Rose refused to give up. A headstrong girl, she cultivated the patience of a saint. She read the books and saw the plays Simon enjoyed, memorized the rules of the sports he played, and even grasped the fundamentals of his railroad business. Strand by tenuous strand Rose wove a bridge across the gulf that separated them. She loved Simon with a ferocity that sometimes startled even her and used it to cleave herself onto his heart, penetrate it, and finally fill it with a love from which Simon couldn't escape. She overcame his reluctance and kissed away every argument he could muster: that he was too old for her, that their interests were so different, that he would somehow be inadequate to her fantasies of him. In the end, nothing had stood up to her determination to make Simon hers.

"Come along, m'amselle," Mathilde Lebrun scolded her. "It is time to fix the train. We must hurry!"

Obediently Rose followed the seamstress into her sitting room. On the way, she glimpsed maids carrying the wedding presents that had been arriving all week, sent by the three hundred guests who would be attending. Among them were senators, congressmen, two Supreme Court justices, and the governor of New York, all of whom were coming as much to pay homage to Jehosophat Jefferson as to watch his granddaughter get married. Rose was sure the gifts would be wonderful but she was equally certain that none could possibly match the one she would receive from her grandfather.

Bereft of a mother and father, Rose had grown up in what was more a kingdom than a home, where an aging patriarch, Jehosophat Jefferson, ruled over the empire he had carved out of the American Dream. By day she was

13

tutored in Greek and Latin, mathematics and literature. In the evenings, when other children were having stories read to them, her grandfather would sit Rose down and tell her all about Global Enterprises, the express company he had started in 1850 with three carriages and twelve horses and which had become one of the country's transportation giants.

Later, while her girlfriends worried about freckles and pimples and wiled away pampered days dreaming about boys, Rose Jefferson accompanied her grandfather to Global's Lower Broadway offices in the Wall Street district. Her Saturdays were never so happy as when she spent them seated in his enormous leather chair, her feet not quite touching the floor, plowing through company ledgers, brochures, and pamphlets. From the time she had first scrambled onto that chair Rose thought it suited her perfectly.

Rose was fascinated by Global's history. The express business dated back to the ancient Persian couriers, described by Heroditus, who let nothing stand in the way of their mission. Bestowed with royal sanction because they carried the messages of kings and queens, these couriers also conveyed spices and fish, vestments and silks, perfumes and oils to and from the farthest reaches of the empire they served.

In the early 1850s Jehosophat Jefferson saw a similarity between a burgeoning America and the once-glorious Roman Empire. Like the Empire, the United States was a far-flung, virtually untamed land that was being settled as quickly as people could travel west. Jehosophat Jefferson undertook a year-long study that confirmed what he had suspected all along: in the eastern and southern corridors the demand for a reliable express service was already apparent.

In 1856, the Manhattan-to-Rochester express, served by teams of stagecoaches, became an instant success. Trunk lines soon fanned out to Erie as well as other bustling industrial trade ports along the Great Lakes. Over the next few years, Global Express more than lived up to its motto: EFFICIENCY, RELIABILITY, COURTESY. Its reputation was such that during the Civil War it was the only express company that guaranteed delivery of packages to both combatants.

After Appomattox, Global expanded in another direction. The cost of mailing a letter between New York and Rochester was twenty-five cents, a princely sum for many people. Jehosophat Jefferson believed he could offer a cheaper and more efficient service. He developed a plan for Global to carry mail and issue its own postage stamps. The artist J. C. Wyatt made the engraving for Global's blue six-cent stamp, bearing the likeness of Rose's mother in profile.

Within a year Global was swamped with mail delivery orders, shipping a thousand sacks to the United States Mail's one. The government finally intervened to protect its monopoly, threatening dire consequences for Global's operations. Jefferson stuck to his guns and financed his court battles through a fraction of company profits. Because of the tremendous public support for Global, the government backed down and instituted an across-the-board postage rate of three cents. Jehosophat Jefferson gracefully bowed out of the postal business but took with him thousands of small businessmen and entrepreneurs who would remain loyal customers for years to come.

As the nineteenth century drew to a close, Global steamers plied the Great Lakes and the artery rivers like the Hudson, the Ohio, and the Mississippi, carrying the lifeblood of an expanding nation's commerce. West Coast businessmen relied on the famous Global Overland Express to deliver goods from the American heartland to the shores of the Pacific. To protect its passengers and cargo, especially gold bullion, the company organized its own security force of grim-faced lawmen whose uniforms consisted of range coats, Stetsons, and Winchester rifles.

But Rose learned early in life that success can extract a cost, sometimes a very cruel one. When she was nine years old her father, mother, and grandmother perished in the sinking of a Global vessel caught in a storm on Lake Superior. It was a tragedy that Jehosophat Jefferson never forgave himself for. The day she stood before her parents' grave Rose silently promised her grandfather that she would become worthy of the legacy that should have passed to her father. Everything she had done since then had been to prepare herself to inherit the mantle. Now, that day had arrived.

When Rose looked at herself in the full-length mirror, she didn't see an anxious bride but a young, poised woman who was about to take her place beside her grandfather in the office on Lower Broadway.

"I'm ready," Rose announced calmly.

She knew that Madame Lebrun didn't have the faintest idea what she was talking about.

The drawing room was in the east wing of Dunescrag, well away from the principal rooms. Nevertheless, some of the conversation of arriving guests filtered through the corridors, sliding under the door. Seventy-five-year-old Jehosophat Jefferson wondered what the ghosts who sat around him were thinking of the occasion.

Jehosophat Jefferson loved this room, decorated by his late wife, Emma. The walls were finished in satinwood, decorated in gold and ebony and covered with rich, tufted damask bordered in red at the corners. The light in the room came through a panoramic, heavily mullioned bay window facing the Atlantic Ocean. Here his children had played around the heavy furniture and Emma had sat on the ottoman, her feet tucked under her legs, patiently working on her embroidery, a soft smile on her lips. In the emptiness and silence Jefferson saw his son as a boy, who had changed into a young man and finally a husband, bringing home his young bride who would soon become a mother. And Emma, sweet Emma, with her grandchildren around her . . .

The old patriarch blinked back tears. They were all gone, long dead beneath the icy waters of Lake Superior. But he had never stopped carrying them in his heart, and now he asked himself, *What do they think? Would they agree with the decision I've made?*

There was no one in the world Jehosophat Jefferson loved more than his granddaughter, Rose. After the death of his family he had sworn that not even the demands of Global would intrude on the time he would devote to her. Throughout the years that promise had been kept. Now it came back to haunt him.

Jefferson had always believed that his grandson, Franklin, eight years younger than Rose and the only male heir, would eventually succeed him as head of the company. Girls were reared to become wives, mothers, and hostesses, devoting themselves to home, hearth, and charitable works. Even in this progressive day and age it was unthinkable to consider a woman running a modern, complex organization.

But Rose had broken that mold. To the untrained eye she was a beautifully turned-out young lady, cultured and well versed in the ways of her social class, ready to become a splendid mate for the right husband. But beneath the refinement was a girl who, after the first day he had shown her Global's offices, badgered him to take her there again. And again. Until ten-year-old Rose had become something of a permanent fixture, fussed over by the secretaries and indulged by Jehosophat's executives.

Although he had been amused by Rose's attachment to the company he was sure that in time she would become bored and move on. She had, but not the way he'd expected. By the time she was sixteen Rose knew the company history backward. Her grasp of the day-to-day operation, the complicated routings, schedules, and tariffs, never failed to amaze Jefferson. Facts and figures that brought yawns even to the most diligent accountants were a delight to her.

She couldn't have made it any clearer to me.

Rose had never asked, in so many words, to be involved in Global, but her attitude and commitment made her intentions unmistakable. Then, on her eighteenth birthday, when other girls were consumed by thoughts of making their debuts, she announced that she wanted to work full-time for Global.

"There's so much I have to learn," she had told him. "I want you to be proud of me, Grandad."

Jehosophat Jefferson had been shocked. Rose's fierce determination and proprietary pride left no doubt as to what she wanted: to become an active

16

partner in Global, the Jefferson who would one day take his place at the head of the family business.

That's the dowry she expects, Jehosophat Jefferson said to his ghosts. *How am I supposed to tell her that I can't give her the only thing in the world she really cares about?*

The patriarch was startled by the knock on the door.

"Excuse me, sir," the manservant said. "Miss Rose is ready. She is waiting for you downstairs."

Jehosophat Jefferson slowly got to his feet. He paused, hoping that his ghosts would, at the last minute, tell him how he should explain his decision to Rose. But as he walked out, Jehosophat Jefferson left only silence in his wake.

On his way back from a breakfast thrown by friends in New York after the evening's revels, Simon Talbot managed to slip into Dunescrag without running into any of his numerous relatives. Given their attitude, Simon was relieved. Ever since he had announced his engagement to Rose he had endured everything from tearful regrets to dire warnings about marrying into a northern flock.

As he passed through the largest of Dunescrag's ten guest suites, Simon noted approvingly that Albany, his black valet, had already packed up the steamer trunks and suitcases for the honeymoon. Simon threw off his soiled evening clothes, the shirt smudged with lipstick and reeking of cheap perfume, and tested the temperature of the bath water. He was a tall, heavyset man, with thick arms and legs, but he carried his weight well. At thirty-five the first gray had appeared in his curly, chestnut hair, accenting his high forehead and the aggressive slant of his cheekbones, his strong jaw. Even as he lowered himself into the hot bath, Simon could not completely relax. His eyelids closed over deep black pupils, but behind them, the dreams that fueled his restless ambition sped on.

Simon Talbot presided over a sprawling collection of brothers and sisters, cousins, aunts and uncles who were members of a southern aristocracy once ruled by his father's iron hand. Upon his death, Simon had overseen the family's dwindling cotton and tobacco operations. In its collective heart the clan believed the Civil War had never been lost. It stubbornly refused to acknowledge the new industrial age with its fierce competition and cutthroat business practices. As far as Simon was concerned, his family was doomed, by their myopia, to become relics. He had no intention of sharing their fate.

There had been anger and disappointment when Simon had struck north. Beginning with a few old spur lines, he had, in less than a decade, built up a substantial railroad network in the heart of Yankee territory. His family looked upon his achievement with indulgence rather than pride, and they forgave him his trespasses when, as a true son of the South, Simon took a Georgia belle for his bride.

His marriage changed nothing. Working like a man possessed, Simon tripled his holdings in the first few years of the new century and made New York the hub for thousands of Talbot Railroad locomotives, freight, and passenger cars that ran as far north as Vermont and south to Florida.

Simon had been very happy during the first years of his marriage. Nicole was an exemplary wife. She knew exactly what was expected of her and ran the household with unerring efficiency. She never questioned her husband about his business or demanded explanations for his overnight absences from home. In return for such obedience and docility Simon gave Nicole a vast new house on Fifth Avenue and an unlimited budget. It was a social contract with which Simon felt very comfortable.

In spite of Nicole's love for her husband, there was one thing she had been unable to give him: an heir. The day the doctor told Simon that Nicole was barren, the light went out of fortune's smile. Shortly afterward, Nicole succumbed to influenza. Those who knew her whispered that she had died as much from grief and shame as from the epidemic. Whether this was true, Simon couldn't say. As far as he was concerned, he had lived up to a husband's duties. Nicole's death had freed him to find a wife who would live up to hers.

Simon Talbot rinsed his face with a cold washcloth, toweled himself dry, and placed himself in Albany's competent hands to be shaved. Over the last few years he had gotten along nicely without a spouse. In fact, Simon had discovered that the cachet of widowerhood was an attractive lure to even the most respectable women. But his many affairs did not bring him what he wanted and believed he had earned.

In spite of his meteoric rise in the world of commerce, Simon felt shunned by a New York society as clannish and inbred as any in the South. No matter how lavish his home or how generously he contributed to the right charities, Simon was always conscious of being an outsider. He could never hope to rise any further unless he broke into the charmed circle of New York's ruling Four Hundred families. Money alone would not do it. He needed a wife who already belonged to that world, one whose pedigree guaranteed him acceptance.

Simon quickly discovered that almost all the eligible women had been spoken for. The few available widows were substantially older and he avoided them as assiduously as he did the spinsters. Simon would be damned if he'd settle for leftovers. Then he opened his eyes and saw Rose Jefferson.

Simon had not been oblivious to Rose's schoolgirl infatuation with him. But in time Rose had outgrown that. Her promise had been fulfilled by a fiery beauty that tantalized, and the more he saw of her the more conscious he

18

became of the effect she had on him. His skin tingled whenever her fingertips grazed his hand, and her eyes glittered with an eroticism that left him breathless.

Nonetheless, Simon was very careful not to encourage Rose; Jehosophat Jefferson and the business he brought Simon's way were much too valuable to risk on a fling. Simon retreated into the persona of the solitary, burdened widower, expecting that Rose would soon tire of him. Instead she asked him to be her escort to the season's cotillion.

Rose's boldness sent Simon Talbot into a frenzy of wanting her. Evenings, no matter how gay or glamorous, lost their sparkle without her throaty laughter and bold, challenging stares. Yet Simon remained convinced that if he accepted Rose's invitation he would incur Jehosophat Jefferson's wrath. And that would be the end of him in New York.

"Rose tells me you still haven't given her an answer," Jehosophat Jefferson said as he and Simon were walking by the seawall at Dunescrag on one of Simon's visits.

"Sir?"

"About the cotillion."

Simon swallowed hard. "I'm not sure how you'd feel about my escorting her, sir."

The patriarch grunted and marched on.

"I can see how Rose feels about *you*," he said after a while. "She's a headstrong girl but she has good judgment." Jefferson stopped short and faced the younger man. "How do *you* feel about *her*?"

Simon realized that he was about to give the most important answer of his life. He looked Jehosophat Jefferson right in the eye.

"I love her, sir."

Jehosophat Jefferson nodded and stared out to sea.

"I like you, Simon. I liked Nicole and admired the way you treated her. Rose will be needing someone like you when I'm gone. There are a lot of things she isn't prepared for yet, things which you'll have to teach her, help her with. Do you understand what I'm saying?"

Simon's mind was racing. He had always known that Rose's dowry would include a share of Global, however large or small. He was equally certain that no matter who the husband might be, Jehosophat Jefferson would never allow him any controlling interest in the company. Franklin, Rose's younger brother, would surely be groomed as successor.

Simon forced himself to remain calm and chose his words carefully.

"I'll do whatever I can to help Rose," he said. "I will honor any arrangements you choose to make for her."

Jehosophat Jefferson looked at him for a long time.

"I believe you would," he said finally, and drew out a sealed envelope.

"There will be papers for you to sign, of course, but this is part of my dowry to the two of you. Go ahead, open it."

Simon found himself looking at a contract which gave Talbot Railroads the exclusive right to carry Global freight. The magnitude of the gesture overwhelmed him. Jehosophat Jefferson had just given him the wherewithal to challenge such giants as Vanderbilt's Pennsylvania Railroad and Morgan's TransAmerica Lines, allowing Simon to take what he had always believed was his rightful place among the pantheon of America's great industrialists. More, he was getting a wife who would give him not only unquestioned respectability but what Nicole had failed to provide: an heir.

"I want you to look after her, Simon," Jehosophat Jefferson said. "If something happens to me before I can teach her everything she has to know, you must promise to finish what I began. Global is in her blood. One day, she'll be running it. I know that as surely as I know anything."

"I'll do whatever you say, sir," Simon replied solemnly.

"Good. Let's get back to the house. We have a lot to talk about."

Ten days later, at the cotillion, Simon Talbot formally proposed to Rose Jefferson and was accepted. From the joyous expression on her face and her passionate kisses, Simon realized Rose had no idea his mind was already on other things.

Albany held out a dove-gray suit coat with tails for his master. Simon Talbot slipped it on, fixed the pearl stickpin in his cravat, and examined the result in the mirror.

He glanced at his watch. "I guess it's that time."

Albany held out his hand. "Congratulations, sir, and good luck."

Simon left his suite and walked along the balcony to the top of the staircase, where he stopped and looked down. The three hundred guests were all seated. The minister was behind the altar, waiting. In the gallery, the musicians were playing softly. Simon surveyed the scene like a feudal lord, its power intoxicating him. He wondered if Jehosophat Jefferson had told Rose about the agreement he and Simon had struck. Simon had found it ludicrous even to consider that an eighteen-year-old girl would expect to have anything to do with a company as complex as Global. The last thing he needed was a headstrong young wife telling him his business, especially since he had already mapped out how Global operations would be absorbed into Talbot Railroads.

It will be all right, Simon assured himself. With that, he took a deep breath and proceeded down the staircase to embrace his victory.

– 2 –

"Do you, Rose Alice Jefferson, take this man, Simon Horatio Talbot, to be your lawfully wedded husband, to love, honor, and obey . . ."

Rose Jefferson stopped listening to the Episcopal minister's drone. She was struggling to ignore the chafing caused by the voluminous folds of her wedding gown. The multilayered creation weighed a ton. Rose had scarcely been able to walk down the aisle, much less move her arms to reach the itch near her backside, hidden somewhere under the lace train.

Do I love Simon? Of course I do! Honor . . . ? Well, I certainly respect him. Obey?

Rose's eyes lifted to Simon's face as she murmured demurely, "I do."

Rose felt a tug as Simon slipped the ring on her finger.

Very carefully she executed a half-turn and steadied herself on Simon's arm. Together, they sailed out the grand double doors onto the perfectly manicured lawn that ran all the way to the seawall. The laughter and applause of her guests roared in her ears. Rose threw the bouquet over her shoulder at the gaggle of bridesmaids, not caring in the least who managed to snatch it out of the air.

Now I have become a woman and given up childish things. Now my real life begins.

Silently Rose began rehearsing what she would say when her grandfather publicly announced her dowry.

While the photographers began snapping pictures for the bride and groom, their families and guests, and the newspapers, the ballroom was transformed into a fairyland banquet hall, complete with ice sculptures of Cupid and nymphets and a twelve-tier wedding cake. The reception line took so long to pass, Rose thought her hand would fall off. Her face was stiff from smiling and her throat hoarse from accepting congratulations. In spite of a ravenous appetite, Rose only pecked at the dishes that were presented at the luncheon and barely wet her lips with the champagne being poured like water. Although she loved the grandeur of the moment, she waited impatiently for her grandfather to get around to the dowry. As his wedding gift to her Simon had bought a huge neo-Georgian stonepile on Fifth Avenue to be their new home. Rose had had her eye on a more modest mansion on Park Avenue, within walking distance of Global headquarters on Lower Broadway. Rose was certain Simon would eventually agree that her choice was much more convenient.

After interminable toasts, the wedding cake was cut, the service and tables cleared away, and the orchestra ready to play. Standing in front of the mountain of gaily wrapped presents, Simon thanked their guests for their generosity and good spirit, while Rose kept frowning at her grandfather.

What's he waiting for?

Before she had her answer the orchestra struck up. Rose danced the obligatory first waltz with Simon, then passed into her grandfather's arms.

"You don't think I forgot you?" he teased her.

"Of course not, G'andad," Rose replied sweetly, using the nickname by which she had called him when she had been a little girl, struggling with her *rs*.

"I have it right here," Jehosophat Jefferson assured her, tapping his chest.

Rose glided to the side, catching a glimpse of a thick white envelope tucked away in his jacket.

"Hi, sis. Ready to dance with me?"

Rose glanced down at her ten-year-old brother, Franklin, his face scrubbed to a shiny pink, his golden-white hair framing mischievous eyes.

"My, aren't we the gallant," Rose commented, extending her arms so that Franklin could hold her, laughing as they whirled across the floor to the delight of the audience.

Rose looked fondly at Franklin. As far back as she remembered, Rose had taken care of her brother, slipping naturally into the role of surrogate mother, protector, and playmate. When she grew older Rose dreamed how, one day, she and Franklin would work together. Because she was older she would naturally assume her responsibilities first. Then, as Franklin came of age, she would teach him everything he needed to know about the company. Together, they would build on what their grandfather had left them, their destinies inseparable.

Rose was still daydreaming when she collided with what felt like an oak.

"Do you think . . . That is to say . . ."

Rose couldn't help but laugh. Monk McQueen stumbled over his words in much the same way he dealt with girls—with grave uncertainty.

"Come along," she said, taking the lead.

Although only sixteen, Monk McQueen had already shot up over six feet. He was a shambling bear of a youth with unruly brown hair and eyes that sparkled with curiosity.

Rose had known Monk all her life. Her grandfather read Alistair McQueen's *Q* newsletter religiously, considering it the most prescient financial report in the country. The McQueens were comfortably off but far from rich. The money they made from their own investments was minuscule in comparison to the rewards people like the Jeffersons and Talbots gleaned from the same advice.

"How long will you be in Europe?" Monk asked, holding Rose as though she were a porcelain figurine.

"It's our honeymoon, silly!" Rose teased him. "We'll be gone as long as possible."

Monk struggled to maintain his composure but Rose did not miss his crestfallen look. She slipped closer into his arms.

It was no secret that Monk McQueen had been in love with her for years. Even though she was two years older, Monk's physical stature and serious nature erased the age difference between them. As a child Monk had protested his love for her on the widow's walk of Dunescrag. Out of curiosity, Rose had allowed him to kiss her full on the lips. The touching of their flesh had been funny, but also strangely wonderful.

Carried away by puppy love, Monk had showered Rose with gifts: candy, cards, tiny charm bracelets, all bought with an allowance he carefully hoarded. At first Rose had thought McQueen's outpouring of affection cute and was flattered by such largesse. She even liked his curious first name.

At that age girls mature much more quickly than boys and Rose was a sterling example. When she returned to summer at Dunescrag on her thirteenth birthday she discovered that Monk's ardor had become more annoying than amusing. She began avoiding him, preferring to spend time with older boys. When she fell in love with Simon Talbot, Monk passed from a friend into a memory she dismissed with an embarrassed giggle.

"What do you intend to do, Monk?" asked Rose, counting down the bars to the end of the dance.

"Oh, I guess I'll go on to Yale," he replied dubiously.

"That's very nice."

"You'll be living in New York, of course."

"Of course."

Monk beamed. "That's just grand. Yale isn't that far from the city."

"I'm sure we'll both be very busy," Rose said, refusing to give him the slightest encouragement. As the orchestra wound down she glanced around the ballroom.

"Isn't that awful, Monk," she exclaimed.

Rose nodded toward the girls who were standing in knots, one eye enviously on the dancers, the other on the boys across the room who hadn't screwed up the courage to lead them onto the floor.

"There's Poppy and Melissa . . . oh, and I see Constance as well. Be a darling and dance with them."

Before Monk could protest, Rose had guided him over to the young ladies, who began blushing furiously.

"You've been a wonderful friend," Rose whispered, extricating herself from Monk's grip. "Simon and I want you to come and see us as soon as we get back."

Rose had noticed her grandfather beckoning to her and drew away from Monk without a second glance.

He'll get over it, she thought, trying to convince herself that Monk McQueen's heart was no more special than any of the others she had broken in the last few years.

Rose's pulse was pounding as she entered her grandfather's study. Jehosophat Jefferson came around and embraced her.

"I've never seen a more beautiful bride."

"Everything was so wonderful, Grandad. Thank you!"

Jehosophat Jefferson led his granddaughter to the sofa in front of the bay window that overlooked the formal gardens of Dunescrag. He removed the envelope from his suit jacket pocket and handed it to her.

"I want you to read this now."

Rose was puzzled by her grandfather's reticence. When she started reading she couldn't believe the words.

"Go on," he said gently. "Finish it."

"I don't understand," Rose said, bewildered. "I've worked so hard. . . ."

"I wanted you to have security," Jehosophat Jefferson was saying. "If anything were to happen to me—"

"You don't think I can run Global!"

Rose immediately regretted her outburst. It was petulant and childish.

"You know as much about Global as anyone," Jehosophat Jefferson continued. "But that doesn't make up for experience. In the event I'm not here, the arrangement with Simon will give you that experience. He's promised me he will teach you everything you need to know about managing the company. When you're twenty-six, Simon will relinquish custodianship of your fifty-one percent of Global and you'll become the majority shareholder. The balance will be held in trust for Franklin and when he comes of age, I hope the two of you will continue the work I began."

Jehosophat Jefferson looked pleadingly at his granddaughter. "This is just a precaution, Rose. Simon has no say in Global."

By now Rose had managed to settle herself.

"So nothing really changes," she said slowly.

"Your legacy is completely separate from Simon's fortune," Jehosophat Jefferson replied. "I call the arrangement a 'poison pill.' "

Rose managed to laugh. "What's that?"

"Simon is a shrewd businessman and Talbot Railroads is a solid concern. However, if some catastrophe befalls Simon, it's there, in black and white, that

Global assets—your patrimony—will never be used to help or bail out Talbot Railroads. Do you understand what I'm saying?"

Rose's eyes were shining as she flung her arms around him.

"I do, Grandad. I'm so sorry I acted like an idiot. We both know that nothing's going to happen to you."

May God forgive me, Jehosophat Jefferson thought as he held his granddaughter. *It's all for the best. I know it is!*

Jehosophat Jefferson had to believe that. He had made the arrangements with Simon Talbot sound like simple prudent business practice. By so doing he had led Rose to believe that nothing had changed. Yet everything was different. All because of a tiny, malignant growth in his bones that would kill him before the year was out.

Once he had accepted the inevitable and made peace with himself Jehosophat Jefferson had looked to the future. He would not live to see what would become of his empire but he could at least make sure that his granddaughter, who lived and breathed what he had created, would have the chance to leave her own mark. All the sweet lies had been for one person: Rose.

— 3 —

Their suite on the USS *Constitution* was a study in polished mahogany, brass, and beveled stained glass. There were bouquets of summer flowers in the living room, bedroom, and boudoir, and champagne frosting in a silver bucket, compliments of the captain.

"It's heavenly!" Rose cried, whirling through the suite and hugging Simon.

Rose supervised the maids who looked after the unpacking, chose a daring, purple and blood-orange evening dress designed by Poiret for dinner at the captain's table, then had a hot bath drawn. In the privacy of the boudoir she stepped out of her traveling outfit and, sitting naked in front of the mirror, asked herself, *What am I supposed to do now?*

Having grown up in a household where females were conspicuous by their absence, Rose had never had anyone to talk to about sex. Her grandfather certainly never broached the subject, and her maiden aunts crimsoned whenever she asked them what it was the horses were doing to one another in the paddock. She measured real men—or boys—against her grandfather but never understood why she always found them wanting. Her dream beau was a combination of Heathcliff in *Wuthering Heights* and Prince Andrei in *War and Peace*. In Rose's eyes, Simon fit the image perfectly. But now that she had him she quaked at the thought of disappointing him.

Maybe I should drink a lot of wine tonight, she thought. *Simon will dance with me, sweep me off my feet, and before I know it . . .* Rose started when the boudoir door swung open.

"There you are. . . ."

Rose turned to snatch up her robe and froze. Simon was standing in front of her naked, his face shining pink from the steam rising off the bath, his breath reeking of champagne. Rose couldn't tear her eyes away from the matted hair on his chest and the rigid penis that stood out, almost touching her lips, throbbing lightly.

"Take it!" he commanded hoarsely.

"Simon!"

Rose felt Simon's hand curl around the back of her head and jerk it forward. The tip of his penis pushed against her lips and teeth until she felt a warm stickiness in her mouth.

"You'll love doing this, Rose," Simon groaned. "I'll teach you everything!"

Rose struggled to pull back her head but was powerless against Simon's grip. He was jutting against her face, forcing himself into her mouth, threatening to choke her. Rose squeezed her eyes shut until tears flowed. Finally, on the verge of throwing up, she did the only thing she could think of: she bit down, hard.

Simon howled and withdrew, leaving her gasping. Snarling, he dragged her into the bedroom and threw her across the satin spread. Her legs were slapped apart and greedy fingers began exploring, their nails cutting her. Then Simon was above her, panting, guiding himself into her until, with a grunt, he penetrated her completely.

The room began to spin. Rose knew she was screaming but couldn't hear herself. Her fingernails raked Simon's back and her teeth clamped so deeply into his shoulder that she tasted blood. But nothing stopped him. Simon was like some giant, mindless engine, pushing and heaving mercilessly until Rose thought she would be torn apart. Then she felt a gush of warmth surge into her. Simon cried out, thrust his hips furiously, and collapsed, rolling over on his side, gasping.

Inch by inch Rose moved away. The satin spread was wet with her blood, her thighs slick to the touch. And the pain! Rose had never experienced anything so terrible. Slowly she brought her knees to her chest, curling up, her fist jammed against her lips. When Simon finally touched her, Rose quivered.

"The first time is always difficult for a woman," Simon said hoarsely, stroking her arm. "But you enjoyed it, didn't you, Rose? Yes, you're so beautiful I can't wait to do it again. I'm going to show you everything. You'll learn to love it, Rose. Each time it will get better and better, you'll see."

Rose whimpered as Simon slapped her on the buttocks and disappeared into the bathroom. Only when she heard the door close and the water run did she open her eyes.

At that moment Rose was seized with an overpowering desire to kill Simon. Everything he said was lies. Love wasn't supposed to hurt like that. It was gentle and caring, the union of souls as well as bodies.

Maybe it's all my fault. If I had known what to do, it would have been different.

The image of Simon pushing his penis into her mouth flashed into her mind. Is this what Simon had been doing to Nicole? Had she allowed him to punish her like that? Could she have enjoyed it?

Stop it! You're a woman now! You can make it beautiful. You have to try!

But it never became beautiful. For the next seven days Rose dreaded the lovely sunsets over the ocean. They were harbingers of unspeakable pain that left her terrified and ashamed. Each day Rose prayed the maids would tell someone, anyone, about the bloodied sheets. But each morning she returned from breakfast to find the bed freshly made, ready for the torture that would be committed upon it. The journey she had yearned to embrace had become an unspeakable, unstoppable nightmare.

The summer of 1907 was a golden season on the Continent. Europe was prosperous and at peace. In every country there was a carnival-like atmosphere that the local people were eager to share with visitors.

As soon as the *Constitution* docked in Southampton, Rose began searching for an excuse to return home. She drafted a dozen cables to her grandfather but tore up each one. Her cheeks burned with shame when she read back the words. They were filled with so much pain that they sounded incredible even to her. Deep down, an ugly doubt gnawed at her. Given how highly her grandfather regarded Simon and the trust he had placed in him, would he believe her?

I'll run away, Rose thought fiercely. *I'll go back myself and make him believe that Simon's a monster!*

She never had the chance. At the dock Rose and Simon were greeted by friends he had made during his previous trips, and Rose quickly found herself surrounded by aristocratic ladies who had already organized her introduction into British society.

Gradually, Rose lost her dread of the night. Simon took to staying out with his friends until all hours. More often than not she found him snoring on one of the sofas, his bloated face buried in a mountain of pillows. Rose was quick to notice that Simon's sex drive diminished in direct proportion to the amount he drank, and she made sure that their suite was stocked with the best liquor and wines.

However, there was nothing Rose could do to cut short the honeymoon. Simon had mapped out their three-month exploration of Europe; business associates and friends were ready to receive them at every stop. He bought a magnificent silver-plated Rolls-Royce Silver Ghost with Roi des Belges coach-work, as well as two other cars to ferry the servants and luggage. After two weeks in London, their entourage set out for the countryside, wending its way through Oxford, Winchester, and Canterbury, the seats of England's greatest cathedrals. By now Rose felt relatively safe. In London, she had bought a large supply of a powerful sleeping powder. If Simon was planning to stay in that night, she laced his predinner drinks with quantities that would knock out a horse.

After crossing the Channel, the couple motored to Paris for the great European Exhibition, then into the mist-laden valleys of the wine country where they were feted by dukes and counts whose family names appeared on some of the greatest vintages in the world. As September passed into October, Rose and Simon's itinerary took them across the Swiss Alps into Germany's Rhineland and ultimately to Berlin.

Everywhere they went, Rose impressed her hosts as the perfect guest. She said little and listened attentively. Although she spoke only English she made the effort to read up on the history of the country and family she was staying with. The grand dames who met her were charmed by her obviously first-class upbringing and took the young bride under their wing, agreeing among themselves that she should be forgiven for having been born American.

Behind her polite smile Rose was busy learning other lessons. Living among Europeans, she finally understood why wealthy Americans emulated their grace and charms and borrowed their mannerisms and affectations. Rose had no quarrel with proper etiquette. However, she wondered if American society ever noticed what lay beneath the European facade. As far as Rose was concerned, continental nobility was brittle. It relied on inbreeding to perpetu-ate itself and turned a haughty eye on the changes taking place right under its long nose. Everywhere she looked Rose saw irreversible decay. She was con-vinced it was just a matter of time before this grandiose structure collapsed on itself.

No matter how fascinating her travels were, Rose never stopped counting the days to the end of the tour. She also watched Simon like a hawk. In public Simon was charming, witty, and gracious, a man who invariably caught the eyes of other ladies at the table. When they were alone he was alternately silent and indifferent, or grasping and demanding. If she couldn't find the oppor-tunity to doctor his drink, Rose discovered other ways to keep him away from her. She pleaded severe cramps and dizzy spells and lay motionless while he pawed her. Her lack of response drove him crazy. On those occasions when

Simon refused to be put off, Rose would knick the inside of her thigh with a razor. As soon as Simon put his hand between her legs and discovered the blood he turned away in disgust, complaining about her seemingly constant menstrual periods.

Back in London, Rose steeled herself for the return trip home, her mind full of the brutal images from the first voyage. Mercifully Simon took to spending his nights in the smoking lounge, where the men played bridge and poker until dawn. But Rose didn't let down her guard. She slept in long nightgowns with enough folds to embalm a mummy.

As the *Constitution* sailed toward New York, Rose was determined to deal somehow with the terrible mistake she had made in marrying Simon. Although she hated the thought, she knew she had no choice but to speak to her grandfather. Rose firmly believed that even though Jehosophat Jefferson held great store in her marriage, he would listen to her and help her find a way out.

During their last dinner at sea, a steward appeared beside Simon and handed him a sealed envelope. Rose barely noticed the interruption, her attention held by the captain, who had a penchant for telling very amusing, if slightly salty, anecdotes. After the captain was through, Simon startled Rose by excusing himself and motioning for her to come with him.

"Simon, what is it?"

Without replying, Simon guided Rose to a secluded table in the deserted first-class cocktail lounge. Silently he handed her the cable from Mary Kirkpatrick, her grandfather's private secretary for thirty years.

MR. JEFFERSON PASSED AWAY TWO DAYS AGO.
CABLES SENT TO INFORM YOU. PLEASE AC-
KNOWLEDGE RECEIPT SOONEST.

"How could you do this?" Rose raged. "Why didn't you tell me?"

"Because there was nothing you could do," Simon replied, trying to keep up with Rose as she half-walked, half-ran through the formalities of customs and immigration. "I didn't want things to be any harder on you—"

Rose whirled around to face him. "Don't patronize me, Simon! Don't ever do that!"

"I've taken care of everything at Global," Simon assured her. "The company's on track—"

"That's another thing," Rose snapped. "I don't want you to do a thing with Global until I know exactly what's going on."

The immigration inspector recognized her name and touched his cap in a two-finger salute.

29

"I heard about Mr. Jefferson, Mrs. Talbot. I'm very sorry. You go along now. I'll see to it there's no problem with your luggage."

Rose's vision was blurred with tears. "Thank you. You're very kind. My husband will look after my things. I must get home."

Before Simon could stop her, Rose was running through the customs hall toward the regal black carriage drawn by four horses, their heads capped with black plumes.

Rose was sitting in her grandfather's chair, her feet planted firmly on the ground. She was intensely aware of his presence in the room, filled with the smell of tobacco he liked, the broad canvases of raging oceans that he enjoyed looking at, the medals, plaques, and congratulatory letters from presidents and statesmen mounted in glass cases. The office stirred memories that instead of hurting her, soothed and comforted.

Perhaps because I was so happy here . . .

"That's really all I can tell you, Rose . . . Mrs. Talbot, I mean," Mary Kirkpatrick was saying. "Please believe me that he went as peacefully as a lamb. I know. I was with him to the end."

"Don't address me as Mrs. Talbot, Mary," Rose said gently. "You've always called me Rose, or Rosie."

Mary Kirkpatrick balled up her handkerchief and managed a smile. Born of "black" Irish parents who had fled to America during the potato famine of 1846, Mary had been Jehosophat Jefferson's first and only personal secretary. Even though she was in her fifties her face retained the lustrous white skin and brilliant blue eyes of her ancestors. Her thick hair, generously streaked with silver, was braided and pinned.

Mary thought she knew Rose better than anyone else in the world did. Over the years she had watched her grow up, scolded her when she was a terror in the office, brought her milk and cookies when she worked beside her grandfather, diligently scribbling numbers in crayon on sheets of butcher's paper. Mary knew that if the good Lord had allowed her to have children they would have been as pretty and precocious as her beloved Rosie.

"Have you seen Franklin, Mary?" Rose asked. "Is he all right?"

"He's a brave little man," Mary Kirkpatrick said stoutly. "Mrs. Mulcahey calls me every day to say he's bearing up well."

"I must go to Dunescrag," Rose said vaguely. "There's so much to do. . . ."

Rose glanced down at the single piece of paper on the green leather blotter of her grandfather's cherrywood desk. In flawless Parker script, Mary Kirkpatrick had noted everything Rose would need and had stacked the appropriate folders on one side of the desk. There was the medical file from Roosevelt Hospital, listing the cause of her grandfather's death as "advanced carcinoma of the bone." A letter from the attending doctor assured Rose that Jehosophat Jefferson had been on a regimen of morphine and had suffered very little pain.

Another file contained Jehosophat Jefferson's last will and testament and was covered with a letter from his attorney. In spite of advice to the contrary, wrote the lawyer, the founder of Global Enterprises had not permitted anyone to tell Rose the nature of his illness or how serious it was. Even before Rose's wedding Jehosophat Jefferson had known he was unlikely to live to see Christmas.

The last file held the details of the funeral, where and when it was to be held, a list of pallbearers, and the particular scriptures Jehosophat Jefferson wished to have read over his grave.

"You've taken care of everything, Mary," Rose said. "Thank you. I know you loved him very much."

Mary Kirkpatrick's lip trembled and she began to weep. Rose came over to her and hugged her tightly.

"I'll need you, Mary," Rose whispered. "We have to carry on what he left us. You'll help me, won't you?"

Mary Kirkpatrick nodded. She had prayed that Rose would ask her to stay. There was really nowhere else for her to go.

Five days later, as the bitter autumn winds capped the long, gray waves of the Sound, Rose Talbot buried all but the last of her kin. She stood apart from the hundreds of other mourners—Jehosophat Jefferson's friends, business associates, and government representatives—a tall, lonesome figure draped in black, like a tenacious, solitary tree on some rocky bluff. Her arm was wrapped around the shoulders of her younger brother, Franklin.

The kilted piper blew his mournful dirge while the casket was lowered into the ground, and Rose accepted the condolences of the men and women as they filed by.

"You all right, sis?" she heard Franklin ask between sniffles. His eyes were bloodshot from tears, his cheeks reddened by the wind.

Rose smiled wanly. "Are you?"

Franklin hesitated. "I guess." He paused again, then asked, "What are we going to do now?"

"Exactly what Grandfather would have expected and not one thing less."

Rose was as good as her word. She moved Franklin, along with his tutors, in from Dunescrag and installed him in the Fifth Avenue house Simon had bought. Then she returned to Long Island and oversaw the closing of the great estate. Furniture, ancient rugs, and paintings were carefully stored away. Antiques, silver service, and bric-a-brac were catalogued and packed. Letters of recommendation were written for departing staff and arrangements made for those staying on to maintain the house and grounds. In spite of Simon's repeated suggestions, Rose would not consider putting the estate on the market. It was hers, to do with as she pleased. One day she would return to Dunescrag and restore it to its old glory.

Before attending to her family duties Rose had left a set of explicit instructions for Mary Kirkpatrick. When she returned to Global headquarters on Lower Broadway she was pleased that the secretary had seen to everything. Mary showed her how Jehosophat Jefferson's office had been touched up for her arrival and where Mary's own workstation was located, and introduced to her the recently hired stenographers and typists. Rose examined and approved the new letterhead Mary had had printed, checked the last-quarter figures, and noted the date of the next board meeting.

"I want to meet with all Global executives," she told Mary. "And please call Mr. Talbot at his office. Ask him if it's convenient for him to pick me up on his way home."

When Simon arrived later that afternoon he regarded the changes Rose had made with a skeptical eye.

"I see you've installed yourself quite nicely," he said. "May I ask the purpose?"

"You promised my grandfather you would teach me everything I needed to know about Global," Rose told him evenly. "I expect you to live up to your word."

"And I will. In fact, I was thinking of moving Talbot Railroads into this building. There's enough space. That way I can be here whenever you need me."

"As long as we can agree on a suitable rent," Rose added.

"Are you considering any other changes?" asked Simon.

Stung by his supercilious tone, Rose was tempted to tell him about the separate bedrooms she had arranged at Talbot House. But she thought she'd let Simon find that out for himself. "Simon, I want to meet with my executives as soon as possible."

Rose leaned on her desk, supporting herself with one arm, her head bowed. Her words echoed dimly in her ears. Suddenly she lurched forward, clutching her abdomen.

"Simon . . ."

Before he could reach her Rose felt herself falling deep into some mysterious void. All she could hear were her own terrified screams.

– 4 –

Rose regained consciousness to find herself in a large daffodil-yellow room at Roosevelt Hospital. She could scarcely see the young doctor hovering over her for all the flowers.

"What . . . what happened?"

The doctor patted her hand reassuringly. "You fainted, that's all. Mr. Talbot is waiting outside—"

"Fainted?" Rose said angrily. "I felt perfectly all right this morning."

She would die before admitting that right now a thousand drummers were staging a parade drill in her head and that it was all she could do to fight back her nausea.

The doctor chuckled. "I'm not surprised. But since this is your first, I guess you don't know how these things work."

"How *what* things work?"

"Pregnancies, of course. Congratulations, Mrs. Talbot, you're going—"

Before the doctor could finish his sentence or leap out of the way, Rose rolled over and threw up.

When Rose came to a second time she found herself surrounded by several older, distinguished-looking men.

"Will someone please tell me what's going on?" she demanded, exasperated.

One by one the specialists gravely announced their conclusions. Rose was indisputably pregnant. Arrangements had already been made for the necessary test although the consensus was that she was in good health and should have no difficulties carrying the child to term. Mr. Talbot had, of course, been kept informed. Regrettably, he hadn't been able to remain at the hospital to speak with his wife; he had pressing business to attend to. However, he had signed the required papers giving the medical staff full powers to do whatever was necessary.

He did, did he?

"How did I get this way?" Rose demanded.

Eyes blinked, jaws dropped, and an embarrassed collective silence descended on the room.

"I was taking precautions. I want to know why they didn't work."

"Mrs. Talbot, no single contraception method is foolproof," one of the

33

doctors replied. "Besides, it was our understanding that you and Mr. Talbot wished to have children."

"*Your* understanding and *his*. Certainly not mine! I want to see that young doctor."

There was a shuffling of feet and some murmured questions.

"Exactly who would that be, Mrs. Talbot?"

"Young man, blond hair, going bald around the crown. He wore rimless spectacles."

"Young Simmons," a voice offered.

"An excellent physician," one of the elders said. "But he's been with us for only two years. Rest assured we in this room will do everything we can for you."

"Then start by bringing in this Simmons! Otherwise I'll walk out of here and find him myself."

A few minutes later a very nervous man poked his head into Rose's room.

"You asked to see me, Mrs. Talbot?"

Sitting up in bed, Rose waved him in.

"What is your full name?"

"Bartholomew Simmons, Mrs. Talbot."

"Tell me about yourself."

The fact that Simmons had a tendency to trip over his words didn't detract from his impressive qualifications. He was twenty-eight years old, had graduated at the top of his class from Harvard Medical School, and was married and had two children.

"I want you to look after me," Rose told him.

Simmons gaped. "That's a great compliment, Mrs. Talbot, but I don't think the supervising doctors would agree—"

"Are you incompetent?"

"Of course not!"

"Then the matter is settled."

"Mrs. Talbot," Simmons asked slowly, "would you mind telling my why you want me to help you with your baby?"

Rose looked him straight in the eye but her voice betrayed her.

"Ever since puberty I have had doctors just like your supervisors, poking and probing me. They look upon a woman's body as either a nuisance or some arcane mystery they alone can decipher. They have a thinly veiled contempt for precisely that gender which constitutes their lucrative practice. They tolerate no contrary opinions from their women patients, expect their instructions to be followed without question, and spend more time reassuring the husband than the mother."

Rose paused, the anger leaving her voice. "I'm not expecting very much from my husband, Simmons. You look like a kind man. That you have children of your own helps, I think. I very much want to trust you because I really don't have anyone else to . . . to tell me what's happening to me and what I'm supposed to be doing."

Simmons reached over and patted Rose's hand. The imperious young woman was gone, replaced by a frightened mother-to-be who had yet to come to terms with her condition. Simmons also discerned a smoldering resentment, and that troubled him greatly.

"I'd be only too happy to attend to you, Mrs. Talbot," he said gently. "Now if you would just lie back I'll examine you myself. Later we'll talk about a diet and the appropriate exercise regime."

"Anything but swimming," Rose said. "I hate swimming." She paused, then added, "I'd be more comfortable if you called me Rose—and I'm awfully sorry I threw up on you."

Rose did not surrender easily to her pregnancy. She thought it a cruel twist of fate that because of the few times Simon had had her, she was now effectively trapped. Rose was certain that Simon would use her condition as an excuse to keep her away from Global.

There was, however, one saving grace: Simon lost all interest in her as a woman. The groping and fondling stopped. Simon created a life that, except for social occasions, did not include Rose. Often he was gone by the time she came down for breakfast and returned home after she had gone to bed. Rose had no illusions that a child would temper or change her husband. He was too old, too set in his ways for that. But his indifference still cut her to the quick, especially when he asked about her latest checkups and what the doctors had to say. All Simon Talbot was concerned about was Rose's giving birth to a healthy male heir. To him, she was nothing more than a vessel.

It was then that Rose discovered something terrible happening to her. All the blame, anger, and frustration she had been directing against Simon began to turn against her baby, as though simply by existing it too had betrayed her. The realization shocked Rose, and she was determined to change her attitude. At first Bartholomew Simmons wasn't keen on his patient's solution, but he too had become concerned about Rose's listlessness and dark moods. He agreed that instead of her rattling about Talbot House, she needed something to keep her occupied.

Turning to the one person she knew she could count on, Rose brought Mary Kirkpatrick up from Lower Broadway. She instructed her secretary to find and hire the best tutors in accounting, business management, and economics. Mary quickly arranged this and more: she rummaged through Global's library and hauled back all of Jehosophat Jefferson's personal notebooks, a day-to-day history of Global Enterprises from its inception as a delivery service to its current status as a nationwide express giant.

"There's more in here than any professor or book can teach you," Mary declared.

Reading her grandfather's accounts, Rose was inclined to agree. But she also insisted on learning modern business principles and techniques. Life, as she had painfully discovered, could change quickly and drastically, and Rose was determined to be prepared.

By her sixth month, a virtual branch office of Global had been set up at Talbot House and Mary became not only a secretary but Rose's lifeline to Lower Broadway. Very few things happened in the company that Mary didn't know about. Rose soon learned that it was the support staff—the secretaries, clerks, typists, salesmen, and managers—who were the root of Global's strength. Executive policy was only as good as the people who ultimately carried it out.

While Rose devoured text after text and spent hours preparing herself for her tutors' ruthless questioning, Mary kept her abreast of what was happening on Lower Broadway, sharing tidbits of employees' gossip. Rose was astounded by how much the average worker knew about the company—where it was strong, which areas needed improvement, which executives were fine people and which were lazy, petty tyrants. Privately, Rose started compiling a list of those men who seemed like dead wood and those who deserved promotions.

In spite of Simon's initial disapproval of and then outright hostility at what she was doing, Rose kept up her hectic schedule until her eighth month, when the demands of pregnancy finally exhausted her. On a sweltering July afternoon, in 1908, when everyone in New York tried to move as slowly as possible, she went into labor. Eleven pain-filled hours later Dr. Simmons delivered a healthy, seven-pound baby boy. Still wearing his bloodstained surgical gown, Simmons wearily passed the good news to a Talbot Railroads messenger who had been pacing nervously in the hall outside the bedroom, telling him to inform Mr. Talbot that both mother and child were doing well.

Two days after the birth of her son, Steven, named after her father, Rose began scouring the employment agencies for nurses and nannies. Once satisfied that Steven was in the best hands, she returned a few weeks later to Lower Broadway.

That year Rose had the opportunity to witness firsthand the difference between business theory and its application in a corporate world that did not play by textbook rules. Several months earlier a rival express organization, the Merchants Consolidated Group, had been formed by a coterie of financiers determined to break Global's monopoly and carve out for themselves a part of that business's immense profits. A rate-slashing war developed, almost ruining

Global. Only the company's powerful network of railroad contractors, led by Talbot Railroads, saved the day. Time and guaranteed delivery were the criteria by which customers chose one express company over another, and the Merchants Consolidated Group's horses and carriages couldn't compete with Global's contracted steam locomotives.

In spite of her cold indifference toward Simon as a husband, Rose had to admit that he was an excellent administrator and was fiercely protective of Global's interests. Putting in hours that exhausted even his most seasoned executives, Simon was able to run both Global Enterprises and Talbot Railroads. The barons of Wall Street showered him with praise, and his personal stock soared.

But if Simon kept that promise to Jehosophat Jefferson, he neglected the other. He refused to give Rose any substantial responsibilities within the company and barely tolerated her suggestions and comments. While she couldn't argue with his success, Rose knew that Simon, not she, was becoming identified as the head of Global. If she didn't stand up for herself, Simon would eventually take over the company by default. A bold, new initiative, based on an idea all her own, had to be taken.

Rose spent endless hours examining projects and ideas her grandfather had left behind. In 1912 she fixed her sights on her target and presented the Global board with a revolutionary new idea: the Global money order. Rose thought its potential was so obvious that the last person she expected objections from was her husband.

"You're crazy to think you can compete with the postal order," Simon told her shortly. "The government will bury you and the investment you make in it."

"Postal orders are issued at a profit," Rose shot back, slapping a thick ledger on his desk. "Look at the figures."

"Of course the Post Office is making money," Simon replied. "It charges a ten-cent commission on every hundred-dollar order. Out of that dime, eight cents are eaten up by administrative and security costs. Not much of a profit."

"Maybe not for the Post Office," Rose argued stubbornly. "But we're a lot more efficient than they are!"

"Remember what happened with Jehosophat's mail-carrying operation? The Post Office undercut him by reducing the cost of their stamp to three cents."

"Our network is far more widespread, not to mention our reputation for on-time delivery. We can beat the Post Office at its own game!"

Nonetheless, Simon's decision prevailed. Global would stay out of the money-order business.

Other proposals Rose brought up were shunted aside. Global was renting office and warehouse space in twenty major cities across the nation and in a host of smaller communities it served. Rose argued vehemently that the country was expanding at such a phenomenal rate that land value couldn't go anywhere but up. The thought of paying rent, which financed someone else's stake, galled her. But again Simon blocked her. Capital was needed to maintain and improve Global's express services, purchase more express cars, hire new employees, and pay its carrying charges to the railroads.

Privately Rose began to wonder if Simon wasn't more interested in keeping Global tightly bound to Talbot Railroads than in seeing the company grow and expand. She took Mary Kirkpatrick aside and shared her reservations. Mary's comment startled her.

"There are some executives who would agree with you," the secretary told her. "Not the senior men. They all think Mr. Talbot is doing a wonderful job."

"Who, then?" Rose pressed her.

"I can't say for sure," Mary replied. "These gentlemen are very careful about what they say, as you can appreciate."

"Find out who they are," Rose urged her. "I need their opinions." She paused. "Later on I may need their help."

Simon Talbot had every reason to be pleased with his lot in life. In spite of Rose's presence at Global he retained a firm hand on the company tiller, effectively blocking what he believed were her harebrained schemes for expansion. He met often with board members and senior executives and made sure they understood where the real power in the company lay. He also moved the Talbot Railroad offices into Global's Lower Broadway building so that he could keep a closer eye on Rose as well as make his presence felt among the employees. Simon knew that many of these remained loyal to the memory of old man Jefferson and had transferred their allegiance to Rose. He was determined to identify them and ease them out of the company. The future he envisioned for Global—or what would be left of the express company—demanded it.

Simon Talbot was also confident that he would gradually nudge his wife out of Global completely. Rose could not continue to be a mother and still spend the time she did at the office. Simon was very proud of the fact that he now had a son. At least in that respect Rose hadn't disappointed him. The rest of his marriage he had already written off as a bad investment. The woman he thought he could mold into the image he wished had proven stubborn and unmanageable. Still, Simon reckoned he could live with that. There was a host of willing young ladies who regularly satisfied his needs. Even if Rose were to find out about them, she was scarcely in a position to complain.

As European monarchies teetered and collapsed and the shadow of war lengthened across the Continent, Rose watched America's industrial might grow with each passing year. Yet, the more time and energy she put into Global, the less her contribution really counted.

Far from being listened to by Simon and his senior executives, Rose was barely tolerated. Everyone expressed polite interest in her ideas. Her suggestions were tabled on agendas and discussed. But nothing she advocated was acted upon. Nothing she had learned seemed to count.

The worst of it was that Rose perceived Global's profits to be on the decline. When she confronted Simon with the figures he laughed them off.

"Of course our investments have eaten into profits, but they'll pay off in the long term. All we have to do is stay on track," Simon chuckled at his own pun. "If you see my point."

"What I see, Simon, is a company which is stagnating," Rose replied angrily. "I see investments being made which pay one or two percent instead of six or seven. I see money being thrown out the window because we're still renting thousands of square feet of space across the country."

"Rose—"

"But what I truly resent is the way you presume that I'm too incompetent to have any say in Global's affairs. You would do well to remember that you don't own a single share in the company. In another two years your custodianship is finished and I take control of Global. It would be nice to have something left to run!"

"And perhaps you will remember that you're my wife and the mother of my child!" Simon shot back. "Long ago I gave up any expectations as far as your wifely duties are concerned. You also seem quite content to hire strangers to look after Steven. Is that how responsible you can be?

"And while we're on the subject of responsibilities," Simon hammered on, "what about our social commitments? We haven't given a dinner party in months. We're total strangers at the theater, opera, and fund-raisers. Our political commitments have been ignored. In short, my dear, thanks to you the Talbot reputation is suffering."

Rose's eyes stung with tears. She couldn't believe Simon would stoop to such an unfair accusation. Rose loved her five-year-old son as deeply as she had loved anyone in her life. She had never forgotten the horrible circumstances under which Steven had been conceived and her resentment during her pregnancy. Everything young mothers experience—the warmth and overwhelming tenderness toward a new life, the joy of the miracle of birth—had been foreign to her. Only after Steven was born had Rose slowly come to appreciate the wonder that had overtaken her.

Simon is so wrong. He doesn't know how deeply I love Steven or what I'll do to protect him.

Rose bridled at the thought that anyone, least of all Simon, would dare to accuse her of indifference toward her son simply because she had chosen to go to work every day. She spent as much time as she could with Steven when she was at home, which was a far cry from the time offered by Simon—gone early in the morning and back long after Steven was in bed. The expensive toys he showered on the boy could never make up for the time his father wouldn't give him.

Nor the time he stole from her! Continually fighting Simon had drained both time and energy that Rose had craved to devote to Steven. Yet, in a way she didn't fully understand, Steven had come to play a large role in her determination to stand up to Simon. The blood of Jeffersons ran in his veins, and the future she created was the one he would inherit.

Listening to her husband, Rose was struck by the realization that an out-and-out conflict between them was inevitable. She shuddered when she imagined her son in the middle of a divorce battle, the horrible things he would see and hear. Worst of all, everything he would be exposed to but would not understand would leave painful scars. Rose asked herself whether wresting control of Global from Simon, at the risk of losing Steven, was worth the prize.

If it comes to that, I'll fight for him too!

— 5 —

Of all the New York clubs, the Metropolitan was the most exclusive. Founded in 1891 by J. P. Morgan after a friend of his had been denied membership to the Union Club, it adhered unswervingly to the four freedoms that governed its brothers: freedom of speech against democracy, freedom of worship of aristocracy, freedom from want of tipping, and freedom from fear of women.

Here, more than anywhere else, Simon Talbot felt at home. The furnishings were comfortable, the service unobtrusive and discreet, the wine cellar the envy of New York. Best of all, when a member told the manager he was "not in," that member could not be reached, even by the most hysterical wife.

"Hello, Simon. Sorry I'm late. Been waiting long?"

Paul Miller was a tall, heavy man with a florid, weather-beaten face that looked as if it belonged to a farmer rather than a successful financier and Talbot Railways board member. In fact, Miller's people, when they were known as Müller, had been farmers in Minnesota. Like Simon Talbot, Miller had accumulated a modest fortune close to home before coming east to turn New

York banking on its ear. He too had been considered an outsider by the eastern establishment. The friendship of the two men was rooted as much in their struggle to become accepted in New York as in common business interests. They were natural allies.

"Good to see you, Paul," Simon said, signaling a waiter. "How about sampling some of this port? They tell me a couple of bottles fell off the back of the truck on its way to Buckingham Palace."

Miller grinned. "I'll even put it on my tab."

"You must have good news," Simon commented.

Miller waited until the waiter had brought him his drink, then leaned forward conspiratorially.

"It's only good if you're ready to act on it. How would you like to cut the Commodore off at the knees?"

The Commodore was Cornelius Vanderbilt. Simon thought the title ostentatious, bestowed upon Vanderbilt only because he had once owned a ferryboat empire. But his dislike of the railroad magnate was founded on more than scorn of his vanity.

In addition to the Pennsylvania Railroad, Vanderbilt had created the New Haven, the Harlem, and the Hudson railroad lines, a powerful triumvirate that operated out of his centerpiece, Grand Central Station. Together with the Harrimans, who owned the Southern Pacific Railroad, Vanderbilt had fought bitterly against the expansion of Talbot Railroads into the Northeast. Simon had been forced to spend millions of dollars challenging Vanderbilt in court as well as buying influence among senators and congressmen. Each step of the way he vowed that one day he would make the Commodore pay.

"Tell me more," Simon suggested casually.

"Friends of mine in Washington have let slip that the government will be carving up new areas of railroad development," Miller said, "mostly in the Midwest grain belt. The territories will be open to bids and the Commodore is going to go after them. He's trying to get a deal done under the table even before there's a public announcement."

"Why should I want them?" asked Simon, already knowing the answer.

"Because whoever controls the Midwest will carry everything the world's richest breadbasket can produce. An exclusive contract, Simon . . ."

Simon pretended to consider. "What kind of money are we talking about?"

Paul Miller scribbled a figure.

"That's very rich," Simon murmured, slowly tearing up the paper. "Very, *very* rich."

"No question," Miller agreed. "Still, you've always wanted to butt heads with Vanderbilt. You won't get a better chance."

Simon silently agreed. Ever since Vanderbilt had tried to poach on his reserve by attempting a takeover of Talbot Railroads several years earlier, Simon had been watching for an opportunity to turn the tables. To deprive the Commodore of something he badly wanted would not only give him immense personal satisfaction; in one stroke Simon Talbot could shed the image of upstart, which, for all his achievements, had dogged him since the day he had arrived in New York.

But the cost . . .

As though he had read Simon Talbot's mind, Paul Miller said quietly, "There's always Global Enterprises in your war chest. . . ."

With her customary diligence Rose prepared for what she believed was an inevitable confrontation with Simon. Together with Mary Kirkpatrick she carefully examined the roster of Global executives, eliminating those who had clearly aligned themselves with Simon, as well as the junior staff members who were likely to bow to pressure from above when it came time to make a choice.

"Doesn't leave much, does it?" Mary Kirkpatrick said, dispirited.

"Just the best," Rose replied. "And that's all I want."

Having made her decision, Rose surprised both Eric Gollant and Hugh O'Neill, the two executives she most wanted on her side, by calling on them at their homes one evening.

Eric Gollant was a trim young man in his mid-thirties with an infectious grin and a mind second to none when it came to numbers. When he opened the front door, he was surrounded by giggling children and an adoring sheep dog.

A junior in Global's accounting department, Gollant's rise through the ranks had been slow, in spite of his obvious talents. Rose saw one reason why that was the case: Gollant was clearly devoted to his family, not at all a company man who sacrificed all his time and energy for his work.

In the privacy of the accountant's den, Rose outlined her proposal.

"In a little over a year I will assume full control of Global," she said. "For various reasons, it's likely that my husband will oppose such a move. I'm aware of the people I cannot count on to stand behind me. I want to know whom I can trust. I'm not saying this support won't have a price. It will—and it could be high. But I won't forget those who choose to help me."

Eric Gollant scratched the sheep dog's head and pushed his wire-rim glasses farther up his nose.

"Mrs. Talbot, I'd grab the chance to work with you. But there's something you should consider."

"And what's that?"

"I'm a Jew," Eric Gollant replied quietly. "It may not be in your best interests to have me on your side."

"My grandfather worked with blacks when it was less than fashionable to do so," Rose replied evenly. "On the West Coast Global's best managers were—and still are—Chinese. I don't care about the color of a man's skin or what religion he practices. All I'm concerned about is whether he's good for Global. And you are."

Eric Gollant studied the intense young woman facing him. Slowly a grin spread across his face.

"Well, if you put it that way, I accept."

Rose's meeting with Hugh O'Neill was quite different. A lean, serious-natured Irishman, O'Neill knew the legal workings of Global Enterprises even better than Rose did and was devoted to the company.

"I'm more than happy to go along with you, Mrs. Talbot," he said, brewing a fine tea he called Irish Cradle.

He passed a cup to Rose and to his wife, a lovely, dark-haired colleen.

"But I also think you're in for more of a fight than you realize. Anyone who sides with you is entitled to know everything that's involved."

"I agree. Which is why I also want you to handle my personal affairs. After all, you'd be much more effective that way."

The lawyer sat back and his eyes twinkled.

"I couldn't agree more, Mrs. Talbot. And in this case I think I can even waive my usual retainer."

By summer of 1914, one year before her twenty-sixth birthday, Rose had her strategy worked out. She was convinced that she could counter any hostile move Simon chose to make against her. However, an event she could not have foreseen and that was destined to change everything overtook her. On June 28, Archduke Ferdinand was assassinated in Sarajevo. Several weeks later, what called itself the civilized world plunged into all-out war.

To millions across the Atlantic, World War I brought untold misery. To American enterprise it was a godsend. Vast quantities of supplies—everything from boots and shoelaces to bullets and barges—found eager, even desperate, customers in the allies united against Germany, principally Britain and France. American factories worked overtime to fulfill the demand, and what was being manufactured had to be shipped. In less than six months Global's business trebled. The very weapon Rose had intended to use against Simon, the company's lethargy, had been neutralized. Listening to Simon report how Global profits were going through the roof was the biggest crow Rose had ever had to swallow.

But it won't last! she told herself fiercely. *None of the basics has changed. The management is riding a wave of sheer, blind luck and doesn't even know it!*

Unfortunately, Rose had to admit that hers was the only such opinion. As far as the business community was concerned, Simon and his team could do no wrong. Frustrated and isolated, Rose lost her meager input into Global's day-to-day operations. None of the senior executives even bothered to pay lip service to her suggestions but deferred everything to Simon. Employees used to dealing with her became embarrassed to act on her instructions, knowing they would be overruled. Men she wanted to see couldn't be reached, and messages were never returned.

Patience had never been her strong suit but Rose managed to rein in her resentment. Short of killing her, Simon could not forestall her twenty-sixth birthday. After that, things would be very different.

The New Year's gala ball at Talbot House was a New York institution. For the occasion Rose wore an Elspeth Phelps evening gown whose diamanté-edged train was cut in one with the bodice while the white tulle bouffant skirt ended in silver-threaded lace. She was determined to make an unforgettable entrance, to make her presence felt among the bankers, financiers, and Washington power brokers, give them a taste of the kind of woman with whom they would very soon be dealing. Judging from the way these men tripped over one another to talk to her, Rose thought she was leaving a very definite impression indeed.

"Quite the party, Rose," Paul Miller said, edging out the undersecretary of commerce and moving into the knot of people around his hostess.

"I'm glad you're enjoying yourself, Paul."

"I think you should entertain more often," Miller commented. "You certainly have the touch."

"I've been very busy at Global," Rose replied sweetly.

Paul Miller laughed. "You're an amazing woman, Rose. How you could be so interested in dull business affairs is beyond me."

"When they're *my* affairs, Paul, I find them very interesting. Now if you'll excuse me . . ."

Such a waste, thought Miller, watching Rose disappear into the crowd.

Ever since he had been introduced to her, Paul Miller had found Rose bewitching. To his eye, she possessed all the qualities a man could possibly want in a woman—grace, flair, and exquisite taste. Unlike Simon Talbot, Miller also appreciated Rose's formidable business acumen and, despite Simon's jokes about her ideas for Global, thought that she had a great deal to offer the company—if Simon would only let her.

Paul Miller was very careful to keep his feelings for Rose to himself. Although it was no secret that the Talbots lived virtually separate lives, Miller wasn't about to jeopardize his business relationship with Simon by trying to seduce his wife. He was a patient man, convinced that, regardless of the social stigma, there was every chance that divorce would split the Talbots. And if that didn't happen, other circumstances might come about that would leave Rose a free woman. Until then, Miller would do his best to have Rose accept him as a friend, someone she could trust and confide in.

Paul Miller checked his watch. It was time to settle some business. To do that he had to get hold of Simon before the New Year's celebrations turned him into a drunken lord.

Paul Miller closed and locked the doors to the study and watched as his host walked a little unsteadily to the sideboard.

"Paul, what's so damn important that it couldn't wait until 1915?" Simon Talbot asked petulantly.

"I warned you that the secretary could make the announcement about the new railroad territories at any moment," Miller said. "Well, he will. First thing Monday morning, January second."

Miller took the drink Talbot handed him but didn't touch it.

"We can't keep our friends in the Capitol waiting any longer, Simon. It's time to shit or get off the pot. I can file the papers in Washington the same time the government makes its announcement. The Commodore won't know what hit him."

Simon Talbot stood with his back to Miller, sipping his whiskey, staring out into the cold deep night filtered with giant drifting snowflakes. Over the last few months there had been secret meetings on yachts drifting in the Potomac, in the private boxes during the running of the Kentucky Derby, at the polo grounds on Long Island. The people involved were some of the highest officials in the government; the amount of money that had changed hands was staggering. Now Simon Talbot found himself on the threshold of something that had once seemed very far away.

In order to raise the money for his bid on the new railroad territories, Simon was prepared to mortgage his holdings to the absolute limit. But it wasn't enough. He was still five million dollars short. He couldn't borrow that money without tipping his hand; neither could he expect even the most trusting banker to advance him the amount without some explanation or security. That left only one alternative.

Simon unlocked the top desk drawer and pulled out two agreements. The first surrendered half of the 51 percent of the Global shares under Simon's custodianship, or a quarter of all shares issued, to Paul Miller. The second detailed Miller's consideration for the shares: five million dollars.

Simon kept telling himself that such an arrangement was a mere formality. As soon as he had the new routes locked up, any bank in Manhattan would throw money at him. He would repay Miller his five million and Miller would then return the Global shares. Rose would never know a thing about it.

"Is there a problem, Simon?" Paul Miller asked softly.

Simon Talbot couldn't answer Miller any more than he could himself. He was far from a saint. In business he employed whatever tactics worked, bending the law, sometimes stepping over the line. To cheat, falsify, bully, intimidate, and threaten were acceptable practices as long as one conducted them like a gentleman and didn't get caught.

But to do this to your own wife . . .

Simon Talbot had no illusions about his marriage being one of mere convenience. As time went on, he found Rose more and more bewildering. He didn't understand her obsession with Global. He couldn't fathom why she refused to be satisfied with being a society figure who could twist New York around her little finger. He was also aware of Rose's intention to take over stewardship of Global on her twenty-sixth birthday. The thought infuriated Simon, because he believed that not only was Rose incapable of running the company, but that she would quickly undo all the work he had put into it and drive it irretrievably into the ground.

And I need Global for this deal. Damn it, Global's ten times the company it was before I came along. I have a right to use what I helped make!

"To hell with her!" Simon muttered, recklessly scribbling his signature on the agreements.

Before the ink was dry the night exploded with cheers, horns, and whistles. Across the city, church bells tolled in the new year. The merriment was lost on Simon. He couldn't rid himself of the feeling that in some profound way things would never be the same again, that for all his foresight and experience he had crossed over into inhospitable, alien territory.

"Cheers, Simon!"

The two men saluted each other. Paul Miller gathered up the documents and reached for his coat.

"Don't tell me you're not staying for supper," Simon objected.

"You've got all the reason in the world to celebrate," Miller replied. "I have to call on a few people and make sure everything is ready for Monday. We've come this far, Simon. I don't want any last-minute surprises."

Simon Talbot fervently agreed with that.

On his way out, Paul Miller succeeded in finding Rose in the crush of guests and apologized for having to leave so soon. He promised to call early in the new year.

Miller drove quickly down a deserted Park Avenue to the Waldorf, left his car with the doorman, and hurried through the lobby to the elevators. As the car rose, he searched his coat pocket for the keys to the seventh-floor suite.

"Good evening, Mr. Miller. Happy New Year."

The young man sitting in the wing chair under the lamp by the window didn't get up.

"The same to you, Mr. Smith."

Miller knew that the man's name wasn't Smith, that this wasn't his suite, and that the registration desk had no record of his being here.

The young man held out his hand and took the papers Miller had brought. Delicately wetting his finger, he began to leaf through the pages, checking the signatures. Paul Miller continued to stand in front of him.

"Everything appears to be in order," the young man said. "Our thanks for expediting this matter."

Paul Miller breathed a sigh of relief. Nothing could stop him now. Within a few weeks, probably less, the Global shares Simon Talbot had signed over would be his, free and clear.

Miller knew all about the "poison pill" clause old man Jefferson had added to the agreement with his son-in-law. Talbot had conveniently forgotten to tell Miller about that and instead had pretended to agonize over whether to cheat Rose. What he never suspected was that Miller had bribed the secretary of Jehosophat Jefferson's lawyer and had had a look at the agreement himself. Simon Talbot had been out to double-cross him. He believed the "poison pill" clause made the shares valueless, so in effect he was giving Miller something that wasn't collateral at all. Miller had another opinion. His lawyers were positive the "poison pill" clause could be broken but only if Simon Talbot was not in a position to contest it. If everything worked the way it was supposed to, he wouldn't be.

Not that Miller wanted Talbot Railroads. He had no interest in the rail business. It was Global he coveted. The 25 percent stake would be enough for now. Once Talbot had been removed from the picture, the rest would follow.

"Mr. Miller, our business is concluded—unless you have something else. . . ."

Paul Miller broke out of his reverie.

"No . . . That is, I was wondering if he—"

" 'He,' Mr. Miller?" There was a cold, sharp edge to the young man's voice.

"I just wanted to wish . . . to say Happy New Year."

"Thank you for the sentiment."

Paul Miller left the suite and stood motionless in the corridor. He saw the latch turn and a moment later heard faint voices.

So the bastard was there all the time!

A few days earlier, Paul Miller, at great expense, had learned that the seventh-floor suite had been leased in perpetuity to one Commodore Cornelius Vanderbilt.

47

- 6 -

The oak swivel chair creaked ominously as Monk McQueen sat back and planted his size 11-D shoes on his desk. He rolled up the typewritten story into a cylinder and addressed his financial editor, Jimmy Pearce, a Princeton graduate who had a bloodhound's nose for business news.

"You're absolutely certain Talbot is going after those new railroad territories?"

"My sources in Washington will call the minute he files," the editor replied.

"It doesn't make sense," McQueen said, scratching his head. "Simon Talbot doesn't have that kind of money."

"He does if he mortgages all his holdings," Pearce chirped.

McQueen shook his head. "That still leaves him a few million short."

"He has a rich wife."

McQueen regarded his editor sourly. "I don't think he'd get anything there."

"Then he went out on the street for it—"

The phone jangled and Pearce snatched it up. A self-satisfied smile appeared on his face.

"That's the confirmation. Talbot got his bid in before the rest, met the criteria, and was awarded the contract."

"What about Vanderbilt? He was in the running too."

"Dunno. In fact, Vanderbilt's people never put in an appearance. Guess they heard what was going on and backed out."

Maybe, McQueen considered. *And maybe not.*

He tossed the story to his editor. "Run with it—as a lead."

Monk McQueen tested the chair's tolerance by leaning back even farther and pondered the ceiling. His gut nagged him that something wasn't right. Everything he knew about Simon Talbot told him that he wasn't the kind of man to risk a lifetime's work—and more—on one roll of the dice. Yet, clearly he had.

"So besides reporting it, what are you going to do?" Monk asked himself aloud.

In the years after Rose's wedding Monk had gone on to graduate from Yale, traveled the width and breadth of Europe, and, upon his father's passing, assumed the helm of his financial newsletter. In three years *Q* had grown from ten pages to a full-fledged financial magazine. Monk scoured the country for the best writers and analysts and created a nationwide network of correspondents. He poured profits into the latest wireless and telephone equipment and expanded his printing facilities. As a result, *Q* magazine was completely independent. Monk gave his reporters a free hand to ferret out news wherever it might be, encouraged investigations of malfeasance in Wall Street and Washington, and printed the results for the world to see. In his short time as publisher Monk had made his share of enemies. But no one could accuse *Q* magazine of bias or favoritism.

In spite of his long hours at the Chelsea brownstones—two buildings combined to create offices and living space for himself—Monk had kept track of Rose Talbot. He attended Jehosophat Jefferson's funeral and sent an enormous bouquet of flowers when Rose gave birth to her son. On both occasions he received a polite thank-you card.

Given his business, which attracted both financial and social gossip like a magnet, Monk knew that all was not well at Talbot House. He was appalled by the way Rose had been excluded from Global's day-to-day operations and cheered her dogged determination to keep her hand in. He watched carefully as Simon guided the company but couldn't fault his business judgment or decisions. By Monk's reckoning, Rose would soon take control of a company worth a great deal more than it had been eight years earlier.

However big a fool Monk thought Simon was, and as much as he wanted Rose to be happy, he vowed that he would never do anything to drive a wedge into the Talbot marriage. Over the years Monk had had his share of women. His mantelpiece was littered with invitations from New York's great houses whose mothers were eager to introduce him to eligible daughters, hoping to sow the seeds of an engagement between shrimp in aspic and crème brûlée. But as much as he enjoyed the company of these young ladies, Monk always kept his distance. He tried to tell himself that he had long ago stopped measuring every female against Rose. Privately, he admitted this was untrue, which was why the mysterious source of Simon Talbot's money continued to nag.

With a sigh Monk picked up the phone and called Global, asking Mary Kirkpatrick if Rose was free to meet him for tea at the Plaza that afternoon.

"Of course I know about Simon's having gotten those territories," Rose said. "Who doesn't?"

She watched with amusement as Monk McQueen struggled with the impossible task of making himself comfortable in the Palm Court's delicate rattan chairs.

Monk's invitation had completely surprised Rose, as had her own pleasant reaction. She had seen Monk occasionally, at parties and other social gatherings, where their paths crossed just long enough to exchange pleasantries. Rose had not forgotten his infatuation with her and was pleased to see that it was still alive. There weren't many like him, Rose thought, who were gentle and genuinely caring.

"Don't tell me you wanted to see me for some inside information on Simon's coup," Rose said, playing the coquette.

Her teasing flew right over Monk's head.

"No, not at all," he replied hastily. "It's just that . . . well, there's something I don't understand."

"What's that?" Rose asked, enjoying the strains of the quartet in the background.

"Where Simon got the money," Monk replied bluntly. "You're aware that he must have mortgaged Talbot Railroads to the hilt."

Rose frowned. "No, I didn't know that."

"And that even so he would have been five million dollars short."

Rose put down her teacup and leaned forward.

"What are you really asking, Monk?"

Monk McQueen fidgeted in his seat, wishing he could disappear into the Court's rich foliage of palm trees and giant ferns.

"Did Simon come to you for the money?" he blurted. "Did he use Global funds to finance the balance of the transaction?"

Rose threw back her head and laughed. "Of course not! Simon couldn't do that because of the poison pill."

"Poison pill?"

Rose bit her lip, realizing she had said too much.

"As long as you promise me this is in strict confidence," she warned him. "Jefferson family affairs are none of the public's business."

"You have my word."

Rose explained the provisions her grandfather had laid down separating Global from Talbot Railroads and the papers Simon had signed to that effect.

"So you see, there's no way Simon could have dipped into the company funds," Rose concluded.

"I'm sorry," Monk said, shaking his head. "It was just one of those things that didn't add up. I didn't mean to upset you. . . ."

Rose patted his hand. "No harm done. In fact I thoroughly enjoyed myself. I'd very much like for us to do this again."

Monk beamed.

"Mr. McQueen!"

All across the Court heads turned as a young man, scarf and coattails flying, barged through the tables. Monk struggled out of his chair to greet Jimmy Pearce.

"Jimmy, what the hell—"

"It's all over the Street, Mr. McQueen," the editor gasped. "The Commodore is making a run at Talbot Railroads—the lines, warehouses, rolling stock, everything!"

Monk gripped him by the shoulders. "Are you sure?"

The young man gulped. "Positive!"

"Monk . . ." Rose began.

Rose's assurances sounded hollow to Monk but he refused to alarm Rose until he had proof of his suspicions.

"Find out where Talbot got that five million!" he whispered to his editor. "I don't care what it takes. I want to know and I want documentation. Drop everything else, take whoever you need from the office. Go!"

Monk turned back to Rose.

"I think you'd better return to Global," he suggested quietly. "Call your lawyers and get them to go over your grandfather's codicil."

"Why?"

"Just a precaution, Rose, that's all." Monk paused. "Do you know where Simon is right now?"

"In Washington. He left yesterday."

Monk McQueen smiled tightly. He knew for a fact that Simon Talbot was nowhere near the nation's capital.

"Are you sure your wife thinks you're in Washington?"

Marie Jackson, born Anna Maria Jaunich, put the question to her reflection in the full-length mirror. She wet her finger with perfume and ran it between her naked breasts, across a smooth, supple belly, and underneath her silk underpants. When she touched herself she found she was dry.

It isn't the first time, she reminded herself, suppressing a sigh. She shifted her attention to the man lying on the bed behind her, propped up by over-stuffed pillows.

When Marie had first met Simon Talbot two years ago, at the Flamingo Club, she had thought him one of the handsomest men she had ever seen. Just imagining what he looked like without his clothes had been enough to make her wet. Marie recalled that she hadn't been disappointed. But she quickly learned that Simon was a demanding, ruthless lover. Having installed her as his mistress, he expected her to be available to him whenever he wanted her.

Careful not to draw his attention, Marie stroked herself until she was moist. No sense breaking any illusions. Simon Talbot believed that all he had to do was touch her and she'd be panting. Fine. He wasn't the first man whose fantasy she had indulged. But he was the richest and most generous. The allowance he gave her had almost bought her the dream of opening her own place. Marie had calculated that she would need to stay with Simon Talbot another six months. By then she would have saved enough and could begin

51

gradually to wind down their relationship. If she was careful, Simon wouldn't prove difficult. On the contrary, Marie was counting on his help later on, when she would need a good word with police captains, liquor inspectors, and the bank.

Marie took one last look at her ruby-red lips ("bee-stung lips" some men called them), perfectly painted eyebrows that accented her jade-green eyes, gave a light toss to her chestnut ringlets, and walked slowly toward the bed.

"You're sure your wife doesn't know?" she teased, running her fingers through the pelt on Simon's chest.

Simon reached out and cupped one pear-shaped breast, his thick fingers squeezing the nipple.

"I'm sure," he said lazily, drinking in the sight of her. "What's bothering you? You've never mentioned Rose before."

"I'm just being a silly girl," said Marie. "Don't you fret, honey. I'm going to look after my daddy. . . ."

Simon grunted with pleasure as Marie's hand at last reached its goal.

Women! he thought sourly. Still, he had to admit that Marie was a cut above the rest. She made no bones about what she wanted and expected, and what she was prepared to offer in return.

The arrangement suited Simon perfectly. The Aerie in upstate New York was registered as a hunting club, guaranteeing that women, defined as wives, would never be admitted. Other ladies were most welcome, which was what the founding fathers had had in mind in the first place. At the Aerie, service and discretion were bought and royally paid for.

Which was why Simon Talbot didn't immediately register the soft but insistent knocking on the door to his suite until Marie's bobbing head almost brought him to climax.

"Son of a bitch!"

Simon pushed away the startled Marie and leaped out of bed.

"What the hell do you want?" he yelled, sliding back the bolt, his eyes burning into the face of a terrified porter.

"There's someone to see you, sir," the porter replied timorously.

"Who is it?"

"A Mr. McQueen, sir."

"Honey, is anything wrong?" Marie called from the bed.

"Shut up!"

Simon grabbed his robe, whipped the belt around his waist, and threw open the door. Barefooted, he brushed by the porter and was heading for the staircase when he saw Monk McQueen standing on the landing.

"Good evening, Simon," Monk said civilly.

"You've got a lot of explaining to do!" Simon warned.

Monk stood his ground before the older man, wondering if he pitied Simon Talbot more than he was disgusted by him.

"So do you, Simon," Monk said. "You might begin by telling me what you know about Vanderbilt's raid on your railroad holdings. For the record, of course."

News of the Commodore's lightning strike on Talbot Railroads jolted the financial community out of its post–New Year's Eve hangover. Simon returned to Lower Broadway to find his offices besieged by reporters. It took a contingent of burly New York policemen to escort him safely through the shouting mob. Simon quickly discovered that his being back didn't make matters any better.

His somber lawyers outlined the situation: in spite of Simon's secretiveness, Vanderbilt had somehow learned just how heavily the Talbot interests had been mortgaged. With Simon committed to make good on his bid with cash, Vanderbilt had seized the opportunity. He had contacted the banks holding the assets—the profitable Talbot lines—and was offering to buy them up.

"The banks will never sell!" Simon declared. "They wouldn't dare undercut me."

"They will if you don't meet the repayment schedule," the senior lawyer advised him. "We can honor our obligations as long as the government lets us start building those lines right away. Which means the Senate has to override those land claims the settlers and Indians have filed."

"It will," Simon said confidently. "Senator Ridgemount of Minnesota has promised to deliver."

The lawyers raised a collective eyebrow at that. No one had been told of that particular deal. At this point, no one wanted to know the details, either.

Three days later, Senator Mathias Ridgemount from the Ten Thousand Lakes state announced to the chamber his retirement, pleading ill health. Immediately upon his resignation from the chair, the subcommittee on transportation voted unanimously to study further the question of railroad expansion in the Midwest and served a temporary injunction on Talbot Railroads, preventing it from beginning work on the new lines.

"You told me—promised me—that Ridgemount was bought and paid for!" Simon Talbot raged. "What the hell happened?"

"He retired, Simon, that's what happened!" Paul Miller replied acidly. "Or don't you read the papers?"

"Then you had better *un*retire him! Or find someone else to steer that committee into giving us the green light!"

"There isn't anyone else." Miller sighed. "You know that. Ridgemount was our lock on the committee. No one else has his muscle."

"Look, Paul," Simon said, his tone threatening. "The banks came in on this because of the repayment schedule. I agreed to it because you promised me I could start building right away. Any delays and I can't meet the schedule. You know that. The banks know that. Vanderbilt *certainly* knows that."

"You have to persuade the banks to restructure the payment schedule," Miller replied. "It's as simple as that."

"If it's that simple, you do it!" Simon exploded. "I goddamn moved heaven and earth to get the banks to go along. Now, when I need more time, they get on their Yankee high horse and tell me no. You have a vested interest in this, Paul. It's *your* turn to talk to them!"

"All right," Miller said, holding up his hands in surrender. "I'll do what I can."

What Paul Miller ended up doing was having a first-class lunch the following afternoon in the suite on the seventh floor of the Waldorf.

Rose had never seen this side of her husband. To her Simon had always been a man in charge of his destiny. In a few short weeks this image crumbled, replaced by that of a man who had aged twenty years, barricaded himself in his office like a thief, and needed police escorts to see him safely from home to work. Under constant hounding from reporters and ominous silence from the banks, Simon quickly lost his southern charm and manners. He flew into a rage at the slightest real or imagined wrong. The servants at Talbot House quickly learned to walk on tiptoe.

As she watched the forces around Simon tighten their grip, Rose wondered if he was now regretting the road he had allowed their marriage to take. When she looked inside herself Rose didn't see the tiniest spark of emotion for her husband. His opposition to her dreams and needs had bled her dry. And now she was his last hope.

They were sitting opposite each other at the long "family" dining table, eight feet of brilliantly polished cherrywood. It was the first time Simon had been home for dinner since Vanderbilt had dropped his bombshell. He had lost a great deal of weight and his clothes hung on him as they would on a scarecrow. Rose noticed that his hand trembled whenever he reached for his wineglass.

After the service had been cleared away Simon said, "You know what's happened, don't you?"

Before Rose could reply, he answered his own question: "Of course you do."

Rose could tell he was trying hard to keep the bitterness from his voice—and failing.

"Do I have to explain the situation to you, Rose?" Simon asked.

"No."

Rose could have added that Hugh O'Neill, now in charge of Global's legal division, was continually monitoring the debacle unfolding at Talbot Railroads. Together with other lawyers he had scrutinized Jehosophat Jefferson's "poison pill" clause and declared it ironclad. If Simon wanted to use Global assets to fight Vanderbilt he had no choice but to go through Rose.

"Since that's the case I may as well come right to the point," Simon said. "I need to borrow money from Global. A short-term loan, nothing more, just to cover the repayment schedule."

"It would take only one payment to wipe out the company's profits," Rose pointed out. "What happens after that?"

"By then I'll be building the lines."

"You can't guarantee that, Simon. The Senate subcommittee can hold up its recommendation indefinitely, and you've lost your clout with them."

She watched him drink the last inch of burgundy. The crystal pealed out as he set down the glass sharply.

"Then I want to pledge Global stock. The banks will accept it."

Anger welled up in Rose. "It's not a question of whether they'll accept it or not."

"Of course not," Simon replied. "The issue is whether you'll sign it over." He paused. "Will you?"

Even though she'd known Simon would ask, Rose was furious. After the way he had treated her, he had no right even to suggest such a thing. Yet, the sense of obligation that had been drilled into her—that a wife is supposed to defer to her husband, obediently follow his lead—lingered. Rose became more angry with herself than with Simon.

"No, Simon. I will not allow you to commit Global to the banks."

Simon must have been expecting as much because he showed no surprise.

"If you don't, I could be ruined."

"And if I do, *everything* could be ruined. Don't try to practice emotional blackmail on me, Simon. Not after all this time. I'm not going to risk the future, mine and Steven's"—she couldn't bring herself to say "ours"— "because you made a bad business decision."

Simon looked at her for a very long time, then without a word left the table. Rose felt her body tremble and go limp, as though she had finally gotten rid of a millstone she had been carrying too long. She had no idea what Simon would do now. Maybe there was family money he hadn't told her about. Perhaps selling off a fraction of Talbot Railroads would buy him the time he needed. Rose believed that either way, the future was out of her hands and beyond Simon's grasp as well.

As the deadline for the first repayment drew near, the financial community held its collective breath. Simon Talbot virtually disappeared from public view. Rumors as to his whereabouts and doings flew up and down Wall Street. There was speculation about a last-minute loan from Europe, the creation of a consortium bankrolled by wealthy South Americans, even a meeting with the president to plead for White House intervention. In the lounges of private clubs, members debated the subject and made gentlemen's bets on whether Simon Talbot would survive Valentine's Day, 1915.

After Paul Miller had quietly placed his own wager he decided it was time to tilt the odds in his favor. He called Monk McQueen and invited him to lunch at the Metropolitan Club.

"I don't suppose you've seen any more of Simon than anyone else has," Miller said casually.

"No," Monk replied. "Should I have?"

"Not at all. Just wondering. Your phones must be ringing off the hook with tips and rumors."

Monk smiled politely. It wasn't like Paul Miller to go fishing. As a board member of Talbot Railroads he should have known where his president and chairman was every minute of the day during the crisis.

"Obviously you don't have a clue where Simon might be," Miller said. "No harm in asking, though. I don't have to tell you a lot of people are getting very nervous."

"Including you, Mr. Miller."

"Please, call me Paul. Frankly, yes. I've stood by Simon as long as possible, longer than financial prudence would dictate. I thought he might be able to pull a rabbit out of the hat, but . . ."

"Are you saying that Simon won't be able to meet his obligations to the banks?"

"It's possible he might," Miller conceded. "And I truly hope he does. However, I have to look at the long term."

In other words, you don't want to be associated with a potential loser and bankrupt.

"So I've decided to resign from the board." Miller dropped an envelope on the cocktail table. "Effective immediately."

Monk was shocked. "Aren't you jumping the gun?"

"I think of it as protecting my interests."

"If you're resigning, what interests do you have left?"

Miller smiled, his eyes gleaming like cold hard buttons.

"Substantial ones. Anyone who can do arithmetic knows Simon was short five million on his bid for the railroad territories and that he managed to make that up."

Monk stirred uneasily, waiting for Miller to drop the other shoe.

"He got that money from me."

Monk was thoroughly puzzled now. "If that's the case, then why are you pulling out? The loan is obviously unsecured. Your only chance of getting your money back lies with Simon's meeting his obligations."

"Why would you presume the loan is unsecured?" Miller asked softly. "In fact, it isn't."

He added a sheaf of papers to the envelope on the table. "Go ahead, read it."

Monk's curiosity became incredulity as he scanned the pages: in return for the five-million-dollar loan, Simon Talbot had given Paul Miller half the Global stock he held in custodianship for Rose.

"He had no right to do that!"

"I beg your pardon?" Miller said sharply.

Monk cursed his indiscretion. "Nothing," he muttered. "I don't see how—"

"No," Miller interrupted, bearing down on him. "You said Simon had no right. What do you mean by that? He swore he had complete control of the stock. Are you saying he lied to me, took the money under false pretenses?"

"I can't comment on that," Monk replied.

Miller seemed not to have heard him. "Because if that's the case, I'm going to sue Simon Talbot. If it turns out he's bare-assed, then, if I have to, I'll fight to hold on to the stock."

Monk was sickened by the Pandora's box he had accidentally opened. Yet he detected a false note; Miller sounded a little too smug.

Did he know from the very beginning that Simon never had the authority to pledge the stock?

"Monk, I'm afraid I have to get to the bottom of this," Miller said, his expression suitably grim. "Feel free to print what we've talked about. You have the supporting documentation. I'll be in touch as soon as I can."

Monk watched the financier hurry off, the perfect image of an innocent man who had suddenly realized he might have been duped. That too bothered him, because Paul Miller was neither innocent nor anybody's fool.

Monk pushed this twisted skein to the back of his mind. The crucial thing was to tell Rose immediately that Simon had betrayed her. Then he would have to decide whether to print the gist of his conversation with Paul Miller—and ruin Simon Talbot in the process.

* * *

57

Simon Talbot arrived home late that night. He shed his beaver-collared overcoat and made himself comfortable in front of the fireplace in his library. The crackling of dry birch soothed him as much as the first sip of a vintage Bordeaux.

Simon opened the copy of Q magazine on his lap. The issue was devoted entirely to the raid on Talbot Railroads, its difficulties with the banks, and the imminent scandal concerning Simon's illegal assignment of Global shares. Simon had read the story a dozen times and wondered why he was punishing himself like this.

Without taking his eyes off the page Simon clipped and prepared a cigar for himself. He had to admit that Monk McQueen had exercised judicious restraint in his reporting. Still, the facts were damning enough. Paul Miller's comments about his resignation were there, along with the text of the agreement Simon had signed. Next came a short interview with Rose, who vehemently denied that Simon had had any right to enter into such a bargain. As proof, Rose had given Q the text of the "poison pill" clause. Simon's written acknowledgment of the clause and promise to act only as custodian of Rose's fortune was also reproduced.

The Manhattan district attorney added his two cents' worth, stating that if Mr. Talbot could not satisfactorily explain what had happened, fraud and embezzlement charges would have to be considered. Meanwhile, lawyers for Paul Miller announced their intentions to subpoena all Jefferson estate papers relating to the will and launch a suit for the recovery of Miller's five million dollars. They were also petitioning the courts to hold the 25 percent of Global shares in trust, pending the outcome of the district attorney's investigation.

Through Hugh O'Neill, Rose counterattacked, stating that Miller had no claim on the shares.

Simon Talbot drew deeply on his cigar and closed his eyes. It had taken him a long time to see the truth but now it appeared clear and simple: Paul Miller had betrayed him.

At first Simon thought that Miller, having discovered the "poison pill" clause Simon never mentioned, had bolted. But in the interview with Q magazine Miller hadn't come across as a frightened, cheated man. Somehow he'd known about the "poison pill" all along but had been waiting for just the right moment to express his surprise about it. If he had been truly outraged, surely he would have confronted Simon and demanded an explanation.

And who would benefit by that? Certainly not Paul Miller, who stood to lose his five million if Simon went bankrupt. Only Vanderbilt would gain. With Simon already facing financial ruin, a scandal like this would utterly destroy him, leaving Talbot Railroads open prey for the Commodore to feast on.

No, Simon corrected himself. *That isn't quite right*. Others besides Vanderbilt would benefit: those the Commodore had coerced with threats or bought
with promises of rewards. Simon wondered how many pieces of silver Miller
had settled for. Certainly much more than thirty.

A slight draft penetrated the cracks in the windowsills. Simon poked the logs,
sending a shower of sparks up the chimney. Settling back, he asked himself if,
had he the chance, he would do anything differently. No. Not one thing. He
could never have been satisfied living in the South with its tattered dreams of
glory and graciousness. His energies had been too strong, his vision too great.
But for all the changes he had forced upon himself, he had to admit that at
heart he remained a son of the South. A Yankee would declare bankruptcy,
brush off the stigma of failure, and start again. Simon had never been a Yankee
and never would be. He had come in as an outsider and, as Rose and the
eastern bankers had made so clear, remained one. They would never give him
a second chance.

"Father . . . ?"

Simon was startled to see his seven-year-old son standing in the doorway,
barefoot, dressed in pajamas covered with pictures of cowboys chasing Indians.
He looked very fragile, rubbing his enormous dark eyes with small sturdy fists,
his hair tousled from sleep. Simon beckoned to him and Steven rushed
forward, throwing his arms around his father's neck.

A bitter regret twisted Simon's heart. He had never been overwhelmed by
children of his own, as most men were. He remembered the first time he had
held Steven, a tiny, squirming, red-faced human being screaming at the top of
his lungs. The noise and smell had been horrible and Simon had abruptly
handed his son back to the nurse.

Simon told himself it wasn't because he didn't love his son. In his own silent,
distant way, he had always been working for his son. His own father had left
him a legacy so inbred and worm-eaten that nothing could ever be built upon
it. Simon had sworn he would create something Steven would be proud to
continue.

For years Simon had been waiting for Steven to grow up so that he could
explain all this and much more to him. Now, just as the moment was almost at
hand, he had nothing left but his dreams. Nor any way to say how terribly sorry
he was . . .

Steven Talbot had no way of knowing about the remorse his father was
struggling with. Ever since he could remember, Steven had carried a burning
love for his father. In his eyes Simon was a giant, who filled a room when he
came into it, to whom other people bowed, who was like a king, granting favors
or handing out punishment. Steven's favorite pastime had been to squirrel into

his father's study and sit there, drinking in all the things that were a part of him, rejoicing in the smells of tobacco, leather, and port, dreaming of the day he could share this special world.

But as Steven grew older reality began to chip away at his fantasy. Even in a home as large as Talbot House, voices carried. Steven became the consummate spy, finding hiding places from which he could watch his parents quarrel. He couldn't understand why his mother kept arguing with his father because the thought that his father could be wrong never crossed his mind. When he listened to the fights he wanted so much to rush to his father's defense. Yet, his courage always deserted him, and so his love was buried a little more deeply after each quarrel. Until Steven came to hate his mother.

"Way past your bedtime, isn't it, sport?" Simon murmured.

Steven clung fiercely to his father.

"I want to be with you, Father."

"You'll always be with me. You're my son and you'll do all the things I was never able to finish. The world will be proud of you, son. It will know your name."

Gently Simon pried his son's arms from around his neck and put him down. "Do you want me to come and tuck you in?"

Steven shook his head. "That's okay. I'll go by myself," he said manfully.

Simon leaned forward and kissed his son on the forehead. He watched as Steven hesitantly raised his hand.

"Goodbye, Father."

Steven Talbot heard the click of the door closing. He stood motionless in the hallway, scarcely daring to breathe. Then he knelt and pressed one eye against the keyhole. The brass felt cold against his skin.

His father had gotten out of his chair and was standing in front of the gun cabinet. He unlocked the glass doors and removed a beautiful gun with two long barrels and a polished stock. He broke the barrels and slipped in two cartridges. Then he returned to his chair.

Steven didn't know what to make of it. He had always been told that guns were never to be loaded until they were ready to be fired. Now his father was taking off his right shoe. He removed his sock, rested the gun butt against the floor, and curled his toe around the trigger. Then he put both barrels in his mouth.

The blast was deafening and Steven flew away from the keyhole as though struck by the shot. By the time his mother and the servants came running he was on his feet again, standing in front of the door like a statue. He thought it was what his father would have expected of him.

— 7 —

I still can't believe it. . . .

Beyond the drawing room window Rose could see mounted policemen keeping back the crowds of reporters. When she heard the chimes of the mantelpiece clock she was struck by the thought that somewhere in the last two hours she had lost an entire world.

The door opened and Dr. Henry Wright emerged.

"How is he, Henry?" Rose asked, her voice trembling.

Wright was a man of generous girth whose stern disposition belied his gentleness with children. With them he was a miracle-worker.

"He's asleep," the physician rumbled. "I've given him a strong enough sedative so that he'll rest well into the morning. The nurse will be with him every minute."

"Thank God," Rose murmured.

Ever since the nightmare had occurred, Rose's overwhelming concern had been for Steven. Her thoughts were fixed on that instant when, running down the hall, she saw Steven standing motionless in front of the door to Simon's library. As soon as Rose threw the door open and saw her husband's body, with half his head blown away, she clamped her hand over Steven's eyes. The boy immediately spun away and glared at her.

"I know what Father did!" he screamed. "You made him do it! You killed him!"

Rose was so horrified by her son's accusation that she just stared after him as he ran off. Later, when Henry Wright arrived, Steven refused to unlock the door to his bedroom until the physician promised him his mother wouldn't come in.

"He's suffered a terrible shock," Wright was saying. "The truth is he *was* peeking through the keyhole and saw Simon shoot himself. His observations are so in keeping with what the police say happened that I have to believe him."

Rose struggled to keep her tears in check. "What do I do now?"

"I recommend round-the-clock observation by nurses. He'll undoubtedly have very bad nightmares for some time." Wright paused. "We have no way of judging the severity of the trauma. I've seen cases in which children have recovered from a shock like this almost immediately. Others take much longer. . . ."

Rose knew he was holding back. "What else, Henry?"

"In the worst cases, the child only appears to have recovered. That is, for years he behaves quite normally. Then, usually in adolescence, there are inexplicable headaches—severe ones—or other physical manifestations that have nothing to do with bodily health. It's the mind trying to come to terms with a long-buried but never-forgotten pain."

Rose had never hated Simon more than she did at that moment. The way he had chosen to face adversity had been cowardly. But to have tried to punish her by using their son was beyond forgiveness.

But what if you had acted differently? a quiet voice suggested. *Perhaps if you had agreed to help Simon, none of this would have happened. . . .*

Remorse cut Rose to the quick. Maybe she shouldn't have refused Simon so quickly. Perhaps there had been a way to help him without losing her newly found grip on the company.

That's what you want to think, because of what Steven's been through. But there isn't anything else you could have done. If you had given Simon what he wanted, you would have lost your one chance to get Global back. In the end you would have perpetuated your own misery. . . .

"Somehow I'll make it up to him," Rose said aloud.

Wright shot her a curious look. "What's that?"

"I said somehow I'm going to make this up to Steven."

The physician hesitated. "I'm sure you will, Rose, but—"

"Over time, Henry. I know."

By breakfast that morning the whole city had heard the grisly details of Simon Talbot's suicide. New York society's outrage over Simon's flagrant breach of trust concerning Rose's share of Global immediately faded. The press followed suit, running eulogies to Simon's civic achievements, patronage of the arts, and bequests to charity. Vanderbilt's lawyers and bankers dropped their threats, expressed suitably moving public condolences, then quietly proceeded to dismember Talbot Railroads. *By the time they and the tax department are through,* Rose thought, *a lifetime's work will have been picked clean, leaving the heirs almost nothing at all.*

Because of the public's insatiable, lurid curiosity, Rose barricaded herself in Talbot House. The police posted a twenty-four-hour guard to keep the press and onlookers at bay, allowing only Global executives and the doctors through.

Those who thought kindly of her mistook Rose's silence for grief and lauded her courage. Others who were not so charitable openly called her a cold-hearted bitch. Rose didn't care. She closed off the entire world because she needed time to think, to understand how Simon's death had affected her. No one else, just her.

Simon had cheated her of love, she knew that now. When she married, she didn't know what love could be. She was too young. She had wanted him to show her everything—tenderness and passion, the joy of two people sharing, learning from each other. But there was no room in his heart for that. Instead he had cheated her of trust . . . and hope.

When the tears finally came they were born of fear, not grief. Rose was terrified of the abyss of loneliness she now faced, and certain that in it she saw the rest of her life.

For the first time in memory Rose acknowledged that she needed somebody to help her. The hours seemed out of control, with hundreds of details demanding her attention. She was frantic about Steven and worried sick about what would happen to Global in the wake of Talbot Railroad's demise.

Rose was at her wit's end when, four days after Simon's death, Franklin Jefferson finally arrived at Talbot House from a fishing trip in Canada. The minute he walked through the doors Rose caught and held on to him tightly, reassuring herself that he wasn't a mirage.

"I need you here, Franklin," she said. "I can't handle everything by myself. I'll teach you everything you need to know about Global. Grandfather left it to both of us. Now we must live up to our responsibilities."

Because he loved his sister, because he mistook her intensity and fierce determination as a measure of her sorrow, Franklin, who had always been careful to keep Global at arm's length, said, "Yes."

Until the death of Simon Talbot, Franklin Jefferson had led a blessed, carefree life. Just shy of his nineteenth birthday, he was a tall, loose-limbed man who moved with the grace of a natural athlete. He had retained the white-blond hair of his boyhood and his hazel eyes still sparkled with mischievousness and wit. Franklin had been one of those rare children whose sunny disposition had not been eroded by the trials and tribulations of adolescence. When he looked upon the world he saw only its beauty and the promise of everything wonderful within it. In return, the world smiled upon such innocence and protected it.

While Rose had been waging her own private war in the trenches of Lower Broadway, Franklin graduated from a prestigious private boarding school, St. Clement's, and moved on to Yale. His money allowed him to indulge himself and his friends in a variety of activities, from polo to sailing. A diligent student, he was naturally attracted to the humanities and discovered a facility for languages. By his second year Franklin was fluent in both Spanish and French and immersing himself in that potluck supper called European History.

Franklin visited Europe twice before the outbreak of the war. Each time he fell more in love with the Continent, and with the girls who made pilgrimages with him to the great cathedrals of France, the museums of Italy, and the ruins of Greece. Back at Yale his professors were surprised and impressed at the quality of his essays. They honed his style and encouraged his explorations. In their eyes young Jefferson showed the markings of an academic diamond in the rough.

As for Franklin, he had no idea what he wanted to do with his life, only that Global would play no part in it. He had begun traveling at an age when youth sees the world through a poet's eye. Fed by an insatiable curiosity, Franklin looked upon his life as one long, discovery-filled journey in which there was so much to learn that every minute was precious. But he never shared these feelings with anyone, fearing that one way or another, Rose would find out about them.

As much as he loved Rose and as often as he visited her, Franklin had been very careful not to become enmeshed in the twisted skein of the lives at Talbot House. To him it was a matter of self-preservation. If he allowed himself to come too close, Rose would try to mold him in order to prepare him for his responsibilities at Global, making what he had to do all the more difficult.

Franklin knew that the day would come when he'd have to tell Rose that he had absolutely no interest in Global. As far as he was concerned, she could have his share anytime she wanted. It would be difficult, and he would need more resolve than he had now in order not to buckle under the force of her disappointment and persuasive arguments. But with Simon's death, that time had been denied him. When he felt his sister trembling in his arms, Franklin was terribly afraid that the moment of his declaration had slipped away, possibly forever.

On a cold, clear February morning Rose finally emerged from Talbot House. With Franklin beside her and her arm around Steven, she made her way through a phalanx of police toward the Silver Ghost for the drive to St. Patrick's Cathedral.

"Is Father with the angels, Mommy?" Steven asked in a low solemn voice.

Rose squeezed his hand. For days Steven had barricaded himself behind a wall of silence. Then, miraculously, he began to talk and in a short time seemed completely normal. Rose was as overjoyed as the doctors were cautious.

"Yes, darling, he's with the angels," Rose said. "Are you all right?"

Steven nodded. "You did love him, didn't you, Mother?"

Rose swallowed hard. "Of course I did, darling."

Steven looked straight ahead. Since his father's death he had felt himself changing. He couldn't say how or why but he was sure something about him was different. At first, when the doctors kept asking him all those stupid questions, he refused to answer. But when he realized that this only made them more persistent he began to talk and quickly grasped what it was they wanted to hear. Steven thought their questions about how much he loved his father, what they had done together, and whether he thought his parents were happy, were boring. But he replied to each one carefully, and he discovered that the more he talked, the happier the doctors were and the shorter the sessions became.

This experience taught Steven a great deal about the gullibility of adults. Whenever he fooled either the doctors or his mother, he felt a tremendous power within him that he thought could get him anything he wanted. Right now Steven had to make his mother believe he had never meant those things he had said to her. She must never suspect how much he hated her.

"Are you sure you're all right, darling?" Rose asked as the car approached the cathedral.

Steven looked up at her and smiled. "Yes, Mother."

Rose breathed a sigh of relief. She was so proud of her son. In his new suit, his black hair parted in the center and eyes looking straight ahead, he appeared more a little man than a child. Looking at him, she was convinced that Steven was both the past and the future, a reflection of Jehosophat Jefferson and the model of a man to whom she would leave a mighty empire. Her son would be worthy of everything she did for him.

The memorial service was brief. At its conclusion Rose accepted the condolences of New York's Four Hundred, the financial community, and government leaders. She bore the silent hostility the Talbot relations had brought with them and was relieved when the hearse and its retinue of horse-drawn carriages finally disappeared down Fifth Avenue. In keeping with her agreement with the Talbots, Simon's final resting place would not be Dunescrag. Instead, the Talbots would take their son home to the South.

"Rose, it's time to go."

Rose looked up to see Monk McQueen towering over her, his moon face heavy with sorrow. She squeezed his hand and whispered, "Thank you."

Shepherding Steven ahead of her, Rose walked in the shadow of her brother and Monk. At the car she turned to Franklin.

"Will you take Steven home?"

"Sure, but—"

Rose laid a hand on his arm. "I have to go to the office."

Franklin couldn't hide his astonishment and was about to protest when he caught Monk's warning glance.

"I'll drive you to Broadway," McQueen said.

* * *

65

Since most of the employees had been given the day off to attend the funeral, Global Enterprises was all but deserted. But Hugh O'Neill and Eric Gollant, who had left the funeral service earlier, were already there, along with a third man, Isaiah Phipps, Simon's personal lawyer.

"Hello, Isaiah, thank you for coming," Rose said.

The grizzled attorney, dressed in a black morning coat, offered her a frosty smile.

"Simon was a good friend," he said. "I shall miss him."

If he was such a good friend, why didn't you stop him from risking a lifetime's work?

Instead Rose said, "Is it safe to assume there aren't any further surprises?"

"Simon's will is quite straightforward. Aside from a few holdings that go to Steven and other heirs, you are left with Talbot House. With the railroad gone there's really nothing else."

"I don't agree, Isaiah. There's the matter of Paul Miller's claim on my shares. What do we do about that?"

"There's nothing *I* can do," Phipps replied. "It was a matter between Simon and Paul Miller."

"You mean to say you let your client—and friend—sign a five-million-dollar pledge without checking it?" Hugh O'Neill demanded.

"As you're well aware, sir, a lawyer isn't always privy to his client's actions. In this case I'll swear on a stack of Bibles that I didn't know a thing about this contract."

"Let me see if I understand this," Rose said. "My husband pledged shares that did not belong to him. In so doing he broke his contract with my grandfather. Now Simon is dead. Vanderbilt has what used to be Simon's assets. Miller is left holding twenty-five percent of my company, which he says he won't return without a fight. Isaiah, are you telling me I may have to buy back what is already mine?"

"Whether your grandfather's 'poison pill' clause is enforceable may be hard to determine," Phipps reflected. "It could take months, even years, for a judge or jury to reach a decision. After all, Simon was responsible for Global at the time. He made tremendous profits for the company, and was able to do so precisely because he had a free hand. In fact, your own people will tell you that Global prospered on the coattails of Talbot Railroads. So there was a connection—some would argue a very strong one—between the two companies that could negate the 'poison pill' clause."

Rose glanced at Hugh O'Neill.

"It's always possible," the Irishman said grudgingly. "We'd fight, and undoubtedly win, but it would take time."

Which I don't have!

"Isaiah, there's something I don't understand," Rose said slowly, hoping she sounded genuinely puzzled. "What does Miller think he's going to do with twenty-five percent of Global? He's not an express man."

Phipps smiled frostily. "Perhaps that's a question you should ask him yourself."

"Is that professional advice, Counselor? Paul Miller wouldn't happen to be a client of yours, would he?"

"As a matter of fact, yes."

"A recent one, no doubt."

Phipps ignored the contempt in Rose's voice. "I took the liberty of asking him to join us—with your permission, of course. He's downstairs right now. Shall we have him come up?"

Before Paul Miller was shown in, Rose asked both Phipps and O'Neill to wait in the boardroom. She wanted Miller to face her, a widow dressed in mourning, alone. However slight, it would still be an advantage.

Paul Miller was appropriately somber. He hovered over Rose and held her hand a little too long while gushing condolences. Rose managed to extricate herself and slipped behind Jehosophat Jefferson's desk, forcing Miller to sit across from her like a petitioner.

"I thought it would be best if we cleared the air as quickly as possible," Miller said.

"I couldn't agree more," Rose replied.

"I'm sure you understand how shocked I was to learn that Simon had no authority to pledge Global's shares," Miller continued. "However, the fact is he did."

"Paul," Rose interrupted, "I realize Simon borrowed five million dollars from you and that given what's happened to Talbot Railroads you're not going to get your money back from Vanderbilt. I'm willing to repay the loan personally. It'll mean working out a fair interest rate and some kind of schedule we can both live with, but it can be done."

Paul Miller crossed one leg over the other and pretended to study his perfectly manicured nails.

"Rose, I've always admired you, especially the way you've worked so hard for Global. Frankly, I thought Simon underestimated your talents. When I accepted the Global shares it wasn't only because they were solid collateral. I believed—and still do—that I can make a valuable contribution to the company. I don't want to fight you, Rose. I want to work with you."

"I'm flattered, Paul," Rose said carefully. "But you haven't had much experience in the express field, have you?"

Miller inclined his head. "True. But I am a businessman. We could work together, Rose. Between my financial savvy and your knowledge of Global we could make the company twice as big as it is now."

"It's a generous offer, Paul, but frankly, I never considered taking on a partner."

"I'm talking about something more than a partnership," Miller said in a low voice. "This is very awkward for me, Rose, and I know how it must sound, especially right now. But I have to say it. It's no secret that you and Simon had been . . . estranged for a long time. The whys and wherefores aren't important. The point is that I do care for you, Rose, and I'd like to give you the kind of life, a full life, that you and Simon never had."

Rose could hardly believe what she was hearing yet she managed to contain her outrage. She must find a way to hang Paul Miller with his own words.

"I'm touched, Paul. But there are proprieties to be observed."

"Of course," Miller said quickly. "I just wanted you to be aware of my feelings."

"Regardless of them, Paul, we should still work out a repayment—"

Miller held up his hand. "I don't want you to worry about a thing. I'll hold on to the shares and instruct my lawyers to wait. I don't want to fight you on this, Rose," he repeated.

And there's the steel fist beneath the velvet glove, Rose thought.

"I appreciate your candor, Paul," she said, certain he would not detect the sarcasm. "I'm sure you also realize that I need time to think about this."

Miller smiled. "Of course. I want you to call me if you need anything, anything at all. I'll be there for you, Rose."

"I'm sure you will be," Rose said softly.

That evening Rose held a council of war at Talbot House with Franklin, Hugh O'Neill, and Monk McQueen. The three men couldn't believe that Paul Miller intended to hold on to the shares.

"Miller's a first-class, opportunistic son of a bitch," Franklin said, perfectly summing up the others' sentiments.

"But a son of a bitch who's holding on to twenty-five percent of Global," O'Neill added.

"So what?" Franklin protested. "That's not enough to hurt us. We'll get it back eventually as long as we pay back the five million dollars."

"In the meantime we can't move ahead," Rose said. "We've been riding a lucky wave. With the war in Europe it's impossible *not* to make money. But we have to look ahead now. The plans I have for Global won't wait."

Franklin looked keenly at his sister, surprised and disturbed by her cold-blooded comments. Obviously Rose had never read the horrifying accounts of the butchery taking place in the trenches of France and Belgium.

"The first thing to do is to make sure we can repay the loan," Rose continued. "Hugh, I want you to talk to the banks and see what needs to be done to extend our line of credit. Franklin, I want you to work with Eric. He knows the company inside out and can teach you everything you need to know."

"Is there anything I can do?" Monk asked.

Rose touched his hand. "There is, but I'd like to discuss it privately."

O'Neill and Franklin took the hint. When they were alone Rose poured Monk another glass of port and placed it on the coffee table in front of the fireplace.

"I think we'll be more comfortable over here," she suggested.

Monk thought Rose had never looked more beautiful than she did at that moment, with flames bringing a pink glow to her skin, making her jet-black hair shine brilliantly. The feelings she stirred in him seemed so out of place in the circumstances.

"There's something I didn't tell the others," Rose said. "It doesn't really concern Hugh, and Franklin . . . well, I think he would overreact. But I need to tell someone, a friend. . . ."

"Yes, of course, Rose. Anything . . ."

Slowly, with just the right amounts of gravity and reserve, Rose explained what it was Paul Miller really wanted. Monk reacted exactly as she had hoped.

"I can't believe it," he exploded. "The day you bury your husband, Miller says he's in love with you!"

"Well, he didn't come out and say that exactly," Rose reminded him. "But he made his intentions very clear."

"He's blackmailing you!" Monk stormed. "There's no other word for it."

"I suppose that's true," Rose admitted, grateful that Monk had reached the conclusion by himself.

"I won't let him get away with it," Monk declared. "Paul Miller has to be stopped."

"But how?" asked Rose. "I don't know very much about him. He's rich and influential. . . ."

"Leave that to me," Monk said grimly. "I can find out anything you want about Mr. Paul Miller!"

"That would be a great help."

"I'll get to work immediately. But if Miller starts making any . . . any advances toward you, I want you to tell me right away."

"I will, Monk," Rose said solemnly.

Only then did she allow Monk to gather her up in his arms and hold her.

- 8 -

Spring was nudging winter out of Manhattan and Simon Talbot had been in the ground for two months. New York society was quick to bury those whom it found embarrassing and instead focused its attention on the beautiful Rose Talbot, who carried her widowhood with such flair and chic. The gossip mills were already hard at work, speculation flying not as to whether Rose would remarry but when and to whom. As far as Rose was concerned, nothing could have been further from her thoughts.

Since her first meeting with Paul Miller, Rose had been walking a tightrope. Her days were filled with the hundreds of details that had to be looked after if Global was to survive. Talbot Railroads had been Global's sole freight carrier. After Vanderbilt had taken over the lines, Rose petitioned the courts to force the Commodore to honor Talbot's existing contracts and won. But this bought her only breathing space. Global's agreements with Talbot Railroads would expire in a few months. Clearly these would not be renegotiated, much less renewed pro forma, unless Paul Miller had what he wanted.

Miller himself presented a host of problems. The financier had made it very clear that he intended to use the stock he held as a stumbling block. Miller urged Rose to meet with Vanderbilt and hammer out a long-term pact to carry freight. He even offered to conduct the negotiations for her, which Rose politely declined. She saw all too clearly the path Miller wanted to start her on: once she agreed to trade with Vanderbilt she would be at his mercy. All sorts of "acts of God" could be manufactured to delay, lose, or destroy Global shipments. As soon as word got around that Global was unreliable, customers would flee in droves.

Paul Miller's interference also prevented Rose from implementing the new ideas she had labored over so hard and so long and had never given up on. One day she put them to Theodore Coolidge, her grandfather's banker of many years.

"Your idea to create what you call a money order is nothing short of brilliant," he said after hearing her out. "I wish I had thought of it myself because you're going to make so much money it'll be sinful."

"There's a big *but* hanging over what you say," Rose observed.

"You know as well as I do what it is," Coolidge told her. "First of all, the banks won't go near you until you control Global absolutely. They don't want to cross Miller, much less his éminence grise, Vanderbilt. Second, if either of them gets wind of what you're thinking they'll jump all over you. There's too much money to be made from your scheme, and if you're not very, very careful they'll steal it out from under you."

Theodore Coolidge paused. "I think the world of you, Rose, and I'll help you any way I can. But you have to do something about Miller."

That, Rose thought, was proving to be a maddening conundrum.

Paul Miller had become her shadow. He called her at the office at least every other day, asking her out to lunch or inviting her to a dinner party some "mutual friends" were giving. Rose, who had paid little attention to the frivolities of New York's Four Hundred and had been ignored in turn, suddenly found herself deluged with invitations to the sort of small, private evenings acceptable for a widow to attend. She was certain Paul Miller was orchestrating this but she could scarcely refuse everybody. It was clear they all believed that Rose Talbot looked upon her husband's demise as a godsend and was positively grabbing the new life being offered her. Some matrons even went so far as to include a winter wedding on their social calendars.

Through all this Rose blushed sweetly and made the appropriate comments. Meanwhile her blood was boiling. She felt as though Paul Miller had slipped around her neck a golden leash that, for the moment, he chose not to tug too hard. But Rose knew that Miller's patience had its limits. He was investing a good deal of time and even more money in pursuing her and he expected something tangible in return. At night Rose lay awake, tortured by the thoughts of what she would have to give him to buy more time, time for Monk to help her as he'd promised. If he could help her at all . . .

The moment Rose had made her appeal, Monk McQueen's world changed. The infatuation he thought time and distance had put behind him resurfaced with a vengeance. Monk was convinced that if he could help Rose, nothing could possibly keep them apart any longer.

In the weeks following Simon Talbot's funeral, Monk debated how he should go about freeing Rose from Paul Miller's hold. One plan after another broke apart on the same rocks: Miller was a wealthy, powerful man who seemed not to have a single chink in his armor.

As Paul Miller's pursuit of Rose became the favorite subject of New York gossip, Monk was plagued by a sense of helplessness. He hated the proprietary way Miller escorted Rose about and the smug, self-satisfied expression he wore as others silently envied his prize. Even worse was Rose's reaction. There were times when, in the middle of a society event, her eyes would search him out across the room. Sometimes her look carried with it the smile of hope. More often there were questions in those eyes, and worse, a disappointment that cut Monk like a blade.

The breaking point came during the Memorial Day weekend when Rose held a small party on Long Island to celebrate the reopening of Dunescrag. Monk was one of the first guests to arrive, coming early especially to have some time alone with Rose. As he was shown in he saw Paul Miller walking down the grand double staircase. Miller couldn't hide his surprise but quickly recovered and welcomed Monk as though he were the host. Monk smelled the fresh aftershave on Miller's face and noticed that his hair was still damp. All Monk could think of at that moment was the location of the upstairs bedrooms where he had played as a child.

Before Monk could bury his suspicions he saw Rose on the balcony. From her expression he knew immediately that she had read his thoughts. The welcome in her eyes died. Rose gave a tiny shrug and held her chin defiantly high as she passed him, as if to say, "What did you expect?"

Monk knew then what it was he had to do.

Alistair McQueen had taught his son that information was a priceless asset. During his distinguished career as a financial adviser Alistair McQueen had compiled personal histories on hundreds of America's entrepreneurs. Some were men who had, for one reason or another, lost their fortunes or had them squandered by careless heirs. Others had risen to eminence and remained undisputed captains of industry. Shortly before his death Alistair McQueen had shared his observations and secrets with his son. He showed Monk how some great fortunes had been built on the bones of competitors, how young men, eager to make their mark, had lied, cheated, and stolen to create their first big stake, parleying it into greater assets, taking advantage of others' misfortunes, sometimes even creating those misfortunes to suit their own purposes. He explained how, after their money bought respectability, these no-longer-young men quietly buried their sins and rewrote histories to suit their place in society.

Alistair McQueen catalogued sins but never profited from them. What he referred to as his Doomsday Book had only one purpose: to maintain the freedom and integrity of his newsletter. In his editorials and special reports he exposed questionable practices, challenged legislators' bills, and called for public inquiries when private enterprise conflicted with the common good. Whenever his commentaries provoked a response and he was urged to moderate his views or drop them altogether, Alistair McQueen quietly reminded the petitioners that he could say a lot more if he wished. A few facts and figures were enough to counter veiled threats and hints of bribery.

The Monday after the holiday weekend Monk McQueen arrived at the Gotham Bank and removed the safety deposit box his father had purchased thirty years ago. In the privacy of a cubicle, he opened the Doomsday Book, quickly finding the references he was looking for.

Alistair McQueen had carefully documented Paul Miller's rise from obscurity to fortune. Set in the chronology were disturbing questions about Miller's business practices. Several times Miller and Alistair McQueen had confronted each other, yet as far as Monk could tell from the notes, his father had never followed up on the information that hinted at malfeasance.

Why? What else had his father known about Miller that had made him shy away? The notes were silent on that point. Monk couldn't shake the feeling that something was not what it should be.

Monk closed the Doomsday Book, staring at its cover. He remembered how Rose had looked at him that moment at Dunescrag—the self-contempt draped over her like a shroud, the resignation and accusation in her eyes as she had brushed past him.

Monk made his decision. His father had left him a starting point. He would dig as hard and as deep as necessary to find out what Miller had been involved in, and he would print whatever he found, no matter who might be hurt by the truth. Because, Monk was convinced, that truth would set Rose free.

Monk began his quest in Minnesota where Paul Miller had been born and raised. In talking to the townspeople he quickly discovered there was no love for the native son who had made good.

While still in his early twenties, Paul Miller had organized the building of a small meat-packing plant. He convinced farmers that they would make more money if they processed their small herds of cattle, pigs, and sheep locally rather than shipping them to the Chicago slaughterhouses. The plant was structured as a cooperative, built, run, and owned by the farmers, with Miller as general manager.

From its first day the cooperative was operating in the black. Flushed with success, its members agreed to let Paul Miller buy expensive machinery and new buildings and to sign binding delivery contracts with suppliers in the East. No one seemed to notice or care that the cooperative's debt far exceeded its income.

The day the banks came knocking on the cooperative's door Paul Miller was nowhere to be found. Repossession quickly followed, and men who had fiercely prided themselves on being independent owners/operators discovered that they were debtors. The final blow came when one of the giant Chicago meat-packers made an offer the banks could not refuse. The cooperative was bought, lock, stock, and barrel, at thirty cents on the dollar and promptly reopened the following month. Its members, stripped of their property and investments, had no choice but to accept whatever price the new owner set for their livestock. Throughout all this no one ever saw or heard from Paul Miller. Much later, a Twin Cities newspaper noted that the same Chicago concern had recently appointed him junior vice president for the Midwest.

Monk resurrected Paul Miller's first business coup in flawless detail, concentrating on the human drama, the hopes, dreams, and lives destroyed because of one man's ambitions. When he was satisfied with the story, Monk sent it to Q with instructions to run it "as is," the first in a series of articles that would appear under the heading PROFILES IN PROFIT. McQueen wondered if the irony would be lost on his subject.

Throughout that summer Monk doggedly followed the trail left by Paul Miller over the years. Stretching from Minneapolis–St. Paul to Duluth, Chicago, Washington, and finally New York was a history of buyouts and sellouts, broken promises, takeovers, and mergers that chronicled Paul Miller's dues for admission into the pantheon of American robber barons.

Monk interviewed small bankers ruined by Miller's financial manipulations, families left destitute because their businesses had been swallowed whole by giant concerns Miller fronted for, and daring entrepreneurs whose ideas and inventions, born in basements, stables, and garages, had been stolen by Miller and then promptly patented as his own. The emerging portrait of Miller resembled the one of Dorian Gray. In life, Miller was a sterling example of success. But hidden away in the past was the true man, grasping, manipulative, and profoundly greedy. And if his readers' letters were any yardstick, Monk thought they saw Miller in exactly the same light.

With every article he wrote Monk twisted the screws a little more. He was certain that if he could apply enough pressure, someone somewhere would come forward with information so damaging that a formal investigation of Miller and his practices would have to be launched. Meanwhile, he rebuffed Miller's attempts to contact him, and when Miller's lawyers filed a defamation suit, he ordered his counsel to fight it. Later, in Washington, two private detectives accosted him on the steps of the Capitol. Monk loudly demanded what they wanted and whether they were working for Miller and were here to threaten him. The detectives fled, but their pictures and an account of the incident appeared in the next issue of Q magazine.

"I need your decision, Rose. Time's running out."

They were sitting opposite each other in the formal garden of Dunescrag, a fantasy of topiary animals and meandering rose bushes punctuated by splashes of color from beds of geraniums and tulips. Beyond the stretch of green lawn was Long Island Sound, the sailboats a study of white on sparkling blue.

Rose poured more tea. "What decision is that, Paul?"

"Global's freight contracts with the Vanderbilt lines will expire in three weeks. You haven't even begun to renegotiate them."

Rose studied him carefully. The strain caused by Monk McQueen's articles was telling. Miller's once charming manner had become abrupt, even when he was around her, while at the same time his ardent courtship had fallen off. These days Paul Miller had other things on his mind.

Rose had been thrilled to read Monk's articles. She knew what he was trying to do and silently, across the miles, urged him on. She watched Paul Miller carefully, searching for signs of weakness, waiting for the moment he would falter, surrender the shares voluntarily, and accept the loan repayment. Nothing less would get him out of her life—and Global—permanently.

"I'm not sure Vanderbilt is the best man to go with," Rose said, running a brilliantly painted red fingernail around the rim of her cup.

"He's the only one!" Paul Miller replied sharply.

"At the terms he's offering?"

"No one's come up with better ones."

That's because no other carrier dares to make a bid. Vanderbilt has spooked them.

"If the deal isn't made, Rose, Global may lose its carrier. You know as well as I do that if that happens, the value of the company will plummet."

You mean the value of the shares you hold.

"I don't want to force you into a decision, Rose," Miller said. "But if you can't see your own best interests then I'll have to instruct my lawyers to petition the courts to validate my claim on those shares. Once that's done you won't be able to dismiss my advice so easily."

In spite of the summer sun, goosebumps broke over Rose's arms.

"Do you really feel that's necessary, Paul?" she asked softly. "Have I done anything to deserve this? You've given me the time I asked for and I'm grateful for that. But I've reciprocated. In spite of what's been written about you I never questioned your integrity. Doesn't that tell you something?"

Paul Miller licked his lips. "I'm not sure. That is, I don't know what you mean."

Rose laughed, covering his hand with hers. "Men can be so dense. Can't you see that I'm falling in love with you, Paul?"

An hour later Rose lay in her canopied bed, looking up at the intricate design of Flemish lace but not really seeing it. Paul Miller lay beside her, snoring lightly, spent.

Quietly Rose slipped out of bed and went into the bathroom. She locked the door, then examined her naked reflection in the mirror. Aside from a soreness between her legs, where Paul Miller had pounded himself into groaning ecstasy, there was nothing different about her. What had taken place was many things—a mechanical act, a ploy to distract, an attempt to buy time, a down payment, a sacrifice for the future of something she would never, ever surrender to another human being. What it hadn't been, would never be, was an act of love.

Rose stood in front of the mirror for a long time, naked and shivering, looking at herself as if to burn the image into her mind so that she would never forget what she had done and what it had cost. Only when she was convinced that she wouldn't falter, did she pick up the sponge and begin to cleanse herself.

The juggernaut was building. Newspapers across the country, including the influential dailies in Washington, New York, and Boston, were picking up Monk's stories and running with them. Editorials demanded an accounting of Paul Miller's interests while financial writers speculated on the reasons for his silence and why he was hiding behind his attorneys. Monk added Q magazine's voice to the others and offered Miller its front page if he wanted to defend himself on the record. The reply Monk received was startlingly different from the one he had expected.

Senator Charles Humbolt of Delaware had spent more than half of his seventy years in the Senate. He had written some of its most effective legislation and ensured speedy passage for every bill he thought would benefit the nation. At the time of his retirement Humbolt had been chairman of the powerful Senate Finance Committee, and his gracious Dupont Circle mansion was filled with tributes to a lifetime of public service.

"Even your daddy had a few good things to say about me." Humbolt chuckled, wrapping his gnarled, arthritic fingers over the silver knob of his walking stick.

"And rightly so, Senator," Monk replied, nudging his wing chair forward.

Humbolt's hearing was every bit as good as Monk's but the senator tended to speak very softly. It was a technique that forced people to listen carefully to what he said.

Monk was still bewildered by the call from Humbolt. The legislator's reason for wanting to meet with him was a mystery.

"Now that you've paid me all the right compliments and I've made the appropriate noises, we can get down to business," Humbolt said. "You've been writing a lot about Paul Miller. Mind telling me why?"

Monk began with the reply that he had repeated many times over the past months. He had become intrigued by Paul Miller's role in Talbot Railroads and the highly questionable, if not outright illegal, arrangement between him and

Simon Talbot. Naturally, this had prompted him to investigate Miller's history as a businessman.

Senator Humbolt rapped the floor sharply with his walking stick.

"I'll thank you for the courtesy of the truth, Mr. McQueen. If I want entertainment I can read the funnies. Let me help you out a little. You dredged all this up because you wanted to help Rose Talbot stop Miller from getting his hands on Global."

Monk crimsoned. "That's true, Senator," he conceded.

"And you've done a pretty good job of it so far, haven't you?"

"If you mean I uncovered a few skeletons, yes. But I've backed up every word I've written and Paul Miller hasn't exactly rushed out to contradict me."

"Do you know why?"

"Because I print the truth, Senator," Monk said quietly.

"The truth," Humbolt murmured. "You refer to it with a certainty only the young and the righteous can muster. Let me tell you something, Mr. McQueen, you're only getting close to the truth. You haven't reached it yet. Nor may you want to."

"I'm sorry, Senator, I don't understand."

"You've carved up some very rotten apples but you haven't quite reached the bottom of the barrel," Humbolt said sadly. "You've accused Miller of unethical conduct, thievery, deception. And he's guilty, no doubt about it. But you see, young Mr. McQueen, we knew about it a long time ago. Hell, some of us even profited. Given your sense of mission and prodigious talents, you would have learned that soon enough."

Monk swallowed hard. "Who is 'we,' Senator?"

"Why, some of the most august members of the United States Senate." Humbolt raised his jaw defiantly. "Including myself. And I'm going to tell who, when, where, and why."

The words were still reverberating in Monk's mind as he heard himself say, "Senator, I hope you don't mind if I take this down. . . ."

Humbolt smiled wanly. "I insist on it."

Three hours later Monk felt as though some giant force had drained the very lifeblood out of him. His incredulity must have been written across his face.

"Got a little more than you bargained for, did you?" Humbolt observed.

Senator Humbolt had been as good as his word. From an encyclopedic memory he had plucked out names, dates, places, and amounts. Paul Miller's tentacles stretched further than Monk had ever imagined, touching people he believed were above influence. The list of favors bought and sold, government investigations quashed, quiet words whispered from Wall Street lips to Washington's ears, seemed endless. Contrary to public myth, Paul Miller's meteoric rise hadn't been a combination of luck, skill, and daring. Every move he made had been covered in advance—for a price.

"I hope you won't take offense, Senator," Monk said. "But do you have any documentation to support what you've told me?"

Using his walking stick, Humbolt pushed an ancient briefcase toward Monk.

"You'll find what you need in there. Many who helped Miller have passed away. There are records, of course, in archives, family collections, estate lawyers' files. It would be quite a task for one man to get at them all but I don't think you'll be needing to do that."

"Why is that, Senator?"

"Because you know as well as I do what's going to happen if you go to press."

Monk had no illusions on that point. He was going to unleash the scandal of the decade across the front page of Q magazine.

"There's bound to be a congressional investigation, Senator. Public outcry will demand one. You'll be implicated and eventually called upon to testify."

"Only if you choose to print what you know."

Monk hesitated, uncertain what Humbolt was intimating.

"You see, it wasn't only politicians and legislators who helped create men such as Paul Miller," Humbolt continued. "We didn't think that what we were doing was terribly wrong or unethical. A favor in return for a market tip, a quiet word in exchange for support in the next campaign, these appeared to be small, inconsequential things, taken one at a time over the years. And of course the conscience doesn't like to keep track of these things so you never quite get around to adding them all up. Until one day you wake up and have to face the fact that what began as a single favor has become an institution. Having succeeded in corrupting you once, the same men return to the well, knowing they can't be refused."

"You mentioned there were others involved," Monk said, his throat dry.

Charles Humbolt sat back in the wing chair. He regarded the young man carefully and finally indicated the briefcase.

"Alistair McQueen, your father, was one of the others who was beholden to Paul Miller. It's all in there, as you'll see for yourself. That's why I said 'if' you print the story. Because you, my young friend, might very well change your mind. And who would blame you if you did?"

— 9 —

It was all there in black and white. Monk McQueen couldn't ignore it, couldn't make it disappear.

Monk had gone from Senator Humbolt's home to the Willard Hotel, where he rented a suite and left standing instructions not to be disturbed. He stared at the black, weathered briefcase for a long time before he found the courage to open it. Finally he began to read.

The senator had kept meticulous records. His correspondence and notes were neatly filed, complete with names, dates, and places. Together, they told Monk a story about his father he had never heard before.

There had been a time when Alistair McQueen, struggling to get his newsletter off the ground, was on the verge of losing everything to creditors. Everyone refused him, except, at the last minute, a fledgling financier named Paul Miller.

By today's standards the amount was laughably small—a few hundred dollars. Alistair McQueen had taken the money and, when Q was turning a profit, repaid it with interest. Except the payments didn't stop there.

Over the years Alistair McQueen had investigated numerous accounts concerning Paul Miller's business activities. He had discovered payoffs, bribery, blackmail, and stock manipulation. He had written up the stories, which, even as Monk read them, still retained their anger and demand for an accounting. Except for one thing: Alistair McQueen never published any of them.

Instead McQueen expressed his outrage to a promising young politician named Charles Humbolt, railing at Miller's sly suggestions that if any of the material ever saw the light of day, he would be ruined. Q, which was synonymous with integrity and fair reporting, would become a laughingstock, its founder looked upon as a hypocrite who now wanted to destroy the man who had once saved his dream. Charles Humbolt had counseled Alistair McQueen to leave Miller alone. "There are plenty of other targets more deserving of your attention," he had written. "Forget Miller. Believe me, he wants nothing to do with you."

Monk could only imagine the terrible conflict that must have raged within his father. But in the end he had left Miller alone. The stories, however, were still there, waiting to be told.

The telephone jangled and Monk let it ring for a long time before he picked it up.

"Good evening, Senator."

"Hello, Monk. I suppose you've read everything by now?"

"Yes."

"Are you going to go ahead and publish?"

Monk didn't know what to say.

"Think about your father. What this will do to his memory . . . This isn't your fight, Monk. Rose Jefferson can look after herself. She has the big battalions. But if you carry the flag for her, you're the one who'll pay. Don't do it, son."

Anger surged through Monk. How dare Humbolt presume to tell him what he should or shouldn't do for Rose!

"I know what you're thinking," Humbolt continued. "You're the only one who can help her. She's put all her trust in you and you're not about to let her down. Stop and think, Monk. Alistair had plenty of opportunities to use what he knew about Miller. He saw a lot of good people get hurt by that bastard. But he never did. Do you know why? Because in the long run Q had to remain strong and influential so that he could go after bigger fish than Miller. As much as your pa hated compromises, he realized this was one he had to live with. And so do you."

"Is that why he gave you all the notes on Miller?" asked Monk. "Because he knew you'd make sure no one ever got to see them?"

"That's exactly why," Humbolt replied softly.

"I don't believe that, Senator."

"Monk—"

"Another thing. Did Miller tell you to show me this material?"

Humbolt's silence told Monk that his question had caught the senator off guard.

"He thought that under the circumstances I could explain things a whole lot better, what with your pa and I being friends. But that doesn't matter a tinker's damn. Don't publish, Monk. You know I'm not asking for myself. I'm trying to look out for you."

"I appreciate the thought, Senator," Monk said. "I'll keep in touch."

Monk didn't sleep at all that night. He sat by the balcony with the French doors ajar, smoking cigars and staring at the lights of the Capitol as though seeking to divine the answer. He tried to look at the issue objectively and weigh the pros and cons. Instead, all he could think about was Rose.

At five o'clock in the morning, Monk called the floor valet and ordered a large pot of coffee, a typewriter, and two hundred sheets of bond. It was time to go to work.

*   *   *

Rose sat on the back terrace of Dunescrag, at a white wrought-iron table shaded by an enormous red-and-blue-striped umbrella. She glanced across the lawn to the Sound where Steven was in the middle of a sailing lesson. She was proud of how quickly her son was mastering the twenty-foot craft as well as the capricious waters with their currents and tows.

"This just came for you, ma'am," Albany said, handing her a large envelope.

Rose's heart was pounding as she scanned the front page of Q magazine, then she started reading, forcing herself to concentrate on every word.

"Albany, please get Hugh O'Neill on the telephone."

Something must have been different about her voice, because the manservant immediately said, "Is everything all right, ma'am?"

Rose smiled at him. "It's better than all right." She paused. "Call Mr. Gollant as well."

A hundred thoughts whirled through Rose's mind as she hurried to the house. She never saw her son waving at her as he neatly executed a sharp turn or heard him calling to get her attention.

The odor of a rich cigar hung in the air of the seventh-floor suite of the Waldorf. Yet, the young man facing Paul Miller did not smoke and the ashtrays were clean.

"Can you explain this?" he asked in a neutral voice, tapping the front page of Q magazine.

Paul Miller shook his head. He appeared in command, freshly barbered, nails manicured, his smartly cut blue suit a perfect fit. But his eyes kept darting around the room as though searching to escape.

Miller cleared his throat. "I've been calling the Q offices all morning. McQueen's people claim he's not there and won't say where I can find him."

"We've been told the same thing," the young man observed. "Nonetheless, you can appreciate that Mr. Vanderbilt is concerned."

"And I'm not?" Miller shouted. "That bastard is hanging me out to dry. I need help. I know goddamn well Vanderbilt is in the next room. Why doesn't he come out and talk to me?"

The young man appeared not to have heard the question.

"You're aware of the repercussions," he said. "There's going to be an investigation. Obviously Mr. Vanderbilt cannot be connected to you in any way."

"It's a little late in the day for that, don't you think?" Miller retorted.

"Not at all. Mr. Vanderbilt had nothing to do with your earlier transactions. His only relationship to you is through Talbot Railroads. I'm sure you'll agree that connection must be severed."

Miller's eyes narrowed. "What are you saying?"

81

"You must cease to have any interest in Global Enterprises, which is your link to Talbot Railroads."

"You mean I should return the shares?" Miller demanded incredulously. "The whole point of my lending Talbot the money was to get leverage in the company so that eventually Vanderbilt could take it over as well."

"Plans change, Mr. Miller. We're prepared to settle with you once you're out of the public eye, so to speak."

"I'll be out of the public eye, all right. I'll be in jail!"

Paul Miller tried to rein in his emotions. Now, more than ever, he needed to keep his wits about him.

"What kind of settlement did you have in mind?" he asked cautiously.

"Fifty thousand dollars, cash."

Paul Miller reeled. The amount was worse than a pittance. It was insulting. Then Miller saw the truth behind it.

"You're cutting me loose, aren't you? You want to get the hell away from me as fast and as far as possible."

"We're offering you something for your old age," the young man said callously. "Think about it, Mr. Miller. Carefully."

Paul Miller nodded as though weighing the decision. Then without warning he leaped to his feet and crashed into the door of the adjoining suite. In spite of his bulk and momentum the door didn't budge.

"Come out here, Vanderbilt!" he roared. "Come out and tell me yourself how you're going to sell me down the river!"

The young man drew the gun he carried, then, as Paul Miller began sobbing, put it away. He had been prepared to shoot Miller had it become necessary. Now he could only pity him.

"Well, I'm glad I caught you in time."

Paul Miller stepped into the orangerie and reached forward to kiss Rose.

"Paul, please," Rose said, pulling away.

Miller laughed. "Aren't we shy all of a sudden."

Paul Miller was not the same man he had been just a few hours earlier. After the debacle at the Waldorf he had fled to his Park Avenue home and, as calmly as possible, looked at his options. They had been reduced to one: If Rose hadn't seen the article, he could still push her into the deal with Vanderbilt. His only blessing was Rose's being at Dunescrag on Long Island. Chances were better than even that Q magazine hadn't been delivered out there yet. Which meant he had to get there first.

Paul Miller brought out a tiny box wrapped in silver paper and placed it on the desk.

"Go ahead, Rose. Open it."

Rose removed the top of the box, then opened the Cartier's velvet case. A tear-drop diamond solitaire, mounted on a gold band, shot its brilliance into her eyes.

"Why, Paul?" she asked quietly.

"Because I love you, Rose," he replied, not taking his eyes off her. "Everything that's happened between us these last few weeks only confirms what I already knew: I want to marry you, be a husband to you."

Rose closed the case with a loud snap. She reached over and dropped a copy of *Q* on the table.

Miller flinched. "I assumed you'd already seen this," he said, keeping his voice as level as possible. "Please believe me, there's nothing to McQueen's allegations. I've already spoken to my lawyers. They're going to slap him with a lawsuit first thing in the morning."

Rose was surprised by Miller's tactic. She had expected him to bully her into a decision concerning Vanderbilt, not present her with an engagement ring. Unless Vanderbilt was no longer in the picture . . .

Silently Rose pushed a single piece of paper toward Miller. She uncapped a fountain pen and handed it to him.

"This is a waiver, Paul," she said tonelessly. "Sign it and you give up all claims to the Global shares you now hold."

Miller stared hard at her. He'd be damned if he'd let this woman threaten him.

"Why should I, Rose?"

"Because very soon you're going to be brought up before a Senate judiciary committee. Then there are the criminal indictments for bribery, extortion, and fraud. If you sign now, Paul, I won't add mine to the long list of complaints against you."

"You don't know what you're asking me to do, Rose."

"Yes, I do," Rose replied, offering him a second piece of paper. "Here are the charges against you that Hugh O'Neill is prepared to file in federal court tomorrow, along with a petition to strip you of the shares. Given your circumstances, I doubt any judge in his right mind will side with you."

Rose paused. "Of course, you might choose to take your chances and go to Vanderbilt. As I see it, that's your only option."

Paul Miller stared at the two papers for a long time as though trying through sheer willpower to change what was written on them. Then he looked at Rose, at the total emptiness in her eyes. He had seen that same fathomless expression, devoid of joy, after they had made love and she thought he wasn't looking, or didn't care. At the time he had thought Rose was frigid. Now he knew the really cold thing about her was her heart.

"How much?" Paul Miller asked hoarsely. "How much are you offering for the shares?"

"Not one cent!" Rose snapped. "You had every chance to settle with me. You chose not to. You wanted more and in the end you got it. But I'm going to prove the most expensive fuck you ever had. Sign and leave!"

Paul Miller gaped. "You whored yourself for a company, a . . . a thing?"

"Sign, Paul," Rose said softly. "Before I change my mind and call the police."

Paul Miller stared at her uncomprehendingly. His hand shook as he snatched up the pen and scrawled his signature across the bottom of the waiver.

"God help you, Rose," he whispered. "Because one day it'll be your turn!"

"If that makes you feel better, Paul, then by all means, believe it!"

The revelations in *Q* magazine were carried by newspapers across the country. In their wake followed demands by legislators, governors, and citizen groups for a congressional investigation.

Amid the uproar sweeping Capitol Hill, Monk McQueen returned to New York. He found the atmosphere in the *Q* offices subdued, with a hint of mourning in the air. Monk gathered his staff together and asked them what was wrong. Jimmy Pearce answered for all of them.

"We believe it took incredible courage to do what you did, sir. We'd like you to know that every one of us is proud to be a part of this magazine and that we'll stand behind you every step of the way."

Monk was on the verge of tears. The support of all his employees, right down to the copy boys, meant the world to him. A few days later he discovered just how precious their faith in him was.

Most editorial and financial writers lauded the fact that Monk had revealed how and why his father had chosen not to pursue investigations into Paul Miller's corrupt business practices. They agreed that Alistair McQueen had allowed himself to be compromised and that this threw a shadow over his otherwise exemplary journalistic record. However, they added that McQueen's lifetime work more than made up for this one lapse.

Other papers, the scandal sheets and tabloids, were not so generous. There were accusations that over the years Alistair McQueen had profited handsomely by keeping Miller's name off his pages. Some reporters insinuated that this secret fortune had been swelled by contributions from other robber barons McQueen had secretly protected. Monk vehemently denied every accusation but there was always one question, which cut him to the quick:

"Why did you do it, McQueen? What made you finally turn in your old man? What do you think he'd say to you if he were around?"

"My father was an honorable man," Monk declared. "But he wasn't perfect.

84

He made mistakes. I believe that at some point he would have printed these stories."

The hoots and jeers broke Monk's heart but he carried on.

"I think he would approve of what I've done."

"Sure he would," a reporter called out. "Every father wants to be stabbed in the back by his son!"

Monk's face was burning with shame and anger. When he had written the first sentence of his articles, he had been so sure that his father would have agreed with what he was doing. But now, whenever he silently pleaded to be given some answer, the ghost of Alistair McQueen was conspicuously silent, leaving Monk only one other person to turn to, to ease his burden.

"Monk, you're back!"

He thought Rose had never looked more beautiful, her rich black hair piled high, held in place by tiny diamond pins, her arms, sheathed in white lace, held out to him, her mouth rich, red, and laughing, her fingertips cool.

"Hello, Rose," he said softly.

She took his arm and led him into the formal parlor, where Albany was supervising the tea service.

"Had I known you were coming I would have canceled the whole thing," Rose chattered on. "As it is, thirty members of the city's fine arts endowment committee will be here any minute."

"I can't stay long," Monk said. "I'm dead on my feet. But I wanted to come by . . ."

For the first time in weeks, words failed him.

"Well, you look exhausted. And no wonder, all those terrible things the gutter press has been saying about your father. It's disgraceful."

"Rose . . ." Monk faltered. He wanted to say so much, needed to hear so much! "Rose, have you been reading the articles?"

"Of course I have. They're brilliant!"

"Has everything worked out with the shares?"

Rose smiled triumphantly. "They're back where they belong."

"Then everything's all right . . . ?"

Rose looked at him curiously. "Of course it is. Paul Miller is finished, thanks to you."

Monk winced but immediately forgave Rose her unfeeling words.

"I was wondering . . . that is, if you're not doing anything, maybe we could have dinner."

Rose clapped her hands in delight. "My dear, dear, Monk, you sound just like you did at my wedding, so serious and shy. Yes, of course we can have dinner. Franklin's dying to see you."

"I thought just the two of us—"

"Oh, Monk, please," Rose said, a touch of exasperation to her voice. "You're not going to start that again."

"Start what?"

"That nonsense about being in love with me."

"But I am in love with you!" he blurted.

Rose stood up and came very close to him.

"I haven't had good luck with men," she said quietly. "You of all people must know that. I'm very fond of you, Monk. I always have been. But I don't love you, not in the way you would like. I don't know if I'll ever love anyone again. I've learned that one shouldn't be too greedy. I have my work, which I treasure, and a future to build. For now, perhaps always, that is enough."

Monk didn't dare look up as Rose was speaking. He heard the words but somehow they didn't register. They weren't real or believable. His tears were.

The door chimes sounded.

"Those must be your guests," he said hoarsely. "I must be going. Goodbye, Rose."

"Monk!"

But he kept walking, not to the front door but farther into the house, down corridors he remembered so well, past maids and cooks who quickly got out of his way. He passed through the garden, out the gate, and onto the street, running now, not knowing, not caring where he was going.

The revelations Monk McQueen unleashed on the front pages of Q magazine focused the nation's attention on Washington. A blue-ribbon commission appointed by President Woodrow Wilson began hearings, and a week before Christmas tabled its recommendations: the evidence against Paul Miller was to be turned over to a federal prosecutor, while Charles Humbolt, whose supporting testimony had been crucial, was given immunity from prosecution.

As far as the public was concerned that was the end of it. Attention was once again focused on the war in Europe. Across the country debates were raging between isolationists who wanted to keep America out of the conflict and interventionists who saw a duty to support the Allied cause. When Paul Miller was sentenced by a District of Columbia judge to three years in a federal penitentiary for bribery and corruption, the news merited a three-inch column buried deep in *The New York Times*.

– 10 –

Franklin Jefferson bounded up the steps of the Metropolitan Club, shouldering his way through the incipient blizzard descending on Manhattan. Handing his oversized racoon coat to the porter, he hurried to the bar, where members seeking refuge from the storm were amiably debating the prospects of an overnight stay. They reminded Franklin of a pack of schoolboys excited by the prospect of being snowed in and having to spend the night away from home.

Drink in hand, Franklin threaded his way through the tables, acknowledging and returning greetings until he came upon Monk McQueen sitting by himself at an alcove table.

"Is this Devil's Island or are you carrying the plague?" he asked cheerfully.

Monk raised his glass. "A little bit of both, I suppose."

As a regular at the Metropolitan Club, Franklin knew that in recent weeks Monk McQueen had been the sole topic of conversation among the members. While financial New York collectively applauded his actions, individuals took a dim view of what Monk had done to Paul Miller; there were many more skeletons rattling around Wall Street. As a result, members effectively ostracized Monk, remaining coolly polite but never asking him to join them.

"We have to stop meeting like this," Franklin said, trying to lighten the atmosphere. "People will start talking. Besides, Rose has been asking about you. She's afraid you're becoming a hermit."

Monk shrugged and looked away. For the first time in years he had missed both Christmas Eve and New Year's dinner at Talbot House. There had been other invitations as well, and each had ended up in the wastebasket. The pain Monk carried was still too raw, too deep even to contemplate facing Rose.

Franklin saw it all too clearly, and his heart went out to Monk. He had always looked upon him as the older brother he'd never had. Monk was part of his earliest memories, the boy who had played with him in the nooks and crannies and secret places of Dunescrag and later guided him through the quandaries and uncertainties of adolescence. It was Monk who had shown him how big, beautiful, and grand the earth was and how much promise it held for the man who could make himself a citizen of the world. Together, they had debated and resolved the great issues of their time and made grandiose plans for the future. On a more practical note, Monk, who was six years older, was able to get an underaged Franklin into the best clubs, no questions asked, and,

87

when Franklin turned sixteen, he introduced him to the earthly delights to be found in Madam Katrina's discreet and sophisticated bordello.

Franklin was also keenly aware of how much Monk loved Rose. He had never understood why his sister had refused Monk's affection and instead had married Simon Talbot. After Simon's death, Franklin had thought that Rose would finally see the light and accept Monk.

Franklin had never asked himself why Monk had gone after Paul Miller with such single-minded ferocity. He believed that Rose had revealed the problem of Miller's having the shares only to himself, Hugh O'Neill, and Eric Gollant. Even when Monk's headline-making articles began to run in *Q*, Franklin failed to make the connection. Then he heard the whispers circulating among Metropolitan Club members that Monk McQueen had charged after Paul Miller in some misguided act of chivalry to help Rose Jefferson.

It finally dawned on Franklin that everyone in New York except him knew the real reason for Monk's actions.

Franklin found himself in a quandary. As much as he wanted to talk to Monk he was afraid he'd end up embarrassing his best friend even more. He was also angry with Rose, who was behaving as though Monk hadn't lifted a finger to help her. Franklin couldn't understand this thoughtless part of his sister's personality.

"How is Rose?" asked Monk.

He sensed Franklin had something on his mind that he couldn't quite bring himself to articulate.

"Going full bore," Franklin replied a little too quickly. "You wouldn't believe the changes around Global."

"Oh, yes, I would."

Although Monk hadn't written a word about Global for months, his editors had been keeping track of how thoroughly Rose was cleaning house. The Talbot Railroad personnel Simon had brought with him had been given their pink slips. Executives he had hired for Global had also been dismissed. Rose evaluated, promoted, or fired employees in every department. Anyone whose loyalty she doubted didn't stand a chance.

Rose had moved just as swiftly and decisively outside the company. She had made peace with Vanderbilt and had even cajoled the Commodore into making a public appearance with her to sign the new contract. The message to other railroad owners was unmistakable. The hatchet was buried; Rose Jefferson was back in business. The next day railroad lawyers were beating a path to Global's door, their briefcases bulging with new agreements.

"What about you?" Monk asked. "Is Eric Gollant teaching you everything you need to know?"

A frown drifted across Franklin's face. "I'm learning," he admitted. "It's interesting enough."

"But . . ."

Franklin drained his brandy. "But it's not really me. It never was and never will be."

"Have you talked to Rose about the way you feel?"

Franklin shook his head. "I'm all she has, Monk. What's she going to do if I say that I don't want to be part of something that's her whole life? Besides the company, she's so worried about Steven. . . ."

Franklin paused. "Do *you* think I should tell her? Do you think she might understand?"

Oh, she'll understand, Monk thought. *And she'll do whatever she feels she must to bring you in line.*

"You're going to have to decide what's best for both of you," he said noncommittally.

Franklin's disappointment at this ambiguous advice was clear but Monk refused to be drawn in.

"I guess you're right," Franklin said at last. He laughed. "You know what? Nothing's going to change, but somehow, in the end, everything will work itself out."

Afterward, whenever Monk recalled those words, he couldn't be certain whether they had been tinged with bitterness or whether it had just been his imagination.

"Well, what do you think of it?" asked Rose, impatient for Franklin's opinion.

It was the morning after the storm and they were sitting in Rose's office, watching as Manhattan slowly dug itself out from under the snow. Rose and Franklin had made morning coffee at Global a ritual, a chance to talk about the day before them. Franklin held up the pale blue rag paper to the light, letting the sun dance across the embossed gold lettering across the top.

"It's my Christmas present to myself," Rose added.

"Rose Jefferson . . ." Franklin murmured. "I do like the sound of that."

Rose threw her arms around him. She had been dying to tell Franklin her decision to take back the name she had given up by marriage. Rose hoped he would agree, because she had already instructed the supplies department to order fresh company stationery and get rid of all the old Talbot letterheads.

"You really like it?"

"I really do," Franklin assured her.

Rose smiled with satisfaction. In spite of everything that had happened, she had managed to hold on to what was truly precious to her: Steven, Franklin, and, of course, Global.

Of the three it was Franklin whom Rose feared she would, in one way or another, lose. While Rose challenged each new day, Franklin embraced it, enjoying society, sport, and young women with equal delight. She was afraid of this freedom because it was so far removed from the unerring vision that governed her life . . . because, when all was said and done, she had no control over it. Rose kept careful track of Franklin's progress under Eric Gollant's tutorship, both pleased and surprised at how quickly he grasped the fundamental workings of the company. But in spite of Eric's reassurances she was never quite convinced of his dedication. She was like a woman who, having taken a younger lover, condemns herself to live in the fear that one night he won't return to her bed.

Still, he's here now, and I'll do what I must to keep him.

"I said I think we ought to shift focus. Rose?"

Good God, I'm daydreaming!

"I'm sorry, Franklin. Shift focus—how, where?"

Franklin had never expressed interest in general company policy, a domain Rose had reserved for herself. His strength lay in dealing with people, and Rose, who had been quick to recognize this ability, had placed him in charge of personnel. Franklin proved a genius when it came to handling everyone from the girls in the typing pools to the endlessly demanding regional managers.

"You had your mind set on buying the properties and warehouses we now rent," Franklin said. "I don't think there's a better time to do that than right now. Pretty soon the war in Europe is going to throw a lot of people on our shores. The demand for real estate will drive up prices. If we were to lock in our commercial holdings now, we could even pick up extra property to sell later on."

Franklin handed her some papers.

"I've examined our liquidity position, which, as you well know, isn't all that great. However, we could raise the money easily enough by a public stock offering."

"*Go public?*" Rose exclaimed. "The last thing we want is to be responsible to a lot of interfering investors who would presume to tell us how to run our business."

"We're going to need the capital down the road anyway," Franklin reminded her, "to finance development of your money orders. If we buy now, when real estate is cheap, we can always sell later, if necessary. Whatever profit we make means we borrow less later on."

"And just whom would we offer our shares to?" Rose asked suspiciously.

90

"We're a joint stock company, not a limited corporation," Franklin replied. "We're not required to publicize our assets or disclose our profits. We pay taxes on what we say we make, not on what we're worth. Don't you think there are a lot of investors out there who would leap at the chance to buy what would be substantially undervalued shares? And of course they would have a vested interest in keeping their mouths shut."

Franklin smiled. "It's all in my report. Along with a list of blind brokers we could use to pick up the real estate. I think we'd like to keep Global as far removed as possible from the actual transactions. No point in prices going up just because people learn we're in the market.

"Now—" Franklin consulted his watch— "I must be off."

"Off where?" Rose asked, bewildered by this smooth recital.

"I'm taking my new secretary to breakfast."

"Franklin, you know how I feel about your fraternizing with the staff!"

Franklin winked. "I just hired her away from our biggest competitor. She used to take dictation for old man Adams himself. I'll bet she knows as much about what's going on in that company as he does."

Rose could only shake her head. Maybe she had underestimated just how much Franklin was learning.

After Franklin left, Rose amazed Mary Kirkpatrick by canceling her morning appointments.

"No calls, no interruptions," she instructed.

Rose went through her brother's report with the eye of a hawk. She would have died before admitting that she was searching for errors. Nonetheless, Rose was afraid that Franklin's natural optimism had blinded him to business realities. After three readings she had to admit that Franklin's analysis and reasoning were sound. Rose was overjoyed.

"Bring me the files on our leases," Rose told her secretary over the intercom.

"All of them, ma'am?"

"Every last one. And call Delmonico's. Tell Murphy to surprise me with one of his special menus. Mr. Jefferson and I will be dining out tonight."

That spring and summer Franklin Jefferson traveled the width and breadth of the nation, calling on brokers he knew were discreet—if the price was right. In the southern ports of Miami, New Orleans, and Galveston, in the great waterfront cities of St. Louis, Buffalo, Detroit, and Chicago, Global Enterprises began buying up miles upon miles of warehouses and shoreline property.

For Franklin, the journey became much more than an extended business trip. Although he had traveled widely in Europe he, like so many young men of his class and upbringing, had never set foot beyond the eastern seaboard. America was a revelation.

Stepping out into his own country, Franklin met people from all walks of life. For the first time, he saw the industry and strength of the men and women who were building America. They had faces and a voice, each one distinct but sharing the same dream of a better life. Franklin found himself thinking back to his circumscribed New York world with distaste. The financial manipulations of Wall Street and the back-room deals of the city's clubs had no place here. The men who created and oversaw them arrogantly believed that they alone ran the country from their Fifth Avenue homes and Lower Broadway offices. They knew nothing of America's heart.

Throughout his travels Franklin kept a diary filled with comments, observations, descriptions, and snatches of conversations. Over the weeks and months it became an old, familiar friend he could talk openly to, express what he felt and believed and the way he was changing. But Franklin never mentioned this to Rose. His letters to her were carefully worded, written in cool, businesslike prose that betrayed nothing. Until now Franklin hadn't realized just how much of him he had allowed Rose to take over. Slowly he started reclaiming bits and pieces of his life, building on ideas and feelings he knew she would resist and inevitably try to do away with. Franklin understood he could not allow that. But neither could he let her see how he was moving away from her and the values she held dear. Not until he was much stronger, until he had worked out what his life was to be.

In New York, Rose carefully followed Franklin's progress and backed his real estate purchases out of funds generated by stock offerings. She picked her investors carefully, choosing men who had no illusions about participating in the running of her company.

By the end of 1917, Global had trebled its assets without creating a ripple in business circles. Although freight still accounted for the bulk of company profits, money was pouring in from space Global rented out, most of it to smaller express companies and railroads. The company had changed from tenant to landlord, and by year's end had a total surplus of almost $27 million.

"That," Rose announced, raising her champagne glass, "makes our resources second only to the National City Bank of New York. Next year—or rather, this year—we're going to surpass them!"

Franklin laughed. "Hear, hear!"

They were sharing a celebratory drink before going out to a party. As he helped Rose with her cape, Franklin said, "But before you make any grand schemes we had better talk to Commissioner Alcorn. I keep hearing that there's something brewing as far as he's concerned."

Rose squeezed his arm. "Whatever it is, it can wait!"

Rose didn't want anything to spoil this moment. For her it was the realization of her dream—she and Franklin working together, taking Global to limitless horizons. From this point on, nothing would stand in their way.

Commissioner Matthias Alcorn was a short, ascetic man in his mid-fifties who favored dark blue suits and polka dot bow ties that gave him a professorial look. Rose knew that beneath the mild-mannered academic demeanor lurked a brilliant mind.

Matthias Alcorn may have been richer than Croesus but he was no friend to his social class. Riding the wave of populist and progressive movements that had swept the nation at the turn of the century, Alcorn had made himself a spokesman for "the little man." He continually demanded government regulation in business and the breakup of monopolies, and railed against what he considered disgracefully lenient sentences handed down in the Miller-Humbolt affair.

To Rose, meeting with Alcorn was akin to poking a snake with a stick. But there were persistent rumors that the commissioner was sniffing around the express companies' business. She had to know what Alcorn was after.

"Thank you for taking time out of your busy schedule to meet with us," Rose said, making sure that Alcorn's glass was filled with his favorite sherry.

"You would have been hearing from me sooner or later, Mrs. Talbot," Alcorn replied, polishing his bifocals with an outrageous purple and pink polka dot handkerchief.

"Indeed," Rose murmured, gritting her teeth at the use of her married name.

"Yes, I'm afraid so," Alcorn said. "The Interstate Commerce Commission is very concerned about express industry practices."

Rose almost choked. Created in 1888, the Interstate Commerce Commission, or ICC, had been designed to regulate the railroad business. For years the railroads had monopolized transport and set whatever rates they pleased. In spite of public outrage this practice continued until even the federal government found it intolerable. The ICC mandated that a railroad was a "common carrier" and so had to provide service to anyone who was willing to pay, without discrimination of price or freight. The railroads had had to comply but express companies remained exempt.

"Why is that, Senator?" asked Rose. "Our customers have no complaints."

"Because your customers can't get a better deal anywhere else," Alcorn replied with a thin smile. "You express people may fight like gamecocks between yourselves for routes, but when it comes to rates you get together, fix a tariff, and live by it—no exceptions. That's not exactly in keeping with the spirit of free enterprise, is it?"

Franklin, who had never looked into that part of Global's operations, raised an eyebrow at Rose.

"Whatever arrangements we make," Rose answered smoothly, "and they are not as sinister as you make them out to be, are really in the interests of our customers, to provide them with the best possible service."

"I'll grant you the service part," Alcorn said. "I certainly reserve judgment on whether it's the best and most inexpensive."

"If that's the case, what do you propose?" Rose asked bluntly.

Obviously there would be no way to sweet-talk Matthias Alcorn out of his crusader position.

"Given your resources, Mrs. Talbot, I'm surprised you don't already know," Alcorn said mildly. "The Supreme Court handed down its ruling a few hours ago. As of this moment, express companies, like railroads, are deemed to be common carriers.

"Which means," the commissioner finished, "that the ICC is going to scrutinize your books, rates, and profits."

"That miserable little man!" Rose fumed. "Alcorn knew what the court's ruling would be all along. He came to us only so he could gloat!"

"What of it?" replied Franklin. "The ICC wants us to open our books, we open them. Other express companies will have to do the same. It's not as though we have anything to hide. I mean, all that talk about collusion and price fixing was nonsense, wasn't it?"

"Most of it," Rose said, hedging. "There have been agreements in the past."

"What kind of agreements, Rose?"

"That's not important," she replied. "The question is how we stop him."

"We can't. There is such a thing as the law of the land."

"You're right there," Rose agreed. "Fortunately for us, the law is subject to many interpretations." She paused. "And in this case, the strictest may be the best. Come, there's work to do."

Rose had reached the door before she noticed that Franklin was still by the fireplace.

"Who is 'we,' Rose?" he asked softly. "Which of our competitors have you been dealing with—if they really are competitors? For how long?"

Rose looked straight back at him. "All of them. Our grandfather created this arrangement long before either of us was born."

Franklin was shocked. "Why didn't you ever tell me? More to the point, why are we continuing to do this? It's not like there isn't enough business to go around."

"Before you go throwing stones at glass houses, think back to your little secretary," Rose reminded him, catching the reproach in her brother's tone.

"You didn't have any qualms about using her when the company's interests were at stake."

At that moment Rose had no regrets about such words. She did not recognize their cruelty because she sincerely believed that Franklin would quickly realize the implications if the ICC was successful in prying open the express companies' books: the silent, hidden agreements between the companies, which guaranteed profits for even the smallest carrier, would be subject to public scrutiny, outrage, and ultimately enforced change. That, Rose knew, would be the beginning of the end for the express business.

— || —

As Rose had anticipated, the Supreme Court ruling was applauded by the public but caused outrage among the express companies. In a secret meeting at Talbot House, Rose and the directors of other companies hammered out a plan to form a united front, share legal expenses, and influence public opinion through advertising.

They think they're out of some Dumas novel, Rose thought as the gathering broke up. *One for all and all for one.*

That, she was certain, wouldn't last long under the concerted attacks of Matthias Alcorn. So Rose made her own plans and in the spring of 1917, Global Enterprises quietly began selling off its contracts with the small feeder-express companies. Rose immediately funneled her profits into the nation's railroads. From personal experience she knew that railroads were a capital-intensive industry dependent on banks or bond issues for financing. She approached several lines offering loans on generous terms. On the face of it the railroads couldn't find fault with the agreement. Only when Global accepted massive blocks of shares in the companies as interest payments did it dawn on the officials that Global was in fact running the whole operation, not only the express end of it.

When railroad customers such as the fruit and vegetable growers on the West Coast banded together to complain about rates and threatened legal action, Rose countered immediately. In the case of the grape growers she waited until her advisers informed her that California would have a bumper crop. Rose promptly jacked up the freight rates and informed the growers that if they didn't like her prices they could ship with someone else. Since both sides knew there was no alternative, Rose suggested a compromise: if the growers dropped their threat of a suit, Global would guarantee delivery of their crop to market. Otherwise the best yield in a decade would be left to rot under the blazing California sun.

"You might be able to fend off Alcorn's ICC and buy out individual lawsuits with your battery of attorneys on retainer, but there's one problem you won't solve either of those ways."

Rose watched Franklin close the door to her office and took a deep breath. She had been keenly aware of her brother's disapproval. However, if Franklin couldn't see her point of view, she was certainly no closer to sharing his.

"It's too nice a day for problems," Rose said lightly, eager to avoid another argument. "I think we should finish up early and drive to Dunescrag tonight. It'll be lovely by the water."

Franklin shook his head. "This won't keep, Rose. It concerns our workers."

"Yes?"

"There's going to be a strike."

Rose gave him a sharp look. For months she had been hearing rumors about workers' dissatisfaction with conditions at Global freight yards. On the other hand, regional managers constantly reassured her that there was nothing to worry about. Certainly Rose had heard no rumblings of discontent at the Global offices on Lower Broadway.

"How do you know this?"

"I spend most of my time in the field," Franklin reminded her. "A lot of what goes on there never makes it back to New York."

"But all our managers tell me—"

"Forget them! They tell you what you want to hear. Believe me, Rose, if Global doesn't raise wages fast, the strike will accomplish what the ICC wishes it could do: break us!"

"A strike is out of the question," Rose said, getting to her feet. "Our people would starve."

Franklin stared at her, dumbfounded. "What do you think is happening to them now?"

The following week Rose found the answer on the front page of Q magazine in an article announcing the strike. A day later, Global employees across the country began walking off their jobs.

"How could you write something so irresponsible?" Rose stormed. "You damn well incited my workers to go on strike!"

Monk rose and closed the door to his office.

"I'm not the one making the news, Rose," he pointed out. "You are. I'm just reporting it."

"Don't confuse the issue!" Rose snapped. "Your piece was inflammatory!"

"Rose, the truth is that it's your relationship with your drivers, loaders, packers, clerks, and everyone else who does scut work that's become inflammatory. You should have seen this coming a long time ago."

Monk tilted his chair back to its usual precarious angle. It had been months since he had seen Rose, yet the instant she had swept into his office she had seized his heart. With every passing year, with every new challenge she confronted, the fire that blazed from her gray eyes and crept under her skin in a blush seemed to burn more fiercely. The effect was hypnotic, and Monk still felt himself irresistibly drawn to it.

"Rose, what do you want from me?"

"At the very least you can give my side of the story."

"Do you know what that is?" The door crashed open and Franklin strode in, his face flushed with anger.

"What the hell is this?" he demanded, flinging a piece of paper in front of his sister.

Rose snatched it away. "It's definitely not something we should discuss here."

"You want the public to know your side of the story?" Franklin carried on, ignoring her. "Fine. Let's tell them." He faced Monk. "What my sister doesn't want you to see is the memorandum of agreement she's signed with Arthur Gladstone."

Monk leaped out of his chair. "Rose, you can't be serious!"

Arthur Gladstone was the country's leading private policeman. His squads were legendary for using strong-arm tactics to break up strikes.

"If it comes to that, you're damn right I'm serious!" Rose told them both.

"Won't you at least talk to our people?" Franklin pleaded.

"We've beaten that particular horse to death," Rose shot back. "If I talk to the drivers then the wagon helpers will want a meeting. If I see them, the agents will be hammering on my door. And so on and so forth. There'll be no end to it."

"Oh, there will be an end. A bloody one!"

"For heaven's sake!" Rose snapped. "Don't you understand? The other companies are waiting to see what happens. They support me to the hilt because if I cave in then their employees will walk out too. Before you know it we'll have chaos."

"How long do you think Global can hold out?"

"As long as necessary!" Rose said grimly.

"There has to be another way—" Franklin began.

"If you're so damned concerned about these . . . these Bolshevik agitators, why don't you go and talk to them," Rose cut in.

"Maybe I'll do just that," Franklin replied coldly.

"And while you're at it, remind them that there are a dozen men lined up for every job vacancy. It's not as though we can't do without them!"

Rose whirled around and left the office, marching past the stunned Q employees in the outer office.

"You know I can't hold back this particular story," Monk said.

"I don't care," Franklin replied. "I can't believe Rose would do something like this. These people aren't our enemies!"

"Then you'd better talk to them. If you don't, no one will. This may be your last chance to prevent violence."

Franklin lit a cigarette. "I never asked for any of this. I never wanted any damn part of Global!"

Monk's heart went out to his friend. He wanted to tell him that he didn't have to live up to other people's idea of what was the responsible and right thing to do. Unfortunately, in this case the other person was Rose Jefferson.

"Whether you wanted it or not, it's yours now. If something happens, you'll never forgive yourself."

Franklin looked up at him. "If anyone gets hurt, I'm not the one who's going to need forgiveness."

Given the bitterness and hostility Global workers harbored toward the company, Franklin approached them cautiously. He was surprised at the welcome he received and quickly discovered that employees were as eager to air their grievances as he was to listen to them.

In smoke-filled meeting halls, the back rooms of freight warehouses, and the bowels of Global's huge sorting facilities, Franklin Jefferson was shown a side of Global that seemed a million miles away from the regal offices of Lower Broadway. Although Franklin knew wages throughout the industry were low, he had no idea they were barely at subsistence level. On the bottom rung were the wagon helpers, some of whom earned as little as seventeen dollars a month. The best made less than fifty dollars. Drivers brought home a paltry nine hundred a year. In addition, fifteen-hour workdays were routine, along with required work on holidays and one Sunday a month.

The figures were appalling but Franklin didn't really understand what they meant until, at the workers' insistence, he visited their homes and saw firsthand how little that money bought: noisy, overcrowded tenements where entire families lived in two rooms while sharing a kitchen and toilet with three others. The sight of children in rags and pregnant wives sewing piecemeal goods by candlelight broke his heart.

"Can't you find other work?" he once asked one of the drivers.

The man stared at him incredulously; then, realizing Franklin was serious, he laughed bitterly.

"You don't understand, do you? Express'n' is all I know. Your people told us we had to sign a paper when we were hired. If we work for Global we can't move to another company."

"You mean you're indentured!"

"If you're sayin' the company owns me and my family and I work for it the rest of my life, that's right."

Franklin checked the employees' list of grievances against the contracts they had signed, as well as agreements between workers and employers in similar industries. The conclusion was inescapable: Global and the other express companies had an ironclad hold over their workers. Convinced of the employees' legitimate grievances, Franklin drew up a list of remedies.

"Higher wages, shorter hours, better working conditions," Rose said, ticking one point after another. "Is there anything they *don't* want?"

"For heaven's sake, Rose, go out there. Talk to these people. *Your* people. See how they live. Then you'll understand that what they want is no more than a pittance."

"I offered all the strikers their jobs back if they return immediately," Rose told him. "The deadline is tomorrow. If they don't come back, they have only themselves to blame for the consequences. But one way or another Global will be open for business!"

As the deadline came and went, trucks carrying scab labor appeared at Global warehouses along the Hudson. They were greeted by hundreds of pickets, each man carrying a club, length of pipe, or chains.

"What is your pleasure, madam?" asked Arthur Gladstone.

He was a short, barrel-chested man with a waxed walrus mustache and furry muttonchop sideburns that hid most of his face. Except for the eyes. They were a policeman's eyes, impassive yet constantly surveying. From his rooftop vantage point, Gladstone watched as Global security guards somehow managed to keep open a corridor between the strikers lined up against the warehouse fence and the row of trucks carrying the scab labor.

Beside him Rose Jefferson shivered as the wind swept in from the river.

"Damn them!" she muttered. "Why did it have to come to this?"

Gladstone had heard the question a thousand times, from mine operators, textile-mill owners, and steel men. There wasn't one major industry in America where his force hadn't been needed, sooner or later. He said nothing. Rose Jefferson would come to the inevitable conclusion just as others before her had.

Rose was thinking of all the freight that had to be moved, the disruptions in service that had already been caused, the bottlenecks that were developing across the country as goods piled up in depots, some to rot and perish.

99

I have a responsibility to my customers. To what Global stands for. Because Global must survive.

She wished to God that Franklin were there, to support her decision. The fact that he had broken ranks and considered her the enemy tore at her heart.

"Go ahead, Mr. Gladstone," Rose said clearly. "Send in your men to protect my property."

The strikers kept a wary eye on the trucks in front of them. A few hurled epithets at the men inside. The leaders paced the line nervously, swinging their clubs. They, like their fellow workers, were not fighters but family men whose faces reflected a lifetime of toil. On one hand they wished desperately to avoid violence; on the other, they still had their self-respect. That, more than money, more than anything, had become the issue.

"Jesus, Joseph, and Mary!"

At the cry, all eyes riveted on the trucks. Dozens of men began spilling out, each armed with a long billy club and wearing the distinctive green cap that identified a Gladstone enforcer. The men on the line began to mill around but found there was nowhere to go except up against the fence. The Global security officers who had patrolled the no-man's land fled.

"Don't panic! Don't leave your positions!"

Heads turned as Franklin Jefferson ran across the lot.

"They won't hurt you!" he shouted, putting himself between the workers and the advancing Gladstone force. "I'm on your side. There's still a way out of this. We don't need to fight!"

"Whaddya think they came for?" a man behind him yelled.

Franklin held up his arms. "It's all right. I'll talk to them. There's nothing to be afraid of."

He turned and boldly stepped forward toward the leader of the Gladstone troops.

Rose grabbed Gladstone's arm. "That's my brother! You've got to stop them."

Gladstone continued to watch the unfolding drama.

"It's too late, madam," he replied. "Mr. Jefferson has no business being there, and my men have their orders. Rest assured they'll be carried out."

Rose couldn't help herself. With all her might she screamed, *"Franklin!"*

"Sir, my name is Franklin Jefferson. My sister and I own these premises. I must ask you to stop where you are—otherwise I shall have the police arrest you for trespassing."

The red-haired Irishman towering over Franklin blinked as though he couldn't believe what he was hearing.

"You with them?" he demanded at last.

"Yes, sir, I am," Franklin said. "I realize your intentions—"

"If you're with 'em then this is for you!"

The Irishman flicked his wrist and his billy club smashed into Franklin's ribs. Another blow struck his kidneys, and a third, to the groin, sent him rolling in agony to the ground.

A giant roar shattered the air. Franklin felt himself being kicked and pummeled, then mercifully something hard struck his jaw and he was borne away, drifting high above the screams and carnage. His last thought was of Rose, and without his knowing it, tears filled his closed eyes.

At the end of the day, after the cries of battle had faded, fifty-two men were taken to the hospital. Three died before the night was out.

Nor did the violence stop there. All month, battles raged from one Global property to another. As casualties mounted and martyrs were interred, New York's mayor, William Gaynor, intervened, threatening to impound wagons and trucks driven by scabs, and used the police to enforce his intentions. Both sides relented and under Gaynor's watchful eye a settlement was hammered out. Rose grudgingly agreed not to fire striking workers other than those whom the police had arrested for rioting. She also appointed representatives to meet with the men to settle their grievances. For their part, the workers returned to their jobs and soon Global freight was once again moving across the land.

"Forty thousand dollars," Rose mused, checking Eric Gollant's final tally on the strike.

There had been a time when she would have considered the settlement cheap at twice the price. But she could no longer measure the cost in money alone.

Rose had raced to Franklin's side when she saw him fall. She led a squad of Global security men to the fringe of the battle and helped drag Franklin to safety, holding on to him all the way to the hospital.

Franklin Jefferson was one of the lucky ones. He had suffered no internal injuries, his broken ribs mended, and the brilliant yellow-blue lump on his jaw faded. In spite of Rose's daily visits, Franklin refused to see her. Instead he wrote letters of condolence to the families of the men who had been killed and a note to Hugh O'Neill asking him to make sure the wives and children were compensated. His only stipulation was that the funds were to come out of his private income. He did not want Global involved.

For the first time since he had started working for Global, Franklin found himself completely alone, beholden to no one. The only person with whom he shared his thoughts and his doubts was Monk McQueen.

"Rose is worried sick about you," Monk said, swinging himself onto the windowsill, completely blocking the dramatic view of the East River and beyond, the autumn colors splashed across Roosevelt Island. "She can't forgive herself for what happened. Not until you do."

"I'm not the one she should ask," Franklin replied. "I'm still alive."

"Then you have to forgive her," Monk said. "You can't believe she ever meant for any of that to happen."

"Maybe not. But she was the one who hired Gladstone and his thugs. She knew what they were capable of. I can't work with Rose anymore. I can't go back to Global and pretend none of this ever happened. I care about our people, Monk. I'll never be able to face them again."

Monk saw the struggle going on inside his friend. Franklin had followed the dictates of his heart and conscience without realizing that no matter how noble these were, they still had their price. To pay it meant turning his back on every hope his sister had ever invested in him.

"I've always tried to do the right thing," Franklin went on. "I believed what Rose said about my responsibilities to my grandfather and the company, so I came to Global. I believed the picture of it she painted and stepped into the fairy tale of Lower Broadway, which was as far from reality as what happened that day by the Hudson. I tried to do the right thing. . . . And I failed."

Monk was uneasy about the turn the conversation had taken.

"Don't make any hasty decisions. You have a lot to think about. It'll take time to put everything in perspective."

"Oh, I've already done that," Franklin said softly. "I know where I have to go and what I must do."

Monk was puzzled. "Where?"

"To the same place you're going."

At first Monk didn't understand the reference. When its meaning finally dawned on him he was dismayed, less by the notion than by the unshakable resolution in Franklin's voice.

Steven Jefferson loved the grand parties for which Talbot House was justly famous. Although only nine years old, he put on a very serious air when his mother introduced him. The rule was he could only stay for an hour, and as much as Steven resented this he made the most of his time. He walked among the throngs, avoiding the women who invariably wanted to hug him and tousle his hair, and tried to get close to the men. He loved the odor of cologne and cigar smoke. He learned to recognize that hearty laughter was often a sign of a man wounded, trying to keep up appearances, while those who were secure in their power spoke softly, easily, with unmistakable authority. In such men Steven saw his father.

When his mother had announced that, because Franklin was still recuperating, she was canceling the Thanksgiving Day party, Steven had raged for days. But no one suspected a thing. Steven had become a master at hiding his emotions. The stuffed animals that he viciously hacked apart with scissors to unburden himself were quickly disposed of after the fury passed.

As he sat at the dinner table next to his mother, Steven glanced resentfully at his uncle. Steven knew all about the falling out between Rose and Franklin, how his mother had called in the strike breakers, and how his uncle had tried to stop them. Steven had never had any affection for his uncle. In fact he considered him a weakling and couldn't understand why his mother worshiped the ground he walked on. How could she not see the kind of man he was? Steven worried the question until he arrived at the inescapable answer: people had illusions that they refused to surrender. In Steven's mind this was a weakness, one to be remembered, possibly used, always guarded against.

Steven ate in silence, listening to the strained conversation between his mother and Franklin. He knew that what they really wanted to say to each other wouldn't come out until he was gone. Steven gobbled up his pumpkin pie, finished his milk, and excused himself from the table. He smiled and said he was going to his room. Naturally, they believed him.

"Rose—"
"Franklin—"
They looked at each other and laughed, embarrassed.
"Go ahead, you first," Franklin said.
Rose took a deep breath. She had been practicing this speech for days. Now the words deserted her.
"I want to say, I'm sorry," she blurted. "For what happened to you . . . for everything."
"That's all in the past," Franklin told her. "You did what you felt had to be done. Things got out of control. . . ."
Rose sighed with relief. She had never been good at apologizing. Especially when she knew she was right. She seized the olive branch Franklin held out.
"It's time for you to come back, Franklin. I need you."
"I can't do that, Rose. I've made other plans." He paused. "I've enlisted in the Marine Corps."
Rose set her coffee cup in its saucer, intensely aware of the delicate ring of bone china. *This can't be happening.*

"The Marine Corps?"

"I'm going to fight in Europe. My ship leaves in three days."

Whatever you do, don't lose control. He'll be sure to go away if you do. . . .

"Don't you think we should have discussed this?" Rose asked as calmly as possible.

"No. This was my decision to make. Not yours. Not anyone else's."

"I don't suppose Monk had anything to do with this. I heard he's going over."

"He didn't. In fact, he tried to talk me out of going."

"Not very successfully," Rose said sarcastically.

Franklin rose. "I'm not going to get into a fight with you, Rose. I have an obligation to my country . . . and myself. I hoped you could understand that."

Rose couldn't hold back her words: "What about your obligation to me? To the company? To everything I've done to make you part of it?"

"After what happened, I don't owe you or the company a damned thing."

For the first time in her life Rose realized that this was something she couldn't change. Not in three days. To press meant to push Franklin even further away, perhaps lose him forever.

"This is a terrible shock for me," she said at last.

"I'm not doing this to hurt you, Rose."

Rose looked back at him, smiling wanly.

"Of course you are. That's the only reason you could possibly have."

Rose did not sleep at all that night. She raised one argument after another and rejected them all. By dawn, Rose knew she had only one hope. She dialed Monk McQueen's number.

"I'm not calling to quarrel," she said as soon as a sleepy voice answered. "Franklin told me he's enlisted and . . . and that you had nothing to do with it. Just promise me one thing, Monk: that you'll bring him back alive, whole."

"Rose—"

"Promise me that, Monk!"

"Of course I promise."

The line went dead. Rose pushed the telephone away and stared out at the majesty of the late fall dawn. Then the sun pierced the windows and warmed her tears.

It's up to me now. Again. To do what has to be done. Alone.

In his bedroom with an illuminated globe casting shadows across his face, Steven Jefferson was sleeping peacefully. After eavesdropping on the conversation between his mother and uncle, he had gone to bed a very happy boy. Franklin was one of two adults he somehow had to overcome in order to claim what his father had left him. Steven didn't know how he would accomplish this but suddenly he understood that perhaps he wouldn't have to do anything at all. He was old enough to know that when men went off to war they were often wounded. And sometimes they didn't come back at all. . . .

PART

—————

TWO

- 12 -

Even with his eyes closed he could see the sun, a fiery yellow disk against a curtain of crimson. Its heat was an invisible weight upon him, streaming through his skin, permeating the flesh and bone, warming him before it passed into the loamy earth. He inhaled deeply, heady from the yellow mustard, blue cornflower, and scarlet poppy that made his bed. The scent of crushed flowers mingled with the musky odor of sun-drenched spring grass, rising in the heat, overwhelming his senses, carrying him away on a symphony conducted by cicadas, crickets, and grasshoppers. His head rolled to one side, his lips breaking into an unconscious contented smile.

Franklin Jefferson's eyes flew open and he raised his forearm to cover them from the sun. But there was no sun, only gray-black clouds, heavy with the grim promise of still another storm, boiling across the morning sky.

Franklin rolled over, groaning as his canteen, ammunition canister, and backpack webbing gouged his body. There was no sweet meadow grass beneath him, only the mud of a deep, angled trench. The smell did not come from flowers but from the damp, chilled bodies of tired, hungry soldiers huddled against the packed earth, their shoulders hunched over bayoneted rifles gripped by white-knuckled fingers.

Carefully Franklin pushed himself up and peered over the lip of the trench. Across a cratered field, once heavy with wheat and rye, he saw the German positions. It was only there that flowers grew, roses which had miraculously survived the fury of war, been severed whole from their stems and strewn across the battlefield to be caught on the tangle of barbed wire that surrounded the enemy's position.

Franklin Jefferson sank back into the trench. He knew exactly where he was now. No dream could dispel the reality of a place called Belleau Wood, in France, in a season he faintly recognized as June, in the seemingly endless year of 1918.

"Come on, McQueen, time to get some food into that belly of yours."

Franklin Jefferson stepped over two Marines sprawled across the narrow path at the bottom of the trench. He squatted, balancing tin plates of greasy stew topped with a crust of moldy bread.

Monk McQueen took a tentative sniff and shook his head. "Please, not first thing in the morning."

"We're lucky to get this," Franklin replied cheerfully, thrusting the plate against Monk's chest. "The Germans are surviving on rat sausage."

Monk dipped the bread crust into the stew to soften it and chewed silently. He gazed up and down the trench where soldiers were waking up from what precious little sleep had been stolen from the fear, cold, and nightmares. The wind shifted and the trench was filled with the noxious odor from a nearby latrine.

"What do you think?" asked Franklin, using his bayonet to spear his meat. "Will the Hun be coming over the top today?"

"Not today. It's going to rain like hell and the Germans won't risk a fight in the muck."

For six days the Second United States Marine Division had been pinned down at Belleau Wood, north of the bloody fields of Château Thierry. Their orders were unequivocal: hold the position at all costs until American and French support units arrived. A week ago the German advance had been stopped in its tracks by the First and Second divisions at enormous cost to American lives. General "Black Jack" Pershing had made it clear that these men would not have died in vain.

"That's exactly why the Germans will counterattack!" Franklin said, his voice sparkling with excitement. "They always counterattack in lousy weather, at exactly the time we think they'd dig in."

Before Monk could argue, the platoon sergeant, a grizzled, beefy veteran of the war against Spain, slid into the trench.

"Well, boys, looks like another shitty day in the land of gay Paree. Any patrol volunteers to see what the Kaiser's boys are up to?"

Franklin raised his hand. "Count me in, Sarge."

And doesn't old Sarge know it! Monk thought angrily.

Ever since the platoon had gone into combat, on December 6, 1917, Franklin Jefferson had volunteered for every hazardous assignment that had come along. Miraculously, he had completed each one without so much as a scratch on his once-fair city skin. To the men in the platoon, superstitious as only soldiers can be, he had become a talisman. It was a side of the man Monk had never seen before.

The transformation of Franklin Jefferson had begun soon after the ancient troop ship *Hatteras* left the algae-covered pier of the Brooklyn Army Terminal. Before the vessel was halfway across the storm-ridden Atlantic almost every Marine in the Division was experiencing agonizing seasickness, made all the worse by the constant groaning and squealing of hull plates as the *Hatteras* rolled in interminable swells. Even though he was an experienced sailor, Monk succumbed to nausea. But not Franklin. Frankie, as he was dubbed by the men of Bravo Company, became their guardian angel, emptying bedpans and chamber pots, changing sheets, and washing sweat-soaked clothing. He listened to the innermost secrets of ailing men who were convinced they were going to die and even assisted the Division surgeon during an emergency appendectomy.

By the time the *Hatteras* docked in Le Havre, Franklin had more friends than he could count. Everyone knew his background, but if a stranger made a cutting remark about a rich boy playing at war, he was quickly told to shut up. As far as the men were concerned, Frankie was one of their own.

Monk had never thought Franklin a leader, yet when the company moved out to the American forward positions the men naturally clustered around him. They may have listened to officers' orders but it was Franklin they followed when the call came to go over the top. As the American offensive rolled over France, pushing the Germans back mile by bloody mile, Franklin's reputation grew into legend. In St. Amiens, where the company encountered fanatical resistance, Franklin singlehandedly charged an oncoming tank, destroying its tread with a hand grenade, then proceeded to finish off its crew. On another occasion he stayed in the field, firing back as German bullets tried to cut down him and the two wounded Marines he was dragging back to safety.

By early spring, accounts of such exploits were on the lips of every man in the Division. Yet, when soldiers came up to congratulate him Franklin was embarrassed by all the fuss. General Black Jack Pershing, who personally decorated Franklin in the field, spoke of his modesty. Others thought Franklin shy. Only Monk, who was keeping careful records of both the battles and his friend's extraordinary actions, knew that what Franklin had told him at the Brooklyn Army Terminal was indeed the truth: he had gone to war to meet his destiny. But whatever it was, Monk was convinced that it did not include Franklin's dying in blood-streaked mud under a foreign sky.

"Right, boys, are you ready?"

There was no lack of volunteers to accompany Franklin on patrol. Every man was convinced that nothing would happen to him as long as he was at Jefferson's side.

"Has there been any movement in their trenches, Sarge?" asked Monk.

"Not enough to shake the pee off your dick," the veteran replied. "But we got to know if the bastards are still there or if they pulled out during the night."

"Oh, they're there, all right." Franklin grunted, adjusting the straps on his backpack. "They're just sleeping late."

"If they are, we'll wake 'em up nice and easy like."

The third soldier in the patrol was a nineteen-year-old private from Kentucky with hands callused and yellow from the tobacco fields. The men had nicknamed him Bluegrass Boy.

"Don't go looking to be a hero," the sergeant warned him. "Just get over to that hill there and have a look. If they're in the trenches, signal back. Let artillery do the dirty work."

"Hell, ol' Frankie here is all the artillery we need!" the Kentuckian said, laughing.

The three men clambered up the side of the trench and began crawling on elbows and knees across the cratered field, their rifles rocking in the crooks of their arms. After a hundred feet Franklin signaled a stop.

"Very quiet," he whispered.

"Not even a morning fart," the private agreed. "We could probably go right up and knock on their door."

"We go to the hill," Monk said firmly.

The hill was nothing more than a large mound of dirt thrown up by four years of constant shelling. The three men hugged one side, then slowly proceeded to creep up the face. As they peered over the top they saw the German trenches not twenty yards away.

"Well, I'll be," the Kentuckian drawled. "They skedaddled on us."

Franklin raised himself for a better look. The trenches were empty.

"I don't know," he said softly. "If they're gone we should have heard them during the night. The only place they could have moved to are those trees. That would have caused a racket."

"Ah, hell, Frankie, even if that's so it's okay for us to take their holes."

Franklin hesitated. The shallow trenches appeared empty, but from their vantage point they couldn't see into all of them. There could still be men hiding in them.

"No!"

Franklin's warning came too late. The Kentuckian had signaled back to their lines and Marines began pouring over the trenches, running across the field, not bothering even to crouch.

"Something's wrong!" Franklin shouted to Monk.

His words were cut short as he saw the private rise to his feet to better survey the landscape.

"Bluegrass Boy!"

The private looked down at him with a wide grin. He opened his mouth to reply, but instead of words Franklin and Monk heard a sharp crack. The Kentuckian's eyes widened in surprise and his hand flew to his throat. Slowly he pitched forward, crashing against Franklin.

"No!"

Franklin rolled the private over, his hands slippery from the blood pouring from the Marine's throat. The Kentuckian was staring at him in horror, his lips working feverishly. Franklin cradled the private's head in his hands. "You'll be all right! I'll get you out of here, I promise!"

At that moment the sky erupted in artillery, machine gun and carbine fire. Franklin and Monk pushed their backs up against the mound of dirt, dragging the dead Marine with them. Franklin looked back in disbelief. One by one, then in pairs, and finally in whole groups, Marines were falling to the earth as shells and bullets found their mark.

"I've got to stop this!"

"Stay down!" Monk yelled, jerking his friend to the ground. "There's nothing you can do! Nothing!"

McQueen watched Franklin's eyes glaze over. Throughout the fury he just kept staring at that field of death, knowing with a certainty only the damned can experience that his destiny was about to reveal itself to him at last.

– 13 –

The three hundred souls who remained in the village of Saint Eustace, a mile behind the American lines, barely took notice of the shelling. They had lived with the war for years and during that time the armies of five nations had left their mark on Saint Eustace.

The native sons of France had been the first to march along the centuries-old cobblestone streets, on their way to the frontier, proud and cheerful, confident of their invincibility. A few months later, as French casualties slowly turned the village into a makeshift field hospital, the Belgians came, followed by the Canadians and British. The villagers watched somberly as fresh-faced troops, led by buglers, pipers, and drummers, crossed the stone bridge that spanned the local brook, whistling at the girls who lined the street, shouting brave words to the older men and women silently gazing at them through open windows of leaf-shaded houses. The villagers had seen it all before, and if the soldiers mistook their tears for joy and relief it was only natural. They could not have known that in their shining faces the people of Saint Eustace saw not defenders but the ghosts of sons, husbands, and fathers.

The war spared Saint Eustace until the second year. In the fall of 1915 a German offensive swept across a fifty-mile front, swallowing up a third of France. After September hundreds of cities and towns fell under the German yoke. But once again Saint Eustace escaped devastation. Wounded Allied soldiers who had been left behind in the evacuation because of lack of transport were quickly dispatched to camps in Germany. Overnight the empty beds were filled with German casualties, and Berlin, like the Allied High Command before it, declared Saint Eustace a fire-free zone.

When they heard the news the villagers crossed themselves and gave silent thanks. The able-bodied men who remained continued to tend the fields and pastures. That the Germans demanded more of the land's bounty was a small price to pay for peace. For the women the change was even less noticeable. Sheets still had to be washed, bandages changed, broken limbs set in splints, and the instructions of the German field doctors carried out quickly and efficiently. The only difference was that the faces gazing up at them from the beds and cots belonged to the enemy. But after a time the women all agreed that the fear and resignation of these young men were no different from what they had seen in the eyes of the broken soldiers who had been there before them.

With this same stoicism Saint Eustace greeted the Americans when, on January 16, the occupying troops changed for the third time.

When will it finally end?
Michelle Lecroix stepped away from her patient and looked anxiously out the window as the bombardment started. She was a petite, slender woman with bountiful red hair that cascaded in waves around her shoulders. Although her high cheekbones gave her face a heartlike quality, her chin hinted at strength and resolve. But it was her deep blue eyes, so startling a contrast against her hair, that captured and held her image in the eye of the beholder. Gazing into them, many a soldier had felt his heart lurch. Amid so much horror and bloodshed the eyes of Michelle Lecroix made them remember that a thing called beauty still existed.

Since the first casualties had begun pouring into Saint Eustace four years ago, Michelle, then fourteen, had been working at this makeshift infirmary, once a cheese storehouse. She was the daughter of a French farmer whose family had lived in the village for generations and a British woman who had turned her back on her ties to England for a man who not only loved her but encouraged her to devote herself to her passion: sculpting.

Michelle had started out as a nurse's aide. Even though she had seen her share of nature's brutal side on the farm, nothing had prepared her for the carnage swept in by the war. Men with severed arms and legs, missing eyes, faces reduced to monstrous caricatures by shrapnel, all passed through her care. At first she shrank from the horror but as the fighting intensified and the trickle of wounded became a deluge, Michelle steeled herself. When sheer numbers overwhelmed the efforts of army doctors and the one physician native to Saint Eustace, Michelle began to assist in surgery. By the time she was sixteen she believed she had seen every cruelty men were capable of inflicting upon one another.

During the days, which more often than not stretched to forty-eight hours, she was able to maintain a calm that fooled everyone. In her eyes the soldiers saw a tenderness and concern that gave them sanctuary from their ordeal, if only for a little while. But the facade was not without its price. Michelle's sleep was plagued by relentless nightmares. Overwhelmed by what was going on around her, she stole precious moments, retreating to a hidden glade near a pond upriver from the village. There, alone, with her arms wrapped around her knees and her head bowed, she reflected on the terrible waste she was witnessing.

Michelle longed to pour out her heart to another human being, to be embraced by strong arms and feel whispered breaths telling her she was not alone. But as much as she craved such shelter she pushed away every soldier's attempt to court her. Although many were dashing and handsome, she had only to glance at one of a dozen beds to see what would inevitably become of her would-be lover.

"Hey, you're as cold as ice. What's wrong?"

Michelle looked down at the soldier who was grinning at her, holding her hand. She banished the shadow that had fallen across her face.

"Nothing at all," she replied lightly.

"This has to be my lucky day," the Marine said. "We've been holding hands long enough to be engaged."

A new barrage of gunfire erupted, rattling the hospital windows. Michelle shivered.

"Nothing to worry about," the Marine reassured her, his voice easy with the confidence of a single-engagement veteran. "Our boys probably decided it was time to push old Fritz closer to Berlin."

Michelle moved to the window.

"No, I don't think so."

"What do you mean? Whose guns could they be?"

Michelle turned to him. "They belong to the Germans. Believe me, I've heard enough to know the difference." She looked into the soldier's innocent and suddenly fearful eyes. "It's the counterattack. It's finally come."

The next twelve hours were the most chaotic Michelle had ever lived through. As soon as the Germans broke through Allied lines, the Americans ordered an evacuation. One by one the beds were emptied. Every available truck, carriage, and cart was pressed into service. Michelle worked feverishly, trying to impose some order on the mayhem. She decided which casualties could leave on their own and which had to wait for proper ambulances. She gave instructions to queasy soldiers about changing dressings and bandages and thrust packets of sulfa and rolls of gauze into their packs.

"Don't think, just do!" she repeated over and over again. "If you don't treat a wound or change a dressing, infection will set in. After that comes gangrene. Then your friend will lose a hand or arm or even die!"

As the hours flew by, Saint Eustace was reduced to bedlam. Men, horses, and vehicles clogged the narrow streets, struggling to cross the humped bridge that was the only exit to the main road. The exodus was further impeded by a violent storm. Cold driving rain caused trucks to become stuck in mud. Horses bolted in terror at the thunder and lightning while the men cursed, trying to control the frightened animals and put their shoulders to half-buried wheels.

The rage of the guns drove them on. Those who had spoken valiantly of American doughboys beating back the counteroffensive fell silent as the shelling reached its crescendo, moving closer with every clap. Finally the moment

116

Michelle had been dreading was upon them. In the midst of flight, fresh casualties began to appear on the outskirts of Saint Eustace. Singly, in pairs, then in ragged groups, men supporting one another emerged from the smoke of battle, silent, broken ghosts seeking shelter.

As soon as she saw them Michelle hustled her last patients aboard the remaining trucks. She returned to the hospital and began stripping the dirty bedding. By the time the first soldier stumbled through the door Michelle was ready. What caught her unawares was the utter defeat on the young Marine's face. Michelle's heart sank with her hopes. The Americans had not held. The Germans were coming back.

Ironically, it was their forward position on the side of the small hill that saved their lives. As the barrage intensified and the first German infantrymen materialized out of the trenches, Franklin came to his senses and threw himself at Monk, knocking him away from the hill. A second later a direct hit landed on the very spot Monk had occupied, the shock waves tearing the breath out of the two soldiers. Franklin heard Monk scream and clawed his way toward him.

The sky was spinning madly as Franklin lay there, his chest laboring for precious air. Through the haze of pain he reached out, fingers searching for his friend. Just as he found Monk's hand and held it tightly, the sky exploded. A rain of dirt, stones, and debris poured down on Franklin, sending his body jerking in pain. With a final superhuman effort he rolled over and covered McQueen's body with his own. Then something with the weight of a smith's hammer hit him behind the ear. Franklin gasped as the pain cut through his skull. In his last lucid moment he wondered why he was screaming so much.

As his eyes closed Franklin Jefferson realized that the cries were not his. Through the mists of battle he saw the Germans, their long greatcoats flapping around their boots, their bloodstained bayonets rising and falling as they worked their way through the Allied dead and dying, making certain no one survived the hellish caldron.

They're coming for us, Franklin thought wearily. And he understood that for all the profundity and importance he had placed on his destiny it really was to be no different from that of the young Kentuckian or Monk or any other ordinary mortal.

The swiftness of the German counterattack took both the Allied armies and the French population by surprise. In twenty-four hours the Kaiser's troops had pushed forward thirty miles across a two-hundred-mile front. By dusk, as the last American Marines were pulling out, the citizens of Saint Eustace saw enemy infantrymen emerge cautiously from the woods surrounding the village.

Like everyone else, Michelle Lecroix expected this occupation to be no different from the one that had preceded it. The Germans would take over the hospital facilities of Saint Eustace and fill the empty beds with their own casualties. Life, as normal as it could be under the circumstances, would continue.

But this time was different. Watching the troops enter the village, Michelle shivered uneasily. These men were not callow youths but seasoned veterans, grim, unsmiling men who moved swiftly from house to house, conducting searches, barking orders, dragging out Allied soldiers they found hiding in root cellars and attics. The civilians who had sheltered them were driven into the village square before the church.

After the Allied soldiers and civilians had been formed into two ragged rows and the population of Saint Eustace herded into the square, the regiment commander, a tall, mustachioed officer with the erect bearing of a Prussian nobleman, stepped forward. Silently he went up and down the ranks before stopping in front of a man Michelle recognized as the postmaster.

"Do you deny you were hiding the enemy in your home?" the Prussian demanded in thickly accented French.

The postmaster, cap in hand, head bowed, shook his head, not daring to look up.

"Are you hiding anyone else?"

"No, Major, I swear it!"

The officer regarded the postmaster silently, then took two quick steps back.

"You swear it?"

"On my life, Major!"

"On your life . . ." the Prussian murmured.

He turned to the villagers and shouted, "You heard him, all of you! He swore on his life that he hides no enemy."

The officer raised his hand. Two infantrymen emerged from the post office, dragging a wounded American airman between them, dropping him at their superior's feet. The Prussian stared down at the semiconscious flyer, who was groaning in agony. He took out his pistol and pointed the barrel directly between the prisoner's terrified eyes.

"On your life!" the Prussian shouted. "That was what you said, wasn't it?"

The postmaster stared at the German in horror. "But, Major—"

"That was what you said!"

The postmaster nodded, unable to tear his eyes away from the airman, who had only seconds to live.

Forgive me, he thought, crossing himself. *I did what I could*.

"You all heard him!" the Prussian roared, turning to the villagers. "You

118

heard him say he harbored no one. You see for yourselves that he lied. Now you will witness the penalty for such deceit!"

The Prussian brought the gun barrel forward until it almost touched the airman's forehead.

"I hope you have made your peace with your Maker," he said in a ringing voice.

The single shot exploded in the silence that had enveloped the square. Men and women who hadn't flinched under the worst bombardment shuddered and squeezed their eyes shut. Then a collective gasp broke. Miraculously the airman was still alive, shivering and sobbing, his body huddled like a baby's. Two hundred pairs of eyes followed the rigid arm of the Prussian officer, to the hand that held the smoking pistol. A few feet away lay the postmaster, blood streaming from the gaping hole in his chest where the bullet had torn into his heart.

Slowly the Prussian holstered his weapon.

"I do not shoot helpless, wounded men who have fought honorably," he called out to the crowd. "I will shoot liars and enemy agents without mercy. That, people of Saint Eustace, is the only thing you need to know about Major Wolfgang von Ott!"

Michelle Lecroix, Major Wolfgang von Ott, and Emil Radisson, Saint Eustace's sole physician, who had ministered to three generations of villagers, were standing by the entrance to the infirmary. Michelle watched the activity around her, impressed with the efficiency of the Germans, an efficiency she knew would save lives. Even before sentries reached their posts the medical field teams had taken over the rudimentary surgery and were hard at work. Meanwhile, less serious wounds were being treated by orderlies. Although dozens of soldiers waited their turn outside, the major had yet to put Michelle and the other six nurses, or even Dr. Radisson, to work.

He doesn't trust us.

Michelle slipped the major a sidelong glance. Even if the noble "von" hadn't preceded his surname she was certain she would have recognized his lineage, evident in the arctic-gray eyes, the contempt on the thin, unsmiling lips. Wolfgang von Ott, Michelle thought, was a very hard man.

"You are Mademoiselle Lecroix."

The statement, not question, startled Michelle. "I am, monsieur," she replied, forcing herself to be calm.

How does he know my name?

"Your reputation precedes you," Major Wolfgang von Ott said, smiling faintly. "As does that of the good doctor here. I received a full report from the previous commander who passed through here. He spoke very highly of your work."

119

Neither Michelle nor Radisson said anything.

"Tell me, mademoiselle," von Ott continued. "Do you feel outraged by my action in the square?"

Michelle felt Radisson's gnarled fingers on her forearm but she ignored the warning.

"I found it despicable, Major."

"Was the postmaster a relative of yours?"

"No. But he had a wife, daughter, and grandchildren."

"We all have families, mademoiselle. Mine was killed when French troops overran Alsace-Lorraine." The German paused. "I gave him his chance to live. He should have taken it."

"What threat was he to you?" cried Michelle. "He was an old man trying to protect a wounded soldier."

"I don't have to tell you what my men have been through," von Ott said, sweeping his arms across the room. "That much you can see for yourself. I will not tolerate any danger to them. You French think that because the Americans are here the war has been won. I tell you this is not so. Your people will respect my troops. They will obey my orders. As long as they do we will get along peaceably. But if they try to betray me then they are aware of the consequences in store for them."

Von Ott looked keenly at Michelle.

"I have to trust your people, mademoiselle. I have to trust you to nurse my soldiers. Can I do that?"

Michelle stared straight back at him.

"I am a nurse, Major," she said. "My duty is to give help to whoever needs it, German or French, soldier or civilian. I promise you we will do our best."

Wolfgang von Ott stared deeply into the brilliant blue eyes of the woman before him. He had not failed to notice the upthrust breasts, slender waist, and full hips that even the baggy makeshift uniform couldn't hide. The first time he had looked at Michelle Lecroix he had felt the stirring of lust. Yet he realized there was far more to her than the attraction of a beautiful woman. At another time, another place, he might have slaked his curiosity.

"You will do your best," he repeated slowly. "Very well, mademoiselle. That is all I can ask of you. I only hope, for both our sakes, that the rest of Saint Eustace shares your sentiments.

"Now it is late. I suggest you return to your home and rest. My medical corps can look after the men we have here at the moment. But come morning we will need you. Very much."

I can't be alive. . . . But I am!

Monk McQueen's eyes snapped open. Franklin was lying beside him, one arm stretched across Monk's chest. Monk winced, his eyes watering from the stinging, acrid smoke drifting over the battlefield. The silence around him was deafening, unnatural. There wasn't a man-made sound to be heard, not a groan, a whisper, a plea, or a prayer.

Carefully Monk moved first his feet, then his legs. Nothing was broken. Next he felt his chest and arms and finally his face. When his hands came away they were covered with blood.

That's why they didn't gut me, he thought. *They took one look at me and thought I was dead.*

Gently Monk pushed Franklin's arm off his chest and rolled over. Monk found no wounds on his friend's body but when he removed Franklin's helmet he spotted a deep, crimson gash at the temple above the right ear.

Oh, dear Jesus!

Monk probed the wound with his finger, parting the hair until the furrow disappeared into the skull. Gently he turned Franklin's head. There was no exit wound.

The bullet's lodged in his skull!

Monk pressed his fingers to Franklin's jugular and breathed a mighty sigh of relief when he discovered a strong and steady pulse.

"Hang on, friend," he whispered. "I'm going to get you out of here."

Without warning Franklin groaned and his eyes fluttered open. Monk clamped a hand over Franklin's mouth, raising a finger to his own lips. Franklin blinked. Cautiously Monk raised his head, peering into the cordite-laden mists. As far as he could see the landscape was littered with the corpses of Marines. When he was certain there was no enemy, he staggered to his feet.

No prisoners . . . They mowed us down and then bayoneted the survivors as they advanced. No time to take prisoners during a counteroffensive . . .

The utter brutality of the scene made him vomit.

Monk heard Franklin groan again and bent over him, raising him by the shoulders.

"Franklin, you've got to stand up!"

"Don't know if I can . . . head hurts . . . feel like I'm drowning . . ."

"Get up! You should be dead right now but you're not. So, damn it, you're going to get up and both of us are going to walk out of here. We're not going to die in this godforsaken shit heap!"

Incredibly, Franklin's lips creased into a smile.

"You always had to have your way, didn't you?" he rasped, raising himself inch by agonizing inch until he was standing, leaning heavily on Monk's shoulder.

"One step at a time, one foot in front of the other," Monk whispered under his breath, his eyes restlessly surveying the charnel house around him.

"My God . . ."

"Don't look at them! They're dead. There's nothing we can do for them. Come on, Franklin, one foot in front of the other . . . one in front of the other. . . ."

When they reached the woods, Monk felt safer. But he knew that the Germans, having overrun the American positions, would have swept through the forest as well. Depending on how far their advance had taken them, they could have set up a new front line anywhere between his present position and Saint Eustace. In that case he would have to find a bolt hole through that line to reach the safety of the village.

The going was excruciatingly painful but in spite of his exhaustion and Franklin's raspy breathing, Monk refused to stop or even slow the pace. He half-dragged, half-carried his friend, knowing that he might well be killing him by his effort. But to stop meant certain death.

One foot in front of the other . . .

After what seemed an eternity Monk guided Franklin into the safety of dense brush and gently laid him on the ground.

"Strange, this doesn't look like Paris," Franklin whispered, coughing hoarsely.

"Shut up and drink this," Monk said, holding a canteen to Franklin's lips.

After a few minutes they were moving again. Monk found a hunter's path and stayed on that. It was a calculated risk because the Germans would be using it too. But it was far safer than the road and allowed them faster progress than did the brush.

After they had gone about a mile Monk suddenly stopped. He could have sworn he had heard footsteps moving along the forest floor. He listened keenly and heard the sound again. This time it was louder, indicating at least several men. Monk pushed Franklin in among the trees and laid him down.

"Don't even breathe!" he whispered.

Franklin gripped his hand, his eyes burning feverishly.

"If something happens," he said in a tortured voice, "promise me you'll leave me . . . save yourself. . . ."

"The hell I will!"

"Someone's got to tell Rose." Franklin grimaced in pain. "It hurts so much. . . ."

The footsteps came closer. Monk unclipped the bayonet from beneath his rifle barrel and crawled to the edge of the path. In crablike fashion he moved toward a tall maple and slid up against its side. The footsteps had almost reached him. As a shadow fell across the path Monk stepped out from behind the tree, jamming one arm underneath the chin, choking off a scream. The other, holding the bayonet, was raised high over his head. It would be over within seconds.

— 14 —

As night fell the curfew imposed on Saint Eustace by Major Wolfgang von Ott took effect. The streets were deserted and the windows dark. Only in the major's office, behind thick blackout curtains, did lights continue to burn.

"All right, get him out of here and escort him home!"

The apothecary was the second-to-last man of the dozen who had been rounded up for interrogation. For thirty nerve-racking minutes he had answered the questions snapped at him, praying that his words would be believed. Since he spoke no English and so had had nothing to say to the *Amis* when they had occupied his village, how could he have overheard conversations about Allied war plans?

The apothecary bobbed furiously before von Ott and backed out of the office. His heart went out to the last man waiting to be questioned, Serge Picard, the jovial, rotund baker whose breads and pastries had, in better days, added a special touch to the tables of Saint Eustace. Right now the sweating Picard appeared as white as the dough he kneaded.

"Close the door," von Ott ordered after Picard had been marched into the room and pushed into the chair before the mayor's expropriated desk.

Von Ott tried to hide his disgust with the gross, porcine-faced baker. Serge Picard slouched in the chair, passing his hands over his jiggling belly and extracting a cigarette from his stained shirt pocket. Lighting it, he carelessly tossed the match across the desk into an ashtray at von Ott's elbow. Von Ott ignored the impudence.

"So, *mon capitain*," Picard said expansively. "Did you catch any fish to fry?"

"You know as well as I do the interrogations were only a charade to maintain your cover," von Ott replied.

"I'm glad you appreciate my importance," the baker said. "I am the reason Saint Eustace is free of traitors who would work with the *Amis*."

Except for you, von Ott thought. *You are the worst kind of scum, a Judas to his own people.*

But the major grudgingly admitted that over the years Picard had earned his

123

blood money. He had read the reports of his predecessors praising the baker's actions.

"Will you be staying long this time?" Picard asked, his words mocking.

"Long enough to keep you busy," von Ott retorted. "Which I assume you've already been."

"Except for the unfortunate postmaster, no one is hiding any *Amis*," Picard boasted. "Of that I am certain."

"What about arms caches?"

"The Americans took everything when they left."

Picard omitted the fact that he had stored in the bakery cellars precious sugar, flour, and even butter cadged from the quartermaster during the turmoil of retreat. Such provisions were worth their weight in gold. One could not eat bullets or gun powder.

"Are you certain no one in Saint Eustace suspects where your true loyalties lie?" von Ott asked.

"Absolutely," Picard replied emphatically.

"Good. During this offensive it is vital that I have any—I repeat, any—information relating to American troops or their movements."

"Rest assured, Major, I am at your service. Now, if there's nothing else I will be on my way."

"You will need one of my men to see you home because of the curfew."

"A *laissez-passer* signed by you would be much more convenient," the baker suggested.

"A pass issued to anyone would be exceptional and therefore dangerous—for both of us," von Ott objected.

"Not if it stated a valid reason," Picard replied smoothly. "Such as having to get up in the middle of the night to bake for your troops."

Von Ott was too tired to argue. He called in his adjutant and had him prepare the papers. When Serge Picard stepped into the darkness from the mayor's office it was with slumped shoulders and a bowed head. He shuffled down the street, giving any prying eyes the impression of an innocent man wronged. But Picard's heart was singing and the *laissez-passer* burned in his palm. He couldn't wait to see the expression on Michelle Lecroix's face when he appeared at her door.

Two things registered in Monk's mind at the same instant: the bayonet in his hand was swinging down for a killing blow yet his intended victim had long red hair and startling blue eyes.

The blade stopped just short of Michelle Lecroix's neck.

"*Qui êtes-vous?*" Monk whispered savagely.

Michelle twisted in the overpowering grip of the giant who had swooped

124

down upon her out of the darkness. A strangled whisper emerged from her throat.

"Lecroix . . . my name is Michelle Lecroix. . . ."

Monk slackened his grip, amazed to hear her speak English. With a pronounced accent but English nonetheless.

A branch swished in the darkness. The soldiers were behind him, closer now. Monk dragged his prisoner off the path into the brush.

"How many Germans in the patrol?" he demanded.

"I . . . I don't know."

"Where is their main force? How close are they to Saint Eustace?"

Michelle stared at him as though he was mad.

"How close? Monsieur, the Germans have *occupied* my village."

Slowly Monk released his grip on the frightened woman. Saint Eustace occupied . . . The Germans all around, Franklin's untreated wound killing him a little more with each passing moment . . .

Michelle reached out tentatively and touched the *Ami*.

"You can't stay here, monsieur. The patrol will surely find you."

"I can't leave either!"

Monk pushed aside the brush and let the Frenchwoman see Franklin. Michelle knelt and quickly examined the unconscious soldier.

"He needs medical attention," she said. "Right away."

"And where's he going to get it? Not from the Germans, that's for sure!"

"No, monsieur, from me. I'm a nurse and I live not far from here. If we can get around the patrol we can bring your friend to safety, where I can look after him."

Monk was torn. Was she really a nurse? Could he trust this beautiful woman whom, seconds ago, he had been ready to kill? If he did and she betrayed him, Franklin would die. But if he did nothing . . . The crunch of German boots made the decision for him.

"What do you plan to do?"

"I will go back on the path," Michelle explained quickly. "The Germans will challenge me, but chances are, one or two will recognize me from the village hospital. They won't bother me. I will try to distract them, get them to pass by this point."

Monk looked at her keenly. He couldn't think of a better alternative.

"I hope you're not a collaborator," he whispered, squeezing her wrist. "If you turn us in I'll make sure you die first."

Michelle refused to flinch. "I believe you've made that perfectly clear, monsieur," she said calmly, prying back McQueen's fingers one by one.

The next moment the darkness swallowed her up.

* * *

Just as Michelle had hoped, one of the soldiers did remember her. After the initial challenge the patrol clustered around her, lanterns casting young, friendly faces in pale yellow. Michelle gently turned away their eager offers to escort her to her farmhouse. Once she had led them away from the area in which the *Amis* were hiding, Michelle said good night, watching the patrol disappear up the path toward Saint Eustace.

"Clever girl!" Monk said, stepping out of the thicket.

Michelle ignored the compliment. "We must get your friend to safety."

She examined the *Ami's* wound again and bit her lip. The American soldier's breathing was much too rapid, his skin feverish to the touch. The bullet was deeply lodged and Michelle was certain this meant surgery. Without it, he would die.

Michelle propped up the soldier and slipped an arm underneath his shoulder. "Help me stand him up."

"If you take his pack I could carry him," Monk volunteered.

"If he's walked this far, it's best we keep him going. There's no telling what would happen if you were to put him over your shoulder and let the blood run into his brain."

After leaving the commandant's office, Serge Picard had gone to the infirmary only to learn that Michelle Lecroix had already left. No matter. He would stop off at the bakery to get her a fresh loaf and use a shortcut to reach her farmhouse before her. Picard huffed his way down the moonlit road, moving as quickly as his bulk permitted.

The son of a baker, Serge Picard had fallen in love with Michelle when they were still children. He was convinced that one day he and this freckle-faced girl with the titian hair would be man and wife. The fact that Michelle had remained polite but distant to him didn't bother him in the least. Picard, who had ballooned as an adolescent, had convinced himself that in spite of her reticence, Michelle truly loved him. After all, wasn't she the only one of the village children who never teased or made fun of him?

Serge Picard was secretly overjoyed the day war was declared. The young men of Saint Eustace, who had begun to court the blossoming Michelle, were swallowed up into the army ranks while Picard, because of his obesity, was exempt from conscription. Given his fawning nature, he quickly toadied up to the quartermasters and received a lucrative contract to provide bread for army regiments stationed around Saint Eustace. The bakery, his father's legacy, had left him well off. The war was going to make him a rich man.

But as the fighting dragged on and opposing armies won and lost the same bits of ground, Picard watched his dream slipping through his fingers. Instead of rushing to his side at the first sign of danger, Michelle Lecroix became a nurse. The hours Picard felt she should have devoted to him she spent at the bedsides of wounded and dying men. During the four years of hostilities Picard had watched dozens of handsome foreigners fall in love with Michelle. There was more competition than ever before. Serge Picard lived in constant fear that one day a man might be brought in from the field who would sweep away his Michelle.

Eventually Picard found a way to put that fear to rest. He sniffed around and discovered that the Germans had plenty of gold to spend on a man who was reliable and discreet, and, above all, provided impeccable information. Picard didn't consider himself a traitor. After all, the British, Canadians, and Belgians he betrayed were as much foreigners as the Germans. Picard never even saw their faces and found it easy to remain indifferent to their fate. And the German gold meant he would be able to buy Michelle whatever her heart desired.

In spite of the cool night air Picard was sweating as he hurried across a freshly plowed field. Up ahead, in the shallow valley, he saw the silhouette of the Lecroix farmhouse. The thought of Michelle made Picard sweat in anticipation. Soon there would be no more soldiers to threaten him. The day the war ended Michelle would become his bride. They would live in the small apartment over the bakery and during the day she would work behind the counter. They would do everything together and she wouldn't be out of his sight for a minute.

Picard's ardor was so great that he almost failed to notice the three figures moving toward the small barn, the one in the middle being supported by the others. He froze in his tracks.

Soldiers! Ami *soldiers!*

As the clouds parted and the moon bathed the countryside bone white, Picard recognized the third person, Michelle Lecroix.

"Lay him down over here," Michelle said.

She pointed to a straw-filled mattress set in a makeshift bunk in one corner of the barn. Before the war the hired hand who helped her father during the harvest had slept there.

"There's another lantern by the stalls. Bring it to me."

Michelle primed water out of an ancient pump by the feeding troughs and, in the yellow light of the lantern, began carefully cleaning the wound. As she worked she realized that she had never had a good look at this *Ami* soldier. She was struck by his handsome features, especially the thick, white-blond hair and long, curly eyelashes. But she sensed there was more to this man than just physical beauty. There was strength in his spirit, which had willed him to live, forbidden him to cry out in spite of the pain he must have endured in moments of consciousness.

"What is his name?" she heard herself ask.

"Franklin Jefferson. I'm Monk McQueen."

"Franklin . . ." Michelle cupped his face and whispered, "Franklin, you must be strong, very strong. . . ."

"You're a damn good nurse," Monk said, watching her rinse the cloth and cover Franklin with a coarse horsehair blanket. "Where did you learn English?"

"From my mother," she said hesitantly. "And you are a monk, a brother?"

Monk slumped against the bunk and laughed.

"No. It's just one of those odd Anglo-Saxon names some parents inflict on their children." His expression grew serious and he moved closer to her. "How bad's the injury?"

"The bullet is causing pressure on his brain. It must be removed."

"Then I've got to find a way to reach our lines."

"He will never survive the journey—even if you eluded the Germans."

"What choice do I have? If I do nothing, he dies."

Michelle bit her lip. Only when the three of them reached the safety of the barn had she realized what she had done. As the new commandant had made clear, helping the *Amis* was rewarded by death.

"Are you all right?" Monk asked, reaching out to her. He felt her hair, the red strewn with gold thread from the light, brush against his palm. When she looked at him he felt himself swallowed by those enormous blue eyes.

"It's nothing."

"I know what you're thinking," Monk told her gently. "And I don't blame you a bit. You've already risked too much by helping us. Let me get a few hours' sleep. We'll be gone before midnight."

"And where will you go? How far will you get with Germans all around, you not even knowing where your troops are?"

"Those are risks we'll have to take."

"They are risks that will kill Franklin!"

Monk was startled by her vehemence.

"No," Michelle continued. "This is what we shall do. Both of you will stay here. The German patrols have already searched the farm. They won't be back. Tomorrow I will find the doctor and bring him here to help your friend . . . Franklin."

"In broad daylight?"

"Sometimes that is when people don't see—how do you say—the trees for the woods, *n'est-ce pas?*"

In spite of his determination to stay on watch, Monk fell into a dreamless, exhausted sleep. Neither the pounding of the storm-driven rain nor the morning call of birds pierced his consciousness. The rattle and backfire of a vehicle did.

Monk grabbed his rifle and scrambled toward the barn doors. Cautiously raising himself to a grimy window, he peered out to see a German staff car pull up before the farmhouse. Two soldiers got out first, followed by an older man and the girl.

Monk held his breath as he watched Michelle Lecroix say something to the soldiers. Then she pointed at the barn. The Germans began walking.

I believed her and now she's turned us in!

Trembling with fury, Monk jacked a round into the rifle chamber, drawing a careful aim. Whatever happened, the first bullet would be for her.

"Ah, *mon vieux*, you've really done it this time," Dr. Radisson scolded the man sitting on the bed.

His patient, a tall, rawboned farmer, dressed in a weathered chamois shirt, scarred leather overalls, and a single knee-high boot, shrugged noncommittally. He inhaled deeply as Radisson leaned forward and probed the gaping wound on his right calf.

"We're going to have to take him into the hospital for surgery," Radisson said, straightening up. "There's nothing I can do here."

The two German soldiers who had accompanied the physician and Michelle Lecroix to the farmhouse paled when they looked at the bloodstained gash on the farmer's leg and the imbedded jagged piece of a plowshare. The soldiers had no doubt that if it weren't for the brandy reeking from his breath, the old man would be howling in agony.

Michelle came over to her father and carefully draped a blanket over his shoulders.

"You'll be fine, Papa, really," she whispered.

Emil Lecroix cupped his daughter's cheek in a gnarled hand.

"I'll need you to help me get him into the car," Radisson said to the Germans.

"There won't be enough room for all of us," one of the soldiers protested. "We should have brought the ambulance or a wagon—"

"Not enough time," Radisson broke in impatiently. "Take him to the hospital as quickly as you can. Mademoiselle Lecroix and I will follow in the buggy."

The soldiers looked dubious.

"Your commandant was generous enough to loan us his staff car," Radisson said pointedly. "I'm sure he would like it back."

The reference to von Ott dispelled whatever misgivings the infantrymen had. They swung Lecroix onto the litter and covered him with the blanket. Michelle ducked down and kissed her father on the cheek. In return he gave her a broad wink.

"Now we get to our real work," Radisson said, watching the Germans drive off. "You know what to do."

As the physician disappeared in the direction of the barn, Michelle raced to the buggy. Flicking the whip over the dappled mare, she drove down the winding lane, slowing as she reached the main road. Carefully she guided the horse until one wheel was in the ditch. Michelle leaped out and slacked the harness. She struggled with the pin holding the wheel in place until it gave. The buggy, already at a precarious angle, crashed to one side, the wheel spinning away. Michelle tethered the mare and examined her handiwork. Satisfied that the damage appeared accidental, she ran back to the farmhouse.

"How is he?" Michelle demanded breathlessly, closing the double doors and throwing the bolt.

Then she noticed that McQueen had his rifle leveled at Dr. Radisson.

"What's going on?"

"Our American friend would like to know what the Germans were doing here," Radisson deadpanned.

McQueen's grim expression told Michelle what the *Ami* suspected.

"Did you see the man the Germans carried away on the litter?" she asked quickly. "That was my father. He was wounded in 1871, during the Franco-Prussian war. To this day a piece of shrapnel remains in his leg. I needed an excuse to bring Dr. Radisson here so I cut open my father's leg. Once the Germans saw the steel fragment they couldn't very well leave my father like that."

"Jesus Christ!" Monk swore, lowering his rifle.

"That's why Dr. Radisson was able to come out here," Michelle said and then told McQueen about the staged accident that would serve as an explanation for Radisson's prolonged absence from the village.

"Everything you've done may be for naught," Monk said softly.

Seeing Michelle's puzzled expression, he explained, "The doctor says the bullet has fragmented around his skull. He can't get at all the splinters."

Radisson nodded. "Not only that, but I can only guess how deep the main part of the shell casing is buried in the bone. If it's too close to the brain then removing it could cause uncontrollable hemorrhaging."

"If you leave it there he'll die!" Michelle said fiercely.

"Hey, take it easy, will you? I'm not going to die. But I won't have a hand left if you squeeze much harder."

Michelle gasped at the sound of Franklin's cracked voice. She felt the tiny pressure from his fingers and released his hand.

"I didn't mean you had to drop it like a hot potato," Franklin whispered. "Tell you what, since I'm not sure you're real, why don't you tell these guys to fix me a vermouth then get that Hun souvenir out of my skull. My head's killing me. . . ."

Michelle could scarcely hide her relief.

"You're going to live," she promised him. "The bullet will be removed and you will live!"

Monk was overwhelmed by the Frenchwoman's determination.

"How long will the operation take?"

"An hour, perhaps longer," the physician replied. "I won't be able to tell until I start."

Radisson was already preparing a chloroform pad while Michelle drew a syringe of morphine. There were only a few milliliters, not nearly as much as she would have wanted. She prayed it would be enough at least to dull the pain.

Monk looked around in despair. He was agreeing to madness! How could a man be operated on under these conditions—lying on a dirty, straw-filled mattress, with no light except the lanterns and with mice squeaking in the shadows? Even if Franklin miraculously survived the knife, infection would kill him.

"Monk . . ." He turned around at her touch. "I know he is a friend," Michelle said gently. "And how much you care for him. Trust me. Nothing will happen to Franklin."

Monk's heart cried out for reassurance. Then the image of Michelle's father being carried away came into his mind. These people had literally given up their blood for two complete strangers. What more could he ask for?

"You get to work," he said, looking over her shoulder at Franklin. "I'll do something I rediscovered after coming over here."

Michelle raised an eyebrow.

"How to pray," Monk told her.

— 15 —

"The rest is in God's hands."

Dr. Emil Radisson wiped his hands on a bloodstained towel and lit a cigarette. Beside him, Monk watched as Michelle finished weaving a bandage around Franklin Jefferson's head.

"Will he make it?"

Before the physician could reply Michelle said, "Of course he will."

Monk looked at Radisson, whose answer drifted out on a cloud of tobacco smoke. "Some fragments were imbedded deep in his skull. It was impossible to get them out. I can't say for certain they won't put pressure on the cranium."

"What if I were to get him to an army hospital?" asked Monk. "Have him shipped home as soon as possible?"

Radisson shrugged. "With all due modesty, I doubt your field doctors could improve on my work. As for what can be done for him in America, that I cannot tell you. I am not familiar with your techniques.

"The main thing now," Radisson finished, "is to let him rest. He needs to regain as much strength as possible. To move him is out of the question."

"Franklin will be safe here," Michelle promised Monk. "The morphine will keep him asleep for the rest of the day. I will try to get more from the hospital."

"Speaking of which, you and I had better be leaving," Radisson said, consulting his antique timepiece. "Even with our 'accident' we should have been back by now."

Monk helped Michelle gather up the bloodied towels and carry them to the zinc washtub.

"I have to try to reach my lines," he said. "If there are any plans to throw the Germans back, I want to make sure a unit reaches Franklin as soon as possible."

"You can't walk around in broad daylight in that uniform," Michelle protested.

"Your father looked about my height. Give me some of his things. I'll head west, stay off the main road, and hope like hell I don't run into any patrols."

"You would be better off waiting for nightfall."

"I've waited too long already." Monk gripped her by the shoulders. "I'll never forget what you did for us. If there's anything you need, anything I can do . . ."

Michelle pecked him on the cheek. "Well, friend, the best thing you can do is get back safely to your people and return for Franklin. These days we shouldn't ask the Almighty for much more."

Serge Picard was cold, tired, and very hungry. His clothing was soaked through from the rain-laden brush in which he had been sitting watching the Lecroix barn. His stomach rumbled incessantly. Yet for all the discomfort Picard would not budge.

After an all but sleepless night, racked by indecision and doubt, Picard had returned to his vantage point at dawn. When he saw the Germans arrive his spirits lifted. Michelle had come to her senses. Like any good French citizen she was turning in the *Amis*. Satisfaction quickly dissolved into incredulity as the baker watched Michelle's clever ruse unfold.

After the Germans left there was quiet for several hours. Since both Radisson and Michelle had stayed behind, Picard guessed they were tending the *Ami's* wounds. He was sorely tempted to steal away to the village and demonstrate to that Prussian highbrow, von Ott, how stupid his army was. Hundreds of soldiers had passed through the area but none had found two wounded American soldiers.

Only one consideration held Picard back: Michelle Lecroix. He would never be able to convince von Ott to spare Michelle. The thought that Michelle would take such risks galled Picard. But on the other hand, he now knew a secret that Michelle would do anything to guard.

Picard's imagination was so inflamed that he almost missed seeing one of the *Amis*, dressed in a fieldhand's shirt and overalls, step out of the barn. Cautiously he surveyed the area, then slipped off into the woods.

Before Picard could figure out what to do next, Michelle and Radisson left the barn. Picard watched them go down the lane, fix the wheel onto the buggy, and drive off.

How can they leave him alone? He must be unable to travel. Maybe even dead.

Curiosity got the better of Picard. Stealthily he made his way to the barn, eyes darting nervously in every direction. The latches squealed as the doors swung open.

What if the Ami's *armed?* Picard thought, cringing.

He took a deep breath and burst into the barn. There were no telltale signs to indicate that anyone had been sheltered there. The stalls were empty, as was the hayloft. The baker resumed his search, more carefully this time, and found a trapdoor, covered with straw and dirt, cut into the floor. He grasped the ring and pried open the door. Picard wiped the sweat from his brow and peered down. In the sunlight shot through with dust motes he saw the man lying on a cot, his head swathed in bandages. His breathing was shallow and irregular but he was alive.

Picard didn't take his eyes off the *Ami* for a long time, not until he was absolutely certain of what he was going to do.

Michelle Lecroix was exhausted. As soon as she and Dr. Radisson had returned to Saint Eustace they plunged into the work awaiting them. The German counteroffensive was extracting a brutally high price and there was no shortage of wounded. It wasn't until midnight that Michelle was able to help her father, his wound cauterized and stitched, into the buggy and bring him home. As they drew closer to the farmhouse Michelle found her heart beating painfully against her chest. The *Ami's* face haunted her and she was impatient to hold Franklin Jefferson in her arms again.

Michelle helped her father into the house, made sure he was comfortable in his bed, then glided out into the night, carrying a lantern. The oubliette was covered, just as she had left it. Relieved, Michelle set to work opening the trapdoor.

For an instant Michelle thought he had died. Franklin Jefferson lay so still she couldn't detect any movement. Only when she was cradling him in her arms did she feel his warmth. He was alive. Some color had returned to his face. She was convinced that he was on the mend.

Carefully Michelle examined the dressing around Franklin's head and was pleased to find no blood seeping through. She pressed a cloth soaked in cold water to his lips and watched as he sucked on it, all the while continuing to sleep.

What is it about him? Michelle asked herself. Where did such feelings of tenderness for a perfect stranger, with whom she had exchanged less than a dozen words, come from? And why?

Michelle was so caught up in her reflections that she did not hear the barn door open. Then her ear caught the sound of boots crushing straw underfoot.

The Germans! They must have seen the light.

Terrified, Michelle scrambled to her feet only to realize there was nowhere to run. She didn't even have a weapon with which to defend herself.

A shadow loomed over the oubliette. Michelle's clenched fists flew to her mouth, her teeth digging into the knuckles. But the sharp cry that escaped her throat was one of relief as she recognized the familiar face of Serge Picard.

Monk McQueen covered six miles in as many grueling hours. For the first while he stayed in the woods, using hunters' paths, always alert for any sound

134

other than the natural sounds of the forest. As the woodland thinned he waded into a stream, staying close to the bank where brush and trees could provide cover the instant he needed it. At midafternoon McQueen took refuge in a small ravine and ravenously attacked the bread and cheese Michelle Lecroix had packed for him.

Although his body cried out for rest McQueen doggedly kept on. He skirted the periphery of Saint Eustace and quickly worked his way west. Nightfall found him within a stone's throw of the German lines. Monk's heart sank as he realized how far the enemy had driven. He wondered where he would find an opening into the no-man's land that separated the German troops from the Americans.

Monk pressed on, his luck riding on the clouds that obscured the moon. He crawled across fields oozing with mud and hid among sleepy pigs when he was forced to run from oncoming patrols. He moved as close as he dared to the German lines, sometimes able to see the machine gunners slumped over their barrels or smell the warming aroma of burning tobacco. Finally, at the foot of an abandoned grist mill, Monk surrendered to his fatigue. With his last ounce of strength he crawled into a crevice beneath the motionless waterwheel and curled up.

"My God, Serge, you scared me half to death!"

Michelle was so relieved her knees buckled. She was scarcely able to climb the ladder out of the oubliette.

"What are you doing here this time of night?"

Picard licked his lips nervously. With her disheveled hair lying across her breasts Michelle looked more beautiful than ever.

"Who is that?" Picard demanded.

Breathlessly Michelle explained.

"Serge, I'm so glad to see you," she said when she had finished. "Do you think you might be able to get us some food? There's nothing left in the house."

"For you, Michelle, anything," Picard replied fervently.

Michelle smiled and pointed to Franklin Jefferson. "For him, not me."

The baker looked over her shoulder at the unmoving soldier.

"Michelle," he said hesitantly, "what you're doing is very dangerous. . . ."

"What choice do I have? I couldn't very well turn him over to the Germans."

"That's exactly what you should have done," Picard said, surprised by his firm tone. "And you can still do it. All you have to say is that you found him near the barn and cleaned his wound before going to the authorities."

"Serge, you can't be serious!" Michelle exclaimed. "The minute a German doctor removes the bandages and sees the stitches he'd know about the operation. Since Radisson is the only French surgeon for miles around he'd be arrested immediately. So would my father and I."

"No, Michelle, it doesn't have to be that way," Picard said, grabbing her hands. "Not if you did your duty, explained to von Ott—"

"My duty?" Michelle cried out in disbelief. "My duty is to help throw out the *boche* who have raped my country."

"Michelle, please, listen to me," Picard begged. "Sooner or later von Ott will find out you're hiding the *Ami*."

"How, Serge? How will he find out? Three people besides myself know he is here. I can trust two of them. Please tell me I can trust you too."

Picard faltered. Maybe he could stay silent, become a hero in her eyes.

A hero as long as you're the only man she has, a malignant voice whispered to him. *How long do you think she will stay with you after the other men come home? Besides, are you willing to jeopardize the fortune you've harvested?*

"No, Michelle," the baker heard himself say. "I can't let you endanger yourself like this. If you won't tell von Ott, I must."

Michelle couldn't believe what she was hearing. She grabbed Picard, forcing him to face her.

"Serge, you're not . . . not working for the Germans. . . . You can't be!"

Everyone in Saint Eustace believed that Picard supplied the enemy under duress. It was a condition of war that all the people understood. But what if that wasn't the case at all?

Michelle forced herself to listen to Picard's protestations of love for her, how he idolized her and had done it all for her. As the confession poured out Michelle was stunned and sickened.

"Enough!" Michelle screamed. "Get out of here! Now! I don't ever want to see you again!"

"Michelle, I love you!" Picard said miserably. "You are mine—"

"Yours! How can you say such a thing? I thought I knew you, Serge. How could you betray the people you grew up with?"

For a moment there was silence between them.

"I love you, Michelle," Picard repeated at last. "Is that so wrong?"

Michelle shook her head. "But I don't love you."

"You will, Michelle—"

"After what you've done?"

"But it was for you. For us . . ."

"No, Serge, you did it for yourself. Only yourself." Michelle paused. "You'd better go now. We have nothing more to say to each other."

Because for so long he had believed he walked through hell for her, Serge Picard obeyed. He started to turn away, then stopped.

"No, Michelle," he said softly. "We have a great deal to say to each other. We have a lifetime together. . . ."

When he faced her Michelle began to tremble. Picard's eyes glazed over.

"Serge . . ."

"It's not the *Ami*, is it, Michelle?" he whispered hoarsely. "You haven't fallen in love with him . . . ?"

"Of course not!"

"Then it doesn't matter to you if I turn him in, does it?" Picard said, slowly coming toward her.

"You can't do that!" Michelle cried. "I won't let you."

"But why, my dear Michelle? Why shouldn't I turn him over to my good friend Major von Ott?"

Michelle's eyes blazed, her hands balled into fists as Picard came closer. "Because you would be killing him!"

"I don't care about him," Picard said. "I love only you."

He was close enough for her to smell the rank odor of his body. Michelle shuddered as his fingers reached out and caressed her breast. She knew now what it was he wanted.

"I can't love you if you hurt him, Serge," she heard herself say. "I could never love a murderer."

Dear God, what am I doing to myself!

"I won't hurt him, my lovely," Picard cooed, pressing her into the folds of his body. Michelle dug her nails into his back to stop from crying out.

Fight him! her heart screamed. *Kick, claw, scream! Do something!*

If you resist, Franklin will die.

Michelle felt herself sinking to the floor under Picard's weight. His hands were all over her, lifting her skirt, squeezing her thighs.

"Michelle! Michelle . . ."

Michelle turned her head away, her hair spilling over her face, wet from tears. She squeezed her eyes shut, trying to conjure up Franklin's image. Then suddenly something terrible was happening to her, as though her insides were being torn away. She screamed, mindlessly pummeling Picard's back with her fists. She didn't know how long she tried to punish him before, mercifully, the pain exploded into blackness.

A few yards away, in the darkness of the oubliette, Franklin Jefferson felt the woman's screams ripping his soul apart. He had heard every word and tried to call out to her. But the words, if he spoke them at all, never reached her.

As the pounding and thrashing continued, Franklin cursed his feeble body. Unable to move, he heard himself whisper over and over again, "I'll kill him, my angel. I swear to you I'll kill him!"

— 16 —

The whistling of incoming artillery shells pierced Monk's sleep. Instinctively he pushed himself deeper into his lair, clamping his hands over his ears. Even so the impact was deafening.

The barrage seemed to continue into infinity, the earth quaking and buckling, and the mill disintegrated in a fury of splintering rock, brick, and wood. Then, suddenly, silence reigned, broken only by the groans of the wounded. Cautiously Monk squirmed out from beneath the overhang.

Miraculously the waterwheel was still intact. Monk tested the paddles and climbed up until he was level with the short bridge that spanned the river. He jumped over the parapet and immediately tripped over something. The bridge and path leading to the mill were littered with the bodies of German soldiers who hadn't been able to outrun the barrage. Holding his breath, Monk began to pick his way through the dead and dying.

One foot in front of the other. One step at a time . . .

"Hold it right there!"

Monk stopped and looked over his shoulder. A few feet away, leveling a rifle at him, was a young soldier, his eyes unnaturally white against his grimy face. Monk sat down wearily in the middle of the road.

"Don't point that thing at me, sonny," Monk said. "I'm on your side."

With that he ripped away the dogtags hanging around his neck and flung them at the astonished soldier.

The swiftness and ferocity of the American attack had caught the Germans completely by surprise. They fell back, surrendering by the thousands. The offensive ground to a stop simply because the victors couldn't cope with the sheer number of POWs.

The chaos frustrated Monk. It took an entire day for him to be vetted, re-equipped, and reunited with what was left of his unit. His pleas to be assigned to active duty fell on deaf ears.

138

"We ain't moving an inch," his captain told him. "Christ, we don't know what to do with the bastards we already got!"

Monk had one last card to play. He discovered that General Black Jack Pershing was billeted in one of the forward positions. The general's chief of staff was an old classmate of Monk's who remembered Franklin Jefferson from the time when Pershing had decorated the young soldier for his valor.

"This better be good, son," Pershing glowered, looking up from the rickety table covered with maps.

Quickly Monk explained what had happened to his unit and described how severe Franklin's wounds were.

"He needs help, General," Monk finished. "I'm asking for your permission to go get him."

Pershing was impressed by Monk's determination and loyalty.

"The Jefferson boy, you say."

"Yes, sir."

"The one I decorated in the field a while back?"

"The same, sir."

"Well, son, don't just stand there, take whoever you need and bring him home."

"*Yes, sir!*"

Sitting in the kitchen of her farmhouse, a single lamp illuminating the darkness, Michelle Lecroix wondered what was going to happen to her. Picard had returned every night since that first time. By unspoken arrangement he always came to the barn where, without hesitation, he forced himself on her. Try as she might, Michelle could not shut out his hoarse cries of passion and protestations of love. No matter how hard she scrubbed herself afterward she never felt clean.

Picard's bestiality went further. He would come by the infirmary several times a day and openly kiss and embrace her. It didn't take long for the staff to give her knowing smiles and winks. The story of Michelle's having fallen in love with the young baker soon made the rounds of Saint Eustace.

Throughout it all Michelle kept up a brave front. The Germans wouldn't be there forever, and as soon as the Americans came back she'd expose Picard as a traitor. In the meantime, whenever he touched her, her hate for him deepened.

The saving grace was that Picard had kept his part of the bargain. He seemed to have forgotten about the American soldier in the oubliette. More important, as far as Michelle was concerned, Picard opened up his treasure trove to her.

Michelle was shocked by the bounty he had managed to squirrel away during times when others were starving and dying. But the food and medicine she took from Picard helped Franklin Jefferson regain his strength. Although he was still prisoner to blinding headaches and periodic blackouts, Michelle believed the worst was over. She stole an hour here and there to minister to him and left food for him when she was away. Not for a moment did Michelle suspect that Franklin was aware of the terrible price she was paying. She was wrong.

One evening when Michelle was in the oubliette with Franklin, Picard had come in, calling for her. Franklin had gripped her hand.

"Don't."

Michelle recalled how her cheeks had burned. She tried to put on a brave face.

"It's just my friend."

Franklin would not let go of her hand.

"Don't," he repeated.

He knows, she thought, feeling her heart wither.

The next day Michelle prepared Franklin's meal earlier than usual, well before Picard was to arrive. But when she reached the barn the door was already ajar.

He can't be here already!

Michelle slipped inside and was about to call out Picard's name when she felt a hand clamp over her mouth. A match blazed in the darkness and she found herself looking into the eyes of Monk McQueen.

"Are you all right?"

Michelle nodded quickly.

"Franklin?"

"He's safe."

"Is he well enough to be moved?"

"Yes . . . yes, I think so."

Michelle's heart rejoiced at the sight of Monk and the three soldiers who had come with him. The Americans were back! They would be her salvation. Just as quickly her hopes faded when Monk explained that they had come only to take back Franklin Jefferson. The main American force was still several miles from Saint Eustace. Monk saw her crestfallen expression and quickly reassured her.

"We'll return. It's just a matter of time now before we throw the Germans back."

Time! For me every hour is agony!

She turned to Monk but he was already clambering into the oubliette.

140

"Quit poking me, will you?" Franklin mumbled. "Good God, it *is* you. I thought I was having a nightmare."

"Shut up and tell me you can travel," Monk said gruffly. "Old Black Jack wants to talk to you. Something about another medal."

Franklin Jefferson propped himself on one elbow and felt the bandage around his head.

"I can make it," he said. "But I'm not going anywhere. Not yet."

"The hell you're not! If you think I came all this way—"

"Listen to me!" Franklin whispered urgently. "You don't know what's been going on around here. . . ."

Monk spent a long time in the oubliette, listening to Franklin, fighting to keep the bile from his throat. He couldn't believe what he was hearing, but when he looked up he saw the bitter truth in Michelle's eyes.

"Michelle?"

Serge Picard's plaintive call echoed across the eaves of the barn. The baker had arrived laden with tribute: fresh bread, a leg of ham for which he had paid a king's ransom, cheeses, and a vintage wine he had liberated from the German officers' canteen. But it was the small jeweler's box that was burning a hole in his pocket. With this ring he would bind Michelle to him before the tides of war changed and she had a chance to slip away.

Picard checked the barn thoroughly and was dumbfounded when he discovered the empty oubliette. Where could the *Ami* have gone and who could have carried him? Michelle couldn't have done that by herself.

Picard felt twinges of fear as he ran from the barn to the farmhouse. Finding the door locked, he shambled around the back and peered through her window. The bed was empty. With a sinking heart Picard got back on his bicycle and began peddling laboriously to the village. He couldn't believe she would try to leave him.

As Picard climbed the steps to his apartment, his muscles aching unmercifully, he promised that when he found Michelle she would pay for her transgressions. First he would make her his bride, then he would teach her obedience.

The pounding on his door woke Picard instantly. He groaned and rolled out of bed.

"All right, all right! I'm coming—"

Picard's last words were lost in the crash of splintering wood as his front door flew off its hinges. Armed German soldiers pushed inside, two of them seizing

141

Picard and throwing him against the wall. The rest fanned throughout the apartment, ripping open closets and drawers.

"What are you doing?" Picard yelled.

"We just want to see what special ingredients you use for your bread," Major von Ott said, stepping into the room.

"I don't understand," Picard blubbered, trying to hold up his pajama bottoms. "What special ingredients? What are you looking for?"

Von Ott stepped up to him, smiling coldly.

"We'll all know soon enough, won't we?"

"*Herr Major!*" one of the soldiers shouted.

The Prussian walked quickly into the kitchen and peered into the cabinet beneath the sink. He reached inside and began pulling out what he found there. Von Ott carried the bundle into the bedroom and one by one dropped the pieces of clothing at Picard's feet.

"An American soldier's field jacket, bloodied at the shoulder," he intoned. "A shirt from the same uniform with more blood. Socks and shorts. You've been very generous, baker, sharing your underwear with the enemy."

Picard's head snapped back and forth as von Ott slapped him across the face, then grabbed his hair.

"You scheming, treasonous bastard," von Ott whispered. "How dare you betray me like this?"

"I don't know anything," Picard said, blood and broken teeth reducing his words to a gurgle. "I swear I didn't—"

"I suppose the *Ami* came in here by himself, availed himself of your hospitality while you were with your whore, and slipped away without so much as a thank you," von Ott replied derisively.

"I've never had anything to do with the Americans!" Picard shouted feebly. "I've been loyal to you—"

"Then what are these clothes doing here?" von Ott demanded. "And this?"

He shoved a roll of American military script under the baker's nose.

"You planned a little too far ahead, my friend. We are in command at Saint Eustace, not the Americans!

"Get him out of here," von Ott ordered his men.

Clutching his pajamas and shouting over his shoulder, Picard was hustled downstairs. The minute he saw the citizens of Saint Eustace gathered in the street he forgot about his arrest and the insane situation that had overtaken him. The only thing he could think of was how ridiculous he must look, standing there half-naked, shivering in embarrassment and shame.

"Michelle!"

The cry of her name was mixed with blood and spittle. In a final desperate gesture Picard broke free from his guards, staggered toward Michelle standing in the middle of the street, and collapsed at her feet.

"Michelle, where were you . . . ?"

Picard stared up at her, the answer so very clear in those ice-cold blue eyes.

"Why, Michelle? I loved you. . . ."

As Picard was hefted to his feet by the Germans, Michelle stepped back and spat into his face. "I hope you rot in hell for what you did to me!" The citizens of Saint Eustace recoiled. At the same time they saw von Ott come outside carrying the American's clothes.

"Take him to the square!" von Ott ordered.

He turned to Michelle, clicked his heels, and bowed from the waist.

"Just as you suspected, Mademoiselle Lecroix," he said, holding up the clothes. "Your lover was working for the *Amis*. You did your duty."

Michelle heard neither his words nor Picard's screams of protest as he was marched off. There was a profound emptiness within her that she wasn't sure could ever be filled.

"*Putain!*"

The first stone hit her on the shoulder, making her cry out. The second drew blood on her leg.

"*Collaboratrice!*"

Michelle backed away as one by one the people of Saint Eustace reached down into the dirt for stones.

"How dare you turn in such a decent man?" a woman shouted. "Shame!"

"German whore!" another cried. "Your time will come!"

Michelle began running as the stones pelted down upon her. She cried out as they struck her but it was as though she were moving through a dream, watching this happen to someone else. Only Monk McQueen's voice was real, echoing in her consciousness. She remembered the way he had looked at her after climbing out of the oubliette.

"Picard must pay," he had said with quiet finality.

Michelle had protested, begged him to forget about the outrage the baker had committed against her. But even as she was saying the words Michelle heard their hollow ring. Wherever Picard had touched her, her skin burned. She could still feel him thrusting and tearing her apart inside. So she had listened to McQueen. . . .

"I'll get the clothes and plant them in Picard's room when he's not there. The next morning you go to von Ott, tell him Picard has been hiding Allied wounded. Then just walk away, Michelle. Walk away from it all. The Germans will do the rest."

Michelle kept running, outdistancing the angry mob behind her. She

143

didn't stop when she passed the German patrol dragging Picard into the square.

It happened exactly as Monk had said it would, she thought, and ran even faster, her legs refusing to stop although by now she was safely out of the village. Then a single gunshot rang out, freezing her in midstride. As soon as Michelle heard it she crumpled to the dusty road, sobbing.

When Michelle reached the farmhouse she found her father and Monk McQueen waiting for her. As soon as she explained what had happened in Saint Eustace, Monk said, "You have no choice. You must leave with me. If everyone thinks you're a collaborator your life is in danger. I've told General Pershing all about you. You'll be safe with us."

"I can't leave my father," Michelle protested.

"You can and you must," Emil Lecroix said. "I know these people. No matter how they feel about you, they will not harm me."

In spite of her reluctance Michelle understood that her father was right. Eventually the truth about Serge Picard would come out and she would be vindicated. But until then Saint Eustace would remain hostile and unsafe.

"We're going back to our lines," Monk said, reading the questions in her mind. "Franklin and the others are there by now." His voice softened. "You'll be able to see him soon."

But what will I have to say to him? Why would he want to have anything to do with a woman who whored herself—even if it was for him?

"You'd better get ready," Monk said gently. "We'll be taking a long, round-about route."

Michelle packed her few clothes and personal mementos. Fiercely she embraced her father, tears burning her eyes when he laid his hand upon her head in benediction. Then she and McQueen were on their way, heading west. As hard as she tried, Michelle couldn't shake the feeling that in some profound way her life was changing in a direction she could not alter. She knew only that she had never before experienced such a sensation—just as she had never had her heart opened by love until the day she had set eyes on Franklin Jefferson.

As they passed through the American lines and approached the town of Saint Denis-des-Anges, headquarters of the *Ami* advance, Michelle became more and more nervous. She couldn't get Franklin's image out of her mind. She remembered how tightly he had held her hand and the timbre of his voice when he had told her not to go to Picard. Something had passed between them in that instant, creating a bond she couldn't deny.

Will he still want me?

Michelle longed to convince herself that Franklin would. Yet, as soon as she saw the huge Red Cross flag flying outside the building her steps slowed.

"I'll go inside and see if he's there," Monk told her. "Don't worry, everything's going to be just fine."

But her uncertainty was not put to rest. A few minutes later, Michelle was told that Franklin Jefferson had been transferred to a Paris hospital that morning.

Although Michelle was dismayed at having missed Franklin, part of her was relieved when their paths failed to cross again. Now she could begin to pick up the pieces of her life, put behind her Saint Eustace and everything that had happened.

Here, Monk was a godsend. He spoke to the hospital administrator, who recognized and appreciated Michelle's experience. Before she knew it Michelle was working double shifts and soon was second in charge of the burns and gas wards. Her English improved dramatically from daily contact with doctors and nurses and her skills quickly multiplied as she learned the advanced techniques the Americans had brought. Summer had scarcely started when already it was a memory.

On September 15, 1918, General Pershing's troops launched a new offensive at Saint-Mihiel, taking fifteen thousand prisoners in less than two weeks. By mid-October the battles of Argonnes and Ypres had passed into history and Germany was teetering on the brink of collapse. On October 28, a mutiny broke out at German naval fleet headquarters at Kiel and was followed ten days later by a revolt in the city of Munich. The following day, November 8, Kaiser Wilhelm II abdicated, leaving the way open for negotiated surrender. On November 11 the guns at last fell silent over the Western front.

"You're back—and you're safe!"

Michelle flung her arms around Monk McQueen's neck as he strode into the hospital, looking very handsome in his new sharply creased uniform and gleaming boots.

"And you had me all worried that you were at the front!" Michelle scolded him. "You look like a tailor's mannequin."

Monk laughed, grabbed her, and whirled her around by the waist.

"I'll have you know I was slogging my way toward Berlin until two weeks ago. Then Black Jack got tired of beating up on the Hun and decided to go to Paris. Since I'm on his staff—"

"On his staff!" Michelle exclaimed. "Well, I am impressed."

"Not half as much as I am," Monk said somberly. "I understand you've redeemed yourself as far as Saint Eustace is concerned."

Michelle blushed. "It wasn't anything important."

McQueen knew different. By the time General Pershing recaptured Saint Eustace he had heard all about the bravery of Michelle Lecroix. He was outraged when he was told that the villagers considered her a collaborator and would gladly hang her. Determined to correct such an injustice, Pershing ordered Michelle to be brought to Saint Eustace and there, in front of the entire populace, declared her a heroine. The general concluded the ceremony by presenting Michelle with the President's Medal, the highest civilian award for valor.

"You can go back to Saint Eustace—if you want," Monk said.

"There isn't anything to return to," Michelle told him, her eyes welling with tears. "My father had a heart attack and died a few days after the ceremony."

"I'm sorry, Michelle," Monk said softly. "I had no way of knowing."

She agreed and offered him a quiet smile.

But there is more, my dear friend. You can't imagine how naked I felt standing before all those people. True, for the first time they learned that Serge Picard had been a traitor. But that made me a traitor's whore, not a heroine. You didn't hear those evil whispers, people wondering how much I had managed to take from Picard before I turned him in. That's why I can never go back, will never go back. . . .

"I don't suppose you've heard from Franklin," Monk said, conscious of Michelle's discomfort and changing the subject.

"No, I haven't," Michelle replied lightly.

"You didn't try?"

"Monk, what was there to try? I barely knew him."

"You would have wanted to know if he was all right."

"I'm sure he is." *But how many times have I dreamed of him, woken up thinking exactly that.* . . . "Besides, by now he's home in New York, waiting for you to join him."

"No, he's not," Monk replied.

When he told her the rest, Michelle almost fainted.

Michelle walked swiftly through the thousands of tents that had sprung up around Saint-Mihiel. Most served as bivouacs for soldiers; others were field hospitals, supply depots, and administrative posts. The traffic—human, animal, and mechanical—was equal to the clank and clamor of an army getting ready to stand down. Over everything hung the fine dust thrown up by feet, hooves, and vehicles. Michelle darted in and out of the traffic, ignoring the soldiers' flirting calls and whistles, and raced up the rickety staircase to her apartment.

Franklin Jefferson appeared exactly as she imagined he would, his white-blond hair swept back across his scalp, his hazel eyes matching the easy smile on his lips. He had gained weight, and for the first time Michelle realized what a handsome athletic figure he cut in properly fitting clothes. She almost forgot about the bandage wrapped tightly around his temples.

"Franklin?"

"Hello, Michelle." He turned away from the slanted window, came to her. "I could never have left you, Michelle. I will never leave you. Not unless you send me away."

His words confused her but his fingertips, when they touched her hair and ran along her cheek and upper lip, caused her to shiver.

"How could you believe, after all you did for me, that there could be a single moment when I wasn't thinking of you, dreaming of you?" Franklin whispered.

Michelle gasped as she felt his arms slide around her, his fingers gently pressing her against him until she felt his breath upon her neck.

"I . . . I didn't know what happened to you."

"I would have written but the doctor said I should wait. Michelle, I had to know if I was going to be a whole man for you."

She drew back and touched his temple, feeling the ridge beneath the bandages.

"I'm all right, Michelle. I swear it. I've never stopped loving you. Not since the first moment I saw you."

Michelle raised her lips, her eyes fixed on his, and felt his passion flow into her like an untamed river. Then he scooped her up in his arms and carried her to the bed in the corner. Michelle felt herself being lowered and Franklin's hands tugging at her clothes. With a soft cry she pulled herself away.

"Franklin, please, my love, I want to but . . ."

No matter how hard Michelle tried to banish the horrible image of Serge Picard from her mind, she couldn't. It was as though Picard were in the room with them, leering at her.

"It's all right," Franklin whispered, holding her tightly. "I love you, Michelle. Let me hold you, just hold you. . . ."

She was trembling against him as he stroked her hair, listening to him talk softly about all the wonderful things that lay ahead of them. Slowly Michelle relaxed, pressing her tear-streaked face into his neck.

"We survived, Michelle," Franklin whispered. "We lost and then found each other. Nothing will ever come between us again, I promise."

Franklin felt Michelle's eyelashes flutter against his skin and her lips sought his in a tentative kiss. She believed him. Oh, Lord, she believed him!

PART

———————

THREE

- 17 -

The Rolls-Royce Silver Ghost turned off Overland Avenue and glided through the maze of cobblestone streets that crisscrossed the approach to the Brooklyn Army Terminal. After bumping across the railroad tracks the car came up against a seemingly impenetrable wall of horse-drawn carts, cars, bicycles, trucks, and a crush of humanity that choked traffic all the way to the piers. The burly chauffeur touched his horn. The sound seemed lost in the din, yet people pushed aside, gaping at the Barker Roi des Belges touring body sheathed in gleaming silver plate. The chauffeur guided his charge through the labyrinth of narrow streets fronted by warehouses and sailors' rooming houses. When he reached the Army Terminal the gates to the Harbor Commission building magically swung open and he drew the car up to the reception party at the front doors.

"Miss Jefferson," the harbormaster said, doffing his derby and extending a hand to help Rose alight from the backseat.

"Thank you."

Rose Jefferson stepped out in a swirl of pecan-colored Russian sable. Her doeskin boots were short, in keeping with government regulations to save leather, and were fastened by a row of tiny buttons. The crisp December air made her cheeks glow against a fashionably pale complexion.

"Are all those people waiting for relatives?" asked Rose, looking at the crowds that overfilled the cavernous waiting area beyond the customs and immigration stalls.

"Oh, yes, ma'am. It's been a madhouse for weeks now. But pay them no mind, ma'am. My office is at your disposal. I've already alerted the customs boys to watch out for Mr. Jefferson and escort him upstairs at once."

"You're too kind, sir."

Rose allowed the harbormaster to guide her into a birdcage elevator that rose to the third floor. As they approached his office Rose touched his arm.

"Do you think it would be possible for me to have a look below? I know I won't be able to see my brother, but if you could indulge me . . ."

The harbormaster frowned. "If you're certain the noise won't bother you, Miss Jefferson . . ."

He wasn't sure whether to tell her about the god-awful smell reeking all the way up to the warehouse rafters. Let her find out for herself, he reckoned.

The harbormaster guided his distinguished visitor to the far end of the hall and unlocked a metal-sheathed door. The noise hit Rose like thousands of hammers striking a huge anvil. Stepping out onto the catwalk she saw at least a thousand people packed into the reception area, shouting in a dozen different languages as they searched for their men coming home from the war.

"Some of them have actually been sleeping here," the harbormaster informed her, wrinkling his nose.

The smell of unwashed bodies mingling with that of food going bad from the heat didn't bother Rose in the least. Her heart sang out to the cries below and her eyes darted about as nervously as did thousands of others. The anticipation of mothers and fathers, sisters and lovers roared in her ears.

Beyond the high wooden fence, reinforced by a line of blue-uniformed police, were the customs stalls. Before each one was a long line of young men in uniform, gunnysacks at their feet. Rose strained to catch a glimpse of Franklin but couldn't find him. Then she looked out the high grime-laden windows that covered an entire story of the warehouse and saw the troop ships moored at the piers. The one currently offloading, its gangplank jammed with men eager to step back onto their own soil, was the *Eagle Star*. Unconsciously Rose reached into her purse, her fingers clutching the packet of letters bound by honeysuckle-scented ribbon. In his last letter Franklin had written that the *Eagle Star* would be bringing him and Monk McQueen home.

What if he didn't make it? What if something happened to him in the time it took the letter to reach me?

Rose had endured this unspoken fear for weeks. She couldn't bear to think that the final bullet of the war would be meant for him.

Bring him home to me, God! Just bring him home safe and sound!

Rose uttered a sharp cry, covering her mouth with her hand sheathed in fine black calfskin. It was Monk McQueen stepping into the customs line, his gunnysack resting lightly on one shoulder. Rose couldn't help herself. In spite

152

of everything she had blamed him for and the resentment she still harbored, she shouted his name, hoping he'd somehow hear her through the dull roar of infantrymen shuffling toward reunion.

Don't be silly! He can't see much less hear you.

Then Monk cocked his head and his eyes swept across the warehouse, traveling toward the catwalk below the rafters. When he saw her his arm began moving like a windmill. Rose waved back and glanced in the direction he was pointing, just in time to catch a glimpse of a blond man ducking through the customs stall.

Franklin!

Rose gripped the railing to steady her trembling hands. Relief and dread surged through her at the same time. It was true, it was real. Franklin was home.

But much has changed that he doesn't know about. He's coming back to a company that doesn't exist anymore, not the way he remembers it. . . . So it will be a fresh start for both of us. He'll see that. . . .

In 1918, the great express industry that had helped open and then bind a nation was effectively destroyed. After the bloody strikes of 1917 and the public's outrage over the workers' wages and job conditions, the express companies faced an uphill battle to keep, much less expand, their business. Riding the wave of popular opposition, Matthias Alcorn's Interstate Commerce Commission had attacked the companies at their most vulnerable point: rates. All told, the expresses had over 200 billion separate rates, making accurate bookkeeping and accounting impossible. In one stroke the ICC overhauled the entire system, replacing individual rates with a zonal system that fixed a per-pound rate from quadrant to quadrant. If the express companies wanted to change rates they had to petition the ICC, which was quick to refuse any increases. Profits, especially Global's, nose-dived.

In the summer of that year another telling blow was delivered. The government authorized the U.S. Post Office Department to extend dramatically the parcel-post system it had created in 1913. Global and the other companies fought bitterly but, because of their poor public image and dwindling support on Capitol Hill, failed to stem the tide. Profits were further reduced and companies began failing.

Unlike her competitors, who vowed to fight to the death, Rose had no intention of allowing Global to follow the others' path of self-destruction. As much as it pained her, she began to downscale the size of Global.

A few weeks before Armistice was declared, Global Enterprises closed down 14,000 miles of express lines and 2,600 offices across the country, leaving over 30,000 people without jobs. Rose sold off the remaining lines, which were barely showing a profit, to the government with the agreement that its vast real estate holdings and cash surplus were untouchable. Global neatly sidestepped the fate of other companies that were drowning in the swamps of government regulations. It left behind a dying business, ready and cash-heavy to start again.

"Rose!"

She whirled around at the sound of the familiar voice and saw him at the end of the catwalk.

"Oh, Franklin!"

He was standing with his hands stuffed into his trouser pockets, leaning nonchalantly to one side, a lopsided grin on his lips. She took two steps toward him, then, with her fur billowing behind her, ran to him.

Rose saw Franklin stop. He turned, held up his hand, and looked down another corridor. Puzzled, Rose slowed down. Suddenly Franklin opened his arms wide and swept up a young woman with brilliant red hair who flung herself at him, her arms circling his neck. Franklin laughed and whirled her about and set her down beside him.

Rose couldn't take another step. She was furious that Franklin would have written to some old flame to tell her when his ship was docking. More to the point, who was she? Rose couldn't place the redhead at all.

Rose's question wasn't answered with words. As Franklin draped one arm across the woman's shoulder Rose caught the glimpse of a single gold ring on the fourth finger of his left hand.

No, it's not possible!

Rose's eyes darted to the woman's hand and the blood drained from her face. There was a ring on the woman's fourth finger, a mate to Franklin's.

Dear God, what has he done?

– 18 –

The oyster-gray light of morning barely penetrated the thick, condensation-shrouded windows of the orangerie. Rose Jefferson sat alone in the gloom, a cup and saucer balanced in her lap. None of the help was up yet and she had made tea herself, carrying it into this haven where the lush fragrance of herbs, flowers, and foliage enveloped her. But the quiet beauty brought her no peace nor any answers to the questions that had plagued her throughout that long, long night.

Rose remembered very little about yesterday. Her shock had been so profound that she had found herself doing and saying things in the most mechanical fashion. She supposed she had been gracious enough to this woman. From what she recalled of their three-sided conversation, in the car and at home, Michelle Lecroix was French, a nurse, with no family, who had met Franklin in some place called Saint Eustace and married him in a civil ceremony in Saint-Mihiel. Franklin had carried on about Michelle's being a real-life heroine but Rose dismissed this as a love-besotted exaggeration. The one thing Rose couldn't doubt was that she was his wife. It was bad enough that her brother couldn't stop crowing about his marriage; the rings on the couple's fingers made Rose wince every time she looked at them.

Who is this Michelle Lecroix? What does she want? And what am I going to do?

The plans she had waited so long to share with Franklin, the time she wanted to heal the rift between them, had been stolen. Another person now stood between them. Rose vowed that no matter the time or cost she would learn everything about this seductive intruder. Michelle Lecroix might just be the wide-eyed innocent she appeared. Then again, she could be someone very different, with secret intentions and dark dreams. Rose had to know.

Because he thinks she's family now. Families are included in new wills. New wills can bring an outsider into Global. . . .

The thought petrified and angered Rose, yet it also raised new possibilities. Franklin was so consumed by his love for Michelle Lecroix that he probably never asked himself the obvious question: in spite of whatever Michelle felt for him, could she find her place in this new world he had brought her to? Perhaps the key lay not in persuading Franklin to see the error of his ways but in showing Michelle just how unsuitable she really was and always would be.

Then he could never blame me when she decides to leave, not after everything I tried to do for her.

Michelle awoke abruptly and for a few seconds didn't know where she was. As soon as she touched Franklin she felt comforted. But sleep had fled.

The pale lamplight from the street cast her shadow along the golden-yellow tapestry wallpaper as Michelle slipped out of bed and into a quilted satin housecoat. She looked around, scarcely daring to breathe. At the foot of the bed was a magnificent sculpted fireplace with a brass gate, the mantelpiece almost hidden by delicate Chinese porcelain vases. Beside that was an over-stuffed daybed and, to the right of the door, a large burled walnut dresser with a seven-foot gilt-edged mirror.

Michelle slowly drank in the room. This was the first time that she found herself alone, face to face with Talbot House. Ever since her arrival she had felt like a time-traveler who had stumbled into the royal court of a magic kingdom. Everything was overwhelming and bewildering. Now, Michelle decided to explore.

She made her way along the second-floor hall, down the grand, circular staircase, and through the center hall crowned by a lofty ceiling, mute Greek and Roman statues with their unseeing eyes, and cold Corinthian columns. When she stepped into the picture gallery, its size and grandeur took her breath away. The mahogany ceiling was at least thirty feet high, with a skylight of opalescent and tinted glass. A gigantic rug hid almost all of the parquetry floor, and the collection was hung above ebonized oak paneling. To Michelle, this room could just as easily have been in the Louvre. The paintings had the names of legends inscribed beneath them: Rubens, Titian, and Goya.

The magic continued in the library. Although it was a small room, only some thirty by forty feet, its walls were jammed with bookcases carved from rosewood and inlaid with mother-of-pearl and bronze. Calfskin-bound volumes of world classics stood in long rows behind cabinets with small, beveled glass fronts. As she walked past these gifts of the centuries, Michelle thought of her mother and wondered if this was the kind of life she'd had as a young woman. Her mother had seldom talked about England but from the few references Michelle remembered she thought her youth there must have been an unhappy time. Now she wished she had asked those questions. Perhaps the answers would have given her the measure of confidence she needed so badly, explained how people were supposed to live among such precious things that seemed too delicate to touch much less use.

Suddenly it all became too much. Michelle hurried out of the library, relieved when she reached the enormous kitchen with its warm, lingering smell of bread baked late the previous night. While she waited for the coffee to boil,

Michelle's thoughts turned to Rose. She was not unaware of the reserve with which Rose had greeted her, the way she had cast a measuring eye over her. It was equally obvious that Rose had found her wanting.

Franklin warned you about that. He told you Rose could be very possessive. And why shouldn't she be!

She tried her best to imagine what it would be like suddenly to have to share a brother one had had all to oneself. Besides that, Rose was a widow, not only bringing up a young son but running an enormous business. Michelle told herself these were things she had to understand—or at least try to.

But will Rose do the same? Will she accept me? Will this world accept me?

Lost in thought, Michelle carried her cup of coffee into the orangerie.

"Hello, Michelle. I see you're an early riser too."

Michelle's cup rattled in her saucer.

"Rose! I'm sorry. I didn't think anyone was up. . . ."

For a few seconds the two women faced each other, not knowing what to do next.

Why not? thought Rose, beckoning with her arm.

"Come and sit with me, my dear. This is the perfect opportunity for us to become better acquainted, don't you think?"

"Yes . . . thank you."

Rose settled back in her chair, smiling over the rim of her cup.

"Now, I want to hear everything about you," she said softly. "You can't imagine how interested I am."

The following day America celebrated the "war to end all wars." At Madison Square, veterans paraded through a huge plaster triumphal arch while children gleefully set fire to effigies of the dethroned Kaiser.

For Michelle, the days to Christmas disappeared in a whirlwind. New York overwhelmed her with its noise and bustle, the towering grandeur of its buildings, and the incredible wealth to be found in its streets. It seemed impossible to get a grip on a city that moved so quickly, spoke in a dozen tongues, and stopped for no one.

The pace was even more frantic because Franklin insisted on introducing Michelle to all his friends. Boyhood chums came over to share breakfast, college friends were met at New York's smartest restaurants, and the rest were caught up with late in the evening at 21, which occupied an entire mansion.

The regimen at Talbot House was equally bewildering. When Michelle needed to go shopping to replace the clothes she had brought over in one small suitcase, Rose gave her a list of shops and blithely told her to sign for the purchases. It seemed the Jeffersons seldom paid cash for anything, but if they

157

had to there was always a thousand dollars in the bedroom safe to which Michelle had been given the combination.

Michelle did her best to make herself comfortable in Talbot House, but whenever Franklin was away she felt lost. She tried to get to know the servants but they kept a respectful distance. Rose's son, Steven, had been polite enough when he and Michelle were introduced but Michelle sensed that the boy was suspicious of her. No matter how she tried to make friends with him, Steven remained aloof.

The only time Michelle felt truly at ease in the great house was late at night, when she and Franklin were alone in their second-floor suite. As soon as he took her into his arms the rest of the world might as well have not existed. On her wedding night Michelle had learned that Franklin was an experienced and tender lover who took as much pleasure in giving as receiving. She had been terrified that after the shame Serge Picard had inflicted upon her she could never respond to love. But Franklin was patient and resourceful. Now, every night as she undressed in the boudoir, Michelle felt herself tingle in anticipation. She would step out naked and smile as Franklin beheld her. After so many years of watching young men die beneath her hands, she could at last believe that the one who had opened her up to love would always be there, that she could give herself to him freely and completely, utterly convinced that he would never leave her.

"Isn't that a sight, darling?"

Michelle bit her lip as she wound the screw in her earring too tightly. She took a last look at herself in the rococo mirror and turned to the balcony off their bedroom.

"Franklin, you'll catch cold out here!"

"It's beautiful," he replied, looking at the night sky.

Michelle saw the myriad stars flung across the black heavens, each so bright it was impossible to recognize the one that had guided the Wise Men to Jerusalem. She shivered and pressed herself against Franklin.

"You look ravishing."

Franklin's compliment made Michelle blush, but she had to admit that the hours spent preparing for this Christmas party had been worth it. Her gown was a jade-green chemise suspended from diamanté straps in satin brocade. It swept around every curve of her body, revealing bare, milk-white arms as well as, Michelle thought, a little too much freckled bosom. Her golden red hair was loose, a cascade of ringlets and curls that invited touch. Tiny emeralds glittered from her ears while a diamond necklace with a jade centerpiece burned white-hot at her throat.

"I feel that any moment I'm going to wake up and all this will have been a dream," Michelle said, rubbing the jade between her fingertips.

"Nonsense," Franklin soothed her, slipping his fingers beneath her hair and stroking the fine down at the back of her neck. "This is all yours now." He checked his watch. "Shall we go?"

"Are you sure there won't be many people?" Michelle asked nervously as they proceeded along the second-floor hall, lined with Barbizon landscapes by Diaz de la Peña and Moorish scenes by Mariano Carbo, two of the most popular artists among the Four Hundred.

"Just some family friends," Franklin assured her.

If that's the case, Michelle wondered, *who's going to eat that mountain of food and drink all the wine?*

For the last week Michelle had watched tradesmen and delivery boys come and go. A small army of cleaners had descended upon Talbot House and, under Albany's careful eye, had shined it from top to bottom. Irish maids sat at the formal dining table busily polishing heavy silver, gossiping about presents they had bought. In the Flemish Ballroom, so called because the entire room had been shipped over from a château in Ghent, Belgium, housemen were putting the finishing touches on a twenty-foot tree already groaning with gaily colored bulbs, candles, bunting, and reindeer cookies.

Michelle guessed the preparations could feed and make merry at least sixty people. As she and Franklin descended the grand curved staircase into the main hall she was petrified to discover there were at least twice as many guests.

"Rose, what have you gone and done?" Franklin demanded, pecking his sister on the cheek. "You promised Michelle and me a quiet Christmas. A few friends, you said."

"Oh, Franklin, don't be beastly," Rose said, her smile becoming a pout. "They are our friends. Besides, everyone wanted to meet the bride."

Rose, wearing a shimmering gray gown shot through with silver thread, and a diamond tiara nestled in her coiffed, piled hair, stepped back, appraising Michelle.

"You look absolutely stunning, my dear," she murmured. "I told you green was your color."

Michelle smiled nervously. Rose had insisted on taking her shopping for the Christmas-party gown. They had gone to a brownstone on Madison Avenue that housed New York's most exclusive salon run by the dressmaker Madame Bouchard. Michelle had sat silently as Rose and the woman discussed the most suitable colors and fabrics. Next had come the actual design of the dress, followed by a whirlwind of fitting appointments. When the creation was at last in hand Michelle dared to ask the dressmaker how much it cost.

"Of course, you were very late with your order," Madame Bouchard scolded her in her singsong voice.

It seemed odd to Michelle that the Frenchwoman never spoke her native tongue but chose to address even a compatriot in accented English.

"Usually I accept no commissions under three months."

"Three months ago I was fighting a war," Michelle murmured.

"What's that you say?" Madame asked suspiciously.

Michelle shook her head. "I was just saying how kind it was of you to take the time . . ."

"Time is money," Madame Bouchard pronounced, sounding very much to Michelle like a Breton peasant. "You understand that there will be a surcharge for this creation."

"Of course," Michelle agreed quickly.

"But," Madame Bouchard carried on, "even seven hundred dollars is nothing compared to how you will look."

Michelle almost fainted. "Seven . . . hundred dollars."

"Of course I will put it on Mademoiselle Rose's account. It's understood."

When Michelle had protested the price of the dress to Rose, her sister-in-law only laughed.

"Consider it my wedding present to you."

"Come, my dears," Michelle heard Rose say as she stepped between Michelle and Franklin and proprietarily took their arms. "It's time to bring you out."

During the next hour Michelle found herself being introduced to the elite of New York society. Each man seemed to be wealthier and more powerful than the previous one; each wife and daughter vied to be more beautiful, more stunningly gowned than the next. Michelle couldn't help but notice how quickly Franklin became the center of attention. Young women left their escorts and drifted across the room to be near him, forming a charmed circle of laughter, adoration, and not a little flirtation. Standing alone, Michelle wondered if she shouldn't make her presence felt to serve notice on would-be poachers.

"How are you making out?"

Startled, Michelle turned around to see Monk McQueen next to her, looking very handsome in his tailored white tie and tails.

"I'm having a wonderful time!" Michelle exclaimed. She pointed to a group of older women who sat along the walls, scrutinizing the festivities like crows. "Who are they?"

"Ah," Monk exclaimed. "Those are the Dowagers. They were filthy rich before they married and now control their husbands' estates as well. If they got together they could buy and sell half the men in this room."

160

The thought flabbergasted Michelle.

"Well, if you need anything, holler," Monk said. "Remember, I want you to come visit me at the paper and have lunch."

Michelle didn't understand the reason for the concern that flickered across Monk's eyes. Before she could say anything it was gone, and Franklin had returned.

"You've made quite the hit," he said, grinning. "People are saying I'm the luckiest guy in the room."

Michelle couldn't help herself. She threw her arms around her husband's neck and kissed him deeply. Over his shoulder she saw a knot of young women, several of whom were gazing at Franklin with obvious interest. The rest were looking at her and suddenly began to titter.

"I think it's time we all went in for dinner, don't you?" Rose interrupted smoothly. "Michelle, I've given you a very special place, among my best friends."

Christmas dinner at Talbot House was right out of a fairy tale. As they entered the banquet hall guests were shown to their seats by formally attired waiters. At each setting, behind an array of silver and fine porcelain china, was a card embossed with the guest's name, set in a sterling holder. Michelle found herself between a banker who, after politely acknowledging her existence, turned his attention to a middle-aged woman with spiked, carrot-colored hair, and a younger man who devoted himself to a dowager whose white-powdered face made Michelle think of a Holstein cow.

Michelle was first bewildered and then overwhelmed by the array of food. The meal began with poached oysters complemented by a heavenly and very rare white wine, Barsas. This was followed by Consommé Britannia, Cassolette de foie gras, and Timbales à l'écarlate. *How much more can there be?* Michelle wondered, trying vainly to finish her portions. Then she noticed that the women around the table had scarcely touched their servings. Conscious of their curious glances and one or two outright disapproving frowns, Michelle set down her knife and fork. Nonetheless, she couldn't help feeling guilty about all this food going to waste.

Michelle had three bites of roast partridge but lost track of the number of times the wine steward topped off her claret glass. By the end of dinner, she was feeling pleasantly flushed. The colors around the table were dancing and candles seemed to burn more brightly than before. She looked down the table and saw Franklin regaling the women on either side of him with amusing stories. She wished she could go over and give him a big kiss.

After dinner Franklin led the men out to the billiard room for coffee, brandy, and cigars while the women clustered around Rose to "retire" to the music

161

room where champagne, coffee, and petits fours would be served. On his way out, Franklin came by and brushed his lips across Michelle's cheek.

"Enjoying yourself?"

"I'm having a wonderful time!" Michelle exclaimed.

She failed to notice how loudly she was speaking or that several heads swiveled in her direction.

Franklin patted her hand. "Everyone loves you."

Before Michelle had a chance to reply, Rose was guiding her into the music room, seating Michelle between the two women who had been closest to her at the dinner table.

"I'm Amelia Richardson," the outrageous, orange-haired creature said, squeezing Michelle's hand. "I just know we're going to be yummy friends!"

Michelle watched, fascinated, as Amelia Richardson screwed a cigarette into a foot-long jade holder.

"Do you smoke?"

"No . . . That is, I never tried. It's bad for you."

A glacial debutante drifting by laughed. "Such scruples! My dear, our Amelia doesn't let anyone tell her what's good or bad or what she should or shouldn't do. Why, she's the first woman who ever had a cigarette at the Plaza. When the silly manager came over and asked her to put it out, Amelia said, 'I am led to believe this is a free country and I shall do nothing to alter its status!' Isn't that enough to slay you?"

Michelle was utterly lost. Was this painfully thin, bone-white girl telling her that American women would fight to the death for the right to smoke in a hotel?

"You certainly had an appetite at dinner, my dear," Amelia Richardson was saying. "You're not eating for two, are you?"

Confused by the reference, Michelle's English deserted her. "*Pardon?*"

Amelia winked slyly. "You know. Are you *enceinte?*"

"*Mais, non! Pas de tout!*" Michelle cried, blushing furiously.

Her color deepened as she noticed that she had become the center of attention.

"Tell me," another young woman said. "How did you meet our Franklin?"

"I was a nurse in Saint Eustace," Michelle replied and went on to explain the exact circumstances.

"How very noble!" Amelia Richardson said in a bored tone.

"Yes, yes," interrupted the old cow-faced Dowager on Michelle's left. "But where did you say your people came from?"

"My people?"

"Yes, your people!" the Dowager snapped impatiently. "Where did they come from?"

"You mustn't pay any attention to Constance," Amelia Richardson whispered. "She's deaf as a rock!"

"From the village of Saint Eustace, madame," Michelle answered loudly.

"Don't shout at me, girl! Do they own it?"

"Own it?"

"Don't you understand English? Yes, own it!"

"I think what Auntie means is, do your people own the land?" the beautiful debutante suggested.

"Well, my father had his own farm," Michelle started to say.

"A farm?"

"Yes, it was his father's and his father's before him," Michelle struggled on.

"How many people did he have working it?"

"He worked it himself."

"Oh, so he was a *farmer*," the debutante said, finally making the connection. "How very quaint. Is that where Franklin married you—in Saint Eustace?"

"No. We were married by the mayor of Saint-Mihiel."

The woman regarded her blankly. "How very droll." Then she added, "But how very much like Franklin!"

"It must have been difficult for you making all the arrangements under those conditions," Amelia Richardson sympathized. "Arranging for your trousseau . . . By the way, which Paris couturier did you use?"

"Paris?"

"Naturally you had a Paris designer, my dear."

"I have never been to Paris."

Amelia Richardson let loose her famous braying laugh. "Never been to Paris! My dear, that's priceless!"

"She never has either!" the old Dowager said at once, stirring from her reverie. "She's a bumpkin, not one of us. She can't even speak proper English. For the life of me I can't see why Franklin married her!"

Michelle stared at the woman. She couldn't believe how cold and final her words sounded. Opposite her, two of the debutantes were whispering and giggling to each other.

Why are they doing this to me?

Michelle was so wrapped up in her thoughts she never noticed Rose observing her from the far end of the room, very content with what she saw.

- 19 -

Rose Jefferson was pleased with the way the boardroom had turned out. The dark trappings Simon had considered so masculine had been replaced by warm yellow pine panels, comfortable chairs upholstered in blue leather, and an old refectory table salvaged from a defunct Spanish mission. In place of Simon's dour landscapes there now hung dramatic oils by Remington and other prominent American painters. Rose thought the room reflected perfectly the vitality of a company stepping boldly into the future.

As she waited for Franklin, Rose thumbed through the thick stack of paper in front of her, representing months of grueling work. Rose admitted to herself that there had been times she had all but thrown her arms up in despair. The scope and complexity of the plan almost dwarfed one person's ability to deal with it, even hers.

From its earliest days Global had been involved with carrying cash. At first the company relied entirely on the business of banks, but later Jehosophat Jefferson had extended the service to individuals. As Global and the American frontier expanded, more and more people shipped money across the length and breadth of the United States. Since checking accounts existed only for the privileged few, merchants and traders came to rely on the service, putting their cash into envelopes, sewing them shut, and sealing the flaps with wax. For a flat fee Global guaranteed delivery.

In 1864 Congress enacted a law that created something that would eventually have far-reaching consequences for all express companies: the postal money order, designed to keep postmen from robbing their mail of cash. The charge was ten cents for a ten-dollar order, and by 1880 the Post Office Department had sold $100 million of these negotiable instruments from 5,491 branches.

Rose intended to challenge the government head-on by designing Global's own money order. Since other express companies were scrambling for new sources of revenue, she tackled the job of drafting a prototype of the Global instrument in complete secrecy.

After carefully examining its operations Rose discovered that the Post Office Department had serious difficulties with its money order. Anyone who wanted an order first had to speak English to buy it, then be able to read the language so he or she could fill it out. This represented insurmountable problems for new immigrants and illiterates who were forced to rely on strangers—often swindlers—to write out the particulars for them.

The second weakness lay in forgeries. Post Office orders could be cashed only at a designated office that had been advised in advance of the true amount of the order. This policy was supposed to stop customers from forging a higher amount in place of the original one. In reality the system was an ungainly nightmare in which people waited weeks for rebates on lost or inaccurate orders.

The question of forgery bedeviled Rose but finally she seized on a solution as simple as it was ingenious. On her prototype, which she quickly patented, Rose placed nine columns of figures running from one dollar to ten. Rose figured that when a customer bought the order the agent would write the name of the payee on two stubs, giving one to the buyer, keeping the second for company records. But rather than write in the sum, the clerk would cut off the figures of the amount paid for. For an amount larger than ten dollars, there were larger-denomination orders.

Rose did not expect to make a profit at first. Not only was she going to compete with a known commodity from the Post Office Department, she would have to commit a great deal of money to advertising. After reams of calculations Rose determined that she could make a handsome profit and at the same time undercut the Post Office by two cents on each order. Moreover, she would make certain that all 4,212 Global offices nationwide not only sold orders but promptly cashed them as well.

With her domestic plans honed and ready, Rose turned her attention to taking the Global money order to the world arena. Since the Renaissance the tried and proven way for a traveler or merchant to finance his journey or business was the letter of credit. The letter reflected an amount of cash on deposit at a bank at home that the traveler could, by providing his signature, draw on as needed through a correspondent bank abroad. This method had its drawbacks. There were delays while the signature was authenticated, and only certain banks would cash the letters at all; usually one or two in major capitals and none in small towns. Furthermore, a businessman lost money when his letter, denominated in dollars, was converted to pounds, francs, or marks at whatever rate the correspondent bank arbitrarily set. Exchange complications multiplied, as did expenses, when borders were crossed and currency had to be changed several times.

Rose was determined to cut through such red tape and inconvenience. She had listened carefully to her friends' endless tales of woe about cashing letters of credit abroad, an experience that reduced the stately to the level of ordinary mortals. If that was happening to well-heeled travelers she shuddered to think what the average tourist could expect. And the middle class was a market Global could profit from mightily—if Rose found a way to exploit and service it.

Using her domestic money order as a blueprint, Rose set about creating its international cousin, the traveler's check. From the letter of credit she borrowed the idea of the required signature, although in the TC, as she referred to the check in her notes, she had two places where the buyer would sign—on the upper left-hand corner when he made the purchase, and the bottom left when he cashed it. The handwriting had to match for the check to be cashed.

Rose also did away with the uncertainty of exchange rates. She had examined foreign rates against the dollar over the last two years and found them stable enough to guarantee the traveler's checks at a fixed rate against European currency. This, she reckoned, would be one of the TC's strongest selling points: customers carrying the Global Traveler's Check would no longer be gouged by opportunistic bankers.

Finally Rose compiled a list of British banks with which Global had done business on a regular basis. Having already decided to launch the TC in England, she didn't think she would have any trouble persuading them to accept the check. The key lay in bringing the smaller ones on board, creating a network so extensive that wherever a tourist found himself he didn't have to worry about money.

Neither, Rose calculated, would Global. The company would receive its profit up front, as soon as the purchase was made.

Rose glanced at the ormolu clock on the mantelpiece, wondering where Franklin could be. She forced herself to remain calm. He'd said he would come and he'd be there.

Rose was very proud of Franklin's military record, his medals and citations. She believed the war had forced him to mature and that Franklin had learned that he couldn't simply abandon his responsibilities. In the same way he had had a duty to his men, so too he had to answer to family commitments. Rose was about to buzz her secretary when Mary Kirkpatrick's voice came over the intercom.

"Mr. Jefferson is here, ma'am."

Rose smiled. "Send him in."

Unknown to Rose, Franklin had already spent several hours at Global. He had arrived well before any of the staff and had walked slowly through the halls of a place which, he thought, belonged to another lifetime. At Lower Broadway, nothing had changed. Inside Franklin Jefferson, nothing was the same.

As employees drifted in, Franklin disappeared into his office. Here too everything was just as he had remembered it. His chair even held the familiar indentation on its seat. The photographs mounted on the walls had been carefully dusted. He could just imagine Rose's instructions to the staff: *I want everything ready for Mr. Jefferson's return, exactly the way it was when he left.*

Franklin shook his head, then rubbed his temples as a tendril of pain touched his skull. Rose was going to be disappointed.

Franklin unlocked the top drawer of his desk and took out his diary. From the film of dust on the cover he knew that no one had touched it since he had placed it there. For the next hour, Franklin journeyed back in time, reliving those days he had been on the road for Global, meeting and talking to people all across America. Each page held a different adventure and each brought back vivid memories. But all ended inextricably at the same time and place: that terrible morning at the Global warehouses along the Hudson when Arthur Gladstone's private police had turned on the strikers and men had died on the cold, gritty cobblestones.

As he closed the diary, Franklin became conscious of the familiar sounds outside his office: telephones ringing, typewriters clacking, the light taps of secretaries' heels on the thinly carpeted wooden floor. The great machine that was Global was preparing for another day, just as it had yesterday and would do tomorrow.

As it did every day I was gone.

Then Franklin knew he had his answer to the question Rose would inevitably ask. He slipped the diary into his pocket and held on to it tightly, like a talisman, all the way down the corridor.

"Sorry about the delay," Franklin said, stepping into Rose's office.

Rose offered her cheek for the customary kiss.

"I just got in myself. It's wonderful to have you back, Franklin. Ready to go to work?"

Franklin shrugged noncommittally. "You said you had something you wanted to talk to me about."

"That's an understatement."

For the next two hours Rose described her plan to launch Global into the financial arena, carefully explaining every detail. From her brother's intent expression she saw that he understood and appreciated the opportunities.

"It's a hell of an idea," Franklin said when Rose was finished.

Although he tried to remain phlegmatic, Franklin had been overpowered by Rose's narrative. The potential of what she was talking about was staggering.

Franklin tapped the pile of notes in front of him. "You know that what you're doing is creating a new universal currency. It's a license to print money."

"Exactly!"

"Let me play devil's advocate." Franklin held up a finger. "Potential stumbling block number one: forgery. Like any paper money, both the money order and traveler's check will be an open invitation to copy. A good counterfeiter could bankrupt the company."

"We'd use the best engravers in the country," Rose replied. "Preferably those at the Bureau of Printing and Engraving, which would also supply our paper."

Franklin nodded. "Second: for both to work, appearances must match reality. If Global promises to pay off frauds, it has to keep its word. Banks honoring its checks will have to be covered."

"Global will back every check. If fraud does occur in the system and our correspondent banks take a loss, we'll make good."

"Last but not least there's the customer. You say that if TCs are lost or stolen Global will replace them, no questions asked. I agree with you that that's your strongest selling point as far as the public is concerned. But again, you have to honor that commitment. One mistake on your part and the goodwill you will have built up—and paid dearly for—will evaporate."

"We'll honor our commitments," Rose insisted. "By the time we're through Americans won't want to carry anything but our orders and checks."

"If that's the case, I don't see how you can miss."

"Do you mean that?"

"Of course."

"I can't wait for us to get started!" Rose exclaimed.

"No, Rose."

Rose stared at him, open-mouthed. "No, what?"

"It's not going to be 'us,' " Franklin said gently. "I'm not coming back to the company. Nor did you have any right to expect I would."

Rose sat back in her chair, her heart pounding. "I see. Can you tell me why?"

Franklin handed her the diary.

"This can better than I. Read the first few pages—and the last."

Without taking her eyes off Franklin, Rose accepted the notebook. She read intently for a half-hour before she closed its covers.

"The strike happened a long time ago, Franklin," she said. "It was a terrible thing. The mistakes were awful—on both sides. But I made restitution. You can't keep hanging it over my head forever."

"I don't want to do that," Franklin replied. "But it's not only the strike, Rose. It's the way I feel, the person I am."

"You mean who you've *become.*"

Franklin shook his head. "No, the one I've always been, the one you never wanted to see."

Rose regarded the book silently, then said, "I'm ready to admit that I made mistakes in the past. Are *you* ready to accept *your* responsibilities?"

"There's nothing I can do to help you, Rose. You've proven that to me and yourself by managing Global while I was in Europe. Just look at everything you've achieved. You don't need me."

"What I achieved was meant to be for us," Rose replied quietly. "You make it sound so easy, Franklin, but believe me, it wasn't."

"I'm not suggesting it was. But that's what you chose for yourself. Give me the chance to choose for myself."

Rose was about to press her argument but Franklin's tone of voice warned her off, cautioning her that any further arguments would only reinforce his determination to stand up to her.

"What is it you want, then?"

Franklin let out a deep breath. "I will help you with the money order, setting it up, negotiating with the banks, and so on. After that I'll resign from Global altogether."

Rose placed both hands on the blotter of her desk, fingers splayed.

"I'm sorry, but I can't accept that."

Franklin couldn't believe her words. "It's not as though you have a choice, Rose."

"But I do have an alternative. Will you at least listen?"

"Of course."

"I'm going to have my hands full with the money order," Rose said. "Since the traveler's check is designed as an international financial instrument, I won't be able to deal with it and the money order at the same time. Global will need someone in London to look after the details. Since the negotiations with the British banks will be every bit as delicate as the ones here, there's only one person who's qualified to do the job: you. I'm asking you to help me launch the money order here, then take the traveler's check to London."

Franklin considered the proposal. The more he thought about it, the better it sounded. Three thousand miles of ocean was a long way away. It would be a chance for him and Michelle to start a new life together.

"I accept—but on a trial basis," Franklin said.

"Then so do I."

Rose came around her desk and embraced her brother. She had salvaged what she could under the circumstances. She had also gained a precious commodity: time. It would take at least a year to bring the money order on

169

stream—if everything went well. A great deal could happen during that time to change Franklin's mind.

It was six o'clock and Mary Kirkpatrick was standing in front of the elevator when the door opened and a young officer in uniform stepped out.

"Pardon me, ma'am. Can you tell me where I can find a Miss Rose Jefferson?"

Mary escorted him through the empty work area toward the executive suites.

"Someone here to see you, Miss Jefferson."

Rose experienced a tug on her heart like the one every relative feels when a somber military officer arrives on the doorstep. But the war was over. Franklin was home, safe. Nonetheless, Rose was wary in accepting the sealed envelope.

"I'll be ready in ten minutes," she said quietly, refolding the letter.

"Will you be needing me for anything?" Mary Kirkpatrick inquired.

Rose stared at her, praying her secretary wouldn't notice anything.

"No, Mary, thank you. This is something I have to look after myself."

"I'm sorry, Miss Jefferson, but there's no mistake."

The words, so awful in their finality, didn't suit Dr. William Harris at all. He was a slim, short man with black curly hair sprinkled with gray and sad, kind brown eyes. The wall behind his desk was chockful of framed diplomas, citations, and battlefield commissions. William Harris was a graduate of the Columbia Medical School, had interned at Walter Reed Hospital, and had seen service with Teddy Roosevelt's Rough Riders at San Juan Hill as well as in Europe. His specialties, Rose noted, were neurological and cerebral traumas. He was one of the best, and knowing that took away a little more of the hope she struggled to hold on to.

Rose stared past him, out the window where snow was falling over a city rushing pell-mell toward the new year.

"Please tell me everything again."

Harris took a deep breath. He was out of practice at this sort of thing. Given his rank, he seldom had to break tragic news to relatives. But Franklin Jefferson had been no ordinary soldier. General Pershing himself had written Harris about the young man's exploits and in so many words ordered Harris to speak to his sister personally. After all, Rose Jefferson was no ordinary civilian either.

"There's no way we can get at the shrapnel lodged in your brother's skull," Harris said. "Over the years the metal will cause pressure to build up against the brain. Your brother will be subject to memory loss and dizzy spells. Ultimately he will lose control of his bodily functions. . . ."

"And he will die."

Harris said nothing.

170

"How much time does he have?"

"Impossible to say. A year, two, maybe five. I'm sorry, Miss Jefferson, but it's all guesswork. You're certainly entitled to a second opinion; however, I don't think you'll get a different answer."

Rose noted Harris's professional courtesy but she didn't need more opinions. The stack of medical records on the doctor's desk told her what she had to believe. Every conceivable test had been run on Franklin at the army hospital in Paris.

"In cases like this, the army always contacts the next of kin before informing the . . . the patient," Harris finished. "Would you like me to tell him now?"

Rose raised her head. "Tell him what, Doctor? That he's dying and doesn't even know it? That he will never live to see his grandchildren? Perhaps never even have children of his own?"

Harris was shocked. "Miss Jefferson, that's not fair! Neither to your brother nor to his wife. The two of them have a right to know what the future holds. To mislead them this way—"

"I don't give a damn about Michelle Lecroix," Rose told him, her tone frigid.

"Well, perhaps you should!" Harris replied angrily. "Not only is she your brother's wife but she saved his life. If it hadn't been for the fact that she nursed and took care of him, he'd probably be dead!"

"On the other hand, he might have returned exactly the man he was when he had left," Rose shot back. "I'm sick and tired of hearing about Michelle's heroics, Michelle's quick thinking. If Franklin had received proper medical attention when he needed it, instead of some botched-up barnyard sawing, he would be fine today!"

Harris realized it was pointless to argue. Rose Jefferson was distraught. He had to take the decision out of her hands.

"You may think it's best not to say anything to your brother, but as the attending physician I have a responsibility to him," Harris said firmly.

"Which is?"

"Your brother has a right to know what to expect. He needs to recognize certain symptoms. He'll require constant monitoring and different drugs. Those around him, especially his wife, will have to know what to look out for."

"And what would that be?" Rose demanded. "Can you tell Franklin exactly what's going to happen to him?"

"Not really—"

"That he has precisely two years, three months, and seven days to live?"

"No, of course not—"

"That he'll experience dizzy spells at eleven o'clock Monday, Wednesday, and Friday?"

"Miss Jefferson, you're being unreasonable!"

"No, Doctor. I'm saying that if you don't know what to expect, what can you possibly tell Franklin? You won't have to live with your uncertainties, but if you plant them in his mind, he will. Is *that* fair?"

"It may not be fair, Miss Jefferson," Harris replied heavily. "But it is my duty."

Rose reached across the desk and gripped Harris's arm.

"I'm asking you, pleading with you, not to do this. Besides my son, Franklin is all I have left in the world. I'll take full responsibility for him. Give me the papers to sign. I'll indemnify you, the army, the whole damn government. No one will ever have to lift a finger for or spend a dollar on Franklin's care. I'll see to everything, I swear it."

Gently Harris dislodged his arm. He was convinced that this woman wouldn't let go until she had what she wanted. She would use her influence, which, he had been forewarned, reached as far as the White House, to challenge any decision he made. The possibility angered Harris but he counseled himself to think like a doctor. Would his patient, Franklin Jefferson, be in any way harmed if this happened? The answer was no. When the time came, Rose Jefferson could pay for the best medical services in the world.

Rose sensed what Harris was thinking. A plan crystallized in her mind. It was dangerous because she didn't know anything about the man but her instinct urged her to gamble.

"Dr. Harris, may I ask how old you are?"

"I beg your pardon?"

"How old are you, Doctor?"

"Forty-three."

"I take it then your twenty-year service will be up soon."

"Yes, in a few months."

"Do you intend to go into private practice?"

William Harris shrugged. He had wanted his own practice ever since he had decided to become a doctor. Except there was no way a longshoreman's son could afford Columbia Medical School, no matter how brilliant he was. The only alternative had been the army, which had paid his fees—and demanded twenty years' service in return.

"Doctor, I'm going to ask you to listen very carefully to what I have to say," Rose continued. "I don't mean to insult you, nor do I wish you to misinterpret my words."

Rose gestured at the diplomas on the wall. "Obviously you are an excellent physician. You have served your country honorably. You are in the prime of life and there is a great deal you can accomplish. If you wish to enter private practice I would be willing to fund you through an outright grant. In return I ask for only two things: that you become my brother's personal physician and that you never divulge the true nature of his condition to him or to anyone else. Whatever happens, I am the only one who is to know."

Rose's voice was rock-steady but her hands were in her lap where Harris couldn't see them.

"And because of the circumstances I must ask you for an answer immediately. If you decline, I will have to consider other alternatives."

William Harris was stunned. The woman was offering him a bribe. Magnificent, tempting, but a bribe nonetheless. The words to dismiss her summarily were on the tip of his tongue yet Harris couldn't bring himself to utter them. Rose Jefferson was handing him everything he had ever dreamed of, including the chance to take his place among his peers. Although Harris had risen to the rank of captain and had scrupulously saved a part of every paycheck, he had less than five thousand dollars to his credit. He could never open the kind of practice he wanted on that money. It could never allow him to have the wife and family he had dreamed of throughout his lonely years in far-flung postings. At forty-three, William Harris knew that there were only so many fruitful years left to him. He could spend them in the army until retirement. He could go to work in a hospital. Or he could seize the chance Rose Jefferson was holding out.

"Your offer is very generous, Miss Jefferson," Harris said quietly, "and I accept. However, I must insist on certain conditions. First, you will sign waivers that relieve the army of any responsibility insofar as your brother is concerned. Second, I require a deposition from you stating that I have told you of Franklin Jefferson's true condition and that in spite of my advice to inform his wife, you are placing him in my care for the duration of his natural life. If at any time you disagree with any of my medical recommendations, I cannot be held responsible for the consequences."

"Your terms are acceptable, Doctor," Rose said. "I'll have my attorney draw up the necessary papers for the grant."

Rose held out her hand and William Harris shook it briefly.

"Believe me," Rose said softly, "it's best this way."

"I hope you're right, Miss Jefferson. More for your sake and your brother's than mine."

Rose could not bring herself to return to Talbot House. Little by little she realized just how irrevocably her life had been overturned. Rose wished she had someone to talk to about the feelings churning within her, a friend she could trust to listen. Instead she went to the only place where she could find sanctuary.

In the stillness of her office, Rose sat staring at the row of paintings she had

173

had moved from Dunescrag. This time even the heroic feats of Jehosophat Jefferson failed to comfort her. Global was no longer the vision her grandfather had molded into reality. It was changing, breaking and splitting like a chrysalis from which a new and different entity would emerge. At that moment Rose needed to know if her grandfather would have approved of everything she'd done. She had to be reassured by someone she loved that everything she had struggled for was good and right. But Jehosophat Jefferson's stern expression did not change, nor did the oils magically dissolve and bring him back to life.

Nor can I give Franklin back his life . . .

The thought that her brother was living on borrowed time emptied Rose. She railed against the cold unfeeling words in the medical reports yet ultimately they defeated her. But Franklin would never live with the pain cutting through her, a pain she would learn to endure and hide from the world. When the time came and he had to be told, she would find a way. But not until then.

Which brought Rose back to Michelle. Dr. William Harris assumed that she was unaware of her husband's condition. But was that really the case? After all, Michelle had been the first to tend to Franklin. She was an experienced nurse who might have recognized the long-term consequences of Franklin's wounds. Later, she could have gotten her hands on his medical file. So it was possible, Rose thought, that Michelle knew—had known before she married—just how short her husband's life would be. Maybe she had decided it was an acceptable trade-off: a few years with a man she could bring herself to love; then, after Franklin's death, a whole future stretching before her while she was not only young but very rich as well.

Rose scribbled a cryptic note to herself to make sure that Dr. Harris detailed Franklin's condition very carefully in the indemnity papers. In the event that Franklin changed his will to include Michelle, Rose could, if and when the day came, argue that Franklin had not been of "sound mind or body" when he had added the codicil. She'd be damned if she'd let Michelle Lecroix see a penny of any inheritance.

Rose thought back to the bargain she had struck with Franklin only a few hours ago and felt sick. Had she known about his condition then she never would have insisted that he remain with the company. Nor was it possible for her to go back on the arrangement. Franklin would immediately suspect that something was wrong and inevitably the secret would begin to unravel.

Rose slumped forward and wept softly. All the power, money, and influence at her command couldn't help her now. Nor would they magically remove those few pieces of metal resting in her brother's skull like a ticking bomb.

— 20 —

Michelle poured herself coffee from the service on the table nestled in one corner of the library in Talbot House. Outside, the bitter March winds continued to rattle the windowpanes as they had all month long. The bleak landscape of Fifth Avenue was a perfect reflection of her mood, although this morning, as every morning, Michelle tried to smile through it.

With Franklin gone so much of the time, Michelle, who was used to daily hard work, found herself with nothing to do. Albany ran the house with clocklike precision and politely but firmly rebuffed her offers to help. The ever-present silence of the house also grated on Michelle. Although there were six full-time servants, Michelle seldom saw or heard them except when she needed something. Then, like magic, one would appear. It gave Michelle the uneasy feeling that she was being watched all the time.

Whenever they went out socially Michelle made a point of staying very close to Franklin and always suggested they leave early. During the predinner chitchat and the conversation at the table, she tried to say as little as possible. In return, she got her wish and was ignored.

When Franklin broke the news that they would be going to Europe at the end of the year, Michelle could scarcely hide her happiness and relief. For her, that day couldn't come soon enough. Nevertheless, Michelle continued to watch, listen, and learn. To help pass the time she had created a private world in this little corner of the Talbot library, reading aloud from the great works, careful to pronounce the words correctly. She was tired of people remarking what a lovely accent she had.

"Excuse me, ma'am," Albany said. "Mr. McQueen is here to see you. Shall I show him in?"

"Yes, of course!"

Michelle was thrilled; this was the first time someone had called at Talbot House for her.

"Monk! It's so good to see you!"

She threw her arms around him although his back was so broad her hands never met. Monk McQueen held her at arms' length and smiled.

"You look beautiful—as always."

Michelle blushed. "Would you like some coffee?"

"I'd love a cup. Where's that ne'er-do-well husband of yours?"

"He's already left for the office."

Monk frowned and checked his watch. "That's early for him."

"Not really," Michelle said. "He's been putting in long hours."

Monk caught the wistfulness in her voice. He too had been surprised by Franklin's return to Lower Broadway, given what had happened between Franklin and Rose. Franklin had explained that the arrangement was temporary and by the end of the year he and Michelle would be returning to Europe. He offered no details and Monk didn't press him.

"I brought these for you," Monk said, placing two well-thumbed volumes on the table.

Michelle read the titles out loud. "*American Etiquette and Rules of Politeness, 1886; Hills Manual of Social and Business Forms.*"

Monk grinned. "Indispensable for a New York hostess. Normal children are read Grimm's fairy tales. Bluebloods tuck one of these into their daughters' cradles."

Michelle opened the *Hills Manual* and discovered a gold mine of information on how to decipher the complex rules and regulations that governed New York society. Finally, what no one took the time to teach her, she could learn for herself. Michelle was touched by Monk's thoughtfulness.

"I'm going to start reading these right away. God knows I have enough time."

"That's another thing I wanted to mention to you," Monk said casually. "Don't you think it's time you became involved in something besides your marriage, started getting out a little more?"

"I'd love to," Michelle replied. "But I don't know if there's anything I can do. Unless you're offering me a job."

Monk had told Michelle that his door at *Q* magazine in Chelsea was always open to her and she had taken him at his word. The first time she had gone there she had been overwhelmed by the furious pace of activity. It was like watching an extended family having a mad reunion. People bickered, huddled together, criticized one another, and shouted into telephones. The atmosphere was very different from the sterile one Michelle had felt hanging over Global's offices on Lower Broadway.

Monk winked. "That's not exactly what I had in mind. But here's something to think about."

It took Michelle two days to screw up the courage to put to Rose the first of the ideas Monk had given her. She offered to tutor Steven in French.

"Oh, Michelle, that's so sweet of you," Rose told her. "I'll speak to his headmaster."

The next day Michelle scoured the bookstores and discovered a primer on how to teach French as a second language. She hoped it would help Steven overcome his indifference to her, which, over the months, had crystallized into resentment.

Michelle had never met another boy like Steven. Although he was only ten she thought that he was far too old for his age, a child whose natural spontaneity and curiosity had been bred out of him. At the beginning Michelle had assumed Steven's coldness was directed only at her. But as she saw more of him she realized this wasn't the case. Steven was a solitary boy who seldom invited classmates to Talbot House. When he did, he tended to dominate if not bully the other children. Some were clearly afraid of him.

Michelle was tempted to mention something about this to Rose, yet she always held back. Rose was fiercely possessive of Steven. Also, Franklin had told her about Steven's having witnessed his father's suicide, and Michelle could imagine the deep scar the tragedy had left. Nonetheless, she also believed that far from helping Steven, Rose was hindering his emotional development. She surrounded Steven with everything a rich, enlightened mother believed was necessary—governesses, tutors, music and riding instructors. Everything except her own time, generosity, and love. Not that Rose didn't love Steven. But she loved Global more. Michelle asked herself if Rose saw the kind of human being she was creating, not the perfect heir she had in mind but someone dark, suspicious, and brooding.

When Rose returned home that evening, Michelle told her she was ready to begin her tutorials.

"Oh, I'm terribly sorry, my dear," Rose apologized. "I really did mean to call you from the office. I spoke with the headmaster and I'm afraid he doesn't think Steven is quite ready to take on more work at this time."

"But it wouldn't be so much work as fun," Michelle protested. "I could teach him to live the language, not only speak it—"

"Michelle, really, I'm touched by your offer. But I'm afraid I must abide by the headmaster's decision. Copperfield School is recognized for its progressive teaching methods. I'm sure they know best."

"If that's the way you feel . . ." Michelle said, trying to hide her disappointment.

Rose smiled. "I'm so glad you understand."

Perhaps it was something in Rose's voice but Michelle realized that Rose had never broached the subject with the headmaster of Copperfield School—and had never intended to.

Steven wasn't the only subject on which Rose Jefferson thought herself the final authority. Whenever Franklin and Michelle accompanied Rose to a social affair, Rose would always make some comment on Michelle's choice of clothing.

177

"Aren't you just a little overdressed for a cocktail party, dear?"

Michelle would look down at herself, not knowing what to think, then invariably follow Rose's suggestion and change into a different outfit.

The same thing happened when the Jeffersons entertained at home. Thinking that Rose was too busy to look after the details, Michelle would order flowers and prepare a menu only to be told, politely but firmly, that her help was neither needed, wanted, nor expected.

"Madame really shouldn't concern herself with such matters," Albany informed her dryly. "The florist knows what is required for the occasion, the cook knows Miss Jefferson's preferences, and the rest is my responsibility. Thank you, madame."

Michelle refused to be put off. Having seen how many charities Rose was involved in, Michelle suggested that perhaps she could make a contribution at one of the city's many hospitals.

"I think that's a lovely idea," Rose exclaimed and assured Michelle that she would make all the arrangements.

Michelle prepared herself carefully, going over all the medical texts she had brought with her from the American army hospitals in France. She called on Dr. Bartholomew Simmons, whom Rose had introduced her to, and plied him with questions about the workings of modern American facilities. When she thought she was ready, Michelle accompanied Rose to Roosevelt Memorial Hospital.

Michelle was awestruck by the facilities and dedication of the staff at Roosevelt Memorial. She thought it would be wonderful to work with highly trained people who had the best equipment available. She was also surprised when Rose took her to the twentieth and top floor, to the boardroom instead of to one of the many wards.

Michelle found herself sitting at an oval table with eight other women, all coiffed and dressed as though they were expected for tea at the Waldorf. The meeting started without a single doctor present and Michelle soon learned that no one else would be joining them. But what truly surprised her were the topics of conversation: the next charity ball, where it should be held, how much the tickets would cost, and what the theme would be.

Michelle turned to Rose and whispered, "Aren't we here to work?"

Rose looked at her askance, drawing the attention of the other women.

"What is it, Rose?" one of them chirped.

"Michelle was just asking if we were here to work."

The silence was deafening. Finally Amelia Richardson, whom Michelle had met at the Christmas party, spoke up.

"My dear, we *are* working. Charity balls are a very important and demanding responsibility." She paused. "Or did you think we were here to empty bedpans?"

In the spring of 1919, Rose came as close as she ever had to separating herself from Global's day-to-day operations. What was left of the domestic express business was delegated to capable, longtime managers who answered directly to Eric Gollant. Global's real estate holdings, which had swelled enormously, would be managed by Hugh O'Neill. Franklin had the responsibility of organizing a sales staff and opening discreet talks with New York's major banks to gain their support in accepting the Global money order. The banks' cooperation was critical to Rose's plan.

In June, for the first time since taking control of Global, Rose left New York. Her office booked her the presidential suite in the lavish Willard Hotel in Washington, from which Rose set out to conquer whatever obstacles the federal government put in her way. They were legion.

The director of the Bureau of Printing and Engraving, whose department was responsible for producing both coin and paper currency, took a dim view of what he perceived to be a poacher on his exclusive domain. When no amount of flattery or cajoling softened his refusal to cooperate, Rose assembled a battery of state senators and representatives to convince the director that she had no intention of competing with the almighty dollar.

No sooner had Rose won that particular battle than the Secretary of the Treasury weighed in. Confronted with legislators who approved heartily of Rose's plan, mainly because it would reopen now-defunct Global offices in their home states, the secretary took the matter straight to the White House, intent on burying it once and for all.

Rose replied in kind. Having courted the chief of the President's staff, she was promptly shoehorned into an appointment and spelled out her intentions to a mildly amused Chief Executive. Afterward, during a state dinner at which Rose was seated at the head table, Woodrow Wilson whispered to the Treasury Secretary not to be such a goddamn horse's ass. If this woman wanted to take on the United States Post Office Department, let her.

Having bored through the government bureaucracies, Rose set to work on a prototype of the money order. Artists, engravers, experts in print, handwriting, and paper production filed in and out of the Willard suite. Rose inspected and rejected one design after another. To the dismay of those around her, she couldn't say exactly what it was she wanted but insisted she would know when she saw it. Finally, at the end of July, Rose selected one of the presentations, a large stylized G on the left with the company name running prominently across the top, two places at the bottom for her and Franklin's signatures, all against a cream and royal-blue background design.

"It has strength, solidity," Rose declared.

The next day the mammoth presses on L Street were running flat out. As a gesture of thanks Rose sent the first money order for one hundred dollars to the President, promptly deducting it as a business expense.

All the while Rose was in the capital, she remained in constant touch with Lower Broadway, calling Franklin every second day. Rose couldn't have been happier with her brother's reports but her real peace of mind came with the answers to the discreetly worded questions she put to Eric Gollant and Hugh O'Neill.

"Franklin pitched the money order to the hotel controllers at the Waldorf yesterday," the accountant told her. "I'm surprised he hasn't mentioned anything to you. He had them eating out of his hand, Rose. All the major hotels signed on."

Hugh O'Neill had equally reassuring news.

"Didn't Franklin say anything? The new sales force is almost in place."

Such news was nectar to Rose. She had known all along that doctors, even highly qualified ones like William Harris, were not infallible. Ever since she had been told of Franklin's condition Rose had read everything she could get her hands on about soldiers who had inoperable metal fragments in their bodies. In a great many cases these men lived normal, productive lives. There was no reason in the world why the same couldn't be true of Franklin.

As Rose left her hotel suite to inspect the first run of traveler's checks, her spirits had never been higher.

The day Rose Jefferson had left for Washington, two things happened that changed Michelle's life in ways she had never expected.

As soon as Rose was gone the atmosphere in Talbot House lightened. Michelle actually heard the staff telling funny stories and poking fun at their mistress's habits when they thought no one was listening. Michelle was quick to take advantage of this tiny form of rebellion. As she got to know the servants their reserve melted and soon they were gossiping with one another like old friends.

On the other side of the coin, Rose's friends who had made feeble efforts to include Michelle in their carefully orchestrated schedules stopped calling altogether.

The indifference Michelle had worked so hard to overcome might have wounded her deeply had it not been for Franklin. At dinner the first evening after Rose's departure he at last explained to her what he had been working on all these months.

"I'm terribly sorry about this cloak-and-dagger routine," Franklin apologized. "Rose insisted on absolute secrecy. There was no telling what our competitors would do if they got wind of our plans."

Michelle didn't take offense. On the contrary, she was fascinated by the details of the money order and traveler's check. When Franklin was through, she asked, "Is there anything I can do to help you?"

Franklin burst out laughing. "I didn't think you'd be interested in something so boring."

"I *don't* think it's boring, and I *am* interested!"

Over the next few weeks Michelle read all the books, articles, and clippings that Franklin brought home, making voluminous notes on Global's history and growth. With every detail she became more impressed both with her husband and, albeit reluctantly, with Rose. They were at the helm of an enormous business enterprise that demanded all their skill, courage, and business acumen. Michelle was also convinced that, given a chance, she too could make a contribution.

"I'll tell you what," Franklin said after hearing her out. "Why don't you wait until we get to London and launch the traveler's checks. Believe me, there will be more than enough work."

He paused and grinned sheepishly. "I think it's better that we don't say anything to Rose. As far as she's concerned, progressive ideas—like wives working with their husbands, for example—apply only to her."

Michelle threw her arms around him. She had never loved him more than she did that moment.

The corner table in the library became her office, and there Michelle put in the same hours Franklin did at Lower Broadway. When he came home, they went over the day's work together, comparing notes and trading suggestions. When Franklin thought she was ready he presented Michelle with the ultra-secret intentions Rose had for the traveler's check in Europe.

"Read it through and let me know what you think," he said, handing her the portfolio.

Michelle started in on it even before Franklin was out the door. Drafted in Rose's precise, slanted handwriting, the plans called for Global directly to challenge the world's leading travel company, Cooks. Rose had armed Franklin with the names of men who controlled the great London banking houses and whose influence stretched across the world. The object was to persuade them to honor the new, and as yet untested, traveler's check, thus freeing the American tourists from Cooks's stranglehold. If the traveler's check was widely accepted, a tourist could travel wherever, whenever, and however he chose, instead of being at the mercy of Cooks's package tours.

Rose's second line of attack called for Franklin to persuade steamship and rail companies to consider the traveler's check as legal tender. This would further undercut Cooks's bookings and reservations.

It all came down to two things, Michelle reckoned: stealth and speed. If Cooks got even the faintest whiff of Rose's plan, they could use their enormous cash reserves not only to fight her directly but to pressure their clients into refusing the traveler's checks. The losses to Global would be staggering, if not crippling.

The more she examined Rose's plan the more Michelle was impressed by its audacity. The delicacy of the negotiations would be nerve-racking, the attention to detail and nuance had to be faultless. The pressure on Franklin—

Suddenly Michelle whirled around, her arm knocking over the inkstand, sending a blue-black wave across the pages.

"Steven, you frightened me to death!"

Steven's pale blue eyes were fixed on Michelle, unblinking. Michelle wanted to move but couldn't. This ten-year-old boy, in gray shorts, white shirt, and blue blazer school uniform, mesmerized her.

"What are you doing here?" she asked weakly. "Why aren't you in school?"

"There aren't any classes today," Steven replied. "It's field day."

"I didn't—"

"Of course you wouldn't know. You're a foreigner."

"Steven, that's not very nice—"

"I don't have to be nice to you. You're a foreigner! You're different! You should go away. Don't pretend you want to work. It's just your way to get at our money. I heard you and Uncle Franklin talking about it!"

Michelle's eyes filled with tears. "Why are you so cruel, Steven? What have I ever done to you? And I don't want your money!"

Steven smiled. He came over and lifted the ink-drenched pages by their corners so that the ink ran onto Michelle's skirt.

"I can do whatever I want to you," he said and calmly turned his back on her.

Michelle watched Steven walk away and the library door close behind him. She heard the chauffeur's voice, then the crunch of tires on gravel as the Jefferson limousine drew away.

Her whole body quivering, Michelle rose and cleaned the desk as best she could. Her fear turned to anger as she saw that her clothing was ruined. Michelle ran out of the library and up the stairs to her bedroom, furiously tugging at the buttons on her skirt. Sooner or later Steven had to come home. When he did, she'd get an explanation, and apology, out of him, even if it meant a thrashing.

Michelle was opening one of the closets when she noticed some of her underclothes lying on the bed.

How did they—

Michelle screamed as she picked up the shredded silk and lace. The image of Steven, standing there like a ghost, his expressionless eyes boring into her, tore into her mind.

I can do anything I want to you.

— 21 —

The Copperfield School in Murray Hill was a New York institution, the cradle of men who went on to become the country's leading politicians, attorneys, and businessmen. Franklin himself was an alumnus and he'd had no difficulty in persuading the headmaster to bring Steven Talbot off the playing field so he could talk to him privately.

As Franklin waited he gently massaged his temples, willing the needle-sharp pain to go away. He still could not believe the sight that had greeted him when he had run into Talbot House: Michelle sitting like a statue on the edge of the bed, her face streaked with tears, and behind her, the pile of shredded lingerie, scissors gleaming beneath the lace. . . . His anger mounted as she told him about the encounter with Steven.

The door opened and Steven was led in, his shorts and jersey muddy from the soccer match, his shoes trailing grass and dirt across the spotless floor.

"If you need me, Mr. Jefferson, I'll be in the next room," the headmaster said and excused himself.

"Sit down, Steven."

The boy did not obey him. He remained standing, his feet planted apart, looking at Franklin defiantly.

"Is Mother all right?" he asked.

"She's fine. That's not what I want to talk to you about. Steven, what did you do to Michelle in the library?"

A wisp of a smile creased Steven's lips. "I don't know what you mean, Uncle Franklin."

"You didn't spill ink on her dress?"

"No! She did that herself!"

"Before that happened, did you go into our rooms?"

"No!"

Franklin squeezed his eyes shut as a bolt of pain hammered his skull. For an instant he felt dizzy, as though he were going to black out. His next words came out as a gasp.

"Did you . . . did you take anything from your aunt's drawers?"

"She's not my aunt!"

"That's not what I asked you! Did you take Michelle's underthings and cut them up?"

"I don't know anything about her smelly underwear! May I go now?"

Without bothering to wait, Steven turned toward the door. He managed to take one step before Franklin seized him by the scruff of the neck and shoved him into a chair.

"Did you cut up Michelle's things?" he whispered hoarsely.

Steven was terrified but he refused to back down. "What if I did?"

Franklin grabbed Steven by both shoulders, his fingers digging into the boy's skin.

"I want you to remember this. If you're ever rude to Michelle again, if you ever try to hurt her, I'll punish you myself."

"You wouldn't dare!" Steven screamed. "I'll tell Mother!"

Franklin took a deep breath and relaxed his grip. "You won't have to. I'm going to tell her myself."

Steven didn't know what possessed him. In that split second his hatred for Michelle crystallized into pure fury. Very deliberately he cleared his throat and spat into Franklin's face.

Franklin spun away as though he had been struck. The pain was relentless, blinding him. Through the red haze, the evil grinning face of Serge Picard descended upon him, mocking him.

In the next room, the headmaster jumped to his feet when he heard the sound of breaking glass. He rushed in in time to see Franklin holding Steven in the air, the boy clawing at his face, his legs bloody from where they had gone through the frosted glass set in the door.

"Mr. Jefferson!"

Franklin snarled and with one blow sent the headmaster sprawling.

"You little bastard!" he kept shouting. "You'll never hurt anyone again!"

Horrified, the headmaster watched as Franklin Jefferson heaved his nephew through the glass, the boy screaming as the jagged edges tore into his flesh.

He's insane! the headmaster thought, staggering to his feet and leaping at Franklin as he wrenched open the door once more to get at Steven.

"Keep away from him, sir! If you touch him again I'll call the police, I swear!"

Shielding the boy, the headmaster watched Franklin Jefferson back away, then suddenly whirl around and crash into the corridor, sending other students and teachers to the floor.

"Let him go!" the headmaster shouted. He knelt over Steven, who lay groaning. "Get the nurse in here—quickly!"

"Shall I call the police?" someone asked.

"No, no police!" the headmaster snapped.

In spite of what had happened, this was still the Copperfield School, and more to the point, the family involved was the Jeffersons. The headmaster knew exactly what he had to do.

Rose returned to the Willard Hotel flushed with excitement from her day at the Bureau of Printing and Engraving. The proofs for the traveler's check had been perfect and she had had a very pleasant lunch with the director while finalizing the details of the print run, shipping, and security procedures. In a large black portfolio case tucked under her arm was a specimen sheet containing fifty checks. Rose couldn't wait to show it to Franklin.

Rose was hurrying across the lobby when she was intercepted in midstride by the hotel manager.

"Miss Jefferson, thank God you're back!" he said, then in a lower voice added, "Would you please come into my office. It's urgent."

As soon as he closed the door the manager handed her a stack of message slips. Rose thumbed through them quickly. Three were from Michelle, three from Monk, and the rest from Dr. Henry Wright. The message on all of them was the same: Rose was to call New York at once.

"I need to use your phone."

Ten minutes later Rose's face was ashen.

"There must be some mistake."

"I'm afraid not, Rose," the physician replied, his voice crackling over the wires. "I would suggest that you return as quickly as you can."

"I'll be on the evening train. Thank you, Henry . . ."

Rose dialed the front desk and told the manager she would be leaving immediately. She asked that her bags be packed and a reservation made on the Capitol Express. For a moment Rose sat there trying to make sense of what Wright had told her. It was unthinkable. Unless . . .

Rose signaled so hard for the operator that she broke a fingernail. When she got through to Talbot House it was Monk who answered.

* * *

At one o'clock the following morning Rose was standing by her son's bedside. His face had a bluish cast from the night-light on the dresser. It was all she could do to hold back her tears as she stared at the bandages across his chin and forehead.

"There's no permanent damage," Dr. Wright rumbled. "No broken bones, no scarring, and—" he held up a finger—"most important, none of the glass splinters touched his eyes. He's one very lucky boy, Rose. I've given him a mild sedative to help him sleep through the night. By tomorrow, he'll be full of beans."

"What did happen?" Rose murmured, stroking Steven's hair.

When Rose had arrived home she had ignored Michelle and Monk, who had been waiting for her downstairs, and run directly to Steven's room.

Dr. Wright stared down at his gleaming brogues. "According to the headmaster, Franklin threw Steven through a glass door."

"That's impossible!"

The physician shrugged. "You'll have to talk to the school about that."

"Were the police notified?"

"No."

Rose was relieved. "I assume I can count on your discretion."

It was a statement, not a question.

"Of course." Henry Wright picked up his bag. "He's all right, Rose, believe me. I'll come around tomorrow to look in on him."

Rose didn't hear him go. She sat beside Steven, holding his hand, trying to still the fear that had gnawed at her all the way from Washington.

How could Franklin do such a thing?

Rose considered herself blessed to have such a well-behaved child as Steven. He was a natural leader, popular with the other boys. His teachers and tutors had nothing but praise for his hard work, and none of the household staff ever complained about him.

Although Steven seemed unaffected by growing up without a father, Rose had always kept him close to her, choosing to keep him at Talbot House rather than send him away to boarding school. It was her way of protecting him, showing him how much she loved him. This didn't mean she coddled him. Because Global demanded so much of her time she had taught Steven to be independent, to think and fend for himself. To make up for her absence Rose tried to bring her world to Steven, telling him wonderful stories about his grandfather and the company he had founded, which one day would be his. Nothing gave her greater pleasure than to watch her son's eyes light up when she talked about the future.

"I'm so sorry, my darling," Rose whispered. "This will never happen again, I promise."

186

Rose kissed her son on the cheek and silently left the room. Steven counted to ten, then opened his eyes. The pain from his cuts and bruises didn't bother him at all. In fact, he was very happy. Now maybe his mother would see that Uncle Franklin was crazy and that it was all Michelle's fault. One way or another, Steven was sure his mother would get the Frenchwoman out of their lives. If she didn't, he had a few more surprises in store for Michelle Lecroix.

"Where's Franklin?"

Rose swept into the informal drawing room and confronted Monk and Michelle.

"He's not here, Rose," Michelle answered. "No one's seen him since . . . since what happened at the school. I'm worried about him. . . ."

A tiny spark of fear flared in Rose's belly. "You mean he hasn't even called?"

"Not a word," Monk replied. "When Michelle couldn't reach him at Global, she called me. I've tried his friends' houses as well as all the clubs. No one's seen him."

Rose sat down on the ottoman. "I don't understand. Why would he just disappear?" She looked at Michelle and her voice tightened. "Something happened here, didn't it? What was it?"

Michelle hesitated. She could imagine how Rose must have felt, seeing Steven injured. She didn't want to hurt her any more but neither could she hide the truth. Slowly Michelle recounted what had happened in the library between her and Steven, then what she had discovered in her bedroom.

"I didn't know what to think," she said. "I was terrified. I called Franklin and he came right home. When he saw what Steven had done, he went straight to the school."

Rose couldn't believe what she was hearing.

"You told Franklin that Steven was responsible for cutting up your underwear! Michelle, I've never heard of anything so ridiculous! Steven's incapable of doing anything like that."

Michelle's eyes flashed. "Do you want me to show you what he can do?"

"Michelle, really. You're hysterical."

"Your son hates me," Michelle replied quietly. "He has since the day I came to this house."

Rose sighed. "Now I understand. You made up some farfetched story about an accident that was supposedly Steven's fault, convinced Franklin it was true, and he tore off to punish my son."

"Not punish, Rose," Monk interrupted. "According to the headmaster, Franklin lost all control of himself. I'm relieved Steven's all right, but given Franklin's behavior and that he's missing, I'm worried about him."

187

"I'll get to the bottom of what happened at Copperfield," Rose said hastily. "As for Franklin, he's probably ashamed of what he did."

"I'm sure he is, Rose," Michelle said, "but only if he's *aware* of what he's done. Lately he's been complaining about headaches and dizzy spells. He's never had those before and I've never seen him act the way the headmaster insisted he did. Something's very wrong. I'm going to call Dr. Harris."

"What good will that do?"

Michelle turned on Rose. "If Franklin left the school in a rage, who knows what could have happened to him? He might have been hurt as well. Maybe he's had an accident. . . ."

"Michelle, you're overreacting—"

"Maybe I am, but Franklin's my husband. I care as much for him as you do for your son."

As Michelle hurried away to dress, Rose got up, shaking her head.

"Michelle's overwrought. Franklin's a grown man, for heaven's sake. The two of you are treating him as though he were an invalid."

Rose was horrified by the last word, which had inadvertently slipped out, but Monk attached no significance to it.

"No, Rose," he said. "Michelle's treating him as a husband, and I, as a friend. What about you? Don't you care?"

Rose stared at him coldly. "That was cheap, Monk."

Rose seized the chance to leave. She went upstairs to her suite and lifted the telephone receiver. It was time to remind the good doctor of their contract— and the consequences for him if he was having any second thoughts about honoring its terms.

William Harris's three-story townhouse was on the corner of Park Avenue and Sixty-first Street. Harris had bought it because, with Rose Jefferson's check, not only could he set up his office on the generous main floor but the upper levels made a perfect apartment. Big enough, in fact, for a married couple. When Rose Jefferson had called, William Harris had been dreaming about the lovely Miss Jane Primrose, the eldest and still unmarried daughter of the Murray Hill Primroses. William Harris genuinely liked the shy, willowy thirty-year-old woman who had been unkindly relegated to spinsterhood. Given his new station in life, he thought they'd make a splendid couple. Now, sitting in his office, struggling to stay alert with the help of coffee, he wondered anxiously if that's all it would ever be, a dream.

The doorbell rang.

"Good evening—or rather, good morning, Mrs. Jefferson. Please, come in. Forgive me, but I don't know this gentleman."

"Monk McQueen," Michelle said. "He's Franklin's best friend."

"Of course. I'm an avid reader of *Q* magazine, Mr. McQueen."

William Harris's fear edged up a notch. It was one thing to soothe a distraught wife. That he had perfected a long time ago. But a man of McQueen's reputation mightn't be taken in so easily. Harris would have to tread very carefully.

"Now then," Harris said, once they were seated in his office. "What's all this about?"

William Harris listened with growing dread as Michelle explained what had happened at the Copperfield School, especially when she mentioned the dizzy spells and blackouts.

"Mrs. Jefferson, I gave Franklin some pills to take. Has he been doing that?"

Michelle took a bottle out of her purse. "I found these in the medicine cabinet."

Harris felt sick. He had given Franklin Jefferson a hundred tablets of extremely potent pain reliever, cautioning him to use them only when absolutely necessary. Harris had estimated the supply should last at least a year. Now, only six months later, the bottle was almost empty.

Either he's been overdosing himself or else the deterioration has set in much more rapidly than anyone imagined. . . .

"Please, Doctor, what is it?"

Michelle's plea twisted Harris's heart. Everything he'd been taught and held sacrosanct demanded that he tell this woman the truth.

If I do, Rose Jefferson will ruin me. She'll take away everything she's given me. If anything happens to her brother she'll see to it that the state medical board crucifies me.

Harris looked at Michelle, praying she could forgive him.

"Mrs. Jefferson, I'm sure there's nothing to be alarmed about. Your husband's last physical showed him to be perfectly healthy. I'm a little concerned about these headaches, but for all we know, it's simply the pressures of everyday business. I recall Mr. Jefferson telling me he's been working very hard lately. But under the circumstances I will contact all the hospitals just in case he was involved in an accident and couldn't, for one reason or another, identify himself."

"What about his behavior, Doctor?" Monk cut in. "Franklin's never been a violent person. Do you have any idea why he'd lash out like that?"

Harris put on his best "concerned but calm" physician's expression.

"No, I don't, Mr. McQueen. However, the minute we do find him, I want to give him a thorough examination, no matter how innocent his explanation for what happened."

"Thank you, Doctor," Michelle said gratefully.

"Not at all. If you'd care to make yourselves comfortable in the waiting room, I'll get to work."

"Is there a phone in there, Doctor?" asked Monk.

"Of course. Please, help yourself."

"Who are you calling?" Michelle asked once they were in the waiting room.

Monk put a hand over the mouthpiece. "The major hotels. For all we know, Franklin could have ended up in one of them. I should have thought of it earlier."

Michelle smiled weakly. She was sure that Monk had thought of it. He just hadn't wanted her to see him grasping at straws.

A half-hour later both men had nothing to show for their efforts.

"What do we do now?" Michelle asked anxiously.

"Now," Monk told her, "we hit the streets."

Michelle was stunned by where their search took them.

"Don't tell me you and Franklin went to places like these!" she gasped as they made their way along the narrow sidewalks of the Tenderloin.

Between Fifth and Ninth avenues, as far up as Forty-eighth Street, was a jam-packed collection of boardinghouses, storefronts, nightclubs, gambling dens, and bordellos. The wooden buildings were so rickety that Michelle thought they were ready to collapse on themselves. The streets and sidewalks were strewn with garbage whose stench made her gag.

"We did a lot of exploring in our salad days," Monk replied noncommittally. "Don't worry. Everybody around here knows me."

It was true. No matter how dark and ominous the places they went into, Monk was greeted like a kindred soul. Barkeeps, prostitutes, con men of every color and description saw that he meant business and quickly answered his questions. Nothing, however, led them closer to Franklin.

"Are you sure we're looking for him in the right places?" Michelle asked nervously as Monk led them through the city's night palaces that never closed. At four o'clock in the morning the Silver Slipper and Les Ambassadeurs were still going strong with Jimmy Durante, Eddie Jackson, and Hoofer Lou Clayton holding center stage.

"There aren't many more places he could be," Monk said gently.

Dawn found them on the Lower East Side, on Fourteenth Street past Third Avenue. This was the home of the Jewish immigrants who had arrived from Russia, Poland, and Romania. Michelle couldn't believe how crowded the streets were, even at this hour, jammed with peddlers and pushcarts, women spilling out of small tenements hurrying off with huge sacks on their backs, children in their wake.

190

As they headed uptown Michelle felt the last of her hopes disappearing into the cold, empty morning. There was no choice now. She would call the police as soon as they returned to Talbot House.

"It's the only thing to do," Monk said, reading her mind. "Don't let Rose put you off."

Michelle stopped and faced him. "Franklin's my husband. Rose has nothing more to do with this."

Rose Jefferson's bedroom was the largest in the house. Its walls were lined with creamy silk panels bordered with robin's-egg blue, and the furniture, handcrafted rosewood Tudor, glowed reddish gold from countless polishings. Photographs in silver frames were stacked along the credenza and end tables, and in what had once been a sitting area Rose had created a miniature office whose centerpiece was an elegant Louis XIV desk.

As the fingers of dawn's light tentatively probed the carpet, Rose got up from the daybed and turned out the gasoliers. She hadn't slept a wink. For the first time in years Rose felt that somehow events had raced ahead of her, mocking her efforts to catch up much less control them.

Rose pressed a cold, damp washcloth to her face to bring down the swelling under her eyes, brushed her hair, and went downstairs to make tea. As she waited for the water to boil she wondered where Michelle and Monk were. All night long she had dreaded that the phone would ring. That it hadn't told Rose their search had been fruitless.

Rose carried her tea into the library, where she leafed through her personal directory. She had no choice now. The police had to be called and a search organized. But first a story for the press, which would inevitably get wind of this, had to be agreed upon. Rose was dialing the police commissioner's private number when the doorbell sounded.

"Miss Rose Jefferson?"

She recognized the blue uniform and threw open the door.

"Oh my God!"

Standing between the two policemen was Franklin, his suit torn and muddy, his face scratched and bleeding. His left eye was almost closed because of a wicked-looking bruise that was already changing color. Rose flung her arms around him, running her fingers through his matted hair.

"Help me get him inside!"

Rose led Franklin into the informal drawing room and sat him down. She cupped his face in her hands.

"What happened to you?"

Franklin's vacant stare didn't change. He blinked and slowly two tears coursed down his cheeks.

"I don't know," he whispered. "I don't remember anything. . . ."

The two policemen shuffled their feet, embarrassed.

"We found him wandering around in the Bowery, Miss Jefferson," the Irish officer said finally. "By the looks of things, the damage was done before we got to him. Lucky for us he still had his wallet. The money was gone, of course, but the thief didn't take his driver's license."

"I see," Rose murmured.

She looked again at Franklin and her heart broke. Nevertheless she knew exactly what had to be done next.

"If you gentlemen will follow me, please."

Rose led the two policemen into the library and asked them to wait while she called the commissioner. A few minutes later she handed the phone to the Irishman, who snapped to attention as soon as he heard his superior's voice. From his deferential expression she could see that the wheels were being set in motion.

"I'm indebted to both of you," Rose said after the policeman hung up. "I'll see to it you receive suitable compensation."

Both officers touched their caps. "Just doing our jobs, ma'am. Since no harm's been done really, we won't be making a report."

"I think that's best."

Rose saw them out and hurried back to the drawing room.

"Is Michelle upstairs?" asked Franklin.

"She and Monk went out looking for you. They'll be back any minute. Franklin, please, let me call Albany and have him run you a bath. You need to get out of those clothes. I'll call Dr. Harris as well—"

Franklin held up his hand. "Is Steven all right?"

Rose lowered her eyes and nodded. "So you do remember. . . ."

"Only that he and I were quarreling and I hurt him. After that, nothing."

"He's going to be all right, Franklin. You can talk to him later and—"

"No, Rose. You're the one who has to talk to him."

Rose was taken aback by her brother's sharp tone.

"What do you mean?"

"Did Steven tell you how he behaved with Michelle, what he did to her?"

"I've heard Michelle's version," Rose said coldly. "Quite frankly, I find it outrageous."

Franklin shook his head. "Steven as much as admitted to me that he did those things to her."

"Franklin, that's absurd! We shouldn't be talking about this right now, after everything you've been through."

"No, Rose. We are going to talk about it now. I should have brought it up a long time ago. Don't you see? Steven's taken his cue from you."

"Me!"

"Yes, Rose. From the day Michelle arrived here you've tried to make her life as uncomfortable as possible. You knew she hadn't been brought up the way we were, yet instead of helping her adjust you humiliated her in front of your friends and ridiculed whatever she tried to do. Ever since you decided she wasn't good enough for me you've done everything you could to make that a self-fulfilling prophecy. With the intention, I think, of breaking apart our marriage."

Rose laughed. "That's sheer fantasy! It's true, I was concerned because I didn't know anything about Michelle—"

"You never wanted to get to know her," Franklin broke in. "Let me tell you a few things about my wife that she doesn't talk about. Michelle is more of a hero than I ever was. When I lay wounded in that barn in Saint Eustace, Michelle used her body to protect me."

Rose frowned. "What do you mean?"

"A collaborator discovered she was hiding me. Michelle slept with him so that he wouldn't call the Germans and have me shot. I can't think of a greater expression of courage or love, can you, Rose?"

Rose's eyes went cold. "I see it as an act of a whore," she said tonelessly. "Someone who took advantage of you to emotionally blackmail you into marrying her."

"*How can you say such a thing?*"

"Because it's the truth! Ever since Michelle Lecroix came into our lives we've had nothing but problems." Rose leaned forward and clutched Franklin's hand in both of hers. "I've always tried to do what's best for us, Franklin. We're a family."

"What you refuse to see, Rose, is that Michelle is *part* of our family. If you hurt her, you hurt all of us, especially me."

The sound of voices could be heard in the front hall. Franklin looked at his sister but Rose shook her head.

"I love you so much, Rose. I only wish God had given you a little more charity."

Rose watched him walk slowly from the room, stifling a cry when she heard the exclamations of relief.

The following day Franklin Jefferson and his wife went to see Dr. William Harris. After an exhaustive examination Harris pronounced that Franklin, aside from the cuts and bruises, was in perfect health.

"I warned you about these pills," he said, tapping the blue bottle. "They're very potent. You must have taken one, then had a few drinks. The combination of the two is the only thing that can account for the blackout."

193

Michelle looked at Franklin. "Is that what happened?"

Franklin shrugged. "It must have."

Michelle was unconvinced. Franklin seldom drank anything more than wine with dinner. Still, she respected Harris's opinion. Being military men, he and Franklin got along very well. Besides that, from what she'd seen, Harris was thorough and conscientious.

"Doctor," she said hesitantly. "Please don't think I'm questioning your diagnosis, but is it possible that what happened was somehow caused by Franklin's old injury?"

"Miss Jefferson, I'll grant you that carrying bits of metal in one's skull isn't the most natural thing in the world," Harris replied, smiling tolerantly. "However, there are thousands of soldiers walking around with bullets and shrapnel in their bodies and leading perfectly normal lives. I'm sure that these headaches are nothing more than symptoms of tension and the hours your husband's been keeping at work. I think a short vacation might be just the thing to set matters straight."

"You know, that's not such a bad idea," Franklin said after they left Harris's office. "We never had a real honeymoon."

"Every day is a honeymoon for us."

But underneath her happy words Michelle was still thinking about what Harris had said. She had been a nurse. She knew how doctors sometimes glossed over the truth. What was it about Harris's comments that continued to bother her? Michelle couldn't put her finger on it.

"Well, if you don't want a honeymoon, maybe this will make up for everything that's happened."

Franklin handed Michelle a neatly folded legal document.

"A six-month lease on our own, furnished townhouse. Our home, Michelle."

Michelle looked at him in disbelief.

"Oh, Franklin!"

And at that moment, just as she thought everything was going to be so much better for them, Michelle realized what it was that had been bothering her: for all his reassuring words, Dr. William Harris had never really answered her question.

— 22 —

On a sleet-driven January day, Monk McQueen descended the steps of 21 and elbowed room for himself at the long, dark bar where patrons were gulping down their drinks with grim determination. Monk stared morosely at his reflection in the mirror that stretched the length of the bar, then at the bartenders who were literally crying into the drinks they poured with reckless abandon. *This place will never be the same,* he thought. Nor would millions of saloons across the country. On this day, January 16, 1920, the House of Representatives had passed the Eighteenth Amendment to the Constitution, the Volstead Act, making national prohibition a federal law.

But Monk couldn't have cared less about Volstead or his asinine legislation. The only thing that mattered was that his two best friends, Franklin and Michelle, were gone.

Franklin's decision that he and Michelle would live away from Talbot House had started it all. To everyone's surprise, and Monk's great pleasure, Michelle blossomed when she became the mistress of a handsome townhouse on East Seventy-second Street, a stone's throw from Central Park. On his first visit Monk was delighted at how she had turned an ambassador's stuffy residence into a cheerful, airy home. There were vases of freshly cut flowers everywhere, beautiful antiques, and several small but carefully chosen paintings, including a van Gogh, which had been her birthday present to Franklin.

Once her house was ready, Michelle held an inaugural party attended by almost all of Franklin's friends as well as a smattering of New York society. Rose, however, was conspicuous by her absence.

"I sent her an invitation," Michelle confided in Monk. "Apparently she had a previous engagement."

"More's the pity," he replied blithely, staring at Michelle in open admiration. She was wearing the centerpiece of Madeleine's recent collection, a brocade of black velvet, dull silver, and gray silk, girdled with pearls and emerald beads.

"You're the best-looking girl in the house."

"Why, thank you, kind sir," Michelle replied, trying not to blush.

Although she could easily have afforded them, Michelle did not sign on with the caterers who were purveyors of fine foods to the Four Hundred. Instead, every Saturday she and Monk explored the ethnic markets in Greenwich Village, the Lower East Side, and other nooks and crannies where he himself shopped. As a result, Michelle's dinner parties proved not only unusual but an instant success. She treated her guests to Harlem's finest "yardbird" (chicken), "strings" (spaghetti), corn pone, sweet potatoes, and black-eyed peas. From Moscowitz and Lupowitz on Essex Avenue came unequaled stuffed peppers, while Rappaport's provided the chopped salmon salad, chopped spinach and eggs, and sturgeon salad. Michelle became a familiar face in Pell Street in Chinatown, where the opium and white-slave trades flourished and she shopped for exotic spices and ingredients. Michelle's address became the place to find gifted people from all walks of life—artists, writers, business people, the young rich, and even a few stalwarts from the Four Hundred.

But Monk soon learned that Michelle had far greater ambitions than hosting perfect cocktail parties. She asked him where she could learn more about business and Monk gave her the names of several professors on the faculty of commerce at Columbia. The next time he saw her Michelle had hired three of them as private tutors.

After all she had been subjected to at Talbot House, Monk couldn't have been happier for Michelle. He admired the way she persevered in her studies, helping Franklin, who was swamped with work these days, wherever she could. Monk's spies along Wall Street told him that Franklin was spending long hours negotiating with banks over their commissions on the money order, a process in which a tenth of one percent could mean hundreds of thousands of dollars for either party. At the same time he was screening new candidates for Global's expanding sales force and grooming those already hired.

"Don't you think Franklin's pushing too hard?" Monk asked Michelle on several occasions.

"That's why I'm trying to learn as much about his business as I can," Michelle replied. "I want to do more for Franklin than hold interesting parties."

Because of his intimate knowledge of the financial community Monk was able to provide Michelle with all the little details indispensable to a hostess entertaining her husband's business clients. Michelle knew their favorite dishes, what liquor they preferred, and the cigars they smoked. She kept herself up to date on long-standing feuds and current rivalries and made sure that she didn't invite competitors to her table the same evening. At the same time it was clear that Michelle was being drawn ever more deeply into Franklin's daily work. Whenever Monk joined the two of them for breakfast he found Franklin asking Michelle for her impression about their guests, whether they were the kind of men who would be good for Global to deal with or, if the going got rough, would become wolves at the door. Invariably Michelle's comments were succinct and full of common sense.

As much as Monk enjoyed the time spent with Franklin and Michelle, he never suspected that beneath the warmth and cheer that the three of them shared, something very powerful and completely unexpected was growing. He discovered it only on the eve of the Jeffersons' sailing and the realization shocked him. At the last minute Monk couldn't bring himself to see them off at the pier and instead treated them to a champagne lunch at the Waldorf. Somehow he managed to get through the toasts and tears and promises to write and surrendered them to his driver. The minute they were out of sight, his heart felt empty.

It had been, Monk reflected, propping himself up at the 21 bar, such a wonderful time that he never realized what was really happening. Without knowing how or why, he had fallen in love with Michelle. Thinking of her now, Monk was very glad that the vast expanse of the Atlantic Ocean lay between them.

Although she counted down the days to Franklin's departure, Rose Jefferson never referred to it either at home or at the office. Those around her quickly learned not to raise the subject.

Rose hid the pain of Franklin's leaving behind a veil of furious activity, throwing all her energy into the successful launching of the money order. When news of the agreements with the major banks filtered through the financial grapevine, Rose's phone started ringing incessantly. She noted with satisfaction that the smaller banks were responding exactly as she had hoped, their directors all thinking the same thing: if the big institutions were sure there was profit to be made off the money orders, why shouldn't they get in on it?

Nor had Rose any complaints about the sales staff Franklin had organized. Given his natural ability to deal with people, the group he had brought together was young, eager, and enthusiastic. It was all going so well that Rose sometimes made herself believe it would always be like this.

On the day of the sailing, Rose turned down Franklin's invitation to lunch with him, Michelle, and Monk. Instead, she picked up Steven and together they drove down to the pier from which the White Star liner *Neptune* was to sail. Rose waited until the very last moment, when she was sure Michelle had already gone aboard, before entering the first-class departure lounge.

"You couldn't even bring yourself to wish her good-bye," Franklin remarked sadly.

Rose laid her palm against his cheek. "Please, let's not quarrel." She forced a smile. "You must cable me as soon as you arrive," Rose insisted. "And get to Sir Manfred Smith at Barclay's first. He's expecting you—"

Franklin laughed. "Rose, we've been over this a hundred times."

Rose retreated. "You're right, I'm sorry." Then she added, "Don't forget to check in with your new doctor, Sir Dennis Pritchard. Harris recommended him very highly."

Franklin nodded and his expression became somber. "What about you, Rose? Will you be all right?"

Rose laughed nervously. "How silly! I'll be fine. Why shouldn't I be?"

"I just wish you had someone beside you."

"I have Steven," Rose started to say.

"You know what I mean. Maybe it's time you found yourself another husband."

"I've already had one of those, Franklin, and we both know how that ended."

"That doesn't mean I don't worry about you or keep hoping."

Bells rang out, warning all those not traveling to disembark. Long, deep whistles pierced the gathering fog, their echoes bringing cheers from the passengers lining up along the guardrails. Rose hugged her brother fiercely.

"Good luck!" she whispered.

"I love you, Rose!"

Rose watched as Franklin bounded up the gangplank. When the *Neptune* drew away from her berth, a shower of ribbons, streamers, and confetti descended on the well-wishers. Rose followed the ship's progress as it churned out of the harbor, watching it even after it had become a blur on the horizon.

"Can we go home now, Mother?"

Rose turned to her son. "Of course we can, darling."

You're the only one left, she thought. *You will do what Franklin cannot. You are my bright and shining hope, my son!*

But as Rose walked to the car, she wasn't thinking of the distant future that lay ahead for Steven. There were more immediate problems at hand. Rose thought it ironic what Franklin had said about her needing someone beside her. She did, but it wasn't a husband. As much as she loved Franklin, Rose knew she had no choice but to find someone to replace him. She shuddered when she thought how lonely and cold that search would be.

— 23 —

When Michelle boarded the *Neptune* she felt as though she had not gotten on a ship at all but passed through the doors of a magnificent hotel.

Having consulted her by now well-thumbed etiquette books, she knew that the first night at sea was considered informal. Men were not obliged to wear dinner jackets and women could choose street-length cocktail dresses instead of formal gowns. To make her entrance, Michelle selected a Worth coral-colored velvet dress with brilliants at the waist and pearl rope wings, topped off by a diamond and black paradise-feather headdress. As she examined herself in the mirror, she wondered if the outfit wasn't too avant-garde.

She needn't have worried. Returning to the Continent that January were many wealthy, titled Europeans who far outnumbered the Americans on board. Among the first Michelle was introduced to at the reception was the Duke of Chambord, who insisted on being addressed simply as Christophe, and his blond, vivacious English companion, Lady Patricia Farmington. Later, over dinner at the captain's table, Christophe turned to Michelle and said, "Excuse me, Madame Jefferson, but I'm sure I know you from somewhere. Paris, perhaps?"

"I don't think so," Michelle murmured.

The duke refused to be put off. Throughout the meal he focused his attention on Michelle, his questions never rude but persistent.

"Of course I know who you are!" he exclaimed at last.

Christophe tapped his water glass with his fork to get everyone's attention.

"Ladies and gentlemen," he announced. "I am pleased to say I have at last solved a great mystery. This charming woman on my right, whom you all know as Madame Franklin Jefferson, is none other than Michelle Lecroix, a heroine in my country and a true daughter of France."

Michelle blushed as Christophe proceeded to detail her feats for the other guests.

"Your modesty, madame, becomes you," the duke concluded. "However, as one who served his country I insist that you accept your due."

Immediately the captain had champagne brought out and toasts were raised.

"I'm very proud of you, darling," Franklin whispered.

199

"And let us not forget the brave Monsieur Jefferson," the Duke of Chambord added. "After all, he is the bearer of the Legion of Honor."

Franklin rose and graciously accepted the salutations.

After that first night Michelle and Franklin became the center of the liner's social life. The mantelpiece in their suite was arranged with invitations bearing noble coats of arms or discreet raised printing that highlighted some of the most prominent names in the European social register.

"Franklin, it's impossible to choose which to accept!" Michelle cried.

Franklin's solution was simple. "Accept them all!"

Suddenly Michelle found herself giving advice to European hostesses on the mores of their American guests, helping them select the menus as well as offering advice on the guest lists.

"I don't know what I would have done without you," an Italian countess breathed into Michelle's ear after one such dinner. "These Americans are very strange. Their manners are so *nouveau*, don't you think?"

The first few days on the *Neptune* were heaven for Michelle. There was always so much to do and not enough time to squeeze everything in. Nonetheless, she made sure that she and Franklin had several hours to themselves each afternoon to review the strategy Franklin would employ regarding the traveler's checks. They went over the banks to be approached, their assets, number of branches, and, most important, how closely wedded they were to Cooks. They discussed the personalities and business backgrounds of each director to determine just how favorably he would look upon Global's proposition.

Although these sessions were long and involved, Michelle felt exhilarated. She was struck by the irony that not since the days on the troopship that had brought them to America had she and Franklin shared such perfectly happy moments. With each new day that dawned, Michelle was convinced that nothing could ever again come between them.

The *Neptune* boasted the most luxurious saloon that ever floated the Atlantic. There was a small casino with roulette and chemin de fer, as well as screened-off rooms where card games were played for high stakes.

On his fourth night out Franklin Jefferson sat in a comfortable black-leather chair surrounded by other players around a circular table topped with green felt. The game was five-stud poker, the stakes, measured by red and blue chips, in the hundreds of dollars.

Franklin scrutinized his hand, dropped some chips into the pot, then tossed away one card and asked the dealer for another. As the other players made their decisions he raised his fingers to his temple, massaging it. For a reason he couldn't fathom, the headaches had reappeared, striking more deeply and lasting longer than he remembered. Franklin checked his waistcoat pocket, reassured to find his snuffbox of pills. He hadn't mentioned any of this to Michelle, not wanting to worry her unduly.

The bids were anted up and Franklin took the pot with kings over ladies. As he raked in his winnings Franklin sipped his cognac, drew on his favorite cigar, and watched as a new hand was dealt. Then suddenly he heard the crack of a rifle shot.

"Where's the Bluegrass Boy?" Franklin asked suddenly.

The players around the table looked at him questioningly. A few chuckled, then the game got under way.

"I said where's the Bluegrass Boy!"

Franklin's pulse was racing. The melodies of the band became an artillery barrage, the laughter and voices percolating through the screen, the cries and shouts of soldiers as they raced over the top of the trenches.

"No! It's not safe! Bluegrass Boy, don't show yourself!"

Franklin kicked his chair back and threw himself at the player next to him, knocking him to the floor, trying to cover his body with his own.

"They're waiting for us, don't you see?" he whispered, eyes darting around at the artillery smoke he thought he saw around him.

He seized the man's head and began rocking it in his lap.

"Oh, Bluegrass Boy, why didn't you listen to me!"

"We don't know what happened, Mrs. Jefferson," the ship's doctor said. "One minute he was playing cards, the next it was as though somebody were attacking him, which of course wasn't the case at all."

Michelle watched her husband sleeping fitfully in their four-poster bed. Even the sedatives weren't enough to dispel his terror. Franklin moaned, his fingers raking the sheets as though clutching at imaginary phantoms converging upon him.

Michelle led the doctor out of the bedroom.

"My husband was in the war," she told him. "Like many men, he saw horrible things. Sometimes he can't help himself. . . ."

The doctor, himself a veteran, murmured his sympathies. "Please make sure your husband stays on his medication, Mrs. Jefferson," he said. "I'll square things with the captain."

When the doctor left, Michelle sank into a chair beside the bed. Forcing herself to block out her fear, she ministered to her husband, wiping the sweat pouring off him. Much later, when Franklin finally lay in a deep sleep, Michelle brought out the notes she had painstakingly compiled during her talks with Dr. William Harris. As the gasoliers burned throughout the night Michelle read the pages over and over again, searching for that elusive clue that would help her understand what was happening to Franklin. But no revelation leaped forth. When Michelle slipped into bed, holding Franklin close, she couldn't silence that awful question drumming in her head: what had Dr. William Harris held back from them?

When Franklin awoke the next morning the first thing he was conscious of was his own smell. Quickly he stripped off his sodden pajamas and bathed. While dressing he noticed stacks of poker chips on the dresser, obviously a decent night's winnings. The funny thing was he couldn't remember leaving the table or getting back to his suite.

As Franklin was checking his attire in the mirror he noticed Michelle looking at him.

"Good morning, my love," he said, coming over and giving her a kiss. "Sleeping late, are we?"

Michelle managed a smile. "How are you feeling, darling?"

"Me? Never better. And look—" Franklin held up a palm full of chips— "we can splurge at the gift shop. Will you be down for breakfast?"

"Of course."

"Then I'll see you downstairs."

As Franklin blew her a kiss and disappeared, Michelle sank back into the pillows. Clearly he didn't remember a thing about last night. She didn't know what frightened her more, Franklin's aberrant behavior or his loss of memory. Michelle vowed that as soon as they reached London, she would take Franklin to see this new doctor, Sir Dennis Pritchard.

On their last evening at sea Michelle and Franklin accepted an invitation to a party hosted by their new friends Christophe and Patricia.

Lady Patricia, one hundred twenty pounds of blond, bubbly energy on a five-foot five-inch frame, embraced Michelle three times in the continental manner.

"Would you believe it?" she said gaily. "Before I met Christophe the thought of kissing a perfect stranger made my skin crawl! Not that you're a stranger, dearest . . ."

Michelle genuinely liked Patricia, who seized life with both hands and squeezed every ounce of pleasure from it. And although she tended to be dismissed as flighty, Patricia had a sharp mind, Michelle could see that.

While Michelle helped Patricia with the finishing touches, the guests began to arrive. Soon the party was in full swing and, until Christophe mentioned it, Michelle had scarcely noticed that Franklin still wasn't there.

"Let me go get him," Christophe suggested.

"That's all right," Michelle said quickly.

Christophe took her arm. "Everyone on board knows what happened that night in the salon. Some think that Franklin had too much to drink, others believe he's an epileptic. I've been to the front, Michelle. A man can't simply wipe away everything that happened to him there. Please, let me go with you."

Touched by his concern, Michelle agreed. When they entered the Jefferson suite she was glad she had. The front room was in shambles. Shards of glass from broken mirrors littered the carpet. Furniture had been overturned, curtains, paintings, and wall hangings torn down. A faint moaning could be heard from the bedroom.

"I'll get the doctor," Christophe whispered.

"No! Not until I see him."

Michelle pushed open the bedroom door to witness even more devastation. In one corner she saw Franklin, curled up, cowering. He had been ill and soiled himself.

"Michelle . . . Michelle, I hear them coming. They're going to find me!"

Franklin's rasping voice, the terror in his eyes, jarred Michelle back to another time.

He thinks he's in the barn, hiding in the oubliette from the Germans!

Michelle grabbed one of the sheets and knelt by her husband's side. Speaking softly in French, just as she had in what seemed another lifetime, she wiped away as much of the mess as she could.

"He needs a doctor, Michelle," she heard Christophe say.

"No, he needs me! Please go back and tell everyone Franklin's not well. You know what to say." Michelle paused. "I trust you, Christophe."

"If you're sure . . ." the Frenchman said dubiously.

"I am. Now let me tend to him. If his condition worsens, I promise, I'll call you."

Reluctantly, Christophe departed, not because he wanted to but because he believed that in such circumstances Franklin Jefferson deserved to keep what was left of his dignity.

Michelle shouldered Franklin into the bathroom and ran a bath. She cleaned up their room as best she could, then returned to wash him, slipping two sedatives into the glass of water she gave him. An hour later she collapsed, weeping. She clung to the thought that by tomorrow they would be in London, where Franklin could get the medical attention he needed. Until then she wouldn't let him out of her sight.

Michelle was about to change clothes when she heard a knock on the door. Thinking it was Christophe, she ran to open it.

"Forgive me for intruding, Mrs. Jefferson," the captain said. "May I come in?"

Michelle nodded mutely. To his credit, the captain didn't utter a word when he saw how the suite had been ravaged.

"Mrs. Jefferson," he said gently, "I think it would best for all concerned if your husband was moved to the infirmary."

"I appreciate your concern, Captain—" Michelle began.

"I'm afraid I must insist. I'm terribly sorry about whatever it is that's ailing him, but I think you can see, he is a threat to both himself and the other passengers. Under the circumstances, I have no choice but to confine him until the vessel docks." The captain touched her arm. "If you like, I'll radio ahead to have an ambulance standing by."

"That won't be necessary, Captain," Michelle said clearly. "However, I would like to use your ship-to-shore telephone."

"Of course, Mrs. Jefferson. And the party you wish to speak with?"

"Dr. Dennis Pritchard, Harley Street, London."

— 24 —

Eight days after Franklin's departure Rose received word that he and Michelle had arrived safely and were settling in to their new home. Rose cabled her best wishes, adding a reminder to Franklin to let her know the minute he opened his talks with the British banks. Just as she was leaving the office, Dr. Harris called.

"I just received an urgent message from Sir Henry Pritchard in London," he informed her. "He wants me to send over Franklin's complete medical file as soon as possible."

Rose was unperturbed. "Then by all means send him the results of Franklin's last physical."

There was a hesitation on the other end. "Miss Jefferson, don't you think it would be better for Pritchard to know everything? After all, the information would fall under doctor-patient confidentiality."

That it would, Rose agreed silently. But how discreet could she trust Pritchard to be? She knew him only by reputation. He might not prove to be as accommodating as William Harris.

"The last physical is all he needs," Rose said firmly. "If you feel obliged to add anything else, I'm sure you'll choose your words carefully."

And because the London surgeon's cable hadn't made any mention of what had transpired on board the *Neptune* during its crossing, Dr. Harris saw no

204

reason to get into an argument with Rose, which he knew he would lose anyway.

Within three months the Global money order had become a runaway success. Sales passed the $5 million mark and showed no signs of slowing down. Rose doubled the sales force and bought the building adjacent to the Broadway head office for the necessary support staff.

Although she professed to give her sales managers free rein, Rose kept them on a short, if invisible, leash. She made it a point to get to know each one personally. Besides watching the monthly bottom lines of each account, she kept track of their work habits, matrimonial status, vices and virtues, and goals. All of them, Rose noted with satisfaction, had become dedicated company men, partly because they were getting a percentage of every dollar of business they brought in. There was one, however, who quietly eclipsed all the rest.

A young man by the name of Harry Taylor had taken over the Chicago branch of the money-order business after the sudden death of Franklin's hand-picked manager. The accounts showed Rose that since then, the Chicago bureau had steadily grown to the point where its sales outstripped even those of the head office. Thinking back, Rose realized she had never even met this twenty-five-year-old Harry Taylor. His travel-expense chits indicated that he had never been to New York, not even to attend company conferences. Yet this was a man responsible for making millions for the company. Intrigued, Rose wanted to find out more about him.

Friends of Harry Taylor always said about him, "Things come too easily to Harry. The minute he becomes good at something he drops it and moves on to greener pastures." Harry always smiled at the comment, never taking offense because whoever said it sounded a little envious.

Reared on an Iowa farm, Harry Taylor had carried the values of honesty and hard work to the metropolitan campus of the University of Chicago. Unlike many students from rural communities who felt uprooted and lonely in the big city, Harry adapted. His natural strength, honed by daily childhood chores, made him a superb athlete. Yet the mastery of football or the shattering of a university swimming record didn't seem to matter to him, much to the chagrin of coaches who argued that he was wasting his talent.

The same daily regimen that, on the farm, had taught him to make the most of every hour served to concentrate his mind when it came to studies. Harry made short shrift of essays and papers that took most students hours to write.

Harry left the university with an excellent academic record and began his business career with a commodities brokerage firm, quickly grasping the intricacies of the volatile trading system. In short order he caught a partner's eye and was moved up to the trading offices, where his uncanny ability to predict advances and declines in crop futures made him an overnight success.

At precisely the moment he could have written his own ticket, Harry Taylor walked away from it all. It wasn't the ennui brought on by doing the same thing day after day, or the frantic pace of the business that reduced traders to husks in a few short years. As far as Harry was concerned he had mastered a craft and now it was time to move on.

Harry came to Global entirely by fluke. One of three women he was dating at the time casually mentioned that her boss, the manager of the Chicago office, had just fired his assistant. Harry was certainly qualified for the job, and wouldn't it be delicious if she and he could work together? Harry laughed wholeheartedly at the girl's obvious ploy to truss him, but since he was scouting around for a new job, he agreed to talk to her employer.

"You'll be visiting clients—banks, hotels, railroad and bus companies—and flogging money orders. That's the long and the short of it."

The manager, a bantam-weight Armenian with glasses as thick as Coke bottle bottoms, fully expected to be turned down, given this applicant's over-qualified background.

"I'll take it," Harry announced.

"It's an awful big territory," the manager warned him.

Harry didn't say it but that was exactly what he wanted. He wanted to get out and meet new people, experience new things, see new sights. A company like Global, which had just launched a new financial instrument and whose branch offices stretched across the country, could give him that opportunity. It would also, he thought, provide an excellent excuse to wind down current romantic involvements.

Harry's rise in the Chicago office was as meteoric and seemingly effortless as everything else he had set his mind to. He began selling money orders in the outlying industrial area where Global had few outlets. In three months that territory accounted for a full 30 percent of the regional office's sales. Moving back to Chicago, Harry was put in charge of the accounts with the major banks. He allotted two nights a week to stroking their presidents' egos and spent the rest of his time chivvying business out of the medium and small institutions. By the time his boss succumbed to his third and final heart attack, in the arms of his blond mistress, Harry Taylor had brought fifty more banks into Global's fold. New York took one look at the bottom line and promptly gave him the still-warm manager's chair.

Given a free hand, Harry transformed the midwestern hub into his own image. He took the sales force off the telephones and put them on the roads. In meetings, he stressed the importance of reaching outlets that didn't even know they were outlets. He hired the best secretaries available and paid them handsomely, guaranteeing that he and his top people could be away from the office for days, confident that everything was running smoothly. And it did—until the day Rose Jefferson arrived in Chicago.

Ever since he had lost his virginity to a neighbor's daughter, Harry Taylor had never wanted for women. For Harry, sex was something he gave freely and, because he genuinely liked the female species, received in kind. While the attraction of his mature body was undeniable, the women's true pleasure came with the discovery of the warm, humorous man who was knowing and gentle beforehand, and cuddly and comfortable afterward. Yet, precisely because Harry loved all women he could not choose one and ignore the rest. Women, in their endless differences and shades, were a special joy, to be coaxed and opened, savored and enjoyed, then gently returned to their common stream. And because no woman had ever hurt him, Harry did not know what he was capable of doing to hurt in return.

Harry Taylor was nothing like Rose expected. All her managers were tough, driven individuals who screamed, bullied, cajoled, or bargained as the situation warranted. Harry, on the other hand, was as easygoing as his name implied. Six years her junior, he was tall and rugged, with buttercup-blond hair, clear green eyes, and a flashing smile that hid nothing. He ran his office like an extension of his personality and Rose quickly discovered that his staff would walk on hot coals for him.

"This is a pleasant surprise, Miss Jefferson," Taylor said, leaning back in his chair. "I hope we're up to scratch as far as head office is concerned."

Rose surveyed the office, noticing that with its rolltop desk and Currier & Ives prints it resembled more a country lawyer's den than the nerve center of a million-dollar-a-year operation. She found its quaintness appealing.

"Absolutely, Mr. Taylor. In fact I was wondering if you'd care to share the secrets of your success."

Harry Taylor brought his long legs off the desk and reached for his cap.

"Come on, then."

Rose had expected to be shown the accounts room but instead Taylor whisked her away on a tour of the city. Rose couldn't believe how much Harry Taylor was able to pack into a day. They visited drugstores on the South Side, grocery stores in the Italian district, and book shops on the North Shore. Each business, most no bigger than a hole-in-the-wall, was selling Global money orders, and in each Harry was received like an old friend.

"I remembered what you wrote about the money order being the tool of the common man," Harry explained as they barreled along Michigan Avenue.

"These are the places people go to every day. By setting up branches all over the city, I get the business that misses the banks and our regular outlets."

Rose thought the idea so simple as to be ingenious. That night over dinner she told Harry Taylor as much.

"It seemed like the obvious thing to do," he replied modestly.

Rose had thought that a day—two at the most—would be enough time to scrutinize the Chicago operation. By the end of the week she still hadn't left. Harry Taylor was an excellent host. When he took her to visit clients he made it an adventure. Afterward there was plenty of time for sightseeing.

There was more. Rose found herself looking at Harry as a man. He was undeniably handsome but his attraction wasn't superficial. It rose from a place deep inside him. Rose knew that Harry had been born and bred in the Midwest and had graduated from the University of Chicago. His file reported that he lived on a fraction of his salary and prudently invested the remainder. Harry seemed to have everything he desired from life and was almost indifferent to the rewards that were his already and the greater ones he could reach so easily.

There's nothing he wants or needs from me, Rose thought. *He simply likes what he's doing. And God knows he's the best I've got!*

Rose was in the bathroom doing her hair, getting ready for dinner with Harry, when the chimes to her suite rang. She remembered she was also expecting an important delivery from New York.

"The door's open!" she called. "Just leave it on the table."

Rose finished pinning her hair and entered the living room, looking for the package.

"Is this what you've been waiting for?" asked Harry, holding it out to her.

Rose blushed deeply. She hadn't expected anyone to be there, much less Harry. Suddenly she was embarrassed by how she must look to him, dressed in a thin cotton bathrobe that clung to every curve of her damp body, no makeup, her hair wet and matted. And Harry was coming toward her . . .

"Harry, please . . ."

"Shh," he whispered.

He cupped her cheek in his palm and slowly lifted her face so that there was no running away from the light in his green eyes. Rose trembled when he kissed her, pressing her lips tightly together. She wanted to tell him to stop, that this was wrong, but she was afraid to open her mouth because different words would pour out, that this was wonderful, something she had forgotten existed and needed so badly. . . .

Rose felt his fingertips drawing open the robe, cupping her breasts until his head came down and his lips were kissing every curve. Her knees buckled and slowly Rose lowered herself, her body straining against Harry's as though they were forged together by his kisses. His lips continued to caress her flesh, making her whimper as they moved over her belly, around her thighs, and into the crevices, teasing, tantalizing . . . until she couldn't stand it any longer and seizing him by the hair, guided him to where she knew he was going all along.

Rose closed her eyes and surrendered to the sensations surging through her body. She had no idea her hips bucked or that her legs were tightly clamped around Harry's head. She felt only his coy, gentle touch, the delicate flicker followed by a teasing nibble, driving her toward an explosion that left her shuddering . . . for more, for another, until she started to laugh and cry hysterically, unable to endure the spasms of pleasure.

The room spun as Harry picked her up and carried her into the bedroom. Just when Rose thought she couldn't bear another second of his beautiful torment she gasped as he entered her. She linked her arms around his broad back and clung to him as though he were life itself, letting him lead her, moving with him and finally blending her rhythm to his.

When she awoke, the moonlight was drenching the bed in the palest shade of blue and Harry was beside her, sprawled out, one hand reaching for her. For the longest time Rose stared at him, love, fear, affection, satisfaction, and warmth all pouring through her, colliding, conflicting. Then she left him.

"Hey, what happened to you? I was worried."

Rose slowly let out her breath. "How did you know I'd be here?"

She heard Harry Taylor chuckle at the other end of the line. "Where else could you be? I'm the one in your room."

Rose felt foolish. After running out of her suite she had taken a taxi to the Chicago offices, arriving just as the cleaning staff was leaving. She prevailed upon one of the janitors to get her coffee from an all-night diner and had spent the last three hours at Harry's desk, surrounded by open ledgers. She hadn't read a single column of figures.

"Could I buy you some breakfast?" Harry suggested.

"No! I mean, I'm here already—"

Rose didn't know what to say to Harry Taylor. She had thought of him all morning—and that she had broken her two cardinal rules; *never* again become involved with a man; *especially* never if he's an employee. Harry was both—yet at the same time so much more.

"I understand, Rose," Harry was saying. "I promise I won't embarrass you. Give me thirty minutes and we'll have a breakfast meeting with my sales-people."

"Harry, I don't want you to think . . ." Words failed her. What didn't she want him to think? And what did she want him to know, beyond any doubt?

"It's all right, Rose. We can talk later if you like."

Rose murmured something unintelligible and hung up.

Damn you, Harry Taylor!

As Rose lingered on in Chicago, New York head office began sending memoranda to her on a daily basis. She felt a renewed energy and vigor, dispatching paperwork quickly and efficiently so that there was always time for Harry. Harry, who came to her suite every night, bringing flowers, sometimes a fine wine, or a small, unusual gift. Harry, who did not permit words to break this frail unspoken bond but who knew what she needed, when, and how . . . Harry, who never asked for anything in return, which left Rose wondering if she truly satisfied him or if he was wise enough to be patient, show her, teach her, let her flower. They never spoke before or afterward, and in the light of the early mornings he showed Rose that the glory and the passion hadn't been a dream.

During their days together Harry introduced Rose to a new scheme he was almost ready to unveil.

"People pay monthly utility bills, right? Gas, electric, water, telephone . . ."

"Right," Rose agreed.

"Well, what if we were to get the utilities to accept our money orders as payment? In Chicago alone we have thousands of outlets where people could buy a money order from us, get a receipt as proof of payment, and we, acting like a collection house, would forward it to the utility."

"I love the idea," Rose said enthusiastically. "But will the utilities go along?"

Harry's eyes twinkled. "I just happen to know the man who controls them."

Rose couldn't help but laugh. To her, Harry seemed like a magician who could turn problems into solutions with a flick of his wand. The more time Rose spent with him the more she thought she had found the kind of man she had envisioned on that cold, foggy day when she had watched Franklin's vessel sail away. Very gingerly she reached for the possibility: maybe Harry was a man she could groom to send to London eventually, as a personal representative who could discreetly monitor Franklin's progress. But she had to know a great deal more about him first. Even better, she would have to put Harry under an obligation to her that was so great he would never even dream of betraying her.

The supervisor of the Chicago utility board was a former labor lawyer named Alan Hirsh. Rose was impressed that Harry was on a first-name basis with him and that Hirsh promised them a decision as soon as he had studied the details of Global's proposal. She was so convinced that their application would be approved that, after the meeting, she forwarded Harry's name to the head of Global's security department. Given everything she already knew about him, she was sure that a background check would be nothing more than a mere formality.

If information is true power, then Michelangelo Pecorella was indeed a powerful man. In 1914, a year after his graduation from Yale, M.A., as he was called, was recruited by the State Department and seconded to the Black Chamber, the unit's cryptology section, which deciphered the coded messages of foreign governments and their armies. For the duration of the war M. A. Pecorella was privy to the vices and virtues of world statesmen and generals. What he learned was that they were often the greatest fools. They left him unimpressed.

In 1919, after the Black Chamber had been closed by Secretary of State Henry Stimson, who opined that "gentlemen do not read each other's mail," Pecorella scouted alternative possibilities. He had read and heard a great deal about Rose Jefferson. He scrutinized her operation and quickly saw the Global money order would need protection against intelligent, innovative, and ruthless criminals. Pecorella thought it would be a pleasure to match wits with them—if Rose Jefferson was willing to give him the chance to do so. After one meeting Rose had been convinced that she could ill-afford *not* to have Michelangelo Pecorella working for her. Shortly afterward, the diminutive, soft-spoken Italian became the first director of Global's newly created Inspector's Division.

"Mr. Pecorella, this is a surprise," Rose exclaimed after the hotel manager himself had escorted M. A. upstairs. "Surely my little inquiry about Mr. Taylor needn't have brought you to Chicago personally."

"That's what I thought at first," M.A. Pecorella replied. "And if my investigation hadn't revealed a strong connection between Taylor and the supervisor of utilities, the check would have been routine."

A tiny warning bell sounded in Rose's mind.

"And just what connection is that?"

The security officer handed her a carbon copy. "I believe it's self-explanatory."

It was, painfully so. In his letter to Harry, the supervisor had urged him to quit Global and join him at the utility board, bringing his collection idea with him. He explained that the utility didn't need the Global money order to get its payments but could create its own collection agency, to be headed by Harry Taylor. From that base, there was no limit to how big they could grow.

Rose bit her lip and continued reading. Attached to the letter was a formal contract, signed by the supervisor and dated two weeks ago.

The first time Harry and I made love . . . A coincidence?

"Mr. Taylor's signature isn't on this contract," Rose observed, hoping Pecorella hadn't caught the tremor in her voice.

"It may be on the original, which I couldn't get."

"But what does this contract really mean?"

Pecorella lifted his eyebrows a fraction. Surely that much was self-evident.

"Mr. Taylor came to you with a unique scheme, one that Global could easily implement in other cities. However, if he chooses to take Mr. Hirsh's offer . . ."

Rose didn't have to hear any more. If Harry did that, he would be cutting Global out of a highly profitable venture.

"Under the terms of his contract with Global, Mr. Taylor is required to act in the best interests of the company," Pecorella continued. "Clearly he is in breach of contract and must be dealt with accordingly."

The words chilled Rose's heart. There had to be an explanation! Harry wouldn't do something like this. . . . Or had it been his intention all along to hide the truth from her, blind her with kisses, until it was too late? Rose thought hard. If Harry had indeed tried to cheat her, she'd boot him out of Global immediately. But if there was a good reason for his signature not being on the contract, then just maybe she would give him another chance—on her terms.

"Is there any way we can stop Hirsh?" Rose demanded.

"We have a number of friends in the Chicago area who are looking for a reason to remove him from his current position," M. A. Pecorella said calmly. "I believe this would suffice."

"Could we give them this information on the condition that the Global money order is to be used to pay the utility bills?"

"I don't see a problem with that, Miss Jefferson. However, we must act quickly, before Mr. Taylor makes his arrangement public."

"Do it," Rose said tonelessly.

"And Mr. Taylor, ma'am?"

Rose looked her enforcer straight in the eye. "I will deal with him myself."

"Is there anything else, ma'am?"

"Yes," Rose said. "Have my private railroad car coupled to the next train bound for New York. This city offends me!"

— 25 —

There were six messages from Harry Taylor waiting for Rose when she arrived in New York. She informed her staff that no matter how often Mr. Taylor called he was not to be put through.

Rose threw herself back into work with a vengeance. M. A. Pecorella kept her abreast of the Chicago developments and within a week Rose had the satisfaction of reading about the utility board supervisor's resignation. An announcement followed that effective immediately, the board would accept Global money orders as payment; the company had been given the concession as the board's sole collection agency.

Let's see how Mr. Harry Taylor handles that! Rose thought as she walked past the doorman onto Lower Broadway. She was weaving through the pedestrians toward her car when she felt a hard grip on her arm.

"We have to talk."

Those four words, almost lost in the din, made her heart lurch.

"What are you doing here?"

The outrage in her voice was enough to propel her driver to her side.

"I need to talk to you, Rose," Harry Taylor said, his eyes fixed on hers.

Rose hesitated, then motioned the chauffeur away.

"There's nothing to discuss."

"I don't agree."

Rose noticed that passersby were slowing down to look at them.

"Get in the car."

"Shall I drive home, ma'am?" the chauffeur rumbled from the front seat.

"Yes. I'm sure we can drop Mr. Taylor along the way."

"How did you do it, Rose?" Harry asked softly. "How did you get a copy of the proposed contract?"

"My security people know their business," Rose said, skirting the question. "You breached your contract with Global, Harry. I had to take steps to protect the company's interests."

"I never signed the contract Hirsh offered me," Harry reminded her. "He drew it up months ago. The letter you saw was the last in a long line of inducements. I was never going to leave Global, Rose. If you remember, I brought the idea of Global's becoming the utilities clearinghouse to you. When

213

you discovered the contract, why didn't you talk to me? I would have told you anything you wanted to know."

Rose looked at her reflection in the car window.

"I couldn't take the chance," she murmured.

"The chance? On me? Were you afraid I'd try to damage the company?"

"You might have," Rose said. "Your idea was very good. The company stood to lose a lot of money if you had any second thoughts."

Harry thought about this, then said, "Ask your driver to stop here, please."

The great car glided up to the curb. In one motion Harry swung open the door and stepped outside. Then he leaned back into the car.

"Was it just the company, Rose? Was that the only reason you acted the way you did?"

"Of course," Rose said quickly and immediately realized she had fallen into his tender trap.

"You're lying," Harry Taylor said softly. "What you took from me wasn't yours to steal, Rose. It was mine to give you, as I wanted to and did. You could have trusted me. Why didn't you trust yourself?"

The door closed and the car was back in traffic. Suddenly Rose leaned forward, gripping the top of the front seat.

"Is anything the matter, ma'am?"

He's walking away from me! I'm going to lose him!

The plan she had been so carefully cultivating around Harry Taylor would be nothing without him. The temptation to call him back was almost irresistible.

"No!" Rose said suddenly. "Just get me home."

Rose shivered and hugged herself, looking at the bustle of humanity outside the car window. Any one of those people, whose lives were so predictable and regimented, would jump to trade places with her.

What a cold bed you would find it. So very cold . . .

Rose had the driver drop her at the front door instead of going round to the porte cochere. She was waiting for Albany to let her in when she whirled around, suddenly recognizing Harry's scent, that combination of cologne and male sweat she had been so conscious of in the car.

"Did you really think I was going to walk away from you?" he asked.

Before Rose could reply, Albany had the door open and Harry, holding her by the elbow, was guiding her inside. Without thinking, Rose veered toward the library and firmly closed the doors.

"Harry, what do you want—"

He wanted the same thing she did. His lips and hands made that very clear. A part of Rose couldn't believe what was happening. She was half out of her dress, her fingers clawing at the buttons on Harry's shirt. She didn't care. Nothing else mattered.

He had her down now on the ancient carpet, its knots rough against her buttocks, the smell of floor polish in her nostrils as she whipped her head from side to side. Rose dug her nails into Harry's back and her teeth into his shoulder to stop herself from crying out. Suddenly the image of Albany and the rest of the help watching them flashed through her mind. Each of them had an incredulous expression, as though they couldn't believe what their mistress was doing.

Rose unlocked her teeth from Harry's shoulder and laughed. Even as she strained and bucked against him her laughter rang around the room until she groaned in final pleasure. After that there was only silence and the smile of sweet exhaustion.

After she had bathed and changed clothes, Rose had a cold buffet supper served to them in her sitting room upstairs. She waited until Albany had decanted the wine, then dismissed him for the evening.

"What do you know about me, Harry?" she asked him, piling his plate high.

As it turned out Harry knew a great deal, but this didn't really surprise Rose.

"Where did you learn all this?"

He shrugged. "Newspapers, magazines, shop talk. But that's only the public face behind a very private woman. There's an awful lot I don't know."

"Let me enlighten you," Rose said softly, taking his hand and kissing his fingertips.

Rose chose safe topics, such as her grandfather, Global's growth, and the plans she had for the company. She glossed over her marriage to Simon and her dreams for Steven. The more she talked, the more aware Rose became of the temptation to say more. With every word she spoke, ten others struggled to get out. Rose couldn't help but realize how much she had buried away within herself, how far she had removed herself from other human beings. But as much as she yearned to lose herself in Harry, her reserve, built to protect her and what she'd created, held.

"You're a fascinating woman," Harry said. "But in spite of everything we've told each other, it seems to me we're still not saying what we really want to."

"And what's that?" Rose asked lazily, her fingers running circles around his chest.

"What the two of us are going to do. I couldn't stand to go back to Chicago without you."

"The idea sounds awful to me too," Rose murmured. "That's why I think you should stay in New York."

215

"And just what am I going to do here?"

"Great things," Rose whispered.

Few men could do what came naturally to Harry Taylor, and that was to listen. Women recognized this capacity and were irresistibly attracted to it. They didn't have to endure hours of male preening or be made to feel that their hopes and dreams, desires and fears were insignificant compared to those of the manly warrior. Harry thought that Rose, for all her intelligence and sophistication, was no different.

Harry had followed Rose to New York because she had done something to him no one else ever had: she had stolen an idea that had belonged to him, one which he had been willing to share. In so doing, she had betrayed him, wounding him far more deeply than he had ever believed possible.

Without understanding it, Harry had given Rose something that he too had been withholding for years from his other lovers. It had grown silently, secretly, like a pearl within its shell, a pearl that would one day be discovered, opened, and revealed to the world. For Harry, Rose had been the woman to awaken the love within him. Yet she had taken that pearl and carelessly thrown it into the gutter.

After a time, of course, his anger subsided. In its place grew the need to correct the injustice. Harry had not come to New York to pry an apology out of Rose Jefferson but to settle the score.

Given Harry Taylor's track record in Chicago, no one at Lower Broadway was surprised when he was transferred to the head office. However, eyebrows were raised the day Rose Jefferson appointed him national sales manager at a salary equal to that of her most senior executives.

Outside Lower Broadway, gossip and speculation were lively. Since Rose and Harry frequently appeared in public together the press started dropping hints about a romantic involvement. The fact that Rose did nothing to discourage the rumors only made the talk more piquant.

As far as Harry was concerned, the press could write what it wanted. He remained intoxicated by New York. As soon as he had set foot in the great city he knew that this was where he had been destined to come. Everywhere Harry looked he saw raw potential he could spin into gold, and with Rose Jefferson's help his wheel was already busy.

"The first thing you need is a wardrobe," Rose announced, going through Harry's closet at the Waldorf, which, for propriety's sake, was his official, if temporary, address.

Two weeks and a thousand dollars later, Harry could step out with the best of them. Next on the list was a car.

"Nothing too flashy," Rose advised. "Perhaps a Jaguar . . . ?"

Finally, there was the question of a home.

"It's always better to have something modest at a good address than a jumble of rooms on the wrong side of the tracks."

When Harry looked at the prices for "something modest" he was shocked.

"At the rate I'm spending money, I'll be broke before Christmas," he complained.

Rose laughed. "Don't be silly! Property's always the best investment."

Harry couldn't argue with that and signed a purchase agreement for a Park Avenue apartment.

"There," Rose said to him across her table at Delmonico's. "Now I can come and visit you whenever I want without worrying what the manager of the Waldorf is thinking."

"Rose, the manager of the Waldorf wouldn't think anything unless you gave him permission," Harry said dryly.

Rose smiled. Harry didn't have a clue that he was almost in the same position. Rose had been keeping careful track of the money pouring out of Harry's pockets, money that he didn't yet have and could earn only one way: by doing exactly what she wanted.

— 26 —

Upon their arrival in London, Michelle and Franklin moved into a grand townhouse in Berkeley Square belonging to a friend of Franklin who was currently touring the Orient.

For Michelle, it was love at first sight. The Square's history dated back to 1739 when it had been part of the gardens of Berkeley House. There were beautiful plane trees filled with nightingales, and later in the month the Square would host its annual ball, held outdoors under the stars. There was a "haunted house" at number 50, and the home one door down was currently occupied by Clementine Churchill and her son, Winston.

The servants who came with the townhouse were equally to her taste. Hastings, the butler, was both cheerful and correct. The cook, a motherly woman, immediately wanted to know if the new master and mistress had any favorite dishes. The maids installed the new arrivals quickly and efficiently.

Although Michelle was eager to add her own personal touches to their new home, she was even more eager to dispel the concern that hovered over both her and Franklin. A scant three days after their arrival, she accompanied her husband to his first appointment in Harley Street.

"I'm sorry, Mrs. Jefferson, but I can't tell you what's wrong with your husband. The report of his last physical, forwarded to me by Dr. Harris, only confirms the results of my own examination. Mr. Jefferson appears to be in perfect health."

Michelle regarded the physician somberly. Sir Dennis Pritchard had the sculpted good looks of a matinee idol, with swept-back black hair graying at the temples, a rugged jaw, and glittering blue eyes. He was a distinguished surgeon, a specialist in cerebral traumas, and a Fellow of the Royal College of Surgeons. His brisk, businesslike manner might have put off some patients but Michelle found it professional and reassuring. She sensed she could trust Sir Dennis not to sugarcoat the truth.

"What happened to my husband on board the *Neptune* was not an example of a man in perfect health," Michelle said quietly.

In the room adjacent to Sir Dennis's office, she heard Franklin humming to himself while getting dressed.

"I appreciate your concern," the physician replied. "I've read the ship's doctor's report. Clearly your husband is suffering from some sort of dysfunction. What we do not know is the cause."

"Obviously it's his wound," Michelle protested.

Sir Dennis shook his head. "Not necessarily. There could be a dozen other explanations for his symptoms. I don't want to alarm you unduly, but we can't discount the possibility of a brain tumor."

Michelle paled. "What can you do for him, Doctor?"

"I'm afraid there will be more tests, some of them unpleasant. I am also going to write to Dr. Harris and have him send me your husband's complete case history."

"There's one more thing you might ask Dr. Harris to get for you," Michelle said slowly. "Franklin's army medical file."

"That would be in his case history, Mrs. Jefferson."

"I'm sure it is. But please ask him for it anyway."

Michelle lifted the blue bottle of pills off Pritchard's desk. "Should he continue taking these?"

Pritchard frowned. "That's another thing I find puzzling. There's no record of any prescription in the medical file. Without a laboratory analysis I can't even tell you what these are. With all due respect to Dr. Harris, this is very sloppy procedure."

Michelle was shocked by Harris's carelessness.

"It's worse than sloppy!" she said angrily. "I can't believe he'd forget such a thing."

As she heard the door opening, Michelle, for a reason she couldn't fathom, blurted, "Please, get that army medical file!"

"Well, Doctor, what's the verdict? Will I live?"

Franklin stepped into the room and stopped to kiss Michelle.

"I'm sure you will, Mr. Jefferson," Sir Dennis replied. "But there are a few things I'd like to go over with you. Why don't we chat?"

After they left Harley Street, Michelle and Franklin drove back to Berkeley Square. On the way, Franklin suggested they stop for tea at the Savoy.

"Pritchard tells me that until he's run the tests we'll have to be careful about going out or entertaining," Franklin said after the waiter had brought them their repast. "It wouldn't look good if I fell face first into the soup."

Michelle tried to smile at his lighthearted tone.

"You'll be fine," she said firmly. "We just won't overdo things. I want you to leave all the arrangements to me."

"Maybe I should let Rose know what happened," Franklin said, thinking aloud.

"I don't think that's a very good idea," Michelle replied. "We don't know exactly what's wrong, and that would only worry Rose."

The last thing Michelle wanted was Rose interfering in their lives right now.

"I suppose you're right," Franklin said. "Still, if anything happens to me—"

"Nothing is going to happen to you!" Michelle said fiercely. "After everything we've been through, I'm not about to lose you now."

Franklin gripped Michelle's hand and looked into her eyes.

"How did I ever get so lucky?"

As charmed as Michelle was by London, she dreaded the prospect of establishing her and Franklin's social life in their new home. There were enough expatriate Americans who were Rose's friends to make life miserable. Salvation came from a totally unexpected quarter. The first caller at Berkeley Square was not a Jefferson crony but Lady Patricia Farmington.

"Where's Christophe?" Michelle exclaimed as she embraced her former shipmate.

"Rattling about in his dark, dank château, I expect," Patricia replied with a theatrical sigh. "Or else getting his ponies ready for Deauville. Rank may have its privileges but it also has duties."

Patricia Farmington took the Jeffersons in hand, introducing them to all her fashionable friends. Michelle's acceptance into London's rarefied circles also paved the way for the expatriate contingent to reevaluate their opinion of her. The transplanted Americans who lorded over the great houses in Belgravia and Knightsbridge wondered if their dearest Rose hadn't made a tiny error in judgment as far as her sister-in-law was concerned. After all, in addition to money and prestige, European nobility possess the famous "nose," the ability, with one look or word, to define exactly a person's natural station in life. Obviously Michelle had passed the closest scrutiny and been declared acceptable. As soon as that word made the rounds in the American colony, the invitations poured in.

Throughout the parties and dinners, Michelle kept a careful eye on Franklin. She was pleased by the way he kept to a strict diet, drank sparingly, and always had a graceful explanation for their early departures from parties. Nevertheless, she found Franklin's curbed spontaneity out of keeping with his gregarious nature. It was as though a part of him was always wary.

Sir Dennis Pritchard was unable to give them any explanation.

"Everything Harris sent me contradicts what you've experienced, Mr. Jefferson," the Harley Street physician told Franklin. "According to your case history, you're as fit as a fiddle. However, I still want to conduct further tests."

Franklin groaned. It was a standing joke between him and Michelle that he had become "Pritchard's pincushion." Once a week, at London's Grosvenor Hospital, the doctor supervised blood tests, urinalysis, and other examinations, some of which were not only painful but left Franklin totally drained. As the results proved negative, new, even experimental tests were scheduled. Pritchard had already cautioned Michelle to cancel whatever social and travel activities they had planned for March.

"If we don't find anything in the last batch of samples, I have no choice but to do a spinal tap and a cranium puncture to draw cerebral fluid. It's an exhausting procedure, Mrs. Jefferson. Your husband will need plenty of rest afterwards."

"What about his army medical records?" asked Michelle.

"According to Harris, he's still trying to get them from the military people. Apparently they were never forwarded to him."

Michelle's eyes flashed. "That's not good enough."

"I agree. In fact I've taken the liberty of discussing the situation with a colleague of mine—without mentioning names, of course. He suggested that the hospital in Paris where your husband was treated might have duplicate records."

"I'll write to them immediately," Michelle said. "Or go there myself, if I have to."

Sir Dennis looked at her carefully. "I think the latter is a better idea. You remember those pills you brought me? The laboratory reports arrived the other day. What Dr. Harris prescribed for your husband, Mrs. Jefferson, were the most potent painkillers available. You didn't know that, did you?"

"No!"

"Then that tells *me* Dr. Harris isn't telling us everything he knows—or at least suspects."

Michelle wanted to leave for Paris at that instant. But what was she going to tell Franklin? She couldn't just leave for Paris without some kind of explanation.

By the time she stepped through her front door, Michelle had her answer. Since she would be doing a great deal of entertaining she needed a new wardrobe. No husband, even an understanding one like Franklin, would willingly endure a shopping spree. She ran into the study to tell him the news.

"You're back just in time," Franklin said, hanging up the telephone. "I've been calling a few people from Morgan, First New York, and City National. Everyone's free this Friday. We've got a party to plan."

As February tightened its cold grip over London, Michelle found herself hosting one formal dinner party a week as well as giving and attending cocktail parties and spending weekends in underheated, clammy British country estates, which, for some reason, Americans loved. Nevertheless, she had to admit that Franklin was achieving his goal. As the bankers came to trust and respect him, they began introducing him to their British counterparts. Slowly the faces and accents around Michelle's table changed.

During their hectic schedule Michelle continued watching Franklin for signs of fatigue, restlessness, and other tiny warning signals that Franklin was pushing himself too hard. So far Michelle hadn't seen any, but she never let down her guard. She also went to work trying to run down Franklin's army medical file.

Michelle recalled that Franklin had never told her about the treatment he had received in Paris. However, she did remember the name of the hospital. Michelle had sent letters to Hôpital Notre Dame de Grace in Paris, asking the administrator if the U.S. Army medical records were still in its archives. To date there had been no reply.

In early March, when there was still no word from Paris, Michelle's anxiety turned to desperation. Time was working against her. Franklin's latest and, from what Sir Dennis had told her, most painful tests were about to begin.

There was no way she could leave him now. On the day of his admission, Michelle accompanied Franklin to Grosvenor Hospital and fussed over him until the nurses threatened to complain to the head matron.

"This takes me back to the days in your barn," Franklin said, teasing Michelle as he watched her arrange his toiletries in the bathroom. On a more serious note, he added, "Do you know what to tell people?"

Michelle turned around quickly. "Of course."

They had agreed on a white lie: that Franklin was suffering from a severe flu. This would explain not only his hospitalization but the subsequent convalescence. Under no circumstances could the banking community get wind that there was anything seriously wrong with him. If they did, the image of strength and confidence he had established would be ruined.

Michelle's first night alone at Berkeley Square was a sleepless one. Early the next morning she telephoned the hospital only to be told that Sir Dennis had just begun the procedure. It wasn't until afternoon that Michelle was asked to come in. The sight that greeted her was shocking.

"What's happened to him?" she whispered to Sir Dennis.

Lying in the bed, Franklin looked like a corpse. His complexion was ashen and his cheekbones were sunken, as though overnight he had lost twenty pounds. The sheen of sweat across his face gave off a rank odor.

"He can't hear us, Mrs. Jefferson," the physician replied. "And he's as well as can be expected under the circumstances. There's nothing to be concerned about."

"Is he in pain?"

"I've given him the proper amount of sedative," Sir Dennis replied diplomatically.

"When will you have the results?"

"Two, perhaps three days. We'll take the cerebral fluid as soon as they're in—if we must." The physician paused. "Have you had any word from Paris?"

Michelle shook her head.

"If the tests can't help us, perhaps you should take this opportunity to attend to the matter personally."

"And leave him here alone!"

"Mrs. Jefferson," Sir Dennis said gently, "your husband is receiving the best possible care. The only way you can help him now is by getting us that army medical file." The physician paused. "Unless, of course, you're concerned about something else."

"No, nothing," Michelle said quickly.

But there was something, so private Michelle hadn't been able to share it with Sir Dennis. For the last three months, even before they had left New York,

Franklin had not made love to her. She could see in his eyes and tell by his touch that he wanted to, at times desperately so, yet every time they tried, it ended in humiliation. Michelle couldn't understand what was happening. She tried to make herself believe that Franklin was simply exhausted from the work he was trying to finish before their departure. But then came the incident with Steven and Franklin's bizarre disappearance.

Perhaps I knew all along that the two were somehow connected, Michelle thought. And with that admission a second, even more devastating question broke free: why, for all the times she and Franklin had made love, had she never gotten pregnant?

- 27 -

The cold March rains had arrived in Paris, bringing with them a perpetual fog. Michelle stepped off the train at Gare Montparnasse and after fighting her way to the exit, stood in the pouring rain for fifteen minutes, watching as one taxi after another raced by. Finally she barged in front of an aging Citroen sedan whose driver barely had time to hit the brakes.

"Hôpital Notre Dame de Grace and be quick about it!"

The driver, a cigarette dangling from the corner of his mouth, regarded his drenched passenger with the disdain only French cabbies are able to communicate.

"*Oui, madame!*" he said with mock chivalry, popping the clutch so quickly that Michelle was thrown against the backseat.

At the hospital Michelle tried to make herself presentable before going up to the main desk. The nurse regarded her sourly as she explained whom she had come to see.

"I shall try to find the doctor for you. Sit over there until you're called."

Shivering inside her soaked clothes, Michelle found a seat on a hard wooden bench and slumped back. *Welcome to Paris,* she thought.

An hour passed. In addition to being wet and cold, Michelle became hungry. She screwed up her courage and went back to the front desk.

"The director of archives went to lunch," the nurse informed her. "He will see you when he returns."

With great effort Michelle reined in her anger. "Then perhaps I can get something to eat as well. Can you tell me where the director is having his lunch?"

The nurse regarded her disdainfully. "He *always* dines at the Coq d'Or. However, for you I would suggest something more modest."

Michelle's ears were burning with humiliation as she strode through the front doors. A helpful orderly gave her directions to the restaurant, which was only two blocks away. Michelle thanked him and stepped back into the rain.

The Coq d'Or was all red-and-black-patterned wallpaper, heavy curtains with gold tassels, and gaudy bronze light fixtures. Although the tuxedoed waiters and maître d' gave the impression of class, to Michelle the restaurant's interior resembled a turn-of-the-century bordello. She marched up to the captain and politely but firmly asked to be shown to the administrator's table.

"Monsieur Desmarais is upstairs in the private salon," he said huffily.

Before the captain realized what was happening, Michelle was halfway up the stairs. She raced down the corridor and threw open the door. Six astonished faces, their cheeks stuffed with half-chewed food, stared at her.

"Which one of you is Monsieur Desmarais?"

One of the men swallowed hard and rose. "I am he. And who might you be, madame?"

By this time the captain had run in and gripped Michelle's arm. Without thinking, she lashed back with her foot, catching the captain squarely on the shin.

"I am Michelle Jefferson," she announced coldly. "I have been writing to you for months regarding my husband's army medical records. I want them— now!"

Half the table was looking at the captain hopping around, nursing his injured leg. The other half was watching their colleague, fascinated by this unexpected drama.

"Madame, I haven't the faintest idea what you're talking about," the bureaucrat protested.

Michelle slapped down copies of her letters, almost overturning a silver boat of béarnaise sauce.

"My husband's name is Franklin Jefferson. He served in the American forces during the war and was later treated at your hospital. He is the holder of the Croix de Guerre and the Legion of Honor. Believe me, monsieur, if you do not give me those records I will go to Marshal Pétain himself and request that he deal with you."

Desmarais paled at hearing the name of France's legendary general. As mad as this woman sounded, something in her voice warned him that hers was not an idle threat.

"I regret to inform you, madame, that the records you seek are not at my institution. I wrote telling you this but it seems my letter was misplaced."

"How can you *not* have them? You treated my husband."

"As I explained, madame, all army records were transferred shortly after the war."

"To where?"

Desmarais gave his best Gallic shrug. "As far as I know, the American Hospital in Neuilly."

Adjacent to the Bois de Boulogne, the suburb of Neuilly was created out of what had once been Louis-Philippe's château. As the taxi wended its way through the tree-lined streets, Michelle caught glimpses of stately villas wreathed in fog. After the frenetic bustle of Montparnasse, Neuilly was a welcome relief.

At the American hospital, Michelle, who had girded herself for another round of bureaucratic incompetence, was pleasantly surprised. She was greeted politely and taken to the director's office, where she met a gangly young man whose shock of brown hair and horn-rimmed glasses gave him the appearance of an owl. He introduced himself as Dr. Ernie Stillwater and listened carefully as Michelle explained where she had been and why she had come.

"Well, Mrs. Jefferson, the folks at Notre Dame were right about one thing," Stillwater said. "The records were transferred to us. Unfortunately, they were later moved once more, to the official army archives in Paris. You're going to need military authorization to get them out."

"Is that a problem?"

Stillwater gave her a sympathetic look. "You know how any army does things, Mrs. Jefferson. Every piece of paper is in triplicate, everyone needs someone else's authorization. It could take a long time."

"I don't know if my husband has that luxury," Michelle said quietly.

She outlined what had happened to Franklin in New York and during the crossing and how urgently Sir Dennis Pritchard needed those records.

"I know Pritchard by reputation," Stillwater remarked, obviously impressed.

Michelle seized the opportunity. "Doctor, is there any way you could get those records released to you? After all, they were stored here, and there still are many American servicemen living in Paris. . . ."

The glint in his eye told Michelle that Stillwater knew exactly what she was driving at.

"I suppose that would be a valid request," he said, grinning. "Where did you say you and Mr. Jefferson were living in Paris, just so I can put down a local address, you understand."

Michelle thought frantically but the only place that flashed through her mind was the Coq d'Or.

"Good choice," Stillwater muttered, scribbling notes. "The food's okay but the place looks like a New Orleans cathouse."

That evening Michelle checked into the Ritz Hotel on the Place Vendôme and surrendered herself to its superb staff. Dinner and a half-bottle of Gevry-Chambertin were more than enough to send her off into a deep, much-needed sleep.

The next morning the hotel organized her return to London, looking after everything from a limousine to take her to Calais, to a first-class berth on the ferry. As the vessel ponderously made its way through the choppy waters on the English Channel, Michelle said a little prayer for Dr. Ernie Stillwater. He had promised her he would do his best and she had instinctively believed him. Now all she could do was wait.

Another car was waiting for Michelle quayside at Dover. The foul weather that had dogged her across the Channel persisted all the way to London, causing Michelle to arrive at Grosvenor Hospital far later than she had hoped. She caught up with Sir Dennis just as he was completing general rounds. His expression told her what to expect even before he said a word.

"The spinal tap and cerebral puncture didn't help us at all. Did you have any luck in Paris?"

Michelle told him about Stillwater and what he would try to do.

"Very well, I'll expect to hear from him."

"When can I see Franklin?" Michelle asked anxiously.

"Right now, if you like. He'll be ready to go home tomorrow."

Sir Dennis Pritchard was touched by the radiance that spilled across Michelle's face. As he watched her hurry down the corridor he wondered if he was doing the right thing.

What else can you do?

In Michelle's absence, Sir Dennis had spent a great deal of time analyzing Franklin Jefferson's head wounds and their treatment. He reread Michelle's account of Franklin's condition when she had brought him to safety and the surgery that Dr. Emil Radisson had performed under the most trying conditions. Every fact he absorbed led Sir Dennis back to the same question: What had been done for Franklin Jefferson in Paris?

One possibility that kept crossing his mind refused to go away. The more Sir Dennis considered it, the more likely it became. But he couldn't articulate his

226

suspicion to Michelle Jefferson unless he had irrefutable evidence. If he *was* right, then William Harris, and possibly others, were undeniably guilty of gross negligence.

As part of Franklin's convalescence Michelle wanted the two of them to get away from London and its cold, inhospitable climate. She broached the subject with Sir Dennis, suggesting a week or two in the south of Spain, where the sand and sea would help heal Franklin. The doctor agreed immediately but Franklin wouldn't hear of it.

"I've lost too much time as it is," he told Michelle shortly. He pointed to the get-well notes from the City bankers. "These people know I want something from them. They won't wait forever to find out what it is."

Michelle was dismayed but quietly dropped the idea of going away.

In April, Franklin's schedule became more hectic than ever. Having familiarized himself with the major players in the country's banking community, Franklin turned his attention to the Bank of England, the ultimate arbiter of Great Britain's fiscal policy and money supply. Because these talks had to be absolutely secret, the times and places chosen were both odd and out of the way. Michelle and Franklin would leave a dinner party and on the way home Franklin would instruct the driver to drop him off a few blocks from Threadneedle Street, the bank's headquarters. He'd walk the rest of the way, have his meeting, and sometimes not return home before three o'clock in the morning.

The hours, the necessity for subterfuge, and the painfully slow progress all began to take their toll. Franklin's irregular timetable deprived him of much-needed rest, and when he did retire early his sleep was plagued by nightmares. The headaches followed, beginning as a monotonous pounding around the temples and ending with skewers of pain that made him cry out in agony. One night, when Franklin couldn't stop screaming, Michelle called Sir Dennis Pritchard. The physician took one look at his patient and immediately administered morphine. After that Michelle was given a set of syringes and a supply of the drug in case of emergencies.

Each attack drained a little more life out of Franklin and the recuperation periods became longer and longer. Over the spring, Michelle found herself playing a variety of roles. She continued to organize their social life, paring their commitments to the bone. She also reverted to being Franklin's nurse while at the same time taking on more and more responsibility for preparing his business agenda. By the time England's famous gardens bloomed, Michelle was almost as well versed in the intricacies of British banking as Franklin was.

At the end of some days Michelle wondered how much longer she could stand the pace. She kept praying for some word from Dr. Ernie Stillwater in Paris but every week his answer to her call was the same: no luck yet. In the end it was Franklin, not she, who raised the unspoken subject.

"I don't know how much longer I can work effectively," Franklin said to her one day. "I know you're not happy with the idea of calling Rose. Neither am I. But I don't think we have a choice. Things are reaching a critical point. If I flub the presentation for the traveler's checks, everything Rose has been working on for months will go down the drain."

Everything you've *been working for,* Michelle corrected him silently.

Michelle was torn between her desire to alleviate the pressure Franklin was working under, which Rose could certainly do, and keeping their new lives as separate as possible from the influence of Talbot House. Her doubts and indecision must have been written across her face because Franklin reached out and took her hand.

"Why don't we give Pritchard a little more time?" he suggested gently. "After all those tests he's got to come up with *something!*"

Michelle embraced her husband, holding him close.

"Let's," she whispered.

Michelle cleaved herself tightly to Franklin and as she listened to the steady beat of his heart, her fears slowly dispelled. She had no way of knowing that the feelings she struggled so hard to keep to herself were shared by Rose Jefferson, more than three thousand miles away.

For Rose, the spring of 1920 had been one of most exciting and productive periods of her life. The money order had seized the imagination of the American public and Rose found herself fielding calls from banks across the country, which were falling over one another to do business with her.

Even though business was booming on the domestic front, Rose made a point of keeping abreast of events on the other side of the Atlantic. Through Franklin's letters, she followed his progress avidly. Although she realized it would take time for Franklin to get to know the right people, after a few months Rose began chafing at his apparent lack of progress. She began to worry that Franklin was being overly cautious and might miss the perfect opportunity to launch the traveler's checks.

Her concern deepened when Dr. William Harris informed her that Franklin's London physician kept pestering him for the original army medical file. Rose carefully reviewed all of Franklin's letters but in their cheerful, positive tone found nothing to indicate that the attacks he had suffered had returned.

Maybe he isn't telling me everything. Or else, someone has persuaded him not to say too much. . . .

To Rose, the latter seemed the more likely. And she had no doubt who would be counseling Franklin to keep certain things from her: Michelle.

Damn it all! Rose thought, vexed by her dilemma. She knew she should go to London immediately and find out for herself what was going on. On the other hand, so much more had to be done with the money order. Huge contracts remained to be negotiated. To leave now, even for a few weeks, meant courting the possibility of losing valuable customers. Moreover, Rose was keenly aware that the major banks, even though they were her customers, were covetously eyeing her success. The only reason they weren't creating their own form of money order was that Rose was so far ahead in the game. But if she failed to get the nationwide grip that was almost within her reach, competition would spring up overnight.

The problem continued to chafe her. Rose couldn't send either Hugh O'Neill or Eric Gollant in her place since both had more than enough on their plates. Furthermore, Rose wasn't at all sure just what prejudices the British bankers might harbor against an Irishman and a Jew. She certainly didn't want to find out the hard way. Which left only one person.

But was Harry ready for something like this? And more important, could she trust him with her plans for the traveler's check? If not, was there a way to send him without telling him everything?

The lack of results in London made up Rose's mind. When Harry returned from St. Louis in three days, she would put him on the first ship to Southampton. Rose debated telling Harry about her real target, the British banks, but decided against it.

I can't have him thinking anything's wrong. That would be a weakness. Besides, he doesn't have to know everything.

Rose began to draft a letter to Franklin, telling him of Harry's arrival and exactly how to handle the situation. It pained her to have to lie to her brother, but here too Rose believed she had no choice.

— 28 —

By now Harry Taylor had become accustomed to traveling first class. When his limousine entered Carlos Place in Mayfair he allowed the uniformed doorman to help him from the Rolls-Royce and, watching the alert porters, didn't give his trunks and bags a second thought. Since Rose had made the reservations herself, the formalities at the front desk were minimal. The manager himself escorted Harry to his suite, presenting him with a huge basket of fruit and a bottle of chilled champagne.

When Harry called Berkeley Square he was informed by the Jeffersons' butler that he was expected for dinner at eight o'clock. As he dressed, Harry thought back to his last evening with Rose. During his months in New York he had come to appreciate that Rose was a woman who created and encouraged a sense of mystery about herself. She did this by carefully compartmentalizing what she shared with people. Some were privy to more than others, but only Eric Gollant and Hugh O'Neill knew everything, including Rose Jefferson's "secret project," which was to follow the wildly successful money order.

Wherever he turned, Harry Taylor kept hearing about this mysterious enterprise. There were rumors that Global was about to acquire a major bank, that it intended to go into the brokerage business, or that the company was on the verge of financing some enormous foreign venture. Harry tracked each of these stories, not really surprised that not one had any substance. As curious as he was, he never mentioned anything to Rose, even after they had exhausted themselves in lovemaking and the temptation was almost irresistible. If it was that big, Harry reasoned, then he wasn't about to risk Rose's trust in him by trying to seduce the answer out of her. Harry pinned his hopes on the fact that he was fast becoming an integral part of Global. The higher he rose, the more likely he would become involved in this "project." The evening Rose had announced he would be going to London, Harry was certain the moment was at hand. But, he confessed, not even he had been prepared for just how audacious and far-reaching Rose's secret was.

"That's the background and the plan for the traveler's checks," Rose had told him. "Everything hinges on the willingness of American banks abroad to handle them. That's what Franklin has been seeing to up to now. I want you to help him."

"I'll do the best I can," Harry said, matching Rose's grave tone. "Can you give me some specifics?"

"You're the best salesman I have. As soon as Franklin brings the banks on board, I want you to organize a sales force that will get the traveler's check into every hotel, railroad station, and steamship-line office in Britain."

Harry whistled softly. "That's a tall order. I'd have to get the feel of the territory, see how the Brits do things, find out who has the best people."

"That's why you're going over now instead of waiting until Franklin has everything sewn up."

It seemed to Harry that such a strategy made perfect sense. He never once suspected that by carefully weaving details about Franklin's daily business life into the conversation, Rose had been drawing a picture of exactly what he should expect in London. Or that if this image wasn't exactly the one he found, Harry, her caring considerate lover and the man she had promoted above all others, would naturally tell her what was wrong.

Having heard about Michelle almost exclusively from Rose, Harry arrived at Berkeley Square prepared to be greeted by a French shrew who would see to her social obligations and then go to bed, leaving him and Franklin to discuss their business. He couldn't have been more wrong.

After being shown into the drawing room, Harry was introduced to his hostess, a stunningly elegant woman gowned in a Callot creation of rose chiffon and dull-silver lace. Her brilliant red hair cascaded around white shoulders and her eyes seemed to catch the fire from the electric lamps in the room. Harry was so taken aback by Michelle Jefferson's allure that he was almost tongue-tied as she introduced him to her husband and other guests. One in particular, a young blond Englishwoman, caught Harry's eye and winked at him mischievously. Harry thought it might be a good omen that he and Lady Patricia Farmington ended up sitting next to each other at the table.

Throughout dinner, Michelle carefully watched Harry Taylor. He seemed pleasant and entertained the people around him with amusing stories. He had also, Michelle thought, unwittingly solved her and Franklin's dilemma of whether to tell Rose about Franklin's health problems. But there was something about him she couldn't quite put her finger on.

When Rose's letter informing them of Harry Taylor's arrival had been delivered to Berkeley Square, Michelle was immediately wary.

"I don't understand," she had told Franklin. "This man is her lover. He's also supposed to be a genius at sales and marketing. If he's even half of what she makes him out to be, why doesn't she tell him the truth? Sooner or later, he'll have to know about the British banks. When he does, he may blame you as much as Rose for not being honest with him."

"I don't like it much either," Franklin had replied. "But that's the way Rose works. She must have her reasons. Whatever they are and whether we agree with them or not, I have enough to keep Taylor busy without his becoming suspicious. If and when the day comes to tell him the truth, we'll let Rose explain. By then, we'll be done with Global."

Nonetheless, Rose's subterfuge bothered Michelle. After the rest of the guests had departed, she sat listening to Harry discuss company business. Clearly he appeared both knowledgeable and willing to follow advice Franklin gave him. On the other hand, Harry's attentiveness to an increasingly starry-eyed Patricia made Michelle wonder if perhaps Rose had tired of this handsome young man and had chosen the London appointment as a way to ease him out of her life.

Michelle felt unsettled. With Franklin almost ready to bring his British principals together, the last thing he needed was complications of any kind. Michelle decided that the dashing Mr. Harry Taylor could bear some watching.

Between the expense money Rose had provided and Lady Patricia Farmington's eagerness to help out, Harry soon found himself a luxurious flat in Belgravia. Once he had settled in he became a frequent caller at Berkeley Square. Harry felt comfortable with Franklin and his easygoing attitude but almost immediately he noticed several anomalies. The first was that Michelle often sat in on their discussions and seemed to know as much about the plans for the traveler's checks as her husband did. Given Rose's antipathy toward Michelle, Harry asked himself if she had any idea just how great a role her sister-in-law was playing in Global's affairs.

The second thing was Michelle's unobtrusive but constant concern about Franklin. Whenever their discussions tended to run on, Michelle always found a pretext to cut them off. Harry also noticed that Franklin Jefferson seldom started his day before ten o'clock in the morning and that at dinner parties the Jeffersons always found a reason to leave early.

The last thing that didn't jibe was Franklin's unwillingness to introduce Harry to the American banking community. Whenever Harry pressed him on this, Franklin inevitably replied that there would be time for this later. However, his replies were so evasive that Harry was certain Franklin was hiding something from him.

Although these incongruities puzzled Harry, he kept them to himself. Franklin may not have shared his sister's mettle and drive but Harry found him likable enough, enjoying Franklin's humor and gift of repartee. Soon the Jeffersons, along with Harry and Lady Patricia Farmington, were a familiar foursome on London's social scene.

Traditionally, the Fourth of July party at the American embassy was London's hottest ticket. The festivities were a chance for the diplomatic corps to thank their British hosts as well as give all the American expatriates and visitors the opportunity to celebrate Independence Day. Since every British banker Franklin had chosen to deal with would be there, he and Michelle agreed that it would be the perfect occasion to unveil the traveler's check. The ambassador, well aware that a great deal of horsetrading went on during the outdoor barbecues, made a large, private room available for Franklin's use.

As the days counted down to the celebration Michelle found Franklin becoming more worried and irritable. Although he slept long hours, his concentration span diminished alarmingly. Nonetheless, Franklin insisted he was ready.

"There won't be a better chance," he told her.

The Fourth turned out to be a glorious day. Decked out in their finery, the ladies with gaily colored parasols paraded through the fragrant gardens, while the men, in dove-gray morning coats and top hats, availed themselves of mint juleps and iced tea. Dinner was served early beneath huge awnings so that the guests could relax before the fireworks began.

Michelle stayed close to Franklin and was relieved to see him having such a good time. It wouldn't be long now, she thought, before Franklin's business was finished and they could truly leave Global behind them. Just before the fireworks were to start, Michelle and Patricia stole away to the powder room.

"You and Harry have been seeing a lot of each other," Michelle said, fluffing her hair. From the way her friend blushed, she thought the rumors about Patricia's affair with Harry had at least a grain of truth to them.

"He's awfully nice," Patricia said defensively.

"What about Christophe?"

Patricia gave a tiny shrug. "Don't you like Harry? Franklin seems to think the world of him."

Michelle agreed that Franklin and Harry had hit it off.

"I'm just not sure Harry's right for you," she said lightly, then, not wanting to spoil her friend's obvious infatuation, added, "Still, as long as you're happy . . ."

At the far end of the compound Franklin and Harry were strolling by the brick platform along which members of the famous pyrotechnic family, the Gianellis, were preparing the fireworks.

"It'll be just like home," Harry commented, moving closer to inspect the Roman candles.

As twilight fell, Harry tried to steer the conversation around to the traveler's checks but Franklin would have none of it.

"We don't discuss the subject outside my office," he reminded Harry, an edge to his voice. "Besides, if everything goes well tonight, you're going to be busy soon enough."

Harry pondered that cryptic comment as he knelt to get a better look at the fireworks arrangement. He straightened up and from his jacket pocket withdrew a leather cigar case. He offered one to Franklin and struck a match.

"Signore! Excuse me, please! No fire. No fire!"

Both men turned to see one of the Gianelli brothers rushing toward them, waving his arms.

"What the hell is he talking about?" asked Harry.

At the same time the breeze shifted, fanning the flame, which singed Harry's fingertips.

"No, signore!"

Harry flung the match away. The flame resisted the gentle air current and instead consumed what was left of the stick. It had reached its hottest point when it fell on the priming cord that connected the three tiers of fireworks.

A Roman candle ignited first, rocketing into the sky, its flame and powder shooting back at both men. For an instant the world was blotted out for Franklin, replaced by a sheet of roaring light. Then the sky exploded and he was rolling on the ground. Because the display hadn't been properly completed, there were firecrackers and rockets lying loose around the brick platform. These ignited and raced across the lawn only a few feet off the ground, spinning madly before smashing into trees.

When Franklin raised his head all he saw was a wall of flame. He didn't recognize the figures behind them as the Gianelli brothers, who were frantically trying to cut the priming-cord connectors, but as Germans manning the artillery pieces responsible for the barrage. Somehow his ravaged mind communicated to him that he would die unless the enemy was killed.

Franklin began crawling toward the brick platform on elbows and knees. His outstretched fingertips touched something cold and hard. He wrapped one hand around the sledgehammer head and pulled it toward him. Now he had a weapon. In one motion Franklin was on his feet, the sledgehammer held high over his head, running toward the platform where rockets were still streaking into the night.

On the other side of the embassy compound, the guests, first startled by the explosions, now oohed and ahhed as the fireworks exploded overhead. Standing next to the ambassador, Michelle saw him glance at his watch and mutter that the damned things weren't supposed to go off for another twenty minutes. They also seemed to be exploding willy-nilly instead of in the orchestrated manner that the Gianelli brothers had promised. Michelle looked around to find Franklin, then, seeing neither him nor Harry, slipped through the throngs and began running down the path to where she and Franklin had watched the fireworks being prepared.

How could you have been such a fool? Fireworks! What did you think they would do to him? And leaving him with Harry!

Fighting her rising panic, Michelle darted through the short hedgerow maze. Her eyes stung as she plunged into the acrid smoke. Then, just as suddenly as they had begun, the fireworks fell silent. Emerging from the maze, Michelle saw smoke and ash drifting across the lawn. The Gianelli brothers moved cautiously through the haze, sloshing buckets of water on patches of burning grass. At the end of the platform Michelle saw Franklin on his knees, his hands tightly holding the top of the sledgehammer handle, his head craned back, eyes streaming with tears. She ran up to him and he turned his soot-streaked face toward her.

"I stopped them!" he whispered hoarsely. "There were hundreds of them but I killed them all. . . ."

The sledgehammer fell from his grasp and Franklin collapsed, sobbing. Michelle whirled around to see Harry standing beside her, his face as blackened as Franklin's, his eyes glazed.

"What happened?" she demanded.

"It was an accident," Harry stammered. "The fireworks went off by mistake. Franklin and I were standing right next to them. . . . Then he went crazy."

"Help me get him up!"

"Shouldn't we call a doctor?"

"We will—later!"

Supporting Franklin by the shoulders, they half-walked, half-dragged him to the gate to the parking lot. Michelle found their chauffeur and eased Franklin into the backseat.

"We'll be home soon, darling," she whispered. "Everything's going to be all right."

Franklin clutched her hand. "I have to go back. There's something I have to do. . . ." He squeezed his eyes shut against the pain. "Have to do something . . . Can't remember . . . can't remember . . ."

Michelle realized the car door was still open.

"Go inside and call Sir Dennis Pritchard," she said to Harry, scribbling down two numbers. "One is his home, the other is Grosvenor Hospital. Tell him what happened and ask him to meet you at Berkeley Square."

"What should I say if anyone asks what happened?"

Michelle shot him a blistering look. "Why not the truth? There's been an accident. Franklin's in shock and you're taking him home."

Michelle slammed the door, her arms tightly around Franklin, trying to decide what to do next. Every instinct screamed at her to get Franklin home where he would be safe.

Everything he's worked for comes down to tonight, she thought, remembering the bankers.

Michelle looked down at her husband. His breathing had become shallow and irregular and his skin was cold to the touch. Michelle drew the car blanket around him and held him tightly.

There was a knock on the car window.

"Pritchard's on his way," Harry said breathlessly. "He's bringing his nurse with him, just in case. The ambassador wants to know if Franklin's all right."

Now I have to decide. I can go home with Franklin and all the work he's done will be forfeited. When that happens, Rose will demand explanations and from that moment on our lives will be hell. Or I can do what Franklin can't. . . . Decide, Michelle!

Michelle stepped out of the car and stood very close to Harry.

"I want you to take him home," she said in a low voice. "Tell Pritchard exactly what happened and stay with Franklin until I return."

"You're not coming with him?"

"I can't explain now. I'll be there as soon as I can."

Michelle grabbed Franklin's portfolio case, gave the chauffeur his instructions, and hurried back into the compound. By now a small knot of people were standing around the ruins of the brick platform and Gianelli senior was vociferously bemoaning the catastrophe to the chief of protocol. Michelle carefully skirted them and made her way into the embassy. She buttonholed the ambassador's secretary, who promptly led her into the main office.

"Glad to hear your husband's all right," the diplomat said, getting to his feet. "Got a bit of a shock, did he?"

Michelle gave him her most reassuring smile. "Both Franklin and Mr. Taylor were a little too close for comfort. They've gone home to change."

"Then your husband won't be attending the meeting he scheduled."

"No, Mr. Ambassador, but I will."

The diplomat's eyebrows shot up. "You'll pardon me for saying so, ma'am, but are you sure you want to do that?"

"Very sure," Michelle said firmly.

The ambassador shrugged. "They're waiting in the conference room."

Michelle bridled at his condescending tone and matched him step for step as they walked toward the gleaming double doors at the end of the hall.

What am I doing?

It was too late to retreat. The ambassador swung open the door and announced, "Gentlemen, Mrs. Franklin Jefferson."

236

Their expressions ranged from surprise to mild amusement, and their polished manner couldn't diminish the aura of power surrounding them. These men weren't merely custodians of vast pools of money. They were the bone and sinew that had built and preserved an empire.

Damn them, Michelle thought, angry at being afraid. *They sat at my table. They broke bread with me. Now they'll bloody well listen to me!*

The ambassador made the introductions and bowed himself out of the room. For a few seconds one could hear a pin drop.

"Well, Mrs. Jefferson," Sir Manfred Smith of Barclays said. "We trust that all Mr. Jefferson suffered was a mild fright."

"He's perfectly fine, Sir Manfred."

"And are you empowered to speak on his behalf?"

"I am."

Sir Manfred glanced at his colleagues. Whatever the signals were, Michelle didn't catch them.

"Very well, Mrs. Jefferson. You have our undivided attention."

Harry Taylor had never before experienced such a feeling: he was on the verge of panic. Franklin Jefferson was huddled in one corner of the backseat. He had begun shivering uncontrollably. His hands, balled into fists, were clenched against his temples. From his throat came a high, keening sound of incessant pain. Harry had no idea what to do and sat gingerly on the edge of the seat, watching the car's speedometer, wishing the chauffeur would stop cruising as though he were out on a Sunday drive.

After what seemed an eternity the car finally pulled into Berkeley Square. Harry was relieved to see a woman in a crisp, starched uniform run up, followed by an older, very handsome man who introduced himself as Sir Dennis Pritchard. Harry watched as he and the nurse guided Franklin inside, then slowly followed.

In the library, Harry poured himself a stiff scotch and waited for his nerves to settle. Even so, his mind was racing. Harry realized that what he had just witnessed was proof that Franklin Jefferson was a very sick man. But how many people knew? Michelle. And this doctor. But certainly no one else. Harry had never heard a whisper of Franklin's losing control of himself from anyone.

Not even Rose.

The idea stunned Harry. Now certain things began to make sense: Michelle's constantly hovering around Franklin, Michelle playing such an active role in Franklin's business affairs . . . But in New York, Rose hadn't even hinted that Franklin could be ill, that that was why Harry was being sent to London.

Because she didn't tell me everything? Or else she didn't know!

Harry was convinced that there was something very rotten in the house of

Jefferson and seized the moment. With everyone busy upstairs, he slipped into Franklin's library, which doubled as his office. Harry doubted he'd find anything that would tell him what was wrong with Franklin but he wasn't interested in that right now. He needed to know why Michelle, the loyal, caring wife, had chosen not to accompany her stricken husband home. Only the most compelling reason would have made Michelle act like that. A reason having to do with the traveler's checks project?

Harry began with the most logical place: Franklin's desk. Knowing that someone might walk in on him at any moment, he quickly rifled through the open drawers, then focused his attention on the large bottom one, which was locked. Harry removed a small pearl-handled penknife from his keychain and extracted the blade. As he expected, the lock was more ornamental than functional. Harry reached for the thick ledger bound in blue morocco leather. As soon as he recognized Rose's handwriting he knew he had hit the mother lode.

So she sent me over here on a lie. . . . The American banks had nothing to do with the traveler's check. It was the British she was after. . . . The further Harry delved into Rose's master plan the more he admired her boldness and cunning. But more potent than his respect was his anger. Rose had deceived him from the very beginning. Michelle and Franklin had perpetuated the lie.

Harry's mind was working furiously. The only reason Michelle had stayed behind at the embassy was to talk to the British bankers. Harry was positive Rose had no inkling of either Franklin's illness, whatever that might be, or just how deeply her sister-in-law was involved in a critical Global operation. The possibility of using these elements to his advantage was clear. The key was to choose the most effective way not only to make himself indispensable to Rose but do it in such a way that when this house of cards came tumbling down no one could dare to suggest he had had anything to do with it.

Harry considered his options as he read on. He couldn't believe his luck when Rose's own words handed him the answer.

"Mr. Taylor?"

Harry had been so intent on his reading that he hadn't heard the library door open. With his head still bowed, his expression one of deep concern and his heart pounding in his throat, he turned around.

"Yes?"

"I just wanted to tell you I'm on my way back to Grosvenor Hospital," Sir Dennis Pritchard said. "Please have Mrs. Jefferson call me there as soon as she comes in."

"I certainly will, Doctor. How's Franklin?"

"He's sleeping. I've asked my nurse to stay the night."

Harry heard other movements along the staircase and in the hall. The ledger was burning his fingertips. If only he could take it with him. Franklin might not miss it for a day or two but Michelle would. Aware that the surgeon was still watching him, Harry calmly replaced the ledger in the drawer and pushed it closed.

"Is there anything I can do for Franklin?" asked Harry as he accompanied the physician to the front hall.

"I think you've helped enough as it is," Pritchard replied, looking keenly at Harry. "Not hurt, are you?"

"Just dirt and gunpowder."

"Wash it off straightaway. If there's a cut we don't want it infected."

As soon as the surgeon left, Hastings showed Harry to one of the spare bedrooms. Harry washed up quickly, then went across to the master suite. His work wasn't quite finished yet.

The nurse sitting by Franklin's bed was a young, homely woman with a plain face and thickset frame. Harry wasn't surprised that there was no wedding ring on her finger. He knew that such women could be very receptive to a little kindness.

"Is he all right?" Harry whispered, knocking gently on the door.

"Oh, my goodness, yes. You must be Mister . . ."

"Taylor. But please, call me Harry. It's terrible how this happened to him."

"You know all about it then, do you?"

Harry nodded solemnly.

"It's awful," the nurse went on. "We've tried everything to help him."

"I'd like to be able to help too," Harry said, looking into her eyes. "You know, in case something like this happens again when I'm with him. Maybe you could tell me what I should look out for?"

"That's very sensible," the woman agreed. "You must be a very good friend. Oh, there's no need to whisper. The morphine has put him under nicely."

Morphine!

Harry couldn't wait to hear the rest.

– 29 –

Michelle had never been so nervous in her life. As she walked to the empty chair at the head of the conference table, her heels echoed like rifle shots in the silence hanging over the domed-ceiling committee room. When she sat down she didn't see a hint of encouragement or sympathy in the six faces looking at her.

Michelle placed on the table the file she had brought from the car and opened her mouth. Suddenly, words failed her. She knew exactly what she had to say but the only thing she could think of was Franklin and the terror she had seen on his face. How could she have left him alone like that!

"Mrs. Jefferson, we're all aware how concerned you must be for your husband," Sir Manfred Smith said kindly. "We'd understand if you wanted to be with him at this time."

The Barclays' chairman's word snapped Michelle out of her daze.

"Thank you, Sir Manfred, but I'm sure my husband is perfectly all right. I'm ready to begin."

Michelle spoke for an hour, pausing only when she handed documents and the sample traveler's checks around the table. Even then she concentrated fiercely on keeping her mind from wandering back to Franklin. By now Sir Dennis Pritchard was looking after him. The only way she could help Franklin was by doing what he was unable to do. Michelle concluded her presentation, looked up and down the table, and drew a deep breath.

"Any questions, gentlemen?" she asked, preparing herself for the inevitable inquisition.

No one said a word. Again, it was Sir Manfred who came to her rescue.

"Perhaps you would excuse us for a few moments, Mrs. Jefferson, so we can discuss the matter among ourselves?"

Michelle crimsoned. "Of course."

Michelle made as gracious an exit as she could. Once she was in the hall, she leaned against the wall, struggling to regain her composure. It was over. She had done her best and the rest was out of her hands. Michelle hurried to find a telephone. When Hastings answered, he assured her that Franklin had arrived safely and that Sir Dennis had come and gone. Michelle spoke briefly to the nurse and told her she'd be home as soon as possible.

Walking back to the conference room, Michelle wondered how long the bankers would deliberate. She was surprised to find the doors open and the men starting to file out.

"We were very impressed, both by the proposal and your presentation," Sir Manfred said. "May I compliment you on your grace under the circumstances."

Michelle's heart leaped. "Then you've decided!"

Sir Manfred smiled. "We will study the proposal and let you know as soon as possible." When he saw Michelle's crestfallen expression, he added, "I'm speaking only for myself, of course, but I believe the traveler's check is something Barclays and Global could do very well with together."

"Thank you, Sir Manfred," Michelle said gratefully. "I'll tell my husband."

Michelle quickly said goodbye to the ambassador and left the party. Arriving in Berkeley Square, she immediately went to look in on Franklin. He was sleeping peacefully and Nurse Martin assured her all was well. Sir Dennis would call first thing tomorrow to schedule another appointment. Tired beyond words, Michelle went downstairs to the library.

"You must be exhausted," she said to Harry.

"Glad to have been able to help," Harry replied, getting to his feet.

"My prescription to you is to go home and get some rest." Michelle hesitated. "And, Harry, please don't say a word to anyone about what happened to Franklin. He hasn't been well recently but it's not something we want made public."

Harry held up his hands. "I understand."

As he showed himself out, Harry's conscience was clear. He wouldn't say anything about Franklin's behavior. At least not yet. But there were other matters that he had already decided to act on. His plan was dangerous, but if it worked, both Michelle and Franklin would be cut off from anything having to do with Global. Rose would see to that, just as she would realize there was only one person who could fill that vacuum.

The next morning Harry wrote a letter that he redrafted several times, making sure it conveyed exactly what he wished. After signing it, he sealed it in a thick envelope and hand-delivered it to the addressee's office. Then Harry settled down to wait. He disappointed Lady Patricia by canceling their dinner date but was well rewarded for his patience. At one o'clock in the morning the phone rang and a quiet voice gave Harry his instructions.

In the light of the single lamp that illuminated his office, Sir Thomas Ballantine showed every one of his seventy-five years. His scalp was dotted with liver spots, which the few remaining strands of white hair couldn't hide. His hands, folded on the Chippendale desk, were lined with thick blue veins under translucent skin, the fingers and knuckles swollen by arthritis.

"Your letter intrigues," Sir Thomas said in a hoarse whisper. "It promises a great deal but states very little."

"That's why I knew you'd see me," Harry replied.

Sir Thomas Ballantine let out his breath in a long slow hiss. He did not tolerate impertinence, especially from a foreigner whom he had invited to his home, the most private place in a private, carefully guarded world. Yet, this Harry Taylor, who he was and, more important, what he might be able to do, merited his patience. It was true what Sir Thomas had said: Harry's letter had intrigued him.

> *Although you and I have not had the pleasure of meeting each other, it would be in your interests, and those of the company of which you are chairman, to pay careful attention to what I have to say. . . .*

The writer went on to spell out the success of the Global money order in the United States and Rose Jefferson's intentions to launch the company into the international arena. He concluded by stating that he had valuable information for the chairman of Cooks and requested a reply to arrange a meeting.

Sir Thomas had read the letter a number of times. He knew all about Global and the imperious Rose Jefferson, and was well aware of her success with the money order and the fact that Franklin Jefferson was in London although no one was certain why. Sir Thomas had also taken the precaution of having Harry Taylor's background checked thoroughly. The only blemish on an otherwise distinguished career was his brief suspension from Global's Chicago office followed by an almost immediate promotion to Lower Broadway. Sir Thomas's investigators had suggested that Rose Jefferson's affair with the young executive was the reason for her uncharacteristic change of heart. Sir Thomas conceded it was possible that while Rose Jefferson had forgiven her lover his sins, perhaps he hadn't been quite ready to do the same.

"You imply that Rose Jefferson intends to compete with Cooks," he said in a voice as dry as autumn leaves. "What is your proof?"

Harry crossed one long leg over the other and cocked his head.

"Last night, at the American embassy's Fourth of July celebration, Franklin was to have a little tête-à-tête with the director of Barclays and other City banks. What does that tell you?"

"What *should* it tell me?"

"Jefferson wanted to make an overture, to tell Barclays and the others that

Global was ready to do business in Britain and Europe. The meeting was so critical that when Jefferson was slightly injured in the fireworks explosion, his wife made the presentation instead."

Now Sir Thomas was definitely interested. To have arranged such a meeting, Franklin Jefferson would have had to hold many talks to bring the bank directors together. Sir Thomas hadn't heard anything about this.

"Why is he going after the banks?" Sir Thomas asked, speaking into the darkness.

"Why did Rose Jefferson go to First National, Bankers Fidelity, and the other American heavyweights?" Harry asked rhetorically. "Because she had to make sure they would sell and accept her money orders."

"Are you saying she wants to bring the money order business over here?" The chairman of Cooks sounded skeptical. "We have strict foreign-currency laws in this country. A United States–dollar money order is worthless. No one would accept it over sterling."

"Who said it has to be in dollars?" Harry suggested. "Or that it has to be a money order? Rose Jefferson has created a new international financial instrument called the traveler's check. I'm willing to bet the Bank of England has already agreed to its being issued in English pounds. And if your major banks sign on . . ."

"Tell me about this traveler's check," Sir Thomas said.

Harry obliged, recounting almost word for word what he had read last night in Rose's notes. Although the peer's face remained expressionless, Harry was certain Sir Thomas hadn't missed the implication. If the British banks accepted the traveler's check because there was profit in it for them, then the smaller financial institutions would be next, followed by hotels and steamship and railroad companies, the very heart of Cooks Tours. Instead of paying Cooks for a package tour, a traveler could spend his money as he went, signing checks for transportation, accommodations, even meals.

"I assume you have proof that such an instrument exists?" Sir Thomas said at last.

For Harry this was the tricky part. He had no doubt Sir Thomas believed him but that didn't necessarily mean he would act. Veiled promises wouldn't cut any ice. He had to go with what he had: the truth.

"There is proof," Harry said with quiet confidence. "I saw it last night in Rose Jefferson's own handwriting at Berkeley Square. But there is no way I can bring it to you. I might be able to get it past Franklin but not his wife. And it really wouldn't serve my purposes to get caught."

Sir Thomas believed him. The circumstances under which Harry Taylor had seen Rose's plan were plausible. It followed that the details could not be removed from Berkeley Square without Taylor's jeopardizing himself. But what convinced Sir Thomas that Taylor was telling the truth was the fact that by coming here, he had placed his destiny in Sir Thomas's hands. Taylor didn't need to be caught stealing the plans in order to be thrown out of Global and into prison. Sir Thomas could arrange that with one cable to New York. Which brought up the obvious question.

"Assuming everything you've told me is accurate, what do you get out of all this, Mr. Taylor?"

"Two things," Harry replied quietly. "First, if I can show that Franklin Jefferson is incompetent, I become his successor at Global. Second, if for some reason things do not work out for me at Global, I want to have a comfortable alternative. I'm not asking for any money, Sir Thomas. But I will expect you to remember what I've done if I ever come to you again."

Sir Thomas was mildly surprised. At the very least he had expected Harry Taylor to ask him to set up a Swiss bank account with a generous deposit.

You're very clever, Mr. Taylor, but not hard. There are a lot of things you have yet to learn.

"Very well. Your terms are acceptable. I will investigate what you've told me. You'll be made aware of my decision very shortly."

Harry could not quite believe he had actually gotten what he came for. He sat in the darkened office wondering what else to say.

"Is there anything else, Mr. Taylor?"

"No . . ."

Oh yes there is, Sir Thomas thought, ringing for his evening secretary. *You're just beginning to know what it feels like to be a Pilate. Get used to it, Mr. Taylor. You'll never wash that stain away. You're not a hard man at all.*

Like most septuagenarians, Sir Thomas Ballantine needed little sleep. He did most of his important work through the night. As soon as Harry Taylor left, the chairman of Cooks had his secretary bring in the voluminous file on Rose Jefferson. Sifting through it, Sir Thomas carefully studied every aspect of the money order, then projected what its international equivalent would be. He sketched out the kinds of contracts Rose Jefferson would need with British banks, how and where the checks would be sold, the probable commission the banks would receive, the problems of a central clearinghouse, and, last, how the railroads, hotels, and steamship lines would be brought aboard. When he was satisfied that he had approximated Global's strategy as closely as possible, he was convinced that what Rose Jefferson was on the verge of accomplishing was both audacious and impressive—and for Cooks, potentially ruinous. Pity her dream would never see the light of day.

At five o'clock in the morning, when Sir Thomas finished drafting his notes and instructions, he felt a cold delight. Rose Jefferson wouldn't know what hit her.

It wasn't until noon the next day that Franklin had recovered sufficiently to get out of bed. Michelle thanked Nurse Martin for her care and then took Franklin out into the garden.

"How big a fool did I make of myself last night?" Franklin asked morosely.

His voice was thick with the residue of morphine and his pallor was only one sign of his ever-increasing fatigue.

"Nobody knows a thing," Michelle said firmly and explained what had happened and how fast Harry had brought Franklin home. "Thank God, Sir Dennis got to you so quickly." She paused. "I feel awful about having left you like that."

"How much does Harry know?" Franklin asked, squeezing her hand.

Michelle told him the story she had given Harry.

"He's smarter than that," Franklin replied. "But I think we can trust him."

Michelle wished she could give Harry the same vote of confidence. She couldn't. But right now there were more important things she had to deal with. Michelle went over her presentation to the bankers.

"You're amazing," Franklin said. "We're as good as in."

"We still have to wait for their final word," Michelle cautioned.

"A mere formality, my dear."

Before Michelle could reply, Hastings appeared saying there was a package for her. Michelle followed the majordomo into the house and was surprised when he handed her a cable.

"It's from Paris, ma'am," Hastings murmured. "I thought you would want to see it right away."

Michelle tore open the envelope, devoured the three sentences, and for the first time truly believed that the nightmare might be ending. Not only had Dr. Ernie Stillwater managed to track down Franklin's army medical records, but at this very moment they were on their way to London. In two or three days they would be in Sir Dennis's hands.

By ten o'clock in the morning, Sir Thomas Ballantine had put all his pieces in place. He had called the chairmen of the country's three largest banks and arranged to see each one separately. He savored lunch, tea, and dinner, listening as each man tried to bring the conversation around to the purpose of the meeting. Only at the very last minute did Sir Thomas slip in the knife, informing his guest that he was quite aware of the man's meeting with Michelle, what had been discussed, and what Rose Jefferson's overall plans were. Their identical expressions of shock pleased him enormously.

Satisfied, Sir Thomas sat back and watched his peers backpedal, swearing that they had had no idea their pending agreements with Global would be so upsetting to one of their largest depositors. Afterward, he chose to be magnanimous, reassuring everyone that Cooks's money would remain in their vaults as long as they understood one another; under no circumstances would any of them have anything to do with Rose Jefferson or her traveler's checks.

As he was driven home from the City, Sir Thomas asked himself what, if anything, he should do about Harry Taylor. He had known many men like Harry, adventurers all, to be used once and then written off. They all shared a common and ultimately fatal flaw: they were convinced they could outsmart all the people all the time. Sir Thomas smiled. One way or another, Harry Taylor would get his just reward. He didn't need Sir Thomas's help for that.

For the next forty-eight hours Michelle hardly knew what to do with herself. She jumped every time the phone rang and raced to the door when the chimes sounded.

"Well, you don't have to wait any longer," Franklin informed her on the third day. "That was Sir Manfred on the phone. He wants to see me right away."

"Oh, darling, that's wonderful!"

"I think you should come with me. After all, you were the one who convinced him."

Michelle shook her head. "No, thank you. I've had my share of your wheeling and dealing."

As Michelle walked Franklin to the door, a little voice whispered that she was making a mistake by not going with him.

A case of the jitters! she scolded herself.

"Good luck, darling!" she called after him.

Franklin blew her a kiss and stepped into the car.

Not five minutes after Franklin had left, Sir Dennis Pritchard called.

"I've received the file from Paris, Mrs. Jefferson. I must see you and your husband immediately."

When Michelle told him Franklin was out, the physician said, "Very well. I'll explain everything to you first, then it's imperative we bring Franklin to the hospital at once!"

"This can't be true." Michelle stared at Sir Dennis. "There must be some mistake."

Every physician since Hippocrates has heard those words, Sir Dennis thought. *Why didn't the father of medicine leave us an answer?*

"I wish there were, Mrs. Jefferson. However, the man who operated on your husband was one of France's best neurosurgeons. He was assisted by some top

246

American specialists. It was the best possible care Franklin could have received."

Michelle fought against believing that, against the words, written in French and English, which coldly told her what she had to accept. After being evacuated, Franklin had been taken to Paris, where, because of his battlefield heroism and General Pershing's personal interest, he had been given priority treatment. Dr. de Beaubien's initial notes indicated that the neurosurgeon had considered this a fairly routine operation. But as soon as de Beaubien and his colleagues had a firsthand look at the shrapnel in the skull, they revised their opinion. The metal fragments were embedded far too deep. Some were lodged against the spinal column. Any attempt to remove them would mean paralysis at best or, much more likely, death. Although inevitably the shrapnel would exert more and more pressure and cause severe debilitation, the decision was made to cancel the operation.

"Why didn't they tell him?" Michelle whispered.

"You'll note, Mrs. Jefferson, that de Beaubien passed that particular responsibility on to the army. Perhaps he and the other doctors believed it more charitable for Franklin not to know, at least for a little while."

"Then how could the army not *say* anything?"

Sir Dennis measured his words carefully. "What I'm about to say is nothing more than speculation but this is what I think happened. The army sent some kind of notification to your husband, either directly or through a doctor in New York. For one reason or another, either the message was intercepted or else the facts were deliberately withheld."

"By Harris!"

"Harris had a role to play in this," Sir Dennis agreed. "But I can't believe he was acting on his own initiative."

The full weight of the physician's inference came crashing down on Michelle.

"Rose? Rose kept this from him! But why?"

Sir Dennis shrugged. "It's possible, of course. I'm afraid you'll have to ask her. Believe me, I'd be just as intrigued as you by her explanation."

"I'll get one! What she's done is monstrous!"

"But first we must inform your husband," Sir Dennis said firmly. "He has to know what's been happening to him and why—"

"There must be something you can do!" Michelle cried. "There have been advances in surgery—"

"But nothing that would be of any help to Franklin," Sir Dennis said. As much as it pained him, he would not allow this woman to live on false hope. "We can try to control Franklin's condition, but ultimately . . ."

Michelle's last reserve of strength was sucked away and the pain spilled forth in her tears. She wept for Franklin and herself, for all the beautiful memories of their first weeks and the torment that Rose had subjected them to in New York. She cried for all the things they would never have, that would never be, things fate and Rose Jefferson had cheated them of.

Sir Manfred Smith rose when Franklin entered his palatial office with its vaulted, hand-painted ceiling and tall French windows overlooking the Royal Exchange. Unlike some of his colleagues, the chairman of Barclays genuinely liked the young American. When he saw the enthusiasm and anticipation on Franklin's face, he loathed what he was about to do.

"I take it you've had no ill effects from that unfortunate incident at the embassy?" Sir Manfred opened.

"None at all, thank you."

"I must say, your wife conducted herself most ably," the banker continued. "Unfortunately, after careful deliberation, we at Barclays do not believe we can participate in Global's traveler's check program."

A tremor worked its way down Franklin's body.

"I'm . . . I'm not sure I understand," he stammered. "Michelle told me you liked the idea, that you were going to encourage the others to go along."

"I admit giving Mrs. Jefferson that impression," Sir Manfred said somberly. "I can't tell you how much I regret doing so. I had no right to raise false expectations or presume to speak for my colleagues."

"But what's changed?" Franklin demanded. "You've never before indicated there were any problems. The Bank of England has approved the check. I don't understand. . . ."

"Mr. Jefferson, I'm not at liberty to go into details. I can only tell you that we have responsibilities to other clients, and our commitment to your project would be neither in their best interest nor the bank's."

Franklin had no idea what to say or how to argue. Everything had looked so promising, he had never considered rejection.

"Perhaps we could renegotiate certain clauses in the contract."

"There is really nothing to discuss. I'm sorry, but Barclays will pass on your offer—with regrets."

Sir Manfred rose and ushered Franklin toward the door.

"One last thing, Mr. Jefferson. Please don't blame your wife. She stood you well."

Without quite knowing it, Franklin found himself standing on Bartholomew Lane, buffeted by the pedestrian traffic that coursed ceaselessly through London's famous "Square Mile." When his chauffeur approached, Franklin told him he'd walk and made his way to Cornhill Street where the Westminster

Bank had its headquarters. Thirty minutes later, he emerged even more shaken than before. The chairman of Westminster had been very blunt: there was no hope of Global's doing any business with his institution.

His mind reeling, Franklin walked swiftly toward Gracechurch Street. There he caught the director of the London-India Bank, the third major player, in the lobby as he was leaving for lunch.

"I'm surprised you haven't received our official notice, Mr. Jefferson," the portly director said, obviously eager to get rid of his unexpected visitor. "I had it sent around by messenger first thing this morning. However, since you're here, I can tell you that London-India has no interest in your proposal."

The director tried to brush by him but Franklin grabbed him by the sleeve.

"The least you can do is tell me why!" Franklin shouted.

The director looked around and saw that two beefy porters had noticed the commotion.

"Bank policy," he said loudly, successfully attracting their attention. "Now be so kind as to let go of me!"

Before Franklin had the chance to do so, a pair of strong arms seized him from behind.

"Do as the guv' asks, sir," one of the porters told him. "We don't want a scene, do we?"

Franklin snarled, lashing back with his heel. The porter holding him howled in pain. Franklin pivoted and drove his fist into the other's solar plexus, doubling him over. Before anyone else could touch him, Franklin had the bank director up against the wall.

"What's going on?" he hissed. "Why are the doors closing on me?"

The banker whimpered but said nothing. Franklin's hand moved so quickly it was a blur. Blood erupted from the director's shattered nose.

"Why?"

"You bastard!" the director sobbed. "It's Cooks! No one's going to go against them to do business with you!"

Franklin couldn't believe what he was hearing.

"How? How did Cooks hear about this?"

Before he had his answer Franklin heard footsteps pounding behind him. He released his grip and plunged through a knot of onlookers and into the street, disappearing into the noontime crowd.

A black anger carried Franklin along, pumping adrenaline into his legs as he ran toward Lombard Street. He felt so lightheaded he thought he could go on for miles. He slowed only when he saw the giant advertising sign curving around the top of the prewar building that was Cooks's headquarters.

It was impossible for Cooks to have learned about the traveler's checks! The officials at the Bank of England and the individual bank directors had been sworn to secrecy. Besides them, only he, Rose, and Michelle knew all the details.

Franklin felt the sweat pouring off him. One way or another he'd damn well find out who was responsible, even if he had to beat the answer out of old man Ballantine himself.

It didn't come to that. Crossing the road, Franklin, out of the corner of his eye, saw a gleaming black Rolls-Royce park in front of Cooks. As a uniformed porter rushed up, Franklin headed in the same direction. Only one man merited such instant attention: Sir Thomas Ballantine. Franklin watched the elderly chairman step out of the car. He was about to shout when the words died in his throat. After Sir Thomas came Harry Taylor. The two men exchanged words, shook hands, then Harry started walking away.

Franklin squeezed his eyes shut but couldn't keep the pain away. Suddenly the world went black and he felt himself plunging headfirst down a long, bottomless tunnel where none could hear his screams.

"Tell me again what happened," Michelle said.

The chauffeur quickly recounted the incident at the London-India Bank, how he had run into the lobby and seen Franklin manhandling its director.

"He was out the door in a flash, ma'am. I tried to stop him but he was too quick. With the traffic and all, I couldn't find him."

"Do you have any idea what could have caused the incident in the lobby?" Michelle pressed.

"No, ma'am. But he was out of sorts as soon as he left Barclays."

Dear God!

Michelle turned to Hastings. "You said Franklin came home?"

The butler nodded. "Mr. Jefferson rushed past me as though the devil himself was after him. He went into the library, stayed a few minutes, then left again."

"Couldn't you at least have tried to stop him?"

Hastings lowered his eyes. "I'm sorry, ma'am. I know Mr. Jefferson isn't well. But you had to have seen him for yourself. He was . . . out of control. To be honest, ma'am, I was afraid of him."

Michelle shook her head. "No, Hastings. I'm the one who should apologize. There was nothing you could do." She looked at both men. "Did he say anything, anything at all, that would give you an idea of where he might go?"

When neither ventured a guess, Michelle didn't know what to think. Obviously something terrible had happened at Barclays to trigger Franklin's bizarre spree. It took little imagination to guess what that was. But now she had

250

to concentrate on finding Franklin. Obviously he had come home to get something, something he needed before he went . . . where?

"Hastings, come with me. We're going to look at everything in the library. When we find what it was he took, we might know where he went."

"What would we be looking for, ma'am?"

"I wish I knew. Something out of place, something missing."

Michelle started with Franklin's desk. She went through the drawers one by one, finding nothing amiss until she noticed the scratches on the lock on the bottom one. Michelle frowned. Both she and Franklin had a key.

Or could it have been someone else? Who else had been in the house?

Before Michelle could come up with the answer, Hastings called out, "Ma'am, you'd best see this!"

Michelle darted to the bookcase, watching as Hastings pressed his fingers against what appeared to be a solid panel that then popped back to reveal a secret drawer. The inside was lined with red velvet, with a mold in the shape of a gun.

"Hastings—"

"Ma'am, I swear, I had completely forgotten about it! Mr. Jefferson's friend brought it back as a war souvenir, a German Luger. The gun laws are quite strict in this country, and since he didn't wish to go to the trouble of declaring it as a war memento, and perhaps having it confiscated, he built this bolt hole for it."

"Why didn't you tell me?" Michelle cried.

"Because I don't remember telling Mr. Jefferson about it either," Hastings said miserably. "He must have found it on his own."

Why did you need the gun, Franklin? Who hurt you so badly that this was the only thing you could think of? Sir Manfred Smith . . .

The explanation had a hollow ring to it. Michelle's thought returned to the jimmied drawer. She had opened it last the day of the embassy party. Since then, neither she nor Franklin had needed to unlock it. And they hadn't had anyone to the house—

"Harry . . ." Michelle whispered.

Harry Taylor was in a jaunty mood when he returned to his Belgravia flat, taking the front steps two at a time. This morning the Cooks chairman's secretary had summoned him to Ballantine's fortress-like mansion in St. John's Wood.

"Your information was accurate," Sir Thomas had informed him. "Rest assured that Rose Jefferson will get nowhere with her traveler's checks. If you wish to act on the consequences of this, I suggest you do so now."

Harry fully intended to. All the way home he had been mentally composing

251

his cable to Rose. *And Rose,* thought Harry as he opened the door, *will do the rest for me.*

He knew immediately that something was wrong. An empty apartment gives off nothing. Inside, Harry felt a terrible presence.

"Hello, Harry."

Franklin was sitting in a black leather armchair in the parlor facing the front hall. Harry opened his mouth to speak, then saw Franklin's eyes, lifeless and unblinking. In his hand was a huge Luger pistol, pointed at Harry.

"Franklin—"

"Come closer, Harry."

Harry obeyed, carefully taking three steps into the parlor.

"Why did you do it, Harry? Why did you betray me?"

Franklin's cold, pitiless voice made Harry shiver.

"I've never done anything to hurt you, Franklin," Harry replied carefully.

"Oh? And what were you doing with Sir Thomas Ballantine this morning?"

Harry knew he should answer immediately. But he was human, and as hard as he tried to prevent it, the surprise registered on his expression.

"I asked you a question, Harry."

"He'll tell you, Franklin, but not now. Not this way. He'll tell everything we want to know to the police."

Neither man had heard Michelle come through the front door.

"Michelle, thank God you're here!" Harry exclaimed.

"Don't move!" Franklin screamed.

He looked at Michelle and for the first time his hand trembled.

"Do you know what he did to us?" he whispered.

"I know, darling," Michelle said as calmly as she could. "And he'll pay for that. I promise. But not if you hurt him."

Franklin seemed not to have heard her.

"Do you know how many men I've killed, Harry? Dozens. Maybe hundreds. And they were soldiers. Better men than you. I could kill you so easily, Harry. . . ."

Michelle was terrified by the madness dancing in Franklin's eyes.

"Franklin," she said softly. "Do you remember Paris, the surgery you had there?"

Franklin stared at her wildly. "I was never in Paris! What are you talking about?"

"You were, darling! You were going to have an operation on your wound, only—"

Harry chose that moment to move. Unwittingly, Franklin had lowered the gun and his attention was focused on Michelle. Harry was gambling that he

252

could get into the front hall before Franklin had a chance to react. He was wrong.

The soldier's instinct took over. Franklin saw the blur of a moving man and in the same motion raised the gun and squeezed the trigger. The shot exploded like a thunderclap. By all rights the bullet should have caught Harry in midstride, well before he reached the hall. But instead of going in front of Michelle, Harry had leaped behind her. It was Michelle's scream that shattered the last vestige of Franklin's sanity.

Time froze. Both men stared at Michelle, a red stain spreading over her white satin blouse, just above her breast. Finally Harry looked up at Franklin, his expression one of total resignation. He knew then that he too would die.

The gun clattered to the floor. Franklin took one step forward, hesitated, then took a second and a third. He looked straight ahead and walked past his wife's body as though it were invisible. It wasn't until Harry heard the door open and click shut that he realized he had been holding his breath all this time.

— 30 —

Monk McQueen's six-foot-three-inch frame was stretched along the couch in his office. His arm dangled over the side, fingers trailing on the floor. Except for the ice pack covering his face from forehead to nose, the publisher of Q magazine looked as if he had given up the ghost. He couldn't quite recall yesterday's birthday celebration held in his honor except that the 21 had magically procured some prime Canadian rye whiskey. The rest was history best left unexplored.

"Mr. McQueen!"

Monk cringed as the door slammed.

"Jimmy, don't shout," he said hoarsely.

The editor thrust a cable into Monk's limp hand.

"This just came in. You'd better have a look."

Monk turned his head and the ice pack slid to the floor. He dabbed his face with a towel and tried to focus his attention on the words, which, because of an erratic typewriter, seemed to jump all over the page. The message sobered him up instantly.

MRS. MICHELLE JEFFERSON SHOT BUT IN STA-
BLE CONDITION. SHE URGENTLY REQUESTS
YOUR PRESENCE. NO REFERENCE TO INCI-
DENT TO BE MADE TO GLOBAL. AM UNDER
INSTRUCTIONS TO AWAIT REPLY.

DENNIS PRITCHARD, M.D., F.R.C.S.
ATTENDING PHYSICIAN
GROSVENOR HOSPITAL
LONDON WEST ONE

"When did this come in?" Monk rasped.

"Ten minutes ago."

"Anything on the news wires?"

"Not a peep."

"Calls from Rose?"

The editor shook his head.

Monk heaved himself off the couch. "Get me on the first vessel to Southampton."

"Way ahead of you, Mr. McQueen. There's a ship leaving this afternoon. It's
not the U.S.S. *Constitution*—"

"It'll do. Who else knows about this?"

"The cable operator."

"Tell him to keep his mouth shut. Now go get me some cash and call upstairs
and have my housekeeper pack my bags."

Only when he was alone and had reread the cable did the full impact of the
words strike Monk. Who had shot Michelle? Why? And where was Franklin?
Why hadn't Michelle mentioned him?

As Monk scribbled his reply to London, the questions kept pouring out.
Monk hoped that the ship Jimmy Pearce had booked him on had a good
wireless operator. He would be a very busy man.

The quiet district of Mayfair had been turned upside down. The London
Metropolitan Police flooded the area with men, assisted by Scotland Yard
detectives. Streets were blocked off, alleys, lanes, and mews searched, residents
confronted by grim-faced men who wanted to know if they had seen anyone
suspicious. Even if they hadn't, the residents were politely but firmly asked to
cooperate. Gardens, terraces, and garages were searched.

"I'm beginning to think Mr. Jefferson has given us the slip," Inspector
Geoffrey Rawlins of Scotland Yard said.

While his detectives did their work in the parlor, Rawlins had spirited Harry

254

Taylor into the relative quiet of the kitchen to take his statement. Looking through his notes, Rawlins asked himself why he didn't quite believe that this was as open-and-shut a case as the facts seemed to indicate.

"You're certain, Mr. Taylor, that you can't think of any reason why Mr. Jefferson would want to shoot his wife?"

"No," Harry said wearily. "I've told you everything I know."

Harry gripped his coffee cup with both hands. He was facing a catastrophe that could ruin him, yet he was convinced there was a way to turn it into an opportunity. After Michelle had been rushed to the hospital and Rawlins had taken him into the kitchen to begin the questioning, he saw how he could make this happen.

Harry withheld nothing from the Scotland Yard inspector. He began by explaining what he was doing in London and how long he had known Franklin. He told Rawlins about Franklin's behavior at the embassy party, how he had helped him home, and what Franklin's nurse had later told him about Franklin's previous attacks. Harry was careful to include the fact that Michelle had made him promise not to discuss the incident with anyone and that he had kept his word.

As soon as he was satisfied that he had drawn a portrait of a totally deranged man, Harry began weaving in the lies. He had no idea why Franklin had broken into his home and was waiting for him with a gun. Obviously Michelle had discovered Franklin was missing and had come to Harry's apartment to ask him to help her find her husband. But Franklin was already there, raving about the British banks having somehow betrayed him. Michelle had tried to reason with him but it was too late.

"What I still don't understand," Rawlins said, lighting a cigarette, "is why Mr. Jefferson shot only his wife. Why not you too? Why drop the gun and simply walk away?"

"Franklin's insane, Inspector," Harry replied quietly. "Can you explain what a madman does, or why? I certainly can't."

"Perhaps Pritchard will be able to tell us that," Rawlins said thoughtfully. "Or Mr. Jefferson, if we find him first."

A constable entered the kitchen and whispered something to Rawlins, who listened intently.

"Well, at least when we catch up with Mr. Jefferson, the charge will be reduced to attempted murder. According to Pritchard, Mrs. Jefferson is going to be all right."

"Thank God for that," Harry said fervently. He paused. "Inspector, I've helped you all I can but I also have a responsibility to Miss Jefferson and Global. By tonight this thing will hit the newspapers here. I have to let her know before the same happens in New York."

"Yes, of course, Mr. Taylor. Where can I reach you if I have any further questions?"

"At the Ritz. After what's happened, I can't really stay here. . . ."

And if Michelle starts talking, you'll have a hell of a lot more questions for me!

Upstairs, Harry threw some clothes and his shaving kit into an overnight bag and walked past the bobby standing duty on his doorstep. Thirty minutes later he was installed in a suite at the Ritz, composing his message to Rose. He worked very carefully to create the image he wanted her to see. The situation was grave. Franklin had shot Michelle, whose condition was serious. Franklin himself was missing, the object of a police manhunt. Harry was taking charge of the situation and would do his best to protect the Jeffersons' interests until Rose arrived.

Harry reread the text. He knew that as soon as Michelle could talk, his version of events would be challenged. From what she had said in trying to calm Franklin, Harry was certain that Michelle knew he had done something against Global. But Franklin couldn't have told her that he had seen Harry and Sir Thomas Ballantine together.

But it might be enough for Rawlins to believe Franklin had intended to shoot me all along.

Harry didn't underestimate the taciturn inspector's abilities or intuition. Still, Rawlins couldn't very well accuse him of anything. After all, Franklin had been the one to pull the trigger.

Harry Taylor's cable was transmitted at four o'clock in the afternoon, London time, three hours after Sir Dennis Pritchard's message had reached Monk McQueen. The time difference was crucial. While Harry's cable was being delivered at Lower Broadway, the vessel carrying Monk to Southampton was casting off from its berth at the Hudson River pier. The next British-bound ship, the U.S.S. *America*, would not leave for two days.

In New York, Rose Jefferson was on tenterhooks. The Fourth of July had come and gone and still there was no word from Franklin. On the same day Franklin was meeting with the British bankers Rose had held a spectacular Independence Day celebration at Dunescrag for five hundred friends, business associates, and political figures from all across the country. She hoped that given the time difference and a little luck, he might send word of a successful deal before the festivities ended.

The next day Rose couldn't concentrate on business and looked after some personal affairs. She purchased a stud farm in Kentucky she had had her eye on for some time, as well as a large parcel of oceanfront property in La Jolla,

California, where Frank Lloyd Wright, the architect, would design a West Coast home for her. She placed a successful bid on several Old Masters with Sotheby's and declined a dinner invitation from Randolph Hearst. At the end of the day, with still no word from London, Rose dispatched a cable.

When Rose returned to Talbot House she left instructions with Albany to wake her the minute a reply was delivered. Even though she promised herself not to worry, she did not fall asleep until three o'clock in the morning. Four hours later, back in her office, she sent two more cables, one of them to Harry Taylor.

In her heart of hearts Rose confessed that she missed Harry more than she had expected. Not having him beside her at night had created an emptiness she had never before experienced. But she also longed for the way he made her laugh, and how she felt in his arms when they danced. More often than she wished, Rose, during her nights alone, wondered what Harry might be doing at that moment. At the end of the second day, when no word had come from him either, Rose's conviction of looming disaster grew. One minute she was angry, thinking that Franklin had successfully concluded the deal, then thoughtlessly forgotten to let her know. The next, she was desperately worried about him, certain that he'd had another accident. Finally, Rose couldn't bear the tension any longer. She told her secretary to book her passage on the next liner to Southampton.

"This just arrived," Mary Kirkpatrick announced breathlessly, bursting into Rose's office.

Rose tore open the envelope. The sheer length of the cable made her heart rejoice. It could only be from Franklin!

"Mary, leave me, please."

"Is anything wrong, Miss Jefferson?"

"Just go!"

Rose smoothed the cable out on her desk and, holding her breath, reread the first few sentences. She managed several more before her eyes clouded with tears. Like a swimmer flailing toward shore, she struggled on until she had read every word. Out of the millions of thoughts racing through her mind, one struck it like a physical blow:

What have I done to him?

The room, if it could be called that, was stifling. Located on the top floor of an East End tenement, it was no larger than a closet. The tiny bed frame was pitted with rust, the mattress sagging and stained. Brown water dripped from the faucet into a sink blackened by decay. Above it, a grimy, cracked window looked out on the air shaft and the crumbling brickwork of the building across the way. Wafer-thin walls, covered in water-spotted floral paper, did nothing to keep out the shrill cries from the other rooms. Over everything hung the odor of garbage from the alley below.

Franklin Jefferson lay curled up on the bed, his hands clasped together between his legs. He had his back to the room and stared mindlessly at the flower pattern on the wall. If asked, he could not have said how long he had been lying like this, where he was, or how he had gotten there. The only thing he knew was that some time, long ago, he had shot his wife.

Franklin squeezed his eyes shut and prayed for pain. If the pain was severe enough, he would black out. It was his only relief. Otherwise he remained at the mercy of the grotesque, twisted images that crouched in his mind, like gargoyles waiting to pounce. Sometimes he heard himself whimper but no one came to help him, because, he was convinced, the only person who could have lay dead by his own hand.

Franklin's memories began with the gun shot. He recalled the minutest detail—how the revolver had bucked in his hands, the bitter stink of cordite, the terror and disbelief in Michelle's eyes, how her body had spun away, the blood spreading across her chest. He remembered standing over her for what seemed a very long time. But he couldn't bring himself to touch her. Instead he had simply walked away.

Franklin had no idea how far he had wandered or what part of London he had ended up in. He remembered a huge market, with rows of stalls filled with fruits, vegetables, freshly gutted fish, and bloodied sides of beef hanging on hooks. He was jostled at every turn. All around him, people were squabbling and shouting. And there had been a girl . . . a very young girl with corn-flax hair and painted red lips who had taken his arm and called him "luv." She had steered him out of the market and brought him into a building. Franklin remembered giving the girl, whose name he couldn't remember, his wallet. The girl had brought him into this room and made him lie down on the bed. Then she had taken off her clothes and he saw how thin her body was, all bone covered with pasty skin. He had rolled away. Maybe she had said something and he'd shouted back. The next time he'd looked around she was gone. . . .

Nothing matters, Franklin thought, gritting his teeth against the pain. *I'm safe here. No one will ever find me. Soon everything will be all right. . . .*

At that moment, the steel fragment in Franklin's skull shifted a fraction of a millimeter, adding infinitesimal pressure on an artery. The constriction reduced the blood flow, and the brain, starving for oxygen, began to dim. Another man would have been terrified, but to Franklin Jefferson, the closing darkness was a sweet blessing.

Throughout the afternoon the grim details poured in from London. Rose's conference table was littered with cables from Scotland Yard, Sir Dennis

258

Pritchard, and Harry Taylor. In one corner, Hugh O'Neill sat huddled over the telephone, talking quietly to yet another New York newspaper editor. The press had received the story off their London wires at one o'clock in the afternoon. Since then the Global switchboard had been jammed with calls.

At the far end of the room, Eric Gollant was on another line, talking quietly to the men who represented the British banks in New York, trying to find out what had happened at Franklin's meeting with Barclays. The accountant had a lot of favors outstanding on Wall Street. One by one, he was calling them in.

Amid all this activity, Rose felt worse than useless. Everything possible was being done, leaving her to log the cables as they arrived and watch helplessly as the tragedy unfolded. She was grateful when Sir Dennis Pritchard informed her that Michelle was out of danger. On the other hand, the news from Inspector Rawlins ate away at her. Franklin still hadn't been found. The manhunt would continue through the night, and Rawlins had promised to contact her as soon as he had a break. Rose knew that waiting and doing nothing would drive her mad. She called over Hugh O'Neill and Eric Gollant and informed them that she would sail to England.

"I guess you have no choice," O'Neill agreed. "I've already cabled our lawyers over there. They're ready to act the minute the police find him."

"Then it's settled," Rose murmured.

Mary Kirkpatrick had called the steamship line and learned that the U.S.S. *America* was fully booked. Rose telephoned the company chairman at home, explained the circumstances, and was assured that a suite would be available on the next sailing, the day after tomorrow.

"I'd like to be alone now," Rose said to the two men. "Thank you for all you've done. I couldn't have managed without you."

Rose went over to the ancient French armoire that served as a bar and poured herself a glass of burgundy. Slowly its warmth dispelled the cold shivers that crawled under her skin. Rose curled up in the corner of the sofa. From where she sat she could see the photographs on the sideboard by her desk. Franklin and herself as children, Franklin graduating from Yale, Franklin in his baggy khaki uniform, grinning at the camera.

"Please, Lord," she whispered. "Don't punish him like this!"

- 3| -

The ships carrying Monk and Rose were a third of the way to England when Michelle Jefferson drifted into consciousness at Grosvenor Hospital.

Her first sensation was one of light, then she felt the throbbing in her right shoulder. Her fingers explored and found the surgical gauze bandage.

"You're going to be right as rain," Sir Dennis Pritchard said. He moved from the foot of the bed and took her hand.

"Franklin . . ." Michelle did not miss the concern in his expression. "Please . . ."

Reluctantly Pritchard told her about Franklin's disappearance.

"The police haven't found him yet, but believe me, it's just a matter of time. They're doing all they can."

The surgeon expected a tearful outburst and had medication ready. Instead, Michelle turned away. Pritchard's words numbed her. At the same time, she saw herself walking into Harry's home, seeing Franklin with the gun, Harry flying past her, the awful explosion. . . .

Michelle's hands were tightly clenched in her lap and it was all she could do to keep from trembling. She felt as though the earth had dropped away beneath her feet. What had happened to Franklin was more terrible than she had ever imagined, and her intuition told her that even if he was found alive, the harm would never be undone.

Michelle turned to Pritchard. "I want to talk to the police now."

Four hours after his vessel had docked at Southampton, Monk McQueen arrived at Berkeley Square. Throughout his voyage he had kept in constant touch with Jimmy Pearce in New York. Every time a cable came in, Monk expected to learn ·that the police had apprehended Franklin. He couldn't believe that after six days his friend still hadn't been found.

Monk showed his passport to the bobby in front of the door and was escorted inside. A tall, handsome man rose to greet him, introducing himself as Sir Dennis Pritchard.

"Is she all right?" Monk demanded.

"Mrs. Jefferson is mending nicely," Pritchard assured him. "The bullet— there was only one—caught her in the shoulder, just below the breastbone. It nicked some bone but touched no major arteries or any vital organs. Since it was steel-jacketed, the exit was clean."

From his combat experience Monk knew that Michelle was in no danger.

"However," the surgeon continued, "there's a great deal more involved than a tragic shooting. Mrs. Jefferson has been through a dreadful ordeal. Please don't tire her, Mr. McQueen. She needs as much rest as possible."

Monk took a deep breath and slowly went upstairs. He knocked and pushed the door open.

She was thinner than Monk remembered but no less beautiful. Her hair, a fan of red shot through with gold, shimmered against the embroidered pillow-case. Her eyes sparkled in surprise yet somehow they were different. The luster of innocence and wonder had fallen away, leaving scars that would never heal.

Michelle raised her hand to welcome him. "Monk . . ."

He sat on the edge of the daybed and, careful not to touch her bandaged shoulder, embraced her, stroking her hair while her tears streamed down his cheeks. Seven months had gone by, and not a day that he hadn't thought of her, remembered her scent, heard the delicate peal of her laughter.

"Are you all right?"

"I'll be fine. I can't tell you how wonderful it is to see you."

Michelle wiped her cheeks, curling a tissue into a tight ball. "Franklin . . .?"

Monk shook his head. "They haven't found him yet."

"But you will."

He was taken aback by the emphatic declaration.

"Michelle, I don't know what I can do."

"You know Franklin better than anyone. You'll find him. You have to. . . ."

The last thing Monk wanted was to make promises he couldn't keep. But since the police hadn't made any progress, he had no choice.

"I need to know what happened, Michelle."

Monk winced at the pain that filled her eyes.

"There's so much. You won't believe me but I swear it's all true."

"I'll believe you. Just tell me."

Slowly Michelle took him through the nightmare that had begun back in New York. She recounted the awful crossing and the painful tests Franklin had been subjected to. She spoke about her desperate search for the army medical records in Paris and how, at last, she and Dr. Pritchard had learned the truth. Monk could not believe some of the things he was hearing.

"You mean Franklin still doesn't know what's been happening to him?"

"There wasn't any time to tell him. Everything was happening so fast and then Harry Taylor became involved."

Monk's eyes narrowed. "Taylor? What's he got to do with this?"

261

Michelle explained how Rose had sent Harry Taylor to London to help organize a sales force for the traveler's check, except that, as it turned out, Harry knew nothing about Franklin's dealings with the British banks. She told Monk about her reservations concerning Harry, then about finding the jimmied drawer and suspecting that Harry had, for some reason, broken into it to search through Franklin's private papers.

"As soon as I discovered this, I went to Harry's flat. Franklin was already there, with the gun. He was going on about the way Harry had betrayed him. I tried to calm Franklin down. I know I could have if Harry hadn't run. . . . He was shooting at Harry, Monk, not at me."

Monk struggled to take in what Michelle was saying to him. He knew a great deal about Harry Taylor but obviously not enough.

"What did you tell the police?"

Michelle smiled wanly. "The truth. That somehow Harry had sabotaged Franklin's business deal. When Franklin discovered this, his anger got the better of him. I swore Franklin never meant to hurt anyone, that the gun went off by accident."

"Did they believe you?"

"I don't think so." Michelle squeezed Monk's hand. "I should never have let things go so far. If I had brought him home from the embassy myself, none of this would have happened. It's just that Franklin had worked so hard. . . ."

"It's not your fault. You have to believe that!"

"Franklin knew he couldn't keep going the way he had," Michelle said softly. "He wanted to tell Rose but I stopped him. I couldn't bear the thought of her coming back into our lives." She looked up at Monk. "Do you think she knew about Franklin's condition all along?"

"I'm sure of it," Monk said.

"Then why hide it from him?" Michelle cried. "Why keep it a secret from *both* of us?"

Monk suspected he knew the answer but it wouldn't do Michelle any good right now.

"I want you to rest."

Michelle clung to him as he tried to move away. "Where are you going?"

"To talk to the police."

"But you'll come back here . . . stay with me?"

"I'll be back, I promise."

Downstairs, Monk poured himself a stiff whiskey from a silver flask and tried to make sense out of what he'd learned. Rose's actions were unconscionable. But not only hers. Rose could only have received Franklin's medical file from a qualified army doctor . . . someone like William Harris, who, after becoming

Franklin's physician, had suddenly gotten his hands on enough money to establish an exclusive Park Avenue practice.

She bought him and his silence. . . .

Monk checked his rising anger, trying to think clearly and solve the final riddle: if Rose had known the truth about Franklin's condition, why had she sent him to London? Even with the help of whiskey, the answer eluded him.

Monk placed his glass on the sideboard and left the house. Outside, he asked the bobby for directions to Scotland Yard.

Monk McQueen spent the rest of the day with Inspector Rawlins. He was impressed both by the man and by the kind of search he had been leading, overlooking nothing.

"So you see, we've pretty much eliminated the places someone of Mr. Jefferson's station would frequent," Rawlins concluded. "I've posted men in the railway stations in case he tries to leave London. The newspapers have been running an artist's sketch and the BBC has aired special bulletins. We've also expanded our search to include the less glamorous districts of our city where we have the cooperation of certain individuals."

By "certain individuals," Monk assumed the inspector meant informers.

"There's another thing to consider, Inspector. Franklin's a seasoned combat soldier. He might instinctively search out places that cater to former servicemen."

Rawlins made notes.

"I'd like your permission to place a personal appeal in the newspapers," Monk added. "If he sees it, he may come out. I'd want the same arrangement with the BBC."

"Excellent idea," Rawlins agreed. "If he should contact you, you will of course inform me immediately."

"That depends on a couple of things, Inspector. Will you let me conduct my own search?"

Rawlins considered. "I don't see why not."

"I would also like to know who you think Franklin was shooting at."

"I'm not sure I follow you, Mr. McQueen."

"Michelle told me you weren't convinced things happened the way she said they did. She thinks Harry Taylor told you something else."

"It's not my policy to discuss witnesses' testimonies with the public, Mr. McQueen."

"I'm not asking you to divulge confidential information, Inspector. I'm looking for anything that might help Franklin."

Monk sketched out what Michelle had told him. "All I need to know is whether Harry Taylor's version of events jibes," he finished.

"How well do you know Mr. Taylor?" asked Rawlins.

"Personally, not at all. But I could have my magazine get as much background as you need for your investigation."

"I think that would assist us handily," Rawlins murmured. "To answer your question, what we have are two different accounts based on the same facts. Mr. Taylor doesn't deny that Mr. Jefferson accused him of 'betraying' him, as he put it. However, he insists that Mr. Jefferson was raving and that he has no idea what he could have been referring to. On the other hand, Mrs. Jefferson corroborates her husband's accusation. When I pressed Mr. Taylor on this discrepancy, he insisted that Mrs. Jefferson was only trying to protect her husband."

"Whom do you believe?"

"Mr. McQueen, that's beside the point. The fact is that Mrs. Jefferson has been unable to furnish me with any proof of malfeasance on the part of Mr. Taylor. Given that, I can hardly accuse him of lying."

"At least not yet."

Both men rose. "There's just one more thing," Monk said. "Are you going on the assumption that Franklin may be armed?"

"I must. He managed to get a gun once. He may do so again. And as you've just reminded me, he was a professional soldier."

"I'm asking you for a big favor, Inspector," Monk said. "When you find him, call me. I'll go in and get him. Nobody else needs to get hurt."

"Fair enough," Rawlins agreed. "But I hope for everyone's sake you recognize what kind of man we're up against."

Nobody knows that, Monk thought. *Not anymore . . .*

For the next five days and nights Monk McQueen prowled the city's underbelly. He had worked out his itinerary with the help of local newspapermen who knew the city as intimately as any bobby. Armed with their information and contacts, Monk made his way across the docks, checking every pub, cafe, and flophouse. He stopped at seamen's churches and shelters and spoke with the clergy who ministered to transient flocks. In the gaslit streets of Whitechapel and Notting Hill, he moved from prostitute to prostitute, showing them Franklin's photograph, giving them a number to call if they saw this man, promising a rich reward for their cooperation. In the gritty dawn he visited the fish and meat markets, spreading pound notes, asking still more questions.

At dawn, Monk would return to Berkeley Square, accompanied by the clip-clop of milkwagon horses. Michelle always had breakfast waiting and sat across the table watching him eat, coaxing him for details.

As the days passed Michelle came to crave her time with Monk. Although she was every bit as anxious for word about Franklin, the loneliness and fear she lived with were receding. It was then that she understood Monk was the only one who could give her the greatest gift of all, something which, no matter what happened in the future, she would have forever.

Monk nodded to the bobby on duty and let himself in. This time Michelle wasn't there to greet him. Monk checked the kitchen, found it empty, and decided Michelle was still asleep. Silently he went upstairs, washed, and got ready for bed.

"Monk . . ."

She was standing in the doorway, wearing an ankle-length diaphanous gown with rosebud clasps at the shoulders. Her feet were bare and her hair trailed over her shoulders like the setting sun.

"Michelle . . ."

Her name caught in his throat and Monk shivered as she came toward him.

"You don't know how I've longed for you to be here," she said quietly, never taking her eyes off his. "How much I needed to hear your voice and feel your touch."

"Michelle . . ."

She pressed a finger to his lips. "Don't say a word. Just come with me."

Monk let her guide him to the bed.

"You're going to say this isn't right but that's not true. Nothing is the way you think it is, or the way I wanted it to be. And when Franklin comes back, it will never be the same again. He's dying, Monk, and I have no strength left to see him through it, to give him what he will need. Give me that strength, Monk. Give me the love you've always had. And let me love you. . . ."

His fingers touched her breast and his lips followed and every sense that had lain dormant for so long began to stir within her. Michelle gave herself to Monk with a freedom born of desperation. Hopes and illusions fell away like scales, replaced by a fierce burning that rose from her loins, overwhelming everything except this precious moment.

"I love you, Monk," she heard herself whispering over and over again.

The words flowed with such passion that she never doubted their sincerity. To be able to say them, after everything that had happened, seemed the greatest miracle of all.

Sir Dennis took great pleasure from his hobby, gardening. At the back of his office was a tiny paradise filled with rose bushes, tulip beds, and gardenias. His favorite time was the morning, when, after carefully inspecting his horticultural handiwork, he could enjoy his tea, satisfied that here, at least, everything was well with the world. Except this morning Sir Dennis's keen nose detected an alien smell in his floral kingdom. Frowning, Pritchard began working his way around the garden until he came to the gate.

"Who the devil are you?"

The creature in front of him was little more than a cadaver. The skin had shrunk around the bones of his cheeks, giving him a haunted expression. His hair was greasy and matted and his hands and nails were filthy. Yet the suit, in spite of its grimy condition, was of excellent quality and cut.

"Who are you?" Pritchard repeated, puzzled.

"Don't you recognize me, Doctor? Do I look that bad?"

The voice jogged Pritchard's memory.

"Jefferson? Franklin Jefferson? Good Lord, man, is that you?"

Sir Dennis steered Franklin to a chair and looked him up and down for obvious injuries.

"Where have you been? Are you all right?"

"I don't really know," Franklin replied softly.

"Franklin, do you know what happened to you?"

Sir Dennis wasn't afraid of Franklin's becoming violent. His patient appeared so malnourished, Pritchard would have been surprised if he could lift a spoon.

"I shot Michelle. I killed her. After that I ran away. I came here to surrender myself." Franklin paused. "So I guess you'd better call the police."

Sir Dennis leaned forward on the table. "Franklin, I want you to listen to me very carefully. You shot Michelle but you *didn't* kill her. The bullet hit her in the shoulder. She was taken to hospital and treated but she's made a full recovery. Do you understand what I'm telling you? Michelle is alive!"

Sir Dennis saw the flashes in Franklin's eyes dissolve. His lower lip trembled and his head drooped.

"I didn't kill her?" he whispered.

"I swear to you she's alive and well!"

Franklin Jefferson hunched over, his body racked by sobs.

Sir Dennis seized his arm. "Franklin, do you remember where you shot Michelle?"

Franklin shook his head. "No . . ."

"It was at Mr. Taylor's flat. Do you know why you were there?"

"Harry? I went to Harry's flat? Why?"

Sir Dennis didn't press him. Obviously Franklin had suffered a complete blackout as far as incidents before the shooting were concerned. Some of those might, in time, come back to him. But there were other, equally important things he could tell him.

"Franklin, do you know how long you've been gone?"

"I saw a newspaper with the date on it. Eleven days, I think."

"Yes, that's right. And where were you?"

Franklin looked down at himself. "Somewhere god-awful. I remember a small room. . . . There was a girl. She brought me food." He shook his head helplessly. "I don't remember any more until this morning, when I woke up and found myself like this. I had to come here. I didn't know what else to do."

Pritchard's heart went out to this tortured man. He knew he should call the police immediately. But he also had a duty to try to alleviate Franklin's agony. Pritchard made his decision.

"Franklin, I'm going to tell you something you must know. I want you to listen very carefully."

Choosing his words cautiously, the physician explained exactly what Franklin had been suffering from ever since his return from France.

"Do you understand what I'm telling you?" Sir Dennis asked at last.

Franklin looked up at him. "That the shrapnel can never be removed from my skull without killing me and that eventually it'll do me in anyway."

Suddenly, Franklin threw his head back and cried, "Why didn't anyone tell me? Why couldn't I know what was happening to me? Why didn't Michelle say anything?"

"Because Michelle never knew. Neither did I. Neither of us had any idea this file had been withheld from you."

"Withheld?"

Sir Dennis took a deep breath. "According to army regulations, you should have been made aware of your condition by your doctor."

"Harris? But Harris never told me anything. Every time I went to see him he said I was fine. Rose was there, she knows." Franklin stared at Pritchard in horror. "Rose knew? And she didn't tell me? Harris knew and *he* didn't say anything?"

Franklin rose and walked slowly around the garden. Everything Pritchard had told him made perfect sense. All the doubts and misunderstandings he had labored under fell together like pieces of a child's puzzle.

"Doctor, do you believe that at this moment I am a sane man?"

"Yes, I do."

"Then I'm going to ask you to do something for me."

Sir Dennis considered the request carefully. If he agreed, the implications would be far-reaching. Yet Franklin had every right to what he was asking.

"I'll bring you what you need," he said. "And I'll have my nurse join us. It wouldn't hurt to have another witness."

267

– 32 –

For Rose, the midsummer transatlantic crossing was a humiliating experience. Even before the *America* left the pier, rumors flew thick and fast about Franklin Jefferson, who had tried to kill his beautiful French wife. When Rose boarded, she found herself the object of scrutiny and, worse, pity. She gritted her teeth and managed to get through the sailing-night dinner at the captain's table. After that, she retreated to her stateroom and took all her meals there. Only in the very early mornings, when Rose left her quarters to walk along a mist-laden deck, did anyone catch a glimpse of her. Even then, her defiant solitude served as a warning not to come close.

During the days, Rose threw herself into her work. Stewards hurried between her suite and the wireless office, bringing incoming messages and returning with replies. Through Hugh O'Neill, she established direct contact with Inspector Rawlins at Scotland Yard, who kept her abreast of his attempts to find Franklin. It was also from Rawlins that Rose learned about Michelle's statement to the police implicating Harry Taylor. Rose considered Michelle's allegations absurd, yet they raised questions that bedeviled her. Why had Franklin shot Michelle? Had she been the real target as Harry insisted, or had Franklin been aiming for Harry? If so, why had Franklin, who in his letters had spoken so well of Harry, suddenly turned on him?

Rose remembered that awful morning when the police had brought Franklin home after his attack on Steven. The thought that something like that had happened again consumed her. And if that was the case, Rose couldn't ignore the consequences. The events in London were already having an impact in New York. Banks that had signed on for the money order were calling daily, seeking reassurances. Everyone wanted a statement from Rose Jefferson, clarifying the situation.

On the last day of the voyage, just hours before the *America* was to dock, a cable arrived from Harry Taylor:

> FRANKLIN FOUND AND IS ALL RIGHT. BEING
> HELD AT BELLINGHAM HOSPITAL. WILL BE AT
> THE DOCK TO MEET YOU. COURAGE.
>
> HARRY

Rose was beside herself. As a courtesy to his passenger, the captain of the *America* radioed ahead, asking British customs and immigration to speed her through the usual formalities. Rose was the first person off the vessel and a few minutes later found herself face to face with Harry.

"Is Franklin really all right?" she asked at once.

"Yes," Harry replied, falling in behind her for the long walk to the car. "I arranged for you to be driven directly to the prison."

"Aren't you coming with me?"

"It's best you see him alone. Sir Dennis Pritchard said he'd be there to talk to you. I'll be waiting back at the hotel."

As Rose stepped into the car Harry touched her arm.

"I don't know why he wanted to shoot anyone, Rose. Me or Michelle. That's the truth. And I don't hold him responsible. I wanted you to know that."

"Bless you, Harry."

Rose had expected to be driven into London but instead the chauffeur skirted the city and headed southeast.

"Driver, where are you taking me?"

"Bellingham Hospital, ma'am. It's in the village of Charlton, just beyond Woolwich."

The names meant nothing to Rose but she was confused by the arrangements Harry had made. The car slowed as the driver negotiated the narrow village streets. About a mile and a half from the village center he turned off on a long, winding road, canopied by ancient oaks, and pulled up in front of a Jacobean mansion. The hospital, if that was what it was, seemed more like a prison, with its forbidding spiked fence, dirty red brick turrets, and barred windows.

"Are you sure this is it?" Rose asked nervously.

"This is Bellingham, ma'am."

Inside, Rose expected to be taken by the administrator to his office. Instead, he escorted her through the center hall and down a corridor with heavy wooden doors plated with steel, with peepholes covered by thick glass. The gloom around her was broken by pools of light from flickering gas lamps. From behind the doors Rose could hear faint cries, catcalls, and screams.

"Why can't you bring my brother to your office?" Rose demanded, her voice shaking.

"I'm sorry, ma'am," the administrator told her. "Mr. Jefferson has a history of unpredictable behavior. Our regulations state that he cannot be moved from his quarters. For any reason."

"We'll see about that," Rose said grimly.

At the end of the corridor, two beefy attendants fell in behind them.

"Where are we?" asked Rose.

"This is the medical ward, ma'am."

Something in the administrator's voice disturbed Rose. She stopped and peered through one of the glass slits and couldn't stop herself from screaming.

"What kind of hell are you running here?" she cried.

Inside the cell, its walls covered with filthy canvas, was a man, or what remained of one. He was wrapped in a straitjacket that restrained his arms and upper body but left him free to stumble around the cell and crash against the walls. His pajama trousers were soiled and crusted, his face bloodied from the punishment he inflicted on himself.

"Miss Jefferson, please—"

Rose tore herself away from him and began running to each cell, glancing through the peepholes.

"Where's Franklin?" she screamed. "What have you done with him?"

From somewhere in the gloom, a cracked voice replied, "Hello, Rose. Welcome to London."

Somehow Rose managed to shut out the frightening world that lay beyond the door to Franklin's cell. She calmed down long enough to assess the conditions under which her brother was being kept. The cell was clean, the linen crisp, the blanket freshly laundered. She was alarmed by how much weight Franklin had lost but he convinced her that he was being well looked after. What troubled Rose was Franklin's remoteness. There was no feeling behind his touch and his eyes seemed to look right through her. His voice, once so vibrant and alive, was a monotone.

"I'm going to get you out of here," Rose kept saying. "The minute I get to London, I'll have bail posted. I've hired the best lawyers. In a few days you'll be back in London."

Franklin smiled wanly. "Thank you."

Rose clasped her hands around Franklin's face. "Please, you've got to tell me what happened. I have to know!"

"It's very simple, really. I shot Michelle."

"But *why?*"

Franklin turned away. "I'm very tired, Rose. I want to rest now."

"Franklin, please, don't shut me out. I'm here to *help* you."

Franklin looked up at her, his eyes filled with pity. "Are you really, Rose? Is that what you came to do, to help me the way you did in New York?"

"New York? I don't understand. . . ."

"I know about my medical file. The one you never told me about."

Rose was stunned. The accusation in Franklin's eyes tore at her heart.

"I can explain everything—"

270

"I'm sure you can, Rose. But not to me. Explain it to Michelle. She's the one I almost killed."

Rose flung her arms around Franklin but it was too late. He sat on the cot, unmoving, his eyes lightly closed, silent as a statue. For a long time she held him like that, wondering if she would ever have him back again.

"I don't understand how you could have brought him here," Rose said for what must have been the tenth time. "This is an insane asylum!"

She was in the administrator's office, sitting opposite Sir Dennis Pritchard.

"The police wouldn't have it any other way," the physician replied. "In fact, they wanted to put Franklin in an ordinary jail, in the section reserved for violent offenders. Believe me, that would have been far worse."

"Well, I'm going to get him out!"

Sir Dennis said nothing. He had heard Rose mention Tory, Tory, and Deslauriers, London's most powerful and prestigious law firm. He wished her luck but he doubted that even their influence would obtain Franklin's release before he was brought up in front of a magistrate.

"Doctor, how much do you really know about my brother's condition?" asked Rose, recalling what Franklin had said to her.

"A great deal more than you or Harris chose to tell me," Sir Dennis replied coldly. "You may have had your reasons for withholding the army medical file from Franklin. Not to have shown it to me was inexcusable."

Rose crimsoned at the accusation but let it go.

"I take it you've seen that file?"

"Yes."

"Would you mind telling me where you got it?"

Sir Dennis explained how Michelle had tracked down the information in Paris.

"Your sister-in-law is a brave and caring woman. Perhaps if we had had the information sooner, none of this would have happened."

"Please don't sit in judgment on me, Doctor," Rose said. "My only concern is, and always has been, Franklin. Now that you know the history, is there anything you can do for him?"

"I wish I could, Miss Jefferson."

Rose's knuckles whitened as she gripped the arms of her chair. Then she rose and walked to the door.

"Thank you for everything you've done, Doctor. Please tell Franklin I'll be back in the morning."

"Miss Jefferson, can you at least tell me why?" Sir Dennis called after her.

Rose hesitated. "It really doesn't matter now, does it?"

* * *

271

By the time she arrived at the Ritz, Rose was exhausted.

"Miss Jefferson, there's a gentleman waiting to see you," the manager said, handing her her key. "He's in the Long Gallery. Do you wish to see him now?"

Thinking that it must be Harry, Rose ignored her fatigue and said yes. She followed the manager through a high-ceilinged promenade. Her mouth fell open when she saw Monk McQueen.

"What are you doing here? I mean, it's wonderful to see you, Monk. I just never expected . . ."

Monk embraced her. "Have you seen Franklin?"

Rose nodded. "He's fine . . . or at least he seems to be. But they've got him locked up in an asylum—"

"Bellingham. I know."

Rose looked at him carefully. "Monk, what *are* you doing here?"

Monk explained about the message from Sir Dennis Pritchard, when he had arrived, and how he had helped in the search for Franklin.

"I'm grateful, Monk," Rose said. "But I don't understand why Pritchard contacted you first instead of me."

"Because Michelle asked him to."

"Michelle? Why would she have called for you?"

"I'm her friend," Monk said quietly. "She had no one to turn to. She was terrified, Rose."

It all went back to the war, Rose thought, and what the three of them had shared. She could understand Monk's rushing to a friend's side. That was his nature.

"How is Michelle?" she asked.

"She'll be all right, if that's what you mean." Monk hesitated. "I also know about the medical file."

Rose shook her head. "I don't want to discuss it, Monk. Not now."

"Fine. But what about Harry Taylor?"

"What about him?"

Monk exploded. "Franklin tried to kill him is what! For God's sake, Rose, who is this son of a bitch? Why did you let him loose in London?"

"Harry Taylor is, as you well know, one of my senior executives!" Rose said icily. "He was here on my instructions. As to what those pertained to, that is none of your business!"

"When people start getting shot, it damn well is my business, Rose!" Monk retorted. "And your dealings with the British banks aren't much of a secret either!"

Rose paled. "Who told you about that? It couldn't have been Franklin. It was Michelle, wasn't it?"

"Don't worry, Rose. I'm not going to be the one to print that story. All I want to know is why Franklin shot at Taylor."

"That's what *Michelle* says happened. The police don't necessarily believe her."

"You don't. You believe Taylor!"

Rose gathered up her purse and stood. "Monk, you've always been a good friend. But I'm warning you. Don't interfere. I'll handle this the way I have to."

"And how is that, Rose?" Monk asked sadly. "Too much has happened to be swept under the rug. It doesn't matter whether Michelle or Taylor was the target. Franklin is still facing an attempted-murder charge. But if he had grounds to go after Taylor, the court might take that into consideration. Whatever you do, Rose, don't use Franklin to shield either Global or Taylor. I won't let you hurt him again."

When Rose at last made it to her room, she called downstairs and told the front desk she was not to be disturbed for any reason. A maid drew her a hot bath, laid out her evening robe, and arranged for a light supper to be sent up. When the maid left, she took with her a sealed note Rose had written.

Rose did not emerge from the bathroom until she was sure she was alone. Ignoring the food, she put on the robe and opened the French doors to the balcony overlooking Green Park.

Whom do *you believe?*

The cables Rose had received from Inspector Rawlins indicated that Scotland Yard was far from satisfied with Harry's version of events. The police, like Monk, tended to accept Michelle's word.

How blind could they be? Rose asked herself. Even if Harry knew about the traveler's checks, he wouldn't have dared do anything to jeopardize the negotiations. He had everything to lose and nothing to gain.

No matter how long Rose turned the questions and doubts over in her mind, they all came back to one common point: Franklin. Only he knew what had really happened and why he had gone to Harry's apartment that day. But Franklin couldn't remember. . . .

At least not yet.

Rose heard the door open.

"Hello, Harry."

Rose threw her arms around him and covered his mouth with a deep kiss.

"Don't say anything. We have an hour. I want you to make love to me, Harry, just the way you did that very first time."

- 33 -

At false dawn the groundskeeper at Bellingham Hospital was making his way around the property extinguishing the lamps that had burned throughout the night. By now the patients' shrieks and cries had ebbed away in nightmarish sleep. Only those who had cleverly avoided their medication remained awake. One of them was Franklin Jefferson.

Franklin was waiting for Rose to come back. There was so much to tell her. He kept trying to remember what, exactly, and when he couldn't, he began to cry. Franklin Jefferson had no idea that his sister had left fifteen hours ago.

In his lucid moments, Franklin would wonder why he was still awake. He would stand on his cot on tiptoe to gaze across the deserted grounds and think of Michelle. He had so many things to say to her as well. Franklin thought a great deal about what Sir Dennis had told him. He felt neither anger nor self-pity. In the time they'd had, he and Michelle had forged a lifetime of memories. Now he had to make sure that Rose could never hurt Michelle again.

Then Franklin's thoughts would begin to fragment, like a star exploding in slow motion. He would take out his timepiece and hold the face to the moonlight and wonder when Rose was coming back. . . .

Promptly at seven o'clock Rose made her way across Lincoln's Inn Fields, the largest square in central London, bordered by elegant old houses that now served as legal offices. Rose checked the numbers and found the brass nameplate of Tory, Tory, and Deslauriers.

Jonathan Tory, the senior partner, showed Rose into his cramped office overflowing with books, journals, and legal memoranda.

"I've examined our position, Miss Jefferson, and I believe we will be able to secure a court order to move your brother. However, we must provide a guarantee that Franklin Jefferson will not be a public menace. That is to say, we must have a proper, private location, and a professional round-the-clock staff."

Rose had expected as much. "What if I were to buy a house in, say, Hampstead Heath?"

274

"An excellent suggestion. In fact I took the liberty of ringing a friend who's an estate agent. I'm sure he would have several suitable properties for you to look at."

"Have him call me at the hotel this morning."

"There will also be the question of bail," Jonathan Tory said delicately.

"What's your estimate?"

"Naturally, the Crown will oppose any sum, this being an attempted-murder charge. However, if we can assure the magistrate that your brother won't be a threat to the community and agree to post say, half a million pounds, I think we stand an excellent chance of gaining a ruling in our favor."

Rose's mind reeled. Half a million pounds was an enormous sum.

"I'll arrange it," she said quietly and added, "There's one more thing I need advice on."

Jonathan Tory listened carefully to Rose's request.

"What you're asking for is a restraining order," he murmured. "Would Sir Dennis be willing to provide a testimonial?"

"Let's not bank on it."

"Pity. Would have been easier. However, I think we can find a way to convince the court that such a step would be in your brother's best interests."

"I'm counting on you to do exactly that," Rose said, her tone leaving no doubt that she didn't expect to hear any excuses.

Michelle looked at herself in the mirror and almost burst into tears. For the last hour she'd been trying on one outfit after another, but every one seemed too depressing. Black may have been the color of the season's fashions but she'd be damned if she'd wear something so grim to see Franklin.

Michelle hadn't talked to anyone about her decision. Sir Dennis had vetoed her earlier pleas to visit, saying that Franklin needed time to regain his strength. Michelle might have relented had it not been for Rose Jefferson's arrival in London.

She took one last look at herself in the mirror and hurried downstairs. As she reached the bottom of the staircase, Hastings drew her aside.

"There's someone to see you, ma'am," he said, indicating the front parlor.

"Hastings, I can't now—"

"It's Miss Jefferson, ma'am."

Michelle took a deep breath. "Thank you, Hastings. Have the car wait, please."

Michelle was suddenly aware that her shoulder, still lightly bandaged, was throbbing. Holding her head high, she walked into the parlor.

"Hello, Michelle."

Sitting back in the overstuffed armchair, Rose appeared every bit as poised and calm as Michelle remembered. Her hair was different, though, cut shorter in a becoming style, but the voice was as cool as ever, the eyes appraising, watchful.

"Are you all right?"

"I'm fine," Michelle replied, angry with herself because her voice faltered.

"Were you going out somewhere?"

"To see Franklin."

"I'm glad I came then." Rose uncrossed her legs and sat up. "We have to talk, Michelle, about what happened, what you told the police."

"I told them the truth!" Michelle flared.

"Did you? That Franklin had gone to Harry's house to shoot him. Why on earth would he do something like that?"

"Don't you know?" Michelle demanded. "Haven't the police told you?"

"Why don't *you* tell me," Rose suggested.

Careful to leave nothing out, Michelle explained what had been happening since Harry had arrived in London and why she and Franklin both suspected that he had somehow sabotaged the negotiations with the banks.

"I see," Rose said, her voice going cold. "So it was you, not Franklin, who went to that meeting at the embassy."

"I had no choice. If I didn't, everything Franklin had done would have been wasted."

"It seems to me everything was wasted anyway. What were you thinking, Michelle? How could you believe you had the skills and knowledge to go up against people like that?"

Michelle felt as though Rose's eyes were pinning her to the wall.

"Above all, what right did you have to speak on Global's behalf?"

"I know as much about the traveler's check as Franklin!"

"Obviously it wasn't enough!" Rose got up and began to pace. "All this time I've been thinking that maybe what happened was my fault or Franklin's. But it's yours, isn't it? You took his presentation and botched it. Do you realize how many millions of dollars you've cost Global? And then you tried to shift the blame to Harry."

"Harry Taylor tried to cheat you!" Michelle cried. "Why can't you believe that?"

"Because it's not true! I'll tell you something else you've done, Michelle. By accusing Harry you've put the whole company under a shadow. In New York, the press is having a field day. They love the idea that a Global executive may have turned against his own company."

276

Michelle didn't know if she'd ever intended to say this to Rose but now it seemed like her only defense.

"What about you, Rose? Don't you think that what you hid from Franklin and me had anything to do with what's happened? You knew that he couldn't have surgery to remove the shell fragments . . . that his condition would inevitably deteriorate until . . . until he couldn't manage for himself. But you pretended everything was all right. You brought Franklin back to Global where you wanted him and worked him half to death. What did you think you were doing?"

"What had to be done," Rose said, the determination in her voice tinged with sorrow. "Yes, I knew what had happened to Franklin and yes, I withheld that from both of you. You talk about living with pain, Michelle. Can you imagine what I've been going through? Is that the kind of pain you would have had me pass on to Franklin—or you?"

"It was his life you were playing with, Rose. Franklin had a right not only to know but to decide what he was going to do. It would have been terrible, I know, but I would have been there to help him. Did you really think I would leave him?"

Michelle's eye searched Rose's face for an answer but in the end it was the other woman's silence that betrayed her.

"That's exactly what you wanted, wasn't it?" Michelle said softly. "And if I had gone, you would have had Franklin all to yourself. . . ."

"Well, neither of us will have him," Rose said. "Everything I dreamed of, everything I needed from him, gone because of a few scraps of German pig iron . . ."

Rose paused. "I never loved Franklin any less than you did. But you should have known that Franklin had a tremendous future ahead of him, responsibilities to live up to, a name to carry on. After he came back from the war and I found out about . . . his injuries, I wanted to help him make the most of the time he had left. I wanted him to have a sense of worth, to contribute, and to feel a part of everything that was his. I was only protecting him, Michelle. . . ."

"No, you weren't, Rose," Michelle replied sadly. "You were only after what you wanted. There was no room in your dream for what he needed, nor anyone he loved. What you never understood, Rose, was that I was never a threat to you. Because he loved me doesn't mean Franklin loved you less. As for Global, he never wanted from it what you did. You should have accepted that and let him go."

Rose turned away, her ears burning. "What do you intend to do?"

"I'm going to see my husband and make sure he knows that he has a home and a wife to return to."

"What about your statement to the police?"

"I won't change it. When Franklin remembers what happened, he'll tell you the same thing."

Rose closed her eyes. "If that's the way you want it, Michelle. But I should tell you now that neither you nor anyone else will be able to see Franklin without my permission."

"That's impossible!"

"You're welcome to find out for yourself." Rose picked up her purse. "And when he's better, Michelle, I'll be the one taking him home. Please don't think you can fight me on that and win."

Rose's words, cold, final, unrepentant, chased Michelle all the way to Bellingham Hospital. During the long drive, Michelle tried to convince herself that Rose had been bluffing. After all, what kind of judge would prevent a wife from visiting her own husband?

A judge who could be convinced that it would be in the best interests of justice not to allow an intended victim to see her would-be murderer.

Was Rose's reach that long?

Michelle had her answer soon enough.

"I'm afraid I wasn't told to expect you, Mrs. Jefferson," the hospital administrator said nervously, ushering Michelle into his office.

"These are visiting hours and I want to see my husband," Michelle replied firmly.

"Yes, well, there's a bit of a problem with that."

"And what would that be?"

"I received a court order by special messenger earlier this morning. I'm sorry, Mrs. Jefferson, but I can't allow you to see your husband."

Michelle stiffened. "Show it to me, please."

Michelle examined the court papers, stamped and sealed, and signed by a magistrate. "Does Sir Dennis Pritchard know about this?"

"I'm not aware that he was consulted. In any event, the order doesn't apply to him."

"No, just to me!"

The administrator flushed beneath her gaze.

Inspector Rawlins rubbed his eyes and peered wearily at Monk McQueen, who was sprawled back in his chair, cigar dangling from his fingertips. The two men had been up all night sifting through the clippings, articles, background material, and other information on Harry Taylor that had been sent from New

York. The air was thick with blue tobacco smoke and stained teacups were balanced precariously on the radiator.

Inspector Rawlins yawned. "Not much to go on, is there?"

"Oh, we have enough material," Monk replied. "It just doesn't tell us anything."

Harry seemed a reflection of the all-American success story. That no one had anything bad to say about him disturbed Monk.

"He's a little too clean," Monk muttered, thinking aloud. "Too perfect."

"He may be that," Rawlins agreed. "But that doesn't make him guilty of anything."

He stretched his arms and got out of the chair. "I'm going home to bed. I suggest you do the same."

Monk rose as well. "I'm going to try a different tack. It seems pretty clear that whatever Harry did to Franklin, he didn't plan it back in New York. I think he saw an opportunity over here and ran with it."

"What are you thinking of doing?" Rawlins asked warily.

"I'm a financial-newspaper man, right?" Monk said innocently. "Harry Taylor is an important American executive pursuing business in London. I'm sure my readers would like to know the details."

Rawlins held up his hands in surrender. "I don't want to know a thing." He paused. "Until, of course, you come up with something I can use."

"I thought you might say that."

When Monk returned to Berkeley Square, he found Michelle waiting for him. She didn't have to say much for Monk to realize that her worst fears were coming true. No sooner had Rose arrived in London than she was running roughshod over Michelle and Franklin's lives.

"I don't know how to stop her," Michelle said. "And I'm terrified that Franklin will think I've deserted him."

Monk looked at Michelle and wished he could gather her up in his arms. That one night, when they had feasted voraciously on their love, had never been repeated but its residue clung to them both. Electricity crackled whenever their fingertips met, and their eyes spoke all the words they dared not say. But for all that had passed between them, Monk did not harbor any guilt. When Franklin was back, he would quietly depart, leaving Michelle and her husband in the peace they deserved. The moment he and Michelle had shared would never intrude.

"I'll talk to Rose," Monk promised.

Michelle covered his hand with hers. She would let Monk have his brave words because he truly believed he could change things. He did not share her terrible conviction that the outcome of what had overtaken them was already beyond their power to change.

The courtroom reminded Michelle of a country church. The tall, leaded windows behind the magistrate's bench soared to majestic heights. The intricate scrollwork on the balustrade ringing the second-story gallery where she sat recalled a choir loft. From the polished wood rose the sweet perfume of beeswax.

The courtroom was jammed. On Michelle's left were the newspaper artists who preferred the overview from the gallery. The reporters sat below, along a bench reserved for them directly behind the Crown's table. Michelle's eyes darted to Rose, seated behind the defense table, her face partially obscured by an enormous white hat that curved like an angel's wing. Sitting beside her was Harry Taylor. To the left of the defense was the accused's box, still empty, and above that, the bench, also vacant. Michelle licked a bead of perspiration from her lower lip.

"They'll bring him in any minute now," Monk said, just loudly enough for her to hear him over the hubbub floating around them. He found her hand and squeezed it reassuringly.

For Monk it had been a frustrating, sometimes infuriating week. Rose had not returned any of his calls or replied to his messages. When he had tried to see Franklin at Bellingham Hospital, he like Michelle had been refused. After that, Monk had a top-flight solicitor look into ways to challenge the restraining order.

"I'm afraid there aren't any, Mr. McQueen," the lawyer had told him. "At least, none which would prove effective in the time we have. The hearing's less than a fortnight away. Jonathan Tory could easily delay any petitions we might bring forward."

Monk had done what he could to keep up Michelle's spirits. Watching her now, he thought he had failed her even in that. Michelle's expression was fraught with tension, her eyes roaming constantly.

"It will all be over before you know it," Monk whispered. "Once Franklin is out of the hospital the restraining order will be lifted. Rose won't have any excuse to try to keep it in force."

Michelle seemed not to hear him. All she wanted now was to see Franklin, to give him hope, reassure him that he wasn't alone.

A hush fell over the spectators when Franklin Jefferson walked in, flanked by two court officers who guided him to the dock. Rose watched Franklin's progress intently. She thought he cut a fine figure in the new blue suit she had had delivered last night to Bellingham Hospital.

High in the gallery, Michelle dug her nails into her palms. She couldn't believe how awful Franklin looked. He had lost a great deal of weight and his shirt collar was too large for his neck. He shuffled along like an old man and his eyes were like bright pinpoints of light, as frightened as those of a captive animal.

Oh, Franklin, what has she done to you?

Franklin stepped into the box and looked at the hundreds of faces scrutinizing him. To him, they were just a blur. He focused on the defense table and behind it saw Rose. Then he looked up at the gallery and his eyes picked out Michelle. Franklin held her lovingly in his gaze, his heart soaring.

Everyone rose as the judge made his entry. He mounted the bench, brought the court to order, and indicated that the prosecution should present its arguments.

Franklin paid no attention to the prosecutor's opening remarks about his having attempted to kill Harry Taylor in cold blood and that it would be folly to allow such a man to leave the confines of Bellingham Hospital to await trial. As far as he was concerned, they weren't talking about him at all. Michelle's face swam before his eyes, the same way it had that first time he had seen her, in the barn, in a war that seemed so far away. She had protected him then, but later, in New York, he hadn't been able to look after her when she had needed his help most.

I'll help you now, my love. All I need is the chance. No one will ever hurt you again.

Franklin was mildly surprised to hear that the prosecution was finished and Sir Dennis Pritchard was on the witness stand. He listened as Jonathan Tory had the physician explain exactly what Franklin was suffering from and offer the opinion that his patient's interests would be much better served if he was privately cared for. Rose followed him, explaining what kind of facilities she had arranged for Franklin. The judge listened impassively to the closing arguments and rendered his decision: Franklin Jefferson would be remanded into his sister's custody pending trial. Bail was set at one hundred thousand pounds.

Before Franklin knew what was happening he was being led away by the two wardens. He looked over his shoulder and caught a glimpse of Michelle. Her tears cut him to the quick.

Not long now, my love . . .

Franklin had carefully counted the number of steps when he had been taken from the holding cells in the basement to the long corridor that led to the courtroom. There were forty-six, which meant that the courtroom was on the third if not the fourth floor of the building. At the end of the corridor, just beyond the courtroom doors, was a large window overlooking the street. Franklin could feel the sunlight coming through it warming his back.

They had almost reached the stairs. Franklin began taking smaller steps, letting his bailiffs get just a little ahead of him. He kept his head down and his manacled hands swung in front of him from side to side. When Franklin saw one of the wardens reach out and place his hand on the staircase rail, he threw himself into the man, sending him crashing down the stairwell. The other cried out and lunged at him. Franklin sidestepped neatly, then tripped him. The warden fell to the floor, gasping.

Franklin began running, gaining speed with every loping stride. His arms were swinging wildly as he tried to keep his balance. Behind him he heard shouting and then pounding feet. Franklin kept his eyes fixed on the light. He could feel it on his legs, then on his chest, and finally it hit him squarely in the face. Franklin was blinded by its intensity. His face seemed to be on fire but he kept running, seeing Michelle in that white radiance, hearing her call out to him.

I love you, Michelle!

For an instant the corridor darkened as Franklin's body blotted out the light. Just as it seemed impossible to get any closer to it, he closed his eyes and, smiling, launched himself into the glass to at last touch the woman beckoning to him from the other side.

The reporters were crowding around Rose and Michelle on the courthouse steps. Rose had been expecting this and took it in stride, telling the press how pleased she was about the ruling. Michelle clung to Monk as he shouldered into the mob, ignoring the questions shouted at her. They had almost reached his car when she heard the sound of breaking glass.

Twisting around, Michelle saw a flash of blue as the body burst through the window high above her. For a moment, it seemed to be suspended in midair. Then slowly, as though reluctant to do so, it began falling, tumbling end over end.

"Franklin!"

Michelle felt Monk whirl around and clamp his hand across her eyes. She tore herself from his grip and burst through the crowd, scrambling up the steps. She slipped on something wet, pain shooting up her leg. When her hand came away, it was slick with blood. Sobbing, Michelle crawled the last few feet and cradled Franklin's bleeding head in her arms, whispering his name over and over again. It was all over, finally. No one was going to hurt Franklin again, ever.

- 34 -

For Michelle the distinction between morning and night blurred. She found herself waking up at two o'clock in the morning and wandering the Berkeley Square house like a wraith. Neither the nurse Sir Dennis Pritchard had arranged for nor the sedatives he prescribed kept the nightmares at bay. The instant Michelle closed her eyes she saw Franklin's body hurtling through space, his face contorted by a silent scream.

Monk was Michelle's sole link to the outside world. He went to see Rose and was told that arrangements had been made to have Franklin's remains shipped back to the United States. When she heard this, Michelle told Monk, "I want to see him."

Despite his reservations, Monk called Inspector Rawlins. The detective took care of the necessary paperwork and early one morning drove Michelle to the morgue.

The white-tile floor gleamed, hurting Michelle's eyes as she walked past the autopsy tables, trying not to look at the array of saws, knives, and other stainless-steel instruments used to ferret out the secrets of the dead. The coroner wheeled out a gurney from the huge refrigeration unit and delicately drew back the sheet to just below the chin.

Michelle winced. Franklin's skin was pasty gray, his hair stiff, shot through with ice crystals. For the longest time she stared at him, searching for words to mourn him, to say goodbye. Her whole body ached so hard from her loss that she thought she'd faint. Memories of Franklin's laughter and embrace, his smile and his kisses poured into her heart.

Let him go. You have to let him go.

With her hands clasped in front of her Michelle began to recite a prayer she'd known as a child. She wasn't at all conscious that her fingers kept sliding over her belly or that her words included someone other than Franklin.

The atmosphere in the boardroom of Tory, Tory, and Deslauriers was appropriately somber. Rose, dressed in black, took her now-familiar seat on the right of Jonathan Tory.

This morning, when she had looked at herself in the mirror, she couldn't believe the image staring back at her. Her face was drawn, her eyes enormous against her pale skin. At her widow's peak, a tuft of what had once been jet-black hair was now completely white.

What is happening to me? Why am I being punished like this?

Rose had searched for the answers during long, solitary walks along the Thames and chased them through the nights she lay awake in Harry's arms. But they eluded her, and neither tears, nor rage, nor bitter sorrow seemed sufficient currency to buy them.

"Miss Jefferson," the attorney was saying, "we've made all the necessary arrangements to have your brother's remains returned to the United States. If you would just sign these papers . . ."

Rose glanced at the official documents and scribbled her signature at the bottom. It was time to put the questions to rest. It was time to go home.

"I want to thank you for everything—" Rose began, then suddenly the door opened and a flustered young clerk appeared.

"I'm terribly sorry," he stammered. "Mrs. Jefferson is outside, with Dr. Pritchard and counsel. She says it's extremely urgent."

"Tell her we have nothing to discuss," Jonathan Tory snapped.

"No, let her come in," Rose overruled him. "We might as well hear what she has to say."

Sir Dennis entered first, nodding silently at Rose, followed by a young, smartly dressed young man escorting Michelle.

"Hello, Rose."

"Hello, Michelle."

The two women looked at each other, each realizing how great a gulf separated them. The young attorney, who introduced himself as Neville Thompson, cleared his throat nervously and addressed Rose.

"Miss Jefferson, please believe me that we wouldn't trouble you at such a time unless it was absolutely necessary. However, there is the matter of your late brother's will."

Rose stared at him blankly. "What about it, Mr. Thompson? My brother left his share of the company to me, if that's what you're getting at. In fact, both our wills stipulated that in the event one of us dies, the other inherits everything."

Thank God I checked Franklin's will before he left! Rose thought to herself. At the time she had considered it a prudent business decision. She didn't care if Franklin wanted to leave Michelle some money or property but she had to make sure the provisions regarding Global had been left intact.

"That may have been the case before, Miss Jefferson," the attorney informed her. "It isn't now."

"What do you mean by that?" Rose demanded.

Neville Thompson removed a single piece of paper from his briefcase.

"When Mr. Jefferson surrendered himself to Dr. Pritchard, he requested that prior to calling the police, Dr. Pritchard act as his witness for this codicil. You'll note that this is his handwriting and signature and that the codicil has been dated and duly witnessed by Dr. Pritchard and his nurse."

The words blurred as Rose read them.

"This . . . this is outrageous! Do you really believe this has any validity? Franklin was scared out of his wits when he came to you. He couldn't have had the presence of mind to write such a thing."

"I assure you, Miss Jefferson, that your brother was quite sound when he drafted the codicil," Sir Dennis replied. "If need be, I'll swear to it."

"You can swear all you want! There is no way Michelle can possibly inherit Franklin's share of Global! No court in the world will uphold this!"

"You're perfectly within your rights to challenge the codicil," Thompson said. "However, I do not think you will be successful. The British courts tend to acknowledge the legitimacy of codicils such as this one, especially when heirs are involved."

Rose sagged in her chair. "What heirs?"

Michelle stepped forward and spoke for the first time.

"I'm pregnant, Rose."

PART
———
FOUR

- 35 -

An unseasonably cold breeze swept off Long Island Sound the day Rose Jefferson buried her brother. The sea oats bowed beneath the wind like mourners, and the voice of the minister was whipped away high over the heads of the assembly. Rose and Steven were alone at the foot of the grave as the casket bearing Franklin Jefferson's remains was lowered into its sandy resting place.

Standing behind Rose were Harry Taylor, Eric Gollant, and Hugh O'Neill, and behind them, fanned out across the knoll, the servants of Dunescrag and Talbot House. Rose had deliberately arranged the funeral this way. She couldn't bear the thought of hundreds of people milling around this hallowed ground that was the Jeffersons' last refuge. In a few days, a memorial service would be held in Manhattan so that those who wished to pay their respects to Franklin could do so.

After she had thrown a handful of dirt on the coffin, Rose guided Steven to the Silver Ghost. As she got in, she turned to Harry.

"I want you to go to Talbot House," she said softly. "Have the staff clean out his closets and give the clothing to charity. The trophies, pictures, and personal effects should be packed up and put in the basement."

"There may be things you want," Harry suggested.

Rose shook her head. "What I want has been taken away." She touched his cheek. "Do this for me, Harry, and come back as soon as you can."

For the rest of that summer and into early fall, Rose did not leave Dunescrag. Her days were spent close to Steven, listening to music, taking long walks along

289

the dunes, and talking, always talking, about Global, how much had been achieved and how much remained to be done.

"I'm counting on you to help me," she told him. "You're all I have left."

Steven, now twelve, said, "I will, Mother. I promise."

Steven knew that his mother was an intelligent, intuitive woman. But she was also blind. She could not look into his heart and see the contempt he had for his uncle. In Steven's eyes, Franklin Jefferson had been a weakling. But no matter. His uncle was dead and Michelle would soon be out of their lives. His uncle had been crazy to try to leave her his share—what Steven believed was his rightful share—of the company.

That left only one contender: Harry Taylor, the silver-tongued con man who thought he had managed to slip a golden ring through his mother's nose. There were moments when Steven thought his mother was as weak as anyone else, especially late at night when he stood with his ear to the wall and listened as she begged Harry to do it harder, still harder. . . . By his overnight stays at Dunescrag, Harry had, without knowing it, taught Steven what he thought was an invaluable lesson: women could be slaves of passion as easily as men were.

Even during her retreat, Rose Jefferson kept her finger on the pulse of business, which couldn't have been stronger. Americans embraced the Global money orders, buying more than a million dollars' worth a day, using them to pay for everything from grocery bills to new cars.

But while business editors wrote paeans to her success, Rose found that in spite of her best efforts, the popular press, which had picked clean the grisly details of Franklin's death, continued to feast on an even juicier morsel: one of America's richest men had left his entire fortune to the very woman he had shot.

"I'm terribly sorry, Rose," Hugh O'Neill told her. "There's nothing we can do."

"We can sue these bastards for their last cent!" Rose retorted, sweeping the dailies from the coffee table.

"It wouldn't do any good. I've had our best litigation people go through the stories for anything that even hinted of libel or defamation of character. Once the papers got hold of the codicil, it was easy enough for them to find out about your challenging it in the London courts."

"Damn them!" Rose said bitterly. "Isn't there anything we can do?"

"You're taking the best possible course by staying out of sight. The newspapers can't get at you in Dunescrag."

"I came here because I chose to! I needed time and peace, for myself and Steven, but I'll be damned if I can't return to the office because of these vultures!"

That evening, when Rose and Harry were alone, she asked him what he thought she should do about the press.

"Use it," he said.

It wasn't the reply Rose had expected.

"How?"

"By telling your side of the story. Look, the newspapers aren't going to leave it alone, so you might as well get all the mileage you can out of it. Offer a few interviews. Give a couple of quotes. Let everyone know that Michelle is taking advantage of a situation—no, of a man who committed a totally irrational act. Make her out to be the gold digger she is."

"And what would that accomplish?"

"It would bring public opinion to your side."

Rose placed her palms against his cheeks.

"You can be so clever, Harry," she murmured.

— 36 —

It was a battle the public relished. On one hand stood the country's financial baroness and her battery of gold-plated legal gunslingers. Opposite her was the beautiful widow, Michelle Jefferson, represented by her own cadre of attorneys. Ironically, of the two, Michelle drew more attention because of her absolute refusal to take the fight public. No matter what interviews Rose gave, no matter how clever the maneuvers of her lawyers, Michelle wouldn't utter a word. American readers saw dignity in her stance. To them she became the tantalizing mystery woman.

Contrary to Harry Taylor's predictions, it was Michelle who won the sympathy of Americans. In one tabloid's opinion poll, the public saw her as a female David to Rose's Goliath. The bookies loved it. The smart money was riding heavily on Rose Jefferson but the oddsmakers raked in the heartstring bets as fast as they came in. To them, it just proved that sometimes there were more suckers born one minute than the next.

Michelle Jefferson laughed softly at a joke Monk had made and covered his hand with hers. The gesture drew a knowing smile from the elderly, white-jacketed waiter hovering around their table.

They were sitting in a cafe opposite Place St. Michel, at the foot of the great boulevard of the same name, which ends its meandering through Paris at the foot of the river Seine. It was autumn, and the sidewalks were slick with red and brown leaves. Overhead, the *marronniers* dropped their bounty, chestnuts enclosed in prickly green shells, onto the streets. The air had changed too, losing its tartness to the smoke pouring from a thousand chimneys as oakwood fires were stoked to ward off the evening chill.

"When are you leaving?" asked Michelle.

"The day after tomorrow."

Michelle looked away.

He's been with you for almost three months. You've been lucky. Think of everything you've shared. Keep it, hold on to it. It's your treasure.

With the press hounding her about the dramatic implications of the codicil, Michelle found it impossible to stay in London. She retained the best estate lawyers and issued succinct instructions: "Don't give Rose Jefferson an inch!" Afterward, following Monk, who had quietly gone on ahead to find a place for her to live, Michelle crossed the Channel bound for the French capital.

She had been reluctant to go to Paris. She recalled her first trip there, when she had been hunting for Franklin's medical file. The experience had left a bitter taste in her mouth. Yet, the day she arrived, her trepidations fell away. Here, the sky seemed higher and more majestic than in New York. The smell and feel of city stones a thousand years old spoke of continuity, a sense that come what may, Paris would always endure.

Now, sitting in the bedroom of the grand apartment that Monk had found for her on the Île St.-Louis, Michelle watched the timeless Seine lap quietly through the city on its way to the sea. Across the black waters was the Cathedral of Notre Dame, its arches, gables, and turrets floodlit against the night, reflections undulating across the waves. Beyond that was the Right Bank, the glory of the Marais, Paris's oldest quarter, and farther along, the lights of the majestic hotels of the Place Vendôme.

And there was Monk. . . .

Whenever she woke to see him sleeping beside her Michelle was seized by a happiness that brought tears to her eyes. In Paris, the two of them existed only for each other. Under Monk's gentle caresses, Michelle found herself healing. The wounds she bore lost their pain, and whenever she passed her hand across her belly she realized how much she had to live for. Still, nothing came without its price.

Although Monk spent virtually every night with Michelle, he was careful to keep up appearances. He took a room at the American club and filed reports to

Q magazine from the Paris *Herald* offices. He avoided the overseas press colony as much as possible. He and Michelle laughed about the illusion they had created, and even though both understood that it could not last, each kept coming up with excuses to postpone the inevitable, drawn not only to each other but by a third life, which was stirring in Michelle's womb.

"You don't know how much I want to stay with you," Monk said, stroking Michelle's fingertips, watching as the cafe emptied its noon trade.

"I want you to."

Monk felt the insistence in the gentle pressure of her nails on his skin.

"It's impossible."

The words were cruel, heavy, and final, and he loathed saying them.

"Will it ever be possible?" asked Michelle.

"Someday, yes. I promise you. But right now, with Franklin's codicil being challenged, Rose would seize any advantage. She knows how close you and I are and that I stayed at Berkeley Square all that time. The only reason she doesn't suspect anything is because she can't conceive that I could have fallen in love with my best friend's wife. But if she ever thought the baby wasn't Franklin's, she'd make your life a greater hell than she already has. She'd end up taking away what Franklin left you . . . and your child."

If it weren't for the child, maybe I could let everything go, Michelle thought. *But Franklin left me a legacy. If I wanted to surrender, that would be my choice. But I'll be damned if I'll let anyone steal it!*

Michelle looked at Monk and knew he was reading her thoughts.

"What will you do?" she asked. "How will you feel, tomorrow, next week, next month?"

"How will I feel?" he echoed. "Very proud of you."

"Can you live with that? Will it be enough?"

"No, it will never be enough, but yes, I can live with it. We both have to."

Monk slipped a few francs underneath the saucer with the bill.

"In a way, both of us have much more than we had any right to expect," he said. "We found each other. We found love."

"But she's your child!" Michelle cried.

"And she means the world to me, as you do. And that's what I want her to have—the world." He laughed. "Besides, how do you know we'll have a daughter?"

Michelle managed a tiny smile. "I just do."

Monk McQueen sailed from Le Havre in late October, on board one of the last liners to cross the Atlantic before the winter storms set in. As much as she wanted to, Michelle did not see him off. She could not promise Monk that at the last minute she wouldn't fling her arms around him and beg him not to leave. And that would ruin everything.

In the last months of 1920, Michelle's world contracted. She spent her days supervising the remodeling of the Île St.-Louis apartment and converting one of the bedrooms into a nursery. Once every two weeks Michelle visited her physician, and was told that if every mother was as healthy as she, he would soon be out of business.

As Christmas drew near Michelle realized just how alone she really was. She experienced that sad, strange distance of a person watching helplessly as the rest of the world cheerfully rushes by, secure in the comfort of family and friends.

Next year it will be different, Michelle vowed.

To make the short days of January and February pass more quickly, Michelle carefully reexamined the plans Rose Jefferson had had for the traveler's check. She was convinced that had it not been for Harry Taylor, everything would have worked exactly as Rose had wanted. And still could.

But first the legal battle had to end. As the days counted down to the British court's ruling on the legitimacy of Franklin's codicil, Michelle became more and more nervous. What if Rose won everything? What would happen to her and her baby?

With the time for her confinement approaching, Michelle received a call from the London law firm representing her. As soon as she heard the senior partner's voice, crackling over the Channel cable, her heart sank. For him to bypass his French associates meant that the verdict was in. And against her.

"It's not that at all, Mrs. Jefferson," the barrister assured her. "In fact, the ruling came down this morning—in your favor."

"That's wonderful!"

"It is, but I'm afraid that's not the end of it," the attorney cautioned her. "Miss Jefferson's counsel has filed for a new hearing in New York, claiming that since your late husband's will was drawn up in New York, the codicil should be viewed as being part of it—and therefore subject to validation and interpretation by the laws of that state."

Michelle closed her eyes. "Can she do that, legally I mean?"

"Indeed. However, there is the chance—a very slim one, I warn you—that matters may not reach that stage."

"Why?"

"Because Miss Jefferson has informed us that she wishes to speak to you personally."

Within a few months of Harry Taylor's having been named president of Global's North American operations, the talk on Wall Street centered on the man many assumed to be the undisputed heir to Franklin Jefferson's role in the company.

Harry enjoyed the deference shown him by everyone from the doorman at Global's Lower Broadway headquarters to the secretary of the Gotham Club, where he had recently become a member. The doors to the city's best houses and the offices of the nation's most powerful men magically opened to receive him. He moved into a new duplex apartment on Fifth Avenue. And best of all, Rose, who had returned to steer the company's course, seemed to rely on him more and more—and not only at the office. Almost every night Harry arrived at Talbot House to find Rose waiting for him, hungry, demanding, insatiable.

But after a glorious celebration ushering in 1921, Harry sensed that the bloom was fading. As the court battle in London dragged on, Rose withdrew into a part of herself not even he could reach. Harry kept a close watch on the lawyers' progress and in his private moments with Rose encouraged her to turn the screws. It was inconceivable to him that Michelle might somehow find a way to legitimize the codicil.

Still, it happened.

"Goddamn those British!" Harry raged when Rose told him the news. "You paid them a fortune to get what was yours in the first place! Still, you're right: bringing the case to New York will change everything. No judge in his right mind would rule against you."

Harry turned to Rose for confirmation but she said nothing. Weeks passed, and no matter how many times Harry raised the subject, Rose refused to say a word. Until the day she announced that she was going to France. Then she told him everything.

"You can't be serious!" Harry said.

"I am. Very serious."

"That's crazy!" he shouted. "Do you realize how much that's going to cost us?"

" 'Us,' Harry?"

"You know what I mean! You'll be jeopardizing everything you've worked for."

Rose put down her hairbrush and made herself comfortable on the daybed.

"I'll do anything it takes to remove Michelle from the company. Anything, Harry. Do I make myself clear?"

"There has to be another way!"

Rose's eyes narrowed. "Don't ever use that tone with me. I decide what's best for Global, no one else."

"What about the work I've done? Doesn't that count for anything?"

"Is that what's worrying you, Harry?" Rose asked delicately. "What you're entitled to?"

"You know that's not what I meant," Harry replied quickly. "I'm looking out for you, Rose. That's all."

Rose unbuttoned her blouse. "Come to me, Harry."

"Rose, how can you think of sex—"

"Because I want to. Because I want you. Now come here."

Harry resolved not to move but neither could he stand up to Rose's measured, unblinking stare.

"Now get down on your knees and do all those wickedly wonderful things to me."

Harry felt Rose's fingers gripping his hair, forcing his lips to her breasts, guiding his head across her belly and her parted thighs.

"That's so good," he heard her groan. "Faster, Harry, faster!"

And as he made love to her, Harry Taylor began to understand what it was he meant to Rose Jefferson . . . no more, no less.

The way her meeting with Rose eventually came to pass caught Michelle by surprise. Rose hadn't told her exactly when she would be arriving. One morning, when Michelle least expected it, her housekeeper brought her a hand-delivered card with the morning mail. The message was simple: Rose was at the Crillon Hotel. Would it be convenient for Michelle to meet her there that afternoon?

Michelle dressed carefully for the occasion, keeping her outfit simple and comfortable. It was difficult to look fashionable when you were eight months gone, and she was determined not to sit chafing in some overly tight designer creation.

Michelle arranged for a car to drive her to the elegant Right Bank hotel and was surprised when she drew admiring glances from the men in the lobby. She felt hot, sweaty, and swollen. A porter dressed as an eighteenth-century footman escorted her to the sixth-floor suite and in a grave voice announced her.

Michelle was stunned by the change in Rose's appearance. Although only in her early thirties, Rose seemed much older. She was as beautiful as Michelle remembered, but it was no longer the beauty of a flowering woman. The creases around her eyes and deep lines across her forehead were testimony to an aging that had come swiftly and suddenly.

Rose Jefferson left her chair and held out her hand. "Hello, Michelle."

Did I look like that? she wondered, eyeing Michelle's pregnant figure and the glow of incipient motherhood. *If I did, no one told me. It all seems so long ago. I can't remember the happiness, if there was any. . . .*

"Are you well?" asked Rose.

Michelle nodded.

"Come and sit over here where you'll be comfortable."

Rose led her to a flowered sofa.

"When are you due?"

"Seventeen days, give or take."

"Do you have a good doctor?"

Michelle smiled. "Yes, I have," she said, detecting a stray note in Rose's voice.

She's envious! She thinks I'm carrying Franklin's child, that I have something of his which will never belong to her. . . .

"You've come a long way," Michelle said. "Whatever the reason, it must be important."

Rose sat opposite her, unable to tear her eyes away from Michelle's swollen abdomen.

All because of an heir . . . If she weren't pregnant, none of this would ever have happened.

Rose bit back her anger. She had to choose her words carefully, keep her emotions in check.

"As you know, I'm having the case reopened in New York," Rose said. "It won't take American justice as long to come to a decision as it did the British courts. And to a very different one." Rose paused, letting her words sink in. "However, we still have time to reach a settlement."

Michelle glanced up, surprised. "After all these months? After everything we've said against each other?"

"Michelle, I think that in all this wrangling between lawyers, we've lost sight of the real issue."

"Which is?"

"Why you insist on thinking you have claim on Franklin's share of Global."

"I do because I was his wife," Michelle replied quietly.

"I understand that," Rose said. "But there's a great difference between wanting something—or staking a claim to it—and actually dealing with it. I think it's fair to say that although you know something about Global, it certainly isn't enough for you to be involved in the company. You have no business or financial background, and soon you will have your child to look after and raise. Do you really think you could make any kind of contribution to Global?"

"I was never given the chance to prove myself."

"Be that as it may, the fact is that both you and the company would be better off without each other," Rose said, reaching for her briefcase. "I've had my lawyers establish the net worth of Franklin's share of the company and taken the liberty of having your people in London examine the figures. As you can see, there are no discrepancies."

Michelle accepted the papers but did not glance at them.

"You want to buy me out," she said flatly.

Rose nodded. "The arrangement calls for payments to be made over a period of ten years. You can do whatever you want with the money. There is more than enough to keep you and your child in the style to which you have become accustomed. In short, you gain everything you would should the New York court rule in your favor."

"Except that I would have nothing to do with Global."

"Under the circumstances, I think that's a small enough concession, don't you?"

Michelle picked up the report and opened it to the financial page. The figure at the very bottom, representing the total value of Franklin's shares, was staggering—almost $10 million.

"Why, Rose? Why offer this now, after so much grief?"

Rose's expression hardened. She wasn't about to tell this woman about the sleepless nights and anxiety-ridden days she had endured. All because she knew the moment London had cabled her with the verdict that she could never, never risk challenging Michelle on her home ground. Not when there was even the slightest chance of losing. It would show the other predators in the pool that Rose Jefferson might not be as strong as they thought, that somewhere there lay a weakness that could be manipulated or exploited.

All of which had left Rose with only one course to follow.

"Why?" Rose said, echoing Michelle's question. "Because there's been *too* much grief and waste. Because it all has to stop somewhere."

"There is, however, one condition," she added. "A secrecy clause. When you sign, you agree never to divulge the terms of the settlement to anyone, under any circumstances."

As she said this, Rose thought back to Harry, and how righteous—and greedy—his anger had been when she told him she was going to buy out Michelle.

If he only knew it would be far more than a hundred-thousand-dollar pittance . . .

"I'm waiting for your answer, Michelle."

"No."

"*I beg your pardon?*"

Michelle was as surprised as Rose, even more by what followed. It was as though the words marched out of their own accord.

"I have a different offer to suggest. As far as you're concerned, the traveler's check that Franklin tried to launch is worthless. There's no one here to try and make it work, no one who knows anything about it. Except me."

"What are you getting at, Michelle?"

"Make the traveler's check Franklin's share. Let me finish what Franklin began. I'll need capital to start with but it won't be nearly as much as you're offering. In return, I'll promise never to interfere in Global's American operations, nor anywhere else for that matter."

"What you're telling me," Rose said slowly, "is that in return for the European territory for the traveler's check you will waive all other claims against Franklin's estate?"

Michelle swallowed hard. *Is that what I really mean?*

"Yes," she heard herself say. "But I get to keep whatever profits the checks make. And I can use Global's name."

Rose bridled at the thought of Michelle using the company name. Nevertheless, she sensed an advantage. Michelle was wading far out of her depth.

"How much capital did you have in mind?"

"Two million dollars."

"Two million *and* the use of Global's name?" Rose laughed. "You might as well ask for the moon and the stars as well!"

"Regardless of what you believe, I had nothing to do with the banks' turning down Franklin," Michelle said quietly. "I wanted Franklin to succeed, Rose. I was as much a part of what he was trying to achieve for Global as he was. I've earned the right to that name."

"Not as far as I'm concerned!"

Michelle picked up her purse. "Then we have nothing more to talk about. Please have your lawyers send me the other papers concerning the face value of Franklin's estate."

Rose was thinking hard. In the aftermath of losing Franklin and waiting for the British courts to allow her to bring his body home, she had called the directors of the banks Franklin had been dealing with. Each one had expressed his condolences but when it came to an explanation for their refusal to do business each had stonewalled.

Michelle was right. The checks were finished in England. But if that was the case, where would she sell them? On the Continent? Global's presence was negligible there. So what did Rose really have to lose by letting her use the company name?

"Michelle," Rose called out. "Perhaps there is a way to settle this."

If she takes on the quixotic task of trying to make the traveler's check work she'll inevitably fail. Once that happens, neither she nor her child will ever have any claim on Global again. On the contrary, when she flounders everyone will

299

see that I always had the upper hand. And I'll get back the European territory through a reversion clause.

"I'm listening, Rose," Michelle said quietly.

"What length of time did you have in mind for the loan?"

"Three years."

"No, that's far too long. The interest I'd be losing on that money would be enormous. The most I'd consider is one million dollars repayable in twelve months."

Michelle bit her lip. All her figures and projections indicated that a million was the bare minimum she needed. But a year to repay wasn't long enough.

"Eighteen months," Michelle countered, making her decision. "But I'd want your traveler's-check plates and the sample proofs."

Rose had expected that. "And I would need a license fee for your use of Global's name. Shall we say fifteen percent?"

Michelle shook her head. "The standard fee is seven, Rose. You know that as well as I do."

"Very well. But in that case, I insist that Global receive its percentage out of gross sales. You can pay back the loan out of net."

Michelle felt herself pushed up against a wall. The terms Rose was offering would leave her no margin for error, nothing to fall back on.

"All right," she agreed. "Global gets paid out of the gross."

"Then it's done. I assume you'll call your attorneys to tell them we have an agreement."

"I will as soon as I see the papers."

Rose smiled. "You have my word that the contract will reflect exactly what we decided upon. And you understand the secrecy clause still stands."

Michelle nodded. She was getting to her feet when her face contorted in pain.

"Are you all right?" Rose asked quickly.

Michelle passed a hand over her belly. "Fine . . . The baby kicked. If you don't mind, I should go home. I'm very tired. . . ."

"Of course."

But as she felt her unborn child settle, Michelle was thinking, *My precious love, what have I gone and done? What's going to happen to us now?*

300

With the birth of Cassandra in April 1921, Michelle's life blossomed. When she held her baby for the first time, felt her suckle, and heard her tiny heart beating, all second thoughts, all worries about Rose and the future disappeared. Although she was alone and at times was overwhelmed by the responsibility of this fragile new life, Michelle had only to look into Cassandra's deep blue eyes to wonder all over again at the miracle that had been granted her.

As soon as Michelle had regained her strength, she drafted a long, carefully worded cable to Monk, telling him all about Cassandra. As she read it back, Michelle was bursting to fill the empty words with passion and love, to call Monk a father and tell him how much of him she saw in Cassandra, how the name they had agreed upon seemed to suit their daughter so perfectly. But none of that was possible. Not yet.

As soon as Michelle had Cassandra settled in, she scoured the employment agencies for a suitable nurse. After interviewing ten applicants she finally came across a gem, a middle-aged Swiss woman whose references were impeccable and who spoke French, English, and German. Michelle watched carefully as Fraulein Steinmetz picked up Cassandra for the first time. Cassandra regarded the woman solemnly, then with a sigh, snuggled in her arms and went to sleep. It was the best reference Michelle could have asked for.

For the first six months, no matter how busy she was, Michelle always spent at least several hours a day with her daughter. She took her in the carriage around the Jardin du Luxembourg so that Cassandra could see the brilliant colors of the trees and flowerbeds. In the nursery of the Île St.-Louis apartment, she played with her daughter until Cassandra tired and later, when the baby slept, sat by her crib, working on the traveler's-check scheme. Whenever the night became too long or her eyes too tired, Michelle would touch her daughter, letting her clutch her little finger in her fist. That was all she needed to find the strength to carry on.

For all the happiness Michelle had discovered in her daughter, the doubts about her hasty agreement with Rose Jefferson lingered. The legal papers arrived two months after Cassandra was born, and Michelle had had to devote long hours to them. Not that Rose hadn't kept her word: the contract reflected exactly what the two women had agreed upon. Michelle accepted the bank draft for $1 million, initialed the loan papers, and signed the waiver that closed Franklin's estate to her forever. Now the past was truly just memories, none of which could help her to face the future.

Michelle's immediate reaction was to contact Monk. More than ever, she needed the strength of his love and presence. She longed to talk to him about her ideas just so she could hear the sound of her own voice. Michelle drafted numerous cables but in the end tore up each one. Every time she looked at Cassandra she realized she could not take the risk of involving Monk in what she had to do. That only sharpened her uncertainty and loneliness.

Help came from an unexpected quarter. Among the mountains of gifts that arrived for Cassandra was a lovely silver chocolate cup from Christophe, the Duke of Chambord. In his note the duke mentioned that he would be in Paris and asked if he might call. Michelle was delighted.

"You must forgive me for not having come sooner," Christophe said, sipping a glass of wine in Michelle's living room. "Given how discreetly you have settled in Paris, I didn't want to intrude on your privacy." He paused, then added, "She's a beautiful child, Michelle. You are very, very lucky."

Michelle was touched and caught the wistfulness in his voice. "Have you heard from Patricia?"

Christophe smiled and shook his head. "We had a lovely interlude and it seems to have ended." His tone did not invite further questions, so Michelle dropped the subject. Instead she found herself talking about her arrangement with Rose.

"You made a very good bargain," Christophe observed.

"Except I don't know where to start."

"I think I have just the answer."

Christophe launched into a description of the International Exhibition that would be held in Paris the following spring. Thousands of businessmen and entrepreneurs from all over the world would be attending.

"It will be the perfect showcase for your traveler's check," he concluded.

"What's the good of selling something I don't even have yet?"

"Really, Michelle. Think solutions, not problems. To begin, you must get out more."

Michelle was about to protest but reconsidered. "What do you have in mind?"

"I'm giving a small dinner party tomorrow. I would be delighted to escort you."

The next afternoon Michelle tried Fraulein Steinmetz's patience as she ran through everything that could go wrong that evening. At the last minute, as Christophe's car and driver waited outside, Michelle burst into tears and refused to go.

"Madame," the Swiss nurse informed her, "if you do not leave, I will!"

An hour after arriving at Christophe's Paris residence in the fashionable Sixteenth Arrondisement, Michelle had forgotten her reservations. The cream of society passed through his doors, and the Duke of Chambord was quick to introduce her to his guests, so Michelle discussed life in London with an American envoy who had served there, listened to Jean Cocteau expound on the new directions of French theater, and heard Coco Chanel's pronouncements on the new fashions. The most interesting part of the evening came at dinner. Michelle found herself seated between Emil Rothschild and Pierre Lazard, immensely wealthy and influential bankers who were at the helm of two of France's most prominent financial institutions.

"Christophe tells me you control the license to Global's traveler's check in Europe," Emil Rothschild murmured into his lobster bisque. "Perhaps we might discuss a possibility of a joint venture."

Before Michelle could reply, Pierre Lazard whispered under his breath, "The traveler's check, madame—is it committed to any institution?"

Michelle's head was spinning. Later in the evening she made appointments with both men to talk further about her plans.

"I can't believe they were so interested!" she exclaimed to Christophe after the guests had gone.

Christophe smiled broadly, refilled their brandy balloons, and held his up for a toast.

"This is only the beginning, my dear Michelle!"

It was a promising start, but the negotiations, which dragged on throughout that spring and summer, reinforced Michelle's belief that bankers were the most cautious and suspicious people on earth. It took her until Christmas 1921 to seal the agreements with both Rothschild and Lazard. Even though she had negotiated hard on every fraction of their distribution percentage, the cost was enormous.

Once the contracts had been signed, Michelle scoured Paris until she found what she thought was suitable office space, in a building adjacent to the elegant Lancaster Hotel on rue de Berri. The rent was staggering but Michelle signed the lease, consoling herself with the thought that a good address would reflect the quality of the product she wanted to sell.

As soon as the traveler's-check plates arrived from New York, Michelle met with the directors of the Bank of France. The national bank agreed to sell her the necessary paper as well as to print the checks. Since by law the bank had a monopoly on such services, its fees would have made the greediest pawnbroker blush.

Next came the staff. Michelle spent weeks taking applications and conducting interviews before she realized that former bank clerks, used to dealing with ordinary currencies, couldn't fathom what the traveler's check was all about. Michelle hired the most promising and, in her sparsely furnished offices, began a series of crash courses, teaching her employees what they were dealing with. When she was through, Michelle had lost half her staff, who simply left, convinced that their would-be employer was not unlike the captain of the *Titanic*: doomed to ruin.

By the end of the year Michelle began waking up in the mornings to a now-familiar sensation—panic. In little less than a year she had spent a third of the million dollars she and Rose had settled on. Running expenses such as rent, bankers' and lawyers' fees, salaries for a skeleton staff, and her own household needs were a constant drain on her resources. Looking ahead, she saw that hundreds of thousands of dollars would have to be spent on advertising and promotion in order to get the public's attention. In the meantime she had yet to sell a single check.

Which brought Michelle back to the operation's potentially fatal flaw: an inexperienced, indifferent staff whose rudeness, tardiness, and thinly veiled contempt had become part of their nature. No matter how hard Michelle tried to explain that selling traveler's checks was a *service*, that courtesy, attentiveness, and a helpful attitude were absolutely necessary, her words fell, for the most part, on deaf ears.

"If I don't get the right people I might as well give up," she told Christophe late one evening as they watched the cold, driving January rain turn Paris into a ghost town.

"Perhaps the answer lies in finding those who already know something about the company," Christophe suggested.

At first Michelle was puzzled by his reference, then it dawned on her what the duke was getting at.

"You mean I should try to lure away some of the employees working for Global's European freight operations? Christophe, that would be poaching!"

Christophe shrugged. "From what you've told me about the terms of your contract with Rose, there's nothing to stop you from doing this." On a more serious note, he added, "Michelle, believe me, I have had some experience with poachers. The professional ones I leave to my gamekeepers. But I would never deny a hungry man the chance to shoot a rabbit or land a fish. Besides, what's at stake here is your dream and, more important, your survival, as well as Cassandra's."

The idea was tempting, but the more Michelle turned it over, the more obvious the problems became.

"If I tried something like that, Rose would have a fit. Besides, in most offices, men aren't only the managers but the secretaries and clerks as well. And as I've discovered, men, especially Frenchmen, have a distinct problem working for a woman."

"Who said anything about their having to be men?" Christophe asked innocently. "Take a close look at how the Global branch offices work. You may find a surprise or two."

For the life of her, Michelle had no idea what Christophe was driving at. She thought she knew Global's operations backward. Nonetheless, she took the hint and began a discreet examination of the company's European freight business. What she discovered shocked her.

The express agents, exclusively men, ran their operations as family businesses. Although Rose had a firm policy against hiring women, Michelle learned that the wives and daughters knew as much about the day-to-day affairs of the express trade as did their husbands and fathers. Yet, when the man died, no one thought of allowing these women to carry on with what they did best. The territory was simply given to another man. When she confronted Christophe with her newfound knowledge, Michelle demanded that he tell her why he had gently nudged her in that direction.

"Because many of the widows, having little or no pension, end up hiring themselves out as domestics. Several work for me. That's where I heard the stories." He looked carefully at Michelle. "What do you propose to do now?"

Michelle smiled wickedly. "Watch me!"

Michelle made a list of widows whose husbands had worked for Global and, in the spring of that year, traveled around the country, approaching them. For many of the women, Michelle's offer was too good to be true. She wanted them, and their daughters if they were of age and had the inclination, to come to Paris, where Michelle would teach them the fundamentals of the traveler's check. During the training period, they would be housed in modest accommodations and given an allowance for food and other expenses. If at the end of the program Michelle was satisfied with their performance, permanent jobs would be offered, as well as relocation bonuses.

Michelle chose her candidates carefully. The cost of bringing them to Paris and providing for them would be enormous, and she knew there would be no second chance. She was pinning all her hopes on women who had lived their lives in the shadows of their men. If she could get them to believe in themselves and their own abilities, she was sure they would pay her back with hard work and loyalty. But if, for some reason—incompatibility, homesickness, or just plain lack of skills—most of these women fell by the wayside, then her dreams would fall with them. More than the money, time was working against Michelle; every day the traveler's check was idle was a day closer to the repayment date. And on that score, Michelle knew, Rose Jefferson would show her no mercy.

Twelve of her eighteen months were gone, as was almost half of the staff Michelle had spent two long months training. In the vaults of the Bank of France, millions of dollars' worth of traveler's checks waited for shipment to rue de Berri, and the space they took up cost Michelle dearly each day. Meanwhile, Paris was primping itself for the International Exhibition. All over the city, statues and buildings were being scrubbed and polished, parades were organized, and theme nights planned. Throughout Europe, word had spread that this would be the party of the decade.

"Do you realize what they're asking—and getting—for rents at the Exhibition halls? I'd be down to my last sou if I took space there."

Michelle and Christophe were having lunch in a small outdoor cafe around the corner from her office. Michelle lifted her face to the sun and closed her eyes. Looking over his wineglass, Christophe saw how tired Michelle was. Although she had told him about Monk McQueen and Christophe understood that she was spoken for, he still called on her at least once a week to see how she was faring. More often than not Michelle was at rue de Berri late into the night, poring over charts and figures, trying to find ways to stretch her dwindling resources. On those rare occasions he scolded her into having dinner, Michelle insisted that it be at her apartment. The first time this happened, Christophe understood the reason why. As dinner was cooking, Michelle disappeared into the nursery and didn't come out until the meal was almost ready. That was how scarce and precious her moments with Cassandra were.

Michelle opened her eyes and saw Christophe watching her.

"I'm sorry. I'm not very good company these days."

She stared at her hands, at the thin blue veins beneath white skin. Although she was loath to admit it, Michelle knew she wasn't taking care of herself. She had lost too much weight and ate poorly. At times her mood could turn positively waspish. Yet the frustration of having so much to do and never enough hours in a day to accomplish it all continually ate away at her. The worst of it was that all her commitments robbed her time with Cassandra, time that Michelle knew could never be recaptured.

Christophe recognized the pain in Michelle's eyes.

"You're almost there," he encouraged her gently. "Everything's in place and the Exhibition is around the corner."

Michelle touched the rim of her wineglass with a fingernail, making it peal.

"I'm frightened, Christophe. For the first time since I started all this, I'm really scared."

"You would spend a fortune anyway, to buy space in the newspapers and

306

metro boards," he reasoned. "Even at a time when everyone's attention will be elsewhere. The extra it costs for a booth at the Exhibition . . ." He spread his hands.

"One way or another, I have to decide soon," Michelle said. "By tomorrow, in fact." She leaned over and pecked him on the cheek. "Thank you, my friend. I don't know what I'd do without you!"

"Courage, Michelle. Always courage."

It was well past midnight when Michelle returned to Île St.-Louis. The house was dark and still, and, as always, Michelle went first into the nursery. Much to her surprise she found Cassandra awake, mauling her stuffed animals. Cassandra gurgled a welcome as Michelle picked her up and, rocking her gently, walked through the apartment. Without quite realizing it, she began talking about the Exhibition, all the wonderful things that could come from it as well as the terrible risks involved. On one hand, it was a golden opportunity; on the other, if the checks weren't an instant hit, there would be no second chance.

"So, my darling, what should I do?" Michelle asked, looking down at Cassandra's solemn, blue eyes.

Cassandra smiled happily, shook her tiny fists enthusiastically, then sighed and promptly went to sleep. Michelle couldn't help but laugh.

"Of course. How silly of me."

The next day she signed the lease for the Exhibition space and went off in search of a hot-air balloon. If she was going to spend that much money, she might as well go out in a blaze of glory.

In New York, Hugh O'Neill tapped on Rose Jefferson's door.

"I thought you'd like to see this," he said.

Rose glanced up at him, her expression curious, and took the letter. It was from Global's general manager in Paris, full of self-serving paeans about how wonderfully he'd organized the company's presentation at the International Exhibition.

"The interesting part's at the end."

Rose skipped several paragraphs and smiled.

"My, my. Michelle's decided to play in the big pool."

Rose took out a file of correspondence from her French manager and other contacts. She glanced at the figures, then added the approximate cost of Michelle's Exhibition rent.

"Doesn't leave her much margin for error, does it?"

Hugh O'Neill thought he detected a note of regret in Rose's voice. It couldn't be, he said to himself. Rose had gone into this deal because the odds had been so heavily in her favor. Now that she seemed on the verge of getting back everything she had given Michelle, the sport had gone out of the game.

As though reading his mind, Rose said, "It's not over yet, Hugh. Whatever happens, I have to admit Michelle has gumption. In her place, I don't know if I'd have gambled everything on one roll." Rose paused. "How much longer to repayment date?"

"A little over five months."

Rose shook her head. "On paper, anyway. Keep me posted, Hugh."

"It's magnificent!" Michelle said, gazing around her.

All along the Champs Élysées impressive glass and steel halls had been erected to house the thousands of exhibits that nations from around the world had sent to the French capital. There were diamonds from South Africa, gardens of exotic vegetation from Brazil, the latest industrial machinery from the United States, looms that spun silk and fine fabric from Thailand, enormous brass decoration bowls from India, and ivory sculptures from the African colonies.

"If we could have something like this once a year, the world would learn that it's better to trade than fight," Christophe observed.

Michelle agreed. As she wended her way through the stalls and exhibits, she saw a miniature hot-air balloon rising above the center of the largest pavilion. Stenciled across its canopy was GLOBAL TRAVELER'S CHECKS—ONE CURRENCY FOR ALL! Michelle walked swiftly toward her booth, slipping around the two gendarmes who saluted her.

"Why do you need them?" Christophe inquired.

Michelle pointed to the drawers behind the cashiers' desks. The tills were overflowing with different European currencies and the lines of customers stretched almost to the next exhibit.

"But this is supposed to be an exhibition!" Christophe protested. "Not a bazaar."

"Really?" Michelle replied, raising one eyebrow. "It just so happens, my dear, that there is nothing in the rules and regulations of the Exhibition which prevents participants from selling as well as displaying."

Christophe looked around. "But no one else is doing that."

"Not because they can't!" Michelle shot back. "Most of the exhibitors either never thought of it or assumed it couldn't be done. At least this way, I'm getting back some of the exorbitant rent I've paid out."

Christophe looked again at the line of customers.

"How much are you taking in?"

"Let's just say we're emptying the tills three times a day."

"Touché. Forgive my indiscretion. If this keeps up, you'll have to print more checks."

Michelle smiled lightly. Christophe wasn't privy to the amount Rothschild and Lazard were charging her on every check cashed at either their institutions or at correspondent banks. The percentage reduced Michelle's profit to a bare minimum. The Exhibition would be over at the end of the month. Michelle had already calculated that even if sales remained high, she would be half a million dollars short on her repayment to Rose. With less than four months to make up that difference somehow.

Although she spent long hours around her exhibit, meeting businesspeople from around the world, Michelle worked the floor as well. By now she had her share of imitators and as she moved from pavilion to pavilion, she watched what people spent their money on and how they paid. Most, she noticed, were purchasing gifts for friends and relatives back home. Several days before the Exhibition was due to close, the buying had reached a frenzy.

Too bad they're not taking home traveler's checks.

Michelle stopped short.

Why shouldn't they? Because no one's ever suggested it to them!

Michelle raced home and began going through her notes. The period immediately following World War I had seen a vast emigration wave from Europe to America. From Global's own records Michelle learned that most immigrants arrived carrying only the currency of their own country. Since few banks would accept lira, drachmas, or francs, the newcomers were easy prey for speculators who sold them American dollars at usurious rates. Michelle had no doubt that the practice was still flourishing.

As soon as the Exhibition closed, Michelle posted notices all over Paris stating that Global would sell traveler's checks in U.S. dollars for any European currency at prices 2 percent higher than the daily Paris bourse rate. Within a week the office on rue de Berri was swamped. Francs that had lain under mattresses for generations magically surfaced and were eagerly converted to traveler's checks. As the word spread, Michelle opened two other offices in the city and kept a full-time staff going ten hours a day selling dollar-denominated checks, which visitors and immigrants could cash at any of the thousands of Global offices or correspondent banks across the United States.

"I think Rose Jefferson didn't quite anticipate that particular move," Christophe remarked one evening over supper.

"That's too bad," Michelle replied. "Because under the circumstances Global can scarcely refuse to honor its own currency!"

"I believe this calls for a celebration," Christophe said, signaling for the sommelier.

"No, not yet," Michelle told him. "Not until the debt is paid in full."

Christophe was about to make a remark but caught himself in time. Michelle didn't have to be reminded that her loan was due in less than thirty days.

On the evening of November 13, Michelle personally visited each of her outlets and checked the day's deposits.

"Make sure they're in the bank first thing in the morning," she instructed her managers.

They were perplexed. The deposits were *always* the first order of business.

At ten o'clock the next morning, Michelle presented herself at the offices of Emil Rothschild.

"Such a lovely way to greet the day," the banker said, welcoming her. "It's always a pleasure to see you, Michelle."

"You might change your opinion after you hear what I want."

"For you, Michelle, anything."

"Very well, Emil, but don't say I didn't warn you."

When Michelle told the banker what she needed, he paled.

"But, Michelle, that's impossible!"

"Check your records, Emil," Michelle replied quietly. "And don't forget to include today's deposits."

The banker called his chief accountant, who, a few minutes later, appeared carrying a ledger. Rothschild wet the tips of his fingers and leafed through the pages.

"*Bon Dieu!*"

"I want all of that transferred by cable, as soon as possible, to this account at the Morgan Bank in New York."

"All of it! But what will you live on—"

"Emil, please!"

The banker regarded her carefully. "Very well," he said, and gave the accountant his instructions. "Can I offer you some coffee?" he asked.

"I think something stronger would be in order."

At eight o'clock the same morning, New York time, Eric Gollant called on Rose at Talbot House.

"This is an unexpected pleasure," Rose said warmly. "What got you out of bed so early?"

"A call from the overnight cable department at Morgan," Gollant replied. He handed Rose a sheet with several numbers. "These are the figures he quoted me. Do you have any idea why someone would suddenly send us a million-odd dollars?"

Puzzled, Rose checked the figures. "I haven't the faintest—"

Then she remembered the date.

"The money originated in Paris?"

"According to Morgan, it came from Rothschild."

Rose and Eric stared at each other, arriving at the inevitable conclusion at the same time.

"It can't be," Eric muttered.

"You're damn right it can be," Rose said. The paper fluttered from her hand. "Can you believe it? Michelle actually did it. She really paid back the loan."

Eric saw dark fury cloud Rose's face. He braced himself for the worst.

"She did it!" Rose cried, and then she began to laugh. "I'll be damned if she didn't show us all up!"

— 38 —

In March 1924, Emil Rothschild, Pierre Lazard, and Michelle had a celebratory dinner at the famed La Tour d'Argent. The meal consisted entirely of the restaurant's specialty—duck, served in five different ways.

"To Madame Jefferson," Lazard saluted. "Who, to paraphrase an American statesman, put a traveler's check into the wallet of every European traveler, no matter how humble!"

Michelle accepted the toast graciously. The eighteen months that had followed her repayment of the loan had been almost as hectic and nerve-racking as their predecessors. By scraping together every last centime in order to meet the deadline, Michelle had left herself virtually penniless. Rothschild and Lazard had combined to provide a line of credit for the business but Michelle was loath to dip into it. One of the cardinal rules she had learned was never to give anyone, even your friendly banker, a foothold in your business. Michelle had seen how enormously asset-rich people had been humbled into bankruptcy because they couldn't meet a payment on what seemed like an insignificant loan.

As soon as the Exhibition was over, Michelle extended the office hours at her outlets. She worked Saturdays and holidays and committed her profits to advertising. Within six months her reserves had reached record levels. The French business press began running interviews with her, playing up both her heroism during the war and her intimate connection to one of America's most prominent financial families.

Michelle couldn't help but smile at the last reference. Since the repayment, she had heard from Rose only once. True to her word, Rose's attorneys had forwarded the papers that gave Michelle exclusive control of the Global traveler's check in Europe. Included in them was a brief note, Rose's congratulations couched in terse phrases. Yet for all the humble pie Rose had been forced to eat, her character shone through. She had wagered and lost, accepting defeat as gracefully as possible.

On the other hand, Monk's letters were both a joy and a balm for Michelle. News of her success, he wrote, was the talk of Wall Street, and in every sentence Michelle felt his pride at what she had achieved. But as much as he wanted to be with her to share her triumph, Monk could not go to France yet. He was putting in yeoman's hours organizing *Q* magazine so that very soon it would be able to run itself and he would be free. For Michelle that day couldn't come soon enough. To be ready for it, Michelle consolidated her own affairs. In February, after the existing lease had run out, she had bought the building on rue de Berri, trebled her staff, and brought her entire organization under one roof.

"What is your next coup going to be?" Emil Rothschild asked expansively between courses.

Michelle looked through the windows at the lights of the *bateaux mouches* that plied the Seine ferrying their loads of merrymakers to the tunes of small orchestras.

"I was thinking of expansion."

Pierre Lazard gave a typically Gallic sigh which spoke volumes about man's folly.

"Really, Michelle. You've made such a brilliant start here. Why take unnecessary risks?"

"Because it wouldn't be a risk. Not if you were to help me."

The two financiers ferociously attacked their pressed duck.

"Madness," Pierre Lazard muttered.

"Difficult time to expand," Rothschild agreed. "Too much uncertainty."

Michelle raised her glass and laughed. "Are you both always so gloomy when you're going to make money?"

Michelle launched into her explanation. "What I've succeeded in doing— with a great deal of help from you, gentlemen—is to make Paris the tourist capital of Europe. Every American knows rue de Berri. Usually that's his first stop. I intend to keep it that way, but I also want to expand Global's services. For example, in the next few months I will install desks where our clients can pick up their mail and send back replies. This way, customers will be advertising for us."

Michelle paused as the next course was served. "I've just tallied the latest figures on the dollars Americans spent in Paris last summer, as well as the total for Europe. It was, gentlemen, over fifty million dollars."

Michelle let her point sink in, noticing that both bankers were losing interest in their ducks.

"Fifty million dollars," she repeated. "Where does that money come from? Only two percent of it goes through letters of credit, which the wealthy travelers still insist on carrying. For them, it's all well and good. There's a certain snob appeal to having a banker like Morgan or Harjes. But the bulk of the traffic comes from people those bankers won't deal with: students and middle-class tourists."

Rothschild gaped. "Students?"

"Don't you dare turn your nose up at them, Emil," she scolded. "Tens of thousands of students come to Europe every year. It's become a rite of passage. And a lot of them work to get here, hiring themselves as tenders on cattle steamers to pay their way. As for the middle class, they're just discovering what a bargain Europe is."

"Then what kind of expansion are you looking at in Paris?" Rothschild asked.

"Not Paris."

The financiers stared at her blankly.

"Europe," Michelle said. "I want to duplicate what we've done in Paris in Bordeaux, Nice, and the Riviera. At the same time I want to establish a version of rue de Berri in every European capital."

Michelle's eyes were glittering with excitement.

"And that's where I need you. It would take me months to negotiate with German, Swiss, Italian, and Spanish banks individually. Precious operating time would be lost, not to mention the operational costs. However, if both your banks would give their imprimatur we could expect quick decisions from everybody."

Lazard looked at Rothschild and Michelle could almost see the stream of words passing between them. Both bankers had branches in European capitals. Both had the power and prestige to bring others to the table. Michelle waited for the other shoe to drop.

"What kind of financial arrangement did you have in mind?" Emil Rothschild asked cautiously.

"I propose that in France your percentage remains the same," Michelle said. "However, as far as the rest of Europe is concerned, we work out a straight finder's fee: you bring the banks on board, I make my own deal with them. As soon as it's signed, you collect your share."

"Michelle, Michelle," Pierre Lazard objected. "Surely if we are going to be partners we must participate in the profits."

"Partners only participate if they share in the risk," Michelle said firmly. "In this case, the risk is all mine. I am not asking you for loans to set up the operations or to underwrite the traveler's check. What I do need are your contacts and expertise."

Michelle had had enough dealings with both men to recognize their pointed looks. Each had made enormous profits for his bank because of the few pennies she paid out for every Global check bought and sold through their institutions. Multiply those amounts by six or seven countries, three to four hundred banks, and the figures became staggering. The bankers, she thought, wouldn't surrender Europe without a fight.

"I think we could work out a lower commission for the rest of Europe," Rothschild mused. "After all, your agreements with foreign banks would rest on the fact that we are prepared to back your instrument."

"Nonsense!"

Michelle whirled around at the sound of the familiar voice. Monk McQueen towered over her, both hands on the back of her chair, leaning aggressively toward her dinner partners. It was all she could do not to leap out of her chair and embrace him.

Monk introduced himself although both Rothschild and Lazard knew him by reputation. To Michelle, he bowed and held her hand a touch longer than politeness dictated.

"Gentlemen, I couldn't help but overhear some of your conversation, and while I'm not one to pull the rug out from under honest businessmen, I can tell you that I found Mrs. Jefferson's offer very reasonable. So reasonable, in fact, that if you choose to pass on it, I will personally take it to Morgan himself. I can assure you he won't turn down a chance to make a good dollar just by bringing his friends together in one room."

"Monsieur McQueen," Lazard said silkily. "Naturally we are all aware of your reputation as a publisher. But permit me to say that financial concerns such as we were discussing might well exceed even your abilities to appreciate."

Monk leaned back and shrugged. "We're talking a flat fee of no more than two hundred thousand dollars. Morgan will take less than that because he's already told his people he wants to handle the traveler's checks."

Heads turned toward Michelle.

"Is this true, Michelle?" asked Emil Rothschild.

"It is," Michelle replied calmly, mortified by Monk's ploy. "However, I saw no reason to raise the subject."

Monk casually handed Pierre Lazard a copy of Q magazine. "The proof for the next edition. The interview with Morgan is on the front page."

"Obviously this puts a whole new light on the subject," Lazard said, handing the paper to his fellow banker. "With all due respect to Mr. Morgan, Michelle,

I think that the three of us have developed a relationship and expertise we should continue."

"I'm so glad to hear that, Pierre."

Michelle was thoroughly enjoying herself but she was dying to know where Monk had come from. It was the answer to the dreams she had had every night.

After Emil Rothschild had read the piece, he called over a waiter and ordered that the restaurant's legendary cellar surrender its best bottle of champagne.

"I think it would be appropriate," he said grandly. "After all, to arrive at an equitable figure is a mere formality."

"Gentlemen, I couldn't agree more," Michelle said. When the wine was poured she raised her glass.

"To new horizons . . ."

And then she looked at Monk. "And old friends to share them with!"

"When did you get here?"

They stood in front of the balcony in Michelle's bedroom, facing each other, their hands at their sides, as though they were afraid to touch.

"I still can't believe it," Michelle whispered.

She reached out and cupped his cheek.

"Believe it," Monk said and leaned forward to kiss her gently. When his lips found the nape of her neck, goosebumps broke out on Michelle's skin.

"My God, I'd forgotten how good that feels!" she gasped.

Michelle stepped back and slowly undid the buttons and hooks of her evening dress, letting it spill to the floor. She shrugged off her silk slip, then reached out and took Monk's hand and placed it over her breast.

"I'm not letting you go again," she said.

"I don't intend to leave," he replied hoarsely.

Michelle sighed and threw her arms around Monk's neck, guiding his mouth between the cleft of her breasts. Gently they made love, each scarcely able to believe the other was real.

Afterward, when they lay with him still inside her, Monk cupped her face in his palms, brushing away the tears with his thumbs.

"Why do you cry?" he whispered, gazing into her eyes.

"I always cry, don't you remember? Even that first time . . ." Michelle looked away because she couldn't bear the concern in his eyes. "I love you so much. I will always love you."

Monk gently slid out of bed at first light and padded into the next room. He pulled back the covers so that he could see Cassandra sleeping. For the longest time he stood there, marveling at the small, perfect person before him, listening to her rhythmic breathing, drinking in this vision to which he was inextricably bound.

I will be there for you whenever I can, as often as I can. I promise you no one will ever hurt you or your mother. . . .

When Monk went into the kitchen he found that Michelle had already set out their breakfast of coffee, croissants, butter, and jam.

"She looks just like you," he murmured, kissing her along the nape of her neck.

"If she ever grows up to your size, we'll never be able to feed her."

They laughed together and it was the sweetest sound Monk had ever heard.

"Did you mean what you said last night?" Michelle asked tentatively. "About being able to stay?"

"Of course. The magazine is doing fine without me. I may have to go back once in a while to keep my hand in. But I won't stay away from you or Cassandra. You don't know what that does to me."

Michelle laid her hand on his. "What about Rose? What if she finds out? Everything we were so afraid of . . ."

"Nearly four years have gone by, Michelle. Your widowhood has to end. No one has the slightest reason to think that Cassandra isn't Franklin's daughter. Our being lovers won't arouse suspicions."

He studied her face and amid the joy saw shadows of sorrow.

"Right now it's the best we can make for ourselves," Monk said. "God knows, it will be so much more than we had before."

For a time they ate in silence, then Michelle giggled.

"Were you serious about going to Morgan?"

"You bet I was. The expressions on Rothschild's and Lazard's faces . . ."

They laughed about that too, then Michelle began to ask him about New York.

"Things are pretty much the same except that Global is making pots of money from the money orders and expanding in all directions at once. Profits are being poured into mining companies, paper mills, steamship lines—you name it."

"Then I suppose she's forgotten all about me," Michelle said lightly.

Monk shook his head. "You and your traveler's check were to be dead and buried by now. Instead you've become a runaway success."

"Do I detect a note of concern?" Michelle teased him.

Monk's expression remained serious. "The economy—here and back home—is too volatile. I don't trust it. The stock market is rampant with speculation, there's horrific inflation in Germany. When the situation explodes, I don't want you or Cassandra involved."

"So you're saying that I should rethink my expansion," Michelle said slowly.

"No. Get your offices operating but pay off your debts quickly. That way, no one will ever be able to take away what is yours."

Michelle thought about this for a moment, then looked at Monk with a soft smile.

"That's why you came, wasn't it? You see something no one else does and wanted to warn me."

"I came because I love you and Cassandra," Monk said, then, with a huge grin, added, "The three of us are going to turn Europe on its ear!"

If Michelle had had one concern about Monk's arrival in Paris, it was Cassandra's reaction to him. She needn't have worried. Cassandra took to Monk instantly and without question. While Michelle was busy with her business, Monk, who kept in touch with his New York office via cable and wrote the occasional piece on European financial dealings, had all the time in the world to spend with his daughter.

By the end of June the apartment on Île St.-Louis was shuttered and dustcloths had been draped across the furniture. Monk had bought a huge Mercedes touring sedan that would carry them and the luggage. The Swiss nurse, Cassandra's tutor, and Michelle's European general manager followed in a smaller car.

The first stop was Geneva, which Michelle had selected as her base for Swiss operations. They settled in a villa by the lake, and while Monk taught Cassandra how to swim and took her sailing on Lake Leman, Michelle carefully pieced together her first foreign operation. Within four months its success drew comments even from the skeptical Swiss, who chided themselves for having overlooked the potential business to be had from the American tourist. Even the gold-backed Swiss franc was faltering before the mighty dollar. Americans were to be found everywhere from the hiking trails of the Alps to exclusive shops of Zurich's Bahnofstrasse. Merchants eagerly accepted Global Traveler's Checks, which, having been blessed by the Swiss banking establishment, were considered as holy as the local currency.

Autumn found the family in Italy, where Michelle wanted to establish outlets in Rome, Venice, and Milan. While she traveled up and down the Boot, Monk unveiled the wonders of the ancient city for Cassandra. The following spring, she celebrated her fourth birthday in a Venetian gondola and played with farmers' children in the rolling hills of Tuscany.

In the winter the threesome meandered across southern Europe, beginning in Athens and then skipping along the Algean Islands across the Mediterranean toward Spain and Portugal. After Michelle concluded her business in Madrid and Lisbon, they spent several weeks on the Algarve. There was a brief stop in Paris to check that everything was running smoothly at the rue de Berri headquarters, then they turned north toward Amsterdam, the first stop in a year-long tour that would take them as far north as Scandinavia.

"I never told you my mother was Swedish, did I," Monk said as they stood against the railing of the bridge on the ferry carrying them from Copenhagen to Malmo.

"There are a lot of things I don't know about you, Mr. McQueen," Michelle teased him.

Monk draped his arm around her shoulders.

"Plenty of time to find out about all of them," he said. "All the time in the world."

From the minute they arrived Michelle loved Stockholm. Like Paris, it was a city that breathed history, but instead of imposing grandeur it radiated warmth and charm.

"Looks like they're getting ready to celebrate," Monk observed as they drove from the railroad station in Gamla Stan, or Old Town.

Coincidentally, they had arrived on the eve of Walpurgis Night, a celebration that marked the end of the winter solstice. After putting Cassandra to bed, Monk and Michelle fell in with the crowds in the street and walked through the parks where enormous fires were burning. All around them, people were singing and dancing and Monk swept Michelle off her feet as the revelers applauded. When the dishes were cleared away, the men sat down for the ritual drink. A small silver coin was placed in the bottom of a cup and sweet, hot coffee was poured until the coin disappeared. Then vodka was added so that the coin became visible again. Michelle was aghast at the amount of liquor that went into each round. In spite of the shouts of encouragement from wives and friends, the men at the table passed out one by one until only Monk remained standing. Those who had been watching roared their approval as he downed the final cup.

"I had no idea you could drink so much," Michelle exclaimed as they walked the Norrbro Bridge to their hotel.

"I am a man of many talents," Monk told her gravely.

Monk threw open the doors and stepped onto the stone balcony of their suite, which looked out on Kungsträdgarden and, in the distance, the Royal Palace.

"Are you all right, my darling," Michelle asked anxiously, seeing two tears roll down Monk's cheek.

"I've never been happier in my life," he whispered. He paused, then added, "I've never been able to say this to you either."

Michelle's heart raced. *He's going to tell me he has to leave!*

"Michelle, will you marry me?"

Michelle stared at him, unable to believe what she'd just heard.

"Yes, yes, yes!" she cried, flinging her arms around Monk's neck.

They held on to one another fiercely, both crying now.

"I'm behaving like an idiot," Monk said, wiping his cheek. "Give me a moment, will you?"

Michelle watched him walk into the suite with careful, deliberate strides. Suddenly, there was a crash. Michelle raced into the bedroom to find Monk sprawled on their bed, the end of which had collapsed beneath him, snoring softly, a beatific smile on his lips.

"Oh, you wonderful, impossible man!" she whispered, tugging off his clothes.

Michelle got into bed with him, holding him close. Throughout the night and into the dawn she lay awake, her mind spinning wonderful dreams. Cassandra would at last have her father, and she, a husband. A husband . . . Just before she finally fell asleep, Michelle put in place all the things she would have to do tomorrow.

When Monk awoke the next morning he thought he had been felled by a sledgehammer. In spite of all he had drunk, however, his head was remarkably clear. Noticing that Michelle was gone, he wandered through the suite until he realized he was alone. Michelle and Cassandra, he reckoned, must have gone to breakfast.

Monk was returning to the bedroom when a valet appeared with a new gray suit, white shirt, and navy blue cravat. He informed Monk that he was expected downstairs in an hour and that he was to help him get ready. Monk chuckled at Michelle's pampering him this way and told the valet to go ahead and shave him.

Downstairs, Monk followed the valet through the hotel's formal dining room and out onto the terrace that faced the water. The grounds were beautifully landscaped with fresh spring flowers. Monk breathed in the tangy air, noticing the small gazebo with decked vines at the head of the terrace and the harp standing off to one side.

"Be a great place to get married," he remarked to the valet.

The words were scarcely out of his mouth when Monk realized what he had asked Michelle last night. He looked around in a panic, then saw her come out through another door, wearing a simple white dress accented by pearls and carrying a small bouquet. Behind her, Monk caught a glimpse of Cassandra, also dressed in white, peeking out at him with a mischievous grin. "Oh, my God."

Before Monk knew what was happening, the manager of the hotel was escorting him toward the gazebo.

"No need to worry, sir," he confided. "I have the ring. And Madame took care of the license."

Monk swallowed hard. A cherubic Lutheran pastor appeared, the harpist took her seat, and Michelle was standing beside him.

"You meant what you said last night, didn't you?" she whispered.

"Of course," Monk replied hastily.

"Good. Because I wasn't going to let you get out of it anyway."

Marriage and the joy of at last being with the two people who meant everything to him became the greatest wonders of Monk's life. He was a man who, thinking he had seen most of what life had to offer, suddenly discovered miracles he hadn't dreamed could exist. As soon as they returned to Paris, Monk had official adoption papers drawn up, making him Cassandra's legal father.

"I wish we could tell her the truth," Michelle said.

"One day we will," Monk promised. "But the only reason Rose agreed to your arrangement with her was because you were Franklin's wife, carrying his heir. If Cassandra is to inherit everything you've built, without Rose contesting the legacy, then Rose can never know she's not Franklin's child."

"You mean we might have to wait until Rose passes away before we tell Cassandra?"

"That would be safest," Monk replied.

But such clouds were few and far between in the new family's life. Because he didn't have to go to work in an office, Monk was able to spend a great deal of time with his daughter. Whenever Michelle was away on business Monk looked after Cassandra's lessons, hiring additional tutors as she grew older. By the time she was seven, Cassandra was fluent in English, French, Italian, and Spanish. Her intense curiosity sometimes drove Monk crazy, such as the time she followed him to a newspaper office and, having diligently pecked out a two-paragraph story about Hans Christian Andersen's Mermaid of Copenhagen, promptly added it to the bottom of the piece Monk had prepared for Q magazine.

The success of the traveler's check was overwhelming and by 1928 over $75 million worth had been sold. The profits allowed Michelle to pay off all the notes on her European properties and the balance just kept on growing until Michelle was rumored to be one of the wealthiest women in Europe.

"Just don't go investing a dime in this place," Monk counseled when he accompanied Michelle to Berlin.

As a businesswoman Michelle knew she would have to deal with Germany sooner or later. But old memories of the war had never gone away completely. Twice in forty years the Germans had overrun and occupied France. Fear and suspicion were bred in Michelle's bones.

320

"When the crunch comes, and it will very soon, this is the place it will begin," Monk prophesied.

He, Michelle, and Cassandra were having lunch in a cafe on the Kurfurstendamm, Berlin's Fifth Avenue.

"It's because of that damned Treaty of Versailles," Michelle said. "After the war we humbled them, and they'll never forgive us for the shame we've made them live with."

In spite of her reservations, Michelle found herself courted by German bankers, predominantly Jewish, who were not only eager to do business but who assured her that this "little corporal," as they referred to Hitler, was a nobody.

"The Germans are a civilized people," the financier Abraham Warburg told her. "Your money will be as safe here as anywhere else in Europe."

"It's not my money that concerns me, Herr Warburg," Michelle replied. "It's what may happen to you if you're wrong about Hitler."

She saw the banker hesitate, then he lowered his voice.

"Mrs. McQueen, if, God forbid, some catastrophe befalls us, then everything you do for us now may become even more valuable in the future."

Michelle didn't need to hear another word. She told Monk what Warburg had confided in her and received his unqualified support. By June 1929, Global Travel Offices were open in Berlin, Munich, Frankfurt, and Hamburg, and that summer alone counter clerks processed five thousand letters a day for waiting tourists who jammed the offices to get their mail from home. In spite of the dizzying inflation of the German mark, traveler's checks were sold as fast as the printers could deliver them.

"No one wants the mark," Monk observed. "They're destroying their own currency in order to get as many dollars as they can."

Michelle, who had worked the longest days of her life setting up the German operation, had had enough.

"Let's go home," she whispered to Monk as they lay curled up in their suite at the legendary Kempinski Hotel. "There's no joy in this country and I want Cassandra to stop being a gypsy. It's time she went to a real school and made friends."

"New York or Paris?" asked Monk, although he already knew the answer.

"Not New York, my love. Not yet."

— 39 —

The summer heat wave of 1930 broke all temperature records for the past fifty years. The torpor hung over Manhattan like a heavy, wet shroud, fraying tempers and causing fistfights in hardware stores as customers ransacked the shelves for electric fans.

Harry Taylor didn't need electric fans. His Fifth Avenue duplex was air-conditioned. Except that during the night, a brownout had killed the flow of soothing, cool air, turning the apartment into an oven. Harry had to struggle through a jackhammer headache before he realized that his Filipino houseboy was trying to wake him up.

"What the hell do you want?"

The words came out as a croak instead of a roar. Harry's mouth burned with the aftertaste of whiskey. As soon as his eyes saw daylight, a bolt of pain shot through his skull.

"You instructed me to remind you that you are to be at the Global board-room at exactly twelve o'clock," the houseboy said in perfect English.

Harry stared at his servant's impassive features.

"Time . . . ?"

"Ten minutes after eleven."

"Christ . . . Get out of here and let me shower. Get some clothes ready. Something cool!"

Harry looked over his shoulder at the blonde in his bed, snoring softly. Where had she come from? More to the point, who was she?

Harry staggered into the bathroom and turned on the jets in the shower stall. The water was like a balm and he stood there, eyes closed, letting it purge his abused body. Then, for no apparent reason, he began to weep.

Eight years earlier, when Rose Jefferson had sailed for Europe to confront Michelle, Harry Taylor had resigned himself to the fact that she was making a bad decision. It had turned out to be catastrophic. Instead of quietly buying off Michelle, Rose had given her everything Harry had believed would be his.

"Don't worry," Rose had assured him. "When I get the territory back I want you to finish what Franklin started. You're going to build Global in Europe the way you built it in the Midwest, I promise!"

And Harry had believed her. He threw himself into his work like a man

322

possessed. In two years the number of Global offices selling money orders doubled. The profits poured in, profits Rose used to buy fleets of trucks that carried goods across the breadth of the nation, ships that ferried consignments over the oceans of the world, and whole companies that turned Global into an industrial giant.

Yet the reward Harry had been promised never materialized. When Rose heard of Michelle's arrangement with the French bankers she refused to discuss the subject. Time and again Harry argued that Rose, with her vast financial power, should scare off Rothschild and Lazard by threatening to stop doing business with them if they went ahead and supported Michelle.

"Don't be a fool!" Rose had snapped at him. "We can't bully them precisely because *we* do business with them!"

As the years went by Harry Taylor saw his dream wither away. It died the day Rose received Michelle's check for $1 million, plus interest, repayment of her loan. For all his smartly cut suits, his beautiful home, and his club memberships, Harry realized he was nothing more to Rose than what he had been his first day on the job with Global: an employee.

In desperation, Harry had proposed to Rose on four different occasions. Each time she had rejected him firmly. When he accused her of thinking him good enough to share her bed but not her life, Rose had him barred from Talbot House.

Those few words from her mouth had hurt Harry more than he had believed possible. In his new world of the tightly knit, very rich, Harry had always been regarded as the consort-in-waiting. When Rose started attending society functions by herself, Harry's absence made for juicy gossip in the city's clubs and locker rooms.

"Poor Harry. What's he going to do when Rose turfs him out for good?"

Whenever he overheard such comments Harry put on his bravest face. It had never occurred to him that Rose and Global could do without him. Terrified of the possibility of losing everything, Harry redoubled his efforts at the office. Only in his private moments did he dare dream of revenge. And not on Rose.

The more he thought about it the more Harry became convinced that it was Michelle who had robbed him of what was rightfully his. Obsessively he followed her every move, watching for that one mistake which he could turn to his advantage. But Michelle never faltered, no matter how daring her schemes.

For a time all Harry could do was watch helplessly as Michelle moved from triumph to triumph. Then one day he woke up, looked at himself in the mirror, and discovered that he too had not been immune to time. Except that instead of victory, all he saw were ravages. The features women had once found so attractive were sagging. The body that had been sculpted by honest farm work had withered, the muscle and sinew eroded by too much good food and liquor. Worst of all, there were no more dreams. Somewhere along the way, without his having been aware of it, they had escaped him, like the last wisps of smoke from a candle snuffed out.

Every time Harry thought of his dreams, tears inevitably followed.

Harry Taylor stepped out of the shower, threw back some aspirin, and donned the clothes the houseboy had laid out for him. Then he went into the library and, coming around his handsome desk, studied the thick dossier.

One hand left to play. One chance to save it all . . .

Reverently, Harry opened the dossier and read the first few pages, relieved that the words sounded as strong and confident as he had hoped they would. Years of meticulous work had gone into its preparation, begun the day Global had received Michelle's repayment. It was a blueprint to strip Michelle of her holdings once and for all. The plan was so perfect that Harry was convinced even Rose, who had the only other copy, wouldn't be able to find fault with it.

Now she'll see that Michelle is a threat that can't be ignored. She'll need someone to confront her. And who else does she have but me?

Rose had promised him she'd have the material read by today. As he left his apartment Harry felt lady luck riding on his shoulder. What better occasion for his dreams to be reborn than at a birthday party?

Not even the heavy oak double doors of her office could damper the hum of a celebration in the making. Normally Rose would have found the intrusion annoying. Today, she welcomed it.

Rose turned over the dossier Harry had given her and pushed it away. She wished she could just as easily banish the memories it had brought forth.

Damn you, Harry, for making me relive this all over again!

When she had made her arrangement with Michelle, Rose had been convinced that there was no way Michelle could succeed. Instead, she had watched with disbelief and then anger as whatever Michelle touched turned to gold. At first she'd put it down to sheer blind luck, but as the successes multiplied, it was clear that Michelle had learned many lessons and learned them thoroughly.

The business press, which had lauded Rose's apparent victory, began to change its slant. Led by the editors of *Q* magazine, financial writers gave Michelle more and more space, praising her achievements, daring, and fore-sight. The powerful Wall Street voices that had quietly congratulated Rose on her coup changed their tune. Questions were raised about her tactics, which clearly had backfired. Rose Jefferson could be wrong. She was vulnerable.

Rose listened to whispers with mounting fury, yet the most effective way to stop them was denied her. Hugh O'Neill himself had drafted the contract between her and Michelle. Rose had scrutinized it to make sure the terms would irrevocably trap Michelle. Instead, because Michelle had been able to repay the loan, the trap had sprung the other way. Rose had left herself no opening through which to negotiate an accommodation with Michelle. All she could do was watch as Michelle followed one success with another.

In spite of her grudging admiration for Michelle, to have been so wrong galled Rose, and she vented her anger on those who could neither run nor defend themselves. Throughout the 1920s, Global became an insatiable acquisitions machine. Rose targeted companies, large or small, that she wanted for her empire and went after them relentlessly.

Although this was a time that tested every ounce of her business acumen, Rose never lost sight of Michelle. She was continually overwhelmed by her success, yet, at the same time, none of the rancor she had felt before reappeared. Although she didn't understand exactly why this was, Rose could pinpoint the moment her feelings toward Michelle began to change: when she learned that Michelle and Monk McQueen had married.

It was a love that could have been mine. Was mine. But I chose to use it, ruin it, thinking I could do without it. . . .

Another woman might have heaped scorn upon a man who had been hers for the asking, but not Rose. Instead, the day she learned about the marriage she realized how poor she really was.

Rose tapped the cover of Harry's dossier with a crimson fingernail. She had to admit that the mechanics were brilliant, with flashes of daring and insight that reminded her of the old Harry. His plan called for an alliance between Global, Cooks, and the British banks, the creation of a new traveler's check shared and honored by all three that would eventually challenge Michelle's monopoly of Europe. But his single-minded determination to bring Michelle down had blinded Harry to two vital facts. Because of its licensing fee, Global was receiving millions of dollars annually from Michelle. Second, Michelle's success had inadvertently boosted the company's profile across the Continent, and so she was indirectly responsible for bringing impressive revenues from Europe to Lower Broadway. If Harry was aware of this, it wasn't reflected in his report. He still saw Michelle as the enemy who had succeeded in his place. This obsession, Rose thought, told her everything she needed to know about Harry.

Now it was time to go to the party.

"Happy birthday, Steven!"

Rose stepped forward and, on tiptoes, kissed her twenty-two-year-old son on both cheeks. The executives and staff gathered in the boardroom sang "Happy

Birthday," finishing up with a burst of applause. One by one they filed past to shake hands.

He's such a handsome man! Rose thought, admiring her son.

Steven had indeed fulfilled every hope Rose had had for him. Well over six feet, he had inherited her thick, black hair and his father's cobalt-blue eyes. His face, suntanned from sailing and tennis, was defined by an aggressive jaw and high cheekbones that lent him an almost Roman profile. A graduate of Exeter, he had completed his Harvard studies in three years, winning top honors in business administration, and had spent the past year getting his feet wet in various departments of Global.

Rose had dreamed of this moment, clutching it like a magic amulet. In spite of her schedule she had always made time for Steven, looking out for anything or anyone that might threaten him. But Steven had remained pure. No woman had come even close to stealing him; no accident like the one that had destroyed Franklin touched him. He was perfect in every way.

"Congratulations, Rose," Harry said, approaching her with a glass of champagne. "I'm sure you're very proud of him."

Rose could smell the sour odor of liquor on his breath.

"Late night?"

"Not really," Harry replied lightly. "A lot of work."

"I'm sure," she said dryly.

Rose could not look at Harry without pity. Once he had been everything she had wanted and needed in a man. Now, he was only a husk, empty of the vitality that had so attracted her.

"Have you had a chance to read what I gave you?" asked Harry.

"I did. But this is neither the time nor place to discuss it."

"Of course," he replied expansively. "We can talk about it when we're done here."

Steven felt the generous bosom of the redhead next to him press against his arm but his eyes remained fixed on his mother, now threading her way toward him through the crowd, pausing to accept compliments and congratulations. By any standard, she was a beautiful woman, complete and self-possessed. But not invulnerable.

Although he had never let on, Steven knowingly allowed Rose to mold him into the person she wanted him to be. As much as he resented this he always remembered how the men who had dared go against her had been ruined: his father, his uncle, and, most recently, Harry Taylor. In her private life, as in business, his mother was an unforgiving woman. It was the quality Steven admired most about her.

His mother was only a few feet away when Steven turned to the redhead and lazily said, "I think I'd like to fuck you."

326

The girl's eyes widened and blazed. Then, just as quickly, a saucy smile appeared on her lips.

"Just say when and where, lover."

"Steven!"

Rose slipped in between her son and the redhead, whom she vaguely recognized as a secretary, and took his arm.

"Are you ready for your present?" she teased.

Steven laughed. "Really, Mother—"

Rose clapped her hands. "Attention, everyone! I have an announcement to make."

After the room stilled, she continued. "I'm proud to tell you that today, Global Enterprises welcomes its newest, and youngest, vice president, my son, Steven."

Rose held up her hand against the applause.

"Steven will be going to Europe shortly to oversee our accounts there and find ways to increase our business."

A rush of whispers swept the room. Everyone knew that Harry Taylor had been working on some kind of plan involving Global in Europe. All eyes turned to him and all saw the same thing: a middle-aged man whose face was drained of color and whose eyes stared uncomprehendingly at Rose.

"You can't . . ." Harry said hoarsely.

Rose fixed her gaze on Harry, cutting him off.

"I know you'll all show Steven the same cooperation and loyalty you've demonstrated to me. Thank you."

There was a smattering of applause, which began to grow as executives realized what was happening. Harry Taylor, once considered immovable because of his relationship to Rose, had become a relic. The mantle had been passed, and it rested on the shoulders of the handsome young man who was coolly appraising his audience. Hesitantly, then in a rush, everyone stepped forward to pay homage.

– 40 –

Rose leaned forward and removed a pink dot of confetti from Steven's lapel.

"Did you have a good time, darling?" she asked, settling back in her chair.

Steven crossed one leg over the other to hide his erection. He was supposed to have met the redhead twenty minutes ago. Instead he had dutifully adhered to his mother's summons to her office as the party was breaking up.

"Wonderful. That was quite a birthday present. I think you managed to surprise everyone."

"Timing," Rose mused. "That and luck and the ability to recognize both. Without them, success won't come, no matter how hard you work or how clever you are."

Steven's thoughts drifted back to Harry Taylor.

You forgot the pinch of ruthlessness, Mother.

"Were you surprised?" Rose asked.

"Of course. You never gave me a hint of what you intended to do."

"You saw Harry's report."

"That should have tipped me off," Steven admitted.

"Harry still wants to fight Michelle," Rose said. "He doesn't understand that things . . . have changed."

"You can't tell me that what she's achieved doesn't bother you."

Rose looked closely at her son. He was probing for an explanation, and she approved.

"Bother me? I've never quite thought of Michelle's achievement as some sort of irritating rash. She's done what she's done and we have to accept it. *Deal with it.*"

The magic word, thought Steven. *Deal. A price for everything and everything for a price.*

"You want me to be the one to sound her out about a mutually profitable situation."

Rose laughed at his choice of words but her tone was serious.

"Every check Michelle sells has our name on it. You've seen the books. Our freight business in Europe has trebled in the last five years. If you can convince her that it would be in her best interests to work with us, everyone would, as you said, prosper."

It's as close as you'll ever come to admitting you made a mistake, Mother.

Steven thought back to the days Michelle had lived in Talbot House, how he had scorned and abused and finally terrified her. Obviously his mother had forgotten those incidents. But he hadn't. And he didn't think Michelle had either. It should prove to be a very interesting encounter.

"What do we have that Michelle could want?" he wondered aloud.

"A worldwide transportation network. Cartage agreements with European railroads. One thousand barges that ply Europe's rivers, especially the Rhine." Rose paused. "Two thousand agents and offices to handle the paperwork."

"Which don't sell a single traveler's check because she has her own outlets."

Rose's eye glittered. "Precisely. Someone could explain to her how profitable it would be for her to sell through existing offices rather than rent or build her own. And communications. She wouldn't have to invest a penny in telephones, telegraph, and cable facilities because ours are all in place."

"Advertising," Steven murmured. "We do so much already, she'd save a fortune."

Rose sat back. "You see it, I see it. It's your job to make sure she does."

Steven tapped a cigarette on his thin silver case. "And if she doesn't?"

"I'm counting on you to see that she does. You might not want to approach her directly, at least at first. Talk to her bankers, Rothschild and Lazard and the rest. They're businessmen. They know about these things. Let them do some of the spadework for you."

"I'll need time to put a plan together. Unless you already have one."

"Take as much as you want. We have people in Europe who watched Michelle build from the ground up. Their information can be made available."

At the right price.

"If you want to look at some of her financial records, that can be arranged."

I'll bet!

"I'll get to work on it right away," Steven said.

"Remember one thing," Rose told him, offering him her cheek. "Global can make a great deal out of this. If it does, you, no one else, will take the credit— and the reward."

Believe me, Mother, that much I know!

The party was over and the day was done but Rose found Harry exactly where she knew he'd be. There were papers on his desk and his shirtsleeves were bunched up around navy garters the way they always were when he was working.

"Hello, Rose."

In the flash of his smile, framed by perfect white teeth, she saw the old Harry. For an instant Rose wanted to embrace him, wishing that time could sweep them both back to earlier days. The impulse startled her because memories were not what fed her.

"Have you come to throw me a bone?"

"Don't be like that, Harry. It doesn't become you."

"You could have done it another way, you know. It wasn't necessary to humiliate me."

"You wouldn't have believed me otherwise. You were blind, Harry. That report hung over your eyes like scales. You would have argued with me day and night. *That* would have been humiliating."

Harry sat back, tapping the eraser tip of his pencil against his teeth.

"You know, I never believed you'd cave in to her."

Rose shot him a withering look.

"Circumstances change. Realities too. Some of which you were either unaware of or chose to ignore."

"Like what we're making off the licensing fee?"

"Among other things."

"It's pittance compared to what we could be raking in if we introduce a new instrument and force her to defend her territory."

"No, Harry. And that's my last word on the matter. Be gracious enough to accept it."

Silence crept in between them.

"Do you want me to help Steven at all?" Harry asked at last. "After all, I'm at least as much of an expert on Michelle as you are."

Rose smiled wanly. "I don't think so."

"Neither did I. So the only question is, what do I do now?"

"I hope you'll stay right here, as president of Global North America."

Harry looked at her, and his thoughts traveled back, but not to their erotic moments. He was thinking of London, of how cleanly and cleverly he had undercut Franklin Jefferson. He remembered Sir Thomas Ballantine, that desiccated old man in his gloomy room. Not once over the years had he contacted the head of Cooks. But he knew that Sir Thomas was still alive, still very much the invisible guiding hand behind the giant British tour company. Perhaps the time had come to call in the marker.

"Stay on," Harry echoed Rose. "Under the circumstances I hope you don't expect an answer right away."

"Of course not. But please, don't do anything hasty or rash."

Harry laughed but he couldn't keep the bitterness out of his voice. "Thanks, Rose. I'll take it under advisement."

In the spring of 1931, Steven Talbot sailed for Europe on the *Queen Mary*. He had spent the months since his birthday party studying Michelle's European operation until he knew it backward. As promised, Rose had provided him with the latest financial details, and these gave Steven an idea of how large his task was. Not only was Michelle selling millions of dollars' worth of traveler's checks each day, she was also expanding her base among the Europeans. Italians traveling to Spain, businessmen going from France to Greece, Danish college students vacationing in Portugal—all were buying Global Traveler's Checks.

Steven began his investigation in Paris, calling on Global's forwarding agents, who, since his arrival was unannounced, were shocked to see him. Watching how nervously they scurried around him, Steven promptly seized the books and conducted a spot audit. Two months later he cabled Rose saying that the Paris agents had been skimming at least 15 percent of the business each month. By the time Rose replied, with instructions to prosecute the thieves, Steven had made his own arrangements. He hung the threat of jail over the heads of the guilty and offered a reprieve only if they swore to do exactly what he told them. In one stroke, the agents' allegiance switched from New York to Steven.

Steven also discovered that the Global agents could serve another purpose. He himself spent days watching Michelle's central office on rue de Berri, amazed by the number of people who flowed through it. But that didn't tell him anything he didn't already know. The key was to talk to people who worked inside. Steven admitted he was the wrong man for that job. He had never had a good rapport with hired help and, more to the point, he couldn't speak French. Besides, he didn't want Michelle to think he was snooping. Steven instructed a few carefully chosen people from among Global's agents to befriend employees at rue de Berri. He wanted to know whether they liked working for Michelle, how much they made, the gossip about the other offices—in short, anything that was interesting and might prove valuable.

While his drones took the low road, Steven set out on the high one. From his suite at the Meurice he sent out invitations to the bankers and politicians Global did business with. He feted them in the best restaurants, plied them with vintage champagne, and shared their appreciation of young mistresses. In return he got nothing but glowing tributes to Michelle.

"She has become a symbol, monsieur," one minister said expansively. "Madame McQueen is the consummate Frenchwoman: beautiful, intelligent, successful. Like Coco Chanel or your own Mademoiselle Earhart. And, of course, she is a heroine of France."

Next you'll make her another Joan of Arc! Steven thought.

The reports trickling in from his staff were no better. Although Michelle's people worked hard, they were more than satisfied. Michelle had set up the first employee profit-sharing scheme in the country as well as a series of bonus plans based on sales volume. As far as Steven could tell, Michelle's position in France was unassailable.

Why is he here asking questions about me?

The question had plagued Michelle ever since she had learned that Steven was in Paris and the image of the cruel, silent child of Talbot House had flashed through her mind. She remembered how callously he had humiliated and threatened her and the years it had taken to erase the nightmares. Now, without warning, he was walking the streets of her city and Michelle was damned if she knew why.

Finally Michelle spoke to Emil Rothschild, whom Steven had been to see and who had given the American a frosty reception.

"I have just the solution," the banker said after listening to her. "This is the name of a private detective whose services I sometimes use. He's well connected and discreet. If you want to know Steven Talbot's whereabouts, he's your man."

The next day Michelle met with the investigator, a quiet, nondescript man whose appearance and demeanor reminded her of a postal clerk. He agreed to take the case and gave Michelle instructions.

"Show all your employees a picture of this man. If they see him at any of your offices, they are to call me at once."

A week later, Michelle had her first report. Steven was indeed visiting the traveler's-checks offices. As far as the detective could tell, Steven was behaving like any ordinary American tourist, exchanging Global money orders for French francs. He asked no questions, demanded no special attention. All of which only heightened Michelle's suspicions.

As the weeks passed, Michelle learned that Steven was spending a great deal of time with Global's freight agents. He was also being wined and dined by the powers of the financial community as well as senior government officials. Michelle spoke again with Emil Rothschild, who promised to keep an ear to the ground in those circles.

The idea of confronting Steven, either through a manufactured chance encounter or a direct invitation, crossed Michelle's mind. Perhaps it was the only way to put her questions to rest. Yet, every time Michelle thought she was ready to face him, her courage deserted her. There were, she discovered, things so painful that the mere thought of resurrecting them made one a coward.

"He is gone, madame."

"What? Are you sure?"

"Monsieur Talbot checked out of the Meurice at eleven o'clock this morning," the detective informed her, scanning his notes. "He went directly to Gare de l'Est, where he boarded the Amsterdam express. I waited until the train left the station. He never got off."

Michelle could feel the relief flooding her body.

"But why . . . ?"

The detective shrugged. "One can safely assume that Monsieur Talbot accomplished what he had set out to do in Paris and that there was no reason for him to stay."

But what did he come here to do?

After the detective left, the question drifted back. Michelle glanced at Steven's itinerary, which the detective had mysteriously procured, and decided to alert her outlets in other European capitals. She had a premonition that one day their paths would cross again. When that happened, Michelle vowed, she'd be ready.

"*Maman!*"

Michelle whirled around at the sound of Cassandra bounding into the room, pigtails flying. She ran on long coltish legs but Michelle could see that beneath the prim convent-school uniform a beautiful young girl was flowering. Cassandra's blue eyes were sparkling with excitement as she threw her arms around her mother.

"Guess what, *Maman*," she cried. "Sister Agnes says we can go to St. Paul-de-Vence to see the Impressionist galleries."

"That's wonderful, *chérie*," Michelle replied, laughing at her daughter's excitement.

She could not have asked for a more lovely child. Although only ten years old Cassandra was already fluent in four languages. She loved literature and the arts as well as sports. According to the nuns she was a very popular girl, a natural leader others looked up to. Yet, because of the joy she found in her daughter, Michelle sometimes found her own guilt difficult to bear.

When Cassandra was five she had started asking about her father. Michelle, who had carefully rehearsed what she would tell her, showed her photographs of herself and Franklin and gently explained that her father had been a very great man who had died in the war. She told Cassandra where Franklin had been born and grown up and about his only relative, his sister, Rose. Michelle wept when she came across a photo of him with Monk.

"Don't cry, *Maman*," Cassandra had consoled her. "Papa is with the angels."

As the years passed, Cassandra never referred to Franklin. Even when Monk scolded her she never retreated behind the cruel retort that he wasn't her real father. Instead she poured her child's love for a father into Monk, enriching both of them. Sometimes, when she saw them together, Michelle thought she could almost forget the truth.

"Perhaps I'll come with you to St. Paul-de-Vence," Michelle suggested.

Cassandra made a face. "*Maman*, it's a school trip. I can take care of myself very well."

The confidence of the innocent! Michelle thought. She scooped Cassandra into her arms.

"You're absolutely right. You're a young lady now and I'm sure you'll behave yourself."

Michelle shivered as she watched Cassandra whirl off. Suddenly she was very glad that Steven Talbot had passed through without ever touching their lives.

As he toured the European capitals that fall, Steven discovered that Global's situation in each city was no better than in Paris. The company's agents were second-rate and cared little about its reputation. Michelle, on the other hand, had instilled a sense of purpose in her people. Whether in Copenhagen, Madrid, Amsterdam, or Rome, Steven saw an operation that was geared to people, the staff trusted as much as the traveler's check they sold. As he wrote his reports to his mother, Steven wondered if it was really possible to break Michelle's grip. So far she had succeeded everywhere Global Traveler's Checks were sold. Steven didn't expect the situation to be any different at his next stop, Berlin.

He felt the change as soon as the train from Paris stopped at Munster on the German border. Wherever he had traveled Steven had been conscious of the spiritual malaise around him. Europe, like America, was in the grip of the Depression. There were wide disparities between those who had much and those with nothing at all. In France, Italy, the Low countries, and Scandinavia, the sentiment of the people was furtive and resigned.

Steven had expected Germany to be a wasteland. As he quickly discovered, it was poor, with inflation verging on the ridiculous. Steven was incredulous the first time he saw a smartly dressed young woman pushing a wheelbarrow full of money through the street. Curious, he followed her to a bakery and watched as she carefully stacked the money on the counter, receiving two loaves of bread in return. The baker counted the notes and the woman squeezed the bread, making sure it was fresh. Then each bid the other good morning and the woman departed.

What struck Steven wasn't the ludicrousness of the transaction but the dignity with which it had been carried out. The baker's shelves were almost bare, yet he had chosen those two loaves as if they were his best. The woman, whose clothing, upon closer inspection, was faded from too many washings and mended in too many places, had examined the loaves as if she had dozens of others to choose from. Each must have known it was all a charade, yet their pride refused to let them bow to their circumstances.

334

The moment remained fixed in Steven's mind. As he walked the streets of Berlin he saw it repeated in a hundred different ways, increasing his respect and admiration for the German people. Their economy had been broken by onerous and unjust war reparations yet their spirit had refused to capitulate. Pariahs of Europe, they banded together to face their still-hostile neighbors, expecting neither help nor charity.

They will never accept the latter, Steven thought as he sat over dinner at a small, elegant restaurant on the Kurfurstendamm. *But they need help.*

"Herr Talbot?"

Steven looked up to find a young man standing in front of his table.

"Yes?"

"Please forgive me, *mein herr,* for intruding upon your dinner. My name is Kurt Essenheimer. One of our companies acts as forwarding agents for Global. I wanted to stop by to pay my respects and welcome you to Berlin."

Steven judged Essenheimer to be about twenty-five. He was tall, with blond hair slicked back from a widow's peak. His features were lean, almost lupine, the effect heightened by the washed-out eyes of an arctic wolf.

"Won't you join me?"

"Ah, Herr Talbot, that is very kind of you. But I'm waiting for some friends."

"Then bring your drink over. Unless, of course, you don't want to talk business right now."

"Not at all, Herr Talbot."

Essenheimer snapped his fingers and a waiter appeared with a large, frosted martini.

"Gin," Essenheimer announced. "England's only contribution to man's merriment. *Prost!*"

Steven raised his glass of Reisling, studying Essenheimer. The name had rung a bell the minute the German had introduced himself. The Essenheimers were one of Germany's foremost industrial families, rivaling the Krupps. Steven recalled they had extensive industrial holdings—everything from coal mines to steel works. A minor interest was transportation, which was their connection to Global. Steven had been in Berlin for less than three days, yet for one reason or another Essenheimer had found him. Steven was intrigued.

"It is my understanding that you are on an inspection tour, if I may use the term, of your offices in Europe," Essenheimer said.

"Word gets around."

Essenheimer laughed. "Herr Talbot, compared to America, Europe is very small. What goes on in certain circles of Paris travels very quickly to other such places. You belong to that circle. As do I."

"I'm flattered," Steven replied. "On the other hand, given everything Es-

335

senheimer A.G. is involved in, I have to wonder why you should even remember that you serve as our agents."

"It's true that our mutual interests are, at least for the moment, very small," Essenheimer replied. "However, if we are both satisfied with their operation, perhaps we could move forward together on other projects."

"Perhaps."

"You said you were prepared to discuss business," Essenheimer said. "Naturally I did not bring anything with me since I had no idea we would be meeting. However, I have just reviewed the quarterly report on our agency. The figures are fresh in my mind, if you would care to hear them."

The waiter brought Steven his order of poached pike.

"By all means."

As he ate, Steven found himself more and more impressed by the young German. Essenheimer spoke easily but with authority, quoting rates, tonnage, gross receipts, operating expenses, and profits. Although he didn't show it, Steven was amazed that this battered country was putting more money into Global's coffers than were France and Italy combined.

"I'm impressed," Steven said, as the waiter cleared the table.

Essenheimer shrugged. "We have done well. But there are many other possibilities."

Steven offered him a cigar. "Perhaps you'd care to enlighten me?"

"My pleasure."

Essenheimer launched into a brief description of how thoroughly his country's railroads and highways had been devastated during the war.

"Of course we have rebuilt a great deal, but as you can see for yourself more needs to be done. The problem is compounded by inflation that makes our currency a laughingstock. What we require, Herr Talbot, are men of vision who are willing to make investments. With proper guarantees of substantial profits, of course.

"But there is more. As you know, Germany has tremendous natural resources—coal, iron, timber. However, we are completely dependent on the outside world for other commodities: rubber, bauxite, industrial diamonds, and above all, oil, not only for fuel but for the production of synthetic goods. Given that we lost almost all our colonies after the war, have no merchant marine to speak of, and that, by the Treaty of Versailles, are not allowed to rebuild our navy, there is only one solution. Germany requires a middleman who can help procure what she needs and also guarantee delivery."

Essenheimer regarded Steven carefully. "That is where I believe we can do business."

Steven swirled his Asbach brandy, watching as the liqueur created reddish brown whorls in the snifter. He sensed the German had carefully orchestrated this occasion—the allegedly chance meeting, the topics of conversation, the details. He felt he was three steps behind Kurt Essenheimer and he didn't like it.

"You seem very sure that Global is the kind of partner you're looking for. If that's the case, why haven't we heard from you sooner?"

"Our situation is somewhat delicate, Herr Talbot," Essenheimer replied smoothly. "First, we are in a period of transition. General von Hindenburg is growing old. No one doubts that after the next elections there will be a new chancellor. Second, Essenheimer A.G. has had virtually no contact with anyone in authority at Global, New York. You are the first to visit us since your mother established our relationship before the war. Third, and perhaps most important, is the issue of Frau McQueen."

"Michelle?"

Essenheimer nodded. "Permit me to speak frankly. Your mother is a remarkable woman. However, she gambled with your company's stake in Europe and lost. After that she turned her back on us and Frau McQueen prevailed. I believe your mother has therefore compounded her mistake."

"How?" Steven asked coldly.

"Because people such as myself have no interest in doing business with Frau McQueen, yet, for all intents and purposes, she is Global to us."

"I would have thought that you would have approached Michelle on your own, offered to sell the checks through your agencies. After all, business is business."

"Frau McQueen has been very successful in Germany," Essenheimer agreed. "And in one way, what you suggest would have been natural. However, Frau McQueen has strictly limited her business in Germany. For example, she has only three offices: one here in Berlin, two others in Munich and Frankfurt. Yet the traveler's check is as good as gold in Germany. Day after day those who can afford to buy them line up at the counters. If they don't reach the wicket in time, they are given a number guaranteeing priority the next morning.

"What I am saying, Herr Talbot, is that Frau McQueen could open up a dozen outlets in Germany, make three times the profit she does now."

Steven feigned indifference although he knew that because of her licensing agreement with Global, Michelle was also depriving New York of substantial revenues.

"So what's the problem?"

"Frau McQueen has formed a very close relationship with the Jewish community," Essenheimer told him. "Her banker is Warburg. Her attorneys, accountants, and principal advisers are all Jewish. They are the ones influencing her decisions. They are keeping her out of mainstream Germany. As a result, we do not see Frau McQueen as someone we can deal with."

337

"I see," Steven said noncommittally.

Essenheimer smiled. "However, the fact is that very soon there will be a new order in Germany and Frau McQueen will have to consider Germans in her plans. Or else suffer the consequences."

What the hell is he talking about? Steven asked himself.

Everywhere he'd gone, everything he'd seen and been told only reinforced his certainty that Michelle's hold on Europe was secure. Steven had unearthed nothing that would induce her to come to the bargaining table. On the other hand, he had also seen just how much Rose had given away, not only in money but in power. Now Essenheimer was hinting that perhaps there was a chink in Michelle's armor after all.

"You talk about a new order, a new chancellor," Steven said. "What do you mean?"

"Exactly that, Herr Talbot," Essenheimer replied, looking around.

Steven followed his gaze to the front of the restaurant where the maitre d' and waiters were fawning over a party that had just come in.

"Would you like to meet the future of Germany, Herr Talbot?"

"And who would that be?"

"A man of whom you will soon be hearing a great deal. Adolf Hitler."

Steven had expected Berlin to be nothing more than a whistle-stop on his way back to Paris. After that first night he ended up staying two months, after which he would never again see himself or the world in the same light.

Steven was enthralled by Hitler and arrested by that piercing, unwavering gaze. From the moment he was introduced, Steven felt as though he was in the presence of true greatness. Hitler listened intently while Essenheimer explained Steven's background. Soon the others at the table, Goebbels, Bormann, Himmler, and the rest, began asking Steven questions. Since Steven spoke no German, Essenheimer served as translator.

These men hungered for news from America. They wanted to know everything, from how the Depression was affecting the country to the current popularity of Franklin Roosevelt. When the talk turned to Global they asked dozens of questions about the company and were impressed when Steven described the maritime fleet his mother had established over the last decade. Generalities became specifics: how much did Global ship, to whom, from where, at what rates? What was the capacity of their ships, their relationships with customs officials in various countries, and guarantees to their markets? Steven answered as thoroughly as he could. When he didn't have the facts and figures, he readily admitted it, adding that getting them wouldn't be a problem. Every so often he stole a glance at Hitler. But the man who was clearly *primus inter pares* only stared back silently.

When the discussion finally wound down Steven looked around to discover that the restaurant had closed around them. The waiters had disappeared; there wasn't a sound to be heard from the kitchen. Abruptly Hitler rose. He shook hands with Essenheimer, patting him on the shoulder and murmuring in his ear. Then he clasped Steven's hand in both of his and clicked his heels. One by one, his entourage followed suit and disappeared into the night.

"You made a good impression, Herr Talbot," Essenheimer said, going around the bar and helping himself to a bottle of brandy. "A very good impression."

"He's an incredible man," Steven murmured, draining his snifter. "There's this magnetism about him. . . . I can't explain it."

Essenheimer leaned forward on the table. "Herr Talbot, Hitler *is* a unique individual. Some say he can see straight into a man and touch his soul. Perhaps that is poetic fancy. But I believe it. I think you do too."

Steven nodded.

"Hitler was very taken with you," Essenheimer continued. "He told me that you could have unimpeded access to anyone in the National Socialist Party. Any questions would be answered immediately, without reservation. Anything the Party might offer is yours for the asking."

"National Socialist Party? I don't even know what that is."

Essenheimer laughed and slapped Steven on the back. "You will, my friend. Soon the whole world will know!"

The next morning Essenheimer picked Steven up at his hotel. Over lunch in a Bavarian-style restaurant in the Grunwald, Essenheimer explained the principles of the Nazi party, how, where, and by whom it had been founded. By the time he was through, Steven was even more spellbound by Hitler. For one man to have suffered a near-fatal wound, been repatriated to a country that mocked him, been beaten and thrown in jail, only to rise to such power, was extraordinary.

"And this is just the beginning, Steven," Essenheimer assured him. "See and judge for yourself."

Essenheimer seemed to know everyone in Berlin. Steven hunted with the men who were retooling Germany's heavy industries and rode with generals who spoke of a new military might that would never again allow the ignominy of a Versailles. He dined with bankers who explained why Germany's revival was inevitable, and at the Nazi party headquarters in Munich was received as an honored guest, singled out by Hitler himself for special attention.

It wasn't the proximity to the rich and powerful that intoxicated Steven. He had been weaned on such milk at Talbot House. In Germany he felt he had found a kinship among people who could say what he felt but had never been able to articulate. The idea of a master race, as outlined in Hitler's *Mein Kampf*, made perfect sense to him. What reinforced these beliefs was the attitude Steven saw around him. Desperate and unemployed people, ordinary men and women, turned to Hitler as their last hope. Betrayed by the Kaiser and later the doddering politicians of the Weimar Republic, they reached out to a man who could give them pride, honor, and dignity.

In Hitler and the Nazi party, Steven saw a unique opportunity to create his own empire, secret and apart from Global. He had no illusions about Rose. His mother was a strong, vigorous woman. She would throw him crumbs of power and authority and think that she was truly sharing control of the company. But as long as she remained alive, she would never fully relinquish her grip. Remembering his father, Steven promised himself that Rose would never be allowed to guide or determine his fate.

However, before he could move against his mother, there was one other person who had to be dealt with. Steven was certain his new friends would be more than willing to oblige.

By now Steven and Kurt Essenheimer had become inseparable. In the elegant villas outside Wansee, they sampled the delights of opium and morphine, which aristocratic hostesses served instead of dessert. Then they would move on to smart cabarets and nightclubs where gallows humor was the rage. Persuaded by Kurt, Steven lost his inhibitions in the exotic bordellos that by day were some of Berlin's finest addresses. He discovered the cruel delight that came with bondage and learned to savor a woman's helplessness. He experienced the forbidden joy of black flesh and for a week kept two women as his personal slaves. Once, during an orgy where all the guests were required, for a brief time, to wear medieval costumes, he was astonished to see Kurt servicing and being serviced by a young girl and boy. Afterward Kurt blithely told him, "Steven, my dear friend, I do not discriminate!"

It was a mad merry-go-round that could have spun on into oblivion. But Steven knew it wouldn't last. Sooner or later, the overture he was expecting would come.

"We must make plans, Steven," Essenheimer said over coffee one morning. "For my future, yours . . . ours."

They were in the orangerie of a villa Steven had rented, and the smell of blossoms hung heavy in the crisp morning air.

"So," Essenheimer continued, draping one arm across the back of his chair. "You've seen so much. What do you think?"

Steven looked him straight in the eye. "I think we can do business together. From all the discussions I've had, one thing is clear: Germany needs guaranteed delivery of raw materials essential to your industries. Global has a fleet of ships which can do exactly that. In fact we can expand it. However, we would need to set up a series of dummy corporations throughout Europe that would actually contract for deliveries and pay for them."

"Why is that necessary?"

"Two reasons. First, Michelle must never get wind of what we're doing. She's French. She hates Germans. If she finds out, she'll do anything she can to expose us."

Kurt nodded. "And the second reason?"

"I cannot guarantee that my mother would support us."

Kurt whistled through his teeth. "Nevertheless, you'd be willing to do this on your own?"

"Yes," Steven replied. "And to answer your unspoken question: Can I? You can bank on it." He paused. "That's not to say there aren't a few problems we have to solve."

He went on to explain exactly why Rose Jefferson had sent him to Europe. "I'll tell her what I've found and back it up with figures. Global is so far behind Michelle that we would be negotiating from a position of weakness. My mother would find that intolerable. Then I'll offer a solution. Why not let me return to building Global's European business the way Michelle built the traveler's check? Once that's done, we would have the leverage to deal with Michelle."

"Surely you're not seriously considering going back to her!" Kurt protested.

"Of course not," Steven replied impatiently. "But my mother doesn't need to know that."

Kurt Essenheimer began to appreciate the magnitude of the deception the American was constructing. It was daring, and it could work. But Essenheimer was no fool. What Steven was offering Germany would have its price.

"Steven, I do not wish to insult you or question your faith in National Socialism," he said carefully. "What you are proposing is of immense value to us. Surely we can, as friends, offer something in return."

"Of course you can, Kurt," Steven replied graciously. "You can help me ruin Michelle."

Kurt Essenheimer could not believe what he had just heard. All this time he had thought he was the one who had the upper hand. Now he was seeing a completely different side of this American—someone who knew exactly what he wanted and how he would get it.

"I'm not sure exactly what you mean," Essenheimer said cautiously.

"I think you have a fair idea," Steven replied. "What Michelle has belongs to me and I want it back. How I get it back is my business, except that our working together will make it much easier.

"As you yourself have so often mentioned, Kurt, Germany is an expanding nation. Those who do not stand with her will ultimately stand against her. There's no doubt where Michelle will end up. What I propose, in fact what I must insist on, is this: as the power of National Socialism grows in Germany, certain businesses—presumably, Jewish ones—will be forced to shut down. I recommend that Global's traveler's-check bureaus be added to the list. Naturally, the state doesn't want to lose such a nice source of tax revenues, so those outlets will be handed over to . . . why, to the parent company, Global Europe, which I will by then control.

"As Germany's strength moves across Europe, it will become harder and harder for Michelle to maintain her operation. Subsequently, her offices will fall into my lap one by one. The more I control of Global Europe, the stronger I become, which in turn means we can do a great deal more."

"I can see what you propose being successful in Germany," Essenheimer conceded. "But as for the rest of Europe . . ."

"Kurt, Kurt," Steven chided. "There's already an agreement in principle between Hitler and Mussolini, which means Rome will tumble. Franco is a natural ally, so that gives me Spain. The war will take care of the rest."

"The war . . . ? What war?"

"You should read your *Mein Kampf* more carefully," Steven said coldly. "Do you think all Hitler has in mind is to be the ruler of Germany?"

At that moment Kurt Essenheimer knew that this seemingly innocent, unseasoned American was far more dangerous than he appeared.

"Steven," he said accommodatingly, "I assure you there is no problem we can't resolve. You have my word that each German success will be matched by one for you."

Steven rang for the houseman to bring in the champagne.

"I had it ready, just in case we had something to celebrate."

The two men raised their glasses in a silent toast.

"By the by," Kurt said, as though remembering a minor detail, "I heard something out of London the other day which might interest you."

"Really?"

"You know someone called Harry Taylor? I believe he is your president of North American operations."

"Harry is a relic," Steven replied. "He's on the way down. And out."

"I'm glad to hear that. Because I understand that at the same time your late uncle, Franklin Jefferson, was trying to do business with the British banks, Mr. Taylor was selling out him and his intentions to Sir Thomas Ballantine at Cooks."

"Tell me more," Steven said softly.

Kurt Essenheimer recited the gist of the report Hitler's informants had procured in London. He had been saving it as a trump card if the need ever arose. Now it seemed more important to gain Steven Talbot's trust, as well as a favor owed, if only a small one.

"You don't seem surprised," Essenheimer observed when he was finished. "I take it you knew about this, or at least suspected."

Steven hesitated. The news had stunned him. Was it possible that Franklin had failed because he had been betrayed? If so, then Harry had managed to cover his tracks brilliantly. Otherwise Rose Jefferson would have had his head.

Oh, Mother, what a fool you've been!

"No, I wasn't aware that Harry had done anything like that," he said slowly. "How sure are you of your information?"

"Positive. Otherwise I wouldn't have brought it up."

"Would it be possible to get hard evidence?"

"I'll see what I can do. Anything to help a friend, Steven."

- 4| -

The March winds blew relentlessly along the canyons of Lower Broadway, a sign that the long, bitter winter of 1931–32 was far from over. The city's homeless huddled in doorways or around soup-kitchen fires while in office towers the captains of industry looked in vain for some light, however faint, in that long winter of discontent brought on by the Depression. Among those who saw it, and along with it, hope, was Rose Jefferson.

At forty-one, Rose plotted the course of one of the few major industries in America that had not only managed to survive but actually prosper during the Depression. Goods still had to be moved across the country, and bank collapses had frightened many Americans into putting their cash into a safer place: guaranteed money orders. The few pennies it cost to buy a money order seemed inconsequential when weighed against one's peace of mind. Each day millions of those pennies poured into Global's cash drawers throughout America, creating a glittering road of wealth that led to the heart of New York.

Unlike other major industrial concerns that trumpeted how much of their profit went into goodwill activities, Global kept a low profile. Few of the four million unemployed knew or cared that Rose had fought the Smoot-Hawley Tariff Bill, which raised import duties to historic levels and speeded up

343

the inevitable decline in trade. Rose used every forum and all her influence to convince lawmakers that without trade, industry would languish and jobs would disappear forever.

When the President signed the bill into law, Rose took a different tack. By cajoling and flattering legislators, she helped bring about a public-buildings act, which poured $230 million into construction as well as a $300 million appropriation for state road-building projects. Rose saw the rewards of her efforts every time she traveled along the New York–Washington corridor. Thousands of men who had once languished in poorhouses were busy creating new arteries for future commerce.

Even Rose's closest associates were surprised and puzzled by the actions of a woman who, until now, had been content to donate anonymously to charitable works or arrange for foundations to distribute her grants.

"It's not such a great mystery, Hugh," Rose told her attorney. "If you want to know the answer, come with me."

The last place O'Neill expected to be taken to was the Jefferson resting plot at Dunescrag.

"I think I finally understand what it was Franklin felt for this country," Rose said, standing in front of her brother's headstone. "People like my grandfather and me saw only the opportunity in this land. We seized every chance it gave us and ran with it as hard as we could. Franklin was different. He knew that you could only take so much before both you and the land became bankrupt. He had a conscience, Hugh. When he stood up to those strikebreakers he was also challenging everything I had ever done or believed in."

Rose knelt and placed the bouquet she had brought.

"I didn't understand Franklin then. I didn't want to believe he didn't think like me and I was too scared to admit that he did. I put him through a great deal and denied him even more. What I'm doing now is a pittance compared to what he would have achieved."

"Don't sell yourself short," O'Neill said kindly. "If it hadn't been for you, a lot of what the government's been pushed into doing might never have happened."

The next week, when he read of Rose Jefferson's appointment as chairman of the Committee for Unemployed Relief, Hugh O'Neill wished that Franklin had lived to see it.

Rose stood before the windows overlooking Lower Broadway and shivered from the cold pulsating off the glass.

From the latest figures, it was clear that Michelle was doing proportionally as well in Europe as Rose was in America. Which explained why Steven had sent her the report he had. Rose walked back to her desk and leafed through the carefully typed script. Touching the pages was like touching him. Sometimes she missed him so much she wanted to jump on the next boat to Europe.

I can't do that. I sent him to do a man's work and I won't interfere.

And it was work Steven could justly be proud of. The idea of pumping money into the freight agencies, or buying them out altogether under the banner of Global Europe, would bring the company on equal footing with the European transportation giants. Once Global had presence and stature, it could deal with Michelle from a position of strength. Rose was convinced that Steven could launch and carry the program as president of Global Europe.

Rose picked up her pen and quickly drafted a letter to Steven approving his plan.

"I'm very proud of you, darling," she wrote. "Come home as soon as you can so we can work out the details. I miss you terribly. Love, Mother."

Rose sat back, warmed by her words. Suddenly the March winter didn't seem so cold at all.

"We're over the first hurdle," Steven announced, handing Kurt Essenheimer the letter. "Mother's approved."

"Steven, that's fantastic!"

"That's only the beginning," Steven warned. "Now the real work begins."

The first order of business was to establish suitable headquarters. Naturally Essenheimer proposed Berlin, promising whatever facilities he wished.

"It would be a lot easier to work out of Berlin," Steven acknowledged. "But too dangerous. Remember, Michelle is also set up here. Through Warburg, she's established many contacts. If he were to get even the slightest hint of what we're doing, if her people report seeing me in Berlin on a regular basis, we'd be risking everything."

Essenheimer agreed, and the two men rented a suite of offices in Bern, which had excellent road and rail ties with Germany as well as a first-rate communications network.

"We need staff we can trust implicitly," Steven said. "Everyone has to have been vetted by you personally."

"Leave it to me," Essenheimer assured him. "We'll get whoever we need out of the Party."

"What about bringing them into the country? Won't there be a problem with work permits?"

Essenheimer grinned. "Not if they're coming as embassy staff. That's the other nice thing about Bern."

While Essenheimer was in Germany, Steven met with several of Bern's smaller banks, all of whom were eager to do business with this young American whose funds, posted in Berlin, seemed limitless. The banks' lawyers were more than willing to act as nominal directors for the dozen companies Steven had them set up and didn't utter a word when the purpose of these companies was defined vaguely as "import-export."

As soon as Essenheimer returned with the necessary staff, Steven, who had rented a villa on the outskirts of the city, sent discreet invitations to a number of diplomats. In less than a few months the commercial trade attachés from Egypt, Syria, Iran, South Africa and the Congo, Argentina, Brazil, and Chile had become regular visitors. Once they learned what Steven and his silent German counterpart wanted, and, more important, could pay for in bullion, they sent a stream of their countries' top industrialists to the Swiss capital. Over hard bargaining sessions the lines that would feed Germany the raw materials she needed were forged.

While Steven cultivated potential suppliers, Kurt Essenheimer quietly began buying up oceangoing freighters and merchantmen from the German commercial fleet at ridiculously low prices.

After the ships, newly registered in Panama, weighed anchor, Steven monitored their operations from his Swiss company's offices. Although Essenheimer had assured him that the staff had been carefully screened, Steven was constantly on the alert. Still, even he had his blind side.

Kurt Essenheimer made an unexpected visit to Bern early that summer. He found Steven in a restaurant in the company of a very pretty, dark-haired girl by the name of Anna Kleist, who worked for one of the companies as a junior accountant. As he approached their table, Essenheimer looked at her heart-shaped face and dancing gypsy eyes and sighed. Such a waste. He politely refused to join them but asked to speak to Steven alone.

"Business, fraulein," he said, then winked. "I won't keep him long, I promise."

Essenheimer steered Steven toward the maître d's station.

"I see that you and Fraulein Kleist are becoming close friends."

Steven grinned. "Not as close as I'd like."

"Just as well." Essenheimer gave Steven a dossier with two red diagonal slashes, broken by the Gestapo emblem, on the cover. "Her real name is Anna Baumann."

Steven's mouth tightened. He flipped open the dossier and began to read.

"What's this White Rose organization?"

"A group of malcontents—students, Communists, a few radical priests—who speak out against the Party. They pass information along to British and French intelligence. The Gestapo watches them all, of course. Their leaders have a tendency to disappear. When we took the last one we found this."

He handed Steven some papers that, to his horror, detailed the workings of the Swiss companies, their contract negotiations, the principals involved, the particulars discussed, as well as projected shipping schedules. Among the names mentioned, Steven saw his own.

"How did she get this?" he whispered, his features mottled with rage.

Essenheimer shrugged. "Our friend really couldn't tell us that, no matter how persuasive we were. They're very professional. Each person in the chain doesn't know who passes him the information, and in turn leaves it in a certain place so that he never sees who picks it up."

Steven couldn't help but glance at the lovely young girl he'd been trying to bed.

"I assume you'll get rid of her right away."

Essenheimer held up his hand. "Not so fast. According to our friend, another package is due to be put into the pipeline very soon. I don't want our lovely Anna Kleist to think anything is wrong. Let her take what she intends to and send it on its way. She'll be under surveillance twenty-four hours a day. I want to follow that information and pick up everyone who touches it." Essenheimer paused. "But that means you have to keep up the charade. Can you do that, Steven?"

Steven glanced at the references to him and shuddered. If any of this had gotten out of Germany, into his mother's hands . . .

"Oh, yes. I think I can keep her amused while you sort things out."

For the next several weeks Steven continued to court the woman. He took her to the opera and theater and, on one Saturday, for a ride into the foothills of the Alps. There, picnicking above a beautiful cascading waterfall with a deep gorge below, Steven thought how easy it would be to kill her.

Then one afternoon Essenheimer called from the embassy and asked Steven to come over right away. Using the back entrance, Steven went downstairs to the basement where, in a concrete-lined room, he saw Anna Kleist strapped to a chair, naked, covered in vomit, sweat, and water. The Gestapo man standing next to her wore thick rubber gloves while holding a pair of coiled electric loops.

"She talked," Essenheimer announced, putting out his cigarette. "They always do. We're picking up the rest now. The danger is past."

"What's going to happen to her—to them?" asked Steven, mesmerized by the sight and smells around him. "You can't kill her here."

"True, but once she returns to Germany on medical leave, she'll have a chance to recuperate," Essenheimer replied coolly. "In a place called Dachau."

The experience with Anna Kleist shook Steven. Between her disappearance from Bern and the arrival of the first shipments of copper, gold, and bauxite at the Bremen docks, he stayed away from the company offices. In order to turn in a progress report to his mother, he worked day and night to catch up on Michelle's activities. He finished a scant two days before his ship was to sail.

Steven's farewell party was held at the Zig-Zag Club, Berlin's most spectacular transvestite cabaret. A large, underground room, it was modeled on an Arabian Nights theme, with waiters dressed as harem girls and a floor show that was the scandal of Europe.

"Well, what do you think?" Essenheimer demanded, cigar in one hand, girl in the other, as he watched the female impersonators do their version of Ali Baba and the Forty Thieves.

"Only you could have staged something like this," Steven replied.

He extricated his friend from his girl and maneuvered Essenheimer into a corner behind the bar.

"When will you tell Hitler we're ready?"

"I have already passed along the news to Bormann. He promised me a meeting with Hitler as soon as he returns from Berchtesgarden next week."

Steven felt that cold hard knot in his stomach that every adventurer shares, the slight hesitation, the second thought, before the final commitment.

"We are ready to go, Steven," Essenheimer said. "The hardest part will not be the details but your absence. You will be missed, my friend."

"I'll be back as soon as I can," Steven promised.

The noise and music seemed to disappear. The two men looked at each other and gravely shook hands.

"Come on," Essenheimer said. "Tomorrow you leave, tonight we get drunk. Whatever you want, Steven, it's yours."

Steven was about to plunge into the crowd when he gripped the German's forearm.

"Who is that?"

Across the room, making her way toward the exit, was a young Oriental woman dressed in a startling red and white kimono. Her deep black hair was pinned up in the Japanese way with mother-of-pearl and ivory barrettes. Her skin had a lustrous golden hue. Her face was a perfect oval, with barely discernible cheekbones, red full lips, and eyes the color of ancient jade.

The woman must have felt him staring because she looked directly at Steven. A whisper of a smile appeared on her lips and then she was swallowed up in a phalanx of Japanese men.

"Alas, not even I can bring you her," Essenheimer lamented. "She is Yukiko Kamaguchi, the daughter of one of Japan's most powerful industrialists. Hisahiko Kamaguchi controls shipyards, steel factories, and petrochemical plants. We hope to persuade him to do business with us. I had heard he was in Berlin but never thought he would come by. . . ."

Steven continued to stare at Yukiko's departing figure.

"Forget her, my friend," Essenheimer advised. "You are leaving tomorrow. She goes back with her father the next day."

"You may never see a woman like her again," Steven said thoughtfully. "But you can never forget her either."

Steven left Germany on board the *Siegfried*, the flagship of the Bremen-Hansa Lines. Throughout the six-day voyage he carefully reviewed his notes and proposals. Rose had been keeping a close watch on Michelle ever since the loan repayment, and Steven assumed she would be familiar with most of his figures. Therefore, the projections for Global's business in Europe had been doctored to show only a modest return. Because his mother would invariably question the wisdom of continuing the operations, Steven's task was to convince her that they must. As long as Rose had no inkling just how profitable the continental business really was, the invisible empire he had created would flourish.

Steven had expected the family car and driver to be waiting for him when he disembarked. What he hadn't anticipated was that the chauffeur would take him directly to one of New York's finest restaurants, the Côte Basque.

"Steven!"

Steven brushed by the captain, leaned forward, and allowed himself to be pecked on both cheeks. His mother's eyes were shining.

"You look wonderful!"

"Thank you, Mother. You've never looked better either."

Relaxing on the banquette, Rose was overjoyed to see her son. She had noted with maternal satisfaction how the heads of older women turned when Steven had been shown to her table and how their daughters couldn't take their eyes off him. Europe, Rose thought, had given her son a brilliant sheen.

"I couldn't be happier with what you've done, darling," Rose said as the sommelier poured the champagne. "*Salut!*"

"*Salut*, Mother."

"But I hope you won't be going back to Europe soon."

"It will take a while to get things organized over here," Steven replied. "But I'm afraid there's still a lot left to take care of across the pond."

"Well, it'll be nice to have you home for a change."

Steven laughed. "What's new at Global? From your letters, I got the feeling you've been wanting to tell me something but haven't quite gotten around to it."

A painful shadow drifted across Rose's face. "Harry's gone."

"Gone? You mean you fired him."

"No, darling. Just gone. One day he didn't show up for work. The next thing I know the payroll department is telling me Harry had authorized his own

349

severance pay and cashed in his company benefits. He didn't even leave a forwarding address."

"He's crazy! What's he going to do?"

"I don't know. Maybe he's gone back to Chicago."

"Sounds like he cut his own throat," Steven said bluntly. "He was very good, but not indispensable."

"It bothers me that after all this time he left without even telling me why . . . or even saying good-bye," Rose said softly.

That wasn't entirely true, Rose admitted to herself. Ever since her decision to let Steven build the bridges to Michelle, Harry had lost interest in the company that had once been his life. As his work deteriorated, Rose began to receive complaints from her branch offices across the country until she had no choice but to deal with the situation. She left a message for Harry to call her but he never did. When she heard that he had left, she couldn't believe it. But as the reality set in, her anger was replaced by an aching loss. No matter how estranged she and Harry had become—a distance Rose knew was her own creation—she could never forget those first wonderful years when, under Harry's touch, she had flowered as a woman. Harry was also the closest thing she had to a friend.

"Don't worry, Mother," Steven was saying. "I'll stay as long as you need me."

Rose squeezed his hand gratefully. "Thank you, but I've taken over Harry's work. Besides, you have to concentrate on Europe. I'm expecting great things from you."

Steven smiled. "I won't disappoint you, Mother."

For the next three years Steven Talbot crisscrossed the Atlantic, working with single-minded purpose. At Global offices in Europe, dead wood was cut away mercilessly and the new people who were hired were loyal only to Steven. As Global's rates became more competitive and Steven's connections with European governments grew, the company found itself swamped with freight contracts. Reviewing the figures at their annual year-end meeting in New York, Rose was impressed.

"Even I didn't think you would do this well!"

You don't know the half of it, Mother.

The set of books that Steven displayed to Rose were not the real ones. In fact, European profits were triple what Rose Jefferson thought they were. By now the Swiss companies Steven had created owned a fleet of ships only slightly smaller than Global's.

Even when he was in the United States, Steven capitalized on the opportunity to expand. He became a frequent passenger on the New York–Washington *Capital Express.* In elegant embassy studies he met with financiers, industrialists, and government officials from countries as diverse as Argentina and Brazil, South Africa and Nigeria. Deals running into millions of dollars were consummated with a handshake. Then Steven would go over to the German embassy and from the secure communications chamber in the basement talk to Kurt Essenheimer, telling him that the Third Reich was moving closer and closer to its dream of guaranteed deliveries for badly needed natural resources.

On July 18, 1936, the Spanish Civil War erupted. Steven read the accounts voraciously, relishing every Fascist victory. The oil, rubber, and precious ore he had helped procure for Germany had been forged into an invincible battle machine. That fall, when Steven announced his intention to leave for the Continent, Rose smiled coyly.

"You may not have to."

"What do you mean?"

"I just received this cable from Michelle. She's sailing for New York today. She says she has something very important to discuss with me."

Rose hugged her son. "As if I don't know what that is! Obviously she hasn't been able to ignore the work you've been doing. I think she's coming to us about a merger."

— 42 —

The events that would bring Michelle to the United States in the autumn of 1936 had everything to do with Global but in a way Rose Jefferson could never have imagined.

The portents of tragedy had begun on January 30, 1933, when Adolf Hitler emerged as chancellor of Germany. The party that many had ridiculed as a bunch of misfits and outcasts was legitimized. From then on the Nazis moved quickly to consolidate their hold. Newspapers and radio spewed out propaganda against enemies real or imagined. Nazi bureaucrats drove honest men and women from the civil service and the universities, replacing them with unthinking, unfeeling automatons. Voices of hate began to find a forum, pillorying intellectuals and liberals but especially Jews.

"It's becoming a nightmare," Abraham Warburg, Michelle's German banker, told her that spring. "Yet my people refuse to wake up. We are more

German than the Germans, they say, as though if they repeat that enough times everyone will believe it."

He shook his head in despair.

They were seated on the deck of a beautiful lakeside restaurant in the Wansee district of Berlin. Below, graceful swans drifted by, plunging their heads below the water to retrieve bread thrown by the patrons. Yet in this peaceful setting Michelle saw only latent violence. At every second table was an SS officer in his stark black uniform and gleaming jackboots, or a well-dressed man with a Nazi pin in his lapel. Whenever they saw Michelle and Warburg their eyes would harden. Then a joke, sometimes obscene, would be told in a voice loud enough for them to hear. To ensure the privacy of their discussions Michelle and the banker always spoke English when they met in public.

"You've got to make your people understand they have to get out while they still can," Michelle said.

"I am trying," Warburg replied. "But most refuse to abandon their homes and relatives."

"Then we have to do what we can to help those who want to leave."

God, less than twenty years later I'm fighting the Germans all over again. It's insanity!

"It's becoming harder and harder to get visas," Warburg told her.

"I know. But I think I've found a way around that."

Quickly Michelle outlined her scheme. From her Paris base she would set up a tour company that would offer excursions to various areas of France.

"The Nazis won't have a clue as to what we're really doing," she explained. "These people will have legitimate papers and a fixed itinerary. Only they'll never come back. Once they're in France they can go wherever they please. I'll make arrangements to keep them moving."

Warburg was excited by the plan. "It's ingenious. But many won't be able to pay, and you can't advertise ridiculously low tour prices without the Nazis becoming suspicious."

Michelle shrugged. "Who said anything about making money? Each person will pick up a prepaid ticket at one of our offices, along with some traveler's checks in U.S. dollars. For all the world they'll look like legitimate tourists, as long as they don't try to bring everything they own with them."

Warburg considered her argument. "It could work," he said at last. "However, we have to be very careful about the details."

"Get me people you trust implicitly and leave the rest to me."

By fall of 1933, the exodus began. Michelle carefully screened her current employees, identified the Nazi sympathizers, and found a pretext to let them go—with generous severance pay to avoid ill-will. She replaced them with people Warburg sent her and, when she was sure they knew exactly what to do, returned to Paris to look after the details there. Michelle chafed because the first few tour groups were small, but as word spread there was a backlog for the "Ooh, La La! Paris Excursion." Ironically, that was the beginning of her problems.

Michelle, who had never taken a tour, much less organized one, had badly underestimated both the amount and the kind of help her "visitors" would need. This was partly because the first few groups were composed of engineers, lawyers, and doctors who brought not only enough money to tide them over the short term but who had either relatives willing to take them in or skills that would help them start a new life. Later that year, Michelle found herself confronted by hundreds of lower- and working-class families, bewildered, alone, and penniless except for their fifty dollars in traveler's checks and hotel vouchers.

Realizing she needed help fast, Michelle turned to Emil Rothschild.

"You've done *what?*" the banker demanded, sinking deep into his chair.

"Well, *someone* had to do something!" Michelle replied tartly.

"For all intents and purposes you're engaged in smuggling, the illegal transfer of people. Even if you make allowances for the myopic French bureaucracy, how long do you think it will take some official to discover that the people coming in aren't going out?"

"Really, Emil! Given the number of tourists who cross the border each day, what we're dealing with here is paltry."

"It may seem that way," Rothschild said patiently. "But consider this. What if one of your resettled people sends a postcard or letter home to Germany, telling his friends about the wonderful trick they've played on the German authorities? We both know that mail going to certain names and addresses is being opened by the Germans.

"By the same token, what if some nosy concierge begins to ask questions about why there are suddenly two families living in an apartment where before there was only one? Or one of your people is stopped, for whatever reason, by the police? Their tourist visas will have expired. They have no other papers. What will they say? Whom will they turn to? Only you. And then the authorities will become very interested."

The banker's unerring logic depressed Michelle, yet she stubbornly resisted his arguments.

"You're right, Emil," she said. "I didn't realize exactly what I was getting into. But I can't stop now. I'll need your help and that of others to prevent those incidents you describe from happening. Like it or not, I'm responsible for these people now. I'll try to place as many as I can in my offices, but most of them don't even speak French, for heaven's sake! Emil, you have connections in the

Jewish community throughout France. Use them! Explain to people what is going on!"

"And you, Michelle, have you thought of what might happen to you and Cassandra? You're jeopardizing everything you've built. If the government unravels your scheme, it will haul you into court."

Michelle's eyes blazed. "They wouldn't dare!"

"At the very least, you'd find tax officials poring over your books, immigration people checking all your employees, even building inspectors trying to determine whether your premises are safe. By then, the newspapers will have gotten hold of the story and the Germans will know everything. Even if you manage to fend off the authorities here, Berlin will simply shut down your tour groups on the German end."

Michelle considered his words carefully. She knew that Emil Rothschild was speaking as a concerned friend, not a coward.

"I'm prepared to take that risk," she replied softly. "Are you willing to help me?"

The banker looked grim. "For this alone, they should give you another medal."

As the German "tourists" continued to pour in throughout 1934, Michelle spent less and less time at her office and more at home, working to try to resettle them. Emil Rothschild was as good as his word. Using his connections across France, he enlisted the help of hundreds of people who were willing to take in refugees. These, in turn, contacted friends and relatives they could trust and so the network expanded. By the end of that year, thousands had been spirited into small businesses, predominantly Jewish-owned, whose owners were willing to teach them the trade. In almost every case the new arrivals were introduced to the community as "cousins" or "distant relations" who had come to help out the family.

But Michelle did not stop there. She and the Underground Refugee Council, consisting of Emil Rothschild, Pierre Lazard, and other prominent French Jews, carefully sifted through the French bureaucracy to find sympathetic men and women willing to provide identity papers, work permits, residence cards, and, in some cases, even new birth certificates. These allowed the skilled refugees who spoke some French to resettle on their own, thus easing the crush. Nevertheless, by May 1935 the sheer volume of people was threatening to choke the system.

"We must find a way to keep some of these people moving," Pierre Lazard declared at a committee meeting. "Spain, Portugal, England, the Scandinavian countries—anywhere."

"The problem is that we don't have the same contacts or influence in other countries as we do here," Rothschild observed.

"No," Michelle replied thoughtfully. "But we may have better luck elsewhere."

The greatest strain Michelle worked under wasn't the threat of exposure or the long, grueling hours. It was the absence of her husband.

Monk had returned to the United States, partly to attend to business at Q magazine but also to lend his economic expertise to government programs set up to deal with the Depression. From her husband's letters, Michelle learned that he was closely listened to at the White House and was working day and night to help get the American economy back on its feet. But while the constant stream of words was a balm on their separation, nothing could replace the touch and feel and smell of the man. Even though Monk returned often, Michelle knew that Cassandra pined for him even more than she. She was entering that time when having a father to watch her grow meant everything. No matter how many times Michelle explained to Cassandra why Monk couldn't be with them, her reasoning, accepted one day, was inevitably challenged the next. To make matters worse, Michelle herself had precious little energy or time to devote to her daughter's needs and demands.

When the family was at last reunited during Thanksgiving that year, Michelle told Monk about her refugee program. Monk realized the tremendous strain his wife was working under.

"Our most urgent problem right now is that we can't find room for the new arrivals," Michelle explained.

"What do you propose?"

"We have to find a way to get them to America, Monk. It's their only hope."

Monk let out a low whistle. "That's a tall order. The unemployment rate being what it is back home, the immigration quotas have been cut way back."

"I realize that. But you know people in Washington. . . ."

"Sure, but if I take this on, it'll mean even less time to be with you and Cassandra."

Michelle bit back her tears. "If it were anything else, I would never ask you."

Monk cupped his wife's face tenderly and kissed her. "You're a remarkable woman."

Michelle smiled sadly. "No. No brave face for you, my love. I need you to hold me and kiss me, and tell me everything will be all right."

But during those short weeks in Paris, Monk learned that Cassandra needed him even more. Although she had wanted to, Michelle hadn't been able to bring herself to tell Cassandra about the refugee program. Fourteen-year-old girls loved to share secrets with their friends, and after that, who knew what other ears they would reach? *The least I can do*, Monk thought, *is explain why I can't be here.*

"Why must you leave, Papa?" Cassandra asked him as they sat in the cafe where, years ago, Monk and Michelle had celebrated their love.

Where to begin? Monk asked himself.

"Do you see those people over there, pumpkin?" Monk pointed to a table of middle-aged men who, over an hour ago, had ordered a carafe of wine and, having barely tasted it, sat desultorily playing dominoes.

"Uh-huh."

"Why do you think they're here in the middle of the day?"

Cassandra shrugged. "They're not working."

"And why is that?"

"Because there's nothing for them to do."

"That's right. There are thousands of men like them, Cassandra. Here, all across Europe, America too. Men who want to work to provide for their families but who can't find a job."

"I know," Cassandra said in a bored tone. "It's called the Depression."

"Yes, it is. But it's also called hunger, poverty, sadness, and pain. It means that husbands and fathers go wherever they can, sometimes far away, so that they can find a job. If they can find one."

"But we're not poor!" Cassandra replied angrily. "You don't have to go back to New York." Then, as quick as a ferret, she slyly added, "Or you can take me with you."

Monk refused to be drawn in. "No, we're not poor. But don't you think that's why we should try to help those less fortunate?"

"All the girls at school have their fathers at home," Cassandra said.

The infallible logic of a fourteen-year-old! Monk despaired. All at once, he understood what Michelle had to contend with every day.

"Pumpkin, I want you to listen very carefully," he said quietly, holding her hands tightly. "You, your mother, and I have so much to be grateful for. Maybe right now everything's not the way you'd like it to be, but you can see that we're much better off than most people."

Monk waited until Cassandra nodded, grudgingly.

"Because of our good fortune, we have a responsibility to give something back, to help others when we can. Your mother and I must do what we feel is right, just as one day, when you're faced with choices, you'll look into your conscience and decide which one is best. I'm sorry, Cass, but I can't explain it any better than that. I wish I could."

356

Cassandra lowered her eyes, swinging her legs and scuffing the toes of her shoes. When she at last spoke, her voice trembled.

"But all that means is that you're still going away."

Monk left after Christmas and returned to Washington, where he mapped out his campaign to influence the opinions of senators and congressmen who sat on the government's immigration committees. The work was often frustrating, always grueling, demanding every hour Monk could spare from his responsibilities on President Roosevelt's Economic Reforms Commission as well as from Q magazine, which had become a leading advocate of FDR's policies.

Still, progress was made. Thousands of German Jews who otherwise would have been denied entry into the United States slipped through the loopholes lawmakers had created. Considering the number who now desperately wanted to leave Germany, it was minuscule. Nonetheless, these arrivals to the new world made places for others who could, at least for the moment, go only as far as France, to live on the hope that one day their turn would come.

Inexorably, time was running out as 1936 began. With each visit to her offices in Berlin, Michelle discovered that new and onerous travel restrictions had been added to the Nazi law books. Facing strict currency regulations and interminable waits for exit visas, it became almost impossible for the average citizen to leave the country. The blocks of train seats Michelle had prepaid went unfilled, and it became obvious the tours were losing substantial money. Michelle realized that if she continued to operate at such a glaring loss, the Germans, already hostile toward her, would become doubly suspicious.

"We knew it would happen one day," Abraham Warburg told her the day the traveler's-check offices were closed in Berlin.

"But there's still so much to do!"

Warburg patted her hand. "And we will deal with it as best we can. Think of everything you've done, Michelle. You've helped thousands. They will never forget."

"It's time for you to leave too, my friend," Michelle said. "The situation is intolerable."

"Precisely why I must stay," Warburg replied. "The Nazis won't touch me, at least not yet. I have friends in Switzerland to thank for that." He paused. "Besides, I have stumbled across something which you must know about. It has to do with Global."

Michelle was puzzled.

"For months now I've been hearing talk, just bits and pieces, you understand, about Essenheimer A.G."

Michelle recognized the name. "One of the Reich's top industrial armament conglomerates."

"Yes. But there's more. Information given to me by everyone from book-keepers to cleaning ladies who worked for Essenheimer points to Global's having become the Reich's principal shipper, purveyor of everything Germany needs to wage war."

Michelle was shaken. "Rose isn't the kind of person to deal with Nazis!"

"Who said it was Fraulein Jefferson?" Warburg replied sadly. "It's Steven Talbot, head of Global Europe."

He passed Michelle a thick dossier. "Please, read it, and draw your own conclusions."

As Warburg had told her, the testimonials came from people who had served at all levels of the Essenheimer empire. Michelle could sense both the fear and the truth in their words. But apart from their own observations there wasn't a single scrap of paper linking the German conglomerate to Steven Talbot.

"It's all hearsay," Michelle said. "I believe every word but it's not proof."

"You can't imagine the degree of secrecy and security around this," Warburg replied. "If the Gestapo suspected that these people had told me even this much . . ." He left the obvious unsaid.

"Are there any still working for Essenheimer who have access to records or documents?" Michelle asked urgently.

"Of course. But as I've said—"

"Abraham, you've got to persuade them to get me hard evidence. Steven can't be allowed to continue this!"

"That's going to be very difficult."

"We can do it!" Michelle insisted. "We can bring out the people and their information. Over the years we've developed routes out of Germany no one knows about. Now's the time to use them!"

The banker considered. "You may be right. But have you thought about the risks?"

"To them? Of course. We can—"

"Not them, Michelle. You. If I send these people through to you and if, God forbid, Steven Talbot or Essenheimer or the Gestapo should discover what we're up to, they'll kill you. Believe me, Michelle, given what's at stake, these men would do everything in their power to prevent the truth from coming out."

"Which is exactly what we must bring about," Michelle told him. "Send them to me, Abraham. Tell them to bring me something, anything I can use. I'll do the rest!"

By early spring, Michelle had been forced to close her offices in Germany and had returned to Paris. Every day she went down to the central telephone and telegraph exchange and checked for messages from Abraham Warburg. As the weeks passed with no word, Michelle became not only frustrated but concerned. Her friend was playing a dangerous game of cat-and-mouse in which an errant word or careless move could spell disaster. Over and over again, Michelle told herself that Abraham would move as quickly as circumstances allowed.

Something will happen when I least expect it, she told herself.

Michelle had no idea how prophetic her words were.

"Maman! Maman, wake up!"

Michelle started and sat up. "What is it, *chérie?"*

"Someone's trying to break in," Cassandra whispered. "I heard them scratching at the lock on the door."

"Stay right here."

Cassandra shrank back as she saw her mother remove a gun from her bedside-table drawer.

"Everything will be all right," Michelle said softly. "Don't leave the room."

Closing the door behind her, Michelle made her way to the front of the house. In the moonlight she saw the knob to the front door twist and turn. Michelle stepped behind the door as it opened and, holding her breath, heard the intruders enter. Then she kicked the door shut and jammed the gun into the back of the man closest to her.

"Don't move!" she whispered.

Michelle's fingers searched for the light switch. When she found it, she gasped. Standing in front of her was a young, pregnant woman, a child in her arms.

"Turn around!" Michelle told the man.

"Abraham sent us," the young man said anxiously. "Please, madam, we mean you no harm!"

"Who are you?"

"David Jacobi," the man stammered. "This is my wife, Rachel."

"If Abraham sent you, why didn't I get a message?" Michelle demanded. "And why were you trying to break in?"

David Jacobi regarded her with hollow, pain-filled eyes.

"There were six of us, madam. We all managed to cross the border but the Germans contacted the French authorities. They said we were spies and saboteurs. The police tracked us. Rachel and I were the only ones who escaped. When we finally reached Paris, we weren't sure if the police had been here too."

"What happened to the rest?"

David Jacobi's voice broke with grief. "They were taken back to the border, handed over to the Gestapo."

Michelle was sickened.

"*Maman*, what's going on?"

Cassandra stood by the French doors to the living room, looking frightened and bewildered.

"This is my daughter, Cassandra," she told the Jacobis. Michelle stepped over to her and in a low voice said, "I want you to take Rachel and her child into the guest bedroom. Show her where everything is and help her if she needs anything. Then go to the kitchen and get some food."

"Who are these people?" Cassandra demanded. "What are they doing here in the middle of the night?"

Michelle couldn't believe her daughter's angry words.

"They need our help, Cassandra! Now do as you're told."

My God, at your age I was fighting Germans!

Michelle caught herself. The comparison was unfair. Cassandra had grown up with all the advantages and privileges that came with wealth. *Perhaps,* Michelle thought, *I unconsciously shielded her from the realities of the world, because I remembered what I had already seen at her age. But the world has a way of catching up to all of us. . . .*

"Please, Cassandra," Michelle said gently. "Do as I ask. I'll explain later."

"I'm sure you will, *Maman*," Cassandra said with a toss of her head. Still, she went over to Rachel Jacobi and took the bag out of her hand.

After David Jacobi had washed up, Michelle poured them both a dollop of brandy and waited to hear the rest of his account.

"Do you think the escape route has been compromised?" she asked.

"Those who were returned to the Gestapo won't be able to withstand interrogation," Jacobi replied, staring into his drink.

Michelle shivered. "Were . . . were they carrying any papers?"

The young refugee shook his head. Michelle's hopes rose.

"Did you bring anything?"

Jacobi searched in his suit jacket pocket and removed a sealed letter.

"From Abraham."

"That's all?"

"Madame McQueen," he said, "I used to work in Essenheimer's legal division. Getting the kind of information Abraham wanted was impossible. There are three, even four sets of books. All the information is heavily guarded. You have to have special authorization to look up a contract, never mind sign out for it. God help you if it's not returned at the end of the day."

The lawyer paused. "I risked everything to try to bring some material out. But my supervisor became suspicious. That's why Abraham put us into the escape route. . . ."

He looked pleadingly at Michelle. "I know a great deal about Essenheimer and Global. Please, Madame McQueen, listen to me. Take me to people who can stop this insanity."

"Tomorrow," Michelle said gently. "There will be time enough then."

— 43 —

"Over here!"

Michelle whirled about and ran down the gangplank, throwing herself into Monk's arms.

"My God, I've missed you," Monk groaned, burying his face in her hair.

"And I you."

Michelle clung to him, refusing to let go.

"Who's this?"

Monk looked at Cassandra standing shyly off to the side. Since he'd last seen her, Cassandra had shot up so that she was now taller than Michelle. With paternal pride, Monk noted Cassandra's stunning wool suit in a blue that matched her eyes and set off her long blond hair. Growing up in Paris had its advantages, he decided.

"Come here, darling," he whispered.

The next minute the three of them were crying and embracing one another while other passengers filed by, smiling.

"Come on," Monk said at last, wiping his tears with the back of his hand. "Let's go home."

Monk whisked them through customs and had the luggage packed away in his enormous Cadillac. All three got into the front seat and Monk played tour guide on the way into Manhattan.

"It's all so wonderful!" Cassandra cried, staring at the architectural marvels.

Monk laughed and gave them a short tour. He swung up Sixth Avenue and meandered through Central Park before coming out on the Upper West Side. He parked in front of a tall majestic building with a green and white canopy.

"Home," he announced.

Built at the turn of the century, the Carlton Towers was the largest apartment building Cassandra had ever seen, occupying a full city block and rising more than sixty stories. The outside reminded her of a great castle, all turrets, gables, and leering gargoyles, battened down by a copper-sheathed roof gleaming in the early morning sun. Once inside, Cassandra felt lost. The marble-tile lobby was cavernous, and they had to take two separate elevators to reach the apartment. The door swung back and Cassandra saw a portly black woman waiting to greet them.

"Ah, Abilene," Monk gasped, hauling their suitcases inside. "This is my wife, Michelle, and my daughter, Cassandra. Ladies, this is the woman without whom I'd be lost, Abilene Lincoln."

"Welcome to the Towers!" Abilene said, embracing Cassandra. "I know you'll be real comfy here."

Cassandra stepped forward cautiously and looked around her. She thought her mother's apartment on Île St.-Louis was grand, but this was magnificent. The walls of the living room, where floor-to-ceiling windows faced the greenery of the park, were lined with books. In the far corner was a Victrola phonograph surrounded by hundreds of records ranging from jazz to opera.

"The study's through there," Monk added, pointing to the double French doors. "Behind it is the kitchen. The bedrooms are upstairs."

Cassandra whirled around on her tiptoes, skirt flying to reveal her long slim legs.

"It's wonderful! I could stay here forever!"

Abilene Lincoln caught Monk's eye and said to Cassandra, "How would you like to taste some of the best banana bread north of the Mason-Dixon Line?"

"Mason-Dixon? Who are they?"

Abilene threw back her head and laughed.

"I gotta get you up on yo' history, girl. Come on, let's leave your mama and daddy alone to get accustomed to each other."

When the door closed behind them Monk took Michelle's hand.

"She's almost as beautiful as you are," he said softly. "I never imagined . . ."

"At a loss for words, my love?" Michelle teased him.

Monk stared at the woman he loved, his eye memorizing every fine detail. He felt his hunger for her rising, yet behind the warmth of Michelle's lips and coolness of her fingers upon his cheek he sensed some invisible barrier.

"What's wrong, my love?"

"Not us, darling. We're fine, both of us. It's . . . it's something else."

Michelle took a deep breath and explained how Abraham Warburg had come across extraordinary information concerning Essenheimer A.G. and Steven Talbot. She gave him the details that had been passed along and the role Steven Talbot was playing in the new Germany.

Monk was shocked. The idea that an American of Steven's reputation and influence should be working for the Germans was outrageous. Except for a few misguided individuals such as Henry Ford, Americans laughed at Nazis. Some, like Monk, recognized the potential danger of Hitler's fanaticism and tried to warn their countrymen.

"The problem is, I have no hard evidence to take to Rose," Michelle concluded. "On the other hand, I can't let Steven continue to supply the Reich. So I have to convince her myself."

"Do you have anything?" Monk asked. "A document with his signature on it, individual testimony, an eyewitness?"

"Nothing. It's impossible to take anything out of the company's offices."

"And you've already let Rose know you're coming?"

"I have a meeting with her first thing tomorrow morning."

Monk sat down beside her. "Why didn't you let me know sooner, Michelle? I have a lot of friends in Europe who could have helped. Hell, I would have come over myself."

"That's exactly why I didn't tell you, my love. There's nothing anyone—except Rose—can do. If she believes me . . ."

"And if she doesn't?"

"Then we must find another way to stop Steven."

The next morning Michelle barely had time for a cup of coffee before Monk's driver arrived to take her to Lower Broadway. She pecked Cassandra on the cheek and was off.

I wonder what it would be like to live in this city now? Michelle asked herself as she rode toward Lower Broadway.

As much as she thought of Paris as home, the vitality of New York made it seem almost stuffy by comparison. Here, anything was possible. It was the land of eternal change and opportunity. But Michelle also remembered the humiliation she had had to endure when she lived at Talbot House. Even now, she could hear the mocking laughter of Amelia Richardson and Rose's other friends.

They can't hurt me anymore. This city can belong as much to me as it does to them.

Approaching the financial district, Michelle's thoughts drifted back to Rose. She recalled other times when she had tried to convince her of the truth—the awful incident with Steven, and several occasions concerning Franklin. Every time Rose had chosen not to believe her. Why should now be any different?

Because the stakes are too high!

At the Global Building, Michelle was met by an usher who escorted her directly to Rose's office.

"Michelle, how wonderful to see you. You look lovely."

Rose came around her desk and took Michelle's hand in both of hers. Rose cut an elegant figure in a smoothly tailored beige skirt and jade blouse that reflected a disciplined professional without sacrificing femininity. Yet there was a subtle difference to Rose. The years seemed to have softened her, smoothed away the rough edges of that famous temper and imperious gaze.

"It's good to see you too, Rose," Michelle said.

Rose gestured at the sideboard where coffee and pastries were laid out.

"Can I offer you anything?"

Michelle declined and settled herself on the sofa opposite the desk.

"How is Cassandra?" asked Rose. "I hope I'll have a chance to meet her at last."

"She'd like that."

An awkward silence descended between the two women.

"Michelle," Rose said. "This isn't easy for either of us. There's been a lot of bad blood between us but that's not to say we can't start over. I'm tremendously impressed by what you've done with the traveler's checks, and I think I know why you've come here. I asked Steven to make himself available. Perhaps we should call him to join us."

"Steven . . . ?"

For a moment Michelle thought Rose had anticipated the reason for her visit.

No, that's not it at all. She's talking about Steven's European trip, the reason he went over there. . . .

Of course! Steven hadn't gone to Europe on his own initiative. Rose had sent him there to see how well Michelle was doing. But why? To offer to buy her out? Propose a merger? Whatever the motive, Michelle was certain Rose was in the dark about Steven's dealings with the Germans.

"I don't think we should bring Steven in right now," Michelle said. "It's because of Steven that I'm here."

"From the tone of your voice I take it this won't be a very pleasant conversation," Rose murmured. "I had been hoping otherwise."

"Believe me, Rose, I would have liked nothing better."

"Well, whatever it is, let's get it over with."

Michelle presented her argument, careful not to accuse Steven directly but suggesting that he might be an unwitting pawn in the Nazis' game. To her surprise, Rose listened without interruption. Only when Steven's name was linked to the Nazis did she flinch.

"I find the situation in Germany repulsive," Rose said quietly. "Now you're telling me my son is helping to arm the Nazi war machine."

"If I didn't believe the people who brought me the information, I wouldn't be here," Michelle replied. "It's no less difficult for me to tell you all this than it is for you to listen."

"What do you expect me to do?"

"Talk to Steven. Ask him to tell you the truth."

"The truth, Michelle, is that Steven has turned Global Europe around. I sent him there to build the company, thinking that one day you and I might be able to join forces. I had hoped that was what you had in mind when you came here."

"I'm sorry I disappointed you. If there was any other way—"

Rose held up her hand. "Please, let's not become maudlin about this. I'll indulge you and ask Steven for details about the German operations. But if he proves to me that there's absolutely no relationship between the company and the Nazis, then I think apologies are in order."

Michelle said nothing. She would never apologize to Steven Talbot.

"Thank you, Rose, for listening."

Rose nodded and quietly showed her out.

"It's only as you get older that you learn truly to regret certain things," she said. "And how to avoid making the same mistake twice. I suspect you will reach that point very soon, Michelle."

Ever since he had learned that Michelle was on her way to New York, Steven Talbot had lived with fear. Outwardly, he betrayed nothing. His demeanor remained pleasant and businesslike; his routine never varied. But in the dead of night, as he pored over sets of ledgers, desperately seeking the one false note that would give him away, he felt as though an incubus were twisting his stomach into knots. Now, sitting in his office waiting for Rose's summons, he wished he were invisible so that he could listen in on the conversation three doors down.

Steven jumped as his door swung open.

"That was pretty quick," he said as lightly as he could. "How's Michelle?"

Rose studied him silently.

"She tells me you're shipping for the Nazis," she said bluntly. "I want to know if that's true."

Steven crimsoned, then made a show of reining in his anger.

"No, Mother, it is not true."

"I want to believe that," Rose said. "But I keep asking myself why she's making such an accusation. What can she possibly gain?"

Steven seized the opportunity. "I'll *prove* to you that she's lying."

Steven depressed a lever on his intercom. "Hattie, would you bring all the Global Europe books in here, please? Yes, all of them."

"She's lying," Steven repeated. "The figures won't."

A few minutes later, Steven's secretary and four others struggled through the doors, weighed down with cartons of ledgers and files.

Steven pointed to his worktable. "Over there."

After the secretaries had unpacked everything, Rose said, "Have coffee and sandwiches brought in for lunch. It's going to be a long day."

Eighteen hours later, at four o'clock in the morning, Rose rubbed her eyes, pushed away a cup of cold coffee, and closed the last ledger. Across the table Steven continued to watch her carefully. Rose's stamina and single-minded concentration amazed him. His mother had worked in almost total silence, speaking only when she wanted him to explain an entry or clarify a point in a contract.

"Damn Michelle," she said softly.

Relief surged through Steven.

"I'm sorry this took so long. You've done a magnificent job, Steven. I owe you an apology for having doubted that."

Steven managed a modest shrug. "What do we do now?"

"You go home and get some sleep," Rose said firmly. "I have an appointment with Michelle!"

Cassandra stood on the balcony of Monk's apartment, watching as dawn crept along the tops of the trees in Central Park. Even though she had gone to bed late, she had been unable to sleep, caught up in the pulse of this great city that seemed never to rest.

The chimes of the grandfather clock struck six. From the kitchen drifted the delicious odor of frying bacon and rising pancakes. Cassandra was on her way to get a glass of orange juice when she heard the doorbell ring.

"I'll get it!" she called to Abilene.

Standing in the corridor was one of the most beautiful women Cassandra had ever seen. She wore a tailored blue skirt and jacket with a white silk blouse set off by a Navajo silver and turquoise broach. Only the streak of pure white hair, rising from the widow's peak and startling against the black, betrayed her age. Cassandra stood there open-mouthed, lost for words. The woman seemed equally surprised to see her but as her eyes roamed over Cassandra's face her expression softened.

"You must be Cassandra," she said at last.

"Yes . . ."

"My name is Rose." She paused, then added, "I am your aunt."

Rose stepped over the threshold, unable to take her eyes off Cassandra. She had come here prepared for a quick, decisive confrontation, her anger fueled by what she knew now was an unjust accusation. Yet all of that fell away before this lovely girl in a pink nightdress, with sleep in her eyes.

She has Franklin's hair and his height but that's all, Rose thought.

Cassandra was undeniably beautiful, with her wide blue eyes and straight, white-blond hair. There was a mixture of adolescent innocence and determination, the feeling that one had caught her on the verge of blooming into womanhood. Rose, who in the past had never regretted not having more children, suddenly felt an aching loss. She had seldom enjoyed the company of children, thinking most of them spoiled and loud. Yet she sensed that Cassandra was unique. Something other than mere beauty separated her from the rest, and its promise touched Rose deeply.

"I . . . I'm sorry but I don't know you," Cassandra said, blushing.

Rose laughed. "I'm afraid that goes for both of us. But maybe we can remedy that later on, if you like."

"Yes, I would!" Cassandra said eagerly.

She knew Rose only from one or two photographs, standing with her father. Whenever Cassandra had asked about her aunt, her mother had given only vague replies. Cassandra sensed Michelle's unhappiness when speaking Rose's name and so she had never pursued the subject. But her curiosity remained.

"Cassandra!"

She whirled around to see Michelle behind her, a long terry bathrobe wrapped tightly around her.

"*Maman*, look who's here—"

"I know, *chérie*. Good morning, Rose. You're off to an early start."

Michelle turned to Cassandra. "Your aunt and I have a few things to talk about, and Abilene's ready with your breakfast."

Cassandra recognized the hint but was reluctant to leave. Impulsively, she stepped forward and kissed Rose on the cheek.

"I'd love to go shopping!" she whispered and ran off.

"You made quite an impression," Michelle said, watching as Rose looked after Cassandra, two fingers tracing the spot where Cassandra had kissed her.

"Yes, I suppose I have," Rose said slowly.

"Can I get you some coffee?"

Rose shook her head. "I know it's early and I apologize for barging in on you like this. But I've been working all night and wanted to see you as soon as possible."

"We can talk in here," Michelle said, pointing to Monk's study.

Rose followed her, conscious of that humid, musky scent that clings to a woman who's just made love. It had been a long time for her, too long.

"Michelle, you must tell me why you leveled those accusations against Steven. They're not true. I've gone over all the books myself. Global Europe isn't involved in anything like you suggest."

Michelle drew her robe tightly around herself.

"Rose, those people who worked for Essenheimer A.G. risked their lives bringing me the information I gave you. And no, they couldn't get anything on paper linking Steven to the Germans. But damn it, they'd have no reason to dream up such a connection. They were warning us!"

"Do you really expect me to take the word of people I've never laid eyes on against that of my own son?"

"You know as well as I how figures and reports can be juggled and slanted! Steven is a part of something terrible, Rose, and I can't stop him alone. One way or another, I'll get you the proof. Then it'll be up to you!"

Rose looked at the younger woman and smiled sadly because in Michelle she saw a touch of what had once been herself.

"I wish it didn't have to be this way. I had hoped that your coming here meant that you and I were thinking the same way."

Rose explained her reasons for having sent Steven to Europe.

"I had hoped that once we had built up Global Europe, you'd see the value in combining our resources," Rose said. "I know that in the past I've behaved badly toward you. I'm not asking you to forgive me. But that doesn't mean we have to be burdened by it for the rest of our lives. I hoped this could be a new beginning for both of us."

"I didn't have the faintest idea . . ." Michelle said. "But then why didn't Steven come to see me?"

Because deep down he hates me. He never had any intention of furthering your plan. He was too busy creating his own monstrosity.

Rose got up. "At this point, it doesn't really matter, does it? I wish you the best, Michelle. You have a beautiful daughter whom I'm sure you love as much as I love Steven. Please remember that, if we should ever talk again."

Steven Talbot did not take his mother's advice. He returned to his Park Avenue apartment only for a shower and change of clothes. He caught the nine o'clock express for Washington and was at the German embassy in time for lunch.

"Well?" Kurt Essenheimer demanded, embracing Steven as he was shown into the ambassador's private dining room.

Steven hesitated, then smiled coldly. "She didn't find a thing. Not a damn thing!"

"You're sure?"

"Sure as I'm standing here."

"You can't imagine how worried I was," Essenheimer said wearily. "I barely slept on the way over. At any minute I expected a cable from you telling me that everything was finished."

Steven thought back to those long, dark hours at the office. He saw his mother's hard eyes on the ledger pages, searching, probing, calculating.

"We survived," he said, refilling their wineglasses. "But there's still the problem of Michelle. She's not going to let go of this thing. She'll go back to Europe and ask more questions. Worse, I'm sure that by now she's dragged her husband into this, which means he'll be digging as well."

"We have to stop them," Essenheimer said quietly. "There's no other way. What we're doing is too important, to us and to the Reich."

Essenheimer looked at Steven. "You have something in mind, don't you?"

Steven nodded. "Several things, in fact. But I'll need your help."

"You have only to ask."

On the train, Steven had been thinking of Michelle, dredging up every detail he had ever heard about her. The only thing that seemed out-of-place was that she had not gotten pregnant until just before Franklin killed himself. Given how devoted they were to each other, Steven found this odd.

The anomaly irritated Steven and he couldn't brush it aside. There *was* a child and she was the key.

"First," Steven said, "we must find our old friend Harry Taylor."

- 44 -

"Please, Cassandra, don't make this any harder than it already is."

Michelle felt that everything she tried to do today was like pulling teeth. It was one o'clock. The *Normandie* was sailing late that afternoon and she had just started packing. Cassandra was no help at all, sulking because she hated to leave New York.

"But why do we have to go so soon?" she demanded, fighting back tears.

"Because you have to go back to school. You've missed enough as it is."

"Why can't I transfer here?"

Monk sat Cassandra down. "I don't want you to go, pumpkin, but you have

369

your studies and your mother has her work. Besides, I'll be over in a month or so—before Thanksgiving, probably. The time will go by before you know it."

Somewhat mollified, Cassandra left the room, leaving Michelle to discover that this wasn't Monk's last word on the subject.

"You won't reconsider and wait until I can go with you? I don't like the idea of your tangling with Steven by yourself."

"Please, Monk, I can't let Steven carry on with what he's doing."

"And you're the only one who can do that? Michelle, all I'm asking you to do is wait. I agree with you: Steven has to be stopped. But there are ways of doing this with a lot less risk than you're willing to take."

"Less risk, maybe. But there's not any more time."

Monk saw that no arguments could quell Michelle's determination. But maybe, for her sake and Cassandra's, he could temper it just a little.

"All right," he said. "But promise me one thing: don't go into Germany until I get there. You'll be safe in Paris. Warburg can pass along information to you there. But I don't want you to set foot in Berlin."

Monk's love for her and Cassandra was so obvious and so comforting that for an instant Michelle almost faltered.

"All right. I promise I won't leave Paris until you arrive. But after that—"

"After that, we'll work together," Monk said, tenderly stroking her cheek. "We'll get to the bottom of this."

Michelle nodded, holding him tightly. This was the better way. Four or five weeks wasn't so long, and for her and Cassandra, Paris was the safest city in the world.

The hotel was the kind of sprawling, granite pile that can always be found near the main railroad station of any European capital. The King's Arms, opposite Paddington Station, catered mainly to midlevel business travelers and salesmen. It boasted two hundred small rooms, a pub decorated in mock-Tudor, and a variety of shops. There had been a time when Harry Taylor wouldn't have given the King's Arms a second glance, much less stayed there. Now he had no choice.

"Thanks, buddy."

Harry pressed a pound note into the gnarled hand of a bellhop old enough to be his grandfather. In return he got a quart of gin, some ice—which cost more than the gin—and clean glasses.

"Will you be needin' anythin' else, sir?"

"Not now. Maybe some dinner later."

"We have a very nice roast beef with mash."

The thought of British roast beef, cooked until it was gray, nauseated Harry. "I'll let you know."

The drink was in Harry's hand and over his lips before he sat down in the one comfortable chair in front of the window. From there he could see the grimy, soot-laden glass canopy of Paddington Station. Only in the small hours of the morning did the dull roar of a thousand feet and voices subside. The rumble of the trains, however, never stopped. It continued into the night, the thunder crawling up the building through the stone and mortar, twisting up in the pipes until the wooden floorboards began to hum. At first, Harry swore he wouldn't be able to stand it. But as time went on he found that the rumble became just another accessory in this shabby room with its peeling yellow paint and threadbare rugs. Like so many things, it was just one more he had learned to live with.

After his humiliation at Steven's birthday party, Harry had tried to pretend that nothing had really changed. But while he maintained the facade, those around him didn't. Office juniors who once hung on his every word started to question his instructions. Sales managers bypassed his office, sending their reports directly to Rose. As the months wore on, Harry could not ignore the fact that he had become an anachronism. Soon his workdays were ending at four o'clock, when he headed for one of the hotel bars where he had a monthly tab.

It was after one such evening that Harry, deep into his cups, decided it was time to leave. The next morning, acting with the mulish determination of a drunk, he went down to the payroll office, filled out the necessary forms, and told the startled cashier to cut him a draft on the spot. The next stop was his broker, where he liquidated his portfolio at market price and received another check. Harry's final destination was the Chase Bank, where he left instructions to transfer the funds to Barclays in London.

The next day, Harry arranged for his Park Avenue apartment to be put on the market, then booked a suite on the U.S.S. *Constitution* departing for Southampton the following evening. Packing only what he would need for the crossing, Harry had his last meal in New York at the Oyster Bar and, with a champagne salute, left the New World for the Old.

Harry installed himself in the Ritz and the next morning went for a stroll that took him past the Cooks building. He stood on the corner, smiling at the giant sign that curved around its roof. Harry had a very large marker outstanding at Cooks, or, more precisely, with Sir Thomas Ballantine. If he used it carefully, he could parlay it into a second, even bigger career than the one he had built at Global. Harry did not rush matters. He went to Savile Row and had three suits made. Shirts and ties came from Turnbull & Asser while Llewelyn provided hand-tooled shoes. The agent came through with a beautiful flat in Mayfair. As a final touch, he had personal cards made up. Satisfied that he appeared the model of prosperity and good taste, Harry made an appointment to see Sir Thomas the following afternoon.

The room in which Sir Thomas met Harry was as dark as Harry remembered it. Ballantine, too, had not changed, except that more than ever he resembled an Egyptian mummy.

"What is it you want, Mr. Taylor?"

In his usual, easygoing manner, Harry lied through his teeth, saying he had gone as far as he could at Global and had decided to explore new horizons. Given the wealth of information he had been privy to at Lower Broadway, he was sure he could be a valuable asset to Cooks.

"Indeed?" Sir Thomas said, his voice like sandpaper over dry timber. "Allow me to inform you, Mr. Taylor, that I do not take kindly to traitors. You were useful to me once and you received fair value for your efforts. As far as I am concerned, we have nothing more to discuss. Not now, not ever. Good day."

Harry was about to protest when the door opened and two heavyset men entered.

"Show Mr. Taylor out."

From that moment on, Harry found himself on a long, slippery slope that became more treacherous as time went on. When he called on Lady Patricia Farmington, thinking that to be seen with her would send a signal to the rest of London society, he discovered that she had married and was expecting a child. Many of the people she had introduced him to had changed, and those who remembered Harry were no longer the trend-setters.

Nonetheless, Harry tried to ingratiate himself with those who could, with a few words, open the doors of finance and commerce to him. He threw lavish parties at the Cafe Royale, gambled heavily at Mayfair clubs, and courted the daughters of city men—girls young enough to be his own daughters. Although his charm coaxed a number of debutantes into his bed, Harry quickly discovered that they were only amusing themselves, comparing his prowess with that of other, younger lovers.

Harry's luck was no better when he began making serious calls on his old contacts in the financial district. They were polite enough but each made it clear that there was no place for him in their ranks.

"You shouldn't have pissed off Sir Thomas," one of them said. "I'm afraid the word is out, Harry. That old corpse has made it very clear he'll take a dim view of anyone willing to take you on."

As the months passed, Harry's desperation turned to panic. Instead of the gaming tables he now lost money in the stock market, speculating wildly in a vain hope of hitting the big score. As his capital melted away he was forced to give up the flat in Mayfair and moved back to the Ritz, staying until he failed to meet his monthly bill. From then on it was a steady progression of less and less fashionable hotels until one evening, without quite knowing how or why, he found himself at the King's Arms.

A slow paralysis gripped Harry when he realized that he had sunk almost as low as he could. Using gin to straighten out his logic, he traced back his tragic fall not to himself but to forces that had conspired against him. Through an alcoholic haze he understood quite clearly that Rose had acted as she had out of family loyalty. Steven was her only son. It was right that he be put ahead of everyone else. Harry could not fault her for that. But Michelle . . . That was where the trouble had started, with a little Frog who should have fallen on her face instead of becoming the toast of Europe. Everything Michelle had succeeded in doing, Harry coveted. Whenever he thought of her, his anger swirled inside him like a whirlpool, growing larger and larger as his frustration grew, because in that very anger Harry could not help but see his own impotence.

Harry finished off the bottle of gin the grandfatherly porter had brought him and, taking a few shillings, made his way to the pub downstairs. He would have some shepherd's pie and drink bitter ale until his money ran out. He hoped it would buy him enough to make him pass out.

Harry was carefully spearing the last of the peas when someone slipped into the booth opposite him.

"Hello, Harry. It's been a long time."

The man who had squandered fortune's smile looked up at what surely must have been a ghost: Steven Talbot.

Cassandra McQueen had despaired about leaving New York. Not only had the city seduced her with its magic, but she was hurt because she'd had to leave her father behind. Being with him had brought back wonderful childhood memories of the times the three of them had shared, traveling across Europe. To Cassandra, her father was a friend and confidant, someone who made her feel loved and secure, a man in whose company her mother softened.

The minute she was home in Paris, Cassandra had hung a calendar over her desk and crossed off the days to her father's arrival. As far as she was concerned, it couldn't come soon enough. She was also worried about her mother. Ever since they had returned, Michelle had been working day and night. There was a parade of visitors through the apartment, men and women with frightened eyes and furtive expressions who spoke German and Polish as well as a language Cassandra couldn't identify but learned was Yiddish. Sometimes these people stayed for a night or two, then departed as silently as they came. Whenever Cassandra asked who they were, her mother told her they were friends of friends from Germany.

Walking back from school, Cassandra decided to treat herself to an ice cream at the *glacerie*. As she watched Madame Delamain pile vanilla scoops onto a dish she chatted with her about the goings-on in Île St.-Louis. Madame Delamain, who also ran the bakery and whose husband was the local butcher, had known Cassandra since she was a baby. Cassandra enjoyed the gossip as much as she did.

"*Alors, ma petite*, just a few more days, *n'est-ce pas?*"

Cassandra licked her ice cream, grinned, and crossed her fingers.

"Don't worry." Madame Delamain tapped her forehead. She considered herself an infallible psychic and loved to recount her feats to anyone who'd listen. Cassandra had heard them all.

"*Merde!*" Madame Delamain spat out. "Who is that imbecile?"

A long, black Citroen had screeched to a stop outside the *glacerie*, its powerful engine idling noisily.

"Don't worry, madam," Cassandra said. "I'll see who it is."

Cassandra stepped onto the sidewalk and was momentarily blinded by the afternoon sunlight. She raised her hand to shade her eyes and at the same time heard the car door open.

"*Bonjour*, Mademoiselle McQueen," a guttural voice whispered.

A pair of hands clamped over Cassandra's arms, pulling her into the car.

"No!" she screamed, kicking out.

Her kidnapper cursed as Cassandra's foot connected with his knee. He grabbed her long blond hair and threw her to the floor of the car.

"*Vite, allez!*"

With a screech of rubber, the Citroen fishtailed from the curb, one door swinging wildly. Madame Delamain ran out in time to see a hand reach out and yank it shut before the car, and Cassandra, disappeared around the corner.

Across the city in the fashionable Opéra district, Steven Talbot was indulging in a typical, delightful Parisian lunch that had begun at noon and was just now finishing at four-thirty. There were six people at the table, two men who represented French banks and who raced horses, and three lovely ladies in their midtwenties. Two were mistresses; the third, hanging on Steven's every word, was determined to become this rich, handsome—and, equally important, young—American's companion.

Steven glanced at his watch and signaled for the bill. Over protests that were more polite than sincere, he paid the check and suggested to the blonde that they take a walk along rue du Faubourg-St.-Honoré. The delights to be had in the windows of Cartier, Hermès, and Chanel appealed to the girl. That Steven's hotel, the Meurice, was on the same street was a convenient coincidence.

Michelle was working in her library when she heard the hew-haw wail particular to French police cars. It distracted her because on the Île St.-Louis, unlike the rest of Paris, one seldom heard a siren. This district was considered one of the safest in Paris.

"There is a detective to see you, madam," her housekeeper, Ernestine, announced. "An Inspector Savin."

Michelle looked down at the papers on her desk and, as calmly as possible, said, "I'll be out in a moment."

As soon as she heard the door close, Michelle began to gather up the files she'd been working on. She deposited them behind the secret panels in the bookcase, checked her appearance in the mirror, and drew a deep breath. Had the French authorities finally uncovered her work with the refugees?

Inspector Armand Savin was tall and, despite his middle age, very muscular, with a full head of brushed-back gray hair and eyes that surveyed the world with suspicion rather than compassion. He was, Michelle knew immediately, a very hard man.

"Forgive me for intruding, Madame McQueen," Savin said without preamble, showing Michelle his credentials. "Would you please tell me the whereabouts of your daughter?"

Michelle was bewildered. "Cassandra? Why, she's right here. . . . Ernestine?"

"No, madam," the housekeeper replied. "She has not come home from school."

"But she should be here by now," Michelle began. "There's been an accident!"

"Madame, did you send anyone to pick up your daughter?" Savin asked quietly.

"No! Cassandra walks home every day. What's going on?"

"Please listen to me very carefully, madam. We have every reason to believe your daughter has been kidnapped—"

"No!"

"Madam, listen to me! This occurred less than twenty minutes ago, in front of a *glacerie* owned by a Madame Delamain. She witnessed everything and called us immediately. The kidnappers have a very slight time advantage. If you have any information that can help us, please tell me now. Every minute is precious!"

"I don't know!" Michelle cried. "Why would anyone take her?"

"That's what you must tell me, madam. Have you received any threatening calls or letters? Have you noticed strangers in the neighborhood? Has your daughter mentioned being accosted as she walked between here and the school?"

"No, no, no!" Michelle screamed.

Armand Savin lost the little hope he had allowed himself. If there had been threats of some kind against this woman or her daughter, he might have had a place to start. As it was, without a description of the kidnappers and only a few

375

details about a car whose make was commonplace in Paris, he had to start at the beginning. Savin's expression did not betray any frustration or doubts. He knew that the way he carried himself could make all the difference between despair and cooperation on the part of the mother.

"What was your daughter wearing, madam?"

Michelle stared at him as though he were demented. "My child is gone and you're interested in fashion?"

"Madam," Savin said firmly. "Right now my men are interviewing Madame Delamain. Others are at the school talking to your daughter's teachers. Still others are calling on her friends and classmates to see if anything out of the ordinary happened today. I have a rider waiting to take your daughter's description and photograph to Île de la Cité. The sooner these arrive the sooner we can get her picture across Paris." He paused. "The sooner someone may see her and call in."

Michelle looked up at him, her face haggard.

"Why?" she whispered. "Why?"

"I don't know, madam. Perhaps you do. But first we need to know what she was wearing. Please, help me . . ."

— 45 —

In Roman times, Paris was known as Lutetia, from which came its modern reference as "the city of light." But beneath Paris is another city, a network meandering 188 miles through limestone quarries once used to build the city, a refuge for scoundrels and saints, and the final resting place for the bones of six million souls: the catacombs.

It was there, during the Christian persecution, that Saint Denis, patron saint of France, said Mass to the faithful. During the Black Plague of 1348, when the city's dead outnumbered the living, the survivors fled to the catacombs to save themselves. In more recent times, smugglers used the subterranean warren to ferry goods of every description past custom inspectors who wouldn't dare to venture into the tunnels. Gaston Leroux celebrated the catacombs in *Phantom of the Opera* and Victor Hugo included them in *The Hunchback of Notre Dame*. But no matter how famous they became, only the hardiest Parisian would set foot in the catacombs. In a world of perpetual darkness it was all too easy to get lost. If that happened, one needed a miracle to find a way out, all the more so since the catacombs had their own inhabitants, thieves, murderers, addicts, the insane, all of whom jealously guarded their territory. To the *cataphiles*, any intruder was fair game.

Ninety feet below the heart of Paris, Harry Taylor sat with his knees hunched up against his chest, staring at the pools of light thrown off by four kerosene lamps. Shadows danced along the sand-colored gallery, a domed space forty feet long, twenty feet wide, and twelve feet high. Between them Harry could see the fossils of ancient sea creatures embedded in the walls, as well as the outlines of bones that had fallen away or been wrested from the stone. In one corner rose the fetid odor of an old mushroom bed where an enterprising *cataphile* had grown the famous *champignons de Paris*.

Harry Taylor was cold and miserable. Although he had a warm jacket, bedding and blankets, food and medicine, he could not escape the dampness that cut him to the bone. For the terror that could come at him at any moment, Harry also had a gun.

A few feet away, lying in a sleeping bag, was Cassandra McQueen. Harry checked his watch and opened the small medicine chest. Beside the usual first-aid materials was a set of syringes, each one with a predetermined dose of morphine. Eight hours ago, while the two Germans had held her down in the backseat of the car, Harry had given Cassandra her first injection. It was time now for the second.

Harry bent over the unconscious girl, who appeared to be sleeping peacefully. She was so innocent and vulnerable and, whenever Harry looked at her, he couldn't help but see Michelle. *Dammit!* he thought. What he had wanted from Michelle wasn't to have been extracted this way, by using a child! At that moment, Harry realized how truly little he knew of what he was doing and just how far out of his depth he had really fallen. He hesitated, wondering if another dose of the drug was necessary. But what if he nodded off and Cassandra woke up and fled before he could stop her? He would never find her again in this vast maze. Then everything would be lost.

Harry slid the needle's gleaming tip into Cassandra's limp arm and scrambled back into the comforting light. He would have given his eyeteeth for a drink, but that, of course, had been forbidden. Making sure that his gun hand was free, Harry wrapped a blanket around his shoulders. Forty-eight hours, that was all he had to endure. He kept repeating to himself that it was a cheap price for a second chance in life.

* * *

The plan Steven Talbot had outlined in the London pub was simple and efficient. Harry would take a businessman's holiday to Paris, mingling with the thousands of tourists who crossed the Channel daily. Once in the city, he would go to ground until Steven told him it was time. On a given day, Harry and two other men, whose identity Harry need not concern himself with, would pluck Cassandra off the street and take her to a prearranged hiding place in the catacombs.

"Everything you'll need will be waiting for you," Steven assured him. "Your only job will be to babysit her while I arrange for the ransom."

"Ransom? I thought you said—"

"This is a kidnapping, Harry," Steven said patiently. "The police will expect a ransom demand and they'll get one. The point is to isolate Michelle and tell her that unless she agrees to sell back her business to Global at a predetermined price, she'll never see Cassandra again. Once I have that piece of paper in my hand, you'll free the girl."

Harry's fingers trembled as he reached for his glass of gin, downing it in one swallow.

"No good," he rasped. "Can't work . . . Too dangerous."

"I don't think you understand," Steven replied coldly. "You don't have any choice."

"The hell I don't! I can walk out of here right now—"

"And straight into jail."

Harry stared wildly at the younger man.

"Did you really think I'd come to you without doing a little homework? It didn't take me very long to find you, Harry. Even less time to get the details on your cozy arrangement with Sir Thomas Ballantine. Now what do you think Rose would do to you if she found out that instead of helping her dear brother you were merrily sticking a knife in his back?"

Harry licked his cracked lips. "I don't know what you're talking about!"

"Don't take me for a fool, Harry!" Steven said softly. "If you think you have it bad now, I promise you, when Rose gets through with you this will have seemed like paradise."

Harry knew Steven Talbot was not bluffing. His eyes were cold, with pinpoints of cruel delight.

"If I help you, what's in it for me?"

"Michelle will sell to me, which means I, not my mother, will control the traveler's checks. Since I'm already heading up Global Europe, my time is limited. I'll need someone I can trust to handle the checks. You're going to be my man, Harry. You're going to get Europe, like you've always wanted."

Harry's mind was spinning. Steven reached out and patted him on the shoulder.

"Sleep on it, Harry. I'll meet you here tomorrow at the same time. And don't talk to anyone about this. I'll know if you do, and believe me, I *will* kill you."

Within hours of Cassandra McQueen's abduction the manhunt began in earnest. Radio bulletins interrupted regular programming to give details of the kidnapping and provide a description of the missing girl. In newspaper offices, editors changed the front pages, running both the story and Cassandra's picture. In precinct houses across the city, policemen lining up for the night shift were given hastily made-up posters to hand out along their beat. Teams of detectives swarmed through the city's brothels, gambling dens, night-clubs, and bars, leaning hard on informants. The edict had come from the Interior Minister himself: no effort was to be spared in finding Cassandra McQueen.

Michelle wandered through her apartment, unable to believe how her world had been turned upside down. Two armed men guarded the front door. Inside, a pair of detectives had strung wires to all the telephones in an attempt to triangulate the incoming calls from the kidnappers. Another detective was hunched over a tape-recorder and a fourth was methodically going through everything—from clothing to a diary—in Cassandra's room.

Michelle retreated to her bedroom and there, behind closed doors, stared out the windows onto the moonswept Seine, sending her prayers toward a cloud-veiled moon. Who could have done such a thing? Why? Michelle knew the answers to both questions, made all the more terrible because she couldn't share it with Inspector Savin.

Rose told Steven about my suspicions. He in turn alerted the Germans. . . . And that means they'll want something, something only I can give them, in exchange for Cassandra. They'll keep her safe, otherwise they have nothing to bargain with. . . .

Her reasoning both angered Michelle and gave her hope.

I'll give them anything they want, just as long as Cassandra is unharmed. But once she's away from here, safe . . .

There was a knock on the door and Savin entered, followed by a dignified, older gentleman who was Michelle's physician.

"I asked Dr. Latour to come with me in case there was anything you needed," Savin explained. "Perhaps something to help you sleep?"

Michelle embraced Latour. "Thank you, but I'm fine."

Savin regarded her critically. Given the turmoil of the last several hours, including the relentless questioning he had subjected her to, Michelle was remarkably composed.

"I really think you ought to try to get some rest," Latour was saying gently. "I brought along a mild sedative—"

379

"No!" Michelle said emphatically. "I don't want to be drugged when something happens. And it could, at any moment. Isn't that right, Inspector?"

Savin inclined his head. "On the other hand, you would be more alert if you had some sleep."

Michelle turned away but not before Savin noticed the fierce determination and expectation in her eyes.

She knows something that she's not telling. . . .

Armand Savin called downstairs and told his driver to get himself some coffee. He intended to keep a close eye on Michelle, which meant it was going to be a very long night.

She stirred only once, fingers clawing feebly at the blindfold around her head. There was the sensation of cold and dampness. As she rolled over she felt someone take her arm. Her head jerked back as something cold and sharp jabbed her. At that moment Cassandra felt she had died.

When Michelle awoke the next morning she wished she had taken Dr. Latour's advice. Every bone in her body ached as though she had been beaten. By Ernestine's sorrowful expression Michelle gathered that there wasn't any news. She gave the papers, with their screaming headlines, a cursory glance and pushed them away.

"This came for you early this morning, madam," Ernestine said gravely, handing her a French post office telegram envelope.

"Thank you."

She knew who had sent the message. It was from Monk, full of grief and anger and a promise that he would be on the next vessel for Paris. Yet all she heard was his quiet, insistent voice asking her to wait, not to leave New York without him. Would anything have been different? Would Monk's presence have prevented Cassandra's abduction? The uncertainty gnawed at Michelle.

Michelle was absently stirring her second cup of coffee when she heard a commotion in the living room. Inspector Savin entered, shaking his head in exasperation.

"Good morning, madam," he said. "Please forgive my intrusion but the Minister of the Interior is waiting outside."

"The minister?"

"He wishes to assure himself that everything humanly possible is being done."

Michelle did not miss the contempt in Savin's tone. The last thing the police needed were politicians grandstanding. Michelle felt for Savin.

"Show him in. I'll look after it."

Inspector Savin flashed her a grateful smile and opened the door for the portly, balding minister who scurried in, hands outstretched.

"Madam, I am desolated!" he cried.

But Michelle wasn't looking at him. Behind the minister stood Steven Talbot.

"Steven!"

"Hello, Michelle. I'm terribly sorry we have to meet under such circumstances."

Michelle's eyes blazed. "What are you doing here?"

"I arrived in Paris last week," Steven said calmly. "As soon as I heard what had happened I contacted Rose. She instructed me in no uncertain terms to do whatever I could to help. Monsieur le Ministre was concerned enough to come and see for himself how the investigation was coming along."

Michelle's mind was spinning as she listened to the minister's babble. As soon as she could she turned back to Steven.

"When did you come to Paris?"

"I told you, last week. I was having lunch with some friends when . . . when this happened. Believe me, Michelle, I'm as upset about this whole thing as you are."

Michelle choked back her fury. All her suspicions about Steven leaped back into her mind. Now here he was in the flesh, with a convenient alibi no less.

Michelle was aware that both the minister and Inspector Savin were surprised by her animosity toward Steven.

"Thank you for your concern, Steven," she said coolly. "And please thank Rose for hers. But as you can see the police are doing the best they can."

Michelle quickly translated her last sentence for the minister, who spread out his hands as if to say, "But of course. I would have expected nothing less."

"Please, Michelle," Steven said as he was leaving. "If there's anything I can do, anything at all, call me. I'm at the Meurice."

After he and the minister had gone, Inspector Savin held back, watching Michelle thoughtfully.

"Bad blood between the two of you," he said shortly.

"That was a long time ago, in New York. It has nothing to do with what's happened."

"You're certain, madam?"

"Yes."

The inspector shrugged. Both of them understood that he didn't believe her in the least.

At four o'clock that afternoon, exactly twenty-four hours after the abduction, two things happened simultaneously in different areas of Paris.

In the Faubourg St.-Honoré, a well-dressed man with a dark complexion entered the offices of Rothschild & Fils bankers. He handed the secretary a sealed envelope, saying that the matter was very urgent and confidential. After the secretary took the envelope into Emil Rothschild, she ran out to tell the man the banker wanted to speak to him. The messenger was gone.

The bell over the door of the *glacerie* tinkled just as Madame Delamain was about to close up shop.

"I'm sorry, monsieur, but—"

"This won't take long," the man with dark eyes told her. "I want you to listen well, because if you do not do as I say, *la petite fille* is dead. Do you know who I'm talking about?"

Madame Delamain's head bobbed in terror.

"You will close at your usual hour. After that you will prepare a small cake and take it to Madame McQueen. Underneath the cake you will place this."

He handed her a sealed envelope.

"But the police—" the baker protested.

"The police know you!" the man hissed. "You are the good samaritan, bringing comfort to a grieving mother. You will not have any problem. Be certain to tell madam how delicious the cake is. And to follow the instructions exactly. If she doesn't, if you make a mistake, *la petite* dies!"

"Hello, Emil."

"Michelle! It's . . . it's good to hear from you. Are you all right?"

"Yes. In fact I received some encouraging news."

"So did I."

"Perhaps we can discuss it tomorrow?"

"I think we should."

"Good night, Emil."

"Good night, *ma chère*. Courage . . ."

Michelle woke up at four o'clock the next morning. She donned loose, comfortable clothing she had laid out the night before and, using the back door of the bedroom suite, padded silently into the kitchen. She heard the detective snoring in the living room and Ernestine's telltale whistling coming from the room off the pantry. Gently she opened the door that led to the delivery entrance and made her way down the dark, narrow, circular staircase, shivering as the chilly air of the false dawn crept underneath her sweater.

This is insane!

But it was her only chance. The letter beneath the cardboard in the cake box contained instructions that were brief and explicit; their author left no doubt that if Michelle wanted Cassandra back alive, she would follow them precisely. The thought of sharing this information with Inspector Savin never crossed Michelle's mind. To involve the police would only endanger Cassandra.

Michelle slipped past the garbage bins, skirted the woodshed, and peered around the corner into the street. A police car was parked in front of her building, the driver bundled up against the door, fast asleep. Michelle made sure there was no one else around, then ran quickly down the street, staying well in the shadows.

The Paris subway was not running at this hour but Michelle knew of a place on the boulevard St.-Michel where the nightshift taxi drivers gathered for coffee and calvados before going home. She offered a triple fare to anyone willing to take her to place Denfert-Rochereau and was soon speeding north along the deserted boulevard. Arriving at the square, which was also a major subway intersection, Michelle headed downstairs into the pedestrian tunnel until she came to the accordion-style metal gate. It was padlocked.

"What do we do now?"

Michelle's heart leaped into her throat.

"I didn't mean to frighten you," Emil Rothschild said, embracing her.

"You just took ten years off my life," Michelle scolded him. "Did you bring the money?"

The banker, whose drawn face testified to a sleepless night, handed Michelle a thick package wrapped in white butcher's paper.

"One million francs." He handed it to Michelle. "What happens now?"

Michelle smiled faintly. "The kidnapper has a sense of history. I'm to go into the catacombs."

Rothschild blanched. "No, that's impossible! For God's sake, Michelle, it's a warren down there. You could get lost—"

"They gave me very good directions."

"But you'll be all alone!"

"That's the way it has to be, Emil. I have no choice."

"I can't let you go down there by yourself," the banker said stubbornly. "We must call the police."

"You know what will happen if we do that. The kidnappers chose the catacombs because they could watch me come to them. They'd know right away if someone was following."

"It's diabolical!"

Michelle stuffed the money into her bag.

"I have to go, Emil. You've done your part. I'll call you as soon as I can."

Michelle kissed him lightly on the cheek and, without turning back, headed in the opposite direction.

Just let Cassandra be safe, she prayed, her heart pounding.

The harsh jangle of the telephone shattered Armand Savin's light sleep. "*Oui?*"

"Inspector Savin? This is Steven Talbot."

Savin was alert instantly. "What is it, Monsieur Talbot?"

"I'm not sure, Inspector. I was leaving a friend's apartment when I saw Michelle—Madame McQueen, that is—going into the Denfert-Rochereau subway station. I thought—"

"Hold the line, please, Monsieur Talbot."

Savin bounded off the couch and dashed into Michelle's bedroom, cursing when he saw the empty bed. He raced back to the telephone.

"When did you see her, monsieur?"

"About five minutes ago. As a matter of fact I'm calling you from a phone kiosk in the station."

"The subway's closed," Savin said, more to himself than to Talbot. "Did you see where she was going?"

"Down one of the pedestrian tunnels, Inspector. Something's wrong, isn't it?"

You're right there, mon ami.

Yesterday, he had found Michelle's reaction to Steven Talbot's presence most revealing. So much so that he had quietly checked out the time and place of the dinner party the American said he had attended. The alibi jibed, but that didn't lessen Savin's uneasiness. There was something going on between Michelle McQueen and Steven Talbot, something that had a bearing on the kidnapping and that Savin intended to ferret out. He made a mental note to confirm exactly where Steven Talbot had spent the night. That he had chanced to see Michelle McQueen at Denfert-Rochereau was a fortuitous coincidence. Perhaps too much so.

"Do you want me to go after her, Inspector?" Steven Talbot was asking.

"No," Savin replied firmly. "Don't do anything until I get there. I'm leaving right away."

"But, Inspector—"

"Just do as I say!" Savin slammed down the receiver.

What the hell could she be doing at Denfert-Rochereau?

Although Savin racked his brain for that answer, the rest of what had happened was clear enough. Somehow a ransom demand had been smuggled to Michelle McQueen, along with instructions as to where to go and when. Savin thought back to all the people who had been in the apartment during the

384

last twenty-four hours. The only civilians were Ernestine, the housekeeper, Dr. Latour, and the woman who ran the bakery, Madame Delamain. Savin discounted the first two immediately. The housekeeper hadn't left the apartment, and Latour was a man who would never have jeopardized a patient's life, no matter what the circumstances. The courier had to have been Madame Delamain.

Jamming the telephone between his shoulder and ear, Savin struggled into his jacket. When he was put through to headquarters he ordered two cars to be dispatched to place Denfert-Rochereau.

"Tell the patrolmen to wait for me," he said, and added, "Make sure they are carrying weapons."

Denfert-Rochereau . . . But the subway is closed, so she can't be going into the station. Nor into the train tunnels. What else is there?

Savin's driver was jolted out of his dreams by the pounding on the glass.

"Denfert-Rochereau!" Savin roared at him. "What's there?"

The bleary-eyed detective thought his boss had taken leave of his senses. "The subway?"

"Imbecile!"

The detective yawned. "There's also the catacombs. My son keeps pestering me to take him—"

"That's it!"

Savin grabbed the radio-telephone and spoke with headquarters. Ten minutes and two cigarettes later he had the name of the geologist in the General Inspection of the Quarries, the city agency that had been supervising the catacombs since the eighteenth century.

"Find her address and send a car over immediately," Savin barked. "Yes, now! If anyone gives you any problems, refer them to Minister of the Interior. I want her at Denfert-Rochereau in thirty minutes."

He turned to his driver. "What are you waiting for?" he growled.

If the steel door hadn't been marked as the ransom note described, Michelle would have walked right past it. The door looked as though it were sealed, a plug in the concrete arch that led to God knew where. Michelle planted her feet and pushed. The door moved a few inches. Straining, she managed to create enough of an opening to slip through.

Michelle took two steps in complete darkness and cried out when her foot caught on something. She kneeled down, fingers touching rough canvas. Quickly she unbuckled the strap and reached inside the knapsack to find a large, powerful flashlight. Taped to the handle was a map.

Thank God!

The light helped keep her terror at bay. Michelle forced herself to shut out all the noises whispering to her from the darkness—the scurrying of rats, the slow dripping water from stalactites, the rustle of creatures she didn't want to see. She concentrated on the map. Just as the abductors had promised in their note, it was detailed so that she wouldn't lose her way in the maze. Michelle played the light around her and took her first tentative step.

The going was slow and treacherous. Before each turn Michelle studied the map carefully. Sometimes she walked on limestone that was as smooth as glass, only to come to an opening she had no choice but to crawl through. The deeper she went, the stronger her claustrophobia became.

Cassandra . . . Think only about Cassandra.

Michelle lost track of time. Her progress seemed agonizingly slow but she couldn't go any faster. Twice she almost took the wrong turn. From then on, she held the map to the light, eyes darting from the paper to the path beneath her feet.

Michelle came to the last turn and saw a light playing off the damp, chiseled rock. She plunged ahead, squeezing through a narrow opening, and stumbled into a gallery of sand-colored walls. There, surrounded by kerosene lamps, was a man in a dark hood.

"Who are you—"

Michelle uttered a sharp cry and scrambled forward. She didn't care that he was holding a gun or that he told her to stay back. Next to him she saw a figure bundled in a sleeping bag, her face turned toward her, blindfolded. It was Cassandra.

Steven had no problem finding the gallery. He had memorized the route. It was he who had instructed Harry Taylor exactly how to draw the map. Retracing the steps Michelle had taken only a few minutes earlier, he stooped and entered the gallery. Michelle was hunched over Cassandra, holding her daughter's head in her lap. Cassandra moaned and tossed feebly from side to side.

"I thought I told you to make sure she got the morphine on time," Steven said.

Michelle stared at him, amazed. "Steven!" Then the words he had spoken registered. "Morphine . . . What do you know about this? Who is he?"

Michelle pointed at the mysterious figure holding the gun.

"For Christ's sake, Harry, take off that ridiculous hood!" Steven told him.

"Harry?"

Michelle could not understand what was happening. It was as though the universe had been turned upside down.

"You took Cassandra?"

"That was really clever, Steven!" Harry shouted, flinging off his hood. "You promised me she would never know I had anything to do with this!"

Michelle gasped as Harry revealed himself. She looked from one man to the other, her fear hardening into white-hot anger.

"What in God's name are you doing?"

"Why don't you tell her, Harry?" Steven suggested, moving closer to the lantern light. "And make it quick. The police can't be too far behind."

"Why don't you just give us the agreements?" Harry snarled.

"Agreements? What are you talking about? All you wanted was the money!" She tossed Harry the package. "Go ahead, open it. It's all there!"

Furiously Harry tore away the wrapping. "What the hell is this? We don't want money! You were supposed to give up the traveler's-checks operation!"

"I don't know what you're talking about."

Michelle's heart had leaped at Steven's mention of the police. If in fact they were on their way she wanted to keep these two talking, taking advantage of the obvious confusion between them.

"Well, it looks like we have to change our plans," Steven said.

"What do you mean?"

"Harry, Harry," Steven chided. "Obviously she's double-crossed us. Now she's seen our faces. Even you should understand that we can't let her go."

"There was nothing in the note about any agreement!" Michelle cried. "All you wanted was the money!"

Cassandra lifted her head and groaned. "*Maman* . . ."

"It's all right, my darling. I'm right here. Everything will be fine. We'll be safe. . . ."

Harry was looking at Steven like a man possessed.

"But if we can't let them go, then . . ."

"That's right, Harry. You have to kill them."

Harry shook his head wildly. "I can't! That's not what we planned. No one was supposed to get hurt."

"In France, the penalty for kidnapping a minor is the guillotine, Harry," Steven told him softly. "If they don't die, you do."

As he stared into Steven's pitiless eyes, Harry realized that this was the way Steven had meant it to be from the very beginning. He had believed Steven's convincing details of the kidnapping because he had wanted to. He hadn't asked any questions or listened to his conscience because he had been too afraid.

"You knew it would come to this, didn't you?" Harry muttered, waving the gun. "You wanted her to see me so I'd have to kill her."

"Both of them, Harry," Steven corrected him. "They both have to die."

Little by little the brilliant aura Harry had seen over his future diminished. The promise of a second chance, a new life, was reduced to this damp dungeon, a harbinger of things to come. The idea that he would be thrown into a cell just like this, to endure days waiting for the blade to fall, terrified him. He would rather run to the ends of the earth.

Harry scrambled to his feet. "I'm getting out of here. You can do what you want!"

"Don't be a fool! You can't get out of here alive!"

"You told the police too, didn't you?" Harry said thickly. "They know where to find us. But they're supposed to arrive only after I kill Michelle . . . and Cassandra. Then you'd turn me in and become the hero who had tried to stop me. The police would believe you. Why shouldn't they? I'm a failure and a drunk. Exactly what you were counting on me to be all along . . ."

Steven lunged, his fingers seizing the wrist of Harry's gun hand. The two men crashed to the hard limestone floor, struggling for the weapon. Michelle seized her chance. Groaning, she lifted Cassandra to her feet, throwing one arm around her shoulder.

"Please, *chérie*, you have to walk. Walk, Cassandra!"

Michelle staggered across the slippery floor, her arm around Cassandra's waist, propping her up.

"Just a little farther, my darling, please—"

The explosion was so overpowering that at first Michelle thought one of the lamps had blown up. She was thrown forward, as though violently shoved by some giant hand, and collapsed, spread-eagle on the damp stone floor. There was a terrible burning in her spine.

"Cassandra . . ." she cried weakly, her fingers scrambling over the rocks to touch her daughter.

At the sound of the gun going off both Steven and Harry abruptly stopped struggling. It was Steven who recovered first. He managed to twist Harry's wrist so that the barrel of the gun was pressed hard against the center of his chest.

"Good-bye, Harry!" Steven grunted, staring into Harry's wild eyes as inexorably he tightened his forefinger around the trigger.

The second explosion sprayed Steven with blood. He rolled off Harry's body onto his back. As the echoes of the gunshot faded, he heard a girl's faint cry and, beyond that, men's voices somewhere deep in the catacombs. Scrambling to his feet, Steven made for Cassandra, ready to smash her skull against a limestone outcrop.

The shots tore through Cassandra's mind, shattering the drug-induced web that had paralyzed her. She screamed for her mother, clawing to reach her. Instead her hand touched something very hot and she recoiled.

"*Maman!*"

Cassandra was trying to rip the blindfold away when a terrible weight fell upon her. She felt hot breath on her cheek and her head being lifted up by the hair. Suddenly her face was slammed against the limestone and she almost lost consciousness.

Can't die . . . won't die.

Her fingers clutched for the burning heat she had felt only a moment before. Cassandra screamed as her palm curled around the base of the kerosene lamp. With a final desperate surge, she threw her body to one side, at the same time swinging the lantern high in the air, aiming blindly at the weight pinning her down.

Out of the corner of his eye Steven saw the lamp arching toward him. Cassandra's sudden move had caught him off guard. He threw up his hand but the glass shattered against the side of his face, the kerosene coating his skin and igniting as the flame began to feed.

Steven roared in pain and spun off Cassandra, rolling over and over, screaming and beating his face with his hands. When the police, led by Inspector Savin, poured into the chamber, they were horrified to see a man on his knees, his head craned back as though in prayer, his face all but invisible behind a sheet of flame.

PART
——————
FIVE

− 46 −

Her first sensation was of smell—ointment, disinfectant, and rubbing alcohol. Then touch. Whatever she was wearing was stiff, the fabric irritating the delicate skin of her breasts. The sheet covering her was laden with starch, chafing her bare forearms. Cassandra opened her eyes, squinting against the bright sunlight. She focused on the white enamel of the bedframe, then on the simple wooden crucifix hanging on the opposite wall.

"Cassandra . . . pumpkin."

Cassandra wept softly. Her tears seemed like a miracle because she believed she had gone blind. The miracle continued to unfold when she turned her head and saw her father sitting by her bed.

"You're going to be fine, pumpkin. Just fine."

"Mother . . ."

Her voice was scratchy but she desperately wanted to say the words. Cassandra struggled to sit up and Monk gently slipped an arm around her back. He held a paper cup of water to her lips and she drank gratefully.

"Where am I?"

"In a hospital. You're safe and well. Sleeping like Rip van Winkle."

Cassandra managed a tiny smile before the word *sleeping* opened the door of horrors. She remembered only fragments—the cold and damp floor, the shadows dancing on walls, indistinguishable voices echoing in her mind, the way the light caught the tip of the needle, making the drop on the end glisten.

"It's over," Monk said. "You're safe."

Cassandra looked around the spartan room. "Where's *Maman*?"

Monk's smile faded.

"*Where is she?*"

"The doctors are with her now. She's going to be all right."

But Cassandra saw the light die behind Monk's eyes and knew the real answer.

When the nurse looked in, she saw the large, gentle man hugging the frail blond girl, their arms thrown around each other as though they were the last two people on earth. The nurse remembered her orders but she stopped by to visit three other patients before she finally called the detective waiting in the conservatory.

In another wing of the hospital, Steven Talbot was lying motionless in an identical bed. His hands and face were swathed in gauze, and although he was conscious, he kept his eyes closed. It took every bit of will to fight the pain that clawed through his skin, eating him up like a deadly acid. But beyond the pain was the fear over what had happened in the catacombs. Or what people thought had happened.

"I've never seen anything like it," Steven heard a voice say. "Not even during the war."

"I'm surprised he's still alive," a second opined.

"A fool, going after the kidnappers by himself. A hero, but a fool nonetheless."

"Savin wants to talk to him as soon as he's conscious."

Steven heard the other man snort.

"To hell with Savin! This one has bigger problems than giving a statement to the police."

"Savin will want to know if he can talk."

"Talk? Most certainly. What terrifies me is what will happen when he looks at himself. He has no face left. . . ."

The soft voices died and Steven heard the faint click of the door latch. He lay immobile, feeling only the bitter cold of the jelly on his face and hands.

He has no face left. . . .

It was then that he began screaming.

When Monk saw the blood on the surgeon's gown his hopes plummeted. The physician took him by the arm and guided him into an empty office. Before saying anything, he lighted a cigarette and drew deeply on the tobacco.

"The bullet was the worst kind. It explodes and scatters on impact. It cracked her spine, punctured one lung, and nicked the heart. Only her own will is keeping your wife alive."

Monk bowed his head. "What are her chances?"

"I wish I could tell you, monsieur."

"Can I see her?"

"Of course."

She seemed very small in the bed, her arms, freckles against pale skin, laid out over the white linen. Tentatively, Monk reached out and ran his fingers over her face. Only when he felt her breath did he really believe she was alive.

Oh, Michelle, come back to me!

Monk lost track of the hours. The next time he looked up, it was night. The hospital corridors were silent as he padded down the hall to Cassandra's room. He spoke to the nurse, satisfied himself that Cassandra was all right, and sat with her for a while. Then he left and went into the chapel. Monk was not a religious man but he remembered a schoolboy's prayer. As he recited it, he wept because that was all he had to offer. Later, he walked outside and bought flowers from a gypsy and took them back to Michelle's room. He held her hand and willed himself to believe that even if she couldn't see or hear him, she might smell the flowers and know he was there.

The night drew on. Monk watched the moon ride high over the clouds, spilling its light across Michelle's face. She didn't turn away and reach for him. The moon didn't bother her.

She's gone.

Monk tightened his grip on his wife's hand. No, she was still warm to the touch. He was about to remove his hand when he felt a tug. Michelle's eyes fluttered open.

"Cassandra . . . ?"

Monk brought his face very close to hers. "She's fine. You're both going to be fine."

Michelle reached up and brushed away his tears.

"Mustn't cry," she whispered. "Cassandra needs you to be strong." A grimace of pain crossed her face. "I need you to be strong. . . ."

"I'm here for you, Michelle."

She was silent for such a long time that Monk thought she had lapsed into unconsciousness. Then she spoke again.

"I'm cold, my darling. Please, hold me."

Monk knelt by the bed and, as gently as he could, put his arm around his wife and laid his head against hers.

"I love you, Monk. I always will. Please, be strong."

"I will, my love. I swear to you. . . ."

A long, slow shudder worked its way through Michelle's body. At the last instant, her eyes opened wide and she raised her head. Then slowly she fell back and her lips creased into a smile for him and she was gone.

"I'm terribly sorry to have to do this, mademoiselle," Inspector Savin said. "But anything you can tell us would greatly assist our investigation."

Cassandra's eyes were dry but the salt from her tears continued to burn. *Maman* was dead. She knew that now. Monk had told her. Shot. Trying to carry her out of the cavern. She had died in the same morning light Cassandra had awakened to.

I have to help her now. Just as she helped me. She can't speak now. I have to do it for her.

"Did you see the faces of the men who kidnapped you?" the detective was asking.

Cassandra remembered being thrust into the car, someone hitting her, and that she'd fought back.

"He was wearing a black hood. . . ."

The pain of the needle, followed by oblivion and nightmare.

"I was unconscious. . . ."

"We know that," Savin said gently. "But just before we found you—can you remember anything then?"

"I couldn't see. I heard *Maman*."

"Did she say a name?"

"Harry . . . She said, 'Harry.' "

Cassandra saw Savin glance at Monk and the men's expressions go cold.

"Did she say anything else, Cass?" Monk asked urgently.

"I can't remember," Cassandra whispered. "There was a terrible noise. Someone was hurting me. I grabbed something very hot . . . hit him."

"All right," the detective said quickly. "That's all we need to know. Please, rest now. We can talk later."

"I don't want to rest!" Cassandra cried. "I'm afraid to close my eyes. Monk, please!"

"All right, pumpkin," he soothed her. "You don't have to sleep. I promise you, the nurse won't give you any medication unless you want it. I have to get a few things—" He felt her grip tighten. "But I'll be back. I'll never leave you, Cass. I promise."

Outside the room, Monk McQueen jammed a cigar between his teeth. He waited until he and Savin were on the balcony off the doctors' lounge before he lit it. The detective was watching Monk carefully. Only a few hours ago this man had watched his wife die. Now he was reliving the agony his child had

396

had to endure. Monk McQueen was running on pure adrenaline and rage. Savin wondered how much longer he could go on.

"She doesn't know any more," Monk said flatly. "They fed her enough morphine to almost kill her—"

"They?" Savin inquired.

"Whoever was working with Harry Taylor."

"Tell me about him."

Monk obliged, and when he was through he saw that the Frenchman was convinced Harry Taylor was their man.

"Everything you tell me points to motive." Savin handed Monk a sheet of paper. "A list of what we found in the catacombs. Notice the cross-Channel ferry ticket. Harry Taylor had to show his passport to buy it. His name is on it."

"Which means he's either a fool or he never expected to get caught."

"Was he capable of conceiving and executing such an intricate plan?"

Monk shook his head. "Not anymore. He was a drunkard. I don't know what he was doing in London, but I can tell you he had ruined himself in New York."

"We'll know about London soon enough. Scotland Yard is giving us full cooperation." Savin paused. "But if, as you say, Taylor could not have carried this out by himself, who helped him?"

"Why don't you ask Steven Talbot!"

Savin recoiled at the American's anger.

"There may be a problem with that, *mon ami*." Savin took the cigar from Monk's fingers and carefully extinguished it. "Come."

The men walked swiftly to the eastern wing of the hospital. Monk felt jolted by the sour odor as the doors to the burn ward swung open. The smell reminded him of something long ago, a battlefield on which men had fallen and burned. An abattoir.

Just as they were to enter Steven's private room, Savin touched Monk's arm. "Don't say anything yet. We must first assess the situation."

As soon as Monk went inside he understood Savin's predicament. Standing beside Steven's bed was Rose Jefferson.

This was a Rose whom Monk McQueen had never seen before, lost, bewildered, and very much afraid. In her eyes was a pain too terrible to behold. The accusations Monk had been ready to use to bludgeon the truth out of Steven Talbot died on his lips.

"Oh, Monk, I'm so sorry. . . ."

He embraced her and felt her thin hard fingers on his face. Rose Jefferson looked emaciated, her eyes impossibly large with grief and terror. Over her shoulder Monk saw the Minister of the Interior and another man who, given

397

the deference Savin showed, must have been a senior official in the French police.

"He tried to save her," Rose was saying. "Steven risked his life to save them both. . . . He was a hero, Monk."

Bile rose in Monk's throat but he steeled himself, remembering Savin's advice. The detective was speaking in low tones to the two officials. Monk could guess what was being said.

"How is Steven?"

"Alive."

Monk stared at the bandaged figure, then had to look away, afraid that Rose would see his rage.

"Madam," the minister said gravely. "Inspector Savin has a request. If the surgeons agree, he wishes to speak with your son."

"I don't agree!" Rose replied instantly. "My God, can't you see the condition he's in? He's barely said a word to me—"

"Want . . . want to talk."

The voice could have belonged to a prisoner on the rack. It was nothing more than a tortured whisper, and Rose immediately bent over her son.

"Michelle . . . ? All right?"

Savin ignored Rose's scathing look and leaned as close as he dared to the ruined man.

"Monsieur Talbot, I am Inspector Savin. Can you hear me?"

"Yes."

"Tell us what happened."

Of course I'll tell you. Now, while there is no way you can't believe me.

"Should have listened to the inspector . . . waited instead of following Michelle . . . couldn't take the chance . . ."

Word by agonizing word, Steven told his spellbound audience how he had chased Michelle, following her into the depths of the catacombs. How he had come upon Harry Taylor holding the gun and had seen Cassandra lying there unconscious.

"Tried to stop him . . . The gun went off. Michelle screamed. Couldn't help her . . . Couldn't let go of the gun. Killed Harry . . ."

Before Savin could stop her, Rose interrupted.

"You didn't kill Harry, darling. He escaped."

Steven couldn't believe it. He could still feel the barrel of the gun against Harry's chest, the pressure on the trigger, the roar as the bullet tore into his body. Harry alive! Alive to tell a different story . . .

Steven forced the fear from his mind. He had to say it all, right now. No one would question the testimony of a victim. It would all be put to rest. His mother would see to that.

"Tried to reach Cassandra . . . help her. Must have thought I was Harry. Then the heat, the pain . . . Nothing but pain and fire eating me—"

"That's enough!" one of the doctors cut in sharply. "Everyone will please leave the room. Nurse, a sedative!"

It took both physicians to pry a weeping Rose from her son's body. Monk McQueen looked at Savin. What they had just witnessed was as effective as a deathbed confession.

"What happens now?" Monk demanded once they were in the corridor.

"What do you think? The matter is very clear. We will scour Paris, including the catacombs, for Harry Taylor. If we find him he will be charged with kidnapping and murder."

"Don't tell me you believe what you heard in there!"

Savin turned Monk away from the startled glances of nurses passing by.

"Not a word," he said in a low voice. "Monsieur Talbot is lying. Only an idiot, or someone who knew that part of the catacombs intimately, would have dared follow Michelle McQueen. Otherwise he would have gotten lost immediately. And I do not believe Monsieur Talbot is an idiot.

"Second, why did he charge a man holding a gun on him when he knew the police were on the way? In such close quarters, even if Harry Taylor were a poor marksman, he couldn't have failed to hit him."

"They were in it together!" Monk whispered. "Steven knew Harry would be there. That he had Cassandra—"

"You are reaching, *mon ami*. We have no proof of that."

"You will when you find Taylor!"

"If we find him," Savin corrected Monk. "I don't have to tell you how treacherous the catacombs are. We know that Taylor was shot, whether by design or in a struggle. Perhaps by some miracle he survived, only to die later from his wounds. Or else he was found by the *cataphiles*, in which case no one will ever see him again. No, Mr. McQueen, do not hold out hope of finding Harry Taylor alive—or at all."

"So you're going to take Steven's word?"

Savin spread out his hands. "Cassandra McQueen cannot give us a name other than Harry's. She neither saw nor heard anything to incriminate Steven Talbot. As for the struggle, she might well have tried to fight off someone who was trying to help her. I do not believe that, but again, there is no one to challenge Monsieur Talbot's version of events."

Savin paused. "Believe me, Monsieur McQueen, I understand how you feel. But you saw the power gathered in that room. It has already exonerated Steven Talbot. There is nothing I can do. Even if I had Harry Taylor, how much weight do you think his word would carry?"

The Frenchman's words sickened Monk, yet he couldn't find a way to rebut them. The promise he had made to Michelle now returned to mock him.

"I won't let him go," Monk said softly. "He took my love, my life. He tortured my daughter. Steven Talbot will pay for that."

Four days later Monk brought Cassandra home. As soon as they stepped into the apartment both realized that they could never live there again. Because Michelle had never left. Her laughter echoed from the corners of every room and her smile danced on the dust motes that swirled in the sunlight cascading through the windows. They heard her voice when the bells of Notre Dame pealed and in the shouts of children as they raced on their bicycles along the narrowed, cobbled streets of the Île St.-Louis.

That night Cassandra awoke screaming from nightmares. The next morning Monk moved them both into the Ritz. Alone, he returned to the apartment and, with Ernestine's help, packed.

"Where will you go, monsieur?" Ernestine asked timidly.

"As far away from here as possible. Home . . . to America."

When the paintings and objets d'art Michelle had collected were crated, the furniture covered with dustcloths, and her clothing packed to be given to charity, Monk began the hardest task of all. Hour after hour he sifted through Michelle's financial files. Those that concerned the traveler's checks he put aside. Emil Rothschild and Pierre Lazard would help him sort out the details. It was the material from Warburg in Berlin—the letters, affidavits, and notes that related to Steven's dealings with the Nazis—that preoccupied Monk. He was staggered by the amount of information Michelle had unearthed, and every piece he found tore away a little more of his heart. This was what Michelle really had died for. Cassandra had been merely a pawn.

"I'll finish it for you," Monk said aloud. "I'll find out what you didn't and I'll finish it. My love, I promise you that. . . ."

Monk shuddered. He rose and with both arms leaned against the window and yelled out the question every bereaved person demands an answer for: "Why?"

A week after her death, Michelle McQueen was laid to rest in Paris's oldest cemetery, Père-Lachaise. Everyone from the cabinet ministers who had done business with Michelle to shopkeepers who had served her came. Her employees numbered in the hundreds and wept the same tears as the bankers who had helped found a financial empire. The mayor of Saint Eustace was given the honor of handing Michelle's medals to Cassandra, who saw everything as a dream in which she was both observer and participant.

The reality of her mother's death eluded Cassandra, like a familiar name on the tip of one's tongue. Everywhere she looked she saw her, yet when she called to her or tried to touch her, her mother wasn't there. To make sense of this, Cassandra slowly began asking questions. She demanded that Monk tell her everything he knew about Harry Taylor. Cassandra listened intently, trying to understand what had possessed this man to hurt the people she loved.

"He wanted money," Monk had said. "That's all, just money."

For the first time Cassandra detected a false note in his voice.

"Tell me about Steven."

Cassandra listened to Monk's explanation of how Steven had come to be in the catacombs. This time the false note was stronger. Her father was repeating exactly what she had heard him say to Inspector Savin. He hadn't believed his own words then, either. Did that mean Steven Talbot wasn't the hero everyone made him out to be? Could he have had something to do with her mother's death?

Intuitively, Cassandra knew that her father wouldn't tell her anything more. Nor could she demand he do so. Her heart went out to him for what he had endured. She had to give him time to grieve, to mend, to become whole again.

But one day I will know the truth.

Immediately after the funeral Monk returned to the Ritz with Cassandra. With Ernestine there to look after the girl, he met Abraham Warburg in the manager's office, just as they had agreed.

"She was a very brave woman," the German banker said with quiet dignity. "She helped thousands. We will never forget."

Monk did not miss the concern behind Warburg's sorrow.

"If you're worried about the papers Michelle kept at home, don't be. I moved them all into the hotel vault. Tomorrow I want us to go through them. There's a lot I don't understand."

"Of course," Warburg murmured. "We must tie up loose ends, so to speak."

"We're not ending a damn thing! The work Michelle was doing will be carried on."

Warburg blinked. "By whom? With all due respect, Herr McQueen, you can't take her place."

"I don't intend to. But surely there are people who know what has to be done."

"That's so," the banker replied slowly. "But the details are very complicated. A great deal of money passed through many hands. Michelle created a maze that would confound even the Gestapo's accountants."

"Then we don't have to tamper with it, do we? I promise you, the money for your work—her work—will be there."

Monk paused. "Can you give me your word that the right people will handle it, as she would have?"

"You have my word," Abraham Warburg said. "My life, if you need it . . ."

Monk's second meeting took place in the somber offices of Rothschild & Fils near the Opéra.

"Everything is in order," Pierre Lazard said. "The question is, what happens now?"

"Michelle kept a copy of her will with you as well as with her lawyer," Monk said. "I think we can read the one you have without prejudicing justice."

The bankers agreed. When Michelle's will was produced, no one was surprised that all her assets, personal and professional, went to Cassandra. The stipulation was that the traveler's-check operation would be administered by Monk or by people he chose. Some of the profits were to be used for Cassandra's support, the rest placed in a trust account that, along with control of the company, would be turned over to Cassandra when she turned twenty-one.

"Which won't be for another six years," Emil Rothschild observed.

"Can we talk about this after I've had a chance to settle Cassandra?"

"Of course," Rothschild assured him. "If I may ask, do you have any plans?"

"I wish I did."

Exhausted by the demands upon him, Monk retreated to the Ritz bar. He fortified himself with two pony glasses of Normandy calvados and called Ernestine to make sure Cassandra was all right. The housekeeper told him that Cassandra had nibbled at a salad and then fallen asleep. Thankful for small mercies, Monk presented himself at Rose McQueen's suite a few minutes later.

She was still in the black suit she had worn to Michelle's funeral. When she lifted her head for his kiss, Monk saw the thin blue veins along her neck.

"How are you, Monk?"

"As well as can be expected."

"Cassandra?"

"She'll be all right."

Without asking, Rose handed him a brandy.

"What will you do now?"

"Take her back to New York. There's nothing left for her here."

"I hate this country!" Rose said suddenly. "It took Franklin from me. Now it almost killed Steven. . . ."

Monk couldn't bring himself to say a word.

"You don't believe me when I say how sorry I am about Michelle, do you?" Rose said. "I am, you know. We had a chance, she and I, to right the past. Or at least a little of it. I wanted to do that, Monk. It was important to me. Now it's gone. Missed opportunities . . . they eat at you long after so many other things fade away. I guess that's how you know they were important to begin with."

Monk forced himself to ask the question. "How is Steven?"

Rose's voice was stiff. He could almost see her straighten her back, brace her shoulders.

"The doctors here will do what they can. They had a lot of experience with burn patients during the war. After that he'll go to Switzerland. The reconstructive surgery will take years . . . but he'll never be the same, never."

"Have the police found any leads on Harry?"

Rose looked at him with dead, empty eyes. "Not yet. But they will. I knew him well, Monk. Harry Taylor's a survivor. He's out there somewhere. One day, someone will see him."

Rose did not mention that she had secretly placed a hundred-thousand-dollar price on Harry's head. By now the word had trickled through the European underworld. There was a fortune waiting for the man who brought in this American fugitive alive.

"I know you didn't come to comfort me, Monk," Rose said. "There are things we have to talk about. I imagine you've been to Michelle's lawyer. I can guess the terms of the will."

Monk explained what they were. "So," he concluded, "I control the traveler's checks. But frankly, I don't know if I can cope with the demands of the job. Cassandra will need me. . . ."

"Monk, I would like very much to help you—and Cassandra—if I can . . . if you let me," Rose said.

"What are you suggesting?"

"Let me administer the traveler's checks. I don't want what Michelle built and what rightfully belongs to Cassandra. But I can make sure that Michelle's legacy is properly looked after."

Rose gave him a fleeting smile. "I know you have no reason to trust me. But things have changed, Monk. I've changed. You draw up the terms and conditions, make them as ironclad as you want. Offer me what you think is an acceptable management fee along with whatever dismissal clauses you feel are needed. I'll sign it all." Rose paused. "I just want to help."

Monk accepted another brandy. He had neither the skills nor the time to deal with the financial empire Michelle had created. His focus had to remain on Germany, on Warburg, on keeping the pipeline open and running for all those trying to flee Germany. It was there, among the thousands of refugees, that he would find one, perhaps two, who could bring him the information that would destroy Steven Talbot's unspeakable alliance.

As for letting Rose run the traveler's checks, was there any real choice? She was the creator of the money order. She knew her way around European financial houses blindfolded. But most important, Rose felt she owed Michelle something—perhaps an apology. For that reason alone, to assuage her conscience, Rose Jefferson would be bound by her word.

"We can try it," Monk said. "I don't know how much time we have left in Europe before Hitler gets the war he's looking for, but I can't let everything Michelle's done fall apart."

"I won't leave Europe until I know exactly what's going to happen to Steven," Rose said. "Keeping busy will help me, too."

Rose held out her hand, and tentatively Monk took it.

"We've both lost," Rose murmured. "Please, let's not hurt each other anymore."

— 47 —

Monk McQueen was trying to do the impossible. On one hand, neither he nor Cassandra could leave Paris until he was satisfied that Michelle's traveler's-check operation was in capable hands and running as smoothly as before. This meant long meetings with Rose Jefferson, the bankers Rothschild and Lazard, and a battery of French lawyers. At times it seemed to Monk there weren't enough hours in a day to get everything done. The worst of it was that he had to be away from Cassandra so much of the time.

Although Ernestine had moved in with them at the Ritz and was doing her best to look after Cassandra, Monk was alarmed at how pale his daughter appeared and how much weight she had lost. Cassandra almost never ventured from the hotel, and when they did go out for a bite to eat, she pecked silently at her food. Nothing Monk said or did seemed to touch her at all. It was as though she had retreated into a private world, as far away from the pain and horror as possible.

Late one evening, when Monk was wondering how he could help Cassandra, she curled up beside him.

"Send me home, please."

"Pumpkin, I can't," Monk told her. "I need at least another two weeks here. Besides, there isn't another ship until then."

"There's another way."

Cassandra showed him a newspaper clipping. Monk pushed his half-glasses up his nose.

"You can't be serious."

"I am," she replied stoutly.

"But even if I could get you a ticket, you'd be traveling alone."

"I've traveled by myself before. Besides, Abilene can meet me."

Monk shook his head. "I don't know. It sounds like a very long and rough trip."

"You mean you think it's dangerous."

"That too," Monk admitted.

"No," Cassandra said firmly. "It would be fun. Please, can't you see what's happening to me here? You're gone all the time. Ernestine tries her best to keep me busy but every time I go outside, I remember *Maman*. These were our streets, our shops. . . . It was our city. But not anymore. It will never be that again."

Monk caught the plea in Cassandra's words and thought back to how happy she had been in New York. Who was to say that he, not she, knew what was best?

The next morning Monk called Rose and explained what he needed.

"Consider it done," she replied. "As a matter of fact, there will be two people arriving at the same time whom I want you to meet."

Three days later, Monk and Cassandra boarded the express for the coastal city of Marseilles. They took a taxi to the docks and there witnessed a sight that had drawn thousands of onlookers. Bobbing lightly at the dock was a sleek, silver and blue amphibious plane with the Pan-American logo on its fuselage and tail. Stenciled below the pilot's window in gold lettering was its name: *Yankee Clipper*.

"It's magnificent," Cassandra said excitedly.

"The travel of the future," Rose predicted. "The ride between Marseilles and Port Washington, New York, will take almost twenty-seven hours, but you'll be traveling in the lap of luxury. There's a separate passenger cabin, a dining room, and even a salon for the ladies."

Cassandra's eyes shone with excitement. "What route does it fly?"

"From here to Lisbon, then to the Azores, and a long transatlantic leg home."

"I thought this service wasn't supposed to begin for another eighteen months," Monk said.

"It won't," Rose replied. "This is a promotional flight."

Monk took Rose aside. "Are you sure it's safe? Will she be all right?"

"Monk, the clipper has been flying across the Pacific for years. There's a crew of twelve for just twenty-two passengers. Believe me, Cassandra will be fine."

Seeing the expression on his daughter's face, Monk put his doubts behind him.

"You'll cable me from every stop?"

"Of course!"

405

"And as soon as you arrive in New York?"

Cassandra laid a hand on his cheek. His skin burned beneath her touch because it was exactly the gesture Michelle had used so often.

"Come home soon," she whispered. "That's all I want, for you to be home."

"I promise, pumpkin."

"I love you."

"I love you too, Cass."

The worries that had burdened Monk lifted as the *Yankee Clipper* growled across the bay and hurtled into the sky. On the train ride back to Paris, Rose introduced him to her two friends and closest associates, Hugh O'Neill and Eric Gollant.

"What I propose is that they run the Global Traveler's Checks in Europe," Rose said. "Hugh and Eric know the money-order business backwards. Eric can stay in Paris to look after the financial side while Hugh can troubleshoot problems that come up anywhere in Europe. He still carries an Irish passport. Given Ireland's traditional neutrality, he won't have any difficulties at the borders."

Monk was agreeable. Both men had excellent reputations. But more, he could see Rose was showing him that she intended to keep her word: she was going to be nothing more than an arm's-length administrator.

Back in Paris, it took the three men less than a week to hammer out a satisfactory agreement. Monk then brought together all the European managers and explained the changes that were taking place. Satisfied that everything was in order, he left for Berlin.

"The one thing neither O'Neill nor Gollant knows is the real purpose of the tours," Monk told Abraham Warburg when they met at the banker's gothic-style mansion in the Wansee. "You'll have to find trustworthy people in Paris who can take Michelle's place in France."

"Emil Rothschild and Pierre Lazard have already done that," Warburg replied. "They'll continue placing the refugees once they arrive. In the meantime, I have people in Germany I can trust."

"What about the evidence against Talbot? Time's running out, Abraham. The Nazis have consolidated their hold. If we can't expose Steven soon, it will be too late to stop him and Hitler."

The courtly German placed his walking stick squarely between his knees and, covering its silver knob with both palms, leaned forward.

"It may already be too late, Herr McQueen. The Nazis have a stranglehold on government and industry bureaucracies. Our sources of information dwindle with every passing week. Add to that the fear our few informants work under, and you have an impossible situation."

"Then we have to make it possible," Monk said stubbornly. "Steven and those bastards killed Michelle and I'll see them hang for it!"

Warburg laid a hand on the American's shoulder.

"No one shares your pain more than I. But you must understand the circumstances. . . ."

Monk did understand, better than he had ever wanted to. But knowing how difficult, if not impossible, it was to get information out of Germany did nothing to ease his frustration or quench his desire for revenge.

Patience, that was his only weapon. He had to wait either until Steven made a mistake or he, Monk, got very, very lucky. That was the moment he had to watch for, recognize, and seize. . . .

Monk arrived back in Paris a day before the *Constitution* was to sail from Le Havre. For the first time since Michelle's murder he had the city to himself to make his peace.

Monk walked the streets of Île St.-Louis where he and Michelle had strolled, stopped at the antique stores and art galleries she had loved to browse through. He made his way through the secondhand book stalls that lined the riverbank, where British and American tourists surreptitiously paged through "naughty" French novels. He wended his way across the flea market, with its hawkers and peddlers and pickpockets, and entered the centuries-old silence of the Marais, where, for him, Michelle had breathed life into the history of the French Revolution. At dawn he found himself in Les Halles and watched the endless caravansary of trucks descend on the open-air market, bringing fruit, vegetables, meat, and fish from the most exotic corners of the earth.

As the pace of the city quickened beneath the morning sun, Monk crossed the river Seine and went into the cafe where, a lifetime ago, he had met Michelle on his first trip to Paris. The place was exactly as he remembered it, with its long zinc bar, impossibly small tables, and cane chairs.

"*Bonjour, monsieur.*"

Monk looked up to see the same elderly waiter who had served him and Michelle so long ago.

"*Café au lait, s'il vous plaît.*"

"Just one, monsieur? Won't madam be joining you?"

And then, for the first time since he had lost her, Monk McQueen's great head fell forward under the weight of his tears.

* * *

407

Switzerland's Jura mountain range rises seventeen thousand feet to create a natural defense against Germany. In the spring, after the winter runoff, valleys bloom and the scent of wild flowers is drawn by zephyrs that glide against the alpine slopes.

Snuggled at the foot of the range, on a plateau that stretches all the way to the nearest village, Jarlsburg, is the Hoffmann Clinic, one of the world's finest centers for reconstructive surgery. A three-level T-shaped building houses the medical facilities, and around it are private chalets, each with its own balcony and special amenities, for the patients. The clinic accepts only twenty cases, each one screened by its medical panel. The criteria for acceptance include not only whether the patient can pay the clinic's astronomical fees but whether the surgery will ultimately help. In the case of Steven Talbot, whose petition had received top priority, the surgeons agreed that, given enough time, they could graft onto his ruined flesh something that every human being took for granted: a face.

Steven Talbot was sitting on the porch, his face screened from the sun by a white cotton veil. From below came the lowing of cows and the jangle of their bells as they plodded along. He also heard a car making its way along the winding road toward the clinic. For the first time in months, his heart beat a little faster. Cars were permitted on the property only with special authority. The Mercedes growling toward the Hoffmann Clinic flew the diplomatic pennants of Nazi Germany.

The man who emerged from the backseat wore a long black leather trench-coat. When he saw the figure on the porch he waved and shouted a greeting. Because his mouth was closed by a wire brace, Steven Talbot did not reply.

Kurt Essenheimer bounded up the steps, arms outstretched to greet his old friend. Steven thrust a schoolchild's chalkboard at him. Written on it was, "The first thing to remember is that you cannot touch me and I cannot speak to you. Everything I say must be written down but I can hear you so spare me the dramatics of speaking like you would to an idiot."

"It's good to see you again, my friend," Essenheimer said.

"Is it? But you haven't really seen me. Do you want to?"

Essenheimer nodded without hesitation. He had seen a great many things in the new Germany, at places called Dachau and Buchenwald. Maybe because horror had already eaten into his soul, he didn't flinch when Steven Talbot raised the veil.

Chalk scraped against blackboard.

"That little bitch did a good job, didn't she? So good the doctors tell me the surgery will take years to complete. But I will see her again. I've promised myself that, Kurt. When I do, I'll—"

The chalk snapped in Steven's fingers. He hurled the remaining piece, watching it as it clattered across the floor.

Essenheimer shuddered. Though no stranger to violence, he was afraid of the obsession that had gripped Steven Talbot.

Steven picked up more chalk and continued writing.

"Think of it, my friend, years in Switzerland. The boredom! But we'll be busy, won't we? In fact, it's almost better this way. I have given strict orders to receive no visitors except you or your envoys. And Mother, of course. Here we have all the privacy we need. So tell me, what has been happening?"

Inside, seated opposite Steven in front of a stone fireplace, Kurt Essenheimer began his recital. He spoke for hours, detailing how all the work he and Steven had done was bearing ripe, precious fruit. Everything Germany needed for war was pouring through the pipelines that stretched as far south as the Horn of Africa and east to Malaya.

"Sounds as though everything is working perfectly," Steven wrote.

"It is. There has been one minor development—insignificant, really."

"What's that?"

Essenheimer explained that since Michelle's death, Monk McQueen had been going around asking a lot of questions.

"Last fall McQueen met with the Jew Warburg. Later on he visited the editors of major European newspapers. Since then a few reporters have been nosing around Berlin. As it happens, one of them has a very high regard for Hitler and the Party. He told me that McQueen is intent on proving that you've been supplying Germany through Global. Laughable, isn't it? As though McQueen could hope to get through our security."

Steven didn't share Essenheimer's amusement. He knew McQueen far better than the German ever could.

"Where is McQueen now?"

"Back in America, with his adopted daughter. He can't hurt us."

Steven paced in front of the blackboard, then began writing.

"Don't underestimate McQueen. He's clever and resourceful and he has a big ax to grind. Just because he's three thousand miles away doesn't mean we can afford to get careless."

"Not at all, Steven," Essenheimer assured him quickly. "You know we have sympathizers in America. They will keep an eye on him."

Steven was mollified but far from reassured. Right now, McQueen was merely a nuisance. But later he could prove to be a genuine threat. Steven told himself he would be wise to arrange a contingency plan, in case the newspaperman got out of hand.

However, he now had something more pressing to discuss with Essenheimer, something he needed from London.

Essenheimer was dismayed by Steven's demand.

"To get what you want might jeopardize our most valuable agent in London."

Splinters of chalk flew off the blackboard as Steven pounded out his reply:
"The Führer has always given me the resources I needed."

"But why is this information so important?"

"It's important! I don't need to justify myself to you! Just get my instructions to your man."

Essenheimer shook his head. It was pointless to argue. Nonetheless, Steven had to be made aware of certain realities.

"I'm going to have a difficult time persuading our intelligence people to go along. Then there's the problem of safely contacting our man. Finally, he himself will decide when and how he can act."

"Understood. What I need isn't going anywhere."

"All right, Steven. So *what* is it you need?"

"I believe it is peace for our time . . . peace with honor."

"Like hell it is!" Monk growled and snapped off the large RCA radio. He and Cassandra were sitting in the living room of Monk's apartment at the Carlton Towers. They had been listening to a BBC broadcast of Prime Minister Neville Chamberlain's speech following his return from Munich. Chamberlain proclaimed his appeasement of Hitler a diplomatic coup—as if surrendering the sovereignty of one-third of Czechoslovakia to a dictator were a brilliant victory.

"Does that mean there will be a war?" asked Cassandra.

She looked out the windows at the red and golden foliage of Central Park under the September sun. Amid such tranquillity, it was impossible to think of war—almost.

"There may be, pumpkin," Monk replied. "The more Hitler gets, the more he wants. One day someone is going to have to draw the line."

He pictured Abraham Warburg and wondered what that gentle man was going through now. In the spring of 1938, after the Austrian Anschluss, Monk had urged Warburg to leave Germany. The Nazis had nationalized his bank, plundered its assets, and even requisitioned his home for alleged "back taxes." But Warburg refused to leave.

"Germany," he had written to Monk, "is on the brink of a moral catastrophe. I cannot abandon those who may be swept away."

Monk had tried to convince Warburg that he himself might become one of those who disappeared, but the banker was determined to stay on and fight.

Monk looked at Cassandra, who sat with her legs tucked under her, nibbling her lip.

"Why the frown, pumpkin?"

Cassandra hesitated. "Everyone seems to be talking about war these days, even at school. There are students who think Hemingway and the others who fought in Spain are heroes, and those who believe America should stay out of the next European war. That's how they refer to it, the 'next one.'"

Gently Monk steered her away from that subject. It was enough that Michelle had lost her youth to war. He'd be damned if the same thing would happen to Cassandra.

"What about your studies?"

Cassandra brightened at the topic.

"I'm thinking of concentrating on economics when I go to college."

Monk raised his eyebrows.

"I want to be as good as *Maman* was. I want her to be proud of me."

The minute Cassandra had returned to New York she knew she had done the right thing. Manhattan, with its electric energy and frenetic pulse, cleansed her. Here she did not feel afraid, nor did she have to look over her shoulder while walking down the street. She had the kindness of Abilene to warm her and, when Monk arrived, his love to comfort her.

But even after two years the nightmare of Paris was never far away. All it took was a particular smell or sound, a sudden chill, a child's shriek in the park, the backfire of a car to make Cassandra tremble. Angry with herself for being so vulnerable, she bombarded Monk with questions about the only man who she believed could put her terror to rest.

"Why haven't the police found Harry Taylor?" she demanded. "Where could he have gone?"

"The truth is, probably no one will find him," Monk told her. "You know how dangerous the catacombs are. When people get lost in them, they almost never come out. Besides, we know he was shot. . . ."

Monk stayed away from the subject of the *cataphiles*. Like Inspector Armand Savin, he believed that Harry had long ago fallen victim to them.

"Tell me about him, the kind of man he was."

Monk hesitated, then admitted that if Cassandra was ever to come to terms with what had happened, she had to know as much as possible. He explained to her how Harry Taylor had come to New York, the brilliant Global executive he once had been, and how his ambitions had ultimately ruined him. In telling Harry's story, Monk added the roles others had played. He explained how difficult life had been for Michelle in New York and the long-standing feud between her and Rose.

411

"Now I know why you and *Maman* seldom mentioned her," Cassandra murmured.

"Rose caused your mother a great deal of unhappiness. She had her own dreams and there was no room in them for people she thought didn't belong."

"But she seems like such a kind, generous woman," Cassandra protested, remembering that it was Rose Jefferson who had helped her return to America and who, since then, had made a point of calling several times a week.

"I think in her heart she is," Monk said softly. "Sometimes we do the wrong things for reasons that seem perfectly right to us. It's only later we discover that the reasons were foolish or naïve and we ended up hurting people. Your mother and Rose would have been friends one day. Let me show you what I mean."

Monk went into his study and retrieved the notebooks Michelle had filled, beginning with her arrival in New York right up to a few days before her death.

"Read them carefully. Remember that times and people do change. I think Rose understood her mistakes and wanted to make up for them. She never had the chance to do that with your mother, but I think she wants to do so with you."

Cassandra was both fascinated and repelled by the living history Michelle had left behind. Sometimes her heart soared as she read her mother's descriptions of her hopes and dreams. Then she would come to parts that made her heart ache and she wondered how her mother could ever have endured such hardships.

Because she was a woman who shielded her daughter with her own body and saved her life . . .

There were references to Rose that angered Cassandra, but the more she read the more she found that her mother had secretly admired many things about Rose and had learned a great deal from her. Enough so that when the time came, she had stood up to her and refused to let Rose have what she had built, Cassandra thought, going over the part about Michelle's bargaining for the traveler's-check operation.

For Cassandra the notebooks became lampposts that illuminated the life of a woman she scarcely knew but who had played an important role in her mother's life. When Cassandra asked Monk what had happened to the great company Michelle had founded, he told her, "It's all yours, pumpkin. Or will be in four years, on your twenty-first birthday. Two of Rose's best executives are running it for you now, and believe me, she and I watch every move they make."

Cassandra thought about this, then asked, "What about Steven? I know you don't believe he's the hero everyone thinks he is."

"Steven is very far away and he'll never be back."

"Did he have anything to do with Mother's death?"

"I don't know, pumpkin."

Cassandra saw the pain in his eyes and closed the subject. For now.

Cassandra had turned the three rooms on the second floor of the Carlton Towers apartment into her own little domain. The closets were filled with new wardrobes and the walls hung with her mother's art collection. The few photographs and mementoes she had brought with her found their places on shelves, and after a while she could look at them without hurt or sorrow.

Attending an American school helped to bring her out of her shell. After the strict discipline of a parochial education, the free spirit there was an elixir. Although she couldn't quite understand some of the social customs, such as football mania and "getting pinned," Cassandra soon discovered how glorious a girl could feel when young men made a point of noticing her. She teased Monk about his wary, paternal reaction when they came calling at Carlton Towers.

"Well, it's time to go to work," Monk said after Cassandra's date had brought her home and departed.

As though on cue, the grandfather clock struck midnight.

"Can I come with you?"

Cassandra loved the mad-hatter atmosphere of Q magazine's office. The first time Monk had taken her there, the whole staff had turned out to make her feel welcome.

"There's no one there now, pumpkin," Monk said. "I just have to read the overnight cables from Europe. Boring stuff. Besides, you need some sleep."

Although both of them pretended otherwise, Cassandra knew that Monk was going to the office to check for messages from Abraham Warburg. Not long after Michelle's death, Monk had explained to her what her mother had been involved in. Cassandra had been astonished to learn how many lives her mother had helped save, the sacrifices she had made on behalf of the helpless people who had passed through their home. *People whom I treated with contempt*, Cassandra recalled.

If I could only tell her how sorry I am. Maybe if she'd told me . . .

But Cassandra didn't dwell on the past. Instead she joined clubs and did volunteer work for organizations that spoke out about the dangers of Adolf Hitler, arguing vehemently with those who predicted there would be no war. As far as Cassandra was concerned, when her father left the house at night, he was already fighting it.

413

— 48 —

Preparations for war were being made on other, almost invisible fronts, in the netherworld of secret agents, traitors, and hired killers. Although Sir Dennis Pritchard knew nothing of such men, he unwittingly became one of their targets.

Pritchard looked to the garden behind his Harley Street office as an oasis of peace, a place where he could retreat from the bloodshed of the operating room. Pritchard ran a finger around the delicate rose petals. It was already October but the unseasonably warm weather kept the blooms radiant.

"Good morning, Sir Dennis."

Startled, Pritchard turned around to see a tall, fair-haired young man standing on the flagstones, hands stuffed deep into the pockets of a beige trenchcoat. He spoke with a soft Irish accent.

"How the devil did you get in? My nurse isn't here yet."

"Dr. Pritchard, I've come about a certain file." The man tossed a slip of paper onto the patio table. "This individual's file, to be exact."

Pritchard frowned when he read the name.

"Is this some kind of joke? This man has been dead for years."

"But you do have the file, Doctor?"

Pritchard rose. "I think you had better leave before I call the police."

"In fact I'm *sure* you have it," the man insisted. "You see, I've taken the liberty of having a peek through your records here at the office. Unfortunately I couldn't find it. Then I thought to myself: Hold on, a conscientious fellow like Dennis would have put an inactive file into storage. So I checked the warehouse where you lease space. Sad to say, I couldn't find what I was looking for there either. Which means that you must have a very, very special place for this particular folder, don't you?"

"Get out of here!" Sir Dennis roared.

He did not see the man's hands move, but suddenly his arm was wrenched up behind his back.

"London needs all the surgeons it has, Doctor. It would be a pity to deprive it of one of the best."

Pritchard grimaced as his arm was twisted even higher.

"Now it's my thinking that that file is still here," the man said calmly. "Before

414

you say anything to upset me further, we should go inside and make a telephone call."

Pushing Pritchard forward, the man maneuvered him into the office.

"Please observe the number I'm calling."

Pritchard was horrified as the man dialed his home.

"Now listen—"

"Dennis! Dennis, is that you? Darling, what's going on? There are men here—"

Pritchard squeezed his eyes shut as his wife screamed.

"My associates won't hurt your lovely wife, Dennis. Unless, of course, you think the file is more important than her life."

Pritchard couldn't bear to think of what was happening at his home.

"I have it!" he gasped. "It's locked away. . . ."

"Fetch, Dennis, fetch."

Pritchard scrambled to a cabinet beside his desk. He opened it and removed the file drawer to reveal a built-in safe. Pritchard forced his trembling fingers to dial the combination. When the door swung open, he reached inside and brought out a thick blue file.

The man glanced through it, obviously searching for a particular reference. He smiled.

"You've done well, Doctor. Now I will keep my end of the bargain and see that your wife is left unharmed. But I think you should go over there in any event. She might be wanting a sedative."

"Who are you?" Pritchard whispered.

"Someone who will come back to visit you if you go to the police. Or to anyone else who may be interested in this. Don't do it, Doctor. Forget this ever happened. If someone should ever ask, play the fool. The file was misplaced, lost. Live long and prosper, Dennis. I mean that sincerely."

The man with the Irish lilt in his voice disappeared as swiftly as he had come. Riding the train to the ferry that would take him across the Irish Sea and home, he hoped Berlin would be satisfied. The Germans had been pestering him about Pritchard for eighteen months, but the Irishman had had much more pressing—and demanding—assignments than leaning on a Harley Street civilian. Still, he couldn't help but wonder what was so important about this medical file on a man who'd been dead better than twenty years.

Rose Jefferson was among that tiny minority of Americans who believed that a second World War was inevitable. Throughout the fall of 1938 she made frequent trips to Washington to consult with the Secretaries of Finance and War and even President Roosevelt himself. Global Enterprises was exactly what its name implied—a worldwide industrial and financial empire. The men who occupied the seats of power knew that the ships, railroads, and factories Rose Jefferson controlled would be critical to the nation's defense. But even more important was her awesome financial power.

Because she had the ear of official Washington, Rose was invited to sit on numerous committees that continually revised American strategy and policies as the European situation changed. After the horror of *Kristalnacht*, on November 9, 1938, when marauding bands of Nazis looted Jewish shops and beat up their owners, Rose argued for unrestricted emigration for Jews from Germany to the United States. She was appalled when a number of Roosevelt's cabinet members dismissed the incident as a minor aberration. Rose suggested to Monk that they find ways to get Global's Jewish employees and their families out of Europe altogether, starting with Germany.

"We're way ahead of you on that," Monk said.

Because he had been uncertain as to what her reaction would be, Monk had never told Rose about the pipeline Michelle and Abraham Warburg had set up in Germany. As she listened to the details, Rose was both astonished and impressed by Michelle's humanitarian efforts. She immediately put forward suggestions to make them even more effective.

"We can add to the numbers coming out by hiring people as Global employees and bringing them here for 'retraining.' "

Monk thought this ingenious. He sent the recommendation to Abraham Warburg, who immediately endorsed it.

In the summer of 1939, against the advice of her principal advisers, Rose made one last trip to Europe. Although her business itinerary was crushing, she went first to the Hoffmann Clinic in Switzerland.

As soon as she had accepted the severity of Steven's injuries Rose had been adamant about bringing him home to New York. It was inconceivable to her that Steven could not get the best possible care in the country that led the world in medical achievements. But American specialists who reviewed Steven's case came to a unanimous conclusion: the Swiss, especially the Hoffmann Clinic, were world leaders in reconstructive surgery.

Reluctantly, Rose had gone to Jarlsburg and made the necessary arrangements; then, when Steven was stable enough to travel, she had returned with him to Switzerland. The last time she had seen him his face had been swathed in bandages. Now, she had no idea what to expect.

The director, Joachim Hoffmann, greeted Rose deferentially.

"We have made great progress," he assured her. "But, as I told you in the beginning, nothing can make up for time, the best healer of all."

"Can I see him? I mean really *see* him?"

"I would not recommend it," Hoffmann replied firmly. "Steven knows he has come a long way. We, his doctors, know that. But you would expect to see a face you remember. It's best you wait until we are finished." Hoffmann walked her to one of the guest chalets. "I'll leave you now. Please, don't press your son to show himself if he doesn't wish to do so. You must have as much patience as he has shown."

Suddenly Rose felt paralyzed. What was she supposed to say to Steven? Could she reach out and touch him? Kiss him?

"Hello, Mother."

His voice had a grainy quality to it. She looked up at him, standing on the porch, wearing a cap with a white cloth veil that hung over his face. As he came down the steps she reached for him. Steven caught her wrists. "You can't touch my face."

Rose choked back her tears. "I understand, darling."

Steven offered her his arm. "Why don't we walk? This is the most beautiful time of day, when the sun begins going down behind the mountains."

Steven led her away from the hospital, along a path that led to a small man-made lake with benches arranged around it.

"You should have told me you were coming," Steven said.

"I . . . I thought I'd surprise you."

"So you did."

Rose noticed how stiffly he spoke. Sometimes, when the light caught the cloth in a certain way, she saw blotches of red flesh.

"Are you well?" asked Steven.

"Yes. And you?"

"I'm going to be fine, Mother. As good as I was before."

Rose clung to the resolve in his voice.

"Tell me about Global . . . and New York. Up here, I don't hear very much about the world."

Rose spoke haltingly at first. She was struck at how self-possessed Steven appeared, almost remote. Little by little Rose told Steven everything he wanted to know about Global and its ceaseless expansion, about New York and the new clubs and shows that were playing on Broadway. She spoke of Monk McQueen and the arrangement she had made regarding the traveler's checks and of the committees she served on in Washington.

"Tell me about Washington," Steven asked softly. "It sounds fascinating."

Rose talked through the sunset and into the twilight when the fireflies started to appear.

"Here I am chattering away and you've hardly said a word," Rose scolded herself.

"It's not good for me to speak too much," Steven replied. "The skin has to settle over the muscles, otherwise . . ."

"Of course," Rose said hurriedly.

"Where will you go now, Mother?"

"Berlin first. Then Rome, Amsterdam, and Paris. We're closing all the traveler's-check offices. Monk and I agreed that we couldn't risk keeping our—I mean, his—employees here much longer."

Steven chuckled. "Wise precaution. What about Harry Taylor? Has anyone ever found him?"

"No. And as far as I'm concerned, Harry Taylor died in the catacombs and went straight to hell. I'll never forgive him for what he did to you. Never!"

Steven had heard the rumors about the reward his mother had posted for Harry's capture. Each day he expected to open the newspaper and read that Harry had been found. Even though he and Kurt Essenheimer had a contingency plan ready in case Harry was arrested—a plan whose result guaranteed that Harry would never have a chance to talk to the police—Steven had continued to live with the uncertainty that his co-conspirator might be alive somewhere. Now, he was thinking that if the entire European underworld, which had the best reason to hunt Harry down, hadn't been able to find him, no one would.

Steven reached out and took his mother's hand. "Give me the time I need, Mother. I'll be all right, you'll see."

"I'll give you whatever you need," Rose whispered.

You already have, Steven thought as he escorted Rose to her car. He couldn't wait to see the expression on Kurt's face when he related all those details about American government policy.

As Rose was getting into the car, Steven asked casually, "Have you seen Cassandra at all?"

The question surprised Rose. "I have. In fact we visit quite often. She's a crackerjack of a young lady. Franklin would have been so proud of her."

"I'm sure," Steven murmured.

From his balcony Steven watched the limousine wend its way down the mountain. He tossed his head back and laughed, the sound of his voice echoing across the valley.

His mother was a bigger fool than he had given her credit for. Through the sitting-room windows, lying on his desk, was Franklin Jefferson's medical file, with Sir Dennis Pritchard's name on its cover.

Yes, Mother, a much bigger fool . . .

- 49 -

On September 3, 1939, the "phony war" finally exploded. German U-boats sank the British vessel *Athena* off the Irish coast, prompting Britain and France to declare war on Germany.

"Thank God we got all our people out," Monk said to Cassandra. "Hitler's about to make mincemeat out of Europe."

His grim prediction was accurate. By autumn of 1940, France, Belgium, the Netherlands, Denmark, Norway, and Romania fell to the seemingly invincible German war machine. Cassandra, who wept while watching newsreels of German soldiers strutting beneath the Arc de Triomphe, couldn't believe the American attitude to the war.

"Don't they realize what's happening?" she demanded. "Unless we fight, Britain will be the next to fall."

Monk shared her sentiments. He wrote feverishly day and night promoting American involvement. But he was up against powerful men—former president Herbert Hoover, Henry Ford, and Charles Lindbergh—who advocated isolationism and noninvolvement in what they called "the Europeans' war."

Cassandra pitched in as well. Using her foreign-language skills, she translated Monk's pieces as they came out of the typewriter. French, German, Italian, and Spanish copies were sent via circuitous routes to Occupied Europe to be reproduced in Resistance newspapers and pamphlets.

"How long can the United States wait?" Cassandra despaired as the Battle of Britain raged in the skies.

"Until something so terrible occurs that we won't be able to ignore reality any longer," Monk replied.

On December 7, 1941, the unspeakable happened. Three hundred sixty Japanese carrier-based planes attacked Pearl Harbor. For the United States, the days of waiting were over.

The snow lay in deep drifts across the fields around the Swiss sanitarium. Inside Steven's chalet a fire roared in the hearth. Kurt Essenheimer, who was sitting closest to it, noticed the pans of water set around the room, to add moisture to the air and prevent Steven's sensitive skin from drying up like old parchment.

"Are you absolutely certain this has to be done?" asked Essenheimer.

He had arrived that afternoon, after a long, slow trip through the Alps. Then Steven had told him why he had summoned him and Essenheimer remembered fragments of their conversation about Monk McQueen five years ago. The debate over what to do now had carried well into the night. Essenheimer still had his misgivings.

"What you're proposing can be done, Steven. But it's dangerous, especially now with the war having reached a critical stage. If anything happens to the information our 'traitor' carries over, it will spell the end of everything we've achieved."

"If we don't act, it could still be the end," Steven replied from the gloom. "McQueen has never stopped nosing around, trying to get hard evidence linking me to the Reich. So far our security has held and we've been very, very lucky. No Anna Kleists have slipped by us. But with Hitler bogged down on two fronts, some people might decide that Germany *won't* win. They'll be looking for insurance, something to barter with if the situation gets really tough. McQueen, with his high-level connections, would be someone they'd try to approach."

Steven paused. "There's another reason. As long as the United States was sitting on the sidelines, what I was doing—if it came to light—constituted, at worst, an unsavory business practice. I might have been pilloried and Mother would have tried to shut us down, but that would have been the extent of it. Now it's war, Kurt, and I am collaborating with the enemy. That makes me a traitor and we all know the penalty for treason."

The two men stared into the fire, watching the flames dance.

"We have no choice, Kurt. We know McQueen will never stop carrying on Michelle's work. The time has come to stop him."

Essenheimer lighted a cigarette and tossed the match into the fire.

"All right. We go ahead with the contingency plan. But we'll take some time to put all the details in place. It's February now. Say three months?"

Steven was about to object but then realized the enormous amount of work Kurt was facing. He himself would have asked for no less.

"Fine. Three months. I expect you to keep me up to date, Kurt. And remember: nothing is to be left to chance. Nothing."

One hundred days later, in May 1942, a young man, with dark hair cut en brosse and with the pronounced military gait of an officer, turned the corner of Zurich's principal business avenue, the Banhofstrasse. He scrutinized the gleaming brass nameplates and spotted the one he was looking for: the International Refugee Location Service.

The officer knew that the service was on the sixth floor of the building and that, indeed, some of its activities were humanitarian, trying to bring displaced families together. But beneath the facade lay a much more secret enterprise: the service was in the middle of a financial pipeline that stretched from New York to Zurich, then split off into a thousand different cities, towns, and hamlets across Occupied Europe. Its mandate was as far-flung as its operations. In Switzerland, it paid customs inspectors not to examine entry visas too closely. In Germany it funneled cash or gold into the hands of bureaucrats who controlled exit and travel permits and who, with a stroke of a pen, could transform a Jew into a Christian. It supplied Resistance groups with funds to buy what they couldn't steal from the enemy and kept the underground presses rolling.

The Refugee Location Service, the officer reflected, was as potent a weapon as anything the Allies had devised. And it all rested on the ingenuity and effort of two men: Monk McQueen in New York and Abraham Warburg in Zurich.

"I'm sorry, but we don't have a Herr Warburg working here," the pretty receptionist said brightly. "Perhaps one of our administrators can help you."

The officer removed a thin, oxblood file from his briefcase. It was sealed with wax, bearing the imprint of the double-headed eagle over the Nazi swastika.

"Give this to Warburg," he said, dropping the dossier on the desk. "Tell him not to waste my time."

The secretary, who was Jewish, flinched at the man's glacial tone. She had faced such men before, in Berlin.

"Please wait here."

The officer made himself comfortable, inserted a cigarette into a holder, and smoked quietly. He was only half-finished when the secretary returned.

"Would you come with me, please?"

The secretary showed him into an office whose window faced the street. There was no clutter. The desk was bare except for a telephone. In one corner was a rusty filing cabinet.

"A pleasure to meet you, Herr Warburg," the officer said to the man's back.

When Warburg turned around, the officer noticed that the seal on the file was broken.

"Who are you?" Warburg asked softly.

"Colonel Gunther von Kluge, attached to the Inspector General's office of the Ministry of Finance in Berlin. My credentials."

Warburg carefully examined the identification cards. He had a banker's eye for forgeries and these were real.

"How may I be of service to you?"

Von Kluge nodded at the dossier. "That should be self-evident."

"This is a refugee bureau, Colonel. Your papers relate to some transactions involving an American named Talbot and the deliveries of certain goods to Germany. I really think you've come to the wrong person."

Von Kluge sat down on the hard wooden chair and casually crossed his legs.

"Did you know that in the last week the Gestapo arrested three men?" He gave Warburg the names and was pleased to see the pain in the old man's eyes. "They were taken to Buchenwald. By now I should think they're dead. And do you know why, Herr Warburg? Because they were trying to steal that one piece of paper I brought you."

Warburg felt sweat break out over his forehead.

"I know what it is you and Monk McQueen have been after," von Kluge continued easily. "You see, it's been my job to make sure your people didn't get anywhere near the information they were seeking. But now you can have it all."

"Who are you?" Warburg demanded.

"A realist. Not unlike yourself. Hitler's attack on Russia last year was a fatal mistake. Now Germany will need more supplies than ever before. If I give you evidence that Steven Talbot is shipping for the Reich, you can stop him and so tighten the noose around the Führer's neck. That is what you want, isn't it, Herr Warburg?"

"What about you? Why are you doing this?"

"I have no desire to be buried in the ashes of Germany, so I'm willing to trade: the information on Talbot in exchange for safe conduct to America and one million dollars."

"That's absurd!"

"It's cheap!" von Kluge retorted. "Oh, and one other consideration. I will do business only with McQueen, face to face, here in Zurich."

The German paused. "Shall we discuss this further, Herr Warburg?"

Slowly the banker sat down behind his desk and von Kluge had his answer.

Three hours later von Kluge and Abraham Warburg left the building and went across the street to the Swiss Credit Bank. They were escorted to the safety deposit vaults and given a box and two keys. The material von Kluge had brought with him was deposited and both men turned their keys to lock the box.

Von Kluge held out his hand for Warburg's key. "I'll keep both of them, if you don't mind. Until McQueen arrives."

When they left the bank, the two men separated but von Kluge quickly doubled back and caught sight of Warburg's black bowler hat in the lunchtime crowds. The banker was easy enough to follow and his destination was equally predictable: the American embassy.

Von Kluge slipped into a telephone kiosk and asked the operator to put him through to the Hoffmann Clinic in Jarlsburg. The first part of the plan had gone off without a hitch. Steven Talbot was sure to be pleased.

Cassandra sensed the change immediately. She and Monk were having breakfast on the terrace, surrounded by planters of geraniums, roses, and ivy. Yet, the air of this tranquil setting crackled with Monk's excitement.

"What's up?" she asked brightly, kissing him on the cheek.

"Overnight news. It looks like Hitler bit off more than he could chew when he attacked Russia. The Soviets are going on the offensive."

Cassandra cocked her head, brushing away stray wisps of fine blond hair. She knew Monk wasn't lying to her. He was incapable of doing that. He just wasn't telling her everything.

"Was there anything else on the wire?"

Cassandra could almost see him trying to find the right words.

"Nothing as dramatic."

Cassandra was content to drop the subject—for the time being. Whatever it was, she would learn about it soon enough.

But from that day on, the atmosphere in the house was never the same, as Monk became increasingly absorbed in this mystery. He spent a great deal of time in Washington. When he came home, usually just long enough to change clothes, Cassandra tried to coax out an explanation, which Monk deftly evaded.

One morning, after a particularly restless night, Cassandra awoke with a start. It may have been the stiff morning breeze or the voices she heard distinctly. Naked, Cassandra slipped out of bed and listened. The voices stilled, but there was the scraping of chair legs on the terrace flagstone. Monk was home from Washington, having breakfast. Cassandra splashed some water on her face, brushed her teeth, and donned an old, comfy flannel nightgown.

"Well, it's about time—"

Her lips formed a perfect *o* as she breezed onto the terrace and, at the last minute, saw the stranger. He was taller than she, just under six feet, and a few years older, perhaps twenty-five. He had a full head of curly, chestnut hair and green eyes the color of the sea after a storm. He was a handsome man but for the ridge of broken cartilage on his nose and the thin diagonal scar across one cheek, milk-white against his tanned skin.

"Hello to you, too." His voice was rich with wonder and pleasure. "My name's Nicholas Lockwood."

"Cassandra McQueen," she managed.

"Monk's told me a lot about you."

"I see you two are getting to know each other." Monk padded onto the terrace carrying a tray of coffee, biscuits, and condiments. "You're up early, pumpkin."

"Couldn't sleep," Cassandra mumbled, turning scarlet at Monk's use of her nickname and growing even redder when she saw Lockwood grin.

As she stood on tiptoes to kiss Monk she whispered, "Who is he?"

"Why don't you join us for coffee?" Monk suggested.

The minute she sat down Cass felt the nightgown stretch across her breasts and remembered that she was naked underneath it. As discreetly as possible she tugged at the gown.

"I met Nicholas in Washington," Monk said, pouring coffee for everyone. "He's with the State Department."

Which was technically true. But Monk conveniently omitted that Lockwood worked for General "Wild Bill" Donovan, who had founded the Office of Strategic Services. The OSS, as it was called, was the American fledgling intelligence service and commando group rolled into one. Lockwood was one of its first graduates.

"As a matter of fact, Nicholas and I are going to Europe next week."

"Where?" Cassandra demanded eagerly.

"Zurich," Lockwood replied. "There's an outfit called the International Refugee Location Service. A number of very important writers and publishers, whom the Nazis would dearly love to get their hands on, have managed to escape into Switzerland. It would be very difficult if State tried to bring these people out officially. But if they come because Q magazine needs their editorial skills . . ."

"I think that's wonderful," Cassandra told them.

Lockwood was glad that Cassandra had accepted the white lie. When he had been assigned to accompany McQueen to Europe, his instructions had been maddeningly vague: "make sure that McQueen comes back with what he's going to get." But what was that? Lockwood got the impression that even his superiors weren't sure. Whatever "it" was, the item had to be important to have Lockwood seconded to the case.

"When do you leave?" Cassandra asked.

"In five days," Monk replied, and glanced at Lockwood. "Which means you and I had better go over the details."

As the two men rose, Cassandra said, "It was a pleasure to meet you, Mr. Lockwood. Perhaps we'll see each other again."

His smile radiated through her.

"Count on it."

"I'll hold you to that," she teased.

"I'm counting on that, too."

* * *

The New York–Azores leg of the journey, on a Pan-American clipper leased by Monk McQueen but paid for by the State Department, lasted more than seventeen hours. Nicholas Lockwood had intended to use the time to nudge McQueen into talking about the details of their mission, but two things conspired against him: the older man's ability to sleep over the roar of the engines, and Cassandra.

Nicholas could not get the image of Cassandra out of his mind. He had dated his share of beautiful women but none had had the allure of the McQueen heiress. More than her physical attraction, which Nicholas found very evident in spite of the baggy nightgown, he was drawn to her openness and vitality. She had none of the jaded indifference that characterized the rich women of Washington and New York. Her caring and concern for Monk, for what he was doing, and for the tragedy that had engulfed the world were genuine. Nicholas thought this was all the more remarkable given that Cassandra had survived a kidnapping attempt that had claimed her mother's life. Having experienced adversity firsthand, Nicholas could tell how much character and inner strength it took to put something like that behind oneself.

During the refueling stop in the Azores, Nicholas and Monk had a breakfast of fruit and coffee at the airport counter. It was the chance the OSS man had been waiting for.

"Are you going to contact your people in Zurich before we get there, Mr. McQueen?"

Monk took a bite of his orange. Nicholas was fishing again. McQueen couldn't blame him, but neither did he dare tell Lockwood the truth. Not even the Secretary of War, who had authorized this expedition, knew the whole truth. All Monk had told him was that he had discovered a way to deprive the Third Reich of raw material vital to its war effort. He had said nothing about possibly ruining the Jefferson family.

What am I going to do about Rose?

If the information provided by the German officer, von Kluge, was half as explosive as Warburg had implied, the implications for Rose and Global could be devastating. Monk wondered if Steven Talbot had ever considered that he might one day find himself in front of a firing squad.

Don't get ahead of yourself, he cautioned himself. *One step at a time.*

Monk turned his attention to Nicholas.

"First of all, let's drop the formality. Call me Monk. As far as Zurich is concerned, everything's waiting for us. It's just a matter of picking it up and bringing it home."

Then why do you need me? And what is "it"?

As though he divined the younger man's thoughts, Monk added, "I realize the secrecy bothers you. But it has to be this way."

425

"Mr. McQueen—Monk," Nicholas said, "with all due respect, the OSS wasn't created to be a messenger service. If there's going to be trouble, I want to be prepared."

Monk smiled. He had met a number of OSS officers in preparation for this mission and from the lot had selected Nicholas. The two had taken to each other immediately. In the course of their meetings in Washington a bond of trust and respect had been forged. Monk had sensed that for all his independence and resourcefulness, Nicholas was a sensitive man who placed a high premium on friendship.

"Zurich is probably the safest city in the world," he told Nicholas. "Once we get what we've come for, I'll leave the security decisions to you."

Nicholas knew when to accept half a loaf. He had that rare quality in one so young: he was patient.

The Pan-American clipper took them as far as Lisbon. Using their special Red Cross papers, the two men crossed the Spanish border and traveled into Vichy, France, where, two days later, they connected with another train that, once sealed, rolled across Occupied Europe into Switzerland. In spite of the tedious, uncomfortable journey, Monk insisted that they go directly from the station to the International Refugee Location Service.

"It would be better if I met the principals alone," Monk said as they walked into the office.

Before Nicholas could protest, Abraham Warburg bustled into the waiting room. After the introductions, he steered Lockwood to an empty desk. "One of my people called in sick," he explained. "Please, make yourself comfortable. I'm sure this won't take very long."

Monk followed the banker into his office and for the first time came face to face with the man who could bring down one of the most powerful families in America.

"Herr McQueen," the German said, rising and holding out his hand. "A pleasure. Your reputation precedes you."

"As does yours," McQueen replied dryly.

"I trust you have brought the required papers?"

Without a word Monk handed von Kluge an envelope. Inside were a letter from the Secretary of War guaranteeing the bearer safe passage into the United States and a certified check for one million dollars, drawn on Monk's personal account.

"Excellent," von Kluge murmured.

"Your turn," Monk told him.

The German opened his briefcase with a flourish and handed a file to McQueen.

"The latest shipment figures, as promised."

Monk swore softly as he read the contracts. He had always had his doubts about von Kluge; the man seemed too good to be true, and as much as Monk wanted to get at Steven, he had not let his hope run away with him. Now he saw that as clever and meticulous as Steven had been, he had indeed signed his name to documents that could hang him.

"I trust you are satisfied, Herr McQueen."

Monk nodded.

"In that case, I have a surprise for you."

The German held up a safety-deposit-box key.

"Since I knew I could never return to Germany after this, I brought out a few other things that may interest you. They are safely stored in the bank across the street. If you have no objection I will get them now."

"By all means, Herr von Kluge. We are interested in anything that you might show us."

Von Kluge executed a perfect military about-face and left. As he threaded his way through the desks in the outer office he did not notice the young man who was studying him, his eyes half-hidden by a magazine.

"Well, there you have it," Warburg said.

He had expected to feel elated at this moment of victory. Instead, his heart was empty. Abraham Warburg understood that for his friend the trials were just beginning.

"What Steven did is brilliant," Monk said. "If it hadn't been for von Kluge, he would have gotten away with it." He paused. "Do you have any idea what else he's bringing us?"

Warburg shook his head. "Whatever it is, I'm sure Washington will be interested."

Von Kluge went directly to the Swiss Credit Bank across the street from the Refugee Service. But he did not go to the desk whose officer looked after the safety deposit boxes. Instead he walked up to the teller's counter and stood directly behind another man who had a briefcase by his left leg. The customer finished his business and left. Without the case. Von Kluge chatted with the head teller about opening up an account and then he too left. With the case.

A few minutes later von Kluge was back at the Refugee Service, walking toward Warburg's office. Again, he paid no special attention to the young man studying him. When their eyes met, Nicholas Lockwood smiled politely and looked away. Those few precious seconds were long enough for the German to slip the briefcase behind a large potted rubber plant outside Warburg's door.

Now where's he going? Lockwood asked himself as he saw von Kluge walk back the way he had come. *Maybe he forgot something.*

Or maybe something was wrong. Lockwood's instinct tingled. His eye spied out the thin ridge of sweat on von Kluge's forehead and measured his quick steps. The man was on the verge of running. Nicholas was out of his chair, heading after the German, but von Kluge stepped into the elevator and drew the grille.

Lockwood raced back to Warburg's office. "The guy you were with—what did he want?"

Both Monk and Abraham Warburg looked up at him in astonishment.

"What are you talking about?" Monk demanded. "He left and hasn't come back yet."

"Like hell! He was in here a minute ago. Walked right past me carrying a briefcase."

"Mr. Lockwood," Warburg said reasonably. "I assure you the gentleman in question isn't here. He went out—"

Nicholas bolted out of Warburg's office, looking frantically around the cluster of desks.

Think! Picture him! He's walking past you. He's carrying the briefcase. . . . But he doesn't go into the office. Then he's walking, almost running the other way.

"Everyone, out of here!" Nicholas roared.

When Warburg came out, Lockwood grabbed him.

"Get your people out of here!"

"But—"

"Just *do* it!"

Nicholas saw Monk nod and watched as Warburg began to herd his staff away from their desks.

"Where did you put it, you bastard!" he whispered.

Then Nicholas saw it, the edge of oxblood leather peeking out from behind the planter. He came around the briefcase and froze. A strip of wire was showing where the briefcase came together and closed.

"It's a bomb!"

The words electrified the air and the stampede began. Nicholas dashed back into the office where Monk was stuffing documents into an accordion file.

"There's no time!"

Monk grabbed the rest of the papers just as Nicholas pushed him out the door. They piled in behind the staff crashing their way to the exit.

"Whatever happens, get this to—"

Nicholas didn't hear Monk's last words as the explosion ripped through the office. Wood and glass splintered. Typewriters and telephones became lethal projectiles, hurled by the blast toward the fleeing crowd. Nicholas flung himself at Monk, trying to shield him. He was too late. The explosion was only the beginning. In the aftershock came a wall of flame.

Never in his life had Monk felt such pain. He smelled the sour-sweet odor of his hair burning and heard the crackle and spit as the flames devoured his clothes. Every breath he took set his lungs on fire, yet he remained hunched over, unconsciously protecting the precious contents in the accordion file. Then a terrible weight fell upon him. Monk dropped to his knees, fighting the blackness that threatened to engulf him. His oxygen-starved lungs betrayed him. His last act was to press the file even more tightly against his body.

Dazed but unhurt, Nicholas staggered to his feet. When he saw what was happening he threw himself on Monk, smothering the fire. The blast had leveled the room and there was no way to move forward through the flaming debris. The only way Nicholas could save himself and Monk was to reach the door on the far side of the room leading to the fire escape. Nicholas gripped Monk by his jacket collar.

The journey, measured in feet, seemed endless. The fire was spreading rapidly; worse, smoke blanketed the ceiling. Every time he needed a breath, Nicholas had to duck his head and take a lungful of air through a handkerchief held over his mouth. With the last of his strength, Nicholas threw his weight against the fire-escape door and staggered through it. He dragged Monk's body onto the tiny cast-iron platform and rolled him over.

Don't die on me!

Monk's chest labored mightily and his skin had already taken on a bluish gray tinge as his blood flow slowed. Nicholas bent over him, about to give mouth-to-mouth resuscitation, when the tortured words emerged.

"The file . . . only to Rose. You must do it. . . . Stop Steven . . ."

Nicholas heard the hee-haw wail of the fire engines.

"Hang on, Monk!"

"For Rose . . ."

The windows above them exploded and Lockwood threw his arms over his head to protect himself from the flying glass. When he looked at Monk he saw that his eyes were wide and still.

Nicholas pried Monk's fingers off the accordion file. For a second he hesitated, thinking it sacrilege to abandon a dead man.

For Rose . . .

Nicholas tucked the file under his arm and staggered down the steps.

* * *

Birch logs crackled and curled in the fireplace, their smoky odor a perfect complement to the scent of apple rising from the calvados in the snifter. It was nine o'clock and Steven Talbot was listening to the evening news on the radio. He let the international stories slip by but his attention sharpened when the broadcaster turned to local affairs.

The lead item was the fire in Zurich that had devastated the top three floors of a Banhofstrasse building. Tragically, nine people had died, including the eminent American publisher Monk McQueen, and Abraham Warburg, director of the International Refugee Location Service, in whose offices the fire had started. Witnesses reported hearing an explosion before the blaze and the authorities were investigating the possibility of a gas leak.

Steven raised his glass in a silent toast. It couldn't have been better. In one stroke both McQueen and the meddlesome Jew, Warburg, were dead. Von Kluge, who had personally built the incendiary device, guaranteed that not one scrap of paper would survive the aftermath of the explosion. That had been Steven's gut-wrenching worry. He had convinced Kurt Essenheimer that neither McQueen nor Warburg would ever accept tainted bait. That meant hooking the banker with the real documents with Steven's signature on them and later allowing McQueen to see them as well.

The risk had been enormous but it had paid off. The precious lifelines that girdled the globe would continue to supply Nazi Germany with badly needed war matériel. The money that followed would swell Steven Talbot's personal secret fortune.

And now I can go home.

Steven Talbot picked up a mirror and examined his features, something he did, reflexively, a hundred times a day. His skin was red, polished and hairless, like a bright MacIntosh apple. The lines at the corners of the brows slanted his eyes ever so slightly. On both sides of his face, running from cheek to jaw, were diagonal slashes created by the surgery and which would remain forever. He lifted the hair over his left ear and looked at the wrinkled, purple stump. Hoffmann and his surgical team had done their best. It had taken five years, but they had given him a face. But no matter how soft the light, it remained the face belonging to something from a child's nightmare.

"The time has come for you to pay," Steven said aloud.

He pictured Cassandra and reached out to touch the pain she must be feeling at this moment.

"I've taken Monk," he said softly. "Now I'm going to take the rest."

− 50 −

No one greeted Nicholas Lockwood when he stepped off the Pan-American clipper in Port Washington, New York, that June afternoon. As far as his superiors were concerned, he wasn't due in for another day.

Nicholas took the train to Penn Station and from there walked through Times Square. He felt like a stranger who had stumbled across a glittering, mysterious kingdom where there were lights, laughter, and song. The streets were jammed with servicemen, but in spite of the military uniforms a carnival atmosphere prevailed. There were lines in front of Toots Shor's and 21. Even before dusk had fallen, the doors to the Stork Club and Larue's were jammed. Inside the taverns along Third Avenue, jukeboxes poured out "Praise the Lord and Pass the Ammunition."

Nicholas wandered through all this in a daze. He remembered the gaunt, frightened refugees he had seen crossing into Spain, the suspicious, arrogant officials of Vichy, the cold brutal precision of German border guards a stone's throw from Switzerland. And then there was Zurich . . . Zurich, where he had been bloodied, and a decent, brave man had perished in an inferno Nicholas hadn't been able to stop.

Nicholas crossed Central Park where English nannies were gathering up their charges and putting away the yarn they used to knit sweaters for the troops. He looked up at the gleaming bronze roof of the Carlton Towers and pictured the young woman who lived there. Alone now. His small traveling case suddenly felt very heavy. He had no choice but to see Cassandra. After reading the contents of the file for which Monk had sacrificed his life, Nicholas couldn't ignore the obligation the older man had placed him under.

She was as beautiful as he remembered, but her face was paler and her blue eyes larger against the whiteness of her skin. Eyes ripe with grief, he thought. When she looked at him he felt the questions straining to get out, and behind them, the accusations.

"Please, come in."

She led him through to the terrace where, so long ago it seemed, the three of them had shared breakfast.

"When did you hear?" asked Nicholas.

Cassandra looked away to the park where lamps twinkled in the early evening.

"The day after he died. Jimmy Pearce—my father's editor-in-chief—came over. The minute I saw him, I knew."

Cassandra looked at Nicholas. "Did he suffer?"

Lockwood shook his head.

"Who are you?" Cassandra asked suddenly. "He never talked about you. He never told me anything about you."

Nicholas reached for her but as soon as his fingertips brushed hers, she flinched.

"I know it's no consolation, but he accomplished what he set out to do."

"And what was that?"

Nicholas hesitated. "I can't tell you the details. Only that it was very, very important."

Anger flashed in her eyes. "That's what everybody says! Jimmy's been calling Washington every day, badgering people in the State Department, but no one seems to know anything. For God's sake, Monk had fought his war! Why did you people drag him into another one?"

Cassandra knew her words were unfair but she didn't care. What could Nicholas Lockwood, a virtual stranger, understand about what had been taken from her?

"I have a right to know," she said.

"Yes, you do. And you will, I promise." Nicholas paused. "Have you seen your aunt?"

"Rose? Yes, she came over as soon as she heard. She was very kind, asked me if I needed anything. . . ."

"Do you?"

"Yes. Answers."

"I was with him when it happened. I tried to save him but I couldn't. Maybe if I had done something more . . . I'll never know."

Cassandra watched him struggle with the words, torn between saying enough to violate whatever orders he lived under and too little to satisfy her.

"I'm sorry," Cassandra said. "But he was everything I had. And still I can't be told why he had to die."

Nicholas opened his case and placed Monk's leather cigar wallet, his pocket-watch, and several other personal items on the table.

"I thought you would want these now. The rest will come home with him."

His hand dropped on his briefcase. It took every ounce of strength he possessed not to bring out the file he had carried from Zurich.

"I have to go now. I'll call you from Washington. When I get back—"

"No," Cassandra said quickly. "I don't want you to do that. Not unless you're ready to tell me what really happened."

"I wouldn't have it any other way," he said softly.

The briefcase sat on Lockwood's lap as the train rocked back and forth, carrying him to Washington.

I have the power now. I'm going to have to decide what to do.

Nicholas searched to find some guidance. The answer proved evasive.

Nicholas Lockwood seldom looked back at his life. He had never known his parents. It wasn't until he had reached his teens that the priests at the orphanage told him that he had spent his first few years of life at a Catholic charity home where volunteer nurses and housewives offered their time to raise children no one wanted.

When he was eight, Nicholas was transferred to another institution, one run by priests. By then he knew enough to realize he would never be adopted. Young wives wanted babies, not boys with silent, suspicious eyes. Nicholas kept to himself as much as possible. He stayed away from the gangs other boys formed but was quick to defend his territory with his fists.

Had it not been for his innate intelligence, Nicholas might have been turned out into the world at fourteen to begin a life of menial labor. But the priests saw promise in this strong, taciturn boy who was a natural leader. Nicholas excelled both on the playing field and in scholastic competition and became the first boy from the orphanage to go to Notre Dame on a full scholarship.

University honed Nicholas's character as much as it did his mind. Notre Dame became the home he'd never had and he honored it by winning the intercollegiate boxing title as well as several awards for excellence in mathematics. When asked by the yearbook editor to name one quality he valued above all others, Nicholas unhesitatingly answered, "Loyalty."

It was a reply someone must have been waiting to hear. A few weeks before he was to graduate, Nicholas was called to the dean's office. The man waiting for him introduced himself as Mr. Brown. He was in his midthirties, wore beautifully cut clothes, and had a distinct air of privilege. He tapped a thick file lying in front of him.

"Is loyalty really the most important thing to you?"

"Yes."

Mr. Brown studied him for a long time.

"There is going to be a war," he said at last. "It will be unlike anything we've ever witnessed. We will need men whose loyalty is unquestioned. Do you have that kind of loyalty, young Mr. Lockwood?"

Nicholas thought very carefully before he answered.

"Yes, sir. I do."

The man smiled faintly. "Yes, I think so too. Let me tell you about a little group called the Office of Strategic Services."

The day after his graduation, Nicholas Lockwood traded one home for another. The OSS was headquartered in Washington but had training areas throughout the country. Lockwood deciphered the secrets of cryptography at Foggy Bottom, practiced small-arms marksmanship and lethal hand-to-hand combat in the Virginia countryside, and jumped from airplanes during night drops high over the Adirondack Mountains. He lived with men to whom he entrusted his life and who in turn depended on him. From time to time, Mr. Brown would appear to monitor his progress and offer encouragement.

Having grown up relying only on himself, Nicholas gave what passed for a son's loyalty to this quiet, unobtrusive man. Between training sessions, Brown spoke to him about men who held power, how they had gained it and how they wielded it.

"You are their instrument, Nicholas. No matter how difficult the actions you will carry out, you must always remember there is a reason for and purpose to them. That is the foundation for your oath of loyalty. But there is something equally important that you need to know. Sometimes there will be no one to give you the order. You will have to act on your own. You will decide what loyalty demands under those circumstances."

As the express raced toward the capital, Nicholas remembered those words. By all rights he should hand the briefcase and its contents to his superiors at the OSS. That was his duty. But Nicholas couldn't get either the image of Monk or the sound of his last words out of his mind. A dying man had trusted him with a secret that could scandalize a nation and overturn one of its greatest families. Or, because such powerful people were involved, a secret that might be buried away forever. So why had he demanded that Nicholas take the evidence against Steven Talbot to his own mother, who could easily make it disappear?

You will have to decide what loyalty demands under the circumstances. . . .

The conductor came through the car, announcing that the express would arrive at Union Station in a few minutes. As he watched the Capitol lights come into view, Nicholas made his decision. Monk had grown up with Rose Jefferson. He probably knew her as well as anyone did.

As well as I have to know her . . .

Discovering the kind of woman Rose Jefferson was would be his starting point.

Three weeks after Monk McQueen died, Steven Talbot returned home.

"Good evening, Albany. Is my mother in?"

Steven chuckled at the elderly servant's horrified expression. By now he knew that people who saw his face couldn't help themselves. First there was surprise, followed by fear and revulsion.

"Master Steven?"

"It's me, Albany," Steven said, stepping over the threshold. "The new me."

"But why didn't you tell us you were coming? We would have sent the chauffeur for you—"

"There's a war on, Albany. Getting across the Atlantic, especially on the clipper, is the luck of the draw."

"Of course, sir, of course. If you'll just wait here I'll fetch Miss Jefferson."

Steven took a deep breath and looked around. A thousand memories came rushing back at him. From the little he had seen of New York from the cab, Steven had thought that Talbot House was one of the few such private homes remaining. Others he recognized along the way had been converted into consulates, museums, or, worse, apartments. The cost of maintaining Talbot House must be staggering, Steven realized, but he promised himself he would not let it go, ever. It had been his father's house and soon it would belong to him.

"Steven!"

Rose stood on the balcony that overlooked the foyer, her fingers curled tightly around the railing. All she saw was the top of Steven's head. Ever since she had returned from Switzerland she had kept imagining what her son's face looked like under the bandages. Then Steven looked up.

"Hello, Mother."

Rose shuddered and involuntarily pulled back. Her son was grotesque, his face a shiny pink mask that appeared to be stitched onto his skull.

Look at him. Don't stare. Walk down and welcome him home . . .

"You don't seem very happy to see me," Steven observed.

"No, it's not that at all." Rose laughed nervously. "I just didn't expect you to walk in like this. . . ."

She reached out tentatively and touched Steven's cheek.

"It's all right, Mother. I'm completely healed."

He pressed her hand to the side of his face. Rose cringed. The texture of the skin was rubbery and smooth, like that of a soft plastic doll. Not human but crafted by man.

Oh, my son, what have you made of yourself?

"Well, come on, then," Rose said. "You must be hungry. If I had known— But that doesn't matter. You can join us. I'll have Albany make another setting."

Steven followed his mother into the library. He noted how attractive she remained for a woman in her midfifties. Her back was straight, her head held regally high, her black hair full, with streaks of pure white spun through it. No wonder half of official Washington lived in fear of her and the other half fawned over her.

Then why is she so nervous?

"Company for dinner, Mother?" Steven asked as they crossed into the dining room. "If it's your Capitol Hill friends I'd better wash up—"

Steven froze when he entered the dining room. Seated on the far right of the long cherrywood table was Cassandra McQueen.

It was Cassandra's third visit to Talbot House in as many weeks. Ever since Monk's death, Rose had called her every day to make sure she was all right. Although Cassandra had Abilene, and Jimmy Pearce and other Q staffers came by frequently, she was grateful for Rose's concern. They had spent long hours together sharing memories of the man who had meant so much to both of them. Through Rose, Cassandra came to know a part of Monk he had never talked about, his adolescent crush on Rose, how he had tried to help her during her marriage to Simon, and how, ultimately, he had been rejected.

"Don't make that mistake," Rose warned her. "Don't ever pass love by thinking you'll find it again or that you can live without it."

Each time Cassandra came to Talbot House she truly believed that Rose was trying to make amends for what had happened between herself and Michelle. Up until the minute Steven Talbot walked through the doors.

"Cassandra, what a surprise."

Steven smiled as he watched the fear leap into the young woman's eyes. His homecoming was going to be better than he had ever dreamed.

"Steven . . ."

Albany appeared at Steven's side with a glass of scotch and soda. Steven held the crystal to the light.

"Thank God some things never change. You can't imagine how hard it is to get good whiskey these days." Steven raised his glass. "Cheers!"

Both women followed suit but neither returned the toast.

"I think I'd better go," Cassandra said, pushing back her chair. She felt the walls closing in on her and began shivering, as though Steven had carried with him the cold, wet darkness of the catacombs.

"Not on my account," Steven replied. "You haven't finished your dinner."

"You heard about Monk," Rose said.

Steven nodded. "Yes. Tragic story."

"It was," Rose said faintly. "It's been very difficult for Cassandra. For both of us. Yet it brought us closer. . . ."

"How wonderful," Steven said, unable to keep the sarcasm out of his voice.

"Steven!"

He leaned back, making a temple with his fingers.

"Mother, what would you say if I told you that Cassandra here isn't related to us at all?"

"I'd say you were overtired and not responsible for your words," Rose snapped.

"And if I further told you that I have proof that Uncle Franklin couldn't possibly have been her father?"

Cassandra's fork clattered off the table as her fist smacked the wood.

"How dare you say that!"

"Very easily!" Steven withdrew a sheet of paper from his jacket pocket and handed it to Rose. His eyes bored into Cassandra. "This is part of Franklin's medical record. It lists the childhood diseases he had . . . among them, the mumps. Do you know what mumps can result in, Cassandra? Infertility! Franklin Jefferson was infertile. He didn't father you. He couldn't have had children with anyone!"

"That's not true!"

Rose gripped Cassandra's hand.

"Where did you get this, Steven?"

"When I was in Europe I heard disturbing rumors about Michelle and another man," Steven replied. "Apparently Michelle and he had been lovers for some time, even when she was married to Franklin. Although I knew who this man was, I didn't say anything because I had no proof. On my way back here I stopped in London and persuaded Pritchard to let me have a look at Franklin's medical file. When I saw that he had had the mumps and that Pritchard's own tests showed he was infertile, I knew the rumors had to be true."

"You're a liar!" Cassandra spat out.

"No!" Steven shouted. "You're the one who's been living a lie. And so have the rest of us because of it. You don't belong in this family any more than your slut of a mother did."

Cassandra wrenched her hand free and flung a heavy water glass at Steven. Her aim was wild and the glass sailed harmlessly over Steven's shoulder, smashing on the floor.

"That," he said softly, "doesn't change the fact that Monk McQueen was your real father!"

"Enough!" Rose stood up from the table, glaring at her son. "I want to talk to you!"

"Of course, Mother."

Steven watched as Rose came around to Cassandra and put an arm around her, slowly guiding her from the room. As they left he ran his fingers over the

437

now familiar texture of his skin. The price Cassandra had to pay had been rendered.

Rose Jefferson reached deep inside herself to find the strength to control the rage and questions that hammered at her. She told a bewildered Albany to have the car and driver brought around at once and led Cassandra out to the portico.

"I'm sorry," Cassandra whispered. "I didn't mean to do that. It's just that he was saying those terrible things. . . ."

"Shh, don't worry," Rose told her. "Marcus will drive you home. I'll get to the bottom of this, believe me!"

As the car glided away, Rose marched back into the house. There was no doubt that the paper Steven had given her was part of Franklin's medical file. She recognized Pritchard's handwriting and signature. But infertility!

Rose thought back to her childhood days with Franklin. He *had* been sick with the mumps. She remembered that the doctors had been worried because the illness lingered stubbornly. But as soon as Franklin recovered, everyone had forgotten about it. Was it possible that Franklin never knew he was infertile? That *no one* had ever known?

Why should they have? Or he? He was always so healthy and athletic. Who would have suspected?

However, right now there were other questions that needed answers. Rose turned away from the dining room, walked swiftly to the library, and slammed the door behind her.

"Why did you do this?"

Steven looked up at her from his drink. "Do you believe me?"

When Rose didn't reply, he said, "You do, don't you? Just as well. I'm sorry I shattered your illusions, especially since you and Cassandra were becoming so chummy."

"You haven't answered my question," Rose reminded him tonelessly.

"I thought that would have been self-evident. Michelle's legal claim to Global rested entirely on her being Franklin's wife. When she died she left her legacy to someone we all believed was their daughter. But Cassandra couldn't have been their child. Therefore, the legacy can be invalidated. We'll have the traveler's checks back where they belong, in Global Europe."

"And I suppose you intend to keep running that part of the company."

Steven was puzzled by his mother's caustic tone. "Of course."

"Well, you're not."

Ice cubes rattled as Steven set his glass on a table.

"I beg your pardon?" he said hoarsely.

"You heard me."

Rose steeled herself for what she had to say next. Sentence by cold sentence, she laid out everything she knew about Steven's secret connection to the Nazis. The details shocked him. His mother quoted the names of the shell companies Steven hid behind, how many ships these dummy corporations had leased, the cargo they carried, and who the suppliers were. She named Kurt Essenheimer as Steven's conduit in the Reich, and presented Steven with figures detailing how much profit he had made.

Steven was devastated by the extent of Rose's information. His mind was racing, trying to comprehend how his mother could have unearthed it.

Zurich!

That was the only possible answer. In spite of all the news reports and his agent's personal assurances, the fire that had devastated the offices of the International Refugee Location Service had not destroyed everything. Something in the file with which Steven had lured Monk to the Swiss capital had survived. Enough to convince Rose of his complicity and motivate her to begin the hunt to determine the extent of his guilt.

Steven was tempted to try to bluff his way out, deny everything. One look at Rose convinced him it was too late for that.

"You not only betrayed your country and the company, Steven," Rose said, "you betrayed me. Do you know what could happen to Global, given its government contracts and my seat on presidential commissions, if word of your activities gets out? My God, when I think back to everything I've told you about the decisions and policies that were being made in Washington . . . Did you tell Essenheimer everything?"

Steven's silence spoke for itself.

Rose was on the verge of tears. "Why? For God's sake, why?"

Steven felt his skin tighten painfully across his face, as it always did when he became angry.

"Why?" he repeated. "You have the audacity to ask me that after I grew up in this house, watching you plot and scheme, all for the greater glory of Global Enterprises? You destroyed your husband, *my father*, because of your precious Global. You wouldn't let anything or anyone stand in your way. You killed your own brother as surely as if you had put the bullet in his head. I learned it all very well, Mother. Because I had the best teacher—you!

"Sure I did business with Essenheimer and the rest of them. I wanted Global Europe to be bigger and better than it was before. I did exactly what you would have done. So please, spare me the holier-than-thou attitude. It doesn't become you."

"You're wrong, son!" Rose whispered.

"Look at yourself, Mother," Steven sneered. "I'm exactly what you made me. I learned my lessons well. Power, that's all that matters. And now I have it!"

"Is that so?"

"It is! No one need be any the wiser about what I've done. The Nazis are bound to lose the war, but in the meantime we'll make millions. The invisible empire I created will remain exactly that. After the war, we'll be stronger than ever."

"What about Cassandra?" asked Rose. "How does she fit in to your grand scheme?"

"She doesn't. Our lawyers will see to that!"

Rose drew herself up and placed both palms on the table. "You've had your say, now I'll have mine. I've already decided what you're going to do. God help me that I never saw what was happening to you, but I didn't. I'll have to live with that and pay for it for the rest of my life. But you too have to make restitution.

"You betrayed your country, Steven, so now you will serve it. I'm going to arrange a noncombatant commission for you. You'll be as far away from Germany, Global, and Cassandra as possible. In Japan. As for what you so grandly call your empire, I'm going to dismantle it brick by brick. You were right about one thing: no one will ever know what you've done. But neither will I allow you to perpetuate this horror."

Steven's crimson face became mottled in anger.

"You wouldn't dare do that! You can't!"

"I can and I will," Rose told him coldly.

"But what if something happens to me? I'm the only heir! Your own flesh and blood."

"Flesh and blood, yes. But who are you in your soul? And as for heirs, Steven, there is Cassandra. Yes, it seems that Michelle hid the truth about her daughter's real father from me. But she did it because she felt she had to. She was afraid I'd do exactly what you're suggesting: take away everything she built. I'm not going to do that, Steven. What was Michelle's now belongs to Cassandra."

Rose paused. "As for you, Steven, I'm going to disown you. Since I'll never be able to trust you again, you can forget having anything to do with Global."

Hours later, Rose was sitting in the conservatory of the dark house. Everyone had gone to bed, including Steven. She had made sure of that. In the silence she heard the blood roaring in her veins.

The latch on the French doors leading to the garden turned. A figure entered out of the gloom.

"Mr. Lockwood?" Rose called out.

Nicholas stepped into the light, his face expressionless.

"Did you talk to him?"

"Yes."

"And?"

"I told him I knew everything and that he and Essenheimer were finished. I will also see to it that he joins one of the services and is never again involved with Global."

Nicholas remained silent.

"That is what you wanted, isn't it?"

"Yes."

At first, Nicholas hadn't been able to grasp, much less believe, the magnitude of Steven Talbot's treachery. Given his sense of loyalty, he had been sorely tempted to ignore Monk's plea, hand the file over to his superiors, and watch as Steven Talbot was exposed as a traitor who would pay the ultimate penalty. Yet Monk's last words had held him back.

Did he want me to give Rose Jefferson the file because he never stopped loving her?

In view of Monk's relationship to Michelle, that answer made no sense.

He didn't say, "give." He said, "take."

Nicholas seized the thread. Why would a dying man use the last of his energies to make such a fine distinction?

Because he wasn't about to trust Rose Jefferson completely!

Rose was to be shown evidence of Steven's treachery but it was Nicholas who was to ensure, by the threat of exposure, that Rose would put an end to Steven's madness.

"Are you satisfied that I've kept my part of the bargain, Mr. Lockwood?" Rose asked.

"Yes."

"And I have your word that you'll keep yours?"

"I told my superiors that whatever it was Monk had gone to Zurich for had been destroyed in the explosion. They have no reason not to believe me. But just the same I'll keep the documents in a safe place. If anything should happen to me I guarantee you they'll end up in Washington."

"I surmised as much," Rose said. "And I'll trust you on that. You're not a blackmailer."

"There is one thing you haven't told me," Nicholas said softly. "Did Steven admit that he knew about the bomb in Zurich, that killing Monk was part of the plan all along?"

Rose looked away. "I couldn't bring myself to ask him that. Because, you see, I knew in my heart that if Steven was capable of dealing with the likes of Kurt Essenheimer, he was perfectly capable of murder. And I don't know what I'll ever be able to do about that . . . except live with it."

441

Rose turned back to Nicholas Lockwood. "So if you wanted your pound of flesh, Mr. Lockwood, there it is."

After Lockwood departed, Rose went upstairs, not to bed but to her office. She sat behind her ornately carved Australian lacewood desk and, with her elbows on the blotter, rested her head on intertwined fingers. For the briefest moment a wave of self-pity swept through her.

All my life I have tried to protect and build on what was left to me. Was that so wrong? Were there other things, more important things, that I should have done?

Rose shook off the creeping despair. She was fifty-two years old. She could no more change the decisions of the past than she could turn back her own years. What Steven had wrought had to be dealt with here and now.

As she had promised Lockwood, the pipeline supplying Nazi Germany would be shut down. She would look after this personally, making sure that not even a hint of impropriety would taint Global. If any of Steven's cohorts tried to oppose her she would crush them.

But neither resolve nor ruthlessness helped when Rose faced her second question. Every instinct in Rose told her that Steven had had a hand in Monk's death. But did it end there? Were there other "accidents" Steven could have plotted?

She thought back to Cassandra's kidnapping and the death—or murder?—of Michelle. Could Steven's determination to control Global Europe and hide his secret alliance have driven him to kill the one person who might inadvertently have exposed him? Steven's face, so distorted and unnatural, swam into her mind. She thought of him sleeping upstairs and shivered.

I'm afraid . . . I'm terrified of my own son!

The tiny key rattled in the lock as Rose opened the desk drawer. She withdrew a slim, leather-bound folder and opened it to a marked page.

"I have to know if he had anything to do with Cassandra's kidnapping and Michelle's death. I won't rest until I'm certain. And if he did, then I have to protect Cassandra. Harry, poor Harry who was never found . . . He's the key. He's the one I have to find. He's the only one who knows what really happened in the catacombs. . . ."

And Rose knew just the man to turn to.

The mantelpiece clock struck two. There was one last thing to do. Rose read the final page of her last will and testament. It had been drafted the day, so full of promise, when Steven had joined the company. On his birthday Rose had made Steven sole heir to the Global fortune.

Rose picked up her pen, prepared to cross out his name. The nib wavered.

Her hand began to shake so violently that ink dashed across the page. The pen clattered onto the paper and Rose buried her face in her hands, sobbing.

— 51 —

The scene replayed itself over and over in her mind: Steven's sudden appearance at Talbot House, the sight of his ruined face, the evil words he had unleashed that had dug deep into Cassandra's imagination and become tenacious roots.

It's not true! It can't be true! Cassandra thought as she lay in the darkness in her room. A single question prevented her from believing this: Why hadn't Rose called her? Had she been convinced by what Steven had said?

Am I?

The question whirled in Cassandra's mind. Could Monk have been her real father? If so, why had he and Michelle hidden the truth from her? As she fell into a restless sleep, Cassandra at least knew where she could begin to search for the answer.

Charles Portman was a short, balding man with soft hands and a warm smile that revealed two rows of perfectly formed teeth no larger than baby teeth. He had been Monk's lawyer for years and had drawn up his will. As soon as word of Monk's death had been made official, he had told Cassandra, informally, that she was the only beneficiary to his estate.

"I know how difficult a time this must be for you," Portman said now. "You're bearing up very well."

Cassandra smiled wanly. She had called the attorney to ask if Monk had left any papers with him and whether she could see them. Portman promised to check.

Portman handed an envelope to Cassandra. "We were in luck. The probate court released the contents of Monk's safety deposit box yesterday afternoon. There were some stocks and bonds, which we can look at later. And this."

Cassandra turned the envelope over and saw her name. Monk must have typed this himself. She recognized his typewriter's jumpy *r* in her name.

"I don't have any idea what it's all about," Portman told her. "You can read it in the conference room if you like."

Alone at a table that seated twenty, Cassandra held on to the envelope as though afraid to open it. Finally, she gathered her courage, ran a fingernail under the flap, and removed the folded sheets of paper, smoothing them out. She had read only three words when a strangled cry broke in her throat: *"My darling daughter . . ."*

The paper was twenty years old, brittle at the edges. The black ink was fading to a midnight blue. But the writing was indisputably Monk's.

"You can't imagine how difficult it was for your mother and me not to tell you the truth. But there were reasons for this and we hope that you will try your best to understand them. We never meant to hurt you, pumpkin, never. . . ."

Monk held back nothing. He spoke of the time when, amid the turbulence that had overtaken Michelle, she and he had become lovers.

"It wasn't because she needed Franklin any less but she needed our love more."

Page by page, Monk led her through the terrible legal battles that had raged after Michelle had come forward with Franklin's codicil and the court's ultimate decision to uphold Michelle's claim to the traveler's-check operation.

"She fought not so much for herself but for you. . . ."

Little by little Monk's revelations revealed the answers to all the tiny questions that had sprung up at various stages in Cassandra's life: why Michelle had so seldom spoken about Franklin, why there had been few pictures of the two of them together, why she kept a strict distance from Rose. Once upon a time Michelle had been able to explain all of them away.

Cassandra put aside the letter. She understood so much now. That this man, whom she had loved with all her heart, had really been her father made her heart glow. Not all the love in the world would bring him back, but now, at least, she could mourn him properly.

When Monk's body arrived from Zurich, Cassandra went alone to the docks to claim it. Then she and Jimmy Pearce looked after the funeral arrangements. Afterward, she called on Rose at Talbot House.

"I can't tell you how ashamed I am about what Steven did," Rose said. "But I don't want you to worry. Steven will be going away soon. . . ."

Cassandra caught the deep sorrow in Rose's voice. Something awful must have happened in the house. She wondered if what she had come to tell Rose could wait. Cassandra hesitated, then handed Rose Monk's letter, waiting silently as Rose read it through.

"Why are you showing me this?" Rose asked when she was finished reading.

"So that we both know the truth. Regardless of how Steven might have intended to use what he knew, he was still right. Monk was my father."

"Aren't you afraid that I might petition the courts to have the traveler's-check operations returned to me?"

"Even if you didn't believe Steven, you still would have investigated, to satisfy yourself," Cassandra replied. "And then you would have been faced with the same choice. Do you really want to try to take away what my mother left me?"

The question seemed so simple, yet it loomed as imposing as any Rose had ever faced. She remembered Michelle sitting across from her, her belly swollen, telling her that she was carrying Franklin's child. She had used her pregnancy by another man to keep what she had helped Franklin build.

Would I have acted differently under the circumstances? Haven't I done things exactly like that? If I challenge Cassandra, and win, who's going to benefit after I'm gone? She's all I have left now.

"Your mother and I fought our battles," Rose said. "Remember what I told you about repeating one's mistakes." She came forward and embraced Cassandra. "I don't intend to do that with you."

They buried Monk McQueen in a small cemetery on Long Island, outside the village of Quogue, where he had had a vacation home. Rose and Cassandra stepped out of the Silver Ghost and together walked past the hundreds of mourners from the journalistic, financial, and government communities who had come to pay their final respects. When she reached the grave Rose looked past the casket out onto the waters.

Too many funerals, she thought. *I've buried too many good men.*

Rose, in her diamond-pattern veil, laid a single white rose on the casket and stepped back. She listened to Cassandra deliver the eulogy, letting the world know for the first time that Monk had been her father in so much more than just name.

She'll be just fine, Rose thought proudly. *I'll see to that.*

If it hadn't been for the constant flood of war news, perhaps the revelation of Cassandra's true identity would have created a greater stir. As it was, Cassandra dodged the reporters who pursued her and referred to her attorney those who called her at home.

"You certainly are one for surprises," Charles Portman had said with mock gruffness when he met Cassandra for the reading of the will. "Just like your father. That alone should have tipped me off. But you know, in all these years I never suspected a thing."

Cassandra had smiled and glanced at the stacks of papers and documents. "It looks more formidable than it really is," Portman apologized. "The terms of the will are pretty basic. Monk left almost everything to you. There's a small

445

bequest to Abilene. The day-to-day running of Q magazine passes to Jimmy Pearce and the editorial board. You become majority shareholder with sixty percent of the magazine's shares; the rest is distributed to the employees under a profit-sharing plan. Naturally, the Carlton Towers apartment and all Monk's personal possessions revert to you."

Portman ran a pencil down a column of figures.

"Which means that your net worth is a little over two million dollars." He sat back and folded his hands across his kettledrum belly. "Are you sure there's nothing further you want me to bring up with Rose Jefferson?"

After Cassandra had shown Portman Monk's letter and told him about her discussion with Rose, the attorney had called Rose. The two of them had met alone. Portman had told Cassandra he was satisfied with the outcome.

"No," Cassandra replied.

"How are you feeling now?"

Cassandra smiled. "Better."

It was true. Slowly, the numbness left by Monk's death was beginning to seep from her body, like cold working its way out of flesh warmed by a fire. Cassandra kept telling herself that in the end she'd always had a father and now she had the comfort of his memory. She clung to the last image she had of him just before he'd left for Europe. Monk smiling and confident, with no fear or regret.

"Any ideas as to what you'll do now?" Portman asked.

That was the easiest question to answer.

"Exactly what my father would have wanted."

The next day Cassandra went to the offices of Q magazine to see Jimmy Pearce and the editorial board. The meeting was held in Monk's office, which had been left untouched. It seemed to Cassandra to have become a kind of shrine and she was distinctly uncomfortable when Pearce showed her around the desk. The atmosphere was all the more somber because the usual banter and camaraderie was missing.

"I didn't earn the privilege of sitting here," Cassandra said, tapping the arms of Monk's chair.

"You're the boss now," Jimmy Pearce reminded her.

"But I'm not Monk. I know he's gone, and I miss him every bit as much as you do."

She glanced at the men slouching against the wall, their arms crossed. The spark and hustle had gone out of them. They looked lost and defeated.

"Look at you," Cassandra said, shaking her head. "You seem to think the world's come to an end. Is this how you mourn him, by letting what he believed in and lived for fade away? Or maybe you think I'm going to walk in here and give you a pep talk, tell you what you should be doing? Well, I'm not. I can't hold a candle to any one of you but I'll be damned if I'll sit by and watch this magazine fall apart because he's gone."

"Cass, that's not fair!" Jimmy Pearce protested. "We're like family here."

"Yes, we are! And during the toughest times a family has to pull together. Do you think that if he were here Monk would stand for your attitude? This place has become a mausoleum!"

The men glanced at one another in embarrassment. Cassandra rose and went over to the editor-in-chief.

"Jimmy, get me some boxes so I can pack Monk's things. In the meantime you can all decide whether this magazine is going to carry on or if it too has died."

Cassandra watched with dismay as the men retreated. With tears in her eyes, she opened the glass cabinets and blindly began stacking books on the desk. She lifted the framed photographs, citations, and awards off the walls, careful not to look at any of them. The memories threatened to choke her. She heard the knock on the door and, not bothering to turn around, said, "Come in."

They did, all of them, the entire office staff from Pearce to the copy boys.

"We'd like to help," Pearce said. "If you want us to."

Cassandra's face lit up.

"All of us agreed that this was going to be your office from now on," Pearce continued. "Because we expect you to show up for work. Just like the rest of us. Monk wouldn't have had it any other way."

Someone opened a bottle of wine, glasses appeared as if out of nowhere, and as she raised hers for the toast Cassandra knew everything was going to be all right.

Abilene was waiting for Cassandra when she returned to Carlton Towers.

"You got yourself a visitor," she said, giving her a big wink.

"Who is it?"

"Why don't you go see for yourself?"

Her curiosity piqued, Cassandra went into Monk's study. There was no one in the room. Then she saw a shadow fall across the balcony. Cassandra opened the French doors.

"Mr. Lockwood!"

He turned to her, his green eyes lighting up with pleasure.

"Hello, Cassandra. It's good to see you again."

Cassandra was flustered. After their painful encounter she had never expected to see Nicholas Lockwood again. Yet, she hadn't been able to put him out of her mind. Cassandra remembered her last words to Lockwood and shivered.

"Why are you here?" she asked.

"To pay my condolences."

"The funeral was a few days ago, Mr. Lockwood. I didn't see you."

"I was there." Nicholas placed a briefcase on the patio table. "I have a lot of things to tell you, if you still want to hear them."

Cassandra's heart was racing. "Only the truth, Mr. Lockwood."

Nicholas began by explaining the circumstances under which he had met Monk in Washington.

"The only thing I knew about him was that he was a publisher. I couldn't figure out why the government was interested in him. Until he showed me these."

Nicholas brought out the papers detailing the human pipeline Monk and Abraham Warburg had been running out of Germany.

"My father told me about this," Cassandra said quietly.

Nicholas raised an eyebrow. "Then I guess you also know that it was your mother's money and initiative that saved thousands of lives. When she died, your father kept it running with Rose Jefferson's help."

"*Rose* knew about this?" Cassandra was stunned.

Nicholas nodded. "And she's taken over from your father."

"Is that why the Germans killed him in Zurich?" Cassandra demanded. "To stop him?"

"That's what Washington thinks. But the government doesn't know the whole story because I didn't tell them everything."

Nicholas drew out the papers that revealed Steven Talbot's link to Nazi Germany.

"For years Monk had heard rumors that Steven was one of the Reich's major suppliers but he was never able to get the proof. When the opportunity finally presented itself, he went to Zurich. All he would tell Washington was that he had access to information that could change the course of the war. Because of his reputation, the government took him at his word. They also sent me to make sure nothing happened to him."

Cassandra was touched by the sorrow in his voice. Nicholas Lockwood had not forgiven himself. She was ashamed of the angry words she had said to him the last time they'd met.

As she read the documents that proved Steven's complicity with the Nazis, Cassandra felt herself grow cold.

"Was Steven responsible for my father's death?"

"There's no hard proof."

"But you think he was."

"I'm sure of it."

Cassandra was struck by his words. If Steven had murdered her father, then . . . Cassandra remembered the catacombs, when she had been fighting for her life. She had almost killed a man who, everyone later claimed, had been trying to save her. But Cassandra wondered why no one had asked the question she now thought was so obvious: If Steven Talbot had been trying to help her, who was the man who had been trying to murder her? When she had swung the lamp, it shattered against her attacker's face. It had burned him. Burned *Steven* . . .

"Cassandra, are you all right?"

Cassandra gripped his arm. "Does Rose know about Steven?"

"Everything."

"Then why hasn't Steven been arrested?"

"Because I made a deal with her. I showed her everything and told her it would be handed over to the government unless she threw Steven out of Global and got him the hell away from New York, then used her influence to dismantle everything he had set up for the Nazis."

"But why?" Cassandra cried. "Steven's a murderer."

"So far the Zurich police haven't any leads as to who killed your father. And there's precious little chance they'll get any. The killers disappeared into Germany long ago. One day we may find them and connect them to Steven. But not with the war on."

Cassandra slumped back in her chair, not knowing what to think. After all this, how could she ever face Rose again?

As though reading her thoughts, Nicholas said, "I'm not asking you to forget what Steven did. I'll do everything I can to find the men who killed your father and prove they were acting on Steven's orders. But you mustn't blame Rose for what happened. She had no idea what Steven was up to."

"If we can't do anything, why did you tell me this?" Cassandra demanded.

"Because I promised your father I'd finish what he began. He could have had me deliver these documents to the government, and Rose, along with Steven, would have been ruined. But Monk understood that Rose, with the power at her command, was the strongest weapon against Steven. In effect, he forced a mother to turn against her own son."

"Do you really think she'll do that?"

Lockwood's eyes hardened. "I still have the evidence," he said. "I'd like to believe I'll never have to use it, but if I must . . ." His tone left no doubt that he would carry out this threat.

"I'd better be going now," Nicholas said. "I'm terribly sorry you had to learn all this now. But I felt I owed it to you . . . and Monk."

"Nicholas," Cassandra called after him. "I want you to stay."

He turned around, puzzled. "Why?"

"Because we have to continue what my father and Abraham Warburg started."

"I was very much hoping you'd say that."

- 52 -

By February 1943, the tides of war had turned in favor of the Allies. American and Australian troops pushed the Japanese out of southern New Guinea and Guadalcanal in the Solomon Islands had fallen to U.S. Marines. The air force also stepped up its attacks, sinking twenty-one Japanese troop transports in the Battle of the Bismarck Sea.

At Q magazine, Cassandra chalked up each Allied victory as word came in. She had taken over Monk's office but the heart of the magazine had moved across the hall where Jimmy Pearce and his editorial staff worked. Relieved that Q had gotten its old spirit back, Cassandra busied herself translating editorials and other pieces destined for Europe, putting in the same long hours as everyone else. The only difference was that her day did not end when she left the office.

With Nicholas on leave from Washington, Cassandra was ready to begin. "Since Abraham Warburg is gone, whom do we contact?"

"We start with the employees who survived," Nicholas replied. "Your father and Warburg would have hand-picked them so we know they're trustworthy. They can help us reestablish contact with the underground in Occupied Europe and Germany. We'll also have to find out who Warburg dealt with at the Swiss Credit Bank, how the money was transferred from here and channeled into Germany. I've persuaded the people I work for to let me run with this. Monk and Abraham Warburg provided us with some of the best intelligence Washington ever got out of Occupied Europe. The government would give its eyeteeth to have more. But my staying on depends on our getting results."

"We will," Cassandra promised.

It took Cassandra and Nicholas three months to reestablish the financial pipeline that then fed both the growing Resistance groups in Occupied Europe and the networks that provided escape routes for refugees. The two of them often worked late into the night, going over the intricate details of money transfers, entry visas, and transportation arrangements. Over time Cassandra felt herself more and more drawn to this quiet, intense man who had appeared in her life. She missed Nicholas when he was in Washington and found her heart beating faster whenever she waited for him to get off the train at Grand Central Station. There was a quiet solidity about him that she hungered for. As grisly details about concentration camps and mass slaughter poured in from Europe, he became her only refuge in a world gone mad.

At first, Nicholas was reluctant to say very much about himself. While Cassandra appreciated that a lot of his work with the OSS was classified, she refused to believe that the rest of his life was equally secret.

"It's not fair that you know so much about me and I know next to nothing about you," she told him.

"I'm just an ordinary guy," Nicholas replied lightly.

"Why don't you let me find out for myself?" Cassandra challenged.

"It could be dangerous."

"How?"

"Because I might fall in love with you."

Cassandra blushed. Yet it was true. She hadn't missed the way Nicholas sometimes looked at her, or how his hand rested a little too long on hers when he touched her, and their eyes met and held.

As the weeks passed, Cassandra found herself stealing moments to take herself and Nicholas away from their work. They went for a carriage ride through Central Park and later walked into Greenwich Village to watch the old men play chess in Washington Square Park. She listened carefully as little by little, Nicholas told her about his life.

"One day, when this is all over, I'm going to build a new life for myself," he told her as they strolled along the Hudson piers, watching the troop and supply ships being loaded.

Linking her arm through his, Cassandra looked up at him.

Will I be a part of that life?

As March raced by, Nicholas began spending more and more time in Washington. Cassandra worked long hours in his absence so that they could have as much time as possible when they were together. One day, when she heard the doorbell, Cassandra flew to answer it only to find herself face to face with Rose.

"You look as though you've seen a ghost," Rose said.

"I'm . . . I'm sorry. I thought you might be someone else."

"A certain Mr. Lockwood?"

When she saw Cassandra blush, Rose added quickly, "I didn't mean to tease you, Cassandra. I've heard the two of you have been seeing a good deal of each other." Rose paused. "Is that why you haven't returned my calls?"

After Cassandra showed her inside, she said, "It's not only that, Rose."

Rose lifted her chin a fraction. "I see. Nicholas told you about Steven."

Cassandra nodded.

"Did he also tell you I had no idea what he was doing?"

"Yes. And I'm not blaming you for anything."

"You may think you're not, but I feel you are," Rose said. "I know the kind of work you've been doing with Nicholas and I'm very proud of you. But I don't want you to forget Global. You're a part of it, Cassandra. I want you to be there."

"I don't know if I can," Cassandra began.

"I think you should," said a voice behind her.

Cassandra whirled around and raced into Nicholas's arms.

"Why didn't you call to tell me you were coming?" she scolded.

Nicholas smiled and turned to Rose. "A pleasure to see you, Miss Jefferson."

"Hello, Nicholas." Rose folded up her sable. "I hope the two of you will come for dinner soon."

"Thank you, but I don't think that will be possible," said Nicholas. "You see, I'll be traveling for a little while. . . ."

It was very late in the evening and they were sitting in front of the fireplace in the library. The smell of birch drifted in the room and the wind caked the windows with frost.

"Washington is sending me to the Pacific," Nicholas said, staring into the flames.

"When?"

"The day after tomorrow."

"So soon! Can't you change that? We have so much work to do."

"I wish I could. I wish it more than anything else in the world."

From his tone, Cassandra knew he meant it. "Do you know where you're going?"

"Hawaii first. After that . . ." He shrugged, reached out, and touched her fingertips. "Washington will be shutting down the Zurich pipeline. The OSS found other ways to fund the Resistance movements. But you've made a great contribution, Cass. Monk would have been very proud of you."

"And as a reward, they're taking you away from me. Don't you know I love you, Nicholas?"

The words came out before she had a chance to think and they lay between them like a golden treasure suddenly revealed. His hand cupped her cheek, then slid along to the soft fine hair at the back of her neck as their lips met, and all at once she was holding him tightly against her, her head flung back as his kisses fell like soft rain upon her throat.

452

"That first morning," he whispered. "That's when I fell in love with you. I never stopped."

"Make love to me, Nicholas. . . ."

They fell away together, locked in their embrace. Cassandra's hair cascaded over his face as his hands roamed the length of her body, peeling away her clothes. She shuddered as his tongue ran over her breasts, then began its slow exploration.

Time and place lost their meaning. Cassandra felt herself propelled into an unknown world of heat and light where every second brought with it a new and wonderful discovery. Without realizing it she began rocking, gasping as her pleasure soared and peaked. Then Nicholas settled between her thighs, probing her wetness. Cassandra arched as he slowly entered her. For a moment they lay very still. Then slowly he began to move, guiding her away from the pain into a rhythm that made their newfound glory explode all over again.

"Will I hear from you?"

"I'll write whenever I can. I promise."

They were naked in front of the fire, their skin glistening with sweat, the scent of their lovemaking heavy in the still air. Cassandra promised herself she wouldn't cry but tears overwhelmed her.

"Just when I've found you, I'm losing you."

"You'll never lose me. I'll come back home to you."

Cassandra rolled over, one arm flung across his chest. "I'm going to hold you to that," she said, repeating the words she had teased him with the first time they had met.

Nicholas recognized and smiled. "Count on it."

Nicholas left from Grand Central Station, where Cassandra had so often waited for him. It wasn't until the train was pulling out that she really believed he was going. Then, along with the rest of the lovers, wives, and mothers, Cassandra shed her tears and walked out into the snowy streets alone.

I'm not going to let the war take him. I'm not going to lose him the way I lost Monk.

The next morning, Cassandra called Rose and told her she was ready to come to Global. She would do whatever she could to end this dreadful situation.

Because *Q* magazine had its finger on the pulse of financial America, Cassandra was very much aware that for a handful of people, the war turned out to be a cornucopia filled with riches beyond their wildest dreams. Some, like Rose, found it impossible not to make money.

"We're working flat-out," Rose told Cassandra as she escorted her through the various divisions of the company on her first day.

She introduced Cassandra to her senior executives and explained that from now on Cassandra would be working as her personal assistant.

"There's a lot to be said for working your way up," she said. "But not in your case. I want you to have an overview of the whole operation so that you know exactly what it is we do."

Cassandra was both impressed and bewildered. From the outside Global was just another faceless behemoth that labored in its own mysterious ways. But inside the headquarters on Lower Broadway, hundreds of people worked together to create a huge nerve center that controlled the efforts of tens of thousands of people across the country and in what was left of the free world. Freight rolled across the country day and night, the boxcars and flatbeds, trucks and cargo ships ferrying everything from tanks to uniforms. Industries controlled from Lower Broadway ran three full shifts a day, bringing hundreds of thousands of women into the factory lines. Every week, in newspapers across the country, Global ran ads for skilled managers and technicians, offered on-the-job training, and promised to match wages paid by any competitor. The only parts of the company that didn't share in the boom were the traveler's checks and money orders. The former had come to a virtual standstill because of the occupation of Europe, while profits from the latter plummeted due to domestic war policies.

It took Cassandra several weeks to become accustomed to the hectic pace at Lower Broadway. Since Rose seemed to need almost no sleep at all, Cassandra found herself getting up at five o'clock in the morning to be ready at six, when Rose picked her up. At first, Cassandra simply listened and watched. With the help of Hugh O'Neill and Eric Gollant, who quickly befriended her, she learned about current company projects, which had priority, and which were in the development stage. Using her experience at Q magazine, Cassandra tackled the job of translating everything from instruction manuals to confidential company directives destined for branch offices in South America and Switzerland. Although she seemed to be doing a dozen things at once, Rose kept an eye on Cassandra, helping, advising, and encouraging her.

As Cassandra's confidence grew, she began to deal on her own with Rose's principal advisers, who, unexpectedly, opened the doors to a whole different view of Rose Jefferson. One day Cassandra came across references to a foundation that she'd never before heard of. When she mentioned this to Eric Gollant, the accountant took her aside and showed her the books.

"Rose is very private about this sort of thing so I wouldn't talk about it," he advised Cassandra. "She organized the foundation at the beginning of the war to help our women employees, those whose husbands are drafted and who suddenly find themselves without a paycheck. The foundation also helps the widows and children of Global employees killed in action."

As Cassandra went through the books she discovered hundreds of trust and scholarship funds set up for Global employees and their families. Thousands of dollars were earmarked for retraining disabled veterans, while thousands more were poured into charitable organizations such as the Red Cross.

But there were secrets about Rose Jefferson that not even her intimates were privy to. Rose had promised Nicholas Lockwood that she would break apart Steven's underground empire and she was keeping her word. As soon as she had organized her offensive, Rose summoned the ambassadors of the countries Steven had signed on as Germany's suppliers and told them their contracts were null and void. Diplomats bristled at this impertinent American woman who thought she could dictate their countries' trade policies. Rose convinced most of them that she could—and would—do exactly that. To those who were willing to listen and negotiate, she offered new commitments two and three times the value of the ones signed with Germany. The others she made an example of. Since Rose knew which vessels carried Germany's consignments and what routes they took, she quietly passed the information to the appropriate people in Washington. In short order warehouses, oil depots, and grain elevators were mysteriously blown up. Ships on the high seas were picked off by Allied submarines. Cargo aircraft ferrying industrial diamonds or precious metals were shot out of the sky.

Dozens of Washington officials, including the President, were intrigued by the source of her information but Rose always sidestepped their questions. Her sources, she told them, were always accurate. Nothing else mattered. Washington was miffed but it could hardly argue with the results.

Rose also kept another promise to Nicholas Lockwood. On February 4, 1945, she received word that General MacArthur had retaken Manila. A wire photo followed a day later, showing the general surrounded by his entourage, including Steven Talbot, who was identified as MacArthur's principal aide on commercial redevelopment. Just seeing a picture of her banished son rekindled Rose's pain. She wished that Nicholas Lockwood could share it.

On July 30, 1945, at two minutes past midnight, the heavy cruiser USS *Indianapolis* took three torpedoes from a Japanese submarine and sank in the Indian Ocean in twelve minutes. The navy immediately put a news blackout on the tragedy.

Seven days later, 32,000 feet over Hiroshima, Captain Paul Tibbets, Jr., gave his bombardier the order to drop his load. In the twinkling of an eye an entire city was reduced to ash and the world took an irrevocable step toward the brink of extinction.

On August 8, one day after the second atomic device leveled Nagaski, a quiet, soft-spoken man appeared at Global's offices. He asked to see Cassandra and after he had been shown into her office presented his FBI credentials.

"Miss McQueen, do you know a Mr. Nicholas Lockwood?"

Cassandra paled. "Yes. Yes, I do."

"Perhaps you'd better sit down, ma'am."

As kindly as he could, the federal agent told Cassandra of the *Indianapolis* disaster. Sixteen hundred eighty sailors had perished, some by drowning, others by sunstroke, the rest taken by sharks. All three hundred sixteen survivors had been identified. Nicholas Lockwood, who had been on board the *Indianapolis* on a government mission, was not one of them.

– 53 –

The morning of September 2, 1945, was swathed in blue skies. A burnished-gold sun sparkled off the waters of Tokyo Bay. A dozen warships strained gently at anchor, their guns silent but still pointed toward a ruined city. On the battleship *Missouri* sailors in dress whites hurried along the superstructure, rolling out a red carpet, arranging tables and chairs, and showing civilian cameramen where to set up their equipment. In the crow's nest, next to pennants that crackled smartly in the stiff breeze, lookouts with binoculars scanned the harbor for the launch ferrying the Japanese delegation.

Steven Talbot adjusted his cap to shield his face from the sun. Dressed in full uniform, he held the rank of lieutenant in the U.S. Army. The title, however, was more ceremonial than official.

"If you're going to be working for me, we have to call you something," MacArthur had told Steven when he had been seconded to staff three years earlier. " 'Lieutenant' has a nice ring to it."

Steven thought it did and by now he was used to being addressed by his rank. Although he hadn't seen one day of real combat, he nonetheless felt he had earned that right.

When Steven had reported to MacArthur's Honolulu headquarters in early 1942, he was still reeling from what his mother had done to him. After their confrontation she had refused to speak to him. Steven had had no way of knowing how she'd come about her information, nor, for fear of incriminating himself further, could he contact Kurt Essenheimer to find out exactly what had gone wrong.

After he'd shipped out, Steven still couldn't believe she was serious about disinheriting him, much less sending him off to war. Yet as the weeks and months passed with no word from New York, Steven realized that his mother fully intended to keep her word. And there wasn't a damned thing he could do to stop her.

Hawaii's virgin beauty, which restored the bodies and souls of war-weary soldiers, sailors, and airmen, served only to deepen Steven's rage and frustration. He was forced to live in bachelor-officers' quarters and to make ends meet on his meager army salary. Accustomed to giving orders, not taking them, he had to suffer men he thought were fools, yet who outranked him.

Steven survived by retreating into a world where no one and nothing could touch him. Through MacArthur's office he had access to war news that civilians never saw. Germany was still fighting hard but clearly the Allies were gaining. The Nazis' supply lines were being choked. Badly needed raw materials were impossible to obtain. Ships that carried what was available were systematically sunk. Rose, Steven thought, was keeping her promise with a vengeance, demolishing the invisible empire he had set up.

When American forces began pushing the Japanese back, Steven followed MacArthur across the Pacific. As the general's senior adviser for industrial and commercial rebuilding, Steven witnessed firsthand the devastation the Japanese forces had wrought. But at the same time, he saw beyond the carnage that blinded most Americans to their enemy's achievements. In the Philippines, Indonesia, and Malaya, the Japanese had seized industrial complexes and brilliantly converted them into war factories. They exploited the natural resources left fallow by the local population, created a network of railroads to bring the goods out, and modernized port facilities to ship everything back to Japan. Steven spent long nights going through captured Japanese documents, which were an industrial blueprint for the exploitation of Southeast Asia's rich natural resources. He was impressed at the intricate organization and planning the Japanese military managers had forced upon a subjugated population. The more he read, the stronger he felt that here was a nation and a people to be reckoned with in the future. Where others talked only of destruction and barbarism, Steven saw foresight, determination, and vision. And opportunity.

Steven helped draft plans for the reconstruction of Manila, Singapore, and other great cities. He presented MacArthur with blueprints to rebuild entire industries as well as create new ones on the rubble of the old. The general was so impressed that he encouraged his adviser to start looking at what could be done in Japan after its inevitable surrender. Steven was way ahead of him. He spent nights plowing through Japanese official dispatches, making copious notes, and memorizing the names of top industrialists. Some of these men would be dead by the time Japan gave up the fight. Others, fearing a war-crimes tribunal, would disappear. But a handful would survive. Those would be the ones Steven had to find.

In the little spare time he had Steven studied the Japanese language and customs, finding willing tutors among prisoners of war who spoke English. While fellow officers cheered reports of American bombing raids, Steven worried exactly how much of Tokyo would be left standing when he finally got there. On August 30, 1945, as American forces scrambled ashore at Yokohama, he had his answer: the Japanese capital had been all but leveled. However, surrender was not enough. What was left of Japan's factories and commerce were to be broken apart. Their industrial leaders were to be rounded up and jailed. As far as Washington was concerned, the men who had run Japan's giant *zaibatsus*, or combines, were as guilty of perpetuating the war as were the generals. The war-crimes tribunals would see to it that they paid for their actions.

As he listened to General MacArthur read the terms of surrender and watched the Japanese officials sign the protocols, Steven knew exactly what he had to do: persuade MacArthur to challenge and overturn Washington's decree that would put Japan to the sword.

While the ink on the surrender papers was still drying Steven received MacArthur's permission to create a special office to take charge of Japan's remaining industrial might, determine the guilt of its business leaders, and plot a new course that would include reparations as well as American oversight. MacArthur, who had seen his young lieutenant's efficiency in ravaged Southeast Asia, agreed. With the stroke of a pen Steven Talbot was made Director for Economic and Industrial Concerns.

Steven set up his office in the Dai Ichi building, two floors below MacArthur's headquarters. He chose his staff carefully and worked them hard. Squads of auditors, accountants, and lawyers, accompanied by vetted Japanese translators, fanned out across the country, searching for evidence that would implicate Japanese business leaders in waging war. Steven himself remained in Tokyo, calling upon the major *konzerns* personally. He submitted his carefully worded reports directly to MacArthur, taking care to point out that Japanese companies had behaved no differently from German, American, or British firms that had fueled their countries' war machines.

"You know that and I know that and most American businessmen agree with us," MacArthur told Steven.

He showed him a recent edition of *Newsweek* magazine whose editors predicted that thirty thousand Japanese businessmen would be removed and a quarter of a million barred from ever functioning within the new economic system.

"Personally, I think it's all hogwash," MacArthur said. "We'll be lucky to blacklist a few thousand. But there you have it: Washington wants blood. It's not going to be satisfied with trying only the military. It wants the Emperor to go as well, along with his industrial barons."

The general looked at his director. "You're going to have to come up with a few scapegoats."

Steven had foreseen Washington's demands. There was no way around them. However, deciding which industrialists would be indicted was left up to him. It was a card Steven had to play very carefully.

Steven pored over the reports his field teams brought in, searching the files for that one man who had not only survived but whose prestige was such that others would follow his lead. The work was grueling and inevitably disappointing. Every major industrialist was the target of army investigators. Steven knew that unless he got to the evidence first, and altered or excised the most damaging parts, he would never find the man he was searching for. Heavy-handed military justice would see to that.

Late one evening, just as he was going to call it quits, Steven read a name that struck a faint chord in the back of his mind: Hisahiko Kamaguchi. Steven was positive he had heard the last name before. But the first remained a mystery. Quickly he leafed through the dossier, hoping to find a connection.

Hisahiko Kamaguchi was the patriarch of Kamaguchi Heavy Industries, a *zaibatsu* that had been founded in 1853, the year Commander Perry sailed into Tokyo Harbor. His industrial empire had included steel mills and shipyards, airplane-manufacturing plants, and textile industries. The electronics division had produced everything from radar to radios, while the pharmaceutical arm had been engaged in advanced research in synthetic drugs. Such prominence had inevitably made Kamaguchi a priority target of army investigators. Their reports on him were detailed but always ended on the same note: there was no direct evidence that tied Kamaguchi to the disgraced militants. Yet.

Steven knew that with such a tempting target it was only a matter of time before the connection was found. Should he try to get to Kamaguchi first? Could he be the man he was looking for? The answer came to him on the last page, in the brief about the industrialist's family. Hisahiko Kamaguchi had lost his wife during a bombing raid over Tokyo. He had no surviving relatives except a daughter. Steven's eyes blurred when he read Yukiko's name. Berlin, before the war, a party at a nightclub. He was looking at a beautiful Japanese girl and Kurt Essenheimer laughed and said, "Forget her. She's Yukiko Kamaguchi. You'll never get close to her. . . ."

* * *

459

Unlike most of the Occupation administrators, Steven Talbot made it a point to see as much of Tokyo and its people as he could. While his brother officers preferred the comfort of their offices, clubs, and the PX, Steven took to wandering the streets day and night.

Within months of the "quiet invasion," downtown Tokyo had been transformed into an American colony. Americans were conspicuous by both their height and their color. Fords, Chevys, and Jeeps clogged the streets, while the latest Hollywood offerings adorned theater marquees. At the Hibiya intersection, a stone's throw from the general headquarters, an MP and a Japanese traffic policeman simultaneously directed traffic. G.I.s wandered the streets followed by children singing *Haru ga kita*, "Spring Has Come." Soldiers riding in crowded buses or trams caused mild panic when they offered their seats to Japanese women, who were never publicly deferred to by men. *Tokyo Romance*, written by an American wire-service correspondent, recounted the death of his Japanese wife and became an instant bestseller in both languages.

But beyond Tokyo, which was being rebuilt as fast as American construction supplies could be offloaded, was a very different country. The Japanese economy had come to a virtual standstill.

Finding Hisahiko Kamaguchi in this desolate landscape was far more difficult than Steven had imagined. The address in the intelligence dossier turned out to be a street in a suburb that no longer existed. The Kamaguchi offices in downtown Tokyo were nothing but blackened skeletons from the fire bombing. The main plants in Yokohama had shared a similar fate.

Nor were Kamaguchi's peers helpful. Industrialists netted in the first sweep and placed under virtual house arrest professed to have no idea as to Kamaguchi's whereabouts. Steven received similar replies from the executives and foremen he managed to track down. It was as though Kamaguchi had, like his empire, vanished off the face of the earth.

Steven refused to quit. More than ever he believed that Kamaguchi held the key to unlocking an extraordinary secret that industrial Japan had managed to hide from its occupiers. Steven carefully reviewed every word that had been spoken about his elusive quarry. He listened to the tape-recordings over and over again and read back the transcripts, sifting for that tiny clue that would break the puzzle. He was on the verge of giving up when he noticed that two of Kamaguchi's friends had mentioned the same thing about him: he was a devout Shintoist. Steven plowed through the burial records for the greater Tokyo area. If the *zaibatsu* chieftain was alive, there was one place he would show himself: at his wife's grave.

The Shinto shrine on the outskirts of Tokyo rested in a miniature valley surrounded by cherry trees whose blossoms had long ago faded and fallen.

Winter mists crept around the great ceremonial bell and carried the solemn chants of the priests through the wood and stone edifice. Because he could not wait for Hisahiko Kamaguchi inside the shrine, Steven parked his car on a nearby path, making himself as comfortable as possible. He returned daily for ten days before he saw her.

She was wearing a blue, army-style padded jacket with baggy trousers and felt boots. Her hair was hidden under a woolen scarf wrapped around to cover her nose and mouth. Nevertheless, Steven was sure it was Yukiko Kamaguchi.

"Hello."

She turned around slowly, as though unsurprised to see another person at this early hour, even a *gaijin*. Her nutmeg-colored eyes regarded him thoughtfully. Yukiko removed her tattered woolen mittens and pulled the scarf from her face.

"You are a very patient man, Mr. Talbot," she said in Japanese.

Steven was taken aback that she knew who he was. He was also aware that unlike everyone else who met him for the first time, Yukiko ignored his disfigurement. There was neither revulsion nor pity in her gaze. No doubt she had witnessed far greater mutilations.

"And you are very difficult to find, Miss Kamaguchi," he replied in Japanese.

She was as perfect as Steven remembered. Neither the worn clothing nor her extreme thinness dimmed the fire in her eyes. Yukiko Kamaguchi was, Steven thought, like himself, a survivor.

"You haven't been waiting all this time to see me," Yukiko said.

"But it is an unexpected pleasure," Steven parried.

Yukiko ignored his attempt at gallantry. "You did not come here to chat idly with me. My father has debated seeing you. He asks me what it is you want and thinks it must be important. After all, you found him when even your best investigators could not."

"They didn't know where to look."

"Do you know where to look, Mr. Talbot?"

"Into the future," Steven replied softly.

Silently Yukiko beckoned him to enter the shrine.

Inside, it was very cold. Steven followed Yukiko's lead and removed his mud-caked boots. The air was laden with jasmine incense and somewhere in the back a wind chime punctuated a priest's chants. Steven stayed behind Yukiko as she walked swiftly through the gloom, bypassing the temple itself and stepping into a tiny room where a coal brazier gave off a little light and even less heat. Sitting cross-legged before the brazier was Hisahiko Kamaguchi. The photographs Steven had seen of him indicated a much bigger man. Kamaguchi's wrists and fingers were painfully thin, his face sallow with an unhealthy yellowish hue. In spite of his obvious malnutrition, the industrialist's eyes burned fiercely. Yukiko indicated that Steven should sit opposite her father while she stepped around to his side.

"It is very kind of you to see me."

"You are a persistent man," Kamaguchi replied, his voice crackling like dry autumn leaves being pressed between the pages of a book. "You must have been very cold sitting in your car day after day."

"Discomfort is nothing compared to my reward."

Hisahiko Kamaguchi looked at Steven thoughtfully. "And what is your reward? Is your General MacArthur so keen to see me that he has offered inducement to the one who brings me to him?"

"Sir, General MacArthur is interested in talking to you, as are a great many army investigators. But that's not why I'm here."

Kamaguchi made a temple with his fingers. "No, I think not. It may have taken the skills of Rose Jefferson's son to find me, but if he wanted to make me a prisoner he would have brought others. Perhaps you have come here for a different reason, Mr. Talbot. Tell me, how is our mutual friend, Kurt Essenheimer? Did he survive the fall of Berlin?"

Steven's eyes narrowed. He had no idea how Kamaguchi could have known about his association with Kurt.

"I have not heard from Kurt. I have no idea whether he survived."

"I think he did," Kamaguchi said, with such conviction that Steven believed him instantly. "And you, Mr. Talbot, have found your way to Japan. You have been cut off from your family, but, like any family, it still provided you with shelter. You advise the most powerful man in Japan yet you seek out the weakest. Why is that, Mr. Talbot?"

Steven felt his skin stretch across his cheekbones. He was angered by Kamaguchi's slyness, the secrets he tossed out like worthless baubles, the hint of arrogance and sarcasm in his voice.

"I believe we have something to offer each other."

"Mr. Talbot, you have been disinherited. Once you were a very powerful man. Had fortune looked the other way, you might have become even more formidable. What do you have left to offer?"

"I can protect you. And the secret that the Occupation authorities know nothing about—yet."

Hisahiko Kamaguchi coughed violently, doubling over and clutching his stomach. Instantly Yukiko was at her father's side, covering his mouth with a worn handkerchief. When she slipped it into her pocket her palm was shiny with blood.

"You need medical attention," Steven said. "I would be pleased to get whatever you need."

Kamaguchi waved his hand feebly. "You spoke of a secret. War breeds many secrets. How can you be sure the one you mean is so valuable?"

Steven glanced at Yukiko. He had been surprised that she was permitted to listen to the conversation. Traditionally, a Japanese woman had no role in business discussions.

"I see you are familiar with our customs," Kamaguchi observed. "Nonetheless, you may speak freely before my daughter."

"My apologies for being so presumptuous," Steven said to Yukiko, who merely bowed.

"Secrets," he continued. "Japan is filled with them. Most, the Occupation will never know about. But a few, because they relate to men such as yourself, because they are buried beneath actions that some judge immoral and illegal, may come to light.

"Mr. Kamaguchi, a great many documents cross my desk. In spite of the bombings and your own efforts, we have been able to capture whole sets of records. The information they contain is not very flattering. In most cases it is incriminating. In some, lethal. I am not particularly interested in the role Japan's industrialists played before and during the war. The winners always see them as opportunists or dupes, to be punished one way or another. What I do find fascinating is the Phoenix Plan."

Steven let his words hang but they seemed to have no effect on Kamaguchi.

" 'Phoenix' refers to a bird in Western mythology which resurrects itself from its own ashes," the industrialist said. "It is a quaint fable but it has no meaning for the Japanese."

"Perhaps not for all Japanese," Steven countered. "But certainly for you, and others who had the foresight to make contingency plans in case Japan failed to win the war.

"Allow me to elaborate. The earliest reference I have dates back to 1943. Phoenix was a fallback position, designed by you and funded by Japan's major companies, including Kamaguchi Industries, that created a war chest, a special fund to which all contributed in the event that the unthinkable happened to Japan. These funds, made up entirely of gold bullion, were buried somewhere on the Japanese home islands, in a place so secure that even a full invasion force would never find them. The gold had only one purpose: to resurrect Japanese industry after the Occupation ends."

Hisahiko Kamaguchi's features remained impassive. "Mr. Talbot, truly, I do not know what you are talking about."

Steven continued as though he hadn't heard Kamaguchi.

"What puzzled me about Phoenix was the obsessive secrecy that surrounded it. The only references to it were found in the personal diaries of your compatriots, diaries that, fortunately, were of no interest to investigators who were more concerned with business records. There was no mention of the plan in military papers or even in the royal archives. Frankly, I don't think that more than five or six men knew Phoenix existed—or still exists. And these men chose their hiding place very carefully. The location had to be one that even a *gaijin* occupying power would never suspect."

"I assume, Mr. Talbot, that you have solved the riddle."

"On December 7, 1941, Japanese forces attacked Pearl Harbor. According to your company records, on the same day Kamaguchi Heavy Industries filed a claim with the Nukazawa Maritime Insurance Agency over an iron-ore carrier that had sunk outside the entrance to Yokohama Harbor. The *Hino Maru* came to rest in a hundred feet of water. Since she was no hazard to shipping, had been in service for thirty years, and was, at the time, reported to have been carrying no cargo, the insurance company paid off. And there the matter rested. Except for one thing: the *Hino Maru* was not empty. Welded into her hold were containers of gold bars valued conservatively at five million dollars. That, Mr. Kamaguchi, is your Japanese Phoenix."

A cold wind drifted through the room. Hisahiko Kamaguchi's fingers trembled as he reached for another piece of coal and fed it into the brazier.

"The *Hino Maru*," he murmured, whispering the name as though it evoked the memory of an old lover. "What is she to you, Mr. Talbot?"

"Right now, nothing. But it would be very easy to have her declared a shipping hazard and bring her up."

"Why would you do that?"

"Because I'm gambling that she is your mother lode. She is the down payment on the future, which will never be made once I 'discover' what she's really carrying."

"And you would do such a thing, Mr. Talbot? Are you that desperate a man?"

"I need what the *Hino Maru* has as much as you do. Alone, neither of us gets her. Together we both do."

"You have no claim on the *Hino Maru*," Steven heard Yukiko say. When he turned he saw a small, black gun cradled in her palm, its barrel pointed at his heart. "And you never will."

"There are others—" Steven began.

"No, there aren't!" Yukiko said sharply. "A man like you does not share such things. No one knows you came here. No one has found what you have. And no one will."

"Then your father and I both lose."

"That is not quite true, Mr. Talbot," Hisahiko Kamaguchi said softly.

"You can't get at the bullion without me—"

Kamaguchi held up his hand. "That is not my concern. You see, Mr. Talbot, on August 6, I was in Hiroshima. I was, I suppose, one of the fortunate ones, far enough away from the atomic blast not to perish. But close enough to be eaten up by the radiation. Whatever the destiny of the *Hino Maru*, I will not share it. But my daughter will. If you wish to do the same, Mr. Talbot, it is her you must convince. Not me."

Steven Talbot forgot about the cold and how his buttocks ached from sitting on the hard, coarse mat. He fixed his concentration on Yukiko.

Steven began with Berlin—how he had met Kurt Essenheimer and why he had decided to help the Third Reich. He explained how he had conceived the intricate plan that brought war matériel into Germany and how well the pipeline had functioned until the fiasco in Zurich. He told Yukiko about the confrontation with Rose, the ultimatum she had delivered, and how its consequences had brought him to Japan. Finally, he admitted that now, with the war over, he had no home to return to. Rose Jefferson had forbidden him to return to the continental United States.

Yukiko had been listening carefully and, in spite of her suspicions, found herself impressed by this disfigured American. She had investigated Steven Talbot as thoroughly as possible. Everything he'd said rang true and neatly filled the gaps in her knowledge. Watching him as he spoke, Yukiko thought Steven would never come to terms with the losses fate had dealt him. He was a man possessed by a single thought: retribution at any cost. Yukiko understood now why her father had chosen to listen to what Steven Talbot had to say. Perhaps he was the right man after all.

"Given your position, Mr. Talbot, how do you think you can help us, even if you were successful in secretly raising the *Hino Maru* and her cargo?" she asked.

"No one is certain how long the Occupation will last," Steven replied. "Some Washington officials believe it can be at least five years. Military men would like nothing more than to turn Japan into a vassal state, an American staging base, and keep her that way forever."

Steven was quick to note the anger blazing in Yukiko's eyes at the very idea of her country's subservience.

"What this means is that Japanese industry will be tightly controlled," he went on. "You will be told what to make and how much. Already there are plans for currency restrictions and limits on the amount of money Japanese can invest abroad. Even if you could raise the gold from the *Hino Maru* right under our noses, you would not be able to get it out of the country."

"And you could?"

"Yes. I have all the resources of MacArthur's office at my disposal. Getting the gold out wouldn't be easy but it's certainly possible. Once it is in our possession, there are men in Switzerland who would give us the best prices for it—in American dollars—and, for a small fee, place these deposits anywhere in the world. Attorneys I've worked with can set up companies whose real ownership would be impossible to trace."

"What would you have these companies do, Mr. Talbot?"

"First, I would make substantial real estate investments in Japan—commercial, industrial, as well as residential. Second, we get as many industrial blueprints as possible out of the country. Whatever you were working on—engineering, pharmaceuticals, electronics—everything gets moved offshore. Along with your surviving engineers and scientists. The Occupation won't allow Japan to rebuild an industrial base right away, but later, when the U.S. turns to other problems, you'll be given more freedom. That's when everything that's been developed abroad can be brought home."

"You've given this a great deal of thought, Mr. Talbot," Yukiko said. "But you haven't told us what you expect to receive in return for your efforts."

Steven wet his lips. "I want a fifty percent share in everything we do, beginning with the gold. You need me to act as front man for you. Right now—and perhaps for a long time—you can't afford to be linked in any way to what we do.

"I don't profess to know much about electronics or engineering. My specialty is money. With the stake of the *Hino Maru*, we can create a financial machine in the Pacific that will one day challenge Global Enterprises."

"And where do you propose to make our first investment?" Hisahiko Kamaguchi asked, breaking his long silence.

Steven's smiling lips were cherry red in the light, like a carnival jester's. "Where all this began: Hawaii. There's a certain symmetry to that, don't you think?"

Hisahiko Kamaguchi and his daughter were wary, but Steven had an answer for every question they threw at him. In the end they were not only amazed at how brilliant and daring the scheme was but also convinced that it would work.

"Which brings us to the last question," Steven said. "Do we have a partnership?"

Yukiko glanced at her father and nodded. She was prepared to gamble on this American.

"The bounty of the *Hino Maru* does not belong only to us," she said. "Others are involved. They do not know you as we do. They have no proof of your abilities to do what you say you can. They need to be persuaded."

Steven had prepared himself for just such an argument.

"Tell your people that I will persuade General MacArthur not to try the Emperor as a war criminal."

Yukiko's eyes widened and her breath came out in a long slow hiss. Like

466

every Japanese, she agonized over what retribution the Americans would demand from the Emperor. It was no secret that many Allied officials wanted to hang Hirohito beside his generals. Hitler had cheated them by suicide, but the ruler of the Chrysanthemum Throne was their prisoner.

"You can do this?"

"MacArthur trusts me. If I can convince him that it is in our best interests not to make an example of His Majesty, he might be able to persuade Washington to reconsider. It would be a very difficult—and unpopular—thing to do but I am willing to try. There can be no greater example of my trustworthiness."

Yukiko remained silent. It was sacrilege that the divine person of the Emperor be judged by mortals, must less suffer punishment at their hands. The Japanese people would never recover from such humiliation. It would break their spirit and make them slaves forever. Could this one American really prevent such an indignity? If so, then the price he was demanding was laughably cheap.

"I believe you can do this thing," Yukiko said. She looked at her father and received an infinitesimal nod. "And we agree that if you succeed, we will guarantee that you share equally in the bounty of the *Hino Maru*, as well as anything else that we build together."

"Can you persuade the others involved to go along?" Steven demanded.

"Mr. Talbot," Yukiko replied tonelessly. "If you can help save the Emperor, there is no power on earth that will break our pledge to you."

The cold finality in Yukiko's voice pleased Steven. It carried a promise that would overcome any obstacles, remain potent for years. It was, he thought, exactly the kind of weapon he needed against the woman who, with a few words and the stroke of a pen, believed she had gelded him.

- 54 -

The army information officer at the Pentagon had facts coming out of his ears. What he could not tell Cassandra was what had happened to Lieutenant Nicholas Lockwood.

"I'm awfully sorry," the freshly scrubbed, pink-faced officer said, offering Cassandra an uncomfortable chair in a room that resembled the inside of an avocado. "I wish you'd called me before coming down. There's been no word about Lieutenant Lockwood."

"I have called you," Cassandra reminded him.

She glanced at the file on the officer's otherwise pristine desk, recognizing the pale blue sheets of her stationery.

"I also sent telegrams and letters."

The officer fidgeted in front of this beautiful blond woman with drawn, pale face and eyes that churned in turmoil. He had seen too many such expressions and looked forward to the day when he would be rotated out of this office.

"Can't you at least tell me how the search is going? Where you're looking?"

The officer drummed his fingers on the desk. The USS *Indianapolis* remained a very touchy issue with the navy. Not only had she been carrying the Hiroshima bomb, but after she'd gone down, the survivors had bonded into groups. Only those lucky enough to get into lifeboats had survived.

"I wish I could help you," the man replied sincerely. "But we simply don't have any information that would indicate Lieutenant Lockwood is alive. The nearest island in the area where his ship went down has been thoroughly combed. We've tried to identify any vessels, military or civilian, that might have passed the area at the time. Those that responded say they never picked up him or any other crew members."

The officer hesitated. "I know it's the hardest thing in the world to do. But sometimes you have to let go. . . ."

Cassandra's eyes flashed. "If he were dead, I'd gladly take your advice. But he's not!"

The officer sighed. He'd seen the same terrible, unyielding certainty in mothers, sisters, wives, and fiancées. He noted that this young woman did not wear a wedding band. She was the kind who would carry the torch the longest. She didn't even have memories, only dreams.

The officer rose. "I'm sorry. I'll let you know the minute we have any word at all . . . one way or the other."

What did I expect? Cassandra asked herself as she walked blindly through the Pentagon maze, surrounded by hundreds of men in uniform. She had really believed that if she came to the Pentagon she would magically find him.

For months Cassandra had used the offices of both Global and *Q* magazine in her search. Jimmy Pearce and others had called in favors from all over Capitol Hill.

"We're not going to give up," Pearce had promised her. "So don't lose heart."

Cassandra stepped into the sunlight that smiled upon Arlington, Virginia. A chauffeur opened the door to an immense black Packard and drove her into Washington. At the stately Willard Hotel, an usher escorted her into the terrace restaurant that overlooked the blooms of the Capitol.

Rose Jefferson put down her newspaper. "No news?"

Cassandra shook her head. Rose summoned a waiter and ordered two very dry martinis and lobster salads.

"I had a chat with the head of the CIA," she said, referring to the newly created Central Intelligence Agency, which had replaced the Office of Strategic Services. "He tells me that he hasn't given up on Nicholas. To use his exact words, 'The Agency looks after its own.'"

Cassandra looked at her gratefully. As soon as Rose had heard that Nicholas was missing, she had plunged into her own investigation. Telephones had started ringing all over Washington. Yet even the power she wielded couldn't bring forth a single word about Nicholas Lockwood's fate. It was as though the sea had swallowed him up.

The two women drank silently, and when the salads arrived Cassandra found she had no appetite.

"You won't give up looking, will you?" Rose said.

"Never."

"But you can't hide away either, Cassandra. The war is over. Things have changed. You've become part of Global. I need you there."

It wasn't the first time Cassandra had heard Rose mention this. She knew she had let her responsibilities slide at a time when there was more than ever to do. Rose was predicting a brilliant future for the company. People would be traveling in greater numbers than ever before. With the dollar the prince of currencies, Europe was embarrassingly cheap for Americans. The traveler's check, which Michelle had so skillfully developed, would become a limitless gold mine.

"And who's better qualified than you to run it?" Rose said. "Your name commands unquestioned respect. If anyone can and should take Michelle's place, it's you. I have enough on my plate."

Cassandra knew that was true. Rose was already selling off her railroad empire at a time when its value was highest and investing in civilian-airplane manufacturers. Global vessels, which had been the lifeblood of the transatlantic supply effort, were being cut up for scrap while Scandinavian shipyards were receiving orders for huge new oil tankers. Meanwhile, the profits from the Global money order poured in as America, freed from wartime rationing, went on a spending binge.

"There are a few other things I'm working on," Rose said, pushing away her unfinished salad. "I want you to be a part of it all."

Cassandra noticed the shadow that crossed Rose's smile. In her own way Rose was another of those thousands of mothers whose sons hadn't come back from the war. Steven Talbot was still in Japan, working at MacArthur's Occupation Headquarters. And he would never be returning home. That was the reason Rose wanted her by her side, to fill a void she could neither ignore nor live with.

As though she divined Cassandra's thoughts, Rose changed the subject, leaving behind painful topics. Forgotten, too, when they left, was the newspaper lying on the third chair at their table. Rose had scanned it quickly and Cassandra hadn't even looked at it. Neither had seen the five-line filler at the bottom of page 10 about a salvage operation in Yokohama Harbor. A navy spokesman was quoted as saying that traffic into the port would double as soon as the sunken ore carrier, *Hino Maru*, had been raised from the channel bottom and towed to the scrapyard.

The island was not even a spit in the Indian Ocean. At high tide, the waters surged over the reef and reduced the beach area by half. From the air it would have been difficult to say where the green waters ended and the sparse scrub and few trees began.

Nicholas Lockwood emerged from the ocean naked. He had swum around the atoll three times. By now he was familiar with every current that swirled around this place he had nicknamed Crusoeville—how strong it was, and whether it brought in any fish. Nicholas always fished very close to shore, diving and spearing his prey, then quickly getting out of the water. Indian Ocean sharks are the most savage in the world. He had seen their handiwork in the days after the USS *Indianapolis* went down.

Nicholas gutted and cleaned his grouper and laid it on the bed of hot coals he kept going night and day. He covered the fish with banana leaves and stared across the vast expanse of ocean. There was an eerie calm in the air. The sky

470

was a brilliant blue, unmoving, and the ocean seemed at peace with itself. It was all very deceptive.

Nicholas pulled out his knife, the only man-made tool he had been carrying when he had gone into the water, and carved another notch into the palm trunk lying half-buried in the sand. There were 230 markings, each representing one day. That meant that today was April 2, 1946. Nicholas knew the date wasn't altogether accurate. He had lost track of how long he had been in the water and when exactly he had crawled ashore. Regardless, it was time to leave.

He rose, a thin, nut-brown man whose sun-beaten hide was stretched across ropy muscles. His face was covered by a bleached beard and his hair hung in ragged strings along his shoulders. Civilization had been burned off him, leaving hungry, predatory eyes that reflected a murderous desire to survive.

Once, that had meant finding this atoll, healing himself, building a rickety shelter, and learning to hunt for food in the ocean. As soon as he had his strength back, Nicholas began scouring the atoll for anything he could use to build a canoe or raft. He had neither hammer, nails, nor ropes. But he found young palms whose trunks could be lashed together by creeper vines and fashioned a tiller out of a twisted piece of driftwood.

As he ate his breakfast Nicholas glanced at the shallow pool he had built from coral heads. There were a dozen different fish in it, some chosen because their flesh was rich with fresh water, others for the density of their meat so that even a few mouthfuls could satisfy him. Nicholas calculated he had a two-week supply of food and water . . . if the fish lived in the makeshift tank he had made, if they didn't prey on one another, if he didn't lose them in a storm.

It was the storm that worried Nicholas the most. April was cyclone season in the Indian Ocean. He had seen evidence of past typhoons all around the atoll and reckoned that at worst the fragile island would be completely submerged by the walls of raging water. Which explained why the atoll was probably not on any nautical map or close to any major sea-lanes. As far as maritime navigators were concerned, Crusoeville didn't exist.

Nicholas unscrewed the top of the knife and from the hollow handle shook out a tiny compass whose needle wavered toward the north. He had been one of the dozen men on board the *Indianapolis* who had known her course. But how far had he drifted? In which direction? For how long? Nicholas reckoned his best chance was to head north. The cyclones usually built in the east and swung down in a southwesterly direction. If he got out of their way he stood a chance of reaching the Maldive Islands, maybe even Ceylon. In any case, to stay here meant certain death.

Nicholas threw more stones into the fire and covered them with damp banana leaves. Beside the fire he had built a mound not unlike a simple tombstone. If someone ever came ashore here they might find this man-made marker and beneath it one of his dogtags. It would be proof that he had made it at least this far.

Nicholas pulled on his trousers, tattered and cut off at the knees. He hauled on a cover of woven banana leaves that would offer some protection from the merciless sun, then gathered his fish into a pot he had carved out of a coconut tree trunk. He didn't look back as he pushed the raft into the surf and began paddling toward the break in the reef. Crusoeville had saved his life, given him a second chance. He was determined to use it.

Raising the *Hino Maru* had been the first, and, as Steven was to discover, the easiest part of his operation. Having access to General MacArthur's letterhead, Steven drafted a note to the Yokohama harbormaster instructing him to salvage the wreck so that American warships could safely navigate the passage and enter the vast Japanese drydocks. When he presented the order for MacArthur's signature he explained to the general that the Yokohama facilities would take some of the strain off Tokyo Harbor. MacArthur congratulated Steven on his initiative.

Eleven days later the *Hino Maru* was floated and towed into drydock, where Japanese shipyard workers swarmed over her with welding torches. The engineering machinery was sent to be repaired while the hull was chopped up for scrap. Several large ballast tanks were removed intact and, somewhere between the shipyard and the scrap mill, disappeared. With so much twisted metal arriving every hour, no one noticed the loss.

The tanks were taken deep into the countryside where Hisahiko Kamaguchi himself supervised the cutting away of the pig iron sheets to get at the gold. Others then took over. Under the cover of night the gold was melted down and poured into molds that had once cast the great bells that adorned temples all over Japan. The bullion was later covered with thin sheets of metal and the appropriate inscriptions affixed to the exteriors. For all intents and purposes these bells looked exactly like any of the ones found in thousands of shrines across the country. Except they did not ring. Steven prayed that no Nippophile quartermaster took it into his head to try to make them chime.

The next part of the bells' journey was the most hazardous. While American material was pouring into Japan at a tremendous rate, very little was being shipped out. Export permits were scrutinized by a dozen different agencies, any one of which had the power to scuttle a license. Steven drew up one plan after another, examining each for flaws and ultimately rejecting it. He was on the verge of abandoning his efforts when Yukiko introduced him to a high Burmese official.

"During the Japanese occupation of my country, many sacred artifacts were looted," the official explained. "Among the most valuable were five shrine bells which have great significance for my people. I am told, Mr. Talbot, that you are the man who may be able to persuade General MacArthur to allow me to repatriate this national treasure."

Steven was about to dismiss the fat Burmese when Yukiko took him aside and quickly explained what had to be done.

"It's the only way," she said urgently.

Steven was appalled by the scope of the gamble.

"Can we trust him?" he asked, indicating the Burmese.

"We don't have to," Yukiko replied coldly. "He's been paid well enough. But just to make sure, I am going with him."

The next day Steven introduced the Burmese to MacArthur, explained his rank in the government, and presented official documents the man had brought with him.

"It seems pretty clear, sir, that these bells, besides having tremendous religious significance, were part of the booty the Japanese stole from Burma. It would be an enormous propaganda coup for us to return them."

A clever manipulator of the press, MacArthur readily agreed. But he went one step further and called for a major ceremony, covered by reporters, during which the bells were handed over to the Burmese representative. Steven chafed throughout the pageantry. When the bells had at last been loaded on board the ship for Rangoon, he couldn't believe that no one had asked the obvious question: since the Burmese were devote Buddhists, what possible significance could Shinto bells have for them?

No sooner had the treasure of the *Hino Maru* disappeared over the horizon than Steven Talbot began playing out the last cards of a hand that inextricably fused his destiny with that of Japan.

Ever since the Occupation had begun, Steven had been all too aware of Washington's bloodlust to make Japan pay for her war crimes. The hue and cry was most strident from the President's own men, particularly Under Secretary of State Dean Acheson. Thus far Steven had managed to convince MacArthur that arresting the Emperor and putting him on trial would be a humiliation the Japanese could never endure.

"I respectfully suggest, General, that you remember what happened in the Rhineland after World War One."

The example was not lost on MacArthur. As a young Occupation officer he had experienced the difficulties of controlling a vanquished people without a Kaiser-like figurehead they could recognize and relate to. But as the months wore on Washington's insistence became louder.

"There's only one way to head off a lynch mob," Steven told Hisahiko

Kamaguchi. "You, and others, must persuade the Emperor to make the first move."

"To surrender himself?"

Kamaguchi, whose condition had deteriorated so badly that his skin, giving off a rank, sour odor, barely clung to his bones, stared at the American incredulously. Although he had shared his greatest secrets with this *gaijin*, he always kept a wary eye on him. Yet, Steven Talbot had never caused him to suspect treachery. Even Yukiko, whose keen and clever young senses he trusted more than his own, had developed a grudging respect for Talbot. Now it seemed that the American was revealing his ignorance of Japanese ways at the worst—and most critical—time.

"Mr. Talbot, you promised us that you would find a way to maintain the dignity of the Emperor," Kamaguchi said. "Delivering him up to his enemies does not accomplish that!"

"But what if it were not that at all?" Steven suggested. "Westerners do not place the same importance on face as your people do. What if it were to appear that the Emperor in fact had MacArthur surrender to *him*?"

Hisahiko Kamaguchi coughed hard, his chest sounding like a rattle.

"Is such a thing possible?" he gasped.

"I believe it is."

"A hell of an idea! You mean he really wants to meet me?"

General Douglas MacArthur's voice boomed across his office at the United States Embassy, sending aides and secretaries scurrying for cover.

"Close the door and fill me in!" the general ordered.

Steven quickly explained how the Grand Chamberlain from the Imperial Household Ministry had, through a typically circuitous route, contacted him hinting that His Imperial Majesty desired a meeting with the Supreme Commander.

"It's about time he recognized I was in town," MacArthur said expansively. "What did you tell him?"

"That such a meeting could serve a useful purpose," Steven replied cautiously. "But that even if it could be arranged it would have to take place either here or at your Dai Ichi office."

"Quick thinking," the general said. "Why do you reckon they made the offer now?"

"The Japanese read our stateside newspapers and listen to our broadcasts. They know the pressure coming out of Washington on you to act as far as the Emperor is concerned."

"What you're telling me is I can cut 'em off by seeing Hirohito in public and showing the world who's boss."

474

"Not only that, General. It would be difficult for Washington to try a man with whom you've just shaken hands."

MacArthur reached for one of his many pipes, which he seldom smoked but used as a prop. It diverted attention, giving him time to think.

"I think President Truman is wrong about Hirohito, always has been. We need him. His people need him. Otherwise we'll have a god-awful time with them. But I'm not sure everyone's going to be keen to accept a polite apology for Pearl Harbor."

"The Emperor intends to do much more than apologize," Steven told him. "He's not coming to plead for his own life. His sense of honor would never allow him to do that. What he's demonstrating is the ancient Bushido concept of chivalry, or *migawari*, whereby he offers his life for those of others. Quite literally, he is placing his destiny in your hands. If Washington could be made to understand the significance of this . . ."

Steven sensed that his commanding officer was impressed by the privilege being offered him.

"Tell the Grand Chamberlain that I will see the Emperor at half-past ten the day after tomorrow at my embassy residence," MacArthur said. "Make sure that the sentries follow strict protocol for welcoming a foreign head of state. And one more thing: the meeting between Hirohito and myself will take place in absolute privacy. No household staff—his or mine—no bodyguards, no secretaries, no press. Not even you, Talbot."

"General, if I may suggest—"

"You already have. See that my orders are carried out. And while you're at it, get me Truman on the line."

Steven didn't move.

"That's all!" MacArthur said sharply.

"What about an interpreter, General?"

MacArthur blinked, then laughed. "All right, Talbot, you're in. You and one of his choosing. Don't miss a trick, do you?"

Steven smiled.

Two days after his conversation with MacArthur, at twenty-nine minutes after ten o'clock, Steven Talbot lighted another Japanese cigarette from a pack bearing the gold-embossed sixteen-petal chrysanthemum Imperial crest. Standing beneath the embassy portico he reviewed the MP sentries, uniforms sharply pressed, buttons gleaming. The pebbled driveway had been raked. The curtains over all the windows had been drawn and the staff given strict orders not to go anywhere near them. It was as though the entire embassy held its breath.

One minute later the gates opened. A vintage 1930 Rolls-Royce proceeded sedately along the driveway and drew up beneath the portico. The instant the rear door opened and the Emperor emerged, MacArthur stepped out.

The tableau froze in Steven's mind. He caught the Emperor's eye but divined nothing behind the blank stare. In his peripheral vision he saw MacArthur drumming his fingers along the side of his leg, an unmistakable sign of impatience. It was all Steven could do not to grab the Emperor by the arm and steer him up the stairs.

The two men finally came face to face, the tall, imposing American general and the erect, diminutive man-god twenty years younger.

"You are very, very welcome, sir!" MacArthur boomed out.

It might have been a trick of the light, but Steven was convinced he saw the Emperor smile faintly as he clasped MacArthur's hand and bowed.

"Why don't we go inside?" the general suggested.

Thirty minutes later the doors to the study reopened. The two leaders stepped out, with Steven following MacArthur. The general and the Emperor had talked almost without a break. The 124th Emperor, heir to an unbroken dynasty that had lasted 2,648 years, had offered himself up as the sacrifice for his nation's actions, if the Allies would spare his people. And MacArthur had not refused. He had said nothing.

As Steven watched Hirohito climb into his car a surge of anger ripped through him. He had spent countless hours tutoring MacArthur on Japanese customs and nuances. He had been convinced that the general would understand the enormity of the Emperor's gesture. Steven felt a hand on his shoulder and saw MacArthur staring off into the distance.

"I listened," he said. "I may not have said much, but I listened. And you know what, Talbot? I was born a Democrat and brought up as a Republican, but for me to see a man once so high now brought down so low, grieves me."

They were the sweetest words Steven had ever heard.

They met, as they always had, inside the temple, hidden from prying eyes and whispering tongues. The coldest part of spring was upon them, and both men huddled close to the orange coals hissing in the brazier.

"You have done a great thing, Mr. Talbot," Hisahiko Kamaguchi said. "It is a profound pity that history will never acknowledge your actions."

Steven watched as the industrialist hunched forward, his lungs hacking blood. He had an enormous respect for this man who, consumed by radiation, clung stubbornly to life so that the last piece in the intricate design could be put in place.

"I swear to you your dream will live and prosper," Steven told him. "Yukiko is already in Hawaii—"

476

Kamaguchi raised his hand. "I do not want to hear about the future. To dream of it knowing one can never share it is the most painful thing of all."

Kamaguchi's crimson-veined eyes bored into Steven. "I have placed you under the gravest obligation, Mr. Talbot. I have extended you a profound trust. You have much work ahead of you. Are you prepared?"

"I am."

"Then do what you must," Hisahiko Kamaguchi said, holding out both arms.

From his pocket Steven Talbot took out a pair of handcuffs and circled the steel around Kamaguchi's thin wrists. He helped him to his feet and together the two men left the shrine.

As they shouldered their way through the bitter wind toward the Jeep, Steven was overwhelmed by his prisoner's courage. For months Steven had fed MacArthur and his investigative staff doctored papers that damned Hisahiko Kamaguchi as a firebrand militarist who had used his vast industrial power to arm Japan, then wielded his influence to push the country into war. It hadn't taken long for Occupation investigators to make Kamaguchi the most wanted war criminal in Japan. Yet at the same time Steven had used Kamaguchi's notoriety to convince MacArthur that it hadn't been the Emperor but men such as Kamaguchi who had to be held accountable. And MacArthur had believed him.

All that was left was for Hisahiko Kamaguchi to pay the price he had agreed upon.

- 55 -

The boy was twelve years old, tall and angular. His broad face was the color of old molasses, topped with jet-black hair covered by a faded purple turban that matched the color of his loincloth. He had been fishing all day and his *dohey* was brimming with Pacific snapper, mahi-mahi, barracuda, and two small sharks. Now it was time to return home, to Male, the capital of the Maldive archipelago.

The boy fixed the sail so that he would move farther out into the channel and join the other boats coming in from the northeast. He was watching the current carefully when he saw an unusual sight. From a distance it appeared to be a giant floating nest filled with sea gulls.

The boy was intrigued. He hesitated. The current pulling away from the

477

archipelago was strong. If the wind dropped he could easily be swept out to sea. But the boy believed in his own strength. He adjusted the sail and caught the stiff breeze.

From twenty yards away the boy saw that the nest was really a makeshift raft, covered with foul-smelling leaves, woven matting, and bird droppings. As he came closer he noticed flecks of blood spurting off the sea gulls' beaks as they pecked at whatever lay beneath the leaves. The boy flung a pail of water at them, sending a cloud of white into the magenta sky. He slipped a rope through the rotting beams, secured the raft to the *dohey*, and cautiously balanced himself on the slippery palm trunks.

The boy saw what appeared to be a side of raw meat. When he pushed the matting aside he gasped. Stretched out beneath the brown banana leaves was a man, unconscious, his back riddled with bite marks.

As gently as he could the boy dragged the man over the bow of the *dohey* and laid a tarpaulin over him. Then he judged the wind and current and pointed the bow for the islands.

The dock was ablaze with red, yellow, and green lanterns as the boy steered his *dohey* alongside the jetty. The entire village had turned out to greet him and he showed them the man he had rescued from the sea. His mother carefully examined the almost-dead sailor. Judging by the burns on the man's flesh and the color of his fingernails and lips, she thought he must have gone six days without food or water. Allah was indeed merciful. Usually after three days He would have given the sea its due.

The mother had the man carried to her home, a ramshackle hut of bamboo and mud bricks, and covered his body with a lotion made from shark's liver. She removed the metal bracelet from around his neck and walked to the other side of Male to a small missionary outpost staffed by nuns who looked after the lepers. When the mother superior came out, the woman explained what her son had found and held out the dogtags. The nun squinted to read the name.

"Is he alive?"

"He is."

The nun crossed herself. "I will send two sisters right away."

The nun quickly summoned them, explained what had to be done, and sent them on their way. She herself retreated to the barracks where the nuns ate, slept, and prayed. In this remote outpost, where everything was fashioned from what the land and sea offered, there were only two objects that belonged to the outside world: a powerful shortwave radio and a gasoline-powered generator.

The phone was ringing. Cassandra groped for the chain on the bedside lamp and squinted against the glare.

"Miss McQueen?"

"Yes . . ." Cassandra's voice was thick with sleep.

"Miss Cassandra McQueen?"

"Who is this?"

"I'm sorry to disturb you, ma'am. This is the chief duty officer at Naval Operations Center in San Francisco. Our commander thought you'd like to know that we've located Lieutenant Nicholas Lockwood."

"You *what*?"

"Yes, ma'am. He came ashore on the Maldive Islands about three weeks ago—"

"Three weeks ago! Why did you wait—"

"Ma'am, please. He was in pretty rough shape when we got to him. We moved him to Sydney, Australia, and the doctors say he's going to be just fine. In fact he's on a flight to San Francisco right now. We expect him the day after tomorrow."

"Don't you dare let him go anywhere until I get there!"

The duty officer laughed. "Lieutenant Lockwood thought you'd say that. He wants to know where he can find you."

"Tell him the Stanford Court Hotel on Nob Hill. The bridal suite."

There was dead silence on the San Francisco end.

"Did I hear you correctly, ma'am? The bridal suite?"

"It's the only one in the house. He can't miss it."

For the next few seconds Cassandra sat frozen on the edge of her bed, her palms sweaty, heart pounding.

He's alive! God in heaven, he's alive!

A minute later Abilene bustled into the room to see what all the commotion was about. Suitcases lay open on the bed and Cassandra was flinging clothes into them as fast as she could empty the closets and drawers.

"You mind tellin' me what's going on?" Abilene demanded, hands on hips.

Cassandra ran across the room and hugged her. Silently she pointed to the photograph in the silver frame on her night table. Abilene rushed to the closet and dragged out more suitcases.

The suite at the Stanford Court was a study in pink and blue accented by black lacquer and Oriental motifs. The formal dining table was set for two, a bucket of champagne was on the sideboard, and trays of hors d'oeuvres were in the refrigerator. In the adjoining room the king-sized bed stood on its own pedestal beneath a canopy of blue chiffon studded with silver thread. In the pale light the thread created the illusion of cascading moonbeams.

Cassandra surveyed everything for the hundredth time, pacing nervously, moving an ashtray here, changing a floral arrangement there. As soon as she had arrived that morning she had called the infirmary at the Presidio but was told that Lieutenant Lockwood had already been discharged. The hours dragged on as she waited for him, leaving the room to go downstairs only when she felt the walls closing in on her. She managed a short walk around the block before she ran back into the lobby. By now the desk clerk knew enough to shake his head before the questions poured out.

The worst possible thoughts tumbled through Cassandra's mind: Nicholas had not been discharged. He was gravely ill and the hospital was lying to her. He had gone out with navy buddies and forgotten all about her. He had been run down by a streetcar.

Back in the bridal suite, Cassandra stared at her reflection in the ornately carved rosewood frame mirror.

"Don't worry. You couldn't be more beautiful."

Cassandra uttered a sharp cry and whirled around. He was standing by the double doors, his ill-fitting tan suit obviously new. His skin was the color of ancient teak and his eyes, still red-rimmed, were set in deep hollows. He held out a dozen roses, their long wet stems creating a dark patch on his suit jacket. He moved slowly, like a man who wasn't quite sure of his step. Cassandra ran to him and flung herself against him. The roses came between them, the petals crushing against her breasts, their scent overpowering.

"You're all right," Cassandra whispered over and over again, running her hands over his arms and shoulders, her fingers sliding across his temples and into the thick chestnut hair that she suddenly realized was shot through with pure white. Nicholas framed her face in his hands, thumbs sliding back her tears.

"I always knew I would see you again, Cass," he whispered. "As long as I was alive I knew I would come back to you."

When he spoke her name Cassandra saw the haunted look in his eyes, the look of a man who still could not believe he had reached safe harbor. She took his hand and led him to the bed.

"Sweetheart, I don't know if I can. . . ."

She pressed a fingertip to his lips and in one motion stepped out of her dress. She was naked underneath and she let him breathe her.

"Let me love you," she whispered. "There's nothing you have to do, nothing to be afraid of anymore. . . ."

For the next two days the Stanford Court became their entire universe. Cassandra and Nicholas feasted on the delights of the hotel's famous kitchen, spent long afternoons on the terrace taking in the sun and salt air, and returned to the bedroom to explore each other slowly.

It was a voyage of discovery that both thrilled and frightened Cassandra. As her fingers traveled over every inch of Nicholas's body she felt herself transported into another world. She learned what pleased him and how she could coax and tease him to make their lovemaking explosive. At the same time, she shuddered when she touched the long deep scars across his back or watched as he walked with a painful limp. The navy doctor had assured her that given time and physiotherapy Nicholas would mend.

As soon as the naval hospital's official discharge papers came through, Cassandra and Nicholas headed east on the transcontinental Union Pacific Limited. For four days and three nights, they watched the countryside change from the comfort of the domed panorama car, and made love in their double cabin to the rhythm and sway of the train.

"What are you going to do now?" asked Cassandra as they approached New York.

"Live my life with you."

They were the simplest, most loving words Cassandra had ever heard. She hated to spoil them, but neither could she hold back the question that had been on her lips from the moment she had first seen him.

"What about your work?"

Nicholas smiled. "You mean the OSS? That's finished. I've done my part." He leaned back lazily in the plush seat. "I think I need a lot of tender loving care."

"I think so too," Cassandra whispered.

They went home to the Carlton Towers as naturally as though they had done that all their lives. Abilene greeted Nicholas with hugs and kisses and paraded the best of her southern cooking "to put meat on your bones."

When Rose called, Cassandra was in such high spirits that she immediately accepted her invitation to lunch.

"It's so good to have you back, Nicholas," Rose said. "You can't imagine how worried we all were about you."

"Cassandra told me everything you did," Nicholas said. "It means a lot to me not to have been forgotten."

Lockwood looked around at the perfectly turned-out men and women lunching in the Waldorf's Peacock Alley. The image of the raft tossing helplessly in the waves came back to him, the rotting fish flesh he had forced himself to suck on to extract every precious gram of fresh water. It all seemed like so long ago. It seemed like yesterday. . . .

"Do you and Cassandra have any plans?" Rose asked as their lunch was served.

"None at all," Cassandra replied happily.

"I take it you're not going back to the government, Nicholas."

481

"Not on your life."

"Still, a man with all your experience can't remain idle."

Cassandra's senses perked up. Rose definitely had something on her mind.

"Why not?" Nicholas asked.

"Because you can't," Rose said firmly. "You're not some pretty playboy who wastes his time."

He laughed. "Miss Jefferson, why don't you just put it on the table?"

Rose didn't blink. "I'd like you to come to work for Global, as chief of security."

Cassandra was shocked. This was the last thing she had expected from Rose. But then Rose Jefferson excelled in the unexpected.

"Sounds interesting," Nicholas said casually. "What's the job about?"

"Nicholas!"

Lockwood squeezed Cassandra's hand. "Hey, it doesn't hurt to listen, does it?"

Cassandra couldn't understand why Nicholas wasn't perfectly happy with the way things were. The two of them had everything, starting with each other. They certainly didn't need money. She wondered if all men were like that, eager to keep challenging life instead of taking what came their way—and being grateful for it.

"It's really quite simple, Nicholas," Rose was saying. "I'm reorganizing Global. With the war over, we're going back to basics. The money order and traveler's check. Our expansion is going to be enormous, and along with it, I'm afraid, the problems: theft, forgeries, plant and printing security, just to mention a few."

"Sounds like you need men from the Secret Service's counterfeiting division," Nicholas commented.

"The experience you have is invaluable," Rose countered. "You know your way around Washington and you're a quick study."

Rose wrapped up her offer with what she hoped was a guileless smile.

"It's something to consider," Nicholas said. He glanced at Cassandra. "What do you think, my love?"

Cassandra shot Nicholas a look that could have skewered him and, reaching for a crab leg, promptly cracked it—loudly.

Cassandra had planned to go shopping after lunch. Now all she wanted was to get Nicholas alone and talk some sense into him.

"We'll talk later," he said firmly. "I want you to cool down a little."

Furious, Cassandra turned on her heel and marched straight for Fifth Avenue. Nicholas watched her go and his heart ached. But he had to get to the truth of what it was Rose wanted. He hailed a cab and gave the driver Global's address on Lower Broadway.

"Why, Nicholas, this is a pleasant surprise!" Rose came around her desk and greeted him warmly. "Don't tell me you and Cass have already discussed my offer?"

"What is it you really want, Miss Jefferson?" Nicholas asked quietly.

Rose was taken aback by his hard tone. No one dared speak to her like that. She found the challenge refreshing.

"I'm concerned about Cassandra's welfare. And you should be too."

"How?"

"I think you know, Nicholas, that I've kept my promise to you as far as Steven is concerned."

Lockwood nodded. He had closely followed Steven Talbot's career at Mac-Arthur's side.

"I haven't spoken or written to my son since he left for Hawaii, years ago," Rose continued. "Nor do I expect ever to hear from him again. When you have children, Nicholas, you'll appreciate what this means.

"As you know, Steven was my only offspring, the sole heir. I am fifty-five years old. I will never marry again, much less have another child. I have no one in the world to leave what I've built to except Cass."

Rose paused, her voice softening. "She's changed so much, Nicholas. She's worked so hard and done a great deal that you'd be very proud of. It's time for her to take what Michelle left her. But she needs help, encouragement."

"Is that why you offered me the job?"

"You make it sound so callous. The truth is you *are* qualified. As I said, what you don't already know, you can learn. But the most important thing is that I can trust you. You could have ruined me because of Steven, but you didn't. That says all I need to know about you."

"There's more to this," Nicholas said. "You're still holding out on me."

Rose took a deep breath. "Yes, there is, and in a way you're responsible. You see, you're the one who raised the possibility of Steven's having been involved in Monk's murder and possibly Michelle's. Now I have to know the truth, and you're the only man who can bring it to me. If my son had anything to do with Michelle's death, it means he was planning, a very long time ago, to eliminate anyone who might become a threat to his inheritance. If that's true, and Monk found out about Steven's involvement, then Steven would have had all the reason in the world to silence him as well. But there's only one way we're ever going to be certain. You have to find Harry Taylor."

"Everyone thinks Harry Taylor's dead," Nicholas said flatly. "You don't."

"Do you?" Rose challenged. "Can you afford to make that assumption? If Steven's killed before, Nicholas, he may try again."

The thought turned Nicholas's blood to ice.

"So the job offer—"

"Is genuine. Except no one, even Cassandra, can know about your other activity. As chief of Global security you can travel wherever you please, no questions asked. You'll have resources at your disposal that no police force can match. If Harry Taylor is alive, you'll find him. If not, you'll find his grave. You have the best motive, Nicholas. You love Cassandra."

Nicholas realized how true this was.

"One question. Why not tell Cassandra all this? I think she'd understand."

Rose shook her head. "It took so long for Cass to heal from what was done to her in the catacombs. Telling her what I suspect would plunge her back into that nightmare. I'm doing this for her, Nicholas, but I'm also thinking of myself. I have come to accept that my son is many things. For some of those, he has already been punished. But if he is a murderer then I have to know that too."

When Nicholas walked into Cassandra's apartment he found her in the living room sitting amid bags and boxes from Fifth Avenue shops. There wasn't a hint of pleasure or satisfaction in her expression.

"I was really mad. But don't worry, I'm returning everything tomorrow."

"Why should you? It's probably been a while since you splurged on yourself. You deserve it."

Cassandra looked at him carefully. "You're taking Rose's offer, aren't you?"

Nicholas nodded and then told her half the truth. "I need to work, Cass. I wasn't cut out to sit behind a desk. I love challenge and new experiences. But most of all, I love the fact that we'll be together. You've waited for me for a long time. Things you should have done you've put aside. It's time to get back to them."

"I see Rose managed to convince you that I should take over the traveler's-check operation," Cassandra said, her tone tinged with bitterness.

"You don't have to do anything you don't want to," Nicholas said. "I'd be just as happy if you decided to stay home. But would you?"

Maybe if I were your wife.

As soon as the words crossed her mind, she realized that even that would not be enough. Rose was right: a part of Global belonged to her. It was a trust her mother had died for.

Cassandra shook her long blond hair and sighed theatrically. "You can be a pain, Mr. Nicholas Lockwood. Did you know that?" She hesitated. "And I can be selfish. So why don't you come over here and tell me that you love me madly and are doing all this just for me."

It was then that Nicholas knew he had won. He wouldn't have to convince Cassandra of anything. She would do that herself. Because she loved him.

* * *

484

Upon A. M. Pecorella's retirement, Nicholas was appointed chief of Global's inspectors division. He inherited five thousand files on counterfeiters, bank-note artists, pickpockets, thieves and the lawyers who defended them, and bankers who sometimes acted as fences for stolen bonds, Treasury bills, and commercial paper. The dossiers, Nicholas explained to Cassandra, made up Global's shield. Without them, the company would be prey to every kind of criminal, from a petty thief trying to cash traveler's checks lifted from hapless tourists, to a master forger whose skills could cost the company millions.

Nicholas made frequent trips to Washington, where he exchanged information with his counterparts from the FBI and the Secret Service. Although Cassandra was working closely with Rose on plans to reintroduce the traveler's check in Europe, she occasionally found time to accompany him.

"The Executive Protection Branch wasn't created until after Lincoln's assassination," an agent explained to Cassandra as they toured the Service's private museum. "Our main job has always been to run down the paper men."

Cassandra was fascinated by the number of criminals who, over the decades, had tried to duplicate U.S. bank notes. The glass-enclosed exhibits of paper money, plates, entire printing presses, and samples of dyes and inks were testimony to their ingenuity.

"I imagine they go to jail for a long time when you catch up with them," she said.

The agent smiled. "Don't go telling this to anyone, but it's unofficial Service policy to get the crooks to work for us. If they're that good, we want their trade secrets as well as their eyes. These guys can spot phony paper that even some of our best people wouldn't recognize."

Cassandra quickly came to appreciate the importance of Nicholas's job and the degree of trust Rose had invested in him. As head of the inspectors division, Nicholas had unrestricted access to all parts of the company. Although his sixty full-time investigators reported directly to him, he gave them free rein to pursue their inquiries. Nicholas, Cassandra thought, was a born leader, a man who commanded respect by delegating responsibility.

Cassandra was grateful that Nicholas had not inherited any major problems from his predecessor. He spent long hours at Lower Broadway but seldom would a lunch or dinner date have to be canceled. It helped that, when an apartment became available at Carlton Towers, Nicholas bought it immediately. With Abilene's help Cassandra redecorated it, satisfied that she and Nicholas could now spend all the time they wanted together while still observing proprieties. The simplest things—window shopping for men's clothes, planning a weekend outing, preparing cocktails for the two of them before Nicholas was due to arrive—made Cassandra very happy. They were little things that spoke of continuity and peace in her life. After all that had happened, she had learned to treasure them fiercely.

In the spring of 1947, after Nicholas had been with Global for slightly less than a year, Rose Jefferson was satisfied with both the plan to resurrect the traveler's check and Cassandra's ability to help carry it out.

"As you both know," Rose told Cassandra and Nicholas over dinner, "Global has managed to put its European freight and forwarding systems back on their feet. What we must do is rebuild the traveler's check. The key is the army. There are tens of thousands of American soldiers with the Occupation and they're going to be in Europe for a long time. I want a military banking operation to service all their financial needs. That will eventually serve as our springboard for the traveler's checks."

Nicholas glanced at Cassandra. "You don't want much, do you, Rose?"

"The largest banks in the country have been petitioning the government for a piece of the golden military goose," Cassandra replied tartly. "So far every one has been turned down cold. We've just as good a chance as anyone else."

Rose nodded approvingly. "We need a two-front assault. In Washington and in Europe. Hugh and Eric will handle the combined departments of War, Treasury, and State. Nicholas, I want you to come with Cassandra and me to Europe. Chase and Morgan and the rest didn't get anywhere because the army doesn't believe civilians can cope with the military. We're going to convince General Draper, who heads the Economic Division in Germany, otherwise."

Rose paused. "This would be a good opportunity to meet some of the bureau chiefs in the European police forces. You never know when you'll need their cooperation."

Nicholas Lockwood met Rose's gaze. He knew exactly what she had meant by her last words and how cleverly she had disguised her real purpose for including him.

The three of them arrived in London, their first stop, in early June. Driving into the city, Cassandra was overwhelmed by the devastation. Although many of London's famous landmarks had survived, whole areas had been laid to waste by bombing raids and the infamous V-2 missiles.

"It'll take a miracle to get the city back on its feet," she exclaimed.

"When the Marshall Plan goes through, Europe will get its miracle," Rose said firmly.

By now Cassandra was all too familiar with Rose's work habits and wasn't surprised at their grueling itinerary. There were endless meetings with senior American officers who ran the day-to-day lives of the thousands of G.I.s and civilians still stationed in the city. In the meantime, Nicholas called on high-level officials at Scotland Yard who were responsible for keeping tabs on forgers and counterfeiters.

"You needn't worry about any of our boys duplicating your traveler's checks," a mustachioed Scotland Yard inspector by the name of Rawlins assured Lockwood. "We know who they are and where to get at 'em."

But there were other, more discreet, meetings, held outside police headquarters. On these occasions, the subject was not forgeries or counterfeiters. Instead, Nicholas Lockwood raised the specter of Harry Taylor, asking Rawlins for any information British law enforcement could give him.

"We have a chaotic situation on our hands," Rawlins explained. "Thousands of our own people are unaccounted for and boatloads of refugees are arriving daily. Plus, we're talking about a man who's supposed to have been dead going on ten years."

"I know that, Inspector. Even so, I'd appreciate anything you can give me. This is personal."

Rawlins looked thoughtfully at the younger man.

"I liked McQueen. We tried to run Taylor to ground together once. Very well, Mr. Lockwood. You'll have the files first thing in the morning. I'll ask my people to keep their ears open. Where can I contact you?"

Nicholas gave him a copy of his European itinerary. "Call me anytime, day or night."

Rawlins raised his eyebrow when he saw Cassandra's name. "Is there a chance Taylor might be after her?"

"Not him, Inspector. But the son of a bitch who made him his patsy."

"I'll call," Rawlins promised.

On the eve of their departure for Paris, Cassandra suffered an attack of nerves. This would be her first time back since her mother's death. Memories poured into her that night.

"Don't worry about a thing," Nicholas whispered, holding her tightly. "I'll be right beside you. Nothing's going to happen to you, I promise."

Cassandra wished she could believe him, but the next morning, as the French coastline came into view, she couldn't repress a shudder.

On the afternoon of their arrival, Cassandra and Rose received two callers, Emil Rothschild and Pierre Lazard.

"We heard you were coming to our city and decided we must be the first to welcome you."

Cassandra was charmed by her mother's old friends and appreciated the warm stories they told about her.

"I do not mean to pry, mademoiselle," Rothschild said. "But can we assume that with the war over, you are returning to us to carry on the excellent relationship your mother began?"

"You certainly may," Cassandra replied.

The following morning, after assuring Nicholas that she would be fine, Cassandra made her pilgrimage to Père Lachaise cemetery. She was grateful that in spite of the fighting, someone had seen to it that the grave was properly tended. Cassandra suspected that Rothschild and Lazard were responsible.

For a long time she stood in front of the simple marker, weathered by the elements and seasons, and remembered all the wonderful times she and her mother had shared. Slowly the horror that had tainted her memories of Paris was replaced by the love her mother had felt for this city, a love she had passed on to her daughter, who could not, in her heart, deny it.

After their first meeting with Emil Rothschild and Pierre Lazard, Cassandra and Rose were convinced that the organization Michelle had set up across France could once again become the driving force behind the traveler's check in Europe. The two bankers had already advertised for former Global employees to contact them. The response was overwhelming. Letters and telegrams poured into Paris.

"You'll get back eighty percent of the original staff," Rothschild predicted. "Perhaps more. They are very loyal people."

Going through Michelle's old personnel records, Cassandra was inclined to agree. Michelle had inspired trust among her employees. But would they show her the same respect?

Rothschild seemed to read her mind. "You are your mother's daughter. Continuity is so important to us, especially now."

With the initial details in place, Cassandra, Rose, and Nicholas had a marvelous farewell dinner with the bankers at La Tour d'Argent. Pleading one final obligation, Nicholas excused himself early.

"Don't stay out too late," Cassandra teased. "Our train leaves first thing in the morning."

"I won't."

Nicholas did not have far to go. He crossed the Seine to Île de la Cité and walked in the silent shadows of the imposing Palais de Justice until he came to the sentry box by the front portals. The officer checked Nicholas's credentials and telephoned upstairs.

Nicholas had seen a picture of Armand Savin. The man descending the staircase was older, his face creased with character lines. But the swept-back white hair was the same and he carried himself with a formality befitting the rank of assistant commissioner. Nicholas's sources had told him that Savin had been a key member of the Resistance, whose exploits had driven the Germans crazy and earned him the nickname the White Fox.

"Welcome, Mr. Lockwood," Savin said cordially.

"It's good of you to see me, Commissioner."

"Anything having to do with Michelle McQueen is extremely interesting to me."

Savin led the way upstairs to his office, where Lockwood saw stacks of police reports.

"The kidnapping?"

Savin nodded. "Everything we have on it. Now perhaps you can tell me about your interest in the case?"

Since Armand Savin's cooperation was crucial, Nicholas held nothing back. He explained the mission Rose Jefferson had charged him with and how he intended to pursue it.

"A formidable task," Savin observed. "So many years have gone by, so much chaos has overtaken the world. Do you really believe Harry Taylor could have survived the war?"

"Rose Jefferson believes it. My intuition tells me she's right."

"Intuition is a double-edged sword, my friend. It can lead one to mirages."

"True. But Rose mentioned some specific details that would have been included in your reports. If I may have a look . . ."

"By all means."

Nicholas's French was just passable but he was sure he would recognize what he was after.

"We know that Taylor instructed Michelle to prepare a ransom of one million francs," he said, running his finger down the page. "The bank manager testified that he personally prepared the withdrawal."

Nicholas flicked back several pages. "But later, when you and your men arrived in the catacombs, the money had disappeared. . . . Along with Harry Taylor."

Nicholas looked up at Savin. "If Taylor managed to find his way out of the catacombs, and he was carrying that money, then he could have gone a long way on it. Let's assume for a moment that he did survive. Where would be the first place a wounded man on the run would go?"

"To a doctor," Savin said softly. "A doctor who, for the right price, would treat him and send him on his way."

He paused. "You realize that finding such a man, if he is still alive, won't be easy."

"But not impossible."

The Frenchman shrugged. "If the gods favor us . . ."

* * *

Cassandra had seen the pictures. Everyone had. Documentary footage showed the nightly air raids over Germany and the heroic acts of Allied pilots. What remained on the ground, in broad daylight, was a nightmare beyond imagination.

Berlin's legendary Kempinski Hotel had somehow survived the worst of the bombing and the manager assured Rose, Cassandra, and Nicholas that the water was perfectly safe to drink.

"The lines have all been repaired," he said. "The *Amis* have seen to that."

Nicholas had an army car and driver assigned to him and spent much of his time at the government's military headquarters. Constant shortages of food, clothing, and fuel had created a thriving black market, which in turn had spawned counterfeit rationing cards and military scrip. Army counterintelligence had no idea how to address the problem. As part of her plan to get the military banking contract, Rose had generously loaned Nicholas and his talents to General Draper's office. As a bonus, his work gave him access to existing files on German paper men. This could prove invaluable in the future.

While Nicholas was away, Rose and Cassandra traveled all over the city. Some of the sights they witnessed chilled their hearts. Children, most of them orphans, were living in the rubble, scavenging for food. In alleys and basements, old people died of disease and malnutrition. Girls no older than twelve were selling themselves to soldiers for cigarettes and C-rations.

And Steven had helped bring this about, Rose thought. Could he have known the kind of people he was helping?

The answer was painfully clear. Steven had known because he was one of them.

The ruin of Berlin and its people only made Rose that much more determined to get the banking contract, yet meetings with General Draper, of the Economic Division, proved to be a study in frustration. The general had a low opinion of women to begin with. Bankers ranked just a shade higher. Besides, having six financial institutions competing for the license made him kingmaker, a role Draper relished.

"How are you ever going to persuade him that Global should get the contract?" Cassandra asked Rose.

The older woman smiled and tapped the file Nicholas had gotten for her. It contained Draper's entire career, going back to his cadet days at West Point.

"Pay attention, Cassandra. Sometimes a straight line isn't the shortest distance between two points."

Rose had discovered that Draper considered himself a skilled marksman. He had enough trophies to testify to that. When she learned that Draper also loved to hunt, she told the manager of the Kempinski Hotel to arrange a boar hunt.

"But, Fraulein Jefferson, there are no boar in Berlin," the manager replied.

"Then tell me where I can find some and arrange a shoot. At the very least, your meat lockers will be full."

Three days later the manager told Rose a small party could be accommodated in the forest outside Nuremberg. Rose called on General Draper and made yet another pitch to convince him that Global was the best choice for the banking system.

"You gotta understand, Miz Jefferson," Draper said expansively. "There are other interested parties involved."

"And they're all back in Washington sitting on their duffs," Rose told him. "Do you want civilians to handle your affairs, General, or do you want someone who'll get the job done?"

Draper smiled condescendingly. "And you're the one to do it, am I right?"

"You're a sporting man, aren't you, General?"

"I've done a little shooting in my time."

"Let's make a small bet," Rose suggested. "I've arranged for a boar hunt outside Nuremberg. You and I will be the only players. If I bag one before you do, you promise to cut through the red tape and recommend Global to Washington."

"And if you lose?" Draper asked dubiously.

"Global will withdraw its application. You'll have one less contender to worry about."

Draper couldn't help but smile. He'd have this woman out of his hair in a week.

"I like that idea."

Three days later, Rose, Cassandra, and Draper, along with the general's entourage, drove to Nuremberg. Draper fondly cradled his Remington 360.

"What are you using, Miz Jefferson?"

From a leather sling, Rose produced a hunting crossbow with three wicked-looking shafts. Draper's jaw dropped.

"The boar should have a sporting chance, General," she said and disappeared into the woods.

Draper tracked his quarry with the stealth of an experienced stalker.

"It's in that clearing," he whispered to his aide. "The son of a bitch is probably sleeping in a lair."

Draper crept forward silently until he spotted the unmistakable patch of black bristle. He took careful aim and squeezed off two shots. Then he bounded into the clearing to see a six-hundred-pound boar lying on its side. A few feet away, sitting on an outcrop of rock, was Rose Jefferson.

"Good thing you're a fine shot, General," she said. "Otherwise you might have hit me. You were a little late, though."

"What the hell do you mean?"

Rose pointed to the shaft embedded in the boar's head.

"Better luck next time."

"Did you really get to it first?" Cassandra whispered as they followed the fuming Draper back to the Jeep.

"Certainly seems that way, doesn't it?" Rose said innocently.

And that was her last word on the subject.

General Draper may not have been a good loser but he was a man of his word. In less than a week Rose had a copy of his recommendation letter to the Pentagon.

"Now I can go home," she announced.

The three of them were having their last dinner at the Kempinski. Cassandra ate little and said even less. She and Rose had agreed that Cassandra would return to Paris and reopen the traveler's-check headquarters on rue de Berri. Cassandra was grateful for the vote of confidence but she still had her reservations. Even though Emil Rothschild and Pierre Lazard would be in Paris to advise her, Nicholas had said nothing about coming with her.

Rose noticed Cassandra's glum expression and smiled to herself. When they ordered dessert, she said, "Now, I have a little surprise for you. Although Nicholas has been working very hard, it seems he hasn't quite finished. So unless you have any objections, he'll be staying on in Europe."

Cassandra almost choked on her wine. "When did you two decide this?"

"A few days ago."

"A few *days*?"

"Hey, it was her surprise," Nicholas protested.

Cassandra kissed Rose on the cheek. "Thank you!" she whispered.

"I'm only lending him to you," Rose warned her.

"You may never get him back!"

Cassandra excused herself then and went to the ladies' room. Nicholas watched her go and felt unclean.

"I hate lying to her," he said abruptly.

"You're protecting her," Rose corrected him. "Besides, we agreed she doesn't have to know about Harry." She paused. "Besides, Cassandra will need you. The two of you are good for each other."

Nicholas caught a glimpse of Cassandra weaving her way through the tables.

"So good that we live among secrets."

"Not long now, Nicholas. You'll find him soon. I can feel it. Go to Vienna. Vienna will bring you that much closer."

* * *

492

The Austrian capital was a ravaged city, teeming with spies, agents, informers, and black marketeers. It was, Lockwood thought, the perfect place to set up shop if one was dealing in information. Which was Simon Wiesenthal's stock-in-trade.

Lockwood made his way up the rickety staircase to the offices of the Vienna Documentation Center, presented his credentials to a tough, able young man, and was shown into Wiesenthal's private quarters. Knowing that Wiesenthal was the survivor of numerous death camps, Lockwood had expected to find a ghost. Instead he was confronted by a huge, strapping man with an iron handshake and eyes that burned with the purity of a single, unswerving purpose.

"I'm not sure exactly how I can be of service to you," Wiesenthal said after Lockwood had told him about Harry Taylor and his mysterious disappearance in the Paris catacombs. "After all, this man is not a war criminal. We have no files on him. Our resources are scarce and we must husband them carefully— to search for the right people, if you understand me."

"I do," Lockwood replied. "And I can guarantee that funds—well in excess of what you would spend in your inquiries—will be made available so that you can carry on with your principal work."

"That is a generous offer," Wiesenthal admitted. "Still, my people have other motives besides money."

"Do you know the name Michelle Lecroix, better known perhaps as Michelle McQueen?"

"The woman who worked with Abraham Warburg?"

Lockwood nodded.

"There are hundreds of Jews in Palestine and elsewhere who revere her, Mr. Lockwood."

"Harry Taylor was partly responsible for her murder. If Michelle had lived, she would have done much more. Harry Taylor knows who killed her. He was there. He is the only one who can bring her murderer to justice. Whatever you can do, Mr. Wiesenthal, you'll be doing for her. Not for me or the money."

Wiesenthal stared out the window for a long time.

"Please, tell me everything," he said at last.

— 56 —

Steven Talbot emerged naked from the tidal pool. Three years in the islands had left his skin a nutty brown, while the swimming, riding, and sailing had kept his body trim. His ruined face had healed as much as it ever would, although he was still careful not to expose the red, unnaturally smooth skin, crisscrossed by welts, to the sun. A broad-brim rancher's hat had become his trademark around Oahu.

Steven walked up to the screened gazebo in the back garden, a tropical fantasy overgrown with the dwarf loulu palm, wiliwili trees, pink, yellow, and white frangipani, and a dozen varieties of orchids. He toweled himself off, slipped into a light cotton robe held out by his elderly manservant, and sat down opposite Yukiko.

"How do the figures look?"

"Better than they did six months ago. Much better."

Steven read the balance sheets. The numbers were staggering, all the more so when he recalled that less than three years had passed since he and Yukiko had arrived on the islands. And that had been only the beginning.

The gold, of course, was what had made it all possible. Because of his influence and reputation, Steven had had no problem clearing the Shinto bells through customs in Hawaii at the end of their long, circuitous journey via Burma. Once on the island, Steven reestablished his contacts with influential people who remembered him from his brief stay in Honolulu before he had shipped out with MacArthur. Word of his service with the general and the authority he had wielded preceded his arrival. Steven was immediately welcomed into the tightly knit colony of old, moneyed families and purchased an estate that had fallen on hard times. His criteria were privacy and security, and Cobbler's Point suited him perfectly. Only when Japanese servants and caretakers appeared at the estate, as well as a striking Japanese woman who acted as mistress of the house rather than as a retainer, were eyebrows raised.

Yukiko was not immune to the silent disapproval and sometimes outright hostility that dogged her whenever she stepped outside the estate. She became contemptuous of these Americans who so easily forgot their own history. The sugar and pineapple plantation barons had prospered on the backs of Japanese workers who had first come to Hawaii in 1885, fleeing poverty and hunger.

They worked for nine dollars a month in wages and were given six dollars as food allowance. Entire families were crowded into single houses without cookhouses or toilets. In 1909, when seven thousand Japanese laborers dared to go on strike, the Sugar Planters Association evicted them, herding them into a vast "refugee" camp.

Given a history of exploitation as well as the innate Japanese sense of tribe—the *wareware Nihonjin* or "we Japanese"—Steven had thought it would be simple enough for Yukiko to obtain the silent cooperation they needed from the Japanese community in Hawaii.

"Think again," she had warned him. "Your General MacArthur's constitution may have forced our men to give women equality but in their hearts they haven't changed."

Yukiko's prediction proved accurate. Some leaders of the Japanese community openly snubbed her, looking upon her as a *gaijin's* whore. The more sympathetic ones would not deal with her as long as the community considered her an outsider, belonging more to the West than the East.

"What the hell is it going to take to get them to cooperate?" Steven demanded.

"Stalemates can be broken," Yukiko replied enigmatically. "It is just a matter of time. Be patient, Steven."

That time came at the conclusion of the Tokyo war-crimes tribunal, which handed down the death sentence for General Tojo and others, among them Hisahiko Kamaguchi.

"Now there is no more stalemate," said Yukiko. "Only an injustice—committed against my father—to be righted."

A few days later Yukiko went into the Japanese community once more. Shortly afterward, the first Japanese workers appeared at Cobbler's Point. They were dressed as gardeners and handymen and some in fact worked on the grounds. But others built a small foundry on a remote corner of the estate, prepared the kilns, and began the delicate task of melting down the gold in the Shinto bells. To satisfy his neighbors' curiosity Steven made a production of informing the Honolulu Historical Society that he was reconstructing one wing of the house to its original specifications, which included wrought-iron gates and delicate filigree screens. The neighbors applauded.

When the gold had been melted down into standard size bars, representatives from the Swiss Credit Bank in Zurich arrived to inspect them. Their chemists and metallurgists pronounced the gold 99.9 percent fine and stamped each bar. The shipment was insured, placed on board a Japanese-owned freighter flying the Panamanian flag, and began its journey halfway around the world. By March 1947, a Swiss company, Pyramid Holdings, had been credited with five million dollars.

"Now we begin," Yukiko had told Steven.

Had Yukiko been a traditional Japanese woman she would never have involved herself in Steven's business decisions. But she had been an only child; her mother died before she could give birth to a son. Yukiko's father had been a progressive man who recognized and fostered his daughter's talent. Hisahiko Kamaguchi had seen to it that Yukiko excelled in mathematics, accounting, and business. Where other girls were trained in the arts of family and child-rearing, Yukiko learned about the Kamaguchi *zaibatsu*, how it exercised patience and cunning before its competitors, forged alliances on the basis of strength, and showed no mercy to its enemies. Now she applied everything she had learned to Steven Talbot's master plan.

Within six months Pyramid Holdings controlled a Hong Kong bank and a Philippines shipping line, operated a ten-thousand-acre forest harvesting concern in Malaya, and invested heavily in a petrochemical factory off oil-rich Indonesia. Steven and Yukiko spoke with brokers in Singapore, harangued suppliers in Thailand, cajoled the best rates out of Macao gold traders, and purchased U.S. war surplus planes at a fraction of their real worth.

To maintain his reputation as a businessman, Steven purchased ten thousand acres on the island of Lanai and challenged Bostonian Jim Dole's pineapple empire. The plantation had the added advantage of being an accounting hall of mirrors, allowing Steven to bring some of the profits from the Far East into Hawaii, where they were promptly reinvested in real estate. Along the way Steven made generous contributions to various island societies and established himself as a powerful if discreet patron of charitable works. He entertained Occupation officials who stopped off in Hawaii and who were more than willing to discuss future American policy in Japan.

"What we need are some experienced administrators to take over those old family-run combines we broke up," one official complained. "Problem is, no American wants to put a dime into the place."

"Maybe you should look for Japanese investors," Steven suggested.

The official snorted. "Wish we could. But those guys don't have two yen to rub together."

After the official had moved on, Steven said to Yukiko, "Call your father's friends. It's time."

Yukiko looked across at Steven, then reached out and touched his masklike face. She had known other men who had pursued their goals ruthlessly and single-mindedly. Her father had been one. Those who would arrive at Cobbler's Point in a few weeks were cast from the same mold. Steven was different. Only one thing ultimately sustained him: hatred.

Yukiko had once mentioned this to her father, explaining her concern:

Steven Talbot promised a great many things but how could she ensure that he would keep his word?

"Think of the kind of man he is," her father had advised her. "The rupture between son and mother is irrevocable. He has no other home except his promise to us. His being an outcast will be his bond to us."

Yukiko understood her father and she prepared herself for the day Steven would arrive in Hawaii and expect her to share his bed. He never made such a demand. Their bedrooms were at separate ends of the house and Steven was always careful not to infringe on her privacy. She thought that he might have taken a Caucasian lover somewhere on the island or satisfied himself with the prostitutes in Honolulu's notorious China Strip. When she followed him, she learned this wasn't so.

Yukiko began to watch Steven even more carefully, determined to find that one weakness she could pry open, exploit, and use to bind him to her. Yet Steven remained unfailingly courteous. He enjoyed Japanese customs and knew enough about them to appreciate that he would never fathom them completely. He acknowledged her subtle attempts to seduce him but never reacted to the challenge. For all intents and purposes it seemed to Yukiko that Steven Talbot did not need anything another human being had to offer. And that was the only thing about him which whispered to Yukiko that she would be wise to fear this man, if only a little.

The sun was high over the horizon and the wind had all but died, creating a silent caldron around the gazebo. As Steven retreated into the coolness of the house his houseman came across the lawn and handed him a blue airmail envelope. It was franked by the U.S. Army and the return address was Nuremberg Prison.

Steven read the contents and looked slowly across the horizon. His eyes were still fixed on some distant, invisible point when he handed the letter to Yukiko and said, "We may have a problem."

The autumn air was dense with the scent of pine needles crushed underfoot. The gum had oozed out from the trees and stuck to boots and clothing. As Steven walked up to the forbidding gates of Nuremberg Prison he felt the soles of his shoes tug against the asphalt.

"Mr. Talbot to see a prisoner."

The sentry checked the log for his name.

"This way, sir."

Steven followed an MP corporal through the steel gates that formed the interior barricade around the prison. Once inside, daylight disappeared.

Steven had thought long and hard about making this trip. He and Yukiko had gone over every possible consequence.

"It's a risk," Steven had told her. "But if we don't take it, we'll never know why it was so important for Kurt to contact me in the first place."

"He should never have done that," Yukiko had replied angrily. "Now the authorities have a link between you."

Steven had shrugged. "Plenty of people saw us together in Berlin before the war. If anyone had wanted to make anything of it we would have heard by now."

There was a persistent chill in the prison. Water dripped monotonously from the ceiling, staining the ancient stone surrounded by fresh concrete. Steven was led to a room with a large mirror, a desk, and two chairs.

He closed his eyes and prepared himself for the moment.

It was a ghost, not Kurt Essenheimer, who entered. His face was gaunt and sallow, the fingers bony and nails a deep yellow hue. He shuffled across the floor like an old man and his hand trembled when he reached for the back of the chair to steady himself.

"Kurt—"

"Thank you for coming," Kurt Essenheimer said. "It has been a long time."

He sat down, resting his chin on the knuckles of his intertwined fingers.

"It's good to see you, Kurt."

"Even better to see you, my friend."

"Are they treating you well?"

Essenheimer shrugged. "You know, I can't really say. The monotony of it all dulls the senses. Boredom is the real enemy, the killer." He smiled wanly. "Even more so than the crab."

Steven paled at the mention of cancer. "I didn't know, I'm sorry. I would have come sooner. . . ."

Essenheimer waved his hand in a feeble gesture of dismissal.

"You had no way of knowing. You are doing great things, my friend, even though it's not often I hear your name anymore."

Steven's eyes narrowed. Ever since he had established himself in Honolulu, Steven had taken great pains to keep his name out of both the financial journals and the society pages.

The German turned in his chair so that his back was to the opaque one-way mirror.

"There is something you must know. The Jew, Wiesenthal—the self-proclaimed Nazi hunter—has been asking questions."

Steven felt beads of sweat form along his upper lip.

"Not about you. He wants Harry Taylor. As far as I understand, your mother is the one paying him."

Steven's mind was racing, trying to make the connection.

"Can you tell me anything else?"

"I wish I could, my friend."

Steven forced himself to put the questions out of his mind. There were only a few minutes left.

"How long, Kurt?"

"A few months . . ."

The two men looked at each other quietly. Together they reached back in their memories, to the early days when they had shared the same hopes and dreams, faced and triumphed over the same challenges.

A key scraped in the lock. Kurt Essenheimer rose, hands at his side.

"Thank you for coming, Steven."

"Goodbye, Kurt."

Steven watched as Essenheimer shuffled to the door. The guard took him by the elbow and he disappeared, never looking back. A moment later, a second MP appeared to escort Steven out.

"It's pathetic," Steven said, shaking his head. "The man is dying and the only thing he wants is to see a man with whom he had dinner more than ten years ago."

"He was lucky, sir," the MP replied. "He hasn't had a visitor since I've been here. I guess no one cares anymore."

"I suppose you're right," Steven said softly.

"Do you believe him?" Yukiko asked.

She was walking with Steven along the beach, the mushroom-colored foam running between their toes. He had been back from Germany for over a week, and every night he awoke screaming. The fact that he hadn't been able to help Kurt, couldn't reach out and comfort him one last time, enraged Steven. He vowed that the information Kurt had passed on regarding Harry Taylor would be used in a way that would honor Essenheimer's memory.

"Yes, I believe him," Steven said at last. "There is only one reason Rose would be looking for Harry Taylor. She believes I murdered Michelle and she intends to use Harry to prove it."

"Does she have proof Taylor is alive?" asked Yukiko.

"Not yet. But she has people and resources all around the world. If he survived the catacombs and she's determined to find him, she can do it. You know what that would mean for us."

Yukiko did. In a matter of weeks her father's old partners, the leaders of the *zaibatsus*, would be arriving in Hawaii. Because of Steven's tireless efforts, the giant concerns were ready to be restructured, funded with enormous resources.

It was to be the lighting of Japan's new economic torch. Whenever she thought of it Yukiko saw her father's face in its perfect flame.

"You have to kill Rose."

The words were Steven's but they seemed to have been spoken by the wind, whispering ancient instructions.

"I know," Yukiko said.

– 57 –

There hadn't been many changes in Rose's office at Lower Broadway in the last thirty years. Her desk and the principal furniture, harking back to her grandfather and lovingly tended to ever since, were the same. The paintings along the walls still reflected the glory of the company's origin and growth. The only addition was an oil she had grudgingly agreed to sit for a few years ago, done by Thornton Montgomery. The bric-a-brac along the credenza was testimony to the honors heaped upon her, mementos from kings, presidents, prime ministers, and even the Pope.

I'm fifty-seven. So many have come and gone, and I'm still here. . . .

Rose's eyes traveled to the cluster of photographs tucked away on a rosewood cabinet near her desk.

Cassandra and Nicholas Lockwood were the only people in those pictures. Seated across from each other under the soft light of the dining car on the *Orient Express.* Holding hands on the rugged outcrops of Sardinia with the Mediterranean at their backs. Caught off guard during an embrace when Central Park was in its glory. To Rose they were priceless because in them, she was convinced she saw the future.

Looking at the photographs, Rose felt a measure of something that had eluded her for most of her life: peace. Her decision to nudge Cassandra into assuming her responsibilities in Europe had proved to be the right one. Cassandra's letters had a breathless quality to them, reflecting the excitement she felt as she restructured the traveler's-check operation from the rue de Berri office. Other, more sanguine, reports came from Emil Rothschild and Pierre Lazard. The bankers were very impressed by Cassandra's energy and knowledge and predicted that she would do as well as Michelle. Rose treasured their words. They told her that the wounds she had inflicted so long ago were at last healing.

"Daydreaming again?"

"Come in, Hugh. Don't pay any attention to this senile old woman."

Hugh O'Neill smiled. Rose Jefferson was anything but that. Her skin was as flawless as he remembered, and her dark hair, with its sweeping white streak, remained thick and full. Her eyes could open the world with laughter or arrest it with shrewdness and cunning. Her new designer, Oleg Cassini, understood her complexities. The navy suit spoke of understated but unmistakable authority.

But there was something else to Rose, which lingered in her eyes—pain that would never heal.

"Don't give me that pitying look, Hugh," Rose warned. "We can all be thankful that Steven took me seriously."

She smiled sadly. "A Jefferson becoming a pineapple farmer. Who would have thought it possible? I suppose I should be grateful he's doing something useful."

Hugh O'Neill hesitated, waiting to see if Rose would continue. When she didn't, he decided not to bring up the subject. He had learned of Steven's trip to Nuremberg to see Kurt Essenheimer. But whatever the two men had talked about could not possibly affect anyone. Telling Rose about it would upset her and that was the last thing he wanted.

Ever since the end of the war New York society and the business community had eagerly awaited the return of Steven Talbot. Both expected that after such a distinguished military career, he would resume his duties at Global. When he didn't, tongues began wagging. O'Neill orchestrated the cover story and ran interference for Rose. He let it be known, in strictest confidence, that there had been a falling-out over Global's postwar direction. Much to his mother's chagrin, Steven had decided to strike out on his own. A reconciliation was, of course, inevitable. It was simply a matter of a son proving his mettle.

The financial barons nodded sagely and the mothers of debutantes were silently relieved that Steven Talbot, for all his millions, would not be gracing their salons with a face that "could have been created by Picasso," as one Park Avenue ingenue blithely put it.

"Tell me about the Ho-Ping Bank," Rose said.

"It's small, only ten million or so in assets, most of it in real estate," O'Neill replied, crossing his legs and wincing as he heard the crack of joints. "A few loans to shipping companies secured with proper collateral. The management is sound though not very imaginative."

Rose frowned. "Why is it on the block?"

"There's a little more to it than that. Ho-Ping is owned by Pyramid Holdings out of Zurich. The directors are anonymous, but Swiss Credit, which handles all the finances, tells me that Pyramid has instructed them to sell Ho-Ping. Naturally the Swiss don't concern themselves with the whys and wherefores."

"Sensible people," Rose murmured. "What's your gut reaction, Hugh?"

"You want a building block to move the traveler's checks into the Far East. Ho-Ping fits the bill. Global's having a foothold won't cause the taipans to froth at the mouth, and we can use Ho-Ping to buy other concerns through Southeast Asia. We'll train their managerial talent in New York, then send them back as instructors. I reckon that in five years we could have a lock on the traveler's checks and the Far East tourist business."

"How much does Pyramid want?"

"The asset price. I don't think we should give them a dime in goodwill."

Rose smiled. "Go ahead and make the arrangements."

"There is one thing Zurich asked for—on Pyramid's behalf. The principal at Ho-Ping is Japanese. He has full authority to effect the sale and he would like to meet you."

"That's impossible. I have too many things to do here."

"I know you've been doing things," O'Neill said pointedly. "What they are remains a mystery."

"You'll know soon enough."

"Listen, Rose. It's been ages since you've been out of the country. Even the city, for that matter. Why don't you give yourself a little time."

"Do you know how long it takes to travel to Hong Kong? The ditty about a slow boat to China is true."

"You won't be going by boat. Ho-Ping will fly you out on the clipper. You'll be gone two weeks at most."

Her resolution began to waver. It *had* been a long time since she had seen new sights, tasted and smelled different things.

"Can I tell Ho-Ping you're coming?"

"All right," Rose agreed. "By the way, who exactly am I going to see there?"

"The name is Wataru Fukushima."

Hugh O'Neill sat back, satisfied with himself. "Come on, Rose. It'll be fun. You might even haggle him down on the price."

Much later, Hugh O'Neill would not be able to keep his frivolous words from tormenting him. They would forever mock a lifetime of devotion, loyalty, and affection.

When Wataru Fukushima received Global's cable, he hurried across the floor of his workshop to his office.

The Fukushima family had been associated with the Kamaguchi *zaibatsu* for three generations. Wataru's grandfather had begun a small sheet-metal-manufacturing shop and had been fortunate enough to land a contract with Kamaguchi Heavy Industries. After his death the contract was inherited by his father, who expanded the shop and then passed it on to Wataru.

The relationship between the *zaibatsu* and a subcontractor such as Fukushima was bewildering to outsiders. To Fukushima, Kamaguchi was a customer, financier, and supplier. In return, Fukushima was a processor, manufacturer, and deliverer of the finished product. Kamaguchi dictated what was needed, how much, and by what date. Fukushima in turn did everything to meet Kamaguchi's exacting standards and delivery schedule.

The system was the bedrock of Japan's complicated interdependent industrial world. On his own, without a guaranteed buyer, Fukushima could not have competed with other subcontractors who had a *zaibatsu*'s protection. On the other hand, Kamaguchi made sure that Fukushima had whatever he needed for production and guaranteed to buy his goods. It was a relationship of trust, honor, and commitment.

Wataru Fukushima had mourned the day Hisahiko Kamaguchi had been, as he saw it, murdered. But his passing only reinforced Fukushima's responsibilities to the *zaibatsu*. He had waited patiently for the chance to fulfill them. It had come when Yukiko Kamaguchi summoned him to Honolulu.

Wataru Fukushima, his patron's daughter had explained, was to become director of a bank, invested with full powers to run it. Naturally he would not be asked to do this. He would, however, travel to Hong Kong twice a month, make an appearance at his office, sign some papers, and let his staff know that he was once again leaving on business. The trip would end at his sheet-metal-manufacturing shop.

"One day," Yukiko Kamaguchi had said, "you will receive a cable saying that a certain woman is coming to see you about the sale of the bank. You will contact me immediately, then prepare yourself to receive her."

In his cramped office, surrounded by cartons bulging with paperwork, Wataru Fukushima dialed the overseas operator and waited to be put through to Honolulu. When Yukiko answered, his voice trembled not with fear but with the anticipation of revenge.

It was five o'clock in New York and, because she was traveling the next day, Rose broke off early. Having mixed herself a martini, she took a healthy swallow, then opened her briefcase. Amid the papers was a thin portfolio bound in maroon leather. Unlike other files, this one bore no title. The typing was erratic and the words filled with xs. Every page had been done personally by Rose on her ancient Remington. There were no copies.

Rose had never told anyone about this project, or that she had agreed to the

Hong Kong trip only because it would give her a chance to think through the problems and possibilities in a different environment. She was convinced that what she had in front of her would revolutionize the financial world, making paper and coin currency all but obsolete, historical footnotes to be placed in a museum beside the first Greek and Roman moneys.

The thought excited Rose more than anything else in the world. At one time that alone would have been enough. Now, she needed to share her innovation, to be comforted by the thought that not only would it be appreciated but that it would survive her. The loneliest thing in the world, as she had painfully learned, was to have everything and no one.

I want to show it to Cassandra. I want her to feel the thrill of something new being born. I want her to understand how much I need her.

Yet, sending the report to Paris, even by armed Global courier, was out of the question. The material was far too sensitive.

Perhaps after Hong Kong, when I'm a little further ahead, when Cassandra comes to visit . . .

But Rose wanted Cassandra to have this now, at least symbolically. There was a solution for that, too. On her way home, Rose stopped briefly at Carlton Towers. She chatted with Abilene, then went into Cassandra's study and spun the combination on the vault Nicholas had had installed. Slipping the portfolio inside, Rose was satisfied that it would be as safe there as anywhere in the world.

Rose made the journey across the United States in her private railroad car coupled to the Ocean Pacific *Limited*. In San Francisco she was greeted by the president of Pan-American, who escorted her to the clipper that would fly her to Honolulu on the first leg of her journey across the Pacific.

At the mention of Hawaii's capital, Rose's heart lurched.

"Will it be a long stopover?"

"No, ma'am. The pilot will take on fuel and provisions and you'll be off in no time. Unless, of course, you want to spend some time in Hawaii."

Rose smiled faintly. "No, I don't care to do that, thank you."

Like most people, Rose Jefferson had no idea how limitless the Pacific is. Blue upon blue, dotted with lush green islands surrounded by necklaces of white coral reef, it is primitive and mysterious, captivating and seductive.

As the clipper made stops in Tahiti and in the kingdom of Tonga, then turned northwest toward the Solomon Islands and Guam, Rose's imagination worked furiously. In these thousands of square miles was an unspoiled beauty that would one day draw millions of travelers. Wherever the travelers went, Global offices would be there to serve them.

Rose, who had been enjoying the leisurely, pampered flight, suddenly couldn't wait to reach Hong Kong. In fact, she thought, it mightn't be a bad idea to visit other parts of the East—Thailand and the French colony of Vietnam, Malaya, and the Indonesian archipelago. She began to sense that this journey would bring home with it far more than she had anticipated.

The clipper landed punctually on the island of Guam. Wataru Fukushima greeted the American woman with all the deference and ceremony his instructions had specified. He personally escorted her to the bank's private aircraft and made sure she was comfortable. Rose was impressed by the uniformed stewards and the attention they paid her. She had no way of knowing how carefully Wataru Fukushima had selected them.

As dusk began to fall across the Pacific, the pilot taxied onto the runway.

"What's our flying time to Hong Kong, Mr. Fukushima?" Rose asked once they were airborne.

"Quite a few hours, Miss Jefferson."

"In that case, if you don't mind, I think I'll take a nap."

Fukushima fussed over his passenger until he was sure she was asleep, then he retired to the forward cabin to meditate. Later, when the plane was an hour out of Hong Kong, he had a cup of sake with his men, then entered the cockpit and shared some rice wine with the pilots. In the distance the blurry outline of Hong Kong appeared, the mountains rising from the sea, becoming more defined as the plane lost altitude. Wataru Fukushima returned to his seat and began to pray.

A moment later, as the chartered clipper circled the airport, the engines fell silent. Controllers in the tower saw the wings wobble madly. Radio transmissions carried screams of warning and demands as to what was wrong. The plane drifted in a lazy arc, as though the pilot was trying to gain altitude. Then, like a tethered bird unable to break free, it plunged to the earth, tearing into the runway and exploding in a fireball that boomed across the Crown Colony.

The first word of the Hong Kong crash came over the teletypes at three o'clock, October 8, Paris time. The news was relayed to the Transport Ministry, where the official who saw Rose Jefferson's name on the deceased's list immediately alerted the police. The duty officer at headquarters waited until he had a copy of the Hong Kong teletype, then sent two men to Cassandra McQueen's residence on the Île St.-Louis.

"What's going on?" Cassandra asked groggily as Nicholas slipped out of bed to answer the door.

"I'll be right back," he promised.

One look at the policemen's grim expressions told Nicholas the news couldn't be good. When he read the teletype, his vision blurred. Not Rose! It couldn't be. Rose was indestructible! Nicholas dialed the local precinct and asked the desk sergeant to let the two men stay.

"When the press gets hold of this, they'll be camping on our door."

The duty officer agreed. As the two policemen took up their station outside the door, Nicholas was already on the phone, talking to a French air-charter company. A plane would be ready within the hour to fly them to London. Arrangements would be made for an aircraft to take them to New York via Gander, Newfoundland.

"Nicholas, what's wrong?"

Cassandra stood there in her nightgown and bare feet, rubbing the sleep from her eyes. Nicholas took both her hands in his and held them tightly. "There's been an accident. Rose . . . it's very possible she's . . ."

The next seventy-two hours passed in a blur for Cassandra. Sleep had eluded her for most of the transatlantic voyage. Only when exhaustion set in was she able to sleep fitfully against Nicholas's shoulder.

The nightmare began in earnest at Idlewild Airport. Reporters were out in force, jamming the exits. Mercifully, Jimmy Pearce and others were there to help Nicholas pull her through the crowd. Head bowed, Cassandra plunged ahead, ignoring the questions being shouted at her, shielding her eyes from exploding flash bulbs.

At the Carlton Towers apartment the weariness and loss hung as heavy as the cigarette smoke. Hugh O'Neill, Eric Gollant, and other Global executives were waiting. While Cassandra disappeared into the bathroom, the attorney handed Nicholas a telex.

"This just came in from the British police in Hong Kong. They've positively identified Rose. The . . . the process took this long because the bodies were so badly burned."

"Cassandra doesn't have to know this," Nicholas said shortly.

When Cassandra returned she took her place among the men.

"I want to know what's been happening."

Eric Gollant spoke first. Word of Rose Jefferson's death had stunned the financial community. Besides the outpouring of sympathy, speculation was rampant about a successor. However, no hostile moves were being taken against any Global interests. No one dared to be the first to presume that the company was mortally wounded.

"Legally, the board is empowered to deal with the day-to-day business of the corporation," Hugh O'Neill added. "We've been doing just that. But all major negotiations have been put on hold. We're not taking one step until Rose's will is read."

When Nicholas's turn came, he stunned his audience by announcing that he would be leaving for the Crown Colony the following day.

"Why?" Cassandra demanded. "You keep telling me the Hong Kong police are doing their best to find out what happened."

"I'm head of security for Global. I have to be there."

The pain in his words touched everyone.

"It wasn't your fault," Cassandra said, reaching for him. "A stupid engine didn't work. Something burned out. Nicholas, you can't blame yourself!"

"I have to go and find that out for myself."

"At least let me come with you," Cassandra pleaded.

"That's not a good idea," Hugh O'Neill said quickly. "You're the logical heir, Cassandra. You have to stay here. As far as the public is concerned, you *are* Global. I feel terrible saying this but right now appearances are everything."

Cassandra was tempted to ignore him. Nicholas's pain brought tears to her eyes. She wanted to be there for him.

"How long will you be gone?" she asked finally.

"Ten days, maximum two weeks."

Cassandra closed her eyes. "I need you here, Nicholas."

His silence told her his decision.

As the meeting broke up, Nicholas edged Hugh O'Neill away from the others.

"I want all of Rose's paperwork on the Ho-Ping Bank deal," he said. "Every scrap, even the handwritten stuff. I'll need all your notes as well as anything else you can give me."

"Nick, you don't think that the crash had anything to do with that?"

"Right now I don't know what to think! Except that's the last project Rose was working on. So that's where I start!"

As soon as Nicholas arrived in Hong Kong he was met by the chief of Hong Kong's Criminal Investigation Division and taken to the airport hangar where the remains of the aircraft were stored, each piece undergoing meticulous examination.

"What do you have, Inspector?"

The official, outfitted in khaki shorts, woolen socks, and heavy, kangaroo-skin boots, gestured with his swagger stick.

"My lads have gone over the wreckage with a fine-tooth comb," he said, voice carrying high into the sheet-metal rafters. "We've found a couple of things that might interest you."

The inspector poked a blackened, twisted piece of aluminum.

"Came off the right wing, next to a hydraulic line. Notice how charred it is."

"Meaning what?"

"That the pilot may have been dumping gas just before the crash."

"Why would he do that?"

The inspector's fine blue eyes bored into Nicholas.

"We were hoping you might be able to enlighten us."

The inspector pointed out other bits of debris that were suspicious. Nicholas felt a growing knot of dread in his stomach.

"What do you have on the plane itself?"

The inspector opened a fat ledger. "The aircraft was in tiptop shape. Civil Aviation Department tells us it had less than two thousand hours in the air. Maintenance records show it was serviced thoroughly and on time. The inspections were carried out by our people—that is, British, not local authorities."

"What about the crew?"

"Their documentation was in order. The pilot had logged close to three thousand hours. His copilot almost as much. The stewards had all worked for other airlines. No one had a criminal record."

Nicholas flipped through the pages. "And they were all Japanese."

"Yes, that caught our eye as well," the inspector murmured. "We went around to the Ho-Ping Bank. They were very cooperative, as one would expect, considering that their director was on the aircraft. But there's no law against a Hong Kong bank hiring Japanese pilots or stewards. In fact, we've had

508

quite a few of them over here since the war. Fukushima chose to hire his own kind. Again, understandable."

"Everything seems to be understandable," Nicholas said tightly, "except for these little anomalies you've been pointing out. What are you telling me, Inspector?"

"You understand, Mr. Lockwood, that by themselves these anomalies as you call them do not constitute evidence. Of foul play or anything else."

"But . . . ?"

"But they do indicate that the pilot may have deliberately crashed the aircraft."

Nicholas stared at him, incredulous. "Why?"

"I may not be able to answer that. And neither will you. But let me ask you this, Mr. Lockwood. Your navy chaps in the Pacific had some frightful experiences with Japanese suicide pilots; the kamikazes flew their planes straight into your ships. Or tried to. They had a divine mission. Perhaps you can tell me if our pilot had a similar goal in mind, one so important that he would sacrifice not only himself but his crew and employer as well?"

"Or else he was ordered to crash the plane," Nicholas added quietly.

Nicholas Lockwood spent the next week tearing apart the Ho-Ping Bank. He wrangled an order from the Colony's Controller of Finance and had the bank's books opened up. While a team of hand-picked auditors pored over figures, Lockwood meticulously checked employee records. He put Wataru Fukushima's background under a microscope but found no reason why this unassuming man, whose Tokyo-based sheet-metal plant had given him the wherewithal to open a bank, would want Rose Jefferson dead.

What lay behind Ho-Ping was another matter that incurred Nicholas's wrath. The Swiss principals of Pyramid Holdings arrived from Zurich to express their condolences and, with typical Swiss efficiency, tidied up the mess Fukushima had had the bad manners to create. But there was nothing they could—or would—tell Nicholas about Pyramid.

"Unless you are prepared to bring specific charges against the corporation in a Swiss jurisdiction," they told him, "you must accept the fact that this was simply a tragic accident."

No argument Nicholas marshaled would move the stolid Swiss. The frustration became unbearable. His heart and conscience told him that Rose Jefferson had been murdered. Only one person stood to gain from her death: Steven Talbot.

But that makes no sense, Lockwood argued with himself. *Steven was cut out of Global a long time ago. . . . Then again, this whole damn thing doesn't wash!*

509

But vengeance, Lockwood knew, could carve a very twisted channel in a man's mind.

As he had promised, Nicholas brought Rose's body home with him. He also brought the news that Cassandra and everyone else at Global had been desperately waiting for.

"It was an accident," he told Cassandra, Hugh O'Neill, and the others gathered in O'Neill's office at Lower Broadway. "The Hong Kong police and the Civil Aviation Authority agree that there was a mechanical defect in the hydraulics."

There was silence in the room. All eyes shifted to Cassandra.

"What happens now?" she asked.

"We have a copy of the official investigation," Hugh O'Neill said gently. "We have Nicholas's corroboration. The funeral arrangements have been looked after. Cassandra, if you would stay behind, this would be an appropriate time to have Rose's will read."

The attorney added, "Nicholas, why don't you remain too."

As the others filed out, O'Neill went over to the wall safe. Cassandra remembered another time when death had presented itself to her and demanded an accounting. She hated the thought of receiving anything else from the dead. A legacy from Rose would carry with it an obligation she had no choice but to accept.

Hugh O'Neill returned to his desk with a sheaf of papers bound with red ribbon. The pages crinkled when he touched them, testimony to their age.

"Knowing Rose, it'll all be here on the last page," he said, adjusting his bifocals. "But just to be sure . . ."

O'Neill turned the pages carefully, nodding with the air of a man who had found exactly what he expected.

"Corporate material, bequests to charities, museums, articles of the foundation, everything neat and tidy—"

Suddenly O'Neill's fists smashed down on the pages.

"It's not possible!" he whispered. "She couldn't have meant this. There're . . . there're ink spots all over the pages. She meant to change this!"

Steven Talbot was sitting by the pool, a meandering fantasy bordered by flowers and palms ending at a lava-rock grotto waterfall. Stacked on the patio table were twenty newspapers from around the world. Three weeks had passed since Rose Jefferson's fiery death in Hong Kong but her name continued to dominate the financial headlines. Steven picked up the scissors and carefully

510

cut out another article. He noted the date and slipped it into a folder already stuffed with clippings.

"They're going to be here soon."

Yukiko drifted up behind him. She had been watching Steven for a long time as he whittled, carved, and refined his obsession. When his mother was alive Steven had almost never referred to her. Now that she was dead he couldn't rid himself of her.

"You must allow me my little eccentricities," Steven said, concentrating on his work.

That's all he ever cared about, getting her out of the way.

Steven had never once mentioned anything about the men who had given up their lives so that Rose Jefferson would die. To him, they had been mere tools. But Yukiko had known each of them. She had spent hours with them explaining what had to be done and why. She knew that with every word she was creating widows, orphans, and grieving mothers.

In the end, these men had done their duty to her and paid the ultimate respect to the memory of Hisahiko Kamaguchi. They had gone to their deaths with great honor. Now it was Steven's turn to show them his. The secrets of his past were safe. Global Enterprises had passed into the hands of a young, inexperienced woman who would be easy prey. The men from Japan were in Hawaii. It was time for Steven to surrender what he had created so that every dollar of every investment Pyramid had made would now flow back to Japan, back to the new *zaibatsus*, to the future.

Steven rose at the sound of the wind chimes. He touched Yukiko's cheek.

"Everything will be fine," he said softly. "Believe me."

Yukiko shivered. Something had to be wrong because Steven Talbot had never before laid a hand on her.

He remembered their faces from the Occupation files. Each one had been under suspicion of war crimes. If the investigators had done their work, all would have been hanged. But Steven had seen to it that Hisahiko Kamaguchi had been given up in their place.

The five Japanese, in tailored gray suits, white shirts, and black ties, accepted Yukiko's hospitality. There was no talk about business until tea had been served.

"Gentlemen," Steven said, getting to his feet and walking past the floor-to-ceiling windows that overlooked the Pacific. "As the figures show, the value of the gold salvaged from the *Hino Maru* has multiplied to just over thirty million dollars. We now control financial institutions, shipping, warehousing, raw land, and mines across the Far East. According to our agreement, the time has come to funnel these profits into your *zaibatsus*."

Steven paused and smiled. "But there's been a change of plans."

Steven ignored the excited whispers. Calmly, he handed Yukiko and each man a single sheet of paper.

"This can't be," Yukiko said slowly.

"Is it true, Mr. Talbot?" one of the Japanese asked.

Steven threw back his head and laughed. "Yes! Yes, the old bitch never changed her will. Global Enterprises belongs to me!"

Steven loved the expressions on their faces. Unlike most Westerners, he could discern the emotional changes behind a seemingly neutral facade. Excitement glistened in their sweat. He swore he could feel their hearts beat faster.

"Steven . . . this is incredible," Yukiko said.

"It is a triumph!" the Japanese declared. "What we planned to accomplish in thirty years will now take us half that time, possibly less."

Yukiko felt herself borne away on the enthusiasm sweeping the room. This was victory far greater than anything her father had ever dreamed of. It vindicated everything she had done, what others had surrendered because of their trust in her.

"Steven, we can now use Global's resources to make Pyramid even greater," she said. "Global's worldwide contracts, its financial power, its prestige—we have it all!"

Steven regarded her solemnly. "Or it can be the other way around."

He watched her smile falter, saw the expressions of the Japanese tighten in suspicion.

"What do you mean?"

"Global will be taking over Pyramid. As of now, you are as bare-assed as the day you were born."

The power of his words surged through him and it was the sweetest feeling in the world. Yukiko stared at him and remembered the madness that had danced in his eyes as he was cutting out the newspaper articles.

How long has he known about the will? Was his obsession a charade? Did I allow myself to be so blind?

The questions pounded Yukiko until she felt sick.

"Steven, you can't do this."

"Really? What's to stop me? You needed me because not one of you could afford to have your signature on any check, bill of sale, or lease anywhere in the world. That would have meant questions, too many, too embarrassing. Very dangerous. Pyramid is what I made it. It exists because of my ingenuity. And, of course, mine is the only signature in Zurich."

Steven noted that the shock was becoming anger.

512

"In case any of you think you can stop me, let me remind you that I know every detail of the way you had my mother murdered. The evidence may be circumstantial, but there's more than enough to launch an investigation. I think the American government would cooperate fully with Global Enterprises in determining what caused the death of one of its most prominent citizens."

Steven knew he had them then. As an Occupation officer he had seen the crush of resignation and defeat on thousands of faces.

The men of the *zaibatsus* retreated to the villa that Yukiko had rented for them.

"Have you any explanation?" their spokesman demanded. "Is the *gaijin* serious in his threat?"

Yukiko still could not absorb the words ringing in her ears. If they were true, there wasn't a grave large enough in which to bury her shame.

"He is serious. Make no mistake. I have no explanation to offer you. When he heard about his mother's death, he was elated, but that was to be expected. That was what he wanted. What we all wanted."

"What about telephone calls, cables, messengers," another said. "He had to have been contacted!"

"I swear he did not leave the island," Yukiko told him. "He went into Honolulu, but no more often than before. There were no couriers, no cables, no special calls. It's possible—very likely—that Global used a Honolulu law firm to get in touch with him, in strictest confidence. Believe me, no one, least of all he, expected this."

"We did believe you," the spokesman replied acidly. "And we did not expect this. You should have."

Yukiko was stung by the accusation but made no attempt to defend herself. She had betrayed these men as surely as Steven had betrayed her. There would be a price to pay.

"We all knew that Steven had been removed from Global," Yukiko said. "We had overwhelming proof that"—she added venomously—"all of us agreed was indisputable. That was why he was the perfect tool for us. It was Rose Jefferson who cheated us, by her weakness or oversight."

"No!" another replied. "We placed our trust and our future in Steven Talbot's hands and with a few words he has stolen it from us. His reasoning was correct: we cannot regain what is rightfully ours, nor do we have any way to challenge him."

Yukiko flared. "There has to be a way!"

"There is not. And we shall not allow you to jeopardize our positions any further. There is a time to go forward and a time to retreat. Our choice is obvious."

"So we start at the beginning," Yukiko said bitterly. "In the dust and ashes."

"With one difference," the spokesman said. "You are no longer part of our association."

Yukiko whirled around. "You wouldn't dare leave me out. My father—"

"We all have the greatest respect for Hisahiko Kamaguchi's memory. It is not we but you who have disgraced it. It is you not we who must atone."

"You forget that what is left of Kamaguchi Industries still belongs to me," Yukiko said fiercely.

"No. The Americans would never permit the daughter of a man they hanged as a war criminal to be any part of a future *zaibatsu*. We shall help the Americans dismantle Kamaguchi Industries. Over time, its pieces will fall back into our hands. That way we will preserve your father's memory."

"And what will happen to me?" Yukiko whispered.

The spokesman's face remained impassive. "We have nothing to offer you. There is no place for you among us. You cannot go back to the *gaijin*. You cannot come home to Japan. If there is peace for you in the world, we cannot tell you where to find it. Or even if it exists. That is the uncertain road of your punishment."

A single memory burned in Yukiko's mind as she drove through the darkness back to Cobbler's Point: that night at the Shinto shrine when, after she had brought Steven Talbot to her father, she had drawn a gun to protect Hisahiko Kamaguchi.

I should have squeezed the trigger then. One second and none of this would have happened.

The house was brightly lighted as always but the instant Yukiko stepped inside she felt an emptiness. She found Steven's manservant and demanded to know where his master was.

"In the garden," the servant replied, clearly afraid and confused. "I have already taken the bags to the airport."

Yukiko strode through the back patio and saw him standing facing the ocean.

"I'm going to miss this, the sound and smell of the sea at night." Steven Talbot turned to her. "Did you think I was going to leave without saying good-bye?"

"It might have been more prudent. I could have come back to kill you."

"You wouldn't have gained anything by that. And you don't do anything unless you expect to get something in return."

"Why, Steven?"

In the moonlight his ravaged face took on the bone-white quality of a mask.

"Let me answer with a question: If you had had the chance to do what you wanted without me, wouldn't you have taken it?"

Even as she hesitated Yukiko knew she had confirmed what he believed.

"Of course you would have," Steven said. "Because we're so very much alike. Ultimately one of us would have seized the chance to destroy the other. Mine just came first."

"You don't realize what you've done to me," Yukiko said.

"Of course I do. And there was a reason. I'm not afraid of the *zaibatsus*. They will be too busy picking up the pieces for a long, long time. You were a different matter, though. I had to make sure you could never come after me. So I got them to do what I couldn't—cut you away, make you an outcast. You will survive, Yukiko, but you will never threaten me."

Steven opened an ornately carved chest. Resting on mahogany bridges were two ritual seppuku swords.

"Your father gave these to me shortly before he died," Steven said. "I remember him telling me that if one is skilled, the pain is momentary, even if death isn't. But I forgot to ask him whether women were also expected to use them to regain their honor."

Then, without another word, Steven walked right by her as if she were not even there.

— 59 —

Even before Nicholas had brought Rose's body home, Hugh O'Neill had been frantically searching vaults and safety deposit boxes for a second will or, at the very least, a codicil. At Talbot House and Dunescrag, private files and personal letters were read. O'Neill questioned the staff at both houses but even longtime retainers such as Albany were unable to help him.

"That's enough, Hugh," Cassandra told him when, at the end of the week, the attorney met with her at Lower Broadway.

"Cassandra, do you realize what could happen?"

"Oh, yes, Hugh. Very much so."

Cassandra looked around her. Rose's desk, with its neatly stacked files, remained exactly as it had been the day she had left for the Orient. Behind it, the chair Rose had inherited from her grandfather seemed to wait for its familiar occupant.

The emptiness that had descended upon Cassandra when she lost the last of her family would have been unbearable were it not for Nicholas. She had poured her grief into his arms and kisses and clung to him through the cold nights. Only when the catharsis had passed was she able to look to the future.

"Perhaps Rose never meant for me to inherit," Cassandra said.

"Nonsense!" O'Neill replied emphatically.

"And Steven?"

O'Neill drew a deep breath. "I've contacted his lawyer in Honolulu, as the law requires, but nothing's come back."

"Doesn't he know where Steven is?"

"Doesn't know or won't say."

Cassandra rose and looked out the window at the traffic on Lower Broadway.

"I want to bury her, Hugh. It's indecent to postpone the funeral. Rose deserves better than this." She turned to the lawyer. "I know this is Steven's responsibility. But if he can't or won't look after it, then I must."

The funeral of Rose Jefferson took place in a small Episcopalian church in the village of Prestwick, near the Dunescrag estate. The tranquility of the community was broken by the arrival of hundreds of the nation's most powerful men or their representatives. All the barons of Wall Street were present, as well as government leaders who praised her public service contributions.

After the memorial service, Cassandra followed the hearse to Dunescrag, where, between the graves of her grandfather and brother, Rose Jefferson was laid to rest. Cassandra stepped forward and placed a single white lily on the coffin before it was lowered into the earth.

"Goodbye, Rose."

Flanked by Nicholas and Hugh O'Neill, Cassandra walked toward the snaking line of cars. Along the road, flanked by police, were reporters and cameramen, shouting and snapping photographs as the mourners hurried to their vehicles. Their questions centered on one topic: Steven Talbot. Why hadn't he been at the funeral? Did anyone know where he was? Had he been named Rose Jefferson's successor at Global? So far, Hugh O'Neill had managed to keep the terms of the will secret, but Steven's absence had raised speculation about who would take the helm of Rose Jefferson's empire, Cassandra McQueen or Steven Talbot.

On the way to their car, Cassandra and Hugh were intercepted by a smartly dressed young man. "My name is Joseph Thompson, from Stewart and Delamont," he said. "We've been retained by Mr. Steven Talbot."

Cassandra paled. "Where is he?"

The lawyer smiled at her but addressed Hugh O'Neill.

"Mr. Talbot would like to see you right away."

"You haven't answered Miss McQueen's question," O'Neill replied tightly. "Where's Steven?"

"Where he should be. In his office at Global headquarters."

Steven Talbot sat behind his mother's desk, savoring the trappings around him. All his life he had dreamed of being master of this office. Now it was indisputably his.

Steven laughed softly, remembering the shocked expressions of the staff when he had appeared that morning. He had deliberately waited until the day of Rose's funeral to make his entrance. With most of the executive staff at Dunescrag, he had had the chance to walk through the company and drink in what was now his. Afterward, he had sent his attorney to fetch Hugh O'Neill and gave instructions not to be disturbed.

"Mr. O'Neill is here, sir."

Even over the intercom, Steven detected a tremor in the voice of the secretary.

"Send him in."

When O'Neill entered, Steven saw a tired, dispirited man.

"Hello, Hugh."

"Steven. We missed you at the funeral this morning. Didn't your attorneys notify you?"

"They did," Steven replied coolly. "I'd like to see a copy of the will, please."

Steven didn't miss the anger that flared in O'Neill's eyes, followed almost as quickly by defeat. Carefully, Steven read through the last testament. He imagined how sick O'Neill must have felt when he'd read it to Cassandra.

"I want to convene the board as soon as possible. Say, the day after tomorrow?"

"Steven, there are a lot of details you're not familiar with. The traveler's-check operation, for example—"

"I know all about Cassandra's work with them," Steven replied flatly. "Let me show you what I intend to do about that."

Steven asked the secretary to send in one of Global's security officers. When he arrived, Steven said, "I want all of Miss McQueen's personal effects packed and the lock on her office door changed. Now."

The officer hesitated, glancing at Hugh O'Neill.

"You take your orders from me, not him!" Steven barked. "Get the job done in thirty minutes or else you'll be out too."

The officer retreated.

Steven opened Rose's operations' ledger, an overview of all current and future company projects. He looked up from the pages and said, "That'll be all, Hugh."

Cassandra received Steven's call an hour later. She had been forewarned by Hugh O'Neill that Steven had barred her from her office and had even lifted her authorization to enter Global's premises. Furious, Cassandra had been tempted to confront Steven immediately but O'Neill had urged caution.

"Wait until you know what he wants."

Cassandra thought she knew all about Steven's intentions. Just listening to his voice had made her skin crawl.

Cassandra arrived at Global punctually at one o'clock. She was escorted through the familiar executive suites, and noticed immediately that the office staff avoided her. Cassandra walked into Rose's office without bothering to knock.

Steven looked up from his work, watching as Cassandra's gaze remained fixed on his ruined face. "Still impressed with your handiwork?"

Cassandra didn't flinch. "You were trying to kill me. You killed my mother and you wanted me dead as well."

"If it hadn't been for Harry's bungling you would be dead. On the other hand, this is almost as good. You're finished, Cassandra. As of this moment you don't have a single thing to do with Global."

"I have the traveler's checks," Cassandra replied. "The Paris office is back on its feet. I've rebuilt the organization. Soon I'll reopen the rest of the European offices."

"Will you now? Do you have a contract authorizing you to do that?"

"No, but—"

"That's right. And what are you going to distribute if you don't have the checks either?"

"What do you mean?"

Steven smiled. "I called the Bureau of Printing and Engraving this morning and canceled your order."

"You had no right to do that!"

"Didn't I? The checks are Global property. The minute Rose died, I became Global."

"My mother had a contract with Rose. The traveler's-check operation was hers and she left it to me!"

"Let me refresh your memory about that agreement," Steven said casually, flipping back yellowing pages. "It says here that Rose agreed not to pursue the legal fight over the checks because she and Michelle had come to an agreement. But Rose specifically states that her decision was based on the fact that

Michelle was carrying what she presumed was Franklin's child. Which, as we all know, wasn't the case at all. So by not telling Rose who the real father was, Michelle committed fraud. This contract is worthless, Cassandra."

Cassandra snatched the papers out of his hands. "This doesn't mean a thing!" she said angrily. "My mother was responsible for everything that happened with the traveler's checks. Rose acknowledged as much. When she took over the business, it was only on a temporary basis, until I was experienced enough to run it."

"You may see it that way," Steven said, crossing his arms. "I don't think the courts will."

"Don't threaten to make a public issue out of this, Steven," Cassandra warned. "I know all about your dealings with Kurt Essenheimer and the Nazis. I have names, dates, places, everything!"

Steven laughed. "A lot of good that'll do you. Do you think anyone will believe you or even care?"

"I'll make them believe and they *will* care! I'll talk to Hugh O'Neill—"

"You're forgetting one thing, Cassandra," Steven interrupted softly. "Hugh O'Neill works for me now."

The living room in Hugh O'Neill's Sutton Place townhouse reflected the spirit of the season. A stately blue spruce, decked with twinkling lights, antique ornaments, and loops of gaily colored bunting, stood beside the fireplace, casting its cheer across the room. But neither the tree nor the magic of Christmas dispelled the gloom of the conversation.

"I still say Cassandra should challenge Rose's will in court," Nicholas Lockwood said stubbornly. "It's obvious that when Steven didn't come back to Global after the war, Rose had kicked him out. She never intended him to inherit anything!"

"It's not the intention that counts," Hugh O'Neill replied wearily. "The court will look at what's written in the will. Besides, no one knows what happened between Rose and Steven. There was a lot of speculation and gossip but we managed to hide the truth."

O'Neill sloshed more whiskey into his crystal tumbler. "Hell, we had to hide it. Rose was one of the principals behind the rebuilding of Europe. How would it have looked if the public had learned that Steven had been dealing with the Nazis?

"That's the awful irony," the attorney continued, staring into his glass. "When Rose shut down Steven's operations around the world, she also destroyed any evidence that they had ever existed."

"But some of the people involved must still be alive," Nicholas protested.

"What if they are? Do you think they'll come forward to testify for us? They have as much to hide as Steven has."

"God damn Rose! If she'd just paid a little more attention, none of this would have happened—"

"Stop it, both of you!"

Cassandra glared at both men. "Arguing like this isn't going to get us anywhere."

Unlike Nicholas and Hugh O'Neill, Cassandra could understand how a woman in Rose's position, having created so much but also alone, would have faltered before cutting off the last of her flesh and blood. She imagined Rose holding the pen and staring at Steven's name, remembering all the evil he had been responsible for yet not finding the strength to cast him out completely.

She didn't forgive him. She just needed someone to take his place. I wasn't ready and Rose thought she had all the time in the world to prepare me. . . .

Cassandra went to Hugh O'Neill and squeezed his hand. When she had told him what Steven intended to do, O'Neill had picked up his pen and drafted a brief letter of resignation. They had left the building together.

Thinking back, Cassandra wondered if she had done the right thing. O'Neill had less than a year to retirement. Lately, his health hadn't been the best, and Cassandra knew how much he was looking forward to devoting his time to his grandchildren and his hobbies. When she had mentioned this, O'Neill had said, "I'm not about to let a bastard like Steven steal what's yours. It's going to be a tough fight but I'll be there for you." Cassandra had asked herself if she had the right to expect that from him.

"I'm not going to give in to Steven," she told both men. "But I don't want you, Hugh, to carry the fight all by yourself. Hire as many people as you think we need."

The attorney smiled wanly. "I'll get the best extra hands on the Street."

Nicholas, listening to the exchange, was dismayed by O'Neill's lack of conviction. He had to light a fire under O'Neill, get him to give his best in one last battle. There was only one way to do that. The truth, or what little he could disclose, would hurt Cassandra as well, but Nicholas felt he had no choice.

"What I'm about to tell you," he said slowly, "has to remain in this room."

He looked from O'Neill to Cassandra, both of whom nodded, obviously puzzled.

"There's a real possibility that Rose was murdered." He held up his hand. "Before you ask anything, hear me out. I know what the Hong Kong police report said and that I corroborated it. But I did that because there was no proof—at least not enough to point the finger at someone. I need the time to dig deeper, hunt down some answers."

Cassandra was the first to recover from the shock. "You suspect someone, Nicholas. You wouldn't tell us something like this if you didn't."

"I think the trail will lead straight back to Steven."

"You can't be serious!" O'Neill exclaimed. "Steven was in Hawaii when Rose's plane went down."

"Where was he before then? What is his connection with Pyramid Holdings? With Fukushima and the Ho-Ping Bank?"

"You don't know there were—or are—any!"

"I didn't have a chance to find out. I need more time."

"How sure are you, Nicholas?" Cassandra asked quietly.

"Sure enough to say that you must challenge Steven in court," Nicholas said. "I know it's going to be ugly but we have a lot of ammunition. I'm going to try to get more, enough to bury Steven once and for all."

"If you think Steven engineered Rose's death then I'll do everything I can to nail that bastard!" O'Neill declared, eyes blazing.

"I still find it hard to believe," Cassandra said. "Steven masterminding his own mother's death . . ."

Then she remembered the catacombs. Yes, she could believe it.

As though Nicholas was reading her thoughts, he added, "Remember what Steven did with Essenheimer. Think of how much more harm he can do using Global as his instrument."

Hugh O'Neill's prediction was devastatingly accurate. As soon as Cassandra filed the court challenge, the press swarmed all over her, demanding to know whether she was carrying out a vendetta against Steven Talbot.

"The facts speak for themselves," Cassandra declared. "Michelle McQueen, my mother, single-handedly built the traveler's check in Europe. Rose Jefferson acknowledged that. As well as the fact that I was to take control of the European operation. She also had very good reason not to want the rest of Global to fall into her son's hands. You'll know why as soon as the evidence is filed."

On the first day of the trial Hugh O'Neill weighed in with the evidence of Steven's complicity with the Nazis. Accusations, denials, and threats of lawsuits flew back and forth. Steven Talbot took the high road, shrugging off suggestions of guilt and stating that Cassandra was showing her true colors.

"I haven't the faintest idea where Miss McQueen and her counsel got this so-called evidence or who manufactured it for them. However, there are facts that she chooses to ignore."

Steven produced the French police reports of the incident in the catacombs, as well as the newspaper articles that hailed him as a hero, a man who had risked his life, and been disfigured, in a desperate attempt to save a young girl's life.

521

"And for that she calls me a Nazi," he said quietly. "Gentlemen, I think that tells you everything you need to know about Cassandra McQueen."

The impact of Steven's rebuttals was swift and harsh. Not only did Cassandra lose whatever sympathy and benefit of the doubt the press had given her, but the issue of Steven's heroism cast him in a totally different light. Reporters played on his sterling war record and called on MacArthur, who strongly vouched for Steven's integrity. The tide was turning and there was no stopping it.

For Cassandra, Carlton Towers became a fortress. She seldom ventured out, never knowing where a reporter might be lurking. She received hate mail and threatening phone calls. Hugh O'Neill finally arranged police protection for her, and although this assured Cassandra privacy, it also made her feel like a prisoner.

But Cassandra was more worried about O'Neill than herself. He was working a law clerk's hours, as well as supervising three juniors. Day after day he was advised to drop the case, that Steven Talbot would bury him and, if he chose to bring a lawsuit for damages, cripple him financially. Cassandra did what she could to help, but it was O'Neill who carried the brunt of their offensive. To Cassandra, the toll on his health was becoming intolerable.

As 1949 passed into the bitter grip of February, the news worsened. The judge hearing the case finally ruled that the documents O'Neill had filed purporting to show Steven's dealings with the Nazis, and therefore the reason for Rose Jefferson's intention to disown him, were inadmissible.

"They are not germane to these proceedings, Mr. O'Neill," the justice had declared. "You have no witnesses to corroborate any of the documentation. If you have any other information—or, better, evidence—you would do well to bring it forward at this time."

"Nicholas is our last hope," Hugh told Cassandra. "You'd better call him and tell him we need a rabbit out of a hat."

As far as Cassandra and O'Neill knew, Nicholas was in Zurich, trying to penetrate the secrecy that surrounded Pyramid Holdings. The truth was very different.

St. Julian's was a small fishing village overlooking the bay at the western end of Malta. After the war it was very cheap to live on the island, and the money Harry Taylor had brought with him went a long way. He had a large comfortable house on one of St. Julian's winding streets, with a balcony that overlooked the bay. In the early mornings he liked to sit and watch the green, red, and yellow fishing boats returning with their bounty. Later, he walked to the pier and had swordfish steaks cut from the fresh catch.

But today Harry Taylor was not enjoying the quiet of the morning. He was standing on the deck of a ferry bound for Tripoli, Libya, seventy-five miles to the south. All he had were the clothes on his back, a Gladstone bag, and a money belt.

No one who had known Harry in New York would have recognized him now. His hair had turned snow-white and his grizzled beard had been bleached by the salt and wind. The sun had permanently darkened his skin and created a web of wrinkles under his eyes. The transformation was significant but it obviously wasn't enough.

A few evenings earlier, in the bar of the restaurant where he usually had dinner, Harry had seen a new face, young, European or American, the hard, determined face of a hunter. Later, when the man had gone, Harry chatted with the proprietor, who explained that the man had been asking questions about an American. Protective of their own privacy, the Maltese never volunteered information to strangers. The man had learned nothing.

That was cold comfort to Harry. Ever since the catacombs, flight had become a way of life for him. Even as he had allowed himself to be drawn into Steven's insanity he had never trusted the man. Once he had been told where Cassandra was to be taken and where the alleged exchange was to occur, Harry had carefully researched the treacherous tunnels and plotted a secret escape route.

But getting out alive wouldn't have saved him were it not for the money he had snatched before disappearing into the catacombs. Whenever Harry touched the upper part of his chest, he could feel the scar where a less-than-scrupulous physician had extracted the bullet as well as bits of shattered bone. The procedure had been agonizing because Harry had refused anesthesia, fearful that the doctor might rob him or turn him over to the police—or both. Thirty hours after the aborted kidnapping Harry had managed to get as far as Charenton, where he went to ground.

Harry doubted that he would have slipped through the police dragnet had it not been for luck and the money. He had found a barge whose skipper was more interested in profit than explanations and eventually found himself in Marseilles. Ruled by Corsicans and populated by Algerians and other North Africans, it was a melting pot where men on the run could catch their breath or, if they had skills that were in demand, disappear into the service of any of the hundreds of criminal gangs and enterprises that flourished there. Despite what had been written about him, Harry was not a killer. But he knew a lot about money, stocks, bonds, and other financial instruments. In his broken French, Harry put out the word that he was prepared to be of service to anyone who needed a business adviser. It took three months but he was finally approached by an ostentatiously dressed dandy who showed him some bonds he wanted to dispose of. Harry went to work.

By the time war broke out, Harry was an integral part of a thriving boiler-plate operation. He sold penny stocks in nonexistent African railroads, shares in defunct South African gold mines, and futures in cargoes of raw tuna that were rancid even before they left the dock. His victims were doctors, lawyers, and other professionals eager to make a quick killing. Harry had no compunction about swindling them and sharpening other skills at their expense.

By this time Harry was known under three different names, had established a maze of companies, and had a half-dozen passports stashed in different locations. His reputation attracted others who specialized in white-collar crime—con men, fraud artists, and, most interestingly, counterfeiters. Harry was fascinated by the forger's art. He came to appreciate the difficulty of creating the perfect paper, the importance of grain and texture. He learned the secrets of dyes and inks and admired the intricate work of the graphic artists who designed phony stock certificates. Harry became the hub in a wheel of many spokes. He developed a stock out of thin air, breathed life into it by giving it a provenance, determined the market to which he would pitch it, and described exactly what it should look like. Then his confreres took over, and in the end everyone profited handsomely from the illusion that reaped very real francs, marks, pounds, and lira.

In spite of his success Harry never felt completely secure. When he heard about Steven's disfigurement, he thought it poetic justice. But now Harry knew he had two people determined to find him: Rose, because she believed he had masterminded Cassandra's kidnapping, and Steven, who eventually would take up the hunt because Harry was the only man who knew the truth about what had happened in the catacombs.

Harry kept an eye out for strange faces. He listened carefully to the under-world gossip about new arrivals asking questions or large sums of money being offered for information. In rare quiet moments Harry thought back to Rose, the shining years of his youth filled with such promise, and how, for all his luck, events had conspired against him. But such indulgences were brief because they always brought Harry back to that terrible night in the catacombs where Michelle McQueen had been murdered. Harry knew that if he did nothing else with the rest of his life, he would one day have to find a way to atone for that.

The first word about the stranger had come from one of the counterfeiters. A new face had arrived in Marseilles, not a policeman but someone more capable, who moved confidently through the criminal warrens, a man who did not frighten easily, if at all. He was asking about a Harry Taylor.

Harry didn't wait. He got a glimpse of the man to memorize his face, then packed his essentials, retrieved his papers from the various bolt holes around the city, and left the rest behind. Just hours before Britain and France declared war on Germany, Harry had crossed the Swiss border.

Harry knew better than to continue his activities in Switzerland. He had plenty of money and no desire to run afoul of the Swiss authorities. But his pursuer would not leave him alone. Harry glimpsed him several times in the streets of Lausanne and cursed his fortune. How could the hunter have tracked him over the years? Who was paying him—Steven Talbot or Rose Jefferson? There were moments when Harry was on the verge of confronting his silent tormentor, but each time his instinct for self-preservation prevailed.

After the war Harry spent several years in Rome, living amid that ruined city until the stranger appeared once more. Then it had been on to the island of Capri, and afterward, crisscrossing the Mediterranean in the hope of losing his pursuer. After eighteen months in Malta, Harry had almost believed he had.

Harry leaned on the railing and saw the sun glinting off the red tiles of his house. If his pursuer was there now he'd find nothing to identify the occupant—some clothing, simple furniture, pots and pans.

"Damn you!" Harry muttered.

Harry was tired of running. He craved to feel at home somewhere without having to look over his shoulder. As the ferry's horn resounded across the harbor and the screws churned up the water, Harry vowed that this time he would run even farther. In spite of its diversity, Europe was too small. He needed distant, exotic lands in which to lose himself. Otherwise it was just a matter of time before the hunter brought him to ground.

Nicholas Lockwood leaned against the balcony of the small guesthouse where he was staying, watching the ferry pull out of the harbor. The cable crumpled in his fist was mute testimony to his frustration. Simon Wiesenthal's information had been accurate. He could smell Harry Taylor. Yet now he had no choice but to call off the hunt. The news from New York demanded it.

Nicholas returned to his room to pack. He hated the thought of arriving home empty-handed. Despite what he had told Cassandra and Hugh O'Neill, Nicholas had never fooled himself into thinking he would find any connection between Pyramid and Steven Talbot. Although he was certain one existed, he was equally sure that it would be buried under layers of corporate secrecy. But none of that would matter if he could find Harry Taylor. His testimony would be more than enough to bring Steven to justice—or, because he would be tried in France, to the guillotine. But he had run out of the one commodity no amount of money could buy: time.

Steven Talbot stood on the steps of the courthouse in Lower Manhattan, the folds of his coat snapping in the March wind. Fanned out below him like supplicants were newspapermen hurling their questions.

Steven held up his hand. "Gentlemen, please. I have a brief statement to make. This has been a long, tasteless, and ultimately useless trial. Cassandra McQueen came into it like a thief and leaves it condemned as one. The verdict has proven as much. I only wish that Miss McQueen had had the decency to accept my mother's last wishes. In challenging them, she has cast a slur upon them."

"Will you be taking action for damages?" a reporter shouted.

"There is nothing Miss McQueen has that I could possibly want," Steven replied. "As far as I'm concerned, the matter is closed."

"What do you intend to do with the traveler's checks now that you have them back?" another called out.

Steven smiled. "That, gentlemen, you will have to wait and see."

At the other end of Manhattan, on the Upper East Side, Hugh O'Neill lay in a bed in Roosevelt Hospital. He was barely conscious and his failing eyes discerned only blurred figures. His fingers curled weakly around Cassandra's hand.

"I'm here, Hugh."

Cassandra had been at the hospital for the last three days, ever since O'Neill had been rushed in after a massive heart attack suffered at his office. The juniors he had hired replaced him in court and had brought back the verdict.

"I guess we didn't do so well," O'Neill whispered, his eyelids fluttering.

"You were magnificent," Cassandra told him, fighting back tears.

"All for nothing. None of this would have happened if I had checked the will. It was such a simple thing to remember to do. But I didn't. . . . I brought all this on you."

"Don't say that, please! It's not anyone's fault."

Hugh O'Neill strained to hear her. The darkness was gathering behind his eyes, the light fleeing like the sky before a sinking sun.

"You know Rose . . ."

Cassandra slumped forward, tears streaming across her cheeks. She was losing him and there was nothing she could do.

"Yes, I know Rose."

"No . . . didn't mean that. Rose, the kind of woman she was . . . always had something up her sleeve, a last trick . . . Rose was working on something. . . . Very special . . . Wouldn't even tell me. Before Hong Kong . . . Find it . . . It must be important. . . ."

"Yes, Hugh, I'll find it, I promise. And we'll look at it together, all right?"

Hugh O'Neill smiled faintly and squeezed her hand. For the longest time Cassandra just sat there, holding him, until the nurse finally entered and gently closed his eyes.

* * *

526

The brilliance behind the mansion windows spilled onto Fifth Avenue. Passersby hurried along, looking enviously at the lights, imagining the glamorous party that must be taking place. It was all an illusion. Inside, Steven Talbot was alone. Ever since he had returned to the house where he had been born he had instructed the servants to keep every light burning even after they retired.

Steven loved prowling the house late at night. Each of its thirty rooms held a special memory. He loved its space and silence, the paintings, sculptures, the Persian rugs and Oriental porcelain vases Rose had collected throughout the years. What thrilled him was that it all belonged to him now and no one could ever take it away.

As he walked back to his study on the main floor Steven saw not Rose but his father. This house had been his wedding gift to his bride, a woman who had turned on him, refused to stand by him, who ultimately destroyed him.

You tried to do the same to me, Mother. But you failed.

He wished his father were here to witness the moment.

Steven sat down behind his desk and picked up a personnel file from the stack beside the lamp. He did his best work at night and this was a labor of love: purging Global of Rose's friends and cronies. It was too bad O'Neill had quit, depriving Steven of the satisfaction of firing him. Still, there was Eric Gollant, the chief accountant, as well as a dozen others whose loyalty remained with Rose. A lot of blood would be spilled before he was through.

Steven opened Nicholas Lockwood's file and studied the picture of the head of the inspectors division. He was a purposeful-looking man, with excellent references from the State Department. There were letters of commendation from both domestic and foreign police forces, praising Lockwood's efforts in running down counterfeiters and forgers. The man obviously did his job well.

Several references made Lockwood even more interesting. The first was his report on the plane crash in Hong Kong. From the notes, it was clear that Lockwood had carefully gone over the police and aviation-board inquiry reports. Steven was pleased to read that Global's investigator concurred with their findings. It meant that the case was really closed.

The other two notes, made in Rose's handwriting, counted heavily against Lockwood. His involvement with Cassandra puzzled Steven. Lockwood was a handsome man who traveled widely and lived well. There were ample opportunities to date and bed many desirable women. Although Nicholas Lockwood kept a separate apartment, he was, for all intents and purposes, living with Cassandra.

It doesn't fit. He's not the kind to tie himself down to one woman unless there's a damn good reason.

Steven poured himself a drink and toyed with the conundrum. Only one solution presented itself. Everyone had expected Cassandra to get Global when Rose died. Cassandra was an inexperienced young woman who had no idea what it would take to run an organization like Global. But Lockwood did. As her consort he had positioned himself so that Cassandra would have no choice but to turn to him for help. A sharp player like Lockwood would soon have Cassandra acting as nothing more than a figurehead, without her ever being aware of it.

Well, there's a way to test that theory.

Steven instinctively liked Lockwood and felt that a man of experience, streaked with ruthlessness, would come in very handy in the future. But he had to be absolutely certain where Lockwood's loyalties lay. Asking him about Cassandra was one way to find out. And, just as a surprise, Steven decided he'd throw another name out at Lockwood as well.

Across Central Park, the lights were also burning in the penthouse of the Carlton Towers. Ever since Hugh O'Neill's death Cassandra had been plagued by insomnia. She refused to take even the mildest tranquilizer to help her sleep. She feared not only the nightmares but the possibility that she wouldn't be able to think clearly. And she had to.

Cassandra drifted by the bedroom and saw Nicholas sprawled out on the bed, one arm reaching for the side where she usually slept. It would have been so easy to curl up beside him and let his warmth envelop her. But she couldn't let herself do that, until she had solved Hugh O'Neill's riddle.

"Rose was working on something very important. . . . Wouldn't even tell me . . ."

What was it? What could Rose have been doing that was so secret even her attorney of thirty years knew nothing about it?

If he didn't, how can I expect to?

Cassandra went into the living room and stared at the cold fireplace. She pushed away the hurt and loss these last months had inflicted on her and summoned up every detail she could about the times she and Rose had been together. Images of places came first, followed by snatches of conversation. Cassandra tried hard actually to hear the words, to visualize Rose's expression as she spoke. Memories were all she had to work with. Steven's first official act as president had been to bar Cassandra from Global. There was no way she could get into the notes and files that might have provided a clue, if not an answer.

Think . . .

Cassandra recalled one of the most salient features about Rose's character. She was a very secretive woman. Unlike other creative individuals, she tended not to share new concepts, bounce ideas off others. She worked on her ideas alone, and anything she committed to paper was carefully put away in her private vaults, either at Global or at Talbot House.

Where I can't get at them.

"Cass, why don't you at least try to get some sleep?"

Cassandra looked up at Abilene, her nightgown riding just above the parquet, a cup of steaming chocolate in her hand.

"Drink this. It'll settle you."

Cassandra thanked her and sipped the hot drink.

"You're thinking about Miss Rose, aren't you," Abilene said.

"Yes. I wish I had seen her just once before . . . before the accident. Why is it you always remember what you wanted to say when it's too late?"

"I know what you're sayin'," Abilene murmured. "She had something to tell you too."

Cassandra looked at her curiously.

"What I mean is, Miss Rose came by here the day she left. She had something with her but didn't say what it was."

Cassandra jumped to her feet. *Don't get your hopes up,* she warned herself.

Cassandra pulled back the panel of the wall safe and stared at the gleaming steel face. Rose had known the combination to it. Holding her breath, Cassandra spun the dial, listening to the tumblers click. She pulled open the door and lifted out the contents. On the top, under a pool of lamplight, was a maroon leather folder that did not belong to her. Cassandra flipped back the cover, puzzled by the sloppy typing and the handwritten notes in the margin until she realized that Rose must have typed it herself. She only had to read the first page to understand why.

By dawn Cassandra had gone over the portfolio's contents three times. She could quote parts of it verbatim. There was a secret after all. No one knew it existed because Rose hadn't made any copies. Cassandra slumped back in her chair, her mind reeling at what she'd found. Steven hadn't gotten everything. But he didn't know that.

Cassandra flipped the pages back to the beginning and picked up a fresh pencil. She needed a weapon with which to challenge Steven and Rose had left her one. It would take years to realize what Rose had only imagined, and if Steven got wind of what she was doing before she was ready, he wouldn't hesitate to crush her.

Cassandra imagined Nicholas's reaction to what she was planning. He'd be furious, and with good reason. After all, she would be asking him to betray her.

They sat on the terrace, looking over the spring glory of Central Park. In contrast, the mood around the table was heavy, like a gathering storm charged with thunder.

"Do you know what you're asking me to do?" Nicholas said at last.

In front of him lay the maroon folder. He had read its contents, amazed by Rose's daring and scope of vision. Then he had listened as Cassandra explained how she intended to turn that dream into reality. When he heard the cost, Nicholas had all but refused to listen to anything more.

"I know," she replied tenderly, reaching for his hand.

Nicholas shook his head. "It's crazy, Cass. You want me to butcher everything we've built, to walk away from you and not look back. You're asking me to make the world believe that I never cared for you at all."

"You have to convince Steven I'm not a threat. As long as he believes that, he'll leave me alone. You have to buy me time, love, so I can finish what Rose began."

"How can I do that?" Nicholas whispered. "You yourself said this project will take years to complete, if it can be done at all. And there's not a damn thing I'll be able to do to help you!"

"You'll be helping in a way only you can. Have you any idea what it's costing me to ask you to go away? Please, please try to understand."

Nicholas was used to making hard decisions but none had ever been so difficult as the one he faced now.

Then again, I've never loved anyone the way I love her. . . .

Cassandra read his thoughts.

"I need you to love me, Nicholas, now more than ever."

It was her final plea that tipped the balance.

"We'll need a place," he said slowly. "Somewhere we can meet, which no one knows about . . ."

"In Connecticut," Cassandra murmured. "There's a cabin, on a lake. It's miles from the nearest town. In winter we can skate on the ice and in the summer watch the fireflies dance over the reeds. . . ."

Suddenly Nicholas was beside her, crushing her in his arms, his lips buried in her hair.

"I'm going to miss you so much!"

"Make love to me, darling, right now, so I can remember. . . ."

Nicholas Lockwood had been expecting Steven's call and not only because of the way the pink slips were being handed out. He was aware of how thoroughly Steven was examining employees' records, searching for details that would reveal just how committed these people had been to Rose and how far they could be trusted—if at all. By now, he reckoned, Steven would have realized that as head of the inspectors division, Nicholas knew almost as much about the workings of Global as Rose had. That implied a great trust. Could he convince Steven that he could change allegiance so quickly?

The question wasn't the only one that troubled Nicholas as he walked toward Steven's office. He had no idea what personal papers Rose might have kept relating to Nicholas's hunt for Harry Taylor as well as his connection to Monk McQueen, Abraham Warburg, and Zurich. If Steven had any inkling of this, Nicholas could expect to be unemployed on the spot. And that meant Cassandra would lose her eyes and ears inside Global.

Nicholas steeled himself as Steven's new secretary announced his arrival.

"Have a seat, Lockwood. I'll be with you in a minute."

Nicholas recognized the drill. Steven was behind his desk, pretending to read some papers. He was demonstrating his power, making it clear that there were more urgent matters than Lockwood's future. Nicholas sat back, casually crossed his legs, and let his mind drift.

"You've got an impressive record," Steven said at last. "Like your job?"

Nicholas focused his attention. "Yes, sir, I do."

"Tell me about Harry Taylor."

The question jolted Nicholas but he recovered instantly. Steven watched him carefully.

"There's very little to tell, sir. I haven't found him."

"That's true. But I want to know why you're looking for him in the first place."

"Miss Jefferson asked me to."

"Did she give you a reason?"

"No, sir. I assumed it was a personal affair. Mr. Taylor disappeared a long time ago. Miss Jefferson asked me to use my contacts in Europe to see if I could pick up a trail. She made it clear that this inquiry was not to impede my other duties. It was a sideline investigation."

Steven picked up a silver letter opener and held it between two fingertips.

"And how far has this sideline investigation progressed?"

"Not very, I'm afraid. I had people in England and France looking into Mr. Taylor's whereabouts. There were reports of his having been seen in Lausanne, then Rome. After that the trail got pretty cold." Nicholas paused. "Before I got any further, Miss Jefferson was killed."

"I see. You know, Lockwood, that a lot of things are changing here. Do you want to be a part of that change?"

"If you're asking whether I want to keep my job, the answer is yes."

"I'd like you to stay exactly where you are. You're very good at what you do."

"Thank you, sir."

Steven's eyes narrowed. "But I do have one problem. You and Cassandra have been very chummy. That touching reunion in San Francisco after you were rescued, the convenient coincidence of your living in the same building, it adds up to quite the romance."

"So I've been screwing her," Nicholas said coldly. "What's the problem?"

Steven couldn't hide his surprise.

"You saw what Cassandra tried to do to me in court. I consider any contact with her a conflict of interest. Does that pose a problem for you, Lockwood?"

Nicholas's gaze did not waver. "No problem."

"Just like that? Come on, Lockwood, you're practically living with her."

"You asked me to make a choice. I can understand that you need to know exactly where I stand. Fine. I'm telling you I like this job and want to keep it. That's my explanation. Take it or leave it."

Steven smiled, pleased that he had been correct about Lockwood's interest in Cassandra. "You're a bigger prick than I thought."

Nicholas rose. "Opinions are like assholes. Everybody has one."

For a moment Nicholas thought he had pushed Steven too far. Then Steven laughed.

"All right, Lockwood. I deserved that. Do what you have to do."

As Nicholas was leaving, Steven called out to him, "By the way, I want you to keep looking for Harry Taylor. But very quietly, understand? Whatever you find comes straight to me, no one else."

The next day, Nicholas was in his office when he heard a commotion. The door flew open, the frosted glass rattling in its frame.

"I'm sorry, Mr. Lockwood, I told her you couldn't be disturbed," his secretary was saying as Cassandra pushed by her.

"That's all right, Ethel," he said quietly. "I'll look after it. Thank you."

"What the hell is this?" Cassandra demanded, slamming a newspaper on Nicholas's desk.

The *New York Times* was open to the front page of the business section. The lead story was all about Nicholas Lockwood's having been one of the few survivors of the bloodbath at Global.

"Is it true? Are you going to keep working for him?"

"Cassandra, please, keep your voice down. People can hear—"

"I don't care! I want to know if you're staying."

"Yes, I am," Nicholas replied.

Cassandra shook her head. "I can't believe you're saying that. Not after everything . . ."

"Don't lay all the blame on me," Nicholas said coldly. "I have a future here. If you can't accept that—"

"I can't and I won't," Cassandra retorted. She pushed the paper onto his lap. "Congratulations. I know you'll do very well."

Cassandra turned on her heel and marched out. Nicholas rose and leaned against the door frame, watching her go. Out of the corner of his eye he saw Steven Talbot looking at him, a glint of amusement in his eyes.

– 60 –

Eric Gollant was relieved when an in-house messenger finally delivered his termination letter. He had no illusions about working for Steven Talbot. It would be a hell he could not imagine. Besides, a few weeks shy of his sixtieth birthday, Eric was prepared to retire. While his hair had thinned and the lenses in his glasses had become thicker, the investments in his portfolio had swollen to generous proportions. There was enough money for his modest needs and those of his wife, and plenty left over to indulge a gaggle of grandchildren. Nothing pleased Eric more than the sound of children taking over his house. It was to them that he looked for solace and warmth whenever he remembered his good friend Hugh O'Neill.

As he strolled down Lexington Avenue toward the Empire State Building that warm spring day in 1950, Eric wondered why Cassandra had asked to see him. After Nicholas Lockwood's defection into the Talbot ranks, she had become a virtual recluse. Eric's heart went out to Cassandra. She had lost the two men she had counted on: Hugh O'Neill and Nicholas Lockwood. Eric had genuinely liked Lockwood. It seemed inconceivable that he would change allegiance so swiftly.

He's a gonif, Eric thought, disgusted and angry.

As he walked through the bustling crowd, the accountant thought he saw many Lockwoods hurrying past him, young men with grim expressions, growing old before their time, worshipping false idols.

Jimmy Pearce jammed his Irish houndstooth cap on his unruly red hair. As he wended his way around the desks in the editorial office, staffers pushed slips of paper, each one screaming *Urgent!*, into the pockets of his jacket. When he finally hit the street, he put his long legs into overdrive to get him across town.

Cassandra's phone call had come out of the blue. After the fiasco with Steven and the grief Nicholas Lockwood had caused her, Jimmy hadn't heard a word from her. He had called a few times, to make sure she was all right. He'd even suggested she come down to Q magazine, hinting that it might be better for her to keep busy than to sit around with time on her hands. Cassandra had politely refused and remained noncommittal about her plans.

As he crossed Madison, Pearce wondered why Cassandra had specified the Empire State Building. As a walking encyclopedia of New York eateries, Pearce was certain that the best the city landmark had to offer was a third-rate cafeteria. It didn't seem like Cassandra's style at all.

The five-room suite was in the southwest corner of the building. What linoleum tiles remained were filthy and chipped, the windows coated with grime, and the walls bulging because of countless water-pipe leaks.

"Gee, I guess the card table and chairs fit right in," Jimmy Pearce muttered.

"You're sure we have the right place?" asked Eric Gollant.

"This could never be the right place for anything."

"Thank you, gentlemen, for your candid observations."

Cassandra, dressed in a navy suit and white silk blouse, strode across the room, the heels of her pumps causing little puffs of dust to explode beneath them.

"As a matter of fact, I asked the superintendent to bring these up," she said indicating the rickety table and chairs. "Otherwise we'd be sitting on the floor."

"Great," Pearce said. "I should have brought a picnic basket."

"It's wonderful to see you," Cassandra said, hugging both of them.

The men were impressed by Cassandra's appearance. She had gained a little weight, which filled her out nicely. Her cheeks shone, and her blue eyes sparkled with promise and anticipation.

"All right, I'll bite," Jimmy said. "What is this place?"

"Cheap."

"That much I can tell. What else?"

"My new offices. Or should I say, our new offices."

"All right," the accountant said dubiously. "You have our undivided attention."

"Both of you know what a credit card is," Cassandra said.

"Yeah, a way for its issuers to go bankrupt," the editor-in-chief of Q piped up.

"Thanks for the vote of confidence," Cassandra replied dryly. "In fact, the credit card has been around longer than you might think."

Cassandra went on to explain that at the turn of the century, some hotels offered steady customers cards for room and board. By 1914, a few department stores were issuing metal cards that looked like dogtags, and in the '20s, oil companies printed cardboard ones that were honored at their service stations.

"All that led to was irresponsible debt," Eric reminded her. "Buying stocks on credit—or margin—was one of the causes for the '29 crash. Then during the Depression we had all sorts of cash-down layaway plans and installment payments. That lasted until World War Two, when the government curbed credit spending."

"But all these things—whether charge cards or installment plans—were good with only one merchant or one company's outlets," Cassandra argued. "What if there were a card that could be used in many different stores?"

Cassandra watched carefully as her friends weighed her words. She wished the idea didn't sound so simple, but it was.

"What exactly are you getting at, Cassandra?" asked Eric, polishing his glasses.

Cassandra recognized this fastidious gesture. It meant the accountant was ready to do some serious thinking.

"Steven got everything in Global," she continued. "At least that's what he and everyone else thought. But Rose had been working on a project that she had held back. No one knew about it. No one suspected—or suspects—that it exists. The details are scanty but they're the beginning of something Rose believed could change our whole financial system. I've looked at the notes and I think she was right."

Cassandra paused. "Before I go on, I want to say that neither of you is under any obligation. If you don't feel the idea has merit, you won't hear about it from me again. If you do, then I'm asking you to help me—for suitable compensation, naturally. Either way, I'm going ahead with this."

Cassandra let the words echo through the empty suite. "I know you must think I'm crazy. Maybe I am. But there are debts outstanding and I intend to pay them in full."

Eric cleared his throat. "I think both of us appreciate your feelings, Cassandra. What do you have in mind?"

"United States Express," Cassandra said softly. "USE."

She laid two sets of papers in front of each man.

"The one on the left has Rose's original notes. On the right is what I've added. I'll leave you to it."

Without another word, Cassandra disappeared. She went around the corner for coffee at a greasy luncheonette. The wait seemed interminable but Cassandra felt that she had to give Jimmy Pearce and Eric Gollant enough time to study her proposition, discuss it, and come to a decision. She glanced at her watch. Thirty minutes should be plenty.

On the way back Cassandra deliberately slowed her pace. She wanted so much for them to see what she saw in her proposal, to feel the excitement that

535

tingled through her whenever she glimpsed the possibilities. Cassandra didn't think she had any strength left in her for another rejection.

They were sitting exactly where she had left them. Silently Cassandra handed out the coffees. She was pulling the lid off her cup when it ripped in her fingers, the coffee spilling across the floor.

"Well, at least no one will be able to tell the difference," she mumbled.

"They will once you get the place cleaned up."

Cassandra looked suspiciously at Pearce's irrepressible, boyish grin. "Jimmy?"

"The idea's fabulous!" he crowed.

Cassandra's eyes darted to Eric Gollant.

"I'm signing on as devil's advocate," he said, his voice somber but his eyes twinkling like a leprechaun's. "I'm also serving notice that it's going to take one hell of a lot of work—just to get this off the ground. The logistical problems will be staggering."

He looked at Cassandra keenly. "Are you sure you're ready for this?"

"I've never been more sure of anything in my life!"

Eric sighed. "So much for any plans for a bucolic retirement."

The following day, United States Express was formally registered as a company incorporated under the laws of the state of New York. Both its name and initials, USE, were patented and protected by copyright.

"You'll need a logo," Jimmy told her.

"I have just the thing." Cassandra showed him an artist's rendition of a bust of a heroic, medieval warrior.

With the legalities out of the way, the trio huddled in the suite of the Empire State Building to divide the nuts-and-bolts chores.

"The first order of business is to determine exactly what kind of card this will be," the accountant said.

Jimmy shrugged. "A credit card, what else?"

Eric held up a warning finger. "Not so fast. A credit card implies exactly that: USE will be extending credit. I don't think that's Cassandra's intention."

"Not at all," Cassandra said firmly. "The problem with credit cards in the past has been the issuer's taking on a customer's debt load. When the customer fails to pay on time or skips altogether, the issuer is on the hook. With this card, it's pay as you play. The monthly balance is paid off in full."

"Which means that we have to be careful in targeting the people we want to use it," Jimmy mused. "Folks buying big-ticket items like radios or washing machines want time to pay them off. But traveling salesmen, businessmen, don't. Especially if they're on an expense account."

"Very good, Jimmy," Eric said approvingly. "That means we have the added security of being able to collect from a company instead of an individual."

"So it will be a straight charge card," Cassandra said, more to herself than the others. She looked up at them. "A travel and entertainment card, geared to the businessman who"—she held up three fingers—"travels, stays in hotels, and eats in restaurants."

They looked at one another.

"Now we know who we have to get to accept the card," Jimmy said. "Let's go get 'em!"

The figures didn't lie. For a single, twenty-nine-year-old woman, Cassandra McQueen was a wealthy individual. The value of her duplex penthouse in the Carlton Towers was a shade over a hundred thousand dollars. Her stake in Q magazine added up to five times that amount.

"It's not enough," Eric pronounced.

Cassandra blinked. "What do you mean?"

The accountant ran a perfectly manicured nail along a column in the ledger.

"Although your personal expenses aren't extravagant, they do eat up the Q magazine stock dividends. You can't pledge them as collateral unless you have another source of income."

He looked at her expectantly.

"There isn't any," Cassandra protested.

"The apartment is paid off and you could take out a mortgage for, say, sixty thousand. That would cover the payments for two years. But sixty thousand won't come close to the minimum we need."

"Can I sell the Q stock?"

Eric cocked his head. "Yes, you can. In fact, there will be no shortage of buyers—*Time, Newsweek*, the Hearst people, Katherine Graham of course. But an outright sale will mean you have no control over anything the purchaser might do with Q."

"You mean they can change the format, editorial position, things like that?"

"All of the above, plus, they wouldn't be obligated to keep the current staff."

"The magazine wouldn't be the same without Jimmy and the others! Almost everyone has been with Q for years."

Eric said nothing. Clearly, he had made his point.

"I can't do that to them," Cassandra said at last. "My father brought a lot of those people together precisely because they gave Q its character and vitality. If I tamper with that, I'll destroy everything the magazine stands for."

Cassandra nibbled pensively on her lower lip. "What if I were to sell the shares to the employees? That way, nothing would change."

"It's a possibility," Eric conceded. "But half a million dollars is an awful lot of money. I'm not sure Jimmy and the others can scrape together that much."

He hesitated. "Even if they could and were willing to buy, there's something else you should consider. Once you sell, Cassandra, you've not only given up all stake in Q, but you don't have any income. On paper, the USE card sounds great. But it's going to be a long, hard row to hoe. In the beginning, you'll be hemorrhaging money, wondering where it's all going and why a cent isn't coming back. If, God forbid, this idea doesn't fly, you could find yourself with nothing at all."

The radiance that surrounded her hopes dimmed under Eric's words. Cassandra knew that he was being brutally honest with her, just as he'd promised. Suddenly a black chasm opened up, swallowing the shelter and steady income she had taken for granted.

"How much do I need, Eric? The bottom line."

The accountant smiled sadly. "Almost all of it. You can't cut much closer to the bone than I already have."

Cassandra examined the figures carefully, adding them up as she went along. Rent on the premises, office equipment and supplies, telephones, staff salaries, advertising, transportation, it all added up to $550,000 over a three-year period.

"You don't show any profit!" Cassandra exclaimed.

"You'll be lucky to take a medium loss in the first year," Eric replied. "Maybe a smaller one in the second. By the third, if this thing is still alive, you'll break even."

"Did anyone ever tell you you'd look great in sackcloth and ashes?"

"Cassandra, I'm only trying—"

She laid a hand on his arm. "And I'm only teasing. You're telling me exactly what I have to know, and I'm grateful. So let's take it one step at a time. The first thing to do is to talk to Jimmy and see what he thinks the chances are of the employees buying Q."

"You're willing to take that risk?"

"If they say yes, then I'm committed. Eric, I don't have very much left to lose, do I? If I don't take this one chance that Rose left me, I won't be the only one to regret it. But I will be the one responsible."

"I'm scared, Nicholas."

Cassandra stood on the porch of the cottage overlooking the pond. On the other side, next to the falls, was an old abandoned mill. She listened to the bullfrogs' cacophony as twilight set in, and the soft whirr of the dragonflies as they skimmed the water. The sun pierced the clouds, creating a golden carpet across the pond.

Cassandra heard Nicholas step behind her and felt his hands on her shoulders, fingers stroking the back of her neck. It was the second time they had met here, in the Connecticut countryside, well away from the prying eyes of Manhattan. These were moments Cassandra treasured, clinging to them during the long, lonely intervals.

"You'll do just fine," Nicholas murmured.

He wished he could somehow wash away the turmoil and uncertainty that filled Cassandra. Almost everything she had in the world was now staked. Nicholas himself had spent sleepless nights, worrying because he couldn't be there for her when she truly needed him.

"It will be all right," Cassandra said, as though reading his mind. She turned around. "If the worst happens and I fall flat on my face . . ."

"At the very least you know you'll still have me."

Cassandra held him tightly. Those were the words she had been waiting for. They were what she would take away with her. They were all she really had.

Although Jimmy Pearce was thrilled by the idea of Cassandra's selling Q magazine to its employees, he agreed that many of the staff would have a problem raising the money.

"Let me talk to everybody and see what we can come up with," he said.

The process took months. Everyone from the editors to the secretaries wanted to buy in. To be fair to all, Pearce suggested that each employee be permitted to buy only a hundred shares and that he or she had ninety days to come up with the capital.

"A few of us can buy more than that right now," he explained to Cassandra. "But that wouldn't be fair to the others. The result would be a lot of ill-will, which, in the long run, would prove as damaging as if you'd sold Q to strangers."

Cassandra agreed but chafed under the delay. To keep herself busy, she went ahead and mortgaged the Carlton Towers penthouse, using some of the money to clean and renovate the Empire State Building offices. Next came the necessary furniture and amenities. Cassandra and Eric Gollant spent long afternoons by the pond in Central Park, discussing what kind of people to hire and where best to find them.

"Remember what Monk did," the accountant reminded her. "He took the time to get the right people and he paid them well. No one works better than an employee who feels he or she has a stake in the company."

Cassandra thought back to the wives and widows Michelle had hired as Global Europe spread across France. "I couldn't agree more."

By September, the final papers had been signed and money transferred. The interviews had been held and the staff hired.

"I guess this is it," Cassandra said nervously, glancing around the gleaming, refurbished premises.

It was Labor Day and, as usual, the city had emptied as Manhattanites swarmed to the cottage or beach for one last summer fling. The stillness of New York reminded Cassandra of Paris in August, when it was surrendered to the tourists.

"I hope you're ready to start running," Jimmy said.

Cassandra stared gloomily at the schedule and shook her head. The problem she and Eric had worried to death throughout the summer was as simple as it was fundamental. Cassandra would not succeed in persuading restaurant and hotel owners to accept the United States Express card unless she could convince them that not only would their steady customers use the card but that by offering the convenience, the establishments would draw more business. USE would assume responsibility of collecting the money from the customers, deduct its 10 percent commission, and forward the balance to the restaurants and hotels.

Through his reputation and business connections Jimmy Pearce had come up with a solution to the first half of the problem.

"I can get the restaurant owners and hotel managers together in one room to listen to your pitch. But they'll want to see a client list."

"The proverbial chicken-and-egg situation," Cassandra groaned. "They want a client list; the potential client will want to know where the card will be honored."

"That's why we have to go after the customer first," Eric Gollant told her. "If we can't convince him, we won't convince anybody."

The drill began the following morning. As Cassandra watched, a dozen typists pounded out the first of five thousand letters to sales managers whose names Eric Gollant had gleaned from business directories. As the letters went out by messenger Cassandra manned the phones and began the follow-up calls. Those who ventured even the faintest interest were asked to lunch.

"It'll cost a few dollars to feed them," Eric observed. "But think, you'll be making your point in exactly the circumstances they can relate to: the business lunch. Besides, it's all tax deductible."

After the next sixty days, Cassandra swore she had been to every Manhattan eaterie she had every heard of and then some. Soon she realized many people would simply have to be called on in their offices.

"How many said they'd take it?" she asked, grateful for the Thanksgiving Day weekend, which meant she could rest.

"Three hundred and ten," Eric announced.

"After all that?" Cassandra cried.

"Not bad for first time out."

"But is it enough?"

The accountant knew Cassandra was thinking ahead to next week's presentation to New York's restaurant and hotel owners.

"You'll have to make them believe it is—and that it's just the beginning."

"Right."

Cassandra wished she could slide into a deep, hot bath and disappear underneath the bubbles.

Jimmy Pearce was as good as his word: the conference room of the Roosevelt Hotel was packed with over a thousand men. From the guest list, Cassandra recognized only a dozen names.

"The managers of the Waldorf, Plaza, and other hoity-toity places received invitations but I never expected them to show up," Jimmy explained. "They're snobs to the nth degree. Right now, we don't need them. Later, they'll come to us."

Cassandra saw his logic. Companies never allowed their road people to stay at the most expensive hotels. Neither would they rebate chits from New York's finest restaurants. Judging by the list, this was a strictly meat-and-potatoes crowd.

After the breakfast plates had been cleared away and pitchers of coffee deposited on the tables, Cassandra mounted the podium. Most men were talking and laughing among themselves, others were lighting up, studying whatever business they had brought with them. Cassandra, who had chosen an oatmeal whipcord suit with black braid trim and velvet collar and cuffs for the occasion, smarted under their indifference.

To hell with this!

She threw away her notes and tapped the microphone, hard, getting their attention instantly.

"Thank you, gentlemen, for coming here today," she said sweetly. "Let me explain to you how United States Express is going to put more cash in your pocket this year."

Cassandra spoke nonstop for over an hour. She explained how accepting the card would simplify an establishment's bookkeeping and that payment was guaranteed by USE as soon as its offices had received the receipt. She proudly announced the number of sales managers who had already signed up as USE customers and spoke of a glowing future in which the salesmen these managers sent out would also carry the card. She introduced Eric Gollant as her executive vice president and the director of one of New York's leading banks

541

that had agreed to underwrite the card. She judiciously omitted that the bank's guarantee was good only as long as USE had its own funds in the account sufficient to cover potential losses.

"Ten percent commission sounds kinda steep to me," one restaurateur called out. "Can't we negotiate?"

"Considering the guarantees and services USE is offering, it's not steep at all," Cassandra replied. "But I'll make you a deal. You do fifty thousand dollars' worth of business on the card in one year and we'll renegotiate the percentage."

Out of the corner of her eye Cassandra saw Eric cringe.

"What about fraud?" asked the manager of a midtown businessman's hotel.

"If a member's card is lost or stolen and used without his knowledge or consent, USE will take steps to find the perpetrator. But neither the client nor the establishment will be liable. USE will make good on all charges."

The manager laughed. "That's a hell of a guarantee. Can I have that in writing?"

"Certainly," Cassandra replied. "Because we're one hell of a company."

By this time, Cassandra noted, Eric was grim-faced.

After the presentation, showgirls in cocktail outfits and black fishnet stockings went around the tables presenting each attendee with a USE plate that would imprint the name and code of his establishment on the receipt, as well as a USE card made out in his name.

"The only thing you gentlemen have to do is drop the charge plate in the red box," Cassandra told them. "USE will return it, along with a printer and receipts, the same week we launch our advertising campaign."

"What if we're not interested?" someone called out.

Cassandra smiled tightly. "Just drop the plate in the blue box. But before you do, take a look at what your competition is doing."

There was a scraping of chairs as the presentation broke up and opinions were exchanged. Relieved that it was all over, Cassandra descended from the podium to mingle, shake hands, and offer words of encouragement. She didn't notice Nicholas Lockwood, standing at the very back of the room half-hidden by a curtain, blend into the exodus.

"Maybe they were color-blind."

Cassandra couldn't keep the bitterness from her voice. The huge room was empty, the waiters clearing the tables, snapping off the dirty linen, stacking chairs. On a large table by the podium Cassandra and Eric had been counting the number of charge plates in each of the two boxes. Cassandra had felt the hope drain out of her as soon as she lifted the red box. It was so light she could have carried it in one hand.

"What's the verdict?"

"Two hundred and twenty."

"Could have been worse," Eric said philosophically.

Cassandra sat down on the podium steps. The mailings, the calls, the manufacturing of the charge plates, cards, and printers, the lunches with company sales directors, and now this breakfast extravaganza—it had cost her a fortune. And what did she have to show for it? A couple of hundred establishments and two thousand men who might or might not use the card at these places. Eric had been right: the money was pouring out. She couldn't stop that, nor did she have much to show for it.

"I don't want you thinking like that," the accountant said, taking a seat beside her. "You did damn well your first time out. Now you've got to show those who've signed up that you can deliver."

Cassandra craned her head back and stared at the ceiling.

"I needed to do something more. I don't know why I didn't convince them but I didn't."

"You got a foot in the door. That was the object of the exercise. It's the customers, not you, who'll do the convincing."

Cassandra smiled wanly. "Sure thing."

She stood up and looked around her. The emptiness of the room matched her mood.

"I'm going to the cabin for the weekend," she said. "By Monday, I'll be rarin' to go, promise."

Eric nodded. "An excellent idea."

He was glad Cassandra had found a retreat for herself in Connecticut's lake country. He wasn't even sure exactly where it was, but Cassandra had left him a telephone number just in case. As he watched her walk out of the hall, he hoped that whatever strength she drew from her seclusion would be enough. There would be none to spare in the months ahead.

– 61 –

For all appearances, Global was the same corporation that Steven Talbot had taken over one year ago. Its financial instruments, the money order and traveler's checks, still dominated the domestic and international travel markets. Its trucks and ships continued to move freight across the nation and around the world. The stake Global held in oil, pharmaceutical, and chemical concerns increased, allowing the company to exert a quiet but ever-present authority in over twenty boardrooms.

The directors of charities, museums, and educational foundations breathed sighs of relief when Global's endowment checks not only continued to arrive but with their amounts increased. Park Avenue matrons who organized charity balls for hospitals and other worthwhile causes beamed at Steven Talbot's generous contributions. In the men's clubs of Manhattan, only guests paid any attention to Steven's scarred face. The financial community, which had watched Steven fight for his patrimony and was satisfied with his mettle, accepted him as one of its own.

But beneath the facade fundamental changes had taken place. Over the past twelve months Steven Talbot had quietly sold off what remained of Global's locomotives and rolling stock, leasing it back from the purchasers on short-term contracts. Many of the vast warehouses and storage lots that Franklin Jefferson had bought in the 1920s were broken up, sold to developers, or traded for blocks of stock in companies interested in the property and in which Global wanted a stake. By year's end, Global was a cash-swollen giant, with a war chest the envy of Wall Street.

Inside the Lower Broadway headquarters virtually all of Rose's senior appointees had been dismissed except for two elderly vice presidents, who, upon being summoned to Steven's office, were convinced that they were about to have their heads handed to them.

"I want you to take over the money-order and traveler's-check operations," Steven told them preemptively. "I'm satisfied with how things are running and I don't want any changes. Is that clear?"

The two gentlemen, who were experts in the railroad business, nodded quickly. As soon as they were dismissed they repaired to their club for stiff drinks.

"I don't know a damn thing about the traveler's check. Do you?"

544

"Are you kidding? O'Neill and Gollant ran that operation after Michelle McQueen was killed. I don't think I've even *used* a traveler's check."

"What the hell does he expect us to do?"

"That's obvious, isn't it? Nothing!"

It was true. Steven Talbot had taken one look at the corporate ledgers and spotted the company's profit center immediately. He knew better than to tamper with something he had no interest in but which was a venerable golden goose. Unlike other parts of the company, the money order and traveler's checks needed custodians, not hard, daring innovators. The two codgers, eager to hold on to their jobs and pensions, would do quite nicely.

Given the company's reputation, Steven had the pick of the country's brightest crop of business graduates from which to build a new executive staff. Prospects in other companies were wooed away with wages and benefits no one could match. Steven chose carefully, but the ones who most impressed him never saw the inside of the Lower Broadway headquarters.

Steven's special recruits all shared similar qualities. They were young, energetic, eager to prove themselves, and had no scruples. Upon such individuals Steven affixed his personal stamp, demanding loyalty and unquestioned obedience to his directives. He paid his handpicked soldiers astronomical salaries and trained them in the arts of financial warfare in the privacy and luxury of Dunescrag. Above all, he made certain that no one could ever trace these men either to him or to Global. If anyone checked, as Steven knew would happen, the trail had to begin and end with them.

Steven gave every one of his lieutenants a special assignment and swore each to secrecy. When he was sure they knew exactly what to do, he sowed them across the Orient, in Tokyo, Hong Kong, Jakarta, Manila, and Singapore. There, using funds provided by shell corporations registered in Panama and blind trusts created in Switzerland, these men bought into or created banks and brokerage houses. More money was poured in to make these viable concerns and soon the financial tongues in the Orient were wagging about new sources of capital flooding into new, often struggling industries of the Far East.

Steven fashioned his hook with exquisite care. It had been cast with the gold recovered from the *Hino Maru*. The barbs had been sharpened by the enormous profits from the investments he had made—profits that, but for the sentimentality of an old woman, he would have had to share with the men of the *zaibatsus*. Now the time had come to slip on the bait. The big fish were out there, Steven could sense them circling cautiously. He was certain that eventually they would take the bait. Steven knew the men of the *zaibatsus* very, very well. . . .

Steven was dressing for dinner when his valet appeared with an envelope delivered by messenger. Steven straightened his black tie and examined the result in the mirror. Tonight he would be escorting one of New York's most desirable debutantes, all of nineteen years old, to a formal dinner for sixty. Since his meteoric rise in New York's most powerful circles, Steven discovered a subtle inclination among its women, one that was as old, and potent, as the legends and fairy tales it had spawned: beauty's attraction for the beast.

Steven slit open the envelope and read Nicholas Lockwood's two-page report on Cassandra's little gathering at the Roosevelt Hotel. Lockwood summed it up as a nickle-and-dime operation whose costs and inept management were going to eat up the grandly named United States Express in less than a year. Nothing to worry about. Steven smiled and placed the report in a drawer next to one with an almost identical evaluation. As sure as he was of Lockwood, Steven hadn't told him there would be another man in that audience, with instructions to report back to Steven. It had been an exercise to satisfy his curiosity about Lockwood's commitment. Steven was so pleased it had been a success that he made a mental note to give the chief of the inspectors division a raise.

Tokyo would never again be the city Yukiko Kamaguchi remembered. The Americans had spent millions helping to rebuild the city but at the same time leaving their indelible imprint. The Japanese, in a rush to embrace all things American, had not foreseen the result. Yukiko wondered how many really noticed or cared.

Still, the Americans had done one thing right, the effect of which few people understood or appreciated. Under the terms of the Occupation, the United States had drafted a new constitution for Japan, modeled on its own. One of the most radical provisions concerned women, who were guaranteed the same rights as men. With fewer than a hundred words, America had swept away a thousand years of discrimination and predetermined social status. The irony, however, was not lost on Yukiko. Because she had to hide in the shadows she could not take advantage of the new law. Not yet.

Yukiko had left Honolulu the day after her confrontation with the men of the *zaibatsus*. She knew that those she had failed would take steps to ensure she could never reenter Japan. She had to slip in before they had had a chance to erect their defenses.

During her time in Hawaii, Yukiko had controlled only a small checking account used to pay staff and everyday expenses. Everything else was looked after by Steven. But, unknown to him, Yukiko had built her own reserve of money. There had been nonexistent expenses she had insisted had to be paid in cash, money that she never spent, even bills taken out of Steven's trouser pockets before cleaning. Over time it had added up to several thousand dollars, which, in the Japan of 1950, was a small fortune.

When Yukiko returned to Japan she disappeared into a working-class suburb of Tokyo, renting a modest, one-room apartment. Here, among factory workers and laborers, she was safe from prying eyes and inquisitive strangers.

Yukiko spent entire days wandering through Tokyo, watching what was going on around her. Everyone talked about the rebuilding, how entire factories would be erected from the ground up. On the outskirts of the city Yukiko saw the evidence, for everywhere was the deafening roar of a city rising from its own ashes. She could not compete on the industrial level, however; if the men of the *zaibatsus* were alerted to her presence they would move swiftly to crush her.

But even they cannot stem the tide of the future.

Japan had gone to war because, for all its culture and history, it lacked the one thing its people needed most: land. How often had she heard Americans comment on how polite the Japanese were. What did Americans, coming from such a vast country, know about living side by side with their neighbors, cramped and surrounded, accepting that one could never change such circumstances? Losing the war carried with it more than national disgrace. It had denied the Japanese the space they so deeply craved.

If that is so, then it stands to reason that land in Japan will become even more valuable. Those who own it can make it priceless by building upon it.

Yukiko Kamaguchi knew nothing about real estate or construction, but that did not stop her from going to the Tokyo Central Registry and finding out what land was for sale and where. Most of the lots were in areas where there had been very little, if any, reconstruction. But where other eyes saw only silent devastation, Yukiko imagined shining palaces.

Yukiko now faced a major drawback. Nothing could be bought in her name. The minute she signed a deed or a check, there would be a paper trail for the men of the *zaibatsus* to follow. Yukiko had foreseen this and in the fall of 1950 sent a telegram to Cobbler's Point to summon Jiro Tokuyama home.

Steven's houseman had stayed behind not only to look after the property but to serve as Yukiko's eyes and ears in case Steven returned. He never had, nor had there been a single word from him. Jiro Tokuyama packed his few possessions and quietly left Cobbler's Point, leaving the doors unlocked. It was a small but satisfying revenge.

Upon his return to Tokyo, Jiro Tokuyama moved into a tiny apartment a few streets from Yukiko. Following her instructions, he opened a bank account and deposited six hundred U.S. dollars, which, he explained to the manager, he had earned by working for a *gaijin* in Hawaii. Next, the houseman went to a lawyer who drew up papers for a company.

"What do you wish to call your new enterprise?" asked the lawyer.

Jiro Tokuyama smiled politely. "A number will be fine."

The lawyer called the Title Office and was told the next corporate number was 4780.

A few days later, Company 4780 bought a forty-thousand-square-foot lot, consisting of broken brick, twisted steel, and other debris, for a few hundred dollars. After Jiro Tokuyama had dutifully signed over the deed, Yukiko journeyed to the Shinto shrine where her father had hidden. There, she lighted incense and whispered to his spirit that she had begun to repay her obligation.

Armed with her client and establishment lists, Cassandra was ready for the next step. She wanted to launch the United States Express card just before Thanksgiving weekend, which marked the beginning of the busiest retail season. Hotels and restaurants did a booming business between the end of November and the New Year, and Cassandra wanted USE to get as big a piece of that traffic as possible.

With Jimmy Pearce's help Cassandra found a perfect place to manufacture her cards and printers: nondescript, secure, and close enough to the Empire State Building nerve center so that she could go back and forth between the two. Jimmy had found it on the register that listed abandoned buildings which hadn't been torn down because they had been designated as historically significant.

"It's wonderful!" Cassandra cried as she stood on the corner of Ninth Avenue and Twenty-third Street staring at the small red-brick structure with ornate grilles over the windows and heavy bronze doors.

"Used to be the Maritime Savings Bank," Jimmy explained. "Built at the turn of the century and went bust during the Depression."

The next day Cassandra signed an agreement with the Historical Society to rent the defunct bank on a long-term basis. She agreed to make no alterations to either the interior or the exterior and, over a period of time, to restore the architecture to its original beauty.

"Do you know anyone at police headquarters?" she asked Jimmy as they left the Historical Society.

"A couple of people. Why?"

"By the time I get back from Washington, I want that place wired with the most sophisticated alarm system available. Then, ask a couple of detectives if they want to moonlight for a while. The background of every person we hire to work there will have to be checked all the way back to their first burp."

Cassandra took the train from New York to Washington, then a cab to the Bureau of Engraving and Printing at Fourteenth and C streets. A security guard led her through the factorylike complex until they reached the Metal Room, where plates for everything from the lowly one-cent stamp to million-dollar certificates of indebtedness were intricately hand-carved by master engravers.

"Here you are, Miss McQueen," the director said, passing her a shiny metal plate, eight inches long, four wide, half an inch thick. "You'll see the details more clearly under this microscope."

Cassandra brushed back her hair and pressed her eyes against the twin lenses. The craftsmanship leaped out at her.

The border was done in filigree that resembled fish scales, with two fleur-de-lis anchors at the top left- and right-hand corners. Below that, in bold capitals, were the words UNITED STATES EXPRESS. In the middle was a cameo of a knight in profile, his expression strong and determined, the blind eye looking at some distant point in the future. The symbol of the knight was chosen because the first written account of a "credit card" dated back to the Middle Ages. To protect their valuables, knights wore rings engraved with special insignia. Instead of paying in gold coin, they would stamp an innkeeper's bill, which would later be presented to the knight's lord for payment.

Once the card was printed, the filigree would become black, the lettering white, and the background, undulating whorls that incorporated USE's name, a medium blue. The cardholder's name and membership number would be embossed across the center. Beneath that would run the dates of issue and expiry. On the back was a white strip for the customer's signature.

"It's magnificent!" Cassandra whispered.

"Thank you, Miss McQueen," the engraver replied. "Believe me, it was a welcome change from the usual spate of Madison and Franklin bills. We'll ship this to you right away by Wells Fargo."

Back in New York, Cassandra began advertising for printers who would be responsible for the actual manufacturing process. While two former New York police detectives she had hired checked out the potential candidates, Cassandra interviewed the staff who would assemble the imprinters and those responsible for mailing the cards. By October, all the employees had been vetted and the manufacturing and embossing section sealed off from the clerical. Cassandra turned her attention to the last, but certainly crucial, piece of business.

"Here's what we have," Jimmy Pearce told her as they walked into Q magazine's art room, lined with big, slanted drawing boards.

To save time and money, as well as to keep the details of the advertising campaign a secret, all the artwork and copy had been done by the magazine's in-house artists and writers.

Jimmy showed Cassandra the layouts. "The ones targeting the hospitality industries will run in trade journals and in the travel sections of major newspapers. To reach the clients, we got our hands on as many in-house corporate publications as possible, from IBM and Texaco to the major firms in the garment industry, all the way down to factories making plumbing widgets. Any company with a dozen or more sales reps and an in-house newsletter has been covered."

"How large is the area we're going to cover?" asked Cassandra, studying the layout intently.

"New York, New Jersey, Massachusetts, and Pennsylvania."

The artwork, most of it black and white, was spectacular. A simple rendering of the card followed by the caption: THE UNITED STATES EXPRESS CARD— SECURITY, RELIABILITY, ACCEPTANCE. WORKING WITH YOU TO MEET YOUR GOALS!

Below that, in short, punchy copy, were the details of what the card offered, along with a list of establishments that honored it. The print finished with a bold comment: "The United States Express Card—USE it!"

"It hits you right between the eyes," Cassandra said excitedly. "What else do you have?"

Jimmy read her the radio-commercial copy and told her the amount of air time he had bought. Cassandra blanched when she saw the cost.

"It's expensive," he admitted. "But well worth it. Not only do you have to reassure your clients, you want to get the public to start talking about USE. To do that, you have to let them know it exists."

Cassandra took another look at the bill and signed it. "I know. It's just that it's an awful lot of money."

"Well, cheer up. *Q* magazine has a surprise for you."

Guiding her by the elbow, Jimmy walked Cassandra into her office.

"How does she look?" he asked.

The photographer who was waiting grinned. "Like always—a million bucks."

"Jimmy, what's going on?"

"What do you think? An interview. The cover and a three-page spread in the Thanksgiving Day issue."

Cassandra was overwhelmed. "Jimmy . . . I don't know what to say. . . ."

Pearce waved his hand. "Everyone here wanted to do this, Cass. It's our way of saying thank you—and good luck!"

- 62 -

Like most people, Cassandra had experienced the consequences of the adage, "too much of a good thing" as a child—usually after a second or third helping of a favorite dessert. As she approached her thirtieth birthday, she learned the old lessons in a new way.

By February 1951, the United States Express clearinghouse on Ninth Avenue resembled a lunatic asylum. No one had expected the volume of business that had poured in after the Thanksgiving Day weekend and that continued right through to the end of January. Each day hundreds of receipts arrived in the mail to be processed. Restaurateurs and hotel managers called up screaming for more charge slips. Telephones rang constantly as sales and office managers demanded to be signed up for the card. Cassandra found herself working eighteen- to twenty-hour-days but even that effort barely made a dent in her crammed schedule. She paid her staff double to stay late and come in on the weekends, which kept the operation only a week behind schedule, instead of a month. Cassandra knew that she couldn't fall behind in collecting the money from her clients and at the same time had to make sure the establishments received their payments promptly. The last thing she could afford was a disgruntled merchant.

Another unforeseen problem was claustrophobia. The space in the renovated bank was becoming too cramped. Cassandra hadn't expected the avalanche of paperwork that attached itself to each card. There were files for individuals, summing up their financial history and creditworthiness; others for the merchants; accounts receivable, accounts payable; separate files for salaries and operating expenditures; voluminous ledgers that tracked gross income and the current, always fluctuating, bank balances. Every square inch was being used, yet it wasn't enough. Applications from prospective establishments and cardholders were being processed in Cassandra's own office, literally squeezing USE's chief executive officer into a corner. Although her employees relished their paychecks, fattened by overtime, there were grumblings of discontent at the noise and cramped working conditions. If things got any worse, Cassandra would have a revolt on her hands.

The last weekend in February, Cassandra moved the entire imprinter manufacturing line to a new location near the southern tip of Manhattan. But the worst snowstorm of the winter arrived, and what should have taken one day to accomplish took three. The result was a backlog in the delivery of imprinters to already impatient merchants.

Nonetheless, the move doubled the amount of working space at the clearinghouse. New desks, chairs, and sets of filing cabinets were trucked in and workers swarmed into the area to stake their claims. Cassandra even managed to get her office back.

"It certainly looks like you have everything well in hand," Eric Gollant said phlegmatically, watching the operation hum along.

Cassandra shot him a dirty look. "Everything's just dandy."

"If I might make a suggestion," the accountant continued, "you could do with a few salesmen. I keep getting calls from people who tell me you promised to see them but never showed up."

Cassandra's voice became dangerously low. "Eric, I feel like I'm the warden of a madhouse. People never stop yelling at me. Everybody wants something. If you think I need salesmen, fine—hire them. But first tell me how I'm supposed to pay them."

In spite of the enormous volume of charge receipts, Cassandra's expenses were running far ahead of the income collected by USE from its percentage of each transaction. Leasing the new warehouse and moving the imprinter manufacturing had cost a small fortune. Overtime and new staff had swollen the payroll to the point where Cassandra herself was drawing only enough to cover the payments on her mortgaged apartment and minimal living expenses. Yet, like a barometer forecasting a hurricane, the reserves in the USE bank account were falling ominously.

Eric parted the stacks of paper so that he could look directly at Cassandra.

"Listen to me. Something's happened which no one expected. When you brought the USE card into the market, you tapped something that's much bigger, much more widespread, than we ever dreamed. I get a minimum of thirty calls a day from companies wanting cards for their employees. What about you?"

"Seventy-five, eighty," Cassandra mumbled.

"That's my point!" Eric said triumphantly. "Maybe it was your presentations, maybe the advertising, but whatever caused this interest, you now have something any business would kill for: word-of-mouth publicity. The card's become a conversation piece, an object of curiosity, a fad. Dozens of times I've gone into restaurants and watched someone pay with a card. It's always the same story: the cardholder plunks down his plastic, he has a nice, self-satisfied grin on his face because his clients all look to see what it is. For the next ten minutes this guy talks about the card as if he's the one who discovered it. It makes him feel important; it makes his client believe he *is* important.

"Cassandra, you thought you were giving the public a tool, providing a service. It's gone beyond that now. You're offering them a chance to enhance their self-esteem. You're selling them a dream."

Cassandra had never seen Eric so flushed with excitement. She felt it rubbing off on her, wearing away the fatigue like polish on tarnished silver.

"Then I guess we'd better get those salesmen," she said.

"I have them ready and waiting. All I needed was your go-ahead."

Cassandra laughed. "Of course. But, Eric, seriously, will I be able to handle the overhead?"

The accountant's eyebrows reared up like two caterpillars at the start of a race. "You have no choice."

After Eric Gollant left, Cassandra closed the door to her office and ignored the phone. She was lost in thought, turning his words over and over in her mind. When she came to her decision she still wasn't sure it was the right thing to do.

What the hell, I'm supposed to seize the moment, aren't I?

Cassandra called Jimmy Pearce and told him she wanted to meet with his artists and copywriters at Q magazine to map out a second advertising campaign.

"What's wrong with the first?" Pearce demanded.

"Nothing. It's fine for a piece of plastic. I want to sell dreams."

Having temporarily solved the problem of working space, Cassandra focused her attention on improving USE's cash flow.

"We have too many people using the card in too few places," Cassandra told her new sales force of six. "Since we don't charge the holder any membership fee, our only income comes from the percentage we charge the merchants. In short, our revenue base is much too narrow."

Several of the salesmen made suggestions, but Cassandra rejected them all with a flat "No." She then passed around a copy of their latest advertisement, scheduled to run over the Easter holidays.

"Show them this. Let the prospective merchants see for themselves that when we advertise we include the names of all the establishments that honor our card. That's the full measure of USE's commitment. And let them know that we will do everything possible to encourage our members to patronize these outlets."

"Cassandra, that could be misinterpreted as blackballing," Eric cautioned.

"I can't afford to wait for our customers to prod their favorite restaurants and hotels into accepting the card," Cassandra said fiercely.

"Then give us something to work with," the sales force pleaded.

Cassandra looked at them keenly. "All right. You can tell them, in strictest confidence, that by June, when the American public hits the road for vacation, every Hilton Hotel will be honoring the card. Let them think about what choice John Q. Public is going to make: stay at a place where he has to pay cash or in one where he slaps down a card and ends up spending even more because he doesn't have to pay cash?"

Cassandra surveyed the stunned expressions. "You asked me for an incentive, gentlemen, and you got it. Now it's your turn."

"My God, Cassandra, you should have told me about Hilton!"

Cassandra looked up guiltily. "There's nothing to tell. Yet."

"What do you mean? I just heard you say—"

"Eric, I had to tell them something! They're wonderful young men and probably great salesmen too, but they need something to sell."

"Even if it's a lie?" Eric asked quietly.

"Please don't make me feel any worse," Cassandra begged. "It was the only thing I could give them. Besides, I *thought* about going to see Hilton."

"And what if he refuses to see you? How do you think those boys will feel when you tell them there's no Hilton deal?"

"Not nearly as terrible as I will."

They were silent for a moment, both wrapped in their own thoughts.

"I realize you have to cut corners," the accountant said finally. "But this is an awfully large one."

"Then I'll have to try extra hard to make sure I get the account."

"And how do you propose to do that?"

Cassandra threw up her hands in mock despair. "I'm going to talk to the Kendall people, what else?"

Now Eric Gollant didn't want to think. He certainly had his suspicions, but he refused even to countenance them. The risks involved were too great. Even Cassandra wouldn't try something like that.

No sooner had Eric Gollant left than Cassandra reached for the phone and called Lionel Kendall in Philadelphia. The Kendall name was one of the oldest and most respected in the American hotel industry, but every Kendall hotel operated on cash payment, and although the hotelkeeper was cordial enough to Cassandra, he insisted that he had no intention of changing his cash-only policy. In the course of a half-hour Cassandra managed to persuade him at least to see her.

"I hope you enjoyed your trip here, Miss McQueen," Lionel Kendall said expansively after Cassandra arrived in Philadelphia the following day. "Not likely we're going to do business."

Kendall was a big, barrel-chested man with a mass of snowy hair and an old-fashioned handlebar mustache. But while he could have doubled for Santa Claus, his bright blue eyes reflected shrewdness and stubbornness.

"I suppose it's always easier to say no rather than yes," Cassandra replied.

Kendall chuckled. "Go ahead, I'm all ears."

With the help of brochures, advertising layouts, and a vastly expanded client list, Cassandra spelled out how, by accepting the card, the Kendall chain would not only draw new clientele, but those people would be inclined to spend more money by charging services to their rooms.

"It all sounds pretty good," Kendall told her. "Still, this is a family-run business, Miss McQueen. You have an impressive client list there but I can show you one three times the size. Mine. Hell, I've got repeat customers from all over the country. We know them so well my people have standing instructions to accept their checks. Now you can't get any more personal than that, can you?"

"I guess you're right," Cassandra admitted.

Lionel Kendall came around his desk. "Look, for what it's worth, I think you have a nice little business here. It's just not for me. No hard feelings?"

"None at all, Mr. Kendall. I appreciate the time." Cassandra gathered up her presentation material. "If you don't mind, I'd like to go up to my room and freshen up before dinner."

A slightly lecherous gleam came into Kendall's eyes. "If you're free, I'd consider it an honor if you had dinner with me."

"That's very gracious of you," Cassandra said sweetly. "I'd like that very much."

As soon as she got up to her room, Cassandra threw her materials on the bed and called Jimmy Pearce at Q. In less than five minutes she gave him the gist of her conversation with Kendall, omitting the fact that he had turned her down flat.

"And I'm having dinner with him tonight," she concluded.

"Sounds great, Cass. Any chance of getting a picture of the two of you together?"

"That's up to you. Maybe you could call someone at the Philadelphia *Enquirer.* . . ."

Dinner was wonderful and Lionel Kendall proved to be a generous and entertaining man. He was obviously loved in his hometown, as evidenced by the royal treatment he and Cassandra received at the city's best restaurant and the number of people who stopped by their table to pay their respects. The hotelkeeper smiled hugely and embraced Cassandra when a photographer from the local paper showed up.

"Sure I can't change your mind?" Cassandra asked one last time as Kendall escorted her through the lobby of his flagship hotel.

555

"Not this time. But it has been a pleasure, Cassandra. I hope you won't leave our fair city too disappointed."

"Lionel, I'm not disappointed at all."

The following week, *Q* magazine ran the story of Cassandra McQueen's "business discussions" with Lionel Kendall. The article was vague about what was being discussed, but the picture of Kendall beside Cassandra with a huge grin on his face spoke volumes.

If that doesn't start the ball rolling, nothing will, Cassandra thought, staring at the telephone hooked up to her private line. *Ring, damn you, ring.*

It did, but only after Cassandra's emotions had spent a week on a roller-coaster ride between unbridled enthusiasm and pitch-black despair.

"There's a Mr. Hilton on the line for you," Maddy, Cassandra's secretary, told her over the intercom.

Cassandra almost choked on her breakfast muffin.

"Put him through."

Conrad Hilton came on the line at once. True to his reputation, he didn't mince words.

"Miss McQueen, it would be very advantageous for both of us if we were to meet at my offices at the Waldorf tomorrow afternoon at three o'clock."

"And why is that, Mr. Hilton?"

"I think you already know the answer," Hilton replied dryly. "And I very strongly suggest we keep the meeting confidential. As much as I respect *Q* magazine, there are some things that are best kept out of their pages—at least for the time being."

"Three o'clock will be fine," Cassandra said coolly. "I'll ask my accountant to come with me."

"Forget it, Miss McQueen. In Texas, all we need is a handshake."

"This is New York, Mr. Hilton."

There was a pause and for a moment Cassandra thought she had lost him.

"All right. Bring Gollant along. I like his style. There'll be plenty left over for him and the legal buzzards. Tomorrow at three, Miss McQueen."

The line went dead.

"Thank you too, Mr. Hilton," Cassandra said cheerfully to the dial tone.

"I don't know how you did it. . . ."

A dazed Eric Gollant was following Cassandra as she threaded her way through the tiny tables at the Waldorf's Peacock Alley. It was cocktail hour and the famous watering hole was jammed. The maitre d' escorted them to Conrad Hilton's banquette, well away from the crowds, where Cassandra ordered a double cognac and promptly downed half of it. A slow blush rose beneath her cheeks.

"How *did* you do it?" Eric demanded.

Going into the meeting, Eric had feared the worst. But instead of a blood-bath, he had watched and listened with fascination as, in less than an hour, Cassandra and Hilton had arrived at an agreement whereby every hotel controlled by the magnate would not only accept the United States Express card but advertise the service in all its publicity and promotional brochures.

"So tell me," he insisted. "How were you so sure Hilton would come around?"

Cassandra let out a deep breath as the cognac calmed her. From her purse she took out a wad of USE receipts.

"I wasn't. When I went to see Kendall I knew he wouldn't want the card."

"He was the worst possible choice," Eric broke in. "Kendall has always had a reputation for being a one-man show."

Cassandra shook her head. "Not true. He wanted people to think that, but the bottom line is that our Mr. Kendall is a hard-nosed businessman." Cassandra pushed the receipts across the table. "His establishment may not take the card but he carries one. Look at the places he's used it."

Eric couldn't believe his eyes. He shuffled through the receipts, noting the New York restaurants where Lionel Kendall had used his USE card.

"I asked myself why Kendall would be spending so much time here. Who could he be seeing and why? Then I remembered a profile Jimmy had run on Conrad Hilton. Hilton is based in New York. He plays Monopoly with real hotels. Kendall's business was stagnating. There was a chance, just a chance, mind you, that Kendall was getting ready to sell out."

"That's an awfully long shot," Eric said.

Cassandra grinned. "I narrowed the odds a bit. Before I went to Philadelphia I visited some of the restaurants Kendall had frequented. I told the managers that he had thoroughly enjoyed himself and asked if his guest, Mr. Hilton, had had any comments. Apparently, he had. That's how I knew the two of them were at least talking, if not actually putting a deal together."

"So you went to Kendall to talk to him about taking the card, knowing that he wouldn't. What you were really after was the publicity of the two of you being seen together. Jimmy's article, the photograph—it was all aimed at Hilton, to flush him out."

"If Hilton did in fact have designs on Kendall, he had to show his hand. He couldn't afford for Kendall even to think about taking the card, because the last thing Hilton wanted was someone showing Kendall how he could draw new business."

"And that's why he called you."

Cassandra's eyes shone.

"That's why he was ready to sign his hotels to the card," she corrected Eric.

"No one's ever going to believe this," the accountant said.

Cassandra leaned forward. "No one's ever going to know the details. Think about it, Eric. I used the card receipts to trace a customer's spending habits. If people found out about this, it would create a terrible backlash. USE would be seen as some kind of spy, invading the public's privacy."

Eric Gollant toyed with his swizzle stick.

"I'll grant you that," he said at last. "But you've just come up with a perfect way to stay on top of our customers' creditworthiness. We have to create our own in-house investigation bureau. The files on our clients have to be kept up to date. Once we have an idea of their spending habits, we'll be able to spot something unusual very quickly. Don't forget, Cassandra. The more people who carry the card, the greater the chance for fraud."

Cassandra felt distinctly uncomfortable with Eric's words. What he was suggesting was sensible and prudent. Nonetheless, Cassandra, who knew how terrible invasion of one's privacy could be, felt like a voyeur.

"I need some time in Connecticut to mull this over," she said.

"Take as much as you need," Eric replied; then, with a wink, he added, "As long as you're back in the office first thing Monday morning."

At eight o'clock on April 21, Cassandra breezed through the doors of the USE clearinghouse expecting to be met by the usual hum of business. The converted bank was empty. Not one typewriter was clicking, not a single telephone was ringing. For a moment Cassandra thought she had come to the wrong address.

"Surprise!"

Without warning, balloons, confetti, and streamers rained down. Employees burst from behind office doors and gathered around her. Jimmy Pearce elbowed his way to her side and, with all the aplomb of a Carnegie Hall conductor, led them through a stirring rendition of "Happy Birthday."

Cassandra was so touched she couldn't keep from crying. When the cake was rolled out she had to take three deep breaths before blowing out the candles, after which Eric Gollant, on behalf of the staff, presented her with a solid-gold replica of the United States Express card.

"I can't thank you enough," Cassandra told everyone. "You've all been great and . . . ."

She was at a loss for words.

"Your other present is a day off," Eric announced. "We don't want to see you here or at the Empire State Building all day. Go shopping!"

The impromptu party was over as quickly as it had begun. Cassandra found herself standing outside wondering if she had dreamed it all.

Hell, I will go shopping!

It had been ages since Cassandra had strolled up Fifth Avenue and window shopped just for the fun of it. As she made her way uptown she noted the new spring collections that graced the windows of Saks and Bergdorf Goodman. Two of Paris's most prestigious houses, Dior and Balenciaga, had introduced a Chinese motif to their lines. American designers such as Hattie Carnegie and Norman Norell had followed suit.

Cassandra let herself be carried along with the flow that led to Farraday's. Her pace slowed as she inhaled the heady fragrance of the perfume counters and fingered the silk scarves by Hermès. Clearly the spring shopping mood had hit Manhattan. Even though it was only midmorning, the store was already filled with women gravitating to their favorite departments. Cash registers merrily rang up the sales.

Cassandra watched the women around her, buying everything from handbags to the latest designer outfits. Some were shopping with a purpose—a dinner engagement, a party, or an evening on the town; others, because they needed accessories; still others, because shopping was fun.

But they all need to feel special, to believe that whatever they buy will help them be more beautiful, more desirable. And they're all paying cash.

Cassandra came to an abrupt stop, causing other shoppers to bump into her.

"It's staring me in the face," she said aloud, and blushed when she noticed counter clerks and other women giving her strange looks.

Clothing, jewelry, flowers, dinners. But clothing first! Cassandra headed for the escalators and quickly made her way up to the store's fifth-floor offices. She marched up to the customer service wicket and told the startled clerk, "I need Mr. Farraday's personal number in Los Angeles."

When Cassandra arrived in Los Angeles she was so excited by the prospect of meeting Morton Farraday that not even the balmy Pacific winds or the scent of sea air helped her sleep. The next morning she was a half-hour early for her breakfast meeting with the department store titan.

"We've been hearing a good deal about you, Miss McQueen," Farraday said, as they sat on the terrace of his bungalow at the Beverly Hills Hotel. "That was a nice piece of work you did on Hilton."

"Really?" Cassandra said innocently. "What piece of work would that be?"

Farraday's tanned features were broken by an ear-to-ear grin.

"Don't bullshit a bullshitter, Miss McQueen," he said amiably. "You had Conrad by the short and curlies. Don't know how you did it, but you did."

Farraday ignored the eggs Benedict the waiter deftly slipped in front of him.

"I suppose you want to do the same thing to me."

"I wouldn't dream of doing that to you, Mr. Farraday," Cassandra replied. "I'm just here to tell you something about women."

Farraday's fork never reached his mouth. His romantic escapades were the stuff of West Coast legend. Although Farraday refrained from commenting publicly on his amorous conquests, privately he reveled in his reputation.

"By all means," he said with a touch of sarcasm. "Fill me in on what I've been missing."

Cassandra waltzed through the opening he had given her. "What percentage of your New York customers are women, Mr. Farraday?"

"As far as I can tell, almost a hundred."

"And they all pay cash, is that right?"

The retailer grinned. "Only cash."

Cassandra ignored the taunting in his words. "What do you think of your customers, Mr. Farraday."

"What's to think? I love them!"

"Because they spend a lot of money."

"That's it."

"What do you think of women shoppers as a whole? More specifically, what do you think of your wife when she goes shopping and comes home with two or three bags?"

"Five or six would be more like it," Farraday grumbled. "When she sees something she likes, she goes ahead and buys it. Sometimes I don't know what she was thinking when she put her money down—if she was thinking at all."

He eyed Cassandra suspiciously. "Just what are you driving at?"

"Do you think your wife is unique in the way she shops?" Cassandra asked, ignoring his question.

"No," Farraday replied warily. "I suppose she's your average shopper. . . ."

"What if she saw something she really wanted but didn't have enough cash with her? What if the store was having a sale she hadn't heard about and she saw the chance to save some money? What if she felt sad and needed something nice to lift her spirits?"

Farraday laughed. "Believe me, that wouldn't happen to my wife. Her check is as good as cash."

"But there are very few like her whose name is instantly recognized. What about the millions of women who are by no means poor but who don't walk around with hundreds of dollars in their pocketbooks, who would have to pass up an impulse purchase or bargain?" Cassandra drove her point home. "Don't you think they'd buy right then and there if Farraday's honored the United States Express card?"

Farraday's eyes lost their geniality.

"Is there anything wrong with your breakfast, sir?" the waiter asked anxiously, staring at the congealed hollandaise sauce.

"I lost my appetite," Morton Farraday said, not bothering to look at him. "I think you'd better put some champagne on ice."

Cassandra returned to New York flushed with triumph. It had taken all her willpower not to call Eric Gollant from the Beverly Hills Hotel with the wonderful news. But she had spoken to his secretary and insisted that he meet her at the Plaza for lunch.

"What possessed you to fly to California at the drop of a hat?" the accountant demanded after pecking Cassandra on the cheek. "Hilton's lawyers delivered the agreement papers and we have a lot to go over."

"We'll tackle them right after lunch," Cassandra promised. "But first, listen to this!"

Cassandra explained the deal she had wrangled out of Morton Farraday, and reminded Eric that Farraday's was part of a much larger chain of stores.

"Of course, we're not going to get the entire chain all at once. But when they see Farraday's bottom line, they'll be begging for the card."

Eric regarded her solemnly. "Thank God we're not getting the whole bunch."

Cassandra couldn't believe she had heard him correctly.

"But that's what we were after," she protested. "You yourself pointed out that we had too many members but not enough outlets for them to use the card."

"Yes, I did. But I thought I made it clear we needed more hospitality outlets—hotels, restaurants, nightclubs. Do you realize what you've done, Cassandra?"

"Obviously not," Cassandra replied frigidly.

The accountant grimaced and his tone softened.

"We targeted salesmen and business travelers for two reasons: first, because they have to spend money to make a living, and second, because if they were to default on payments, we could always go after their company to make good the outstanding amount—or at least a fair chunk of it. That was our fallback position.

"Now you've taken us into a whole new arena. As you pointed out, the people you want to aim the card at are women. True, most of them are well off. Nevertheless, each one will have to have her husband's credit checked. The application form for the card will have to be very carefully worded so that if the woman signs, she understands that her spouse or household will be liable for her charges in the event she doesn't pay them off. And what happens if there are problems? You know as well as I that most women do not control the weekly

561

paycheck. The husband is the one who pays the bills. What would happen if he refuses responsibility for her USE charges? Eventually we would make him ante up, but not only would that cost us time and money, it would also result in ill-will."

Having made his point, Eric tried to put as best a face as he could on it. "You had a great idea, Cassandra. But the timing was all wrong."

Always aware that she was in public, Cassandra froze a smile to her lips. "I can't go back on my agreement with Farraday. We'll never get another chance like this."

"I agree. But you have to stretch out the negotiations for as long as possible. Did you give him a firm date?"

"He wants everything in place—imprinters, advertising, promotion—before Thanksgiving Day. He thinks, and I agree, that if the card works, we'll see the results over the Christmas spending spree."

Eric smiled wanly. "Which means we have to target our new members now, give ourselves as much time to sift through their credit records—if any—and pray we cut out the bad risks. Be prepared to spend a lot of money, Cassandra. You have no choice but to at least double your staff to organize, mail, and process the new applications. At the same time, we'll have to hire new investigators. And you know as well as I do that we won't be able to squeeze all the new bodies into the clearinghouse."

"What's our current financial position?" Cassandra asked.

"The billing and accounts receivable are running so smoothly we're able to cover overhead from our percentage of receipts. Over and above that, USE has a rather thin cushion of two hundred thousand dollars."

"Then that's what we're going to have to make do with," Cassandra said quietly.

Dipping into her reserves, Cassandra leased two entire floors in the Empire State Building. She tripled the space for the management and clerical staff, which serviced both cardholders and establishments. The converted landmark clearinghouse was given over entirely to processing incoming receipts and payouts.

While Eric Gollant evaluated and hired new investigators, Cassandra spent innumerable hours with members of her expanded advertising department. One group was given the task of blending together Hilton's advertising with USE's. The second, which Cassandra worried over like a mother hen, was charged with creating a whole new approach to the Farraday market. Cassandra could not tell her new staff often enough that the Farraday's pitch had to be perfect—and effective.

"I know it's going to be a hard slog," she told them. "But remember, if we succeed, we'll get the rest of the chain. And once we have that, we can tailor this campaign to the other stores instead of creating a whole new look."

"Seems like an awful lot is riding on one department store," a copywriter observed.

Cassandra smiled tightly. "I'm going to try to change that."

From the Manhattan Yellow Pages directory, Cassandra tore out the page with the names and addresses of jewelers, florists, and beauty salons. She knew that hundreds of thousands of dollars were spent each week on accessories ranging from pretty-colored glass baubles to gold and diamond bracelets and earrings. Flowers were a staple, and going to the beauty parlor was a favorite way to close the door on the world and its problems for an hour or two.

Her list in hand, Cassandra had her art people create a special advertisement that would run both in the city papers and in national fashion magazines such as *Vogue*. She then had the ad transferred to a flyer that, along with a personal letter, was mailed to each establishment. A week later, just as she was about to send out her sales force on a follow-up campaign, Cassandra changed her mind.

"Why?" Eric demanded. "You have a great idea here. Let the boys do the hard-sell."

"That's exactly what's wrong with it—the boys. Most small jewelry stores, florists, and beauty parlors are run by women. Our boys, as you call them, are good, but they don't have the rapport with women that we need. A woman will seldom be bullied into anything. She needs to be coaxed and convinced that it's right for her."

"I don't like where this conversation is heading," Eric said warily.

"In the only direction it can. We need women who can sell to women."

That, as Cassandra soon discovered, was not so easy. Every employment agency she called told her that their roster of salespeople was almost exclusively male..

"There have to be *some* women in sales!" Cassandra muttered.

Cassandra did indeed find two examples of entrepreneurs who had mobilized women to sell their products for them. The first was David McConnell, a former book salesman, who, in 1886, had founded the Avon Products Company and who now had an army of housewives selling his perfumes and cosmetics part-time. The second was Earl Tupper, a DuPont chemist, who had designed plastic bowls and canisters with a patented seal to prevent the contents from leaking out. Tupper had come upon the novel idea of Tupperware Home Parties through which wives and mothers sold his product to their neighbors.

Cassandra couldn't afford the time to recruit and train housewives. She needed women who already had some experience dealing with the public and with products she wanted to sell them. There was no choice but to do some poaching and hope she wouldn't get caught.

By now Cassandra was a familiar face around Farraday's executive offices. But because she was always seen with the executives, none of the sales staff ever expected to have anything to do with her, much less be asked out to lunch.

Cassandra had had her eye on six saleswomen and very discreetly met with them at the dining room of the Metropolitan Museum.

"From what I've seen," she told them, "I think you're the best salespeople on the floor. I also know what you're earning. I want you to come to work for me, at the same salary but with higher commissions on every sale. The only thing I'm asking is that you keep this strictly confidential. I don't think Mr. Farraday would appreciate what I'm doing."

"Miss McQueen," a pert redhead spoke up. "Mr. Farraday doesn't even know we exist. We could all walk out of there tomorrow and no one would bat an eyelash."

That, Cassandra thought, would be Mr. Farraday's loss.

By the beginning of November, everything had miraculously fallen into place. The Hilton and Farraday projects were running hard. Over fifteen thousand applications had been processed, two-thirds of which had been approved. Five hundred new restaurants and thirty hotels had signed on while Cassandra's Nightingales, as the ex-Farraday's sales force dubbed itself, had sold USE services to four hundred jewelry shops, florists, and beauty parlors.

On the eve of USE's first anniversary, Cassandra held a supper for Eric Gollant, Jimmy Pearce, and the handful of others without whose help she couldn't have come this far. The dining room table was radiant with candles and silver, and champagne chilled in silver buckets. It was almost perfect, Cassandra thought. Almost, but not quite.

She stared out across the lamp lights of Central Park and thought where Nicholas might be at this very moment. His letters arrived sporadically from such diverse and exotic places as Japan and Singapore, Australia and Hong Kong. There were rumors on Wall Street that he had rooted out a major forgery ring in Europe and had been invited to a council meeting of the Cosa Nostra, whose members had wanted to reassure him that their organization would not abide counterfeiting of Global Traveler's Checks. Nicholas was everywhere, the sword and shield of Steven Talbot's empire. He was always in Cassandra's heart. . . .

The chimes sounded and Cassandra let her reverie fly into the night. She opened the door to Eric Gollant.

"For you," the accountant said, presenting her with a perfect orchid and a kiss on both cheeks.

"It's lovely, Eric. Thank you."

While Cassandra went to arrange the flowers in a vase, Eric studied the cheerful plenty of the dining room. He remembered the paper folded neatly in his suit jacket pocket.

How are you going to tell her, he asked himself, *that she's flat broke?*

— 63 —

Although 1952 was only the second year the party had been held, it was already considered one of the highlights of the social season. Bejeweled women escorted by tanned, prosperous-looking men in white dinner jackets strolled along flagstone paths lighted by flaming torches, greeting one another as they gathered around the free-form pool, with its pink, blue, and white orchid of inlaid tile shimmering at the bottom. On the terrace, circular tables had been arranged, each one presenting a feast for the eyes and a temptation to the palate.

Standing off to the side, resplendent in a Hong Kong–tailored silk suit, Steven Talbot watched his guests with a proprietary air. Everyone who counted in the islands was here. There was also a sprinkling of stateside visitors—a senior senator, several industrialists, the governor of California—each carefully chosen so as not to offend the islanders' sensibilities. Steven had learned that Hawaiians were an insular lot; members of their society were judged as much by what they did with their money as by how much they had.

Steven had also cultivated the image of generosity and restraint. He had purchased vast tracts of land on Oahu and in the burgeoning downtown core and constructed a new headquarters, which had become the nerve center for his Pacific empire. He provided jobs for local contractors and construction crews, trained Hawaiians in modern business methods, paid more than fair wages, and helped whenever an employee needed assistance, whether it was to buy a house or send a child to college. Unlike other whites, many of whom were seen as plunderers, Steven Talbot was liked and admired by the locals, who repaid his fairness and generosity with loyalty.

As Steven mingled with his guests he was well satisfied with his achievements. Without anyone's being aware of it, he had slowly turned Hawaii into a refuge where his privacy was guaranteed and protected, where no one asked what he did beyond its shores. And Steven knew that no one really cared, as long as the benefits—pennies to him—continued to be shared.

Hawaii provided Steven with exactly the kind of haven and public image he needed. Both were a world away from the banks and brokerage houses his lieutenants had established, institutions he had weaned and that were finally attracting the fish Steven had been after all along. One by one, the men of the *zaibatsus* were coming to the doors of discreet, powerful banks that had sprung up quietly across Asia to get money to rebuild their cash-starved industries.

And they took as much as Steven's hidden hand could dole out, on terms that were usurious yet nonnegotiable.

They too are fools, Steven thought. *They have no idea that the money they're getting is coming from the man who once cheated them. They believe they are building a house in which, one day, they will be masters. They don't see why my people take thousands and thousands of their shares as collateral, that one day I will own them.*

Unlike most Americans, British, and Australians, who were openly contemptuous of the Japanese, Steven had no such prejudices. He believed that one day the Japanese would be building everything from oil tankers to rubber Halloween masks, their factories going twenty-four hours a day, producing goods at prices the West couldn't begin to match. Steven meant to control as many of these industries as he could, and all he needed was an uninterrupted flow of money to capitalize them.

As long as Global's money order continued to produce record profits, American banks—from whom Steven had borrowed heavily over the last two years—would continue to lend money. Not one financial controller suspected that the profits, so impressive in the ledgers, had disappeared into the coffers of the dozen banks that acted as Steven's fronts, buying into or financing the companies he wanted. For all the might it projected, Global had been reduced to a shell, its profits passing through the body without ever nourishing it. It was a secret that, in the hours of the false dawn, sometimes made Steven tremble.

One mistake, that's all it would take . . .

Steven pushed away the thought. As long as only he knew the whole picture, and trusted no one, everything would be all right. Whenever Steven faced that silent pit of doubt, he always conjured up the image of his father, the twin barrels of the shotgun in his mouth, his toe curled around the trigger, the final awful explosion. Simon Talbot had been driven to his death because he had revealed a momentary weakness that his wife had taken advantage of.

He should have put the bullets into Rose instead.

That thought made Steven smile.

"A private joke?" the head of the Bank of North America asked.

"Just wondering how Cassandra McQueen is faring these days," Steven replied lightly.

"From what I hear, she's this far from going belly-up," the banker replied, making a tiny space between thumb and forefinger.

"Is that so?" Steven said noncommittally.

But he knew very well it was so. Nicholas Lockwood had delivered his quarterly report on Cassandra and USE when he had passed through Honolulu last week.

"You must have someone on the inside," Steven had told Lockwood after reading it.

"Don't ask me for a name," the chief of the inspectors division had replied. "The figures are accurate, take my word for it. The last thing you need to be worried about is United States Express."

Hearing the banker's comments, Steven tended to agree. In fact, it would be a miracle if the credit-card company into which Cassandra had poured her last cent survived to see the end of the year.

Five thousand miles away, in Singapore, it was midafternoon. Heat had descended over the city and now lay silent and unmoving as a predator. On Bugis Street, where transvestites lethargically plied their trade and pigtailed Chinese coolies rested beside their rickshaws, the air was thick with incense rising from Hindu temples and wisps of opium escaping through flues of the underground dens.

The temperature seemed not to bother the white man who sat at a table by the window of an airless teahouse, the brim of his cotton hat pulled over his eyes. A casual observer would have guessed that he, like most of the population, was catnapping. In fact, Nicholas Lockwood was watching the ramshackle shop across the street as keenly now as he had been for the last three hours.

The silence was broken by a distant rumble somewhere up the street. Nicholas went over to the counter and dropped some coins in the metal bowl beside the abacus. By the time the ten-year-old boy had calculated the price of the tea and rice cakes, the rumbling had intensified. Nicholas reached the front door just as the police truck, its grille fortified with steel rods to form a battering ram, smashed through the door of the house across the way.

Pandemonium erupted along Bugis Street. Prostitutes, peddlers, and shopkeepers who lived in tiny rooms above the stores poured into the street. Nicholas elbowed his way through the cordon the Singapore police threw up around the house and quickly made his way over the debris.

"Cover the back!" he shouted at the plainclothes captain.

"No one there, sir," the policeman called back. "Everybody gone."

Nicholas swore under his breath. The front room, laden with bolts of cotton, silk, and madras, resembled any other dry-goods store along Bugis Street. But in the back it was a very different story. Three printing presses, bolted to the floor, their gears shiny from oil, lined one wall. Opposite them were vats of ink ranging from wasp yellow to lime green, zinc tubs in which to mix them, and a long wooden counter, complete with vises and littered with metal shavings.

"Everybody gone," the policeman repeated, slapping his boot with a swaggerstick in his best imitation of a British officer.

"I can see that. Tell your men to search carefully. Something may have been left behind."

But Nicholas's words lacked conviction. The counterfeiters who had been operating out of this storefront were no different from any of the hundreds of others he had tracked in the teeming cities from Hong Kong to Bangkok.

Ever since Steven Talbot had introduced the traveler's check in the Far East, Nicholas's responsibilities and problems had trebled. On numerous occasions he had argued with Steven that he was expanding his operation too quickly. It was impossible to vet all the new employees who were being hired. But that was a minor problem compared to that of the counterfeiters and forgers who saw the traveler's check as a new and very tempting target. Fortunately, most of the illicit operations were shabby, backstreet affairs run by amateurs who lacked the talent to reproduce the ink, design, and paper necessary to manufacture forgeries. The few phony checks that found their way into circulation were of such poor quality that even the lowliest bank clerk could spot them.

Nonetheless, each operation had to be painstakingly ferreted out. Nicholas and his investigators were hampered by unfamiliar languages and customs. Although local police were unfailingly polite and eager to cooperate, raids that promised to net the most precious components of forgery rings—the plates, the watermarked paper, and the engravers—ended up like this one. Counterfeiters were more than willing to abandon the presses, which could easily be replaced. Nicholas suspected that the bribery of high law-enforcement officials, who tipped off counterfeiters, cost substantially more.

While his investigators fanned out across the shop, hunting for clues to the identities of the counterfeiters, Nicholas began a careful examination of the presses. It was his experience that whatever else the counterfeiters might leave behind, they always made sure the presses didn't have a shred of paper stuck somewhere in the rollers. The quality of paper could always tell investigators how close the forger was to making a good copy. Even beginners seldom left anything behind.

For the same reason, police seldom spent any time poking around in the ink and grease. That was why Nicholas had no one looking over his shoulder when his fingertips, brushing the crack between two rubber rollers, suddenly began bleeding. Making sure he was unobserved, Nicholas reversed the rollers, peeled off the single strip of paper, and, like a magician, palmed it.

Three hours later, after the shop had been boarded up, the guards posted and report filed, Nicholas entered the Tiger Bar at the Raffles Hotel, where he was staying. By now, news of his unsuccessful raid had spread among the planters who lounged in wicker chairs, solemnly partaking of the five o'clock gin-and-tonic ritual. Singapore slings, which had been a hotel creation and for which the Tiger Bar was famous, were considered tourist fare.

"Hard luck, old boy!" several called out as Nicholas passed their tables. By now all of Singapore was gossiping about the unsuccessful raid.

Nicholas shrugged and kept on going. As soon as he was in his room, door locked and wooden shutters drawn, he unfolded the bill. It was a one-hundred-dollar denomination Global Traveler's Check. Using a very light solvent and cotton swabs, Nicholas cleaned off the grease and oil. Squinting, he held it up to the light. Then, Nicholas gasped. Not only was the ink exactly the right hue, but the intricate background pattern, right down to the hidden lion's head in the stylized G that Rose had had the original engraver add as an extra identifying mark, was perfect. Rubbing the check between his fingers, Nicholas discovered that the paper was not quite fibrous enough. But how many people besides himself could tell that? Especially since this was the only flaw in an otherwise perfect forgery.

Nicholas rubbed his temples. Somewhere in this city, home to thousands of con men, thieves, and rogues, was a master craftsman who was quietly preparing an assault on the heart of Global Enterprises. Nicholas was certain the counterfeiter wouldn't strike just yet. This man would know that the quality of his paper wasn't perfect. And he would be patient, taking as much time as he needed to get the fiber content exactly right.

And that's precisely the time I have to find him.

But when he did, Nicholas had no intention of letting the authorities know. Slowly, the realization had dawned on him that he had discovered a way for Cassandra to deal with Steven Talbot once and for all.

Less than a mile from Bugis Street, in the oldest part of Chinatown, where two-story, clay-tile houses front the Singapore River, a tall, lean Caucasian stood on the roof garden shielding his eyes from the setting sun.

"He's found it by now," the elderly Chinese behind him murmured.

He was no more than five and a half feet tall, with skin the hue of discolored ivory, wrinkled like the bark of septuagenarian mahogany. His beard consisted of precisely sixty-three white strands and his eyes were as clear as those of a newborn child.

569

"I know," Harry Taylor said, not taking his gaze off the western horizon. "But there was nothing for him to find. He can keep the presses."

The Chinese, who was called Ram, took a Global Traveler's Check from his pocket and idly began to rub it between his fingers. It was a motion Harry had seen thousands of times before. Ram was teaching the nerve ends in his fingers exactly the kind of sensation he wanted them to experience, so that when they did so, he would be certain he wasn't being deceived.

"Is he the same man who has been your shadow?" asked Ram.

"Yes."

"Has he come for you?"

"I don't think so. Too many things have changed."

For one, Harry Taylor was now in his late fifties, although he was still very handsome. His passport identified him as a Canadian who operated a small import-export firm. In Singapore, where a dozen cultures, races, and tongues came together to share the bounty of commerce, it was the perfect cover.

There were other, equally important differences. Harry now knew that the name of his persistent stalker was Nicholas Lockwood, that he worked for Steven Talbot, and that he was very good at his job. He also knew that Lockwood was not here because he had at last run Harry to ground. Somewhere in his trek across the Indian subcontinent Harry had managed to lose his pursuer. Once he had reached Singapore, he had successfully blended into the anonymity of the swollen island city.

"No," Harry said softly. "If he'd wanted me, I'd be his. He's too close to have missed me."

He turned to Ram. "But we always knew that one day he would come—for us, because of what we're doing. Don't worry, Ram. As far as Lockwood's concerned, all he's found is a nickel-and-dime counterfeit operation, no different from the dozens of others he's raided. Tomorrow or the day after he'll be on his way. You'll see."

Both men heard the child's laughter behind them.

"I pray you are right, Harry," the Chinese said softly.

"So do I, Ram. Because the day I met you, I stopped running from Steven Talbot."

Not only stopped, Harry corrected himself. *But decided to go after him.*

Although Harry had arrived in Singapore with a great deal of money, he quickly discovered his options were limited. He dared not risk entering the preserves of the white planters, who would invariably ask too many questions about who he was and where he had come from. The last thing he needed were reports of a new face that might reach his pursuer's ear. Furthermore, Harry spoke neither Mandarin nor any of the dialects Asian shopkeepers used in business transactions. Although English was widely used, Harry knew he'd be at a grave, potentially fatal disadvantage if he tried to duplicate the kind of boilerplate operation he had run so successfully in Marseilles.

Even though he moved around a great deal, Harry made a point of buying all the English papers he could find. Rose's death, so sudden and senseless, had cut him to the quick. So much of his life had been influenced by that indomitable, spirited, complex woman he had once loved. For a time afterward Harry wondered if now, with Rose dead, he might stop running. As soon as he'd read how Steven Talbot had seized the traveler's checks from Cassandra, he knew the pursuit would continue. Steven was the kind of man who would stop at nothing to get what he wanted. And he wanted Harry dead.

So Harry became circumspect. He found himself a modest apartment and made sure his money was carefully hidden but in places where he could get to it quickly. Thus organized, Harry returned to the thorny question of what to do with himself. He found the answer in the most unlikely place.

Saint Andrew's Anglican Cathedral is a city landmark, and it was in its gardens that Harry Taylor quite literally bumped into Ram, making him drop a package that broke apart, spilling out long sheets of very fine-quality paper. The minute Harry touched the paper he knew it wasn't for a lady's letterhead. And when Ram looked into his eyes, he knew that Harry knew.

By way of apology Harry insisted on buying Ram tea. The two men indulged in some gentle verbal fencing before Harry casually mentioned that he needed a job. Ram, having established that he was a printer, replied that he could use a messenger.

"There are hundreds of street kids who would do deliveries," Harry pointed out.

"That's so, Mr. Taylor. But I require an honest, trustworthy individual."

The job wasn't at all what Harry had had in mind but he was intrigued by this elderly Christian Chinese with the unusual name. His sixth sense, which had helped keep him alive this long, tingled. He agreed to take the job on a trial basis.

Over the next few months Harry came to know the city as well as did any native. He made deliveries to the finest hotels as well as to rat traps where only the brave or foolhardy ventured. He learned his way around the Jockey Club and along the waterfront. The only consistencies were in the type of clients Ram serviced—silent, white men who could have been millionaires, seamen, smugglers, or all three, and in the packages, which were always small, the size of a music box. Although Harry ached to open one of them he couldn't find a way to tamper with the wax seal the elderly Chinese affixed to the wrapping. What he brought back was no secret at all. Most of the clients didn't bother to seal the envelopes bulging with the money they paid for their purchases.

Harry continued to bide his time. Although he and Ram became friendly and the Chinese occasionally asked Harry to mind his printing shop—a legitimate if unassuming establishment that catered to other small merchants—Ram never mentioned what he was really involved in. Then one day Harry returned to the shop, his face battered and bleeding, his arm broken.

"The son of a bitch didn't have the money to pay," he gasped. "But he wanted his passports anyway. . . ."

With that, Harry collapsed. When he came to, he was in an infirmary run by a discreet Chinese physician, and Ram was sitting beside the bed.

"I owe you an apology," he said. "Nothing like this has ever happened."

Harry managed a grin. "There's a first time for everything."

Little by little, Ram unveiled the secrets of his little business. Behind what appeared to be solid panels was a workshop worthy of a master forger, equipped with presses, plates, dyes, inks, and paper to produce everything from passports and residence permits to seamen's papers and birth certificates.

"You have been patient and honest with me, Harry," Ram told him. "You had a chance to steal money, sometimes a great deal, but you resisted the temptation. Now I am in your debt. Tell me, how may I repay it?"

Harry thought very carefully about his answer. As soon as he was released from the infirmary he returned to his small apartment and removed some money from its hiding place.

"I would be honored to become a partner in your business," he told Ram, offering the cash.

"But, Harry, you are not a duplicator," Ram protested.

Ram never used the term *counterfeiter* or *forger*, which he considered an insult. He saw himself as someone whose talent, even genius, lay not in creation but in reproduction.

"No, but together we can make a great deal of money—by making our own."

"Harry, the only currency worth duplicating is the American dollar. It is quite impossible to find the necessary inks and paper here."

"I wasn't thinking about the greenback," Harry replied softly.

He reached into his pocket and with the fingers of one hand unfolded a Global Traveler's Check.

By the time Harry's arm mended, Ram knew everything about his new partner. Harry had told him about some very painful episodes in his life, whose shame he still carried.

"Is it still so important for you to hurt this Steven Talbot?" Ram asked.

"He won't stop coming after me," Harry replied. "He knows I'm the only one who can testify that he murdered Michelle. But I'm too old to keep running.

I've never stood and fought back against Steven Talbot. It's time he learned I can."

Harry paused, thinking of Michelle, the terrible thing he had been a party to that had ultimately caused her death, and Cassandra, a child whom he had held hostage.

"I also have a debt to repay," he said softly.

Ram looked at him thoughtfully. He had known all along that Harry was laboring under some terrible load. Now he held the traveler's check between his fingers, rubbing it tightly.

"Whoever designed this was a master. It will take a long time to duplicate, if it is possible to do it at all."

Harry smiled. "I'm not going anywhere."

"Oh, but you are, my dear Harry. With all due respect, there is little that you can do for me here." Ram held up his fine-boned hands. "Unfortunately I cannot transfer the gift from these hands to yours. But there are many things we have to know, and you, being white, can travel to places that are closed to me, talk with people who would not countenance to give me the time of day."

For all the dignity in his voice, Ram could not hide the pain behind his words. Harry, himself a fugitive and outsider, understood perfectly. Ram was a Christian, yet there was a whole world out there with white, God-fearing people who shared his beliefs but who would always turn their backs on him.

For the next several years Harry divided his time between Singapore and places he had never heard of. Instead of Ram's messenger, he became his pupil, absorbing everything there was to know about the art of counterfeiting. He quickly discovered that what he had learned in Marseilles was child's play. Harry studied botany, learning about plants whose secretions made the best dyes. He pored over the chemical formulas used in the manufacture of ink and learned how various acids were used to get exactly the right cut of color into the pigment. He read books on metallurgy to understand how strong yet resilient the metal used in the manufacturing of plates had to be. He came to appreciate the value of a duplicator's tools.

"Each one has to be an original," Ram told him. "My chisel and pick are valueless in another's hands, just as no two violinists can coax the same sound from the same instrument."

Having grasped the intricacies of the duplicator's trade, Harry was sent abroad to complete his education, posing as a commercial buyer for an American publisher of limited editions and coffee-table books. He traveled into the interior of Burma to watch how some of the world's most expensive paper was created from trees that grew only in that region. In the Philippines, he watched delicate rice paper being spun almost literally out of thin air. In

Bombay he discovered the secrets of rag and how the coarse fibers were ground between giant stone mills and finally pounded with wooden mallets until they were invisible to the naked eye.

When he returned to Singapore, Harry found that Ram had broken down the components in the ink in the Global Traveler's Check.

"It is not the new grade of ink used on most currencies," Ram explained. "This surprises me because it implies Mr. Talbot is not staying abreast with technology. However, it is our good fortune."

"What about the background detail?" Harry asked eagerly.

"Three, possibly four months to make the plate. However—" Ram held up a warning finger—"there is the problem of the paper."

"I thought it was very close to what the U.S. mint uses."

"It is much, much better quality. The stock is stiffer, hard yet supple."

"Therein lies the challenge," Harry murmured.

It was one that took over a year to meet. Once more Harry packed his bags and set off for the other regions of the Orient, searching for wood pulp that, when properly treated, would eventually meet the exacting standards Ram had set.

More to the point, which Rose set, Harry reminded himself.

As arduous as some of his travels were, Harry had to smile when he thought of Rose. Only now did he understand why no counterfeiter either in America or in Europe had been able to duplicate her creation. The formula for the paper in the traveler's check was the diadem of Global's crown of industrial secrets.

But what can be done once, can be done again.

In a small village in Thailand, close to the Cambodian border, Harry Taylor at last found proof of the truth in Ram's unshakable belief.

Their laughter was like the peal of wind chimes stirred by prayer chants. The woman who came into the garden was half Harry's age, tall for a Chinese, and slender, with an oval face whose features flowed together in perfect harmony. She brushed back her long black hair as she knelt to scoop up their two-year-old daughter, whom Harry looked upon as the miracle of his life.

"Hello, Harry," the woman said softly.

"Mary, my love . . ."

Harry kissed his wife, Ram's daughter, on the cheek. Their child, Rachel, giggled as her father's beard tickled her.

"Are you ready for dinner?"

"In a few minutes, darling. The sunset is so beautiful this evening. Stay and watch it with us."

"It's not the sunset you're thinking about," Mary said. "You are a poor liar, husband. I will leave you to finish your conversation. But no more than five minutes."

The idea that he might, after all these years, find a lifelong mate had never crossed Harry's mind. Yet, after he had returned from Thailand with the paper, Ram, who had opened his house to Harry, unveiled his most precious secret. The night Harry was introduced to Mary, he had fallen in love with her. The wonder of it all was that she had taken that love and given it back tenfold.

"You wish now that you had never showed me that Global Traveler's Check," Ram said when he was sure Mary couldn't hear him.

Harry turned to face him and the sun bathed the side of his face with the color of blood.

"I'd give anything for that, Ram."

"Perhaps you still can."

Harry shook his head. "Lockwood doesn't stop. Steven Talbot won't let him. So one day he will find me. And I can't afford that.... Can I?"

- 64 -

It was no secret in New York's financial circles that the past year had been even rougher for United States Express than its first. Having sustained a fifty-thousand-dollar loss in the first twelve months, covered only by a remortgaging of Cassandra's apartment, the charge-card company went on to lose three times that amount in its second year of operation.

"This time you really are tapped out," Eric Gollant told Cassandra. "It's going to take a miracle for USE to stay in business."

But Christmas was the season of miracles and Cassandra was convinced that one would come her way. The obvious solution was to go to the First City Bank of New York, where USE had its corporate accounts, and take out a loan. The company had plenty of collateral, beginning with the refurbished landmark that housed its processing center. But Cassandra had deliberately avoided giving First City or any other bank a foothold in her operations. She knew that several banks were keenly watching her progress and, in spite of the losses, saw the potential of the charge-card market. She'd be damned if she'd let them gain a foothold in her operations just so they could choose their moment to foreclose on her and scoop up the assets.

But that left her only one recourse.

"How much is my apartment worth?" she asked Eric.

The accountant made some quick calculations. "Over and above the two mortgages, you could realize about seventy-five thousand dollars."

"And my mother's paintings? The Picassos she bought years ago in Paris?"

Eric frowned. "You'd need an appraiser to tell you exactly. But I read that the last ones sold at Christie's fetched thirty to forty thousand apiece. You're not thinking of parting with them, are you?"

Cassandra remembered meeting the artist at Saint Paul-de-Vence and how she had brought back a small picture for her mother. The paintings were the last of Michelle's personal possessions she had managed to keep.

"I want you to sell everything, including the paintings," she whispered.

Eric Gollant could not believe what he was hearing. The Carlton Towers apartment was more than just a home to Cassandra. It was a place that harbored some of her warmest memories, memories that, Eric believed, had helped Cassandra through the toughest times of the last two years. The same was true of the paintings.

"You don't really want to do that," he said gently.

Cassandra smiled tightly. "Of course not. But I have to. The seventy-five thousand won't cover what I owe, but it'll keep the wolves from the door."

The wolves were the restaurants and hotel owners. Although thousands more people were now using the card, USE's cash flow had declined. Hospitality merchants were slow and careless in sending in their receipts, which meant the company had to wait that much longer for its percentage. But they were quick to demand their checks. Cassandra wasted many precious hours every day listening to their complaints and appeasing their threats to pull out of the program.

"The only reason they won't," Cassandra had told Eric, "is because too many of their competitors accept the card. Still, if there are enough defections, it will start a stampede. . . ."

Although Eric Gollant strongly opposed the practice, Cassandra adopted a policy of sending the restaurants and hotels their share even before her bank had credited to her account the gross amount of the receipts. This meant United States Express was always playing catch-up, juggling accounts receivable with payouts, which made for a bookkeeping nightmare.

The money was out there. Eric Gollant knew that. It was time that was working against Cassandra. Time for Hilton, Farraday's, and all those small establishments—the jewelers, florists, and beauty parlors—to generate the

576

amount of business needed to cover the operating expense of having them in the system. Gollant's figures told him that once they were integrated, Cassandra's worries would be over.

"The hell you'll sell anything," he said at last. "I'll buy the apartment from you. And lease it back to you for a dollar a month."

Cassandra was stunned. Her friend was well off but far from wealthy. Not only that, but he, like Cassandra, had pared his salary to the bare minimum.

"I know you can't afford it, Eric."

"I have a trust fund for my grandchildren's education. They won't be going to college for at least ten years."

"What if I go belly-up?" Cassandra asked quietly.

"Then they'll go to NYU instead of Harvard."

"No, they'll go wherever they want to. On a full scholarship from United States Express. I promise you that, Eric."

The money from the "sale" of her apartment disappeared as soon as it came in, but it bought Cassandra the breathing space she needed. Or so she thought. By 1953, USE had a full-time staff of thirty investigators, led by a former New York City police detective named Kevin Armstrong. A quiet, stolid Irishman, Armstrong had both a sterling career record and a degree in criminal law from John Jay College. This, in addition to his street contacts and old-boy police network, made him invaluable to United States Express.

"There's someone I want you to meet," Armstrong growled as he walked into Cassandra's office unannounced, shaking the snow off his coat. In one hand he had a grip on a much smaller, furtive-looking man whose feet barely touched the floor as he was moved along.

"An associate?" Cassandra ventured.

"Trouble."

Armstrong sat the man down none too gently. He reached into his pocket and dropped a fistful of USE cards in front of Cassandra.

"I don't see . . ."

Then she did, and her heart shrank. All the cards had had their imprinted numbers removed. Cassandra turned on the thief.

"Where the hell did you get these? Who are you?"

The man blinked but said nothing. Cassandra glanced up at Armstrong.

"He's George McKenna, a small-time hood with a record as long as—no, longer than—your arm. A two-time loser but his luck almost changed."

Armstrong laid a heavy hand on the thief. "Do you want to talk to the lady, Georgie? Or shall we begin reading the telephone book?"

Cassandra had no idea that what Armstrong was referring to was, in some New York police precincts, standard procedure for interrogating a suspect:

battering him with a phone directory. The heavy volume left bruises that could have been caused by a suspect's falling down a flight of stairs. George McKenna was well aware of Armstrong's reputation. He didn't bluff.

"It's pretty easy, really," McKenna said. "First, I steal the card. You know, pickpocket, stuff like that. Then I slowly heat it and use the catalyst from polyester resin to get rid of the ink identifying the owner."

Cassandra was bewildered by this con man turned chemist.

"Do you know what he's talking about?" she asked Armstrong.

The security chief nodded grimly.

"Then I press the card with a warm iron," McKenna continued. "To flatten it out, you know."

"Of course," Cassandra said faintly.

"I shave off any bumps with a razor blade, and with an addressograph stamp new names and numbers."

"It's that simple?" Cassandra demanded.

George McKenna nodded enthusiastically. "Yes, ma'am."

"How many cards have you changed?"

"A couple hundred."

Cassandra glanced at the handful on her desk.

"Where are the rest?"

"I break 'em in half after I'm through using 'em. You see, the secret's never to charge too much to one card and not to hold on to it for too long. That way your people don't get suspicious."

"And what do you do with everything you buy?"

Kevin Armstrong supplied the answer to that. "Besides being a thief, our George is also a fence. He sells what he buys—or rather, steals—for half price."

Cassandra slammed her hands on the desk, making Georgie jump.

"I'm going to ask you one more question," she said in a low voice. "Do you know anyone else who's doing this?"

George McKenna nodded quickly.

Cassandra closed her eyes. *This can't be happening. It can't!*

"Well, I guess we're about through here," Armstrong said, hauling the thief to his feet. "Do you want me to bring him downtown, Miss McQueen, or get my buddies to come pick him up?"

"Neither," Cassandra told the astonished detective. "I want you to offer him a job. It takes one to catch one, isn't that what you've always told me, Kevin?"

After George McKenna's startling revelations Cassandra reviewed her entire security system.

"Stealing is bad enough," she told Armstrong. "Would it be possible for someone to counterfeit the card?"

"If you can make it, someone else can," Armstrong replied philosophically.

"I wish you hadn't said that."

"Look, Miss McQueen. So far we've had it easy. The background design on the card is so intricate that it's difficult for anyone except an expert to copy. This guy would not only have to know how to manufacture the actual plastic from which the cards are cut, he'd also need an artist who specializes in silk-screen printing to get the design on the card.

"You also have fine people working for you. You treat them well and they're loyal to you. But believe me, even though we check supplies constantly, anyone who has access to the blank sheets of plastic could push a few out the back door. What we're going to have to watch now is the mailroom."

"Why?"

"Your customer base has expanded so rapidly, things have been a little sloppy as far as the sending out of the cards is concerned. I want the new people in the mailroom vetted as thoroughly as everyone else. Once the cards are packed and ready to be shipped, I want to see them go into the bag and into the post-office truck. Think how easy it would be to grab a handful of envelopes and walk out with them."

Cassandra didn't want to. "Is there anything else?"

"You're going to have to do something about all those files," Armstrong said without batting an eyelash. "There's all sorts of confidential information—or what should be confidential—lying around. Names, addresses, telephone numbers, places of work or business. If a fox gets into that henhouse, he can dummy up cards we'd think really belong to these people."

"I take it you recommend that we act on this immediately."

"The sooner the better. Whatever it takes may cost a few bucks, but in the long run you'll save a bundle."

Cassandra thought about this for a moment. She hadn't discussed her next move with Armstrong because she hadn't been quite ready to commit to it. The picture he had drawn for her changed her mind.

"We're going to meet someone tomorrow," Cassandra told him. "I think you'll find him very interesting."

Thomas J. Watson had been in the numbers business since 1924, the year he reorganized the National Cash Register Company into International Business Machines. Twenty years later, IBM, working with the Harvard Engineering School, produced the Mark 1 Automatic Sequence Controlled Calculator. Now the company was on the verge of launching its second-generation computer.

"What I'm going to show you, Miss McQueen, is a prototype of the new IBM 702, our first business computer," a senior sales executive said proudly. "This unit will do everything you need: keep track of basic cardholder background information, keep an up-to-date list of their purchases and expenditures, alert you to overdrafts or delinquent payments. In fact, we can program it to do virtually anything—better, faster, and more efficiently than the most experienced clerk."

"Can it spot a thief?" Armstrong asked skeptically.

"Perhaps not in the way you think," the executive replied coolly. "But it will alert you to irregularities in an account. Also, if a card is stolen, its number can be logged in the machine. If the thief attempts to use it and the number is called in by the storekeeper, a quick check will tell you the card is invalid. You can ask the clerk to try to keep the customer on the premises until your men arrive or at least caution him to get a good description."

Armstrong inclined his head and looked at the gleaming stainless steel contraption with a touch more respect.

"Tell me a little more."

The IBM representative was only too happy to oblige. For the next hour he explained in detail the functions he had previously outlined.

"What do you think, Kevin?" Cassandra asked.

"If it lives up to its billing, you've got a winner," the security chief said in his customary understatement.

"Then we have a deal," Cassandra said. "I'll expect your people first thing Monday morning."

"Believe me, Miss McQueen, you won't regret it."

Sometimes there is no rhyme or reason why a business suddenly turns the corner and skyrockets. Economists offer theories, financial analysts fall back on trends, bankers tend to overstate their prescience and shrewdness. When asked by the press what it could be in the case of United States Express, Cassandra summed it up best: "We worked hard, we had what people wanted, when they wanted it, we were damn lucky!"

Following business's lead, American consumers fell in love with the charge card and, once smitten, couldn't tear themselves away from it. Form applications run in newspapers and magazines were returned by the thousands. Those who couldn't get one sent in personal letters, including everything from personal references to promises to shop only where the card was accepted.

"You're going to break your first million in profits this year," Eric Gollant predicted, leisurely rolling the ash off his cigar.

"I'll believe it when you show me the books," Cassandra replied dryly.

"You can believe it now," the accountant said, wagging a finger at her.

"Because I'm going to hold you to your promise about scholarships for my grandkids."

When he said that, Cassandra knew it must be true. One million dollars. It seemed like all the money in the world. But it wasn't. It was a beginning. Much more would be needed for what she had to do.

"Since we're celebrating, why don't you ask the lady out to dinner?" she suggested coyly.

"You're young enough to be my daughter—what do you want with this old horse? You should find yourself a nice young man. The last thing I want is for you to suffer the loneliness Rose put herself through."

Cassandra was deeply moved by Eric's words, as well as ashamed. He loved her like a daughter, yet she had kept her greatest secret from him, causing him to worry needlessly.

"I do have someone," she said quietly. "I always have."

Eric's face was lit up by a huge grin. "You've been holding out on me! Who's the lucky guy?"

Cassandra hesitated. "Nicholas. It's always been Nicholas."

The accountant couldn't believe it. "You mean after everything he did, leaving you—"

"He never left me, Eric. That's what we wanted everyone, especially Steven, to believe."

As gently as she could, Cassandra explained the facade she and Nicholas had created, beginning with the "argument" they had had for Steven's benefit.

"So everything was designed to persuade Steven to keep Nicholas on," Eric murmured. "He was your source inside Global, warning you about every move Steven was about to make."

"I had to know whether Steven was going to move against me," Cassandra said. "Nicholas was instrumental in convincing Steven that I was no threat at all. He never would have been able to do that if he hadn't made Steven believe—*really* believe—that his allegiance lay with Global."

"And the times you went up to Connecticut . . . ?"

"Were the only times we had together," Cassandra finished. "I don't think we could have survived without them."

"I don't know how you managed this far. The pain you've deliberately put yourself through . . ."

Eric thought back to Rose, recalling the way she had made the company her life, the sacrifices she had rendered up in its name.

There's a difference. Rose could never bring herself to trust anyone to help her. By the time she realized how wrong she was, she couldn't change. . . .

"I'm sorry I never told you," Cassandra was saying. "After everything you've done, you should have known."

Eric shrugged. "If I had, I might have acted differently. Once you tell someone a secret, it's almost impossible for them to behave as though they don't know about it. Now we'll see how good an actor I really am."

Cassandra was relieved. "Does that mean you're still taking me to dinner?"

Eric's eyes twinkled. "You bet!"

Eric Gollant was seldom wrong about anything having to do with numbers but he badly miscalculated United States Express's profits for its third year. The final tally was close to three million dollars.

The company's explosive growth continued through 1954. More than twenty-five thousand establishments across the nation accepted the USE card. Two hundred thousand clients were logged in the company's battery of computers and more names were being added every day. The contract Cassandra signed with a single hotel association nearly doubled the membership, and the major car-rental companies were quick to follow.

USE's vast growth forced Cassandra to seek more and more space. Her manufacturing plant had been moved to Long Island, and she was already leasing five floors in the Empire State Building. It wasn't enough.

"We're not going to pay rent one day longer than necessary," Eric Gollant fumed.

The accountant scoured the Wall Street district for a suitable building. In early September 1954, he presented Cassandra with four possible sites.

"What's wrong with number five?" asked Cassandra, noting that the last name had been penciled out.

"Look at the address."

Cassandra smiled slowly. "That's the one I want."

"You can't be serious!"

"I am. Eric, please look after the details. I'd like the paperwork completed by the time I return from Connecticut."

The accountant shook his head. This was *meshuga*. He should have known better than to tempt Cassandra like that. Naturally she would choose the building directly opposite Global's headquarters on Lower Broadway.

– 65 –

The erosion had been so gradual that for two years no one at Global suspected what was happening. The first word Steven Talbot received that something was very wrong came not from Lower Broadway but at a meeting called by his lieutenants, who had flown in from their respective headquarters in the Far East.

"We're not getting enough money, Mr. Talbot," their spokesman said. "That's the long and the short of it. The profits from the traveler's checks are not showing up in our accounts. I don't have to tell you, sir, how overextended our positions are. We've bought so heavily into Japanese industries that we're barely able to sustain any kind of float. If word of our liquidity position gets out, there's going to be a run on our banks."

Steven, who had flown from Hawaii to his Long Island estate, was stunned. The last figures for the traveler's checks had indicated that volume had never been higher.

"I'll get to the bottom of this."

When Steven arrived at Global headquarters he ordered his secretary to bring him the financial reports from the sales of domestic and overseas traveler's checks. After poring over the numbers, he discovered that while sales of the checks had indeed risen, associated costs had spiraled. Advertising prices were astronomical, yet there hadn't been a new campaign, with fresh themes and jingles, for years. Theft and pilferage in the various offices had mushroomed horrendously. Inventories showed major equipment purchases yet no resales of old stock.

The picture couldn't have been clearer: because of gross mismanagement the public was losing interest in the traveler's check.

"Get me those two old fools who have supposedly been running the checks division!" he barked at his secretary.

Steven had expected both vice presidents to crawl into his office. Instead, they entered with an air of calm and confidence.

"What the hell have you two been doing—or not doing?" Steven demanded, slamming down the reports in front of them.

"Following your instructions, Mr. Talbot," one replied smoothly. "You said, and I paraphrase, that you were satisfied with the way things were and didn't want any changes. We took you at your word."

"I didn't tell you to run the division from the bar of your club!" Steven screamed. "Does either of you have any idea what's going on?"

"You may not recall, Mr. Talbot, but we did send you memos about the division's problems," the second vice president said. He laid a stack of slips on the desk. "These are copies, dated and initialed. We cannot be held accountable if they didn't reach you."

Steven swept the memos from his desk.

"You're both—"

"Fired, Mr. Talbot? No, thank you. We prefer to resign."

Each man laid his letter on the desk and turned to leave.

"As to the reason for the traveler's checks doing so poorly," one said, "you might find part of the answer out there."

Steven looked where his ex–vice president was pointing and, across the street, saw the bold, blue neon sign of the knight with his sword and shield. For a moment it appeared that the symbol of United States Express was staring directly at him through the window.

"Why the hell didn't you tell me what that bitch was up to? USE is a nickel-and-dime operation, you said. It won't last out the year, you said. Where are your fancy fucking predictions now, Lockwood?"

Steven Talbot was livid. Nicholas Lockwood could see the veins pulsing beneath his facial scars.

"Everybody on Wall Street was saying the same thing," Nicholas reminded him. "I'm your security director, not a financial watchdog. My job is to make sure no one tampers with the checks. And no one has. If you have a problem with that, tell me."

Steven hesitated. He couldn't afford to alienate Lockwood.

"What do you know about USE?" he demanded.

Nicholas shrugged. "Cassandra gambled everything and it looks like she's won. She didn't go belly-up the way everyone predicted. Now the company's in the black. People seem to love the charge card."

"She's cut into the heart of my business," Steven said. "That card is stealing my customers and I want something done about it!"

"USE hasn't broken any laws. It hasn't infringed on any Global patents or copyrights. Maybe your legal people can find a way to go after it, but don't send me. There's nothing I can do." Nicholas paused. "However, I did hear something you may want to run down."

Steven's eyes narrowed. "What?"

"The USE card is as susceptible to counterfeiting as the traveler's check. So far Cassandra has been lucky. No one's tried it, or if they have, they couldn't do it. Now word has it that she's testing a new type of card, one that will be impossible to duplicate."

"What else?" Steven demanded.

"Her computer people have developed a new technology—a magnetic strip to go on the back of the card. The strip will be coded with relevant information about the client. In effect, it's an electronic fingerprint. For the retailers, USE is creating a special verification system. The details are sketchy but I hear that it will be a unit about the size of a shoe box. The card will be run through it, the system will 'read' the magnetic strip and tell the retailer almost immediately whether the card is real, stolen, or if the client is authorized to make the purchase. If it works, and if USE can get the system out to enough retailers, it'll make buying on the card even easier than it is now. And much safer."

Nicholas let the implication of his words sink in.

"USE has already hurt you because it's convinced the public that it doesn't have to pony up cash to buy your checks in order to travel and spend," he finished. "If Cassandra gets this system on-line, the traveler's check may be in for a very rough ride."

Steven turned his chair so that he could look directly at the USE knight.

"Find out everything you can about the new card," he ordered flatly. "I'll expect a report in one week."

As Nicholas rose, Steven added, "And be very, very careful. No one can suspect that Global is asking questions. If word gets out, I'll hang you out to dry."

Harry returned home as he did every day, in time to watch the sun set from his rooftop garden. Today he was feeling especially pleased, and with good reason: the first batch of Global Traveler's Checks, in twenty-dollar denominations, had been run off. Ram had passed each sheet through his fingers before allowing it to be cut and not one had failed this last critical test. They were ready. By the end of the week there would be $10 million in phony checks, bound and packaged for shipment. And that was just the beginning.

Harry heard his daughter's laughter as he climbed the stairs to the roof.

"Mary! Rachel!"

He caught a glimpse of his daughter sitting on the bench, her legs swinging back and forth. There was a shadow across her pretty, white dress.

"Rachel—"

Harry stopped short. His legs began to tremble. Sitting beside Rachel, showing her how to make an origami chicken peck by raising its tail, was Nicholas Lockwood.

"Hello, Harry."

A red haze descended across Harry's eyes. His muscles tensed but he couldn't get them to move.

"Please, don't hurt her," he whispered. "I'll give you what you want, just don't hurt her."

"No one's going to hurt her, Harry."

Harry whirled around and saw Cassandra standing by a tub of sweet frangipani.

"Go on, Rachel," she said. "Show your daddy the bird."

The child giggled and, clutching the origami creation in a chubby fist, raced to Harry, who swept her up in his arms. Hot tears spilled across Harry's cheeks as he rocked his daughter. Then he looked at Cassandra and saw not the beautiful, poised thirty-four-year-old woman but the frightened, helpless girl of fifteen lying on the floor of the limestone cavern in the catacombs.

When Cassandra saw Harry's expression, she realized what he was thinking: that at last the time had come for him to pay for the nightmare he had helped create. And for an instant she wanted that. The years of waiting demanded it.

He's not the one, she told herself. *Look at him. In his own way, he's already paid his price. The only way I can punish him further is by taking him from his wife and child. . . .*

Cassandra knew she couldn't do that. She stepped forward and Harry retreated, holding his daughter tightly.

"I don't mean you any harm," Cassandra said. "Please, believe me."

Her words sounded sincere, but out of the corner of his eye Harry saw Nicholas Lockwood regarding him silently. Harry struggled to make sense of what was going on.

"But you two . . . He works for Talbot. He's been following me for years. . . ."

"Nicholas found you a long time ago," Cassandra told him. She held up an ink-stained hundred-dollar traveler's check. "You were careless once, Harry. That's when Nicholas knew."

Harry Taylor closed his eyes. "What do you want?"

"You've perfected a way to counterfeit the traveler's check, haven't you?"

Harry nodded.

"How much paper do you have?"

"Enough for ten million, maybe more."

Cassandra's eyes widened. "Have you shipped any of the stock yet?"

"Not yet. But I'll give it all to you if that's what you want. Just don't hurt my family."

"I'm not here to hurt anyone, Harry," Cassandra told him. "In fact, I'm here to help you. But first, you have to hold back dumping the counterfeit checks on the market."

Harry's features relaxed. "I don't understand."

"You will, Harry. In time."

In the years since its formation, Japanese Company 4780 had grown from a two-thousand-dollar investment to a multimillion-dollar construction corporation. Its founder and president, Jiro Tokuyama, remained a mystery. Although he now owned whole apartment blocks and office buildings and was a financial force to be reckoned with, Tokuyama lived as a recluse in the penthouse suite of his newest and most luxurious complex. Between himself and the public was a battery of lawyers, accountants, secretaries, and personal assistants. He never gave interviews and dealt severely with those who intruded on his privacy.

Rumors of Tokuyama's secrecy were legion, but in a society that respected privacy as much as Japan did, no one dared infringe upon it. Such circumstances made it easy for Tokuyama to slip away from his office and, after following a circuitous route, end up in a working-class suburb in northern Tokyo. It was there, once a week, in a modest one-room apartment, that he met and conferred with the guiding hand of Corporation 4780, Yukiko Kamaguchi.

Tokuyama was a loyal and cautious man. He understood how important it was that no one link his mistress to Corporation 4780 and he followed exactly the procedure Yukiko had laid down for their meetings. But for all his attention to detail, Tokuyama was still easy prey for the professional stalker.

Tokuyama's error, although he did not realize it, was that he was looking for Japanese shadows. To him, Caucasian faces were unmemorable.

"How do you do, Mr. Tokuyama."

The construction magnate whirled around at the soft voice and found himself confronted by a tall *gaijin* with a blond woman beside him.

"What do you want?" Tokuyama demanded in rapidfire Japanese.

"We're going to the same place you are," Nicholas replied equally quickly. "To see Yukiko Kamaguchi."

Tokuyama blinked, surprised by the foreigner's fluency in Japanese. Fear crawled through his belly at the mention of his mistress's name.

"I don't know anyone by that name," Tokuyama said stiffly. "You will please stop following me."

"We don't have to follow you anymore," Nicholas said.

He walked up to the tiny house before which Tokuyama had stopped and rapped on the door. When it was opened, he said, "Hello, Miss Kamaguchi."

* * *

"You are not here for frivolous reasons," Yukiko Kamaguchi said. "Jiro Tokuyama has been very discreet in all the years he's been coming here, yet you found him out."

The four of them were seated on tatami mats in a room partitioned by a rice-paper screen. Yukiko had been shocked to see Nicholas Lockwood. Because she had detailed files on all of Global's executive staff, she knew him by reputation. Her first thought was that he must have been sent by Steven Talbot. Then she had seen Cassandra. Fear was replaced by curiosity.

"Mr. Tokuyama *was* very careful," Nicholas said. "He just didn't expect foreigners to follow him."

Yukiko glanced at Tokuyama, whose head was bowed in shame.

"But neither of you has come here to exchange pleasantries with me. What is it you want?"

"You are the head of Corporation 4780," Nicholas said matter-of-factly. "No one knows this because after Steven Talbot betrayed you, you were told by the leaders of the *zaibutsus* never to return to Japan."

"Is this leading to blackmail, Mr. Lockwood? If so, it goes against your reputation."

"We are here to give you information, Miss Kamaguchi. And we shall want something in return."

Yukiko knew she had no choice but to hear him out. "Please continue."

"The men who lead the *zaibatsus* have been able to restore much of their industry. Do you know how?"

Yukiko shrugged. "They have borrowed enormous amounts abroad. Beyond that I know very little."

"Do the names of these banks sound familiar to you?" asked Nicholas, listing a half-dozen financial institutions.

"Everyone has heard of them. And yes, I'm aware that they are the lead lenders to the *zaibutsus*."

"But do you know who really owns them?"

"Perhaps you would enlighten me, Mr. Lockwood?"

"Steven Talbot."

"That is not *possible!*"

"Not only possible but true." Nicholas handed her a sheaf of papers. "See for yourself."

Yukiko did.

"Steven Talbot has been silently financing redevelopment in every major Japanese industry," Nicholas said. "The *zaibatsus* think they're dealing with banks run out of Asia. Wrong. They're borrowing from the same man who stole from them. They believe that eventually they'll pay off the loans. Wrong again. When Steven Talbot has them in deep enough, he'll foreclose. Then he'll be the one who runs the *zaibatsus*."

Although her features betrayed nothing, Yukiko was gloating. How sweet it was to know that those who had tried to exile her were themselves unwitting victims! But, Yukiko thought soberly, Steven Talbot was also a threat to her.

"He doesn't have to be dangerous to you," Nicholas said, reading her thoughts.

"And how is that?"

"In the very near future Steven Talbot will experience financial difficulties. Of major proportions. His cash flow, which is already thin, will dry up completely. He will need a great deal of money, and the only way he will be able to get it is by selling off his hidden interests in the *zaibatsus*. I suggest that you and Corporation 4780 will be in an excellent position to buy up those interests. You will end up controlling the men who left you with nothing. Without their ever knowing it, if you so choose."

Yukiko's eyes gleamed but caution reined in her expectations.

"At the beginning you said you would expect something in return."

"Your promise to leave both Steven Talbot and Global alone," Cassandra said, speaking for the first time. "Global belongs to me, and I intend to have it back. As for Steven, there is a personal score I must settle."

Yukiko looked thoughtfully at Cassandra. She had heard a great deal about this woman who, like herself, had created an empire out of ashes. She saw now that it had all been true.

"As you wish," she said tonelessly. "One does not repay the gift of a salmon with a shrimp. You have given me a great deal. I must return in kind."

There was no insincerity in Yukiko Kamaguchi's words. She was quite prepared to surrender her vengeance against Steven Talbot. But her promise did not extend to the one she had made to her father. The personal score, as Cassandra McQueen had put it, would not be settled on Yukiko's behalf but on that of Hisahiko Kamaguchi.

- 66 -

The manager of Barclays Bank in Sydney, Australia, was on his way out to lunch when the head teller intercepted him.

"I think you'd better have a look at this, sir."

He steered the baffled manager to his wicket and showed him a Global Traveler's Check for one hundred dollars. The manager looked closely at the note and rubbed it between his fingers.

"Feels perfectly good to me," he said.

"It is, sir," the teller replied. "Except for the serial numbers." The teller then brought out the control sheet that recorded the serial numbers of the traveler's checks Barclays had received from Global. "According to this, sir, we have the consignment in the series for this check."

"Obviously a customer bought the damn thing here and now someone else is cashing it," the manager snapped.

"That's what I thought, sir. So I went into the vault and checked."

The teller shuffled through a stack of fresh traveler's checks and extracted one. Its number matched that of the one the manager was holding.

"Either Global has sent us a bad lot, sir, or—"

"Jesus Christ!"

The manager looked over the teller's shoulder. "Is the person who tried to cash it still here?" he whispered urgently.

"It's old Mrs. Tompkins, sir. She's waiting over there."

The manager saw a frail, elderly woman, a longtime customer, sitting beside a potted eucalyptus and looking quite perplexed.

"Don't cause a panic but find out where she got this!" the manager said. "And for Christ's sake, don't let her leave!"

With all the dignity he could muster, the manager walked back to his office. He closed the glass door and lowered the blinds. Minutes later, the telephone lines between Sydney and New York were crackling.

It was a nightmare the likes of which Steven Talbot had never imagined. It caught him completely off guard and seemed unstoppable, rolling across the world like some giant tidal wave, gathering strength as it traveled inexorably toward its destination, Global headquarters on Lower Broadway.

The frantic telephone call from Sydney about one check with serial numbers identical to the Barclays' consignment was considered a nuisance by Global's security department. It was logged, and a cable was sent out requesting written verification.

But in the same hour there was another call, this one from London. A third came from Athens, a fourth from Los Angeles. After that the switchboard was inundated with long-distance and international calls. Steven Talbot ordered the operators to stay at their posts. As the deluge continued, the office lights burned well into the night.

By dawn, there was a hint of just how massive the damage was going to be. In less than eighteen hours Global auditors had tallied up over a million dollars' worth of phony checks that had been honored by banks, post offices, hotels, airlines, and other institutions.

"How the hell do we know they're phony?" Steven roared at his auditors. "We haven't seen one yet."

"That's true, sir," his chief accountant conceded. "But that could easily be part of the counterfeiters' plan. The longer we wait to get our hands on a forgery, the more time they have to flood the market. They could be selling or distributing the phonies right now. And since we have a standing policy to make good on all claims—"

"I know what our policy is!" Steven turned on him. "I want to see a phony!"

"I don't think the people responsible for this were stupid enough to drop any in Manhattan," the accountant said miserably. "In fact, I doubt there are any between here and the West Coast. The soonest we'll know is in a couple of days."

"A couple of days? What about the one found in Los Angeles?"

"The bank said they put it in the mail."

Steven couldn't believe what he was hearing.

"But they sent it by special delivery!" the accountant cried over his shoulder as he fled the office.

Steven Talbot spent the next hour on the phone, trying to track down Nicholas Lockwood. No one in the inspectors division had seen him for over a week. No one knew where he had gone or why. Steven's mind reeled. Global was in the middle of a potentially fatal crisis and the man he relied on to keep order was nowhere to be found. Steven was calling the overseas offices in a desperate attempt to find Lockwood when his secretary ran in.

"Mr. Lockwood on line three!" she said breathlessly.

Steven jabbed a button, grimacing as static tore into his ear.

"Lockwood, where the hell are you?"

"Singapore . . ."

The voice was faint and Steven was afraid the connection might be broken at any second.

591

"Do you know what's happening?"

". . . working on it. I have some . . ."

Steven was beside himself. "Forget Singapore! Get your ass back here now! Do you understand!"

"I'll get . . . flight out."

Static jumped along the line, then suddenly there was only the dial tone.

"Thank God for lousy telephone equipment."

Nicholas turned to Cassandra and Harry Taylor, who were watching him from across Harry's living room. "He's running scared. We've hurt him bad."

Nicholas gripped Cassandra by the shoulders. "Are you sure you know what to do?"

Cassandra nodded.

"Harry?"

"We'll be out of the city as soon as the plates and paper have been disposed of."

"Don't stay a minute longer than you have to."

Nicholas cupped Cassandra's face and kissed her gently on the lips.

"Be very careful," he whispered.

"You too," she replied. "You're the one who's going back there. If Steven suspects anything—"

Nicholas placed a finger on her lips. "He doesn't. As far as Steven's concerned, I'm the only hope he has of finding out what's happened. And that's exactly the position we want him in."

Nicholas picked up his overnight bag. "I'll see you soon."

Outside Harry Taylor's house, Nicholas plunged into the traffic of Chinatown streets. He spotted a cab and dove into the backseat before anyone else could claim it. He didn't notice the tall Malaysian in the perfectly tailored tan suit who had been watching him from across the street.

Toward the end of the second day the word about counterfeit Global Traveler's Checks had spread to every major world capital. Banks suspended sales and merchants refused to accept them. Global offices were swamped with customers wanting to return unspent checks and get refunds. Global was hemorrhaging money.

Because customers and merchants alike had begun coming into the Lower Broadway offices, Steven Talbot demanded and received police protection. Only bona fide employees were allowed to enter the building, which, with its cordon of mounted and foot patrols, resembled a castle under siege.

Inside, the fortress mentality was even more evident. Reporters who tried to get through were removed bodily. In retaliation, editors and radio commentators fed the rumors that Global was losing a million dollars a day. The figure was actually higher.

Barricaded in his office, Steven Talbot worked like a man possessed. He had to leave his clients, no matter how big and prestigious, to his staff to deal with. His efforts were directed at the banks. The men who had lent Steven money so gallantly were now calling for reassurances. They had his private number. They could not be put on hold.

Steven mustered every ounce of willpower to keep his voice level. Yes, there was a problem, he admitted. Not as great as the papers or rumors made it out to be, but bad enough. However, both the FBI and the national police in a dozen countries were working hard on the case, in addition to Global's own formidable security force. The essential thing, Steven kept repeating, was for everyone to stay calm. The public was expected to panic; bankers, he implied, were made of sterner stuff. In a few days, things would begin to return to normal, he promised.

"That's fine for you to say, Steven," one banker replied acidly. "But you don't know how much of the stuff those bastards printed, do you?"

Steven forced himself to laugh off that question, yet it was one that continued to burn him.

How much did they print? Ten million? Twenty? Thirty? Enough to bankrupt me?

The flood stopped as abruptly as it had begun. Banks that had been cross-checking serial numbers discovered that after a time there were no more duplications. The counterfeit traveler's checks were logged, bound, and couriered to Lower Broadway by armed messengers from points around the world.

One official delivered several banks' checks in person. He refused to leave until Steven Talbot agreed to see him and listen to what he had to say.

"Thank you for your time," the commissioner of the Singapore police said politely after he was shown into Steven's office.

Steven gave him half a glance, noting that the commissioner's suit was rumpled, as though he had slept in it all the way from Singapore.

"I want to commend you on your sense of duty," Steven said. "But you really didn't have to bring the checks yourself. If you like I'll have one of my people collect them—"

"It is not the checks that I wish to talk to you about, Mr. Talbot," the Malaysian replied, "but about the man who was responsible for printing them."

The commissioner was pleased that he now had Steven's full attention.

"What do you mean?"

"I can give you the name and address of the man who was involved in the counterfeiting."

Steven spread his fingers across the leather blotter, pressing down hard. Was it possible that this flunky actually knew?

"My inspectors-division chief is on his way here right now," Steven said. "He also has information for me."

The Malaysian smiled graciously. He had made sure that Nicholas Lockwood was unable to get a seat on any of the airlines operating out of Changi International Airport until he himself was well on his way. The delays would cost Nicholas at least twenty-four hours.

"You can, of course, wait for Mr. Lockwood," the commissioner said. "Or you can authorize me to apprehend this man."

The commissioner placed a photograph in front of Steven. The picture was grainy, obviously taken from some distance, but Steven recognized the features at once.

Harry Taylor.

Steven's pulse was racing. So Rose had been right all along. Harry Taylor was alive! Neither the bullet nor the *cataphiles* nor even time itself had managed to kill him. *But you're mine now*, Steven thought. *You've run out of lives, Harry!*

Steven composed himself. "Commissioner, I commend you on your brilliant detective work. But as I said, Inspector Lockwood is on his way from Singapore right now. I'm certain he'll be bringing me the same information."

The Malaysian was unperturbed. "That may be so, Mr. Talbot. But with all respect for Mr. Lockwood's abilities, I have several advantages which he does not. For example, my men are watching Mr. Taylor right now. It would be a shame if, for one reason or another, he managed to elude them."

You blackmailing bastard! Steven thought, smiling tightly at the commissioner.

What Steven had no way of knowing was that the Malaysian had given him only half the story. The commissioner had seen Lockwood with Taylor on enough occasions to realize they must be working together. But he would not reveal this to Talbot. The commissioner was certain that both Lockwood and Taylor would pay handsomely to keep their relationship a secret. It was a simple matter of choosing to milk several cows instead of one.

"You mentioned that you have the authority to take this man into custody," Steven said.

"That is so. However, to secure the necessary evidence would prove very costly."

"How costly?"

"One hundred thousand American dollars."

And then Steven saw how he could get his money's worth out of the venal Malaysian.

"That's an outrageous price. If I pay it, I expect more than just an arrest. I think it would be in everyone's interests if this man simply disappeared, don't you?"

Steven went over to his safe and brought out a stack of currency. "Half now, half when I read about Harry Taylor's tragic accident—the story to be accompanied by very clear pictures."

The Malaysian did not take his eyes off the money.

"Singapore's Chinatown can be a very hazardous place," he murmured.

It took Nicholas Lockwood thirty-nine hours to reach New York. He had barely stepped into his office when his secretary rushed in with the news.

"They got him! The Singapore police found the counterfeiter!" She waved a blowup of the grainy photograph of Harry Taylor. "Mr. Talbot wants to see you right away."

Nicholas felt sick. Somewhere, something had gone dreadfully wrong. He had to call Harry immediately and warn him.

"Lockwood! Glad you finally made it back."

Nicholas whirled around at the sound of Steven Talbot's voice.

"We caught the son of a bitch," Talbot was saying. He took the photograph from Lockwood and held it out. "Did you have any idea it could be him?"

"I suspected but I wasn't sure," Lockwood said. He handed Talbot a slip of paper. "That's the address to which I traced the counterfeiting operation. I'm willing to bet Harry Taylor lives there too."

Steven read the address and smiled. "Lived. Past-tense. But you were on the right track, Lockwood."

The minute Talbot was out of his office, Nicholas asked an operator to get him Harry's number in Singapore. The wait seemed interminable.

"I'm sorry, sir," the operator said when she came back on the line. "That number is no longer in service."

Cassandra and Harry were sitting in a small cafe across the street from his house, feasting on crab satay, clams in oyster sauce, and salt-baked prawns.

"I wish Mary would hurry up," Harry muttered, pushing the delicacies around his plate.

Cassandra laughed, pinching his shrimp. "That's why she threw you out of the house, Harry, so she could pack without having you underfoot."

Harry Taylor took a long pull on his Tiger Beer.

"Have you ever forgiven me for what I did to you?" he asked, his words barely discernible over the din in the street.

Cassandra looked away. "It was a long time ago. You said you didn't know Steven was planning to murder my mother and me, and I believe that. If you hadn't helped him, he would have found another way. Don't go back to it, Harry. I think Mary and Rachel are wonderful. They're good for you and you for them. That's all that matters—"

The explosion that threw Cassandra to the ground was so strong that the street and sidewalks buckled. Cassandra heard people screaming. She looked up to see a cloud of black smoke and dirt billow from across the road.

"Harry, are you—"

Harry was already scrambling to his feet. Jumping over pedestrians sprawled on the ground, crashing into those who tried to stand, he raced toward the ruins of what had been his home.

"*Mary!*"

Harry plunged into the burning debris, clawing his way over chunks of stone and splintered timbers. Flames licked at him from all sides but he threw himself forward, disappearing into the inferno. Cassandra stumbled to her feet and ran after him, elbowing her way through the crowds converging on the house and dashing around the back.

"Harry!"

Miraculously, the back of the house was untouched, as though the explosion had neatly cleaved the structure in two. Taking a deep breath, Cassandra forced her way inside. She saw a child's doll sticking out from under the rubble and began to dig furiously.

"Too late . . . too late."

Harry was standing over her, holding Rachel's body. His face was blackened by soot so thick that even his tears did not streak it.

"Mary, Ram . . ." Cassandra began.

"Dead, all dead."

Like a sleepwalker, Harry stumbled out into the tiny backyard and reverently laid Rachel next to the fountain.

"I always knew that one day Steven would find me," Harry said with unearthly calm. "That he would make me pay . . ."

"Harry, we have to get out of here. Whoever did this meant to kill you too!"

"I know."

Cassandra heard the singsong claxons of fire engines and ambulance sirens. "Harry, please!"

Harry turned his back on her and walked back into the destruction. He reappeared carrying Mary's body. Cassandra knelt beside the tangle of bloodied and broken limbs and choked. A moment later, Harry came out with Ram.

"Harry, we can't stay here!" Cassandra gasped, finally raising her head to look at him.

But Harry Taylor, like the happiness and promise of his life, had disappeared.

- 67 -

Thirty-three days after the first counterfeit traveler's check had been spotted, two weeks after the newspapers had reported that a faulty propane tank had exploded in Singapore's Chinatown, killing a young mother, her father, and her infant daughter, the chairmen of America's four largest banks met Steven Talbot at his Fifth Avenue mansion. The financiers had all attended church that morning, as they did every Sunday. But this time each had prayed hard, hoping that God might deign to hear them. If He didn't, their stockholders would certainly make themselves heard.

"All right, gentlemen," the chairman of the Bank of North America, Jason MacTavish, said. "We all know why we're here so let's cut to the chase. Steven, the consensus is that the guys who did this to you cost you a shade over ten million dollars. The loss of business incurred by Global because no one would buy new checks comes to twice that. We estimate that another five million in checks has been returned by nervous Nellie customers who didn't know if they were holding the real stuff or the fakes but weren't about to find out the hard way. Our projections indicate that you'll have to pump out about six or seven million dollars' worth of advertising to regain customer trust but that it'll take at least ninety days before we see any kind of turnaround—which adds up to another forty million, conservatively speaking. By our reckoning, that leaves you eighty-one million in the hole."

The banker looked up from his notes.

"And that's on top of the hundred million you've already borrowed from us," he finished softly.

At the head of the table, Steven Talbot took a sip from his cup, which he held for what seemed a long time before gently depositing it in the saucer.

"Jason," he said, "you've always been good at addition. What are you really getting at?"

"The obvious, Steven," he replied, ignoring the jibe. "You owe us a lot of

597

money. We'd like to see some of it back. There was a time, not too long ago, when your war chest was the talk of the town and your business was solid. But you still kept borrowing from us. It's time to tell us what you did with our money."

"The money is invested," Steven said flatly.

"If that's the case, show us the collateral," another of the men said.

Steven shook his head and smiled, but when he spoke his voice was pure ice.

"I don't have to show any of you a goddamn thing. You're all in so deep to me that you can't get out even if you wanted to. And I don't think you do. Because if word one gets out about how much you've overlent me, your stockholders will kick your collective asses into the street, where the Federal Reserve boys will pick them up and haul them off to jail."

"You can't talk to us like that!" the patrician head of one of the nation's oldest banks shouted. "We acted in good faith—"

"You acted out of greed!" Steven retorted. "This was as close to a no-risk loan situation as you were ever likely to see. The chance was there to make some easy interest and you took it, figuring everything would be repaid and no one would be any the wiser."

Steven paused. "It should have worked out that way. It still can."

Cigarettes and pipes were lighted and a veil of blue smoke swirled over the men.

"Obviously you have something for us," Jason MacTavish said. "We'll listen. But no promises,"

"Very well," Steven said. "It's no secret that United States Express has made inroads into the profits generated by the money order and traveler's check. It represented a danger I had not foreseen and did not act on quickly enough. However, Global has not been the only one to be hurt by USE.

"You gentlemen have been drooling over the income USE is generating and the profits Cassandra McQueen has been pocketing. But what have you done about it? Nothing. Right now the biggest cardplayer is Franklin National here in New York. But there are fewer than a hundred banks in the game. Cassandra is so far ahead of you, she's out of sight—almost."

"What makes you think we want to catch up?" asked MacTavish.

"Each of you has commissioned plans for a card," Steven replied. "In some cases, these plans have been delivered and steps are being taken to implement them."

Steven couldn't help but smile at how each banker stared straight ahead, refusing to meet his neighbor's eyes.

"However," he continued, "you've all committed one error already. Your cards are charge cards—a thirty-day, no-charge basis—just like USE. You want to copy, not innovate. You're ready to commit millions to creating sales and collection departments, plant equipment, new personnel, and advertising in an effort just to try to catch up to USE. There's another way.

"You should be thinking of a credit card, not a charge card. Give the customer more than a month to pay off the balance. Hell, give him as long as he needs, but charge him for it. Make sure he pays, say, ten percent of the bill, and finance the rest at prime plus five percent. That, gentlemen, is what I call profit."

The anger and resignation disappeared from the bankers' faces. Steven knew he almost had them convinced. Patiently, he waited for the obvious objection, calculating how long it would take the brightest of the bunch to come up with it.

"That's a very interesting concept, Steven," MacTavish said at last. "But it doesn't get us around to the fact that even this credit card, as you call it, would face an uphill battle against United States Express."

"Not necessarily."

Steven picked up the phone and said, "Please ask Mr. Lockwood to join us."

Nicholas Lockwood spoke for a half-hour, without notes, his delivery flawless.

"That, gentlemen, sums it up. USE's new card is so sophisticated that if you integrate it into your systems at the very beginning you'll be able to challenge Cassandra McQueen in the marketplace."

Lockwood remained standing to answer questions.

"Has USE patented this strip?" asked MacTavish.

"Yes. But USE is working exclusively with IBM. If you worked out a deal using Remington Rand's UNIVAC, they could design a magnetic code that would be different enough to get around any patent infringement."

"But we don't know what to give UNIVAC to work with, do we?" MacTavish said. "If we wait until the new USE card is on the market before we can study it and, um, make certain alterations, we'll still be very far behind. Simply put, Mr. Lockwood, we need the blueprints for the new card as soon as possible."

Nicholas glanced at Steven.

"I don't think it's necessary or advisable to go into such details," Steven told them. "There may come a time when certain questions will be raised. It would be much better if all of you could say that you have no idea how the new design happened to come into your hands."

Everyone around the table nodded sagely.

"Which brings us to the final piece of business," Steven said. "Once the blueprints are delivered, I'll expect a moratorium on the repayment of all loans, long enough for Global to get its house in order. After that, we'll work out a new schedule to pay back what's owed, over a period of, say, five years."

Steven looked around the table. "And that is the last I want to hear about the matter."

Talbot and Lockwood left the room to allow the bankers to deliberate. Ten minutes later, the chairman of the Bank of North America stepped out of the dining room.

"All right, Talbot. You have your deal. But if you don't deliver, we'll shut you down. It will be hard on us, certainly. But it'll be nothing compared to how you'll end up."

The leaves were turning across the Connecticut landscape, a palette of red, burnt orange, yellow, and brown against a blue sky. It was the time of year Cassandra loved most, when nature released one last burst of glory before the winter sleep.

Nicholas Lockwood mounted the steps of the cabin and sat down beside her. Gently he stroked her cheek with the back of his hand, his touch tingling her as it always had.

"I haven't been able to find Harry," he said, intertwining his fingers with hers. "I'm sorry, Cass."

Cassandra's lips tightened and she looked straight ahead. The elusive Harry . . . Nicholas was very good at what he did, but Harry had managed to keep one step ahead of him for years. Then, just when Nicholas had found him—

"Dammit!" Cassandra cried. "I told Harry how much I was depending on him. He knew that by testifying to what had happened in Paris we could stop Steven once and for all." She turned to Nicholas. "I was there, darling. I saw what happened to Mary and Rachel and Ram. My God, I know what Harry was going through! If he'd waited, I could have given him Steven. . . ."

Nicholas said nothing. He understood exactly what Harry had done and why. Grief enraged and blinded men, yet it also endowed them with a savage cunning, allowing them to accomplish the seemingly impossible. But Nicholas knew he would find Harry. It was just a matter of time. Which was why he didn't object to what Cassandra said next.

"I have to go on. Everything we've done has been to get Steven to come to me, without his ever suspecting that that's exactly what I wanted. I can't lose this opportunity, Nicholas. With or without Harry, I have to take it."

"What do you want me to do?"

Cassandra covered his hand with both of hers. "Exactly what Steven expects."

United States Express's card-manufacturing plant was located in Riverhead, Long Island. A three-story industrial complex, it was protected by a cyclone

600

fence topped with barbed wire, patrol officers with attack dogs, and a state-of-the-art alarm system.

"I don't understand how the bastards got in!" Kevin Armstrong said through clenched teeth. He glanced at Cassandra and added hastily, "Pardon my French."

"Not to worry," Cassandra assured him.

The driveway in front of the main doors was cluttered with police cars. Cassandra watched as detectives, followed by a forensic unit, hurried inside.

"It's got to be an inside job," her chief of security said. "The cops aren't going to find anything to write home about. This was clean, very clean."

"Couldn't it have been a professional burglar?" asked Cassandra.

Armstrong shook his head. "The safe where the magnetic codes were kept was on a time lock. The only way around that was to chop through—which these guys did, using a thermal lance. A thermal lance, for Christ's sake! The only time I've seen one was at the FBI school in Quantico."

"What makes you think any of our employees were involved?"

"Someone had to know the electronic code to the delivery-bay doors," Armstrong replied. "A thermal lance isn't the lightest piece of equipment to carry. It would have taken time to get it out of the truck and into the building. Which means someone knew the patrol schedules. Once they were inside, they didn't go for the vaults where we keep the plastic and blank cards. No, they went straight into my goddamn office, into my safe, and melted it like it was an ice cube."

Cassandra laid a hand on Armstrong's sleeve. She wished he wouldn't blame himself, but the thieves had taken more than just the blueprints for the magnetic strips. They had also stolen Armstrong's pride. Cassandra shuddered to think what would happen if Armstrong ever caught them.

He's not going to think very kindly of me, either, when I finally tell him the truth, she reminded herself.

"And here comes the goddamn press!" Armstrong moaned.

Cassandra prepared herself to make what appeared to be a bad situation a disaster.

In her drab gray dress and mismatching overcoat the woman who entered Tokyo's most fashionable apparel shop appeared a most unlikely customer. As she shuffled to the counter, the saleswoman wrinkled her nose.

For years Yukiko could have afforded the finest clothes but she had not dared draw attention to herself. Nonetheless, that didn't mean she hadn't hungered for the finery she saw around her or anticipated the day when she could step out of her disguise. That day was here at last.

"I want to buy some clothes," she said in a low voice.

The saleswoman, who was also the manager, laughed. "Try the secondhand store, granny."

Yukiko looked at her keenly. She left the store without any fuss and walked to a public telephone, where she made a brief call. Then she waited.

Several hours went by. Yukiko watched the entrance to the store carefully. When she saw a limousine pull up and three men get out, she returned. The store manager was waving her arms in the air, screaming at Jiro Tokuyama and the two attorneys.

"I don't understand. What do you mean the store's been sold?"

"It means that the store has been sold!" Yukiko told her flatly. "And you're fired!"

Before the manager could say another word, Yukiko turned to another saleswoman.

"Dress me!"

Three hours after the robbery at Riverhead, Nicholas Lockwood delivered the stolen blueprints to Steven Talbot's Long Island estate.

"Congratulations," Steven told him. "You made the late-night news."

Nicholas handed him the cardboard shipping tube.

"Will you be needing me for anything else?"

"Go home, Lockwood. You've earned your salary today."

Steven hurried to the back of the house, where one room had been completely cleared and given over to the men waiting for him. They were engineers and technicians, specialists in the latest computer and electronic technology.

Steven passed the tube to the senior engineer, then turned to Jason MacTavish, who had insisted on this inspection by his own experts.

"How about a drink while we wait?"

They had barely tasted their second scotch when the engineer walked into the library.

"Is this some kind of joke?"

"What the hell are you talking about?" Steven demanded, rising from his chair.

The engineer tossed the blueprints on the coffee table.

"These aren't worth the paper they're printed on. It's the circuitry design for Watson's IBM 702!"

"That's impossible!"

"Shut up, Steven," MacTavish told him. "Go on, Dr. Knight."

"As for the magnetic strip"—he held up a foot-long piece of black film—"it's blank. There's no code, no information, nothing."

Steven hurled his crystal tumbler against the wall.

"Don't say it," MacTavish warned him. "I don't want to hear a word out of you. I gave you the chance, Steven, and you failed."

The chairman looked hard at his engineer. "No mistake?"

"None, sir."

"Ten o'clock tomorrow morning, Steven, my office. If you're not there, I'll have a warrant served on you."

Neither the customs nor the immigration officers paid any attention to Harry Taylor as he came off the Pan-Am clipper at Honolulu Airport. His haunted, cadaverous face looked no worse than that of fellow passengers who had endured the rocky, sleepless flight from Sydney, Australia. Harry picked up his overnight bag and shuffled toward the exit.

"Do you know the name of a clean, cheap hotel?" he asked the cabdriver.

"Sure, bro," the Hawaiian replied. "Leave it to me."

Harry did. He didn't care where he stayed as long as it was the kind of place where no one asked questions. He needed privacy and anonymity.

As the cab pulled out onto the two-lane blacktop, Harry saw the lights of Waikiki in the distance, a glittering necklace around the island's throat. The scene reminded him of parts of Singapore. With that, other memories came unbidden. Harry closed his eyes and thought he heard Ram, Mary, and Rachel calling softly to him.

Even before the computer technicians had packed up their equipment, Steven was racing back to Manhattan. He had called Lockwood both at his apartment and at the office and received no reply. Then he had ordered Global's night security officer to get all his people out of bed and track down Lockwood.

"I'm worried that something's happened to him. He was supposed to meet me tonight and never showed up. I expect some answers by the time I get to the office."

But there weren't any.

"He's vanished, sir," the deputy director said. "You have no idea where he might have been or what he was doing?"

"None."

"Then I think it's time to bring in the police."

"No police! I'm paying *you* to find him!"

After the security officer left, Steven turned out all the lights in his office except the green-shaded banker's lamp on his desk. Lockwood had betrayed him, Steven was sure of it. The realization stoked a bitter rage within him, made all the more painful because Steven knew this couldn't have been the first time.

He never left her. It was all a charade. Everything he said, everything he did for me. He was working with her all along.

Steven slammed his fist down on the desk. It was all he could do not to leap up and tear apart his office. He reached deep inside himself and managed to cap the hatred exploding within him. Lockwood's time would come. He would be made to pay. And since he loved Cassandra so much, Steven had already decided on the price.

Steven Talbot alighted from his limousine before Rockefeller Center and took the Bank of North America's private elevator to the forty-sixth floor. A male secretary was waiting and escorted him into the chairman's office.

"Hello, Steven," MacTavish said in a neutral tone. "Take a seat."

Steven's eyes darted around the room.

"We're alone, if that's what you're worried about," the chairman told him. "I've been authorized to speak for the others."

Steven didn't say a word.

"We've had a hard look at your situation, Steven," MacTavish continued. "You were right: the investments you made were pretty good. But getting into the Japanese market meant you were in for the long haul. And you've run out of time."

Steven didn't move a muscle but he knew his eyes had given him away.

"No one was supposed to know you were buying up Japanese industry, right? You wanted that plum all for yourself. And you're asking yourself how we found out. Well, look no further than those bright young cutthroats you had working for you."

"The Japanese assets are no good to you," Steven said at last. "They're not going to get you your money back."

MacTavish smiled. "So one would think. But you're wrong. In fact we've found a buyer who's willing to pay the full hundred million you owe us. Of course, that still leaves you short, but that's another story.

"Now, before you start a fuss, let me tell you that the sale agreements have already been drawn up for your signature. And you'll sign them, won't you, Steven? Because if you don't, there are two federal marshals out there ready to take you into custody. It would be bad for what's left of your business if your clients saw the head of Global being taken out in handcuffs, wouldn't it?

"After the agreement is finalized, you can forget about dealing with any bank in New York again. There isn't a financial institution in the country that would lend you a nickel."

MacTavish turned a sheaf of pages toward Steven.

"Just sign on the last page, by the X."

604

Steven stared at the paper for a long time. "You don't have a buyer. You're bluffing."

"You're going to regret that, Steven," MacTavish warned.

He buzzed his secretary, who opened the door for a smartly dressed Asian gentleman.

"Mr. Talbot, meet Mr. Jiro Tokuyama, who's just bought all your assets in Japan."

A tiny bell went off in Steven's mind. The name sounded familiar and he seemed to recognize the face. Then it all came back.

"He's a goddamn gardener! This bastard used to work for me!"

Even as he spoke the words, Steven realized the truth. *Yukiko!*

Jiro Tokuyama walked up briskly to Steven. Without one sign of recognition, he handed him the morning edition of the *New York Times*. The headline in the financial section swam before Steven's eyes:

UNITED STATES EXPRESS TO BID FOR GLOBAL ASSETS

"I'd say you have plenty to worry about without us on your back," Jason MacTavish said. "Sign the papers and get the hell out of here."

On the way back to Lower Broadway, Steven Talbot couldn't tear his thoughts away from Yukiko Kamaguchi. He had left her destitute. He had learned that the men of the *zaibatsus* had forever banned her from returning to Japan. How had she survived? How was it possible that from nothing she had reaped enough millions to steal his Japanese assets out from under him?

How did she know about them in the first place?

"No calls," Steven snapped at his secretary as he went into his office.

"A Mr. Harry Taylor is on the line," his secretary replied quickly. "He's been calling all morning, insisting to speak with you. He says it's about Singapore—"

"I'll take it!"

Steven slammed the door behind him.

"Harry?"

Static raced across the line and for a moment Steven thought the connection had been broken. Then he heard Harry's voice, sounding very far away.

"I'm waiting for you, Steven. I know what you did and I'm waiting for you. Cobbler's Point."

The line went dead and Steven hurled the telephone against the wall. His heart was racing. Everything that had overtaken him now paled into insignificance before the threat he faced. Yukiko had stolen his dream of being the master of Japan's future economic might. Global was in shambles and needed millions if it was going to survive. But nothing would be regained if he did not survive. Only one person in the world knew what had really happened in the catacombs. Only one, and a few words from his mouth, could, after all these years, still force Steven Talbot to walk to the gallows.

Steven realized that in order to testify against him, Harry would have to admit counterfeiting the checks.

He doesn't care about being arrested and going to jail for that. I took away his wife and child. He doesn't have anything to lose now. . . .

And that meant Harry Taylor had to die.

– 68 –

Cassandra's announcement that United States Express had declared open season on the struggling Global Enterprises caught the financial community by complete surprise. Rumors surged up and down Wall Street, feeding off the banks' and brokerage houses' speculation about the staggering amount of money that had to be involved. Predictably, Global's spokesmen retaliated immediately.

"Mr. Talbot is very familiar with these kinds of tactics," a Global spokesman told the press. "He is studying the best ways to ensure that they don't succeed."

"Have you seen this?" asked Cassandra, holding up the *Wall Street Journal* as Nicholas came into her office. "He can't stay in Dunescrag forever. Sooner or later he has to come out."

"He's already out," Nicholas told her grimly.

"I know. He has a radio interview scheduled in an hour."

"*Two* hours ago, Steven Talbot left Idlewild Airport. He's en route to Honolulu."

"*Honolulu!*"

"I'm sorry, Cass. I should have received word of this earlier. One of the people I had watching Steven slipped up. He never saw him leave Dunescrag."

"But why's he going to Honolulu when . . ." Cassandra looked up at Nicholas. "Harry?"

"It has to be. Steven wouldn't leave New York now unless it was a matter of life or death."

Only after he had boarded the jet at Los Angeles International Airport did Steven Talbot allow his final destination to become public. His timing was perfect. The radio and print reporters were waiting for him when he stepped onto the tarmac in Honolulu.

"I have come here," he declared, "because this is where my home and friends are. The problems that Global has recently faced have all been put to rest. There is no cause for concern. The traveler's check is as sound a financial instrument now as it was the day my mother invented it. I want to assure the public that the check continues to have the full backing of Global's worldwide resources. And in the very near future, if Cassandra McQueen doesn't withdraw her ridiculous attempt to undermine me, she will learn exactly how powerful that backing can be."

The press ate it up. As he walked to the terminal building, Steven fielded the questions reporters kept shouting at him. But his answers were pat. He was already thinking about tomorrow's headlines.

All right, Harry, I'm here. Come and get me.

On the terminal's rooftop balcony, where well-wishers gathered to watch their friends and relatives leave, stood an exquisitely dressed Oriental woman flanked by two silent men. Yukiko Kamaguchi couldn't help but admire how Steven had the press eating out of his hand. He was a master of deceit, a killer and betrayer hiding behind the ravaged face of a hero.

"Welcome home, Steven," Yukiko said softly.

Harry Taylor left his hotel at precisely five o'clock. He crossed the street, heading for the diner on the corner where he would order, as he had over the last week, the blue-plate special. On his way, Harry passed a newspaper vendor who already had the afternoon edition in hand for him. Harry's eyes froze on the headline. Slowly he dropped the change back into his pocket.

"Not today, thanks," he said, managing a smile.

Harry walked past the diner without even seeing it. Suddenly, the gun he was carrying in his suit jacket pocket seemed very, very heavy.

The reception for Cassandra was markedly different from the one Steven Talbot had received. The press was out in force when her plane landed in Honolulu, as was their prejudice.

"Miss McQueen, can you tell us why you keep persecuting Mr. Talbot?" one reporter called out.

"No one is persecuting anybody!" she replied tightly. "Global Enterprises is an empty shell. Steven Talbot has systematically looted its profits and ruined its reputation. I want to change that."

"Mr. Talbot says Global is sound."

"Mr. Talbot is a liar!"

Nicholas, hovering protectively around Cassandra, did his best to clear the way for her. The reporters quickly recognized him.

"When did Mr. Lockwood go to work for you, Miss McQueen?"

"He doesn't work for me!"

"Well, he used to be head of Global's security. And before that the two of you were quite an item. Care to tell us what you offered him to come back?"

Nicholas whirled around, ready to lunge at the man, but Cassandra held him back.

"That doesn't dignify an answer!" she snapped.

"Well, maybe this does: Are you the kind of woman who'll do anything to finish a vendetta?"

"That's a rotten thing to say!" Cassandra cried. "What's happened to Global was brought on by Steven Talbot, no one else!"

Nicholas managed to steer Cassandra to the waiting car, pushed her inside, and slammed the door.

"Let's go!" he barked at the driver.

Nicholas turned to Cassandra. "You're trembling.

"Just hold me," Cassandra whispered. "Please . . ."

They rode in silence all the way to the hotel. Nicholas shepherded Cassandra through the check-in, got her into the suite, and locked the door behind them.

"It was a mistake coming here," he said flatly. "This is Steven's territory. He's ingratiated himself with everyone and they're out for your head."

Cassandra went out on the balcony and he joined her. Directly below were the glistening beaches of Waikiki and beyond that, the limitless Pacific.

"None of that matters," Cassandra said. "It'll all end here, one way or another."

"You don't have to confront Steven," Nicholas said harshly. "He's dangerous. Please, Cass, give me the time I need to find Harry!"

"And what happens if Steven finds him first?" Cassandra asked gently. "I *am* helping you, darling. Steven has to concentrate on me, not Harry. That's what will buy you the time you need." Cassandra saw the turmoil raging in his eyes. "Please, my love, it's the only way."

"All right," Nicholas said at last. "I have several leads to check. Promise me you won't do anything until I call."

"Promise."

For a long time after Nicholas had gone, images of Steven flickered through Cassandra's mind until she couldn't stand it anymore. She thought of her mother and father, of Rose, and reached for the telephone.

"Forgive me, my darling," she whispered as she waited for the hotel operator to put her through to Cobbler's Point.

* * *

Either Harry was getting sloppy or he had stopped caring whether anyone was tracking him. Nicholas thought it was the latter.

Like most soldiers, Nicholas had laid over in Honolulu before heading into the Pacific theater. He remembered enough of the city to know where to look. Harry, on the run, would avoid the tourist strips close to the beach. He needed a lair—a place where no one asked questions, where a man with enough money could buy the weapon of his choice. Nicholas started with the pawnshops and got lucky on his fourth try. The owner slipped Lockwood's ten-dollar bill into his pocket and swore he recognized Harry's photograph.

Nicholas backtracked. The waitress at the luncheonette remembered Harry because he had been a generous tipper. He never said much, always had the blue-plate special, always read the newspaper. Nicholas thanked her and went in search of the closest newsstand.

"Sure I remember him," the newsagent told Nicholas. "Was coming in regular as clockwork."

"Was?"

"Haven't seen him today."

Nicholas held a folded twenty-dollar bill between his fingers.

"I have to find him." he said softly. "It's very, very important."

The money disappeared into the agent's pocket. "He was coming out of that hotel there. I guess that's where you'll find him."

Nicholas was already running.

The hotel was what Nicholas had expected: a third-class way station for military men and transients.

"Don't know about the guy," the desk clerk said, rolling a toothpick between his teeth.

"He's staying here," Nicholas said tonelessly. "Just give me the room number."

"He *was* staying here. The guy paid up this afternoon. Somehow I don't think he's coming back."

"Do you know where he went?"

"Hey, what do I look like—the tourist board?"

Nicholas's instinct told him exactly where Harry was. But that didn't necessarily mean he had gone to Cobbler's Point voluntarily. He prayed Harry's luck had held. If Steven knew he was on the island and had gone after him . . .

Nicholas pushed aside the thought. He jammed some coins into the pay phone and waited as the hotel operator rang Cassandra's suite.

"I'm sorry, sir. There's no answer."

"She's got to be there!" His panic mounted as twilight darkened to night.

"The desk clerk tells me he saw Miss McQueen leave the hotel a half-hour ago and—"

Cursing, Nicholas slammed down the receiver and raced into the street.

Cobbler's Point lay like a streak of phosphorescence against the darkness of the sea and sky. The driveway and paths were lighted and the house itself blazed, as though defying the night. Inside, Steven was alone, standing on the terrace in front of the living room, the ocean breeze pushing back his hair, flapping the tails of his suit jacket. He had dismissed the servants and prepared for Harry's inevitable appearance. What he had not expected was Cassandra's call. Steven had been shocked to hear her voice but he had recovered quickly and agreed to meet her tonight. But only her. Steven had learned that Nicholas Lockwood had accompanied Cassandra to Hawaii. He knew that if he came face to face with Lockwood he wouldn't be able to resist killing him then and there. That wouldn't look like an accident at all.

And if Harry chose that moment to join them, that was fine too. Steven had everything worked out.

Out of the corner of his eye, Steven caught a shadow wavering across the pool. Casually he slipped his hand into his pocket and gripped the butt of the revolver. Steven began walking around the edge of the pool, his eyes fixed on the bushes on the other side. He was certain someone was there.

Steven was near the end of the pool when the doorbell shattered the silence of the night. Steven whirled around, gun in hand.

Then, to his utter incomprehension, something very cold and sharp sliced through him.

Cassandra pulled into the driveway at Cobbler's Point. For a moment she remained motionless, her hands gripping the steering wheel of the convertible, trying to summon the courage to confront Steven Talbot. Every instinct in her screamed, *Go back!*

Defiantly, Cassandra stepped from the car and walked to the front door. Chimes sounded faintly as she pressed the buzzer. Cassandra waited but no one came. Her fingers curled around the handle and, much to her surprise, the door opened.

"Steven?"

Her voice echoed across the wood and stone but there was no reply. Tentatively, Cassandra went forward, toward the cathedral-ceiling living room.

Where is he? Where are the servants?

Before she knew it, Cassandra found herself standing on the terrace. Lights bordering the flower beds glowed all around her, casting the foliage in tones of red, blue, and green. And there was something else, a long shadow by the pool with two sticks, perpendicular to each other, sticking out of it.

"Steven?"

Cassandra's heart was racing. The cacophony of tree toads, crickets, and cicadas roared in her ears. She stepped close to the pool, then froze. The figure lying there was Steven Talbot. Two wicked-looking blades, one longer than the other, were embedded in his chest.

Harry! What have you done?

Slowly Cassandra crouched beside the body, unable to take her eyes off the terrible steel buried in Steven's torso. Involuntarily she reached out and touched the handles.

"Help me . . ."

Cassandra cried out as Steven tried to raise his head. His palm bloodied the edge of the pool as he moved it feebly. Shaking off her fear, Cassandra knelt over him.

"Steven, who did this to you?"

Flecks of blood appeared on Steven's lips, the words lost as he coughed.

Cassandra felt utterly helpless. She didn't dare remove the swords for fear of Steven's hemorrhaging. She scrambled to her feet and raced into the house, snatching up the first telephone she saw. The line was dead.

I have to leave him. I have to get help!

Cassandra backed away toward the door. The thought of leaving Steven helpless like that horrified her. Then she remembered: What if the would-be killer was still here? What if he'd seen her and was waiting to kill her too? Cassandra looked around fearfully, then flung open the door. Taking a deep breath, she raced to her car.

— 69 —

The medevac helicopter touched down on the lawn of Cobbler's Point. Nicholas Lockwood watched as the two male nurses who had wheeled Steven Talbot out of the house on the guerney shielded his body from the rotor wash. One of the nurses helped the doctor load the body, then climbed aboard. The helicopter lifted off immediately.

Nicholas looked around. Half a dozen vehicles, including an ambulance and a fire truck, were parked haphazardly in the circular drive. The white walls of the house were bathed in red from the vehicles' bubble lights. Through the brilliantly lit windows he saw the forensic team methodically searching for clues and dusting for fingerprints. Every few seconds a flash strobe went off. The police photographer was busy.

"I can almost hear you praying."

Nicholas turned around to see Detective Charlie Kaneohe standing beside him. The big Hawaiian, with his gaudy print shirt and woven fedora, lighted a cigarette.

"What did the doctor say?" Nicholas asked.

Kaneohe shrugged. "They'll have to get those knives out of him first."

"Not knives—"

Nicholas stopped short. He had already told Kaneohe that the instruments used to stab Steven Talbot weren't knives but Japanese ceremonial swords.

"Where is Cassandra now?" Nicholas asked.

He already knew that a police patrol had intercepted Cassandra on Platinum Mile as she was heading away from Cobbler's Point. Kaneohe checked his watch.

"Right now she's being booked and fingerprinted."

"What's the charge?"

"Attempted murder."

"You still think she did it," Nicholas said in wonderment. He imagined Cassandra, alone, scared, trying to make sense of the senseless. "I want to see her."

"You her lawyer?"

"No, but—"

"Look, you know the rules. She has a right to a phone call and she's probably made it by now."

To an empty room.

Nicholas felt sick to his stomach. "I've got to go."

"Not too far, Mr. Lockwood," Kaneohe called after him. "You and I have a lot to talk about."

The rented Thunderbird's wheels spewed crushed seashells as Nicholas Lockwood swerved to avoid colliding with a police cruiser. He straightened out the car, took the corner, and hurtled down the highway toward Honolulu. Twenty minutes later he screeched to a stop in front of the government offices that housed, among other departments, the Immigration and Naturalization Service. Nicholas flipped open the Global security identification he still carried and the sleepy guard waved him through. On the third floor, he found the night-duty officer.

"Who the hell let you in?" the officer demanded.

"Someone tried to kill Mr. Talbot tonight," Nicholas said coldly. "I need the immigration cards for everyone who's been cleared into Honolulu for the last week."

The officer gaped. "Mr. Talbot . . . Jesus! Look, I don't know if I should—"

"Right now Mr. Talbot is in emergency surgery. If he survives, you can bet he'll be grateful to anyone who helped track down his attacker."

The officer hesitated. "I should call the police. . . ."

"By all means," Nicholas said, crossing his arms. "Take your time. But we have the name of a suspect. Of course, if he manages to slip out of the islands . . ."

The implication was clear and the bluff worked.

"Follow me," the officer said.

Over a thousand INS cards had been filled out by people entering Hawaii that week. Nicholas ignored the three hundred belonging to military personnel and began sifting through the remainder. He was lucky: the cards had been filed alphabetically by surname. In two minutes he had what he needed.

The Halekulani Hotel had originally been built as a beach cottage at the turn of the century by one of Oahu's wealthiest families. Later it was leased as a hotel and became famous as the *House Without a Key*, after the Charlie Chan novel by Earl Derr Biggers. Even though the Halekulani had expanded, it had carefully retained its patina of sophistication and grace. It was, Nicholas thought as he moved swiftly through the deserted lobby, the kind of place in which Yukiko Kamaguchi would choose to stay.

He wasn't wrong. The desk clerk confirmed that Miss Kamaguchi was registered at the hotel, but after calling her room he told Nicholas there was no answer. Both the restaurant and bar were closed. The clerk suggested that

Nicholas try the veranda, where guests often took their last nightcap. Nicholas thanked him and went toward the beach. He spotted Yukiko at a table next to the large *kiawe* tree, a Hawaiian version of mesquite, sipping a liqueur. There were no other guests about.

As Nicholas walked toward her, two very competent-looking Japanese intercepted him, barring his way. Yukiko looked up and beckoned with her hand.

"Mr. Lockwood, what an unexpected pleasure—I think."

Nicholas was startled by Yukiko's transformation. His last impression of her had been of a drab woman with matted hair and ill-fitting clothes. Now, her perfectly oval face was golden from the sun, setting off her jet hair, which lay across one shoulder. The narrow dress in dusty pink, swathed with satin at the hip, accented her graceful long-bodied look.

"May I ask the kitchen to get you a cup of coffee?"

Nicholas marveled at how self-possessed Yukiko appeared.

"No, thanks. I hate to spoil your night, Miss Kamaguchi, but I'm afraid you did a lousy job on Steven Talbot. He's still alive."

The only hint of Yukiko's surprise was a slight flare of her nostrils. "I have no idea what you're talking about, Mr. Lockwood. Has Steven been injured?"

"Steven's would-be killer stabbed him with a pair of Japanese ceremonial swords used in seppuku. I'm no expert, but I think that if the swords' provenance were to be traced, it would show that they once belonged to Hisahiko Kamaguchi. I wonder how you would explain that to the Honolulu police."

"Very simply, Mr. Lockwood. Those swords were lost during the war. This is the first I've heard of them. If they are part of my father's legacy I would petition to have them returned."

Lockwood wondered at the whisper-soft callousness of the woman opposite him. She was beyond threat and reprisals and knew it.

"Why did you do it? You have everything you wanted. Corporation 4780 has scooped up all of Steven's Japanese assets. You now have leverage in every major *zaibatsu*. But you still broke your word."

"You do not understand, Mr. Lockwood. Taking back what Steven stole satisfied me. In that way, I did not break my promise to you and Miss McQueen. But I wasn't the only one Steven betrayed. He used my father. He persuaded him to offer up his life so that the men of the *zaibutsu* would be spared, so that I would one day have the means to return Kamaguchi Industries to greatness. Such betrayal demanded retribution."

"And you botched that!"

Yukiko was silent.

"Why put the blame on Cassandra? She had nothing to do with what happened between you and Steven. She helped you, for Christ's sake!"

"That Miss McQueen happened to arrive at an inopportune time was—for

614

her—unfortunate. Yet, perhaps such was her destiny. She too wanted to bring Steven down, Mr. Lockwood. She was seeking to redress past injustices that Steven had inflicted upon people she loved."

"Not by murder!"

"All a matter of degree, Mr. Lockwood. One way or the other, Steven Talbot is a dead man."

Nicholas slumped in his chair. There seemed no way to get at this woman. He might be able to persuade the Honolulu police to detain and question Yukiko. But she would tell them even less than she had told him. Eventually her lawyers—the best money could buy—would force the authorities to let her go.

"Cassandra's innocent. You know that. Is it part of your honor code to let her suffer? Is that how you serve your father's memory?"

"Perhaps she is only paying for what she was quite willing to have happen. No, Mr. Lockwood, there is nothing I will do to help Cassandra McQueen. And nothing you can force me to do."

Yukiko paused and held his eyes. "Whatever happens to Steven Talbot now is out of my hands. And remember, killing me would solve nothing."

"Believe me," Nicholas said, "I've already thought of that and come to the same conclusion."

Six messages were waiting for Nicholas when he returned to his hotel suite. One was from Cassandra, and Nicholas closed his eyes, imagining what a bleak and lonely place her words had come from. The rest were from Eric Gollant. Since it was already midmorning on the East Coast, Nicholas called him at his USE office. The normally unflappable accountant was beside himself.

"Nick, what the hell is going on over there? It's all over the news that Cassandra tried to kill Steven!"

Quickly Nicholas explained the events that had overtaken him and Cassandra since they had arrived in Hawaii.

"Obviously she didn't try to kill Steven," Nicholas finished. "But she was at the scene and the police can stick her with a hell of a motive. She needs the best legal representation we can get her."

"I've already contacted someone," Eric replied, giving Nicholas the name. "He'll be in to see Cassandra right away."

There was a pause. "What about you, Nick?"

"Whoever tried to kill Steven is still out there. The police aren't looking anymore. I am."

"Miss McQueen . . ."

Cassandra started at the touch. She opened her eyes to see a moon-faced

615

Hawaiian looming over her. She had never heard his footsteps nor even the rattle of the cell door.

"Who are you?" Cassandra asked, struggling to sit up.

"Detective Kaneohe. It's time you and I had a little talk."

Unsteadily at first, Cassandra followed the matron into the shower area. She splashed her face to wash away the cobwebs and wished she had a toothbrush. When she looked at herself in the mirror, she realized she needed more than that. Cassandra then fell in step between the detective and the matron and followed them upstairs. Kaneohe opened the door to a room with a wooden table and several chairs. Cassandra's stomach churned at the smell of hot coffee wafting up from the two cups on the table.

"I hope you like black," Kaneohe said.

Cassandra took a sip. "It's fine, thank you." She looked at the detective. "How is Steven?"

Kaneohe shrugged. "He's out of surgery. Too soon to tell whether he'll make it."

"And you really think I did it?"

Kaneohe sighed. "Let's take it from the top, Miss McQueen. Why did you come to Hawaii?"

"I have a right to have a lawyer present, detective."

And Nicholas! Where is he?

"Sure you do, Miss McQueen. But let me tell you what we have. Fingerprints off one of the sword handles. I'll bet a month's paycheck they match yours. The switchboard operator at your hotel told us you placed a call to Cobbler's Point shortly before you left. We also know—as does everybody else in Honolulu—that you and Mr. Talbot were not on the best of terms. You tried to ruin him once. Now you were after his company again. Maybe he didn't want to sell. Maybe you didn't like that. Maybe you couldn't take no for an answer. And maybe you thought that with Mr. Talbot out of the way—"

"That's enough, detective!"

The man standing at the door filled the interrogation room with his presence. His tousled hair and sleepy eyes reminded Cassandra of a bear coming out of hibernation.

"My name is Hartley Nathan," the attorney said softly. "I've been asked to represent you."

Cassandra recognized the name immediately. A native San Franciscan, Hartley Nathan had been one of America's foremost criminal attorneys and had an unmatched acquittal record.

"I thought you had retired, Counselor," Kaneohe said.

Nathan yawned. "Just keeping my hand in, Charlie. Now how about a little privacy so I can talk to my client."

The detective shrugged. "You picked a lousy time to make a comeback."

"Who sent you?" Cassandra asked eagerly once they were alone.

"Eric Gollant. He's a very persuasive fellow, even at one in the morning." Cassandra breathed a sigh of relief.

"I want you to tell me everything that happened," Nathan said. "Take your time and don't leave out any details. All right?"

Nathan listened carefully as Cassandra retold her story, interrupting only when he needed a point clarified. While he was studying his notes, Charlie Kaneohe returned and slipped a fingerprint sheet in front of him.

"The prints on one of the sword handles match your client's, Counselor. I'll bring you more good news as soon as I have it."

"They're treating me as though I were already convicted," Cassandra said bitterly.

Nathan shushed her. "Steven Talbot is a powerful man around here. He bought himself an awful lot of goodwill. Everybody liked him. But that will be a good reason to change the trial venue—"

"Trial?"

Nathan leaned forward. "Miss McQueen, you've been charged with attempted murder. The prosecution has motive and opportunity. You were at Cobbler's Point last night. The police caught you leaving the scene of the crime. They have your fingerprints on the weapons. We'll challenge everything, of course. But there will be a trial."

"But I didn't do it!" Cassandra cried. "Why aren't the police looking for the real killer?"

"I'm going to talk to Kaneohe about that," Hartley Nathan promised. "I'm also going to find Nicholas Lockwood and—"

Nathan broke off as Kaneohe slipped into the room. He gestured to the attorney to come to the door. Cassandra watched as the two men spoke in whispers, then she heard Nathan say, "Tell her."

The detective hesitated. "There's been an . . . an incident, Miss McQueen. The Honolulu office of United States Express has been firebombed."

Nicholas Lockwood wasn't one to overlook the obvious. Although he was certain that Harry Taylor wouldn't return to any of his old haunts, he checked both the hotel Harry had been staying at as well as the all-night luncheonette he had frequented. Then he drove to the Good Samaritan Hospital, arriving just as the surgeons were giving the press their update on Steven's condition.

Nicholas hung back, scrutinizing the faces. Harry had come to Hawaii to avenge the deaths of his family and Ram. Someone—Harry had no inkling it was Yukiko Kamaguchi—had denied him the satisfaction. Nicholas reckoned that Harry wouldn't leave Hawaii until he had accomplished what he'd set out to do. And Nicholas wasn't about to stop him. But what Harry wanted had to be done in such a way that Cassandra was completely absolved.

Then Nicholas spotted him.

White lilies. Oh, Harry, you have such a touch!

Nicholas watched Harry write out a card and pay for the flowers. When the clerk stepped away to wrap them, Harry tried to slip out of the shop. Nicholas let him get as far as the door.

"Hello, Harry."

– 70 –

Two days after the near-fatal assault on Steven Talbot, at five-thirty in the morning, Detective Charlie Kaneohe left the sleeping suburbs behind, driving along North Vineyard Boulevard, which would take him into the administrative heart of Honolulu. He found it a mystery that most tourists to the island never set foot in the Kawaiahao Church, built entirely of coral blocks cut from Hawaii's reefs, or the Iolani Palace, America's only royal seat, from which King David Kalakana ruled with his wife Queen Kapiolani. For Kaneohe this part of the city, untouched by the glitter of Waikiki and the pandemonium of Chinatown, was where the ancient spirit of Hawaii dwelt.

Behind the palace, next to the state capitol, was the white-columned limestone building that housed the criminal courts. Kaneohe drove into the empty parking lot and gazed up at the fifteen-foot figures carved from the stone blocks: Solomon, Moses, King Kamehameha, and blind Justice, holding scales. Kaneohe believed that if these deaf and dumb creations could speak, they would show Cassandra McQueen more compassion than she had received until now. Newspaper articles and editorials had vilified her. Demonstrators had besieged the courthouse, carrying placards and shouting for the death penalty. Across the country, there had been vandalism against United States Express offices. After USE's Honolulu office had been firebombed, Kaneohe had arranged for protection of the company's premises and employees. No sooner had he done that than the first anonymous death threat had been received at police headquarters.

The dawn's silence was broken by trucks pulling into the lot. Charlie Kaneohe watched his men jump out and begin unloading orange-painted sawhorses with HONOLULU POLICE DEPARTMENT—DO NOT PASS stenciled in black along the length of the beams. Then another van arrived and the detective carefully examined the passes that would be issued to the press and public attending the arraignment. Hundreds of spectators were expected to try to get a seat in the courtroom, and Kaneohe was leaving nothing to chance. Just as it had been his duty to build the case against Cassandra, so now he had to protect her from the fanatics and madmen.

At seven o'clock, three hours before the arraignment, several vans belonging to a special security detachment pulled up at the courthouse. Kaneohe personally supervised his officers' posting, stationing men along the corridor leading to the courtroom and setting up a screening station in front of the tall mahogany doors. The courtroom itself was carefully checked for anything that might resemble a bomb, as were the judge's chambers and the holding room. Through the tall rounded windows along the east wall of the court Kaneohe saw sharpshooters patrolling the roof of the building across the street.

A few minutes before nine o'clock, Kaneohe had everyone in place. Yet, he was not satisfied. Something he couldn't define kept tugging at his conscience. At face value, this was an open-and-shut case. Motive, opportunity, fingerprints. No conflicting eyewitness testimony, even though Kaneohe had gone out of his way to try to find anyone who had seen or heard anything in the vicinity of Cobbler's Point that night.

So what am I picking at? Kaneohe chided himself.

After almost twenty years in the field, Kaneohe trusted his sixth sense.

Charlie Kaneohe called Good Samaritan Hospital one more time. The surgeon in charge had nothing new to tell him. Steven Talbot was still unconscious, suspended between life and death. The detective whom Kaneohe had posted at Steven's bedside reported that the voice-activated tape recorder hadn't switched itself on once.

Kaneohe hung up. The saving grace, he tried to tell himself, was that this was only the arraignment. If Steven Talbot passed out of the critical stage, if he could utter just a few words, Kaneohe was certain he could put his doubts to rest before the actual trial began.

The detective checked his watch. It was time to bring up his prisoner.

"You look lovely."

Cassandra looked up at Hartley Nathan and managed a smile. She was wearing a navy suit and a rose-blush blouse with an antique cameo pin. Hartley had brought the clothes from the hotel yesterday, and along with them something even more precious—a note from Nicholas, the paper now frayed because of the number of times she had folded and unfolded it.

"Courage," he had written. *"I'm there for you. Everything will work out."*

619

And that was all. No mention of whether Harry had been found or even if he was still alive. No hint as to who had tried to kill Steven.

But he'd never commit that kind of information to paper, Cassandra thought. "Will he be there?" she asked.

The attorney shrugged. He had met with and talked to Nicholas Lockwood, understanding now how important this man was to Cassandra. What Nicholas hadn't told him, and what Nathan, as an officer of the court, didn't want to know, was how Nicholas intended to prove beyond any doubt that Cassandra was innocent.

Nathan heard the door to the isolation block open, and rose.

"It's time," he said, holding out his hand to Cassandra. "Remember, don't expect an ounce of sympathy from the judge. Pukui is one of the few Hawaiians who's had the tenacity to claw his way up a white-dominated judicial system. He has his eye on the governor's mansion as soon as Hawaii becomes a state. The prosecutor, Kawena, is another hot-shot, who wants to be chief district attorney. This case is a political springboard for both of them."

"Thanks for the pep talk," Cassandra murmured.

"Just so you know what you're up against. That won't stop me from getting you bail. Eric Gollant transferred a lot more than we'll need but it's nice to know it's there."

Nathan held Cassandra by the shoulders. "You won't spend another day in this place. Meanwhile, remember that everyone back home is pulling for you."

Cassandra tried to take comfort in that as she and Hartley Nathan followed Detective Kaneohe upstairs to the courtroom.

Inside, the buzz ceased immediately. Cassandra tried not to look at the crowd. Her eyes found tiny details and focused on them: the water stains that blemished the ceiling, the splinter in the giant carved-wood territorial shield above the judge's bench. As she approached her seat behind the defense table, Cassandra heard the soft rustle of charcoal on paper as the newspaper artists focused their attention on her. Finally she dared glance at the spectators. To a person, they were all looking at her, their eyes cold and stony, without a glimmer of compassion.

"All rise! This court is in session. The Honorable Justice Samuel Pukui presiding!"

"Is the prosecution ready?" Pukui demanded.

Daniel Kawena, dressed in a somber blue suit, replied, "The people are ready, Your Honor."

"Defense?"

"The defense is ready, Your Honor," Hartley Nathan said quietly.

"Miss McQueen, you are charged with the attempted murder of Steven Talbot. How do you plead?"

Cassandra gathered up all her strength and looked straight at Pukui.

"Not guilty, Your Honor!"

Yukiko Kamaguchi was sitting on the terrace of her hotel suite, listening as the waters whispered and hissed along the sand. Beside her, Nicholas Lockwood checked his watch.

"Make the call."

Yukiko didn't move. Nicholas placed a telephone on the patio table beside her.

"Make the call," he said softly. "Then it will be time to go."

The Good Samaritan Hospital was the territory's most modern medical facility, thanks in large measure to contributions from Steven Talbot. This fact had not escaped the members of the surgical team that had operated on the philanthropist.

After he had been removed from the operating room, Steven had been taken to a private room on the first floor of the garden wing. Three nurses were assigned to him, one to sit in his room at all times in case of an emergency. Outside the door was a detective whose only job was to be present if, by some stroke of luck, Steven regained consciousness and said anything. A reel-to-reel tape recorder and microphone were ready on the bedside table.

Harry Taylor knew all this and more. Security would have been much tighter had the police not been convinced that they had the chief suspect in custody. Nicholas Lockwood had told him they could count on that.

Dressed in the uniform of a hospital orderly—baggy white trousers, matching jacket, white, soft-soled shoes—Harry stood on the pebbled path that meandered through the garden wing. A few feet away was the window to Steven Talbot's room. The hurricane louvres were partially open and the intruder could hear the clicking of the nurse's knitting needles. Harry checked his watch. Any minute now.

The door to the room opened and Harry heard the detective tell the nurse she had an urgent telephone call. The nurse checked her patient, then hurried out. As expected, the detective did not take her place but remained outside. Undoubtedly he had been told that many more hours would elapse before Steven Talbot regained consciousness—if ever.

Harry went to work. Removing the aluminum window panel took only seconds. The screws had been twisted almost all the way out last night. Harry vaulted through the opening, landed silently, and approached the motionless figure on the bed.

The nurse was becoming impatient. The operator had told her the call was long-distance but that they had been cut off. Now she was redialing and the circuits were busy.

The nurse glanced at the clock above the station. She'd already been gone too long. If one of the doctors saw her, there'd be hell to pay.

On the other end of the line, Yukiko Kamaguchi was also watching the clock. When the second hand finally crawled past twelve for the third time, she hung up.

Very carefully Harry lifted the pillow from beneath Steven Talbot's head. Without an epithet or a prayer, he pushed the pillow against Steven's face and pressed it with all his might. He had counted to fifty before the pulse stopped.

Annoyed, the nurse walked down the corridor to Steven's room.

"Everything all right?" asked the detective.

"I don't know. We got cut off."

The nurse entered the room and picked up her knitting. She made two stitches before she felt a draft. Turning around, she saw that the entire window had been removed. Her immediate reaction was to check her patient. Only when she saw Steven Talbot's bulging eyes did she scream.

The porters had brought the luggage to the car waiting beneath the portico. The bill had been settled by one of her assistants. Yukiko Kamaguchi allowed Nicholas to escort her through the lobby. When he opened the car door, he said, "Go directly to the airport and get on your plane. Don't wait for anyone or anything. All hell's going to break loose here."

"But what if—"

"He'll be there!" Nicholas said fiercely. "All you have to do is fly him to Singapore. He'll look after himself after that. And he's supposed to call me at a predetermined time."

"Rest assured he will, Mr. Lockwood," Yukiko replied.

Nicholas held her gaze briefly. His unspoken message had been acknowledged. With that, Nicholas got into his car and headed downtown to the courthouse.

Cassandra's plea of not guilty galvanized the proceedings. The spectators who had packed the courtroom let out a collective hiss. One or two shouted, "Shame!"

Pukui rapped his gavel sharply. "Order! A plea of not guilty has been entered. As to the question of bail . . ."

Pukui gestured in the prosecutor's direction.

"The people insist that bail be denied," Daniel Kawena said fervently. "Miss McQueen is accused of a major crime, which will become capital if Mr. Talbot dies. She has no ties to this community and her substantial assets would allow her not only to make whatever bail might be set but also to flee the jurisdiction of this court. I therefore request that she be held in custody until the trial date."

"Mr. Nathan?"

"Your Honor, it is true that my client is wealthy and has no specific ties to Hawaii. However, Miss McQueen, as chief executive officer of United States Express, is a high-profile individual. Her business interests, which require her presence, are in the continental United States. It would be silly to think that someone as well known as she could flee—or would want to. I therefore ask that my client be freed on her own recognizance."

Shouting erupted in the audience. Cries of "Murderess!" and "Liar!" were hurled at Cassandra as court bailiffs hurried to station themselves between the defense table and the spectators.

When Justice Pukui finally restored order, he looked at Nathan and asked, "Does counsel believe that this court will grant your client unconditional bail?"

"If it is a just court, yes, Your Honor."

Pukui crimsoned. "Bail denied!" he said harshly. "The prisoner will be remanded into custody of the Honolulu police until the trial date to be set for—"

Before Pukui could finish, a clerk rushed up to the bench. The justice unfolded the note and paled.

"This court is in recess!" he announced, his voice trembling. "The bailiffs will take custody of the prisoner but she is to remain here. Both counsel, in my chambers, now!"

The courtroom murmurs swelled to a roar even before the judge had left the bench. Reporters and spectators surged toward Cassandra. The bailiffs were scarcely able to restrain them. Cassandra ignored the questions being hurled at her and tried to comprehend what was happening. Judging by his expression, Hartley Nathan had been as surprised as everyone else. Then Cassandra caught a glimpse of Nicholas threading his way through the crowd. His eyes reached out for her but it was his calm, emotionless gaze that told Cassandra everything she had to know.

"What do you mean he's dead?" Prosecutor Daniel Kawena shouted. "Where were the police?"

Justice Pukui admonished him with a cold stare. "Remember where you are,

623

sir. And as to the police, you were the one responsible for making sure that Steven Talbot was adequately protected. Obviously your precautions didn't go far enough."

Kawena smarted under the attack but held his ground.

"I'll get to the bottom of this," he promised. "But Mr. Talbot's death doesn't change a thing." He turned to Hartley Nathan. "Except that the charge against your client is now first-degree murder!"

Nathan arched his eyebrows. "Really, Counselor? Mr. Talbot was murdered less than thirty minutes ago. My client was in custody at the time."

"She could have had accomplices," Kawena retorted.

"You have no grounds for that statement," Nathan said softly. "There's no proof Cassandra McQueen entered into a conspiracy to kill Steven Talbot. What you're faced with is murder by a person or persons unknown. The same ones who attacked Mr. Talbot three nights ago." Nathan turned to the judge. "Your Honor, with all due respect, the prosecution has no case. Clearly my client can no longer be held as a suspect."

"Yes, she can!" Kawena thundered. "We have her fingerprints on the murder weapon—"

"Which you know I can explain away."

Before Nathan could go any further, Detective Kaneohe entered the chambers.

"Excuse me, Your Honor, but this was delivered by messenger a few minutes ago. It's addressed to you."

The three men stared at the package, the size of a box of chocolates, clumsily wrapped in brown paper.

"The bomb-disposal boys had to open it, Your Honor," Kaneohe apologized. "Just to be on the safe side." He paused. "If you don't mind, I'd like to be in on this."

Pukui agreed. Carefully he placed the contents of the box on the desk: a cassette tape, the kind used in secretarial dictation, and a water glass carefully wrapped in a plastic bag.

"Obviously someone is sending us a message," Pukui murmured. "Counselors?"

Both attorneys shook their heads.

"Then let's listen." Pukui slipped the cassette into his dictaphone. There was a brief hiss followed by a calm, almost serene male voice.

"*Gentlemen, my name is Harry Taylor. I, and I alone, attempted to murder Steven Talbot. When I didn't succeed the first time, I tried again. By now you're aware of the results. Now I am going to tell you why. . . .*"

Harry, who was as unknown to his listeners as they were to him, held back nothing. He recounted in minute detail the circumstances surrounding the kidnapping of Cassandra, Steven's betrayal in the catacombs, and how he had murdered Michelle McQueen, as well as his subsequent flight, which had ultimately ended in Singapore. He went on to admit that he had been responsible for flooding the market with counterfeit Global Traveler's Checks in an attempt to ruin Steven Talbot and how, when Steven had discovered this, he had had Harry's family murdered. His final words dealt with how meticulously he had planned his revenge.

"*And if you doubt anything I've said,*" Harry's ghostly voice concluded, "*you've only to match the fingerprints on the glass I've sent along with those you will find on the window ledge, night table, and other places in Steven Talbot's room.*"

The spool ran on for a few seconds, then the dictaphone shut itself off. None of the four men spoke. Then at last Justice Pukui raised his head and looked at his prosecutor and detective. Charlie Kaneohe finally knew what his instinct had been trying to tell him.

After an hour's delay, the courtroom spectators began to chafe. Cassandra was bewildered. Hartley Nathan hadn't returned and Nicholas had disappeared. Neither she nor anyone else could imagine the drama that was unfolding behind the scenes.

Detective Kaneohe had spotted Nicholas in the courtroom and had him brought into the judge's chambers. He asked him if he knew a Harry Taylor and, when Nicholas replied that he did, had him listen to the tape.

"Do you have any idea where he might be?" asked Kaneohe.

Nicholas explained how he had been looking for Harry ever since he had arrived in the islands.

"And I haven't stopped, especially after what happened to Steven Talbot," he added pointedly.

"Why didn't you tell us about him?" the prosecutor, Kawena, demanded.

"Because you were all so convinced that Cassandra was guilty," Nicholas replied coldly. "You didn't want to believe it could be anyone else. Besides, I had no proof that Harry had done anything."

"You'd better give me a description," Charlie Kaneohe said. "We'll cover the airport and the docks in case he tries to slip out."

From the resignation in his voice, Nicholas knew that Kaneohe was just going through the motions. He was a professional. From what Nicholas had told him about Harry, the detective was certain this kind of man left nothing to chance—especially his escape route.

Which, Nicholas reflected, was true. Overhead, he heard the faint drone of an airplane and wondered if it was the one carrying Harry Taylor home to Singapore and his ghosts.

The buzz in the courtroom stilled when Justice Pukui and the legal teams marched in. Cassandra looked anxiously at Hartley Nathan, who smiled faintly. Pukui mounted the bench and gazed out over the court.

"I have just been informed that Mr. Steven Talbot has been murdered."

A collective gasp rose from the audience.

Pukui raised his voice. "Accordingly, since there is no evidence that the defendant had prior knowledge of this heinous act, and that she could in no way have directly participated in it, it is my obligation to dismiss all charges against her. Miss McQueen, you are free to go."

Cassandra's knees buckled and she felt herself falling until a pair of strong arms embraced her.

"Nicholas!"

She flung her arms around him.

"I told you everything would be all right," he said softly. "Now we can go home."

EPILOGUE

The first week of September brought a sudden chill that colored the trees of Central Park overnight. The leaves crackled and snapped beneath their feet as Cassandra and Nicholas walked to the Fifty-ninth Street entrance. Halfway through, they stopped. The owner of the coffee and doughnut cart, who could set his watch by them, had their cups ready. He wished them a cheery good morning, and although the woman smiled, it was through a veil of sadness. Cassandra and Nicholas carried their coffees to a bench overlooking the pond. This interval was as much a ritual as the morning walk. It gave them the chance to begin the day gently.

"They still haven't found Harry, have they."

It was a question Cassandra had asked so often that by now it had become rhetorical.

"No."

There was nothing else Nicholas could tell her. After they had returned to New York, Kevin Armstrong—USE's security chief—had flown out to Honolulu to monitor the investigation. Armstrong was impressively thorough but he had little to report. The Honolulu police were no closer to finding Harry Taylor now than they had been two weeks ago. To Nicholas, who had received the prearranged call from Singapore, it was a charade. Harry was gone forever.

"You're going to have to let it go, Cass," he said.

Cassandra brushed away a strand of blond hair, tucking it behind her ear. "I know, but I can't."

At Hartley Nathan's insistence, Cassandra had been allowed to listen to the tape Harry Taylor had made. His words took her back to the madness that had erupted in Singapore and irrevocably set Harry on this road. Cassandra felt nothing at all for Steven but she wished she could see Harry one more time. The sadness and loneliness that poured from his words moved her to tears.

To exonerate Cassandra completely, portions of the tape had been made public the following day. Certain that the press would hound her, Nicholas had spirited Cassandra out of Honolulu on the first available flight.

Back in New York, among her friends and staff, Cassandra began to recover. Everyone sympathized with her and excoriated the high-handed treatment she had received from the Hawaiian officials. But that didn't stop the newspapers and magazines from titillating their readers with accounts about the now infamous Harry Taylor and his role in events that could have cost Cassandra her life. The stories multiplied when, less than a week after her return, Cassandra received an invitation from the board of Global Enterprises. Under the articles of incorporation, the board had full powers to restructure the company in the event of Steven Talbot's death. This included an outright sale, which, the board members agreed, would be the company's only salvation. Global was a rudderless ship, losing hundreds of thousands of dollars a day. Only someone familiar with the operations and with plenty of liquidity could hope to salvage it. The obvious choice was Cassandra McQueen.

Cassandra thought long and hard about the proposal. Part of her wanted to reject it out of hand. She had no doubt that many people would condemn her for capitalizing on Steven Talbot's death.

"You shouldn't look at it in those terms," Eric Gollant had told her bluntly. "It's a straightforward business decision. The banks are licking their chops at the chance to buy in, but they know even less about Global than that board of stooges. Do you think anyone would call *them* cold-hearted? No, they'd say the bankers were making a smart business move—a bargain acquisition. Do it, Cass, before the board changes its mind."

When Cassandra broached the subject with Nicholas, all he said was, "Global was always a part of you."

The next day Cassandra presented her offer and it was accepted immediately. At the press conference that followed, she issued a brief statement.

"There were many people who contributed to the success of Global Enterprises. I owe an obligation to all of them and I intend to pay it in full."

Cassandra refused to answer any questions and, as she had predicted, some journalists accused her of stepping over Steven Talbot's grave to get what she wanted.

"They're wrong, you know," she said softly, sipping her coffee and watching as nannies paraded along with baby carriages.

Nicholas looked at her curiously. "Who's wrong? About what?"

"Sorry, I was just thinking out loud," Cassandra said. "All this time I so badly wanted Steven to pay for what he'd done. To my mother, Monk, Rose . . . To me. Yet when I saw him lying by the pool that night, those awful swords in his chest, he wasn't a monster but a human being who was dying. I wanted justice, Nicholas. Not murder. I wish I could have told Harry that."

"Harry wanted the same thing," Nicholas reminded her.

And did you, my love? Where were you all that time I was in custody, wondering what had happened to you? Did you, in the end, find Harry, just as you said you would?

These were questions Cassandra very much wanted to ask Nicholas, yet as they rested on her lips, she heard Michelle and Rose speaking softly to her.

Whatever he did, he did for you. He alone has to live with that. But he needs you to be there for him, without your ever asking. You never have to be afraid again, Cassandra, because Nicholas gave up something of himself so that you could be free. . . .

Cassandra took Nicholas by the hand and led him out of the park to Fifty-ninth Street. Looking toward Sixth Avenue, Cassandra saw a giant neon sign— USE's knight in blue, gazing resolutely toward the future. Cassandra could not imagine all that lay ahead for her, the trials and victories, the achievements and shortfalls. She knew only that she would never again have to face them alone.

Cassandra reached up and cupped Nicholas's face.

"I love you, Nicholas Lockwood."

"I love you too," he whispered.

They lingered over a kiss, causing passersby to smile, then walked slowly, arms around each other, up the street where the blue knight waited.